Mythic Constantinople

DEVELOPED AND WRITTEN BY
Mark Shirley

EDITING & PROOFING
Brian Pivik, Pete Nash

DESIGN AND LAYOUT
Alexandra James

ARTISTS
Luka Arh, Dean Kotz, Eric Lofgren, Anderson Maia, Chris Yarborough
(Dean Kotz, Eric Lofgren and Chris Yarborough appear courtesy of Outland Entertainment)

CARTOGRAPHY
Colin Driver and Ronan Salieri

COVER BY
David Benzal

SPECIAL THANKS TO
Camo Coffey, Alistair Clamp

PLAYTESTERS
Graham Blake, Alistair Clamp, Camo Coffey, Mike Rudd, Neil Rutherford

Look, Mum – I finished it!

ISBN: 978-1-989028-16-2

FIND US AT
www.thedesignmechanism.com and www.MYTHRASrpg.com.
Facebook: https://www.facebook.com/The-Design-Mechanism
G+: https://plus.google.com/communities/113034383032729983266

CONTENTS

INTRODUCTION

O imperial City, City fortified, City of the great king… Queen of the queen of cities, song of songs and splendour of splendours!

~ Niketas Choniates, c.1210

Kalos 'elthete, philoi! Welcome, friends! Welcome to MYTHIC CONSTANTINOPLE. The Queen of Cities sits like a jewel between Europe and Asia at the crossroads of the world. Seventy thousand people make their home here, although this is just a tenth of the populace at the empire's apogee. The streets of Constantinople were first paved two thousand years ago and it had existed a thousand years before becoming the capital of the Roman Empire. No city in Europe has been continuously occupied by the same (if evolving) culture for as long as has Constantinople, which is why it is sometimes called The Eternal City. Westerners call it the City of Sin, a place of exotic vices and fulfilled lusts, a den of decadence where everything can be bought if you have deep enough pockets. To its inhabitants it is the Holy City, bastion of Orthodoxy and home to three thousand churches and four hundred monasteries; the piety of the people evident in the gem-crusted altars and the gilded ikons. Constantinople is all these things, and more.

In Constantinople you can find travellers from all over the known world: mercenaries from far off England and Russia rub shoulders with merchants from Venice and Tunis; and delegations from the Ottoman Empire and the Mamluk Sultanate face off against each other while the iron-clad Knights of Rhodes debate theology with Neoplatonist philosophers. If you are lucky you many even see fabulous visitors such as the headless *Blemmyai* and dog-headed men. Holy men harangue the crowd in a tongue everyone can understand regardless of their race, and wizards struggle to entertain jaded passers-by with their fire show, levitation or mind-reading spectacular. The sights, sounds, and smells of the city, so familiar to its inhabitants, can be overwhelming to the visitor fresh from the boat.

The year is 1450; or, as the Byzantines reckon it, the 6958th year since Creation. The weight of history contends with wonders of the modern world, such as the waterpowered blast furnace; letter press; the mechanical clock; the magnetic compass and other improvements in navigational aids; scientific advances in optics, hydraulics, and statics; and of course, gunpowder. This is an age of exploration, an age of invention, an age of intrigue, and an age of empires.

This is MYTHIC CONSTANTINOPLE.

RELIGION

Religion is a major feature of the Mythic Constantinople setting. Even if you do not explore these themes directly in your game, the conflicts between Orthodox and Catholic Christianity, and between Christianity and Islam, are powerful shaping forces of the city's past and its future.

As a group, the Games Master and the players should take care not to offend the beliefs of each other in real life. Remember that these are real-world religions which today have millions of followers and you should be sensitive towards the beliefs of others and not run stories that your players would find uncomfortable.

HOW MYTHIC?

Each Games Master should decide the level of supernatural influence there is in their game. The setting works as a purely historical setting, but the default is a moderate level of wonder and mystery, so for games without magic the Games Master will have to make a few adjustments. In the default setting, few people can use magic, but most know of someone who does – a local witch, herbalist, or holy man, for example. Mythical creatures might lurk beneath the surface of the city, but these are mostly tales told to frighten children rather than a daily occurrence. There are non-human races in Constantinople, but they are unusual rather than commonplace – people will stare should a dog-headed man walk down the Mese Odos, for example.

In a game where supernatural magic does not exist, all these things lapse into the realm of superstition. The inhabitants of Constantinople still visit witches and alchemists, but their business is a combination of fakery and pharmacy. The non-human races are reduced to tall tales brought back by travellers, and sorcerers confined to the pages of fairy tales.

If you want to make Mythic Constantinople even *more* mythic, then once again you will need to make a few adjustments. A game like this might have nearby nations populated by non-humans – perhaps Crete has a native populace of minotauroi, for example – and Folk Magic a common tool rather than a rare gift. In a high magic game, the Evil Eye becomes a real threat, causing ill luck and disease with just an envious glance.

TERMINOLOGY

There is a bewildering mess of terminology in fifteenth century Constantinople. Contemporary inhabitants of the city think of "Greeks" as Ancient Greeks, calling themselves *Rhomanoi* ("Romans") and their empire as the Empire of the Romans. However, these designations can be confusing for the modern reader so this book will refer to the Byzantine Empire and Greek culture in defiance of contemporary usage but in common with most modern source material.

Another potential point of confusion is the contemporary term for the people of Western Europe, who are collectively called Franks or Latins by the Byzantines regardless of their ethnic origin. Since the focus of this book is on the Byzantine culture, in this case contemporary usage will be adopted except where it is necessary to make a distinction.

Finally, the difference between culture and ethnicity is worth bringing up. Due to the diversity of the Eastern Mediterranean combined with historical and recent conquests, these two categories can be confusing. A Bulgarian might be ethnically a Slav, culturally Byzantine, but also a subject of the Ottoman Empire. Similar confusion happens on many of the Greek islands, where the Byzantine Greek inhabitants are ruled by Franks; and in the Mameluk Sultanate where the ruling caste is ethnically Turkic but culturally Egyptian.

PRONUNCIATION

Where possible, Greek terms have been used in preference to Latin ones, reflecting the language of the Empire in the fifteenth century.

PLURALISATION

Greek grammar is complex, and the pluralisation of words is not always straightforward. The most common plurals in medieval Greek are as follows:

- *~a* > *~ai*; except where neuter, then *~a* > *~ata*
- *~e* > *~ai*
- *~es* > *~es* (a change from a short 'e' to a long 'e')
- *~on* > *~a* or *~ontes*
- *~os* > *~oi*

PRONUNCIATION OF GREEK

The conventional transliteration of medieval Greek words into Latin script does not always represent Byzantine pronunciation. The following is meant as a rough guide only; ultimately it does not matter how you pronounce a word as long as you can make yourself understood!

- *i*, *oi*, and final *-e* are all pronounced like *ee* in tree
- *-es* at the end of Greek words is pronounced as *ace* in pace, except in plural forms where it is pronounced as *ess* in less
- *au* and *eu* are pronounced respectively as *af* and *ef*
- *b* is pronounced as *v*
- *c* is pronounced as *k*, never as *s*
- *ch* is pronounced as in the Scottish loch
- *d* is pronounced as *th* in then
- *g* between two vowels is pronounced as the *y* in mayor; but otherwise is always as in *goat*, never as in ginger.
- *h* at the beginning of words is silent and sometimes written as an apostrophe
- *rh* is pronounced as *r*.

As a rule, Greek stresses the second to last syllable, or the third to last for longer words.

PRONUNCIATION OF TURKISH

Fifteenth century Turkish is written using the Arabic script. It has been translated into modern Turkish orthography, which has some letters with specific pronunciations. All vowels are short unless indicated otherwise.

- *ö* is pronounced as *e* in learn
- *ü* is pronounced as *e* in new
- *c* is pronounced as *j* in judge
- *ç* is pronounced as *ch* in church
- *g* is pronounced as *g* in goat, never as in ginger
- *ğ* between two vowels puts a *y* or a *w* sound between them but glides the syllables together.
- *ğ* following a vowel lengthens the preceding vowel; so *ağ* is pronounced "aah", *eğ* is pronounced "ay", *iğ* is pronounced "ee", *oğ* is pronounced "owe", *uğ* is pronounced "oo".
- *j* is pronounced as *s* in measure
- *ş* is pronounced as *sh* in fish

Turkish tends to stress the last syllable of a word. Long words which are the compound of shorter ones have multiple stressed syllables.

GLOSSARY

Phonetic pronunciation guides for non-English words are given in parentheses. Stressed syllables are given in capitals.

Allagion (all-AY-ee-on, Greek): the basic unit of the Byzantine army, consisting of 300 stratiotai (q.v.) and lead by an allagator.

Azymos (ah-ZIE-moss, Greek): "without yeast", an insult against Catholics who use unleavened bread for Holy Communion, something that the Orthodox Christians find sacrilegious. Anglicised as "azymite".

Demoi (THEM-ee, Greek): the common people, singular demos.

Devşirme (dev-shur-ME, Turkish): a tax laid on Christian communities in Ottoman territory, forcing them to provide young boys for training as *yeniçeris*.

Dynatoi (thy-NAT-ee, Greek): the ruling class, singular dynatos.

Frankokratia: the period 1204–1261 when the Byzantine Empire was under the rule of Frankish warlords. Constantinople was the home of the Emperor of the Latins.

Gavur (djour, Turkish): "infidel", an insult used to describe Christians.

Kabbadion (kav-VATH-ee-on, Greek): A garment worn as court regalia and indicative of high social status in Byzantine society. It is a floor-length robe with fitted sleeves, made of embroidered silk.

Kephale (keh-FAL-ay, Greek): the head of a district, elected from the people who live there.

Logothetes (loh-yoh-THET-ace, Greek): literally "one who calculates", used as a title for several senior ministers of the Byzantine court.

Makellos (mah-KELL-os, Greek): a covered market.

Mesazon (may-SAZZ-on, Greek): the prime minister of the imperial court.

Mese Odos (MESS-ay OTH-os, Greek): the central street that runs through Constantinople. It divides into a northern branch and a southern branch at the Philadelphion, which terminate at the Gate of Charisios and the Golden Gate respectively.

Mesoi (MESS-ee, Greek): the middle class, singular mesos.

Presbyteros (pres-VIE-ter-os, Greek): an Orthodox priest.

Restoration of the Empire, The: reinstatement of the Byzantine Empire in 1261, when it was recaptured from Latin rule by Michael VIII Palaiologos. His dynasty has ruled ever since.

Sack of Constantinople: invasion and pillaging of Constantinople in 1204 by Frankish soldiers, the most part of the army of the Fourth Crusade.

Stratiotes (stra-TEE-oh-tace, Greek): a Byzantine soldier, plural stratiotai.

Theotokos (thee-oh-TOE-kos, Greek): the Virgin Mary; literally meaning "the God-bearer".

Tzykanion (tzi-KAN-ee-on, Greek): a game like polo, played on horseback.

Vardariotes (var-tha-REE-oh-tace): a military regiment that acts as Constantinople's police force, plural Vardariotai.

Yeniçeri (yen-NI-che-REE, Turkish): elite infantry unit of the Ottoman Empire, recruited via the devşirme (q.v.). Anglicised as "Janissary."

DISCLAIMER

This work is a fictional depiction of Constantinople in the fifteenth century. While best attempts have been made to present a historical setting, this book should not be considered an academic work. There are gaps in knowledge on the specifics of life at the end of the Byzantine Empire, and in building a coherent setting the missing details have been either assumed to be the same as a previous era or else details have been invented to fill in the gaps. Accuracy has been sometimes sacrificed for playability, and the focus has very much been on what would be the most entertaining details for a roleplaying game.

Not all anachronisms, omissions, and inaccuracies are deliberate. Some are undoubtedly accidental and the author takes full responsibility for any errors.

BIBLIOGRAPHY

The following sources were useful in writing this book.

Bartusis, Mark C. ***The Late Byzantine Army: Arms and Society 1204–1453***. 1992, University of Pennsylvania Press

Dawson, Timothy. ***By the Emperor's Hand: Military Dress and Court Regalia in the later Roman-Byzantine Empire***. 2015, Frontline Books.

De Clavijo, Ruy Gonzalez. ***Embassy to Tamerlane, 1403–1406***. Translated by Guy le Strange, 2004, Psychology Press

Harris, Jonathan. ***Constantinople: Capitol of Byzantium***. 2007, Continuum Books

Rautman, Marcus. ***Daily Life in the Byzantine Empire***. 2006, Greenwood Press

HISTORY & GEOGRAPHY

O City, City, head of all cities! O City, City, the centre of the four corners of the earth! O City, City, the boast of Christians and the ruin of barbarians! O City, City, second Paradise planted in the West with every tree abundant in spiritual fruits! Paradise, where is your beauty; where is that copious outpouring of graces so salutary for body and soul? ... what tongue can express the calamity which befell the City and the terrible captivity, and the bitter migration she suffered ... Shudder, O Sun! And you too, O Earth, heave a heavy sigh at the utter abandonment by God, the Just Judge, of our generation because of our sins! ~Doukas, from Lesbos after 1453

The aim of this chapter is to present an overview of the history and setting of Constantinople.

HISTORY

According to legend, the settlement that was to become Constantinople was founded by Byzas in 667 BC as a colony of the city-state of Megara. The subsequent history of Constantinople encompasses over two thousand years, and cannot be given a full treatment here; the key points in this timeline are given below. The bibliography (see Chapter One) lists several resources if you want to delve further.

The great Byzantine Calendar, or *etos kosmou*, charts the passing of time since the Creation, which is dated as occurring on the 1st September 5509 years before the Incarnation of Christ, calculated precisely from Scripture. Byzantines therefore list dates as Anno Mundi (Latin: "Year of the World"); although the more familiar BC-AD system is used in this book for the ease of the reader.

330–364: Constantinian Dynasty. Constantine the Great reunites east and western halves of the Roman Empire and makes Byzantion his new capital (330), which is renamed Nova Roma.

364–457: Valentinian Dynasty. The land walls protecting the city are completed (415).

457–527: Leonid Dynasty. Rome falls (476).

527–610: Justinian Dynasty. The Nika Riots (532, page 15) and plague (541) nearly destroy the city. Code of Justinian reforms the law (533).

610–711: Heraclian Dynasty. War with the Persians ends in Byzantine victory (628). Establishment of the Umayyad Caliphate (661).

695–717: Twenty Years Anarchy. First Arab sieges of Constantinople (674, 717).

717–802: Isaurian Dynasty. The First Iconoclasm (730–787, page 31), commencement of the Byzantine-Arab Wars which last 400 years (780–1180).

802–813: Nikephorian Dynasty. Bulgarian War against Khan Krum (811). Concession of territory to Bulgarian Empire (814).

813–867: Amorian Dynasty. Second Iconoclasm (814–842). Macedonian Renaissance – political and legal reform, blossoming of intellectual thought (840s).

867–1057: Macedonian Dynasty. End of the Byzantine-Bulgarian wars (927). The Great Schism (1054, page 31)

1059–1081: Doukas Dynasty. Battle of Manzikert (1071) marks beginning of Byzantine retreat from Anatolia

1081–1185: Komnenian Dynasty. First Crusade (1096). Rivalry with Venice leads to Massacre of the Latins (1182): sixty thousand Franks killed in Constantinople.

1185–1204: Angelid Dynasty. Fourth Crusade is redirected by the Doge of Venice, resulting in the Sack of Constantinople (1204).

1204–1261: Frankokratia. See boxed text on page 8.

1261–present: Palaiologian Dynasty. Restoration of the Empire by General (later Emperor) Michael Palaiologos (1261). Establishment of the Ottoman Empire (1302–1327). The Black Death (1347). Ottomans conquer Adrianople (1362). Crushing defeat for amassed European army at Battle of Nikopolis (1396) results in loss of Bulgaria and Albania to Ottomans. Ottoman Interregnum after Timur the Lame defeats Sultan Bayezid, ending six-year siege of Constantinople (1402). Byzantine Emperor becomes vassal of Sultan Murad II (1422). Council of Florence (1439, page 32). Constantine IX becomes emperor (1448).

THE LAND

If [Constantinople] did not have these vices [i.e. arrogance, treachery, and blasphemy], she would be preferable to all other places because of her temperate climate, rich fertility of soil, and location convenient for propagating the faith.

~ Odo of Deuil, 1147

Constantinople is located at the easternmost corner of the Thracian plain. Thrace is one of the most fertile parts of the Balkans, crossed by numerous rivers and blessed by a warm climate. Cereals, vegetables, and fruit trees grow well here, and in rocky areas olive trees have thrived for thousands of years. Further inland the hills are terraced for grapevines, and higher elevations are used for the rearing of sheep and goats.

Constantinople lies at the eastern end of a broad peninsula bounded by the Sea of Marmara to the south and the Golden Horn to the north. It is separated from Asia Minor by the narrow strait called the Bosphoros, which joins the Black Sea in the north to the Sea of Marmara.

The whole region is prone to earthquakes: since the founding of the city in 330 there have been 56 significant quakes, of which 20 were severe and seven of these (in 437, 557, 740, 869, 989, 1346, and 1354) were disastrous to the city. The earthquake of 869 was particularly noteworthy – it continued for forty days and nights and caused widespread damage including the destruction of many buildings and the partial collapse of the Hagia Sophia.

CLIMATE

Due to its topology and location, Constantinople has two microclimates. The south of the city on the Sea of Marmara is warm and dry, with an average yearly temperature of 15°C (reaching average highs of 28°C in the summer and dropping to 7°C in January). In the northern half of the city on the Golden Horn temperatures are on average 3°C cooler and humidity is higher (approaching 80% on most days). Extreme events can add 15°C to the hottest summer temperatures and subtract the same from the lowest winter temperatures.

There is nearly twice as much rain in the north of the city as the south: 130mm per month in the winter, with rain occurring 17 days out of 30; and 30mm per month in the summer, with rain on less than 4 days in the month. The high humidity in the north makes fogs rolling in from the Golden Horn a common phenomenon in the autumn and winter. Cold winds from the northwest are balanced by warmer winds from the south, and in the spring these winds can blow on the same day, leading to unsettled conditions.

THE SEA OF MARMARA

An inland sea, separated from the Black Sea by the Bosphoros straits and from the Aegean Sea by the Dardanelles straits. The sea gets its name from its largest island, which is rich in marble (Greek marmaron). An older name for the sea is Propontis, literally "before the Pontos" (i.e. the Black Sea). Several large rivers from both Asia and Europe empty into the Sea of Marmara, which reduce its salinity by about a third.

As well as Marmara Island, there are several other islands of reasonable size, including the Princes' archipelago.

THE BOSPHOROS

The strait takes its name (meaning "cattle strait") from the myth of Io, a titaness who was transformed into a cow and cursed to wander the earth until she crossed the strait. Zeus transformed her back to her natural form, and she became the ancestress of Heracles. The strait is 31 kilometres long and varies from 700 metres to 3420 metres wide. The Clashing Rocks (*Symplegades*) once occupied the hilltops at the narrowest point; they would roll down the hillside and crash between them any ship that attempted the passage. When

THE FRANKOKRATIA

One of the most significant historical events for Byzantium is the Sack of Constantinople and the subsequent conquest of the Byzantine Empire by western lords. The tragic series of events is rooted in the ambitions of the Angelid emperors. In 1195 Alexios III Angelos blinded his brother Isaac II and deposed him as emperor. The future Alexios IV (son of Isaac II) petitioned the Pope for aid against his uncle, offering a huge sum of money plus the submission of the Orthodox Church to Catholicism for aid against the emperor. Meanwhile, the proposed Fourth Crusade to attack Egypt stalled at Venice, because the crusaders could not afford the Venetian fee for transport to the Holy Land. The Doge of Venice suggested a compromise: if the Crusaders go to Constantinople first to collect the money promised by Alexios IV, they could then afford to repay Venice for getting them to the Holy Land.

As the crusading army approached Constantinople late in 1203, Alexios III fled. Isaac II and Alexios IV were incapable of paying the promised funds, and when riots broke out in the city, father and son were both killed. The Crusaders breached the walls of Constantinople in early 1204 and massacred the population, killing perhaps a hundred thousand people, a third of the city's inhabitants. The bodies were piled high in the streets and fires wrecked untold damage to properties. The Crusaders entered the richly decorated churches of the city and stripped them of everything they could sell. Statues were looted from public squares, and they even pulled gilded tiles off the roofs of the palaces.

The Crusade to the Holy Land forgotten, the crusader lords divided up the Byzantine Empire between themselves. The new Latin Emperor was given direct control of one quarter of the Byzantine territory including Thrace and Bithynia, with three eighths going to the Republic of Venice (including three-eighths of Constantinople itself), and the remaining two eighths divided amongst the other parties of the Fourth Crusade. Three Byzantine successor states arose from the ruins of their empire: the remaining Angeloi claimed the Despotate of Epiros while Theororos Laskaris was proclaimed Emperor of Nicaea. The Komnenos family established the Empire of Trebizond in the far east.

It is Nicaea that proved the downfall of the usurping Franks. In 1246 this Anatolian empire recovered Thrace, Macedonia, and Thessaloniki, and in 1259 at the Battle of Pelagonia, Empire of Nicaea defeated the coalition formed of Epiros, Sicily, and Achaea, paving the way for the recovery of the Empire. General Michael Palaiologos, who masterminded Pelagonia as well as several other decisive battles, seized the throne of Nicaea from the underage Laskaris emperor, and, with the help of Genoa, retook Constantinople and the Empire in 1261.

Jason escaped them on his quest for the Golden Fleece they became fixed in place, opening up the Bosphoros from then on.

THE GOLDEN HORN

The *Chrysokeras* or Golden Horn is a major inlet of the European side of the Bosphoros at the point where it meets the Sea of Marmara. Between them the three water bodies form the peninsula upon which Constantinople sits. At its mouth, the Golden Horn is 750 metres wide and reaches 7½ kilometres inland, where two rivers (Cydaris and Barbysis) empty into its northern end.

SHAPE OF THE CITY

This section gives the reader an overview of Constantinople. Games Masters will find more information in the *Constantinople in Detail* chapter about specific places and people.

THE SEVEN HILLS

Like many cities of the ancient world, Constantinople is built on seven hills. The first hill faces the Bosphoros, and has the steepest slope despite being only 40m above sea level. The second and third hills form the bulk of the commercial districts of the city and provide natural boundaries to the administrative districts. The remaining four hills form the sides of the Lycos valley, with the seventh hill forming its southern border and the remaining three hills – the tallest of the seven at 70 metres – to the north.

WATER SUPPLY

The natural supply of fresh water to Constantinople is limited to the small River Lykos, which runs down the central valley north of the seventh hill and empties ultimately into the Eleutherion. From the point that it passes into the bottom of the valley, the river plunges into an underground culvert and travels beneath the Forum of the Ox. There are also some small springs, most prominently in the suburb of Pege (see page 187) and the Church of Saint Mary of Blachernai. None of these sources of water are anywhere near sufficient to support the needs of the city, and in the summer months when there is often no rain for weeks, life in the city would have been untenable without a remarkable feat of Roman engineering.

The Emperor Hadrian began the process of supplying the city with water by building an aqueduct originating 16 kilometres northwest. After extensive improvements from successive emperors, there is now nearly 250 kilometres of underground pipes and complex hydrological mechanisms to the west of the city that feed into Hadrian's Aqueduct and bringing water into Constantinople at the Gate of Charisios. From here it flows into a pipeline, where the excess is stored in the Cistern of Aetios in Petrion and the rest is conducted further into the city via the Valens aqueduct between the fourth and third hills. From thence the water goes into underground pipes, which feed the municipal water supply. Excess water and rainfall is collected in buried cisterns and open air tanks throughout the city.

The system built by the Roman engineers provides high-pressure water to all parts of the city through gravity-fed plumbing. The pipes are made of terracotta and lead, and they run beneath the roads and pavements of the city. There are settling tanks at critical places for the removal of sediment, and manual valves which allow water officers to control the flow of the water to monumental fountains and to flush drains and sewers. Throughout the city are small fountains with basins that provide the daily water of most of the inhabitants, with some richer properties having a personal supply. Responsibility for maintenance and repair comes under the budget of the General Fisc (see page 106), putting them at odds with the Chancellery which controls city governance. When these two squabble about jurisdiction, a whole neighbourhood can be left without a water supply.

THE MANY NAMES OF CONSTANTINOPLE

The original Thracian settlement was called Lygos, which then became Byzantion under the Megarans, Augusta Antonina under the Romans, and then Nova Roma when it became capitol of the Roman Empire. The name Constantinople (or more properly Konstantinoupolis, the City of Constantine) started to be used in the fifth century and has persisted for over a thousand years.

Constantinople also has plenty of epithets. Most common amongst these are Basileouousa (Queen of Cities), Megalopolis (Great City), or just he polis "The City". It is also known as Chrysopolis (the Golden City), Theophylakteopolis (the God-Guarded City), Theotokopolis (City of the Theotokos), and Ateleutopolis (the Immortal City). Other names include New Jerusalem, The Leader of Faith, The Guide of Orthodoxy, and The Eye of the World.

The Norsemen call it Miklagarðr (Great City), the Arabs Rumiyyat al-kubra (Great City of the Romans), and the Persians Tahkt-e Rhum (Throne of the Romans). Constantinople is Tsargrad (City of the Emperor) to the Rus'; whereas the Ottomans call it simply Konstantiniyye, but also Kizil Elma or "the Red Apple" in Turkish.

ARCHITECTURAL FEATURES

Constantinople is an eclectic mixture of architectural styles. The oldest buildings are to the east, and the city gradually spread west as the city expanded, reaching its maximum extent some time in the sixth century. However, riots, invasions, fires, and earthquakes have destroyed parts of the city to a greater or lesser extent, and new buildings have been built amongst the old following these destructive events. There are still buildings standing that are over a thousand years old, but few that are younger than a century old – there has not been a sufficient budget for urban improvement since the civil wars.

TENEMENTS & HOUSES

Constantinople is crowded with residences but not by people; many buildings lay vacant since the city, at one time holding over a million people, now holds barely a twelfth of that. Many residences at the periphery of the commercial districts have long crumbled and become overgrown. Competition for inner city houses can be fierce since these are better maintained than others, but even the most crowded residences are in desperate need of repair.

Most of the population live in tenement buildings rather than houses. These are typically two or three-storey high buildings (sometimes higher), square in nature and built around a central courtyard.

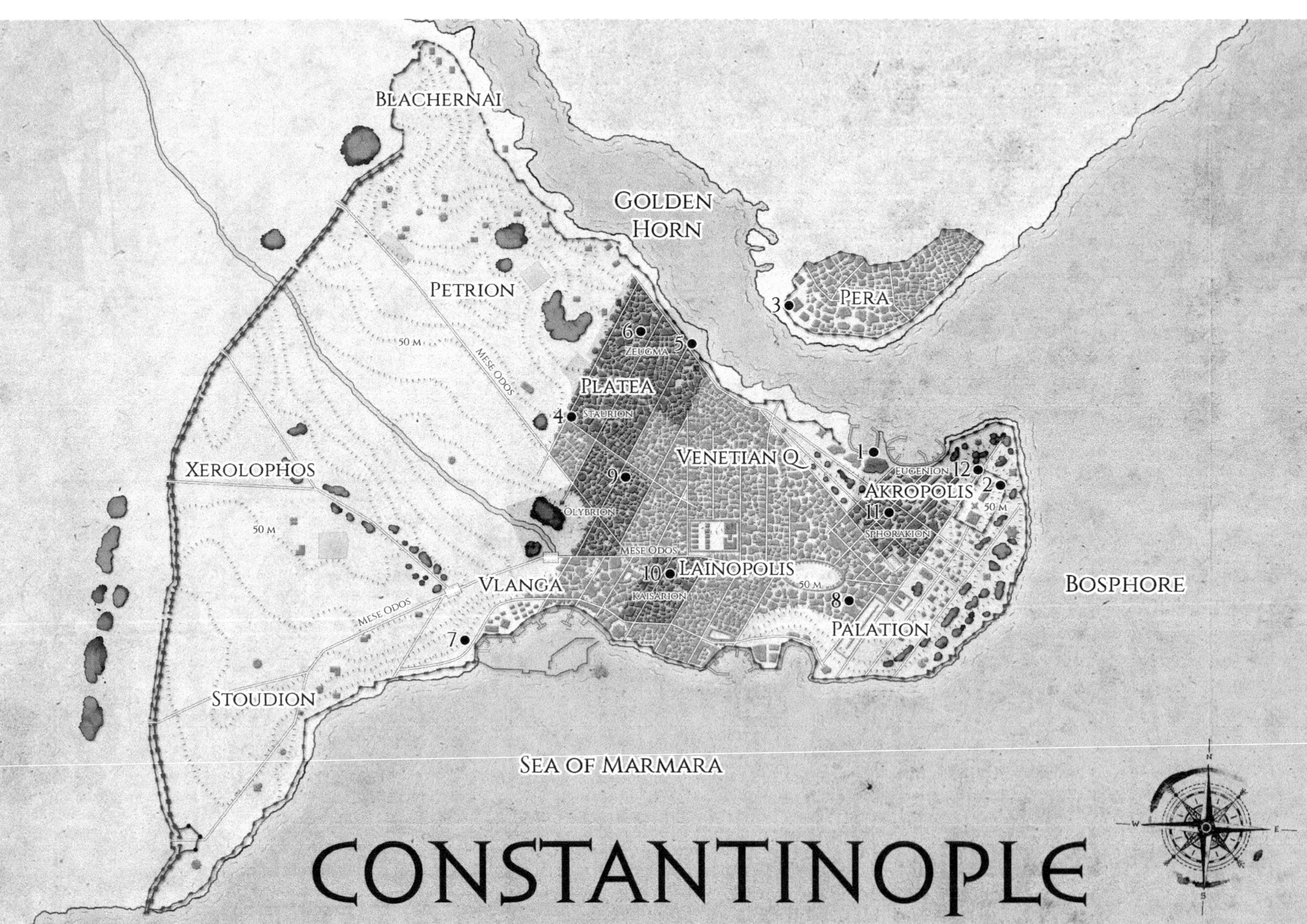
Blachernai
Golden Horn
Pera
3
Petrion
50 m
Mese Odos
6
Zeugma
5
Platea
4
Staurion
Venetian Q.
1
12
Eugenion
2
Akropolis
Xerolophos
9
Olybrion
11
50 m
Sphorakion
50 m
Mese Odos
10
Lainopolis
50 m
Vlanga
Kaisarion
8
Bosphore
Mese Odos
7
Palation
Stoudion
Sea of Marmara
N
W
E
S
Constantinople

Each tenement building is split into up to four to six separate residences. The central court has a sturdy door separating it from the street, and is paved with stone. There may be a covered portico on one or more sides of the court. The tenements are made of mortared brick and stone, with timber roofs covered in pottery tiles. Each residence within the tenement is divided into small rooms by moveable screens and curtains. These are used for storage and for sleeping, and for dining during the winter; the courtyard being the site of most daily activity of the home. Water is supplied from a public fountain, or if the residents are lucky, from a nearby cistern or even the municipal water supply. There is a latrine flushed by roof drains into the public sewer, although these are not reliable in the summer when there is a lack of rain. The tenement buildings are located close to one another with only narrow alleyways in between.

The houses of the rich are found amongst the tenements of the not-so-rich. In Palation (see page 149), all the homes are villas or palaces; everywhere else has a mixture of residence types. That is not to say that the wealthy do not have preferences regarding location; their houses are typically found on the warmer south-facing slopes of the hills, terraced residences with balconies where they can overlook the Marmara. Richer houses are accompanied by substantial gardens, and always have their own water supply. The richest of all houses are set back from the streets behind high walls of stone. Through the gateway will be a courtyard crowded with statues and fountains, with exotic plants and trees providing shade and points of interest. Elite residences have a private chapel, typically decorated with an icon and a jewel-encrusted reliquary.

Large houses can also be found on the busiest streets of the city. The ground floor is a public area and the upper storeys private. The ground floor may be a shop for a middle class family, or else a reception hall for the nobility. Again, the houses are arranged around square courtyards, although in these homes all the buildings around the courtyard form a single residence. Security is an ever-present issue; these houses have bars for the windows and doors, and there is always a porter employed to guard the lower floor at night. Houses of the wealthy always have their own water supply from a fountain or cistern, and usually private latrines. Inside, the walls are coated with plaster and have decorative tiles pressed into them.

STREETS & PORTICOES

Constantinople has well-maintained streets since the city would grind to a halt if merchants could not gain access to the marketplaces. The roads and streets of the city were planned as Constantinople expanded, and as a rule they run parallel to one another or cross at right angles. They tend to terminate at one of the gates in the defensive walls.

The main thoroughfare is the Mese Odos, which runs from the heart of the Palation District westwards through the heart of the city. Throughout the stretch between the Milion and the Philadelphion, the Mese Odos is lined with slabs of gleaming white marble, although where recent repairs have taken place the street has been patched with plain stone. At its midpoint, the Mese Odos is crossed by the Makros Embolos, another cardinal street, which joins the city's two harbours north and south. On both sides of the Mese and the Embolos arise porticoes, covered sidewalks with their roofs supported by rows of columns. These porticoes provide much-needed shade in the summer. The shops that line the main city roads open into these porticoes, which are one of the most distinctive features of Constantinople. The sidewalks beneath the porticoes are paved with marble or mosaics, which have to be maintained by the shop-owners and often advertise the wares for sale inside. By city ordinance, these streets and other key thoroughfares have a minimum width of 12 feet (3.6 metres), and shopkeepers are not permitted to clutter the sidewalks or streets. Underground sewers deal with waste, keeping these streets clean. At night, they are lit by oil lamps outside the numerous taverns, and patrolled by the city watch.

A network of other streets and alleys reach into the neighbourhoods from the main streets. These tend to be irregular winding paths that follow the dictate of the uneven terrain. Many are unpaved, and may suddenly jink to one side or have steep steps cut out of the bare rock. These streets tend to be dark and cramped, overshadowed by the tall tenement buildings and choked with rubbish and waste.

POPULATION

The city boasted a million inhabitants in the 500s, but was riven by plague and war in the centuries that followed. The population was devastated during the Frankokratia, and has never recovered to its former dizzy heights.

350: 300,000
450: 250,000
550: 1,000,000
650: 350,000
750: 125,000
850: 500,000
950: 800,000
1050: 500,000
1150: 250,000
1250: 30,000
1350: 50,000
1450: 70,000

FORUMS & MONUMENTS

In phases of the planning of the city, provisions have been made for public meeting places at the intersection of important streets. Small plazas exist throughout the city, often marked by a fountain or statue. There are also several large public forums on the main streets. The Mese Odos passes through five of these: from east to west they are the Augustaion, the Forum of Constantine, The Forum of Theodosios, the Forum of the Ox, and the Forum of Arkadios. There are several other forums on other streets. Each of these forums is an important public space, serving as market places and commercial hubs. Porticoes line the forum edges and have all manner of specialist shops, often selling wares under Imperial monopoly.

These forums were originally planned as public demonstrations of the Empire's might, decorated with triumphal arches marking military successes, and columns and statues of famous emperors and their families. Some of these structures are still standing, but many have not been repaired from when they were damaged in one of the many disasters that have hit the city. One of the worst such disasters was the Sack of Constantinople, when Frankish crusaders pulled down many of the monuments and stole hundreds of statues to decorate their cities back west.

FORTIFICATIONS

The various walls of Constantinople are a testament to its growth. Starting from the eastern end of the city, the original wall of Byzantion surrounds just the first hill and defines the Akropolis district. Further west are the Severan Walls, built as part of the restoration of the city by Septimus Severus after 196 AD. Very little of these walls still exist since they cut straight through one of the fastest growing and commercially important part of Constantinople. The Constantinian Wall, built by the city's founder, is nearly 3 kilometres west of the Severan Walls. They consist of a single 7-metre tall wall with towers at regular intervals. There are five gates, stationed at the wall's termini and guarding the three main roads. The two gates at either end of the Constantinian wall have been integrated into the two sea walls; the other three gates all still stand, but only the Old Golden Gate is still functional as a defensive structure. The others were ruined in the earthquakes of 437 and 447.

The primary defence of the city is left to the mighty Theodosian Walls. These walls stretch nearly 6 kilometres from the shores of the Golden Horn to the Marmaran Sea, built initially as a response to the threat from the Goth tribes who had attacked along the Danube valley in the fifth century. They were never tested against the Goths, but have proved invaluable in saving Constantinople from at least seventeen separate sieges before the Latin assault in 1204 finally breached their defences. They have since been repaired, but it remains to be seen whether the skills of the fifteenth century masons is the equal of the Roman engineers. Approaching from the west, an invading army is first met by a stone-lined moat some 20m wide. Beyond that are the first line of walls, 9 metres tall. After another 20-metre gap are the second set of walls, this time 12 metres tall and over 5 metres thick at the base. Both sets of walls are protected by more than ninety stone towers constructed from alternating bands of red bricks and limestone blocks. The Theodosian Walls have six main gates and four minor portals, each one guarded by a colossal castle-like gate. An extension of the inner wall surrounds the royal suburb of Blachernai, which wasn't present when the walls were first built.

The Theodosian Walls are continuous with the Propontis Walls, which line the Marmaran shore, and the Blachernai extension joins up with the Golden Horn Walls that guard the city from the north. The Sea Walls were built at about the same time as the Theodosian Walls, and were planned by the same architect. The Sea Walls have been repaired and strengthened since their breach during the Sack of Constantinople. The Propontis Walls were built almost on the shoreline, with the exception of the harbours and quays, they stand at 12–15 metres tall and have a total length of 8.5 kilometres. There are 13 gates and 188 towers, and the Eleutherion Harbour has an additional kilometre of inner wall. The Propontis Walls are as much a defence from the sea as they are defences from attacks by sea: the walls extend underwater with reinforcements against storms. The Golden Horn Wall covers 5.6 kilometres of shore from Blachernai to Saint Demetrios's Cape, with 14 gates and 110 towers. Unlike the Propontis Walls, the Golden Horn Walls stand some 100 metres from the shore. The wall is 10 metres tall and topped with another 2 metres of wooden barricades for the easternmost third.

The Sea Walls are not Constantinople's only defences from a seaward attack. The strong currents of the Marmaran coast prevent the easy landing of ships from the south. The harbours of the Golden Horn are far more sheltered, for this reason a heavy chain across the mouth of the estuary was installed in the eighth century, fastened to the Tower of Eugenios in the Akropolis district and to the Kastellion in the suburb of Pera (see page 157) on the north shore. This chain can be lowered to allow ships to use the harbours, and raised under the threat of invasion.

65 kilometres to the west of Constantinople is another set of land walls commenced by Emperor Anastasios. The Long Walls of Thrace are 56 kilometres long and run from the shore of the Black Sea to the shore of the Sea of Marmara. Although in a poor state of repair, there are many sections of this wall still standing, and the gaps can be defended by a large enough force. In a similar manner to the Theodosian Walls, the Long Walls have a deep outer ditch, a low forward wall, and a taller main wall. There are semi-circular towers every 45–120 metres (depending on terrain), with supporting forts near the main roads.

THE GIRDLE OF THE THEOTOKOS

The persistence of the Land Walls and Sea Walls of Constantinople is not entirely down to the ingenuity of the architects and masons that conceived them. The first recorded vision of the Blessed Virgin Mary on the Walls of Constantinople occurred during an attack by the Avars in 626. Since then she has been seen several times, most recently during the Ottoman siege of 1422. This vision is a manifestation of an Intensity 16 Fortify miracle, presumably cast by the divine spirit of the Theotokos herself. The Inner Walls and every building within 160 metres have 16 additional Armour Points with which to resist damage, and the Intensity of any offensive spell targeting these buildings is reduced by 16. Damage does occur; for example, earthquakes have weakened the mesoteichion ("middle wall" across the Lykos Valley). The miracle allows repairs and upgrades to be made to the gates if done under the orders backed by an imperial mandate, but work must be done in stages to ensure the defences are always continuous, since if a section of the Walls is ever reduced to 0 Hit Points, the miracle will cease immediately.

THE NINE DISTRICTS

Mythic Constantinople is divided into nine main districts. Each district has a kephale (head), a representative of the inhabitants who reports to the praitor, who is in charge of the governance of the city as a whole. In theory, each kephale is elected to lead his community, but in practice this position is generally a result of corruption or politics.

AKROPOLIS

The "old town" consists of the buildings built amongst the ruins of Byzantion. It is a curious mix of ancient and modern: atop the first hill are the remains of the pagan temples of the ancient Greeks who founded the city over two thousand years ago, yet on the Bosphoros shore are the gun foundries and powder factories, which are truly a sign of the current era.

KAINOPOLIS

"New town" is still one of the oldest parts of the city; it was only new when Constantinople became the capital of the Roman Empire.

Still, the name stuck. Kainopolis is the main mercantile district of the city; it is centred around the Mese Odos and takes in most of the workshops and markets. Kainopolis is one of the most crowded parts of Constantinople.

PALATION

In contrast to the noise and bustle of Kainopolis, the Palation district is quiet and serene. This was not always the case; before the Fourth Crusade, the Palation was the centre of the city and the heart of the Empire. The Emperor lived and reigned from the Great Palace in this district (from whence the name), and it is home to the hippodrome and the sports' field. Now, Palation has been left to the bureaucrats; the emperor has moved to the suburb of Blachernai, leaving his courtiers to scheme in the empty corridors of the Great Palace.

PETRION

Famous for its beacon, Petrion is nestled in the shadow of the Fifth and Sixth Hills, and is a middle class residential area. The slopes of the hills are dotted with a huge concentration of monasteries and churches.

PLATEA

"The Flats" lie between the Fourth and Third Hills. This is a crowded commercial district with densely packed tenements vying for space with workshops and markets. Platea has no natural or artificial water supply, since all the springs were redirected into the aqueduct, which is the most distinctive feature of Platea.

STOUDION

Stoudion is mostly given over to the military – most of the regular army is billeted in the houses of the district. This brings them into conflict with the church, since two of Constantinople's most influential monasteries are located in this quarter.

THE VENETIAN QUARTER

More properly called Perama, but nobody calls it that. During the Frankokratia, this district was taken over by the Venetians as their three-eighths of the city. It was surrounded with a wall and there was a great deal of new construction in the Venetian style. It was abandoned after the Restoration, but has gradually become occupied again, mostly with Gasmouli (people of mixed Frankish and Greek origin), who are not welcome elsewhere. It is more common to hear the Venetian language here than it is Greek.

VLANGA

This is the main industrial district; all trades requiring space were relocated here in the 10th century. It is also the main port for fish and livestock, and is home to a ghetto of Romaniote Jews who are mostly involved in tanning hides. All these trades have led to the "Vlanga Stench" which clings to one's clothes for days after merely passing through. Crime is rife here, an odd contrast with some of the richest homes in the city which overlook the sea from their hillside perches.

XEROLOPHOS

Consisting of four villages rather than a single district, Xerolophos is mostly given over to agriculture. The vast fields of Triton grow grain for the city, while the orchards of Olympion supply it with fruit and oil. Paradeison is an English enclave, occupied by the families of the Varangian Guard. Finally, Elebichon is a hotbed of religious sedition. The Lykos Valley, which separates the Seventh Hill from the rest of the city, is famous for its *Kynokephaloi*, although these dog-headed men do their best to stay out of the way of humans.

THE SUBURBS

There are also two suburbs of Constantinople. These don't count as districts, since they are not administered by the praitor of the city but instead are governed separately.

BLACHERNAI

The royal suburb is a comparative recent addition to Constantinople. Since the Restoration of the Empire, Blachernai has been the home to the emperor and his family. By making this move they have divorced themselves from the politics of the court, and lack of imperial supervision has perhaps lead to the proliferation of the governmental departments and the internecine struggle for precedence and power.

PERA

An independent Genoan city ruled by a podestà with no formal ties to the Byzantine Empire, Pera has nevertheless remained a strong supporter of Constantinople. It is a thriving mercantile hub; despite being a fraction of the size of Constantinople, its international trade greatly exceeds that of its much larger neighbour, mostly due to the Black Sea slave trade, which brings wealth to Pera's magnates.

BYZANTINE CULTURE

The Greek inhabitants are very rich in gold and precious stones, and they go clothed in garments of silk and with gold embroidery, and they ride horses, and look like princes. Indeed, the land is very rich in all cloth stuffs, and in bread, meat and wine. Wealth like that of Constantinople is not to be found in the whole world. Here also are men learned in all the books of the Greeks, and they eat and drink every man under his vine and fig tree.

~Benjamin of Tudela, c.1170

In this chapter you'll find information on what it means to be a Byzantine Greek in Mythic Constantinople. The focus is very much on the culture of The City itself, but then there is precious little else of the Empire in the mid-fifteenth century.

THE PEOPLE

In the origin myth of the Greek people, Zeus decided to wipe out the first created race with a great flood. Only one man, Deukalion and his wife, Pyrrha survived. They had a son Hellen, whose three sons were the ancestors of the four ancient tribes of Greece. Aeolus was progenitor of the Aeolians (or Pelasgians), who occupied Thessaly and Aeolia in northern Asia Minor. Dorus gave rise to the Dorians, who were centred on the Peloponnese and conquered Epiros. The third brother Xuthus was father of Achaeus who headed the Achaean tribe of the northern Peloponnese, and Ion who founded the Ionian civilisations on the islands and southern Asia Minor, as well as Euboea and Attica.

The Byzantine people arose from this stock, albeit after nearly three thousand years of interbreeding with the barbarians of Thrace, Macedonia and Illyria, Roman Italics, Coptic Egyptians, and Anatolians. For the most part, they have the olive complexion and dark hair common to Mediterranean peoples, although dark auburn and sun-bleached blond are not uncommon. In temperament, the Platonic cardinal virtues are considered to be the epitome of civilised society and are highly valued by the Greeks; these are restraint (*sophrosyne*), fairness (*dikaiosyne*), courage (*andreia*), and prudence (*phronesis*).

SOCIAL STATUS

Classically, Greek culture was divided in two. The few (*oligoi*, or megaloi "greaters") ruled over the many (*demoi*, or *mikroi* "lessers"), and Aristotle considered this to be the best form of government. These divisions still exist in Byzantine culture, although since the lower class existed mostly in the now non-existent rural communities of the Empire, a middle class (or mesoi) has developed to bridge the gap between. This middle class consists of those who enjoy more wealth and status than the demoi, but who need to work to maintain both.

THE DEMOS

In a political sense the term demos (literally "populace") applies to the largest and poorest sector of the city, those who work for a living. In the past, the demos was one of the three political forces in the city (in addition to the senate and the army), and the approval of the demos was necessary to ratify each new emperor. The Hippodrome was the main meeting point of the demos; here they had the right to freely express their opinion in front of the emperor, a right guaranteed by Constantine the Great. Following the Nika Riots (see "Circus Factions, opposite") the power of the demos was restricted by the emperor, and the political reigns shifted into the hands of the guilds, and thus to the middle class (see below).

Upon the Restoration of the Empire, the Palaiologian emperors re-established the ancient practice of public assemblies. The emperors took to notifying the demos of their plans and asking them for their help, and this process continues today.

Today the lower social strata of the city includes the workers, servants of the aristocracy, fishermen, wandering tradesmen, prostitutes, landworkers, gardeners, and farmers. Refugees form a substantial part of the demos, either descended from those who fled Asia Minor during the Ottoman expansion (1280–1310), or from more recent losses of territory. Another group mostly confined to the poor class are the Gasmouloi, the descendants of mixed marriages between Greeks and Franks during the Frankokratia. By all accounts the Gasmouloi have the zeal and prudence of Greeks and the audacity and impetuousness of the Latins. Two hundred years may have passed since the Restoration, but the memory of the Greeks is longer; and the offspring of miscegenation carry a social taint that has been exacerbated by segregation and propagation of the Gasmouloi.

THE MESOI

The mesoi, or "middle classes" arose in the 11th century during continuing conflicts between the emperor and the aristocracy. Emperors sought to court the men of the marketplace, and bestowed upon them honorary titles to win their support in consolidating imperial power. The mesoi stand between the worker class and the noble families and are characterised by the wealthy business owners and guildsmen. Also amongst the mesoi are the bulk of the civil service, the clerks and petty officials of the machinery of the state. Honorary imperial titles are still moderately common amongst the higher ranks of the mesoi (see page 15).

THE DYNATOI

The dynatoi, or "powerful ones" are members of aristocratic families dating from before the Frankokratia. Upon the empire's Restoration, they were invited back to Constantinople to reoccupy the houses and palaces they owned before the Sack. Membership of the dynatoi is a fluid concept since the class has no official recognition, despite being a powerful political force in the Empire. Descendants of the Palaiologian dynasty and those related to them by marriage certainly fall into this class, and by extension so do the names to which they are related. Ancient and well-attested family names such as Doukas, Komnenos, Angelos, Kantakouzenos, Synadenos, Tarchaneiotes and Tornikes have been joined by the families of those officials who have attracted the emperor's favour, such as the Akropolites, Choumnos, Mouzalones, Metochites, and Rallis. Many of these families maintain the fiction of being provincial governors or military officers, even though the lands to which they pretend have long been in the hands of the enemy, or the units they command have been disbanded. Their rank at court is determined by these hypothetical titles and they still jockey for position and status even though the honorifics are hollow.

Some few noblemen retain the title of autarkes, indicating that they rule in their own right land that has not yet been taken by the Turk, although some will have never actually set foot in their domain. In a previous time, an autarkes ranked highest amongst the dynatoi, and while some of that honour still remains, the majority – who lack land – pretend that it doesn't matter, and commission plays that cast the autarkes as provincial buffoons.

Every dynatos family has an archon, who is the current leader of the family. Being acknowledged as an oikeios of the archon is an important rite of passage for a dynatos male – this confirms one's place in the social hierarchy, legitimises descent, and qualifies one to fight alongside the archon as part of the private household troops. Only acknowledged oikeioi can inherit a portion of the archon's wealth, and it is unknown for a non-oikeios to become archon. Some archontes wield oikeios status as an honour rather than a right, and use it to gain leverage against their families.

The correct form of address for one of the dynatoi is *kyrios* ("lord"), or *kyria* ("lady") for his wife or daughters. This is often shortened to *kyr*, in imitation of the Frankish "Ser", "Sir", or "Herr".

THE PORPHYROGENNETOI

Literally those "born to the purple", the Porphyrogennetoi are the smallest of Mythic Constantinople's social classes, consisting of the Emperor and his closest blood relatives – those who have the potential to become emperor. To be included in this most royal of classes, a person must have been born after his father became emperor and his mother must have been an Augusta. The latter is a title conferred to the legal wives of emperors in a special ceremony, which also grants the empress the right to mint her own coinage, wear imperial regalia, and hold her own court. A Porphyrogennetos must also have been born in the Porphyra, a chamber in the Boukeleon Palace, which is a perfect cube with a pyramidal roof, and veneered entirely with imperial porphyry and bedecked in purple silk.

There are a set of specific court titles that can only be held by a member of this select group.

The title of *Despotes* or Despot is held by the recognised heir to the throne, who is usually brother to the emperor. He is the ruler of the Despotate of Morea, the only remaining part of the Empire outside of Constantinople. By convention the Despotes lives at Mistra in Morea, so if Constantinople should fall the succession does not fail. The term "despot" does not have the modern negative connotation, but instead means something close to "lord".

Sebastokrator ranks directly after Despotes, but is essentially a meaningless title for the third in line to the throne. It is often awarded to other brothers or sons of the emperor.

Kaisar is fourth in importance in the emperor, and the first of the awarded titles. Not a title exclusive to Porphyrogennetoi, the rank of kaisar is conferred on those in great favour, which is often a member of the royal family but not necessarily so. The kaisar is technically

THE CIRCUS FACTIONS

Whether the four circus factions were political institutions first or sporting brotherhoods is unknown, but as well as arranging political rallies amongst their followers, the circus factions also fielded teams of charioteers for the regular races at the Hippodrome. The whole city was divided into four camps according to which faction they supported. The Greens (Prasinoi) were the largest faction: they represented the poorest strata of the city: the farmers, drovers, builders, and labourers. The Greens campaigned for workers' rights, higher wages, the freeing of slaves, social provision of bread, and so forth. The Greens were allied to The Reds (Rousioi) which mostly consisted of soldiers and their families. The Blues (Venetoi) were the principal rivals of The Greens; they represented the business owners and merchant class, who lobbied the emperor for trading rights and monopolies to exclude foreign trade. They were supported by The Whites (Leukoi), who represented the earliest religious brotherhoods who later developed into the trade guilds.

The Nika Riot demonstrated the power of the circus factions. In 532, the demoi were demanding that Justinian pardon two murderers (one Blue, one Green). The emperor held a chariot race to appease them, but commuted the sentence to exile rather than let the criminals go free. The crowd turned ugly, rather than cheering for their teams, they unified under a single chant, "Nika!" ("Win!" or "Conquer"). The crowds broke out of the Hippodrome and rioted throughout the city. Over the next five days half the city was burned or destroyed, and thirty thousand people had been killed.

The importance of the Circus Factions began to wane during the Macedonian Dynasty, when the opinions of the people became less influential in the daily running of the empire. The factions maintained a ceremonial role, which is still seen today in the regulation silks worn by the courtiers; blue and green are never seen together, red still signifies a connection to the armed forces, and white denotes a clerical or financial role.

commander of all the military might of the empire, although these days this is mostly a ceremonial role (and is currently vacant).

Sebastos is a title awarded to junior relatives of the emperor such as his sons and nephews. The female form is sebaste, and is held both by the female blood relatives of the emperor and the wives of the sebastoi.

SLAVERY

The Byzantine Empire was built on the backs of slaves and it is still big business today. Slave ownership in Constantinople is not fashionable due to the campaigns of the Orthodox Church, although it is still common amongst the Venetian and Genoese population, where up to one tenth of the population might be slaves. Throughout the Frankokratia, the Venetians had a stranglehold on the Black Sea slave trade. However, the Genoans were granted these monopolies in exchange for their help in the Restoration of the Empire, and the Republic of Genoa is still the main trader in slaves. According to treaty, Genoese ships are not permitted to bring slaves east of Chios; this does not bar them from trading slaves with the Mamluks and the Ottomans, and in practice the treaty is difficult to enforce. The Black Sea is still the source of most slaves. Slaves brought via this route have many origins: Slavs, Circassians, Serbs, Slovenes, Albanians, Armenians, Mongols, Turks and Turcomans, and Kurds. In theory, slaves must be non-Christian to be legally sold, but included in this definition are heretical versions of Christianity such as Nestorianism. Traders from the Western Mediterranean bring 'Moorish' slaves for sale in the markets of Pera: Berbers and Arabs from North Africa but also other races from beyond the Great Desert.

Although unfashionable, slaves do exist within Constantinople. Some slaves in the city are Greeks who have not been brought from the slave markets but instead have entered into debt bondage. A person willingly indentures himself to an agent, who then pays off the slave's debtors but then owns the person as a slave for a pre-agreed amount of time, which covers the original debt plus the agent's fee and interest, normally coming out to the principal plus one third. Disobedience or laziness results in extension of the indenture. The slave-agent rents out the slave to private individuals or the state in order to recover his costs. Debt-slaves are popular amongst merchants who put them to work on the oar-benches, and this was the main use of all state-employed debt slaves in previous centuries. Another way to avoid a debt is to sell one's own children into slavery – this is illegal, but happens with depressing frequency.

Proponents argue that debt bondage is not slavery, as the person has willingly subordinated himself to the slave-agent. The indenture could end at any time if the slave is able to pay off the debt (and fees, interest, and fines) he owes to the agent. Of course, if the slave had the means to pay his manumission he would have not become indentured in the first place. Some charitable institutions use their benefices to ransom debt-slaves from their agents and set them free.

FOREIGNERS

Constantinople is famous for its cosmopolitan nature. Although the population is mostly Greek, there is a substantial minority population of other races and cultures within its walls.

VENETIANS

Of all the Frankish races, the Venetians are disliked the most by the Greeks. They are still seen as the villains of the Fourth Crusade, manipulating a holy mission in order to destroy Venice's chief trade rival. Due to their role in the Crusade, the Venetians were granted control of a quarter and a half-quarter of the Empire and the same fraction of the city of Constantinople itself. When Michael VIII Palaiologos recaptured the city most of the Franks fled, of those that remained the vengeful population specifically singled out the Venetians, and there were many instances of lynchings. The Venetians returned to Constantinople in 1277 and reoccupied their old quarter, albeit reduced greatly in size.

The Venetian Quarter has its own wall surrounding it, isolating it from the rest of the city. Within that wall, one might as well be in the Serene Republic. The architecture is Venetian, as is the language and the fashions. They even have their own courts under the administration of a bailo who answers to the Doge of Venice, not to the Emperor. For more information, see page 175. The stereotypic Venetian is an avaricious merchant with no morals or conscience, driven solely by profit. Due to the sumptuary laws enacted in Venice and perpetuated in their foreign settlements, most Venetians wear just one or two drab colours of clothing; under these laws more colourful clothing is permitted only to those of higher social status.

GENOANS

In contrast to their rivals, the Genoese inhabitants of Constantinople are treated fairly by native Greeks. The Republic of Genoa has never publically acted against the interests of the Empire, and were not a significant part of the Fourth Crusade. They assisted in the restoration of the Empire and became the heirs to the Venetian trade routes and monopolies.

In 1267 the Genoans moved to Galata on the other side of the Golden Horn, and created their own independent settlement called Pera (see page 157). This caused some friction between the two communities as the Genoans tried to exert influence over Byzantine politics.

OTHER FRANKS

The only sizable contingent of Franks other than Italians permanently resident in Constantinople is the Varangian community of Paradeision, which is mostly English in origin, but has some of Russian and Scandinavian descent. There are no organised communities of other Frankish settlers

JEWS

The Jewish people are spread far and wide through Europe thanks to their diaspora, and several different communities have ended up in Constantinople. There are two Jewish neighbourhoods, and other isolated groups scattered throughout the city. The major Jewish communities in Mythic Constantinople are:

- ***Romaniote Jews*** have lived in the Balkans since Classical times and are the most common Jews in Constantinople. There are significant Romaniote communities in Corfu, Corinth, Patras, Thebes, and Thessaloniki, They speak

Yevanic, a dialect of Greek. They live in a fortified ghetto in Vlanga (see page 178).

- ***The Italkim*** are natives of the Italic city-states, although their origin there extends back as far as the Western Roman Empire. They are a small community, but over-represented in Constantinople in the Venetian Quarter, which has its own Giudecca (Jewish neighbourhood). They speak Veneto.
- ***Ashkenazi Jews*** migrated to Germany and northern France about 500 years ago and since then have spread into eastern kingdoms of Europe. The Ashkenazim speak Yiddish, a dialect of German.
- ***Sephardi Jews*** originate from the Iberian Peninsula, where they predate the Moorish conquest. They speak Ladino, a dialect of Castellano (the principal Spanish language).
- ***Jews originating from Muslim lands*** include the Palestinian, Syrian, and Egyptian communities.

TURKS & ARABS

There has been a mosque in Constantinople since the tenth century, following a request from the Abbasid *caliph* of Baghdad in order to serve Muslim captives brought to the city. Since then, a neighbourhood of Muslims has gathered near the mosque (in the neighbourhood of Leomakellon); this was originally occupied by Arab traders and was vacated during the Frankokratia, but since the restoration has been repopulated by mostly Turkish immigrants.

NON-HUMANS

Not all of Constantinople's foreign inhabitants are human. There are several small communities of other races who have come from exotic lands to the east and the south. Most of these visitors are temporary, consisting of traders and explorers, but the community of Kynokephaloi is a permanent one. These canine-headed men feel at home in this city of dog-lovers, and they have occupied the eastern Lykos Valley where they hunt the deer that live amongst the trees. The other permanent settlement of non-humans are the one-eyed *Arimapsoi* who have become established in the hinterland of Pera in Pegai Krenidai on the northern shore of the Golden Horn. Less frequent sights in Constantinople are the headless *Blemmyae*, the *Minotauroi*, the single-footed *Skiapodes*, and the diminutive fire-spitting *Tripithamoi*. More information on the non-human races of Constantinople can be found on page 56.

MAGIC & SUPERSTITION

Magic is a feature of daily life in Mythic Constantinople. Magical practice falls into three categories: i) protection against adverse forces; ii) manipulation of natural forces, the physical well-being of people, livestock, and crops, human relationships, and supernatural beings; and iii) divination through dream interpretation, looking for patterns in scattered objects, astrology, or gazing into reflective surfaces. Magic is believed to take place via intermediates variously called *stoicheia* ("elements") or *daimones* ("spirits"; *kalodaimones* are good spirits whereas *kakodaimones* are evil ones); and using magic usually requires verbal invocation of these beings, or inscribing their names on amulets or lead sheets. Most neighbourhoods have a witch or herb man who dispenses charms and potions to those willing to pay. Some people make regular visits to a fortune-teller despite the best efforts of the clergy, and the use of amulets to ward illness and bad luck is commonplace. Magic is used by all sectors of society: nobles employ it to try to influence their rivals at court, merchants use it to predict the success of new ventures, and mothers of all social classes use it to protect their babies from demons of disease.

While everyone uses it, most of the magic employed has no actual power – it is mere superstition, herb-lore, and suggestion with no actual supernatural investment behind it. Nevertheless, real magic does exist, and it has been witnessed sufficiently by the people for them to have faith that their superstitions can achieve similar results even if they have no powers of their own. Although most people are familiar with this sort of magic they are still not necessarily comfortable with it, even the subtle manifestation of most Folk Magic.

The populace are even less accepting of overt displays of magic power. A staple of lurid folklore and fireside tales are stories of the witch Circe who turned Odysseus and his men into pigs, or Medea who sacrificed her own children for power. Egyptian sorcerers figure strongly as evil characters in stories, such as Nectanabus, the scheming sire of Alexander the Great who cuckolded Philip of Macedon.

Anyone labelled a sorcerer (Greek *goes*) finds the appellation hard to shake, and while some revel in the supernatural dread it invokes, most find it a nuisance. Note that the common man has no understanding of how magic works and is liable to consider any flashy magic to be sorcery – whether it is Folk Magic (such as Fireblade), an obvious Mystical Talent, a spirit's power, or actual Sorcery.

Christianity teaches that magic is sinful because it leads to other sins. The practice of magic is sinful because it can involve idolatrous acts – indeed, most magic has a pagan origin. Further, if magic eases a person's toil then it can encourage sloth; if it reveals things that are meant to be hidden then this is blasphemous; and if it gives one the ability to do something they should be incapable, then it is questioning God's plan – if He had wanted people to handle hot metal without getting burned or speak directly into another's mind, then He would have given that ability to all without need for spells. These

SPELL CASTING BYZANTINE STYLE

If you want to add some authentic flavour to Folk Magic in Mythic Constantinople, then describe the process of spellcasting based on concepts of Greek magic.

To cast a divinatory spell like Find, the caster should use a mirror or bowl of ink and lapse into a brief trance; or else scatter beans on the ground and examine the patterns they form.

Protective spells such as Avert, Protection, and Spiritshield should involve an amulet hung upon the person or object protected. These items are made in advance and then empowered as the spell is cast.

Manipulation effects also use props, but can take forms other than amulets. These prepared items are inscribed with the name of a stoicheion or spirit. Offensive spells might use figurines or lead sheets covered with symbols, during casting nails are pushed into the prop while invoking malicious spirits. Spells that influence objects (like Bladesharp) use simulacra of the items affected that are bent or crushed during casting. Healing spells take the form of roots or shells tied around the affected body part concerns make most people uneasy around real magic, although only the truly pious reject all "magic" entirely.

Divine magic is the exception to the rule. When exercised by a priest or a monk, any magic is considered to be a miracle. Even without the trappings of the Church, people seem to have an innate sense for the presence of God and the operation of the Holy Spirit, and can recognise it moving through others. Such magic can inspire awe and holy dread at the time, but after the event witnesses will be filled with a sense of wonder, sure that they have seen God's manifest will. This difference is attributed to the *charism*, the gift from God which grants the ability to channel miraculous effects. Possessing Theism is a charism, so too are the gifts given to the Apostles such as the ability to speak in tongues or inspire with a word. More details on charismata can be found on page 77.

THE EVIL EYE

The Evil Eye, or *baskanos*, is a constant threat to health and luck. It is believed that an envious glance and momentary thought of ill-will is sufficient to cause an enduring curse. Children will be dressed in rags or daubed in mud to avoid jealous looks, and one must never praise something too much for fear of accusation of drawing the curse. Many people will employ a charm against the baskanos, which takes the form of an eye crafted in blue glass, and should they catch someone of evil aspect looking their way, a Greek will make the sykon or fig sign – making a fist with the right hand, knuckles downwards, and protruding one's thumb between the index and middle finger – as a ward against ill luck.

As an optional rule, you can give the baskanos a real bite in your campaign. Whenever a target provokes a covetous or malicious Passion in another person, the player of the character making the Passion roll can spend a Magic Point to invoke the Evil Eye. In practice, this expenditure of power is reflexive and unconscious, and is not something that can be caused on purpose. If the target fails a Willpower roll opposed against the Passion, then they suffer a curse. The nature of this curse varies; see the table below. The curse lasts until it is lifted, and the Magic Point does not regenerate until the curse ends. It may be lifted with the casting of the Avert spell, or else with the curser giving an unsolicited gift to the victim.

If a character suspects the laying of the baskanos, they can ward against it with the sykon, which makes the Willpower roll one difficulty grade easier. A character who touches an eye amulet automatically deflects the Evil Eye, but each amulet works only once. Practitioners of Folk Magic learn to control their baskanos; if this optional rule is in place, then everyone with the Folk Magic Skill gains the Curse spell for free, without needing to spend Experience Rolls. Furthermore, anyone with the Folk Magic Skill can figure out a way to remove curses within their magical tradition, allowing them to learn the Avert spell for the normal Experience Roll costs.

Curses

1d10	Curse
1–3	Loss of two Luck Points, and terrible luck where pure chance is a factor
4–5	A fumble occur on any failed Skill roll that is also a double. So with a Skill of 60%, fumbles occur on 66, 77, 88, 99, and 00.
6–7	Lose the Minimum Maintenance Cost (see Mythras, page 55) for your social class every week through a combination of misfortune, theft, and ineptitude.
8	Attract a disease spirit with an Intensity of 1d4-1 (Spirits of Intensity 0 have 1d6 POW and their ailments have no game effects – headaches, coughs, runny noses, etc.)
9	When rolling a certain Skill test, the d100 result is read in the most disadvantageous manner. For example, a roll of 09 is read as 90.
10	Reduce one Characteristic by 1d6 (no lower than the species minimum)

LANGUAGE

Sited as it is at the junction between two continents, there are a lot of different languages spoken in Mythic Constantinople. Greek is the language of the Byzantine Empire, the Aegean and Ionian islands, the southern Balkans and the Peloponnese. It is intelligible with Ancient Greek, although the two languages are distinct from one another. The language spoken by medieval Greeks is a descendant of Koine ("common") Greek, which was imposed by Alexander the Great upon all of his empire. Latin has been replaced by Greek as the language of the imperial bureaucracy, but is widely spoken by the educated; it has the advantage of also being common amongst educated Franks as well.

The Frankish people speak a wide range of languages depending on their origin. The most common languages are English, High German, French, Italian (in north Italy), Veneto (in Venice), and Calabrian (in southern Italy). The three Italian languages are close enough that a speaker of one language can apply a Hard penalty before consulting the Linguistic Fluency table (see Mythras, page 71) when speaking to someone who understands one of the others. The same relationship can be found between Serbian and Bulgarian, both varieties of South Slavonic that have only separated into different languages in the last two hundred years. However, Bulgarian is written using the Cyrillic alphabet whereas Serbian uses the Latin alphabet. The Vlachs have their own language, called Romanian, which is a descendent of Vulgar Latin. The Hungarians speak Magyar.

Turkish is the language of the Ottomans. There are a host of different but mutually-intelligible dialects of Anatolian Turkic, although the dialect spoken by the House of Othman (here called Turkish) is considered the court dialect. A form of Turkic is spoken by the Cuman and Kipchack tribes in the Balkans, this has less commonality with Anatolian Turkic and should take a Hard penalty to determine the degree of intelligibility if two people do not share the same variant. Arabic is the language of Islam, and also the native tongue of the Arab culture. There are several dialects of Arabic, which is spoken from North Africa through Egypt and Arabia and throughout Persia, but they pose no penalties to speakers of different dialects. Khamag Mongol was imposed on the entire empire of Genghis Khan and is still the principal language of its various successor states.

DAILY LIFE IN CONSTANTINOPLE

The daily life of a citizen of the Empire is dependent very much on social class. The majority of peoples still need to work to provide for themselves and their family. Only the upper levels of the mesoi and the dynatoi are rich enough to not have to work, and may spend

their days in leisure. This section details some of the features of the lives of Byzantines.

CLOTHING

The basic item of clothing for all social classes is the *kamision*, a loosely worn draped tunic of undyed wool or linen. It is the sole garment of the lower classes, belted at the waist and with a woollen cloak in the winter months. For the middle and upper classes, the kamision is an under-tunic. The length of a man's kamision (reaching the thighs, knees, shins, or ankles) is usually a good indication of his social status, with the shorter garments being worn by the lower classes because they are cheaper to produce and less constricting for manual work. Unless engaged in heavy labour, men typically also wear trousers (*vrakha*) made of light material with heavier leggings (*touvia*) pulled up over them and fastened to the waistband. Knitted socks are worn with shoes (*tzervoulia*), sandals (*hypodemata*) are also common, often with straps that extend up the calves and bind the touvia close to the leg. A turban (*phakeolion*) is normal headwear if any is worn at all. Lower class women wear an ankle-length himation with fitted sleeves over the kamision; and modesty requires they cover their hair, typically with a folded headscarf called a *savanion*.

As well as a longer kamision, higher status is usually signified by an overtunic called a *delmatikion*. Unlike the kamision, this garment is wider at the bottom, and has fitted sleeves that flare outwards past the elbow. The higher status man might also wear an *epilorikon*, a coat made of cloth brocaded in a tessellated pattern. The epilorikon may be sleeveless or else have under-arm openings. Trousers and leggings are worn as above. Footwear consists of leather shoes or boots, which normally extend to mid-shin (*papoutzia*), but current fashion is knee-high, front-laced, open-toed boots (*mouzakia*). Headwear for the higher status man consists of a fez-like *kausia*, a semiconical cap with a turban wrapped around it, or a skoufia: a headscarf of thick cloth, wrapped around the head in a cylinder then folded backwards and pinned down. An affluent woman wears a kolovion rather than a delmatikion, a sleeved gown made from fine cloth draped over the body and belted at mid-chest height. She also wears a semi-circular cape (*mandyas*). The head is covered by a long wrap or shawl (*velarion*).

Formal dress, worn by the aristocracy at all times and the mesoi if they have a court appointment, consists primarily of a kabbadion, a long belted caftan buttoned up the middle and with fitted sleeves. Over this is worn the *khlamys*, a trapezoidal cloak fastened on the right shoulder and covering the left side of the body. The tablion is a square of cloth sewn onto the khlamys so that it covers the breast; this bears insignia of the person's rank and lineage. The colour and length of the kabbadion, along with the headgear, over-garments, and accessories accompanying it are strictly controlled by court protocol, and it is possible to determine someone's exact rank from their court dress; although differences between two ranks can be as small as the colour of the shoes or whether the baton that the courtier carries has knobs or not. Kabbadia are made of brocaded cloth chosen from a set range of patterns, densely figured in silver or gold on a field of red, green, or blue. Black, white, and purple are reserved for the emperor and his family. Headgear consists chiefly of the conical *skiadion* with a broad brim and the tall *skaranikon*, which is either cylindrical with a domed top or else a truncated cone (like a modern fez). Shoes or boots of soft leather dyed in court-appointed colours are worn on the feet.

Most men keep their hair short in respect for church edicts regarding vanity. Beards are the norm (and indeed mandatory for clergymen), although the only stigma attached to going clean-shaven is the self-same accusation of excessive vanity. Long hair is much admired on women, as long as it is well cared for and hidden from public view with a veil (*maphorion*). Extensions, tints, and perfumed powders are considered vain but employed by some. Attitudes towards personal hygiene have declined since Classical times, although Greeks take baths most weeks and wash daily; they also use soap and hot water to clean themselves, which are both customs that the Franks have yet to adopt. Both sexes may use perfumes to disguise body odours, if they can afford them. Tattoos are worn by convicted criminals, slaves, and barbarians, and expressly forbidden in the Bible; no self-respecting Greek would have one.

Inhabitants of The City do not generally carry weapons unless they are professional soldiers. Such behaviour is unseemly and uncivilised. A Frank might get away with carrying a rapier and dagger, but anything more than this will have the offender reported to the Vardariots (see page 110).

FOOD & DRINK

The diet of the typical citizen of Constantinople is more varied than that of Western Europeans. While wheat forms a substantial part of the menu – as bread, long-lasting wafers (*paximadia*), and porridge (*traganos*) – it is heavily supplemented with rice, beans, lentils, and chickpeas. Bread comes in several qualities depending upon how much you want to pay: clean bread (*artos katharos*) made from carefully sifted wheat, mesoartharos bread from wheat mixed with other grains, and dirty bread (*artos ryparos*) made for the poor from summer wheat, rye, millet, and barley. About a third of the typical energy intake comes from olives and olive oil. Wild-gathered and cultivated greens (cabbage, cress, lettuce, radish, endive, orache, and mangold) are used liberally by the poorer classes, who send their children into the unpopulated areas of the city to gather vegetables run riot from abandoned gardens. Fresh fruit is hard to come by and greatly prized, particularly citrons, pears, and pomegranates. Fish (particularly tuna, bonito, and mackerel) is in abundant supply but most of that landed in the city is intended for export and the lower classes can't afford to buy it. Pale-fleshed species such as bass and turbot are more prized than the darker oily fish. Shellfish is considered a poor man's food and is most often gleaned from the shoreline.

Only the mesoi and dynatoi eat meat with any regularity. Goat, lamb, and chicken are most highly prized, with pork considered fit only for peasants and beef (usually eaten as calves) somewhere in between. For the upper classes, meat is usually cooked with imported spices such as ginger, pepper, cinnamon, cloves, and sumac. Milk products such as cheese and yoghurt are consumed by all, mostly made from goat or sheep milk. Wine is served in all but the poorest households, although quality varies widely. It is usually sweet and heavy, and usually watered to taste. Aristocrats usually serve *konditon*, which is wine flavoured with cinnamon, pepper, and cloves. *Phouska* is wine fortified with spirits and flavoured with fennel, anise, and thyme. It is drunk almost exclusively by the lower classes. Clean fresh water, often boiled with fennel and sage, is drunk throughout the day.

There are two main meals a day: breakfast (*ariston*) eaten mid-morning, and the main meal (*deipnon*) served in the evening. Some people also take an early prophagion at dawn. The Byzantine custom is to have several portions of different prepared dishes rather than a single dish. The Byzantines were amongst the first to have table forks as well as knives and spoons for serving, and their use is still novel to most Franks.

PASTIMES

Visiting the taberna or *phouskarion* is a pastime enjoyed by the lower classes thanks to the state fixing of wine prices. Phouskaria exclusively sell phouska and have a bad reputation as dens of iniquity and prone to violence. Tabernai line the Mese Odos (see page 11) and can be found throughout the back alleys of the city; they are more than just places for drinking, since most tabernai also provide cheap food and provide music for singing and dancing. Some attract customers with plays or mime plays, others operate as brothels, or cock fights.

Tabernai also offer opportunities for gaming and gambling, pastimes of which Byzantines of all classes are very fond. Dice games, knucklebones, checkers, and backgammon are all common games, as is *triodion* (nine men's morris). Chess (*zatrikion*) is popular with the educated classes, imported from Persia in the eleventh century. Unlike modern chess, it is played on a circular board with four rings of sixteen spaces. The game pieces occupy a 4x4 block with the kings and their ministers (i.e. queens) facing each other across the unused centre, with the bishops, knights, and rooks in pairs behind. The pawns guard the two flanks.

Another form of public entertainment are various theatrical performances. Mime shows appeal to the masses; these are retellings of mythological tales danced by characters in grotesque masks. Usually performed accompanied by music, mime shows are redolent with comedy, sexual licentiousness, slapstick, and political satire. Some performing troops enhance their performances with sound and lighting effects, pyrotechnics, water displays, and machinery allowing actors to make flying entrances and sudden disappearances. Religious plays are staged by specialist brotherhoods at the behest of trade guilds. These plays are often thematically linked to the guild through the subject matter or their patron saint, so the Guild of Bakers puts on a play of the Holy Children in the Furnace, and the Moneylender's Guild hosts the Parable of the Talents. Roving bands of illusionists, handlers of exotic animals, acrobats and jugglers, and storytellers roam throughout the Balkans unmolested, making frequent stops at Constantinople to display their acts. The Office of the Drome (page 105) makes frequent use of these performers.

Sporting events are often organised by a given political faction (a guild, deme, or government ministry) wishing to garner support in the city. While these are used as a forum for political rallies, everyone comes for the sport. Horse races are the most popular events of this type, but foot races are also staged. While once famous for chariot racing, this is almost never seen these days. An event inherited from the time of the Frankokratia is *dzoustra* or jousting, which takes place in the Hippodrome. However, the two sports of *Tzykanion* and *Pankration* are by far the most popular in Mythic Constantinople.

TZYKANION

Tzykanion is hugely popular with the aristocracy, a form of polo played from horseback with nets on sticks. Tzykanion is a dangerous sport, routinely ending in injury and occasionally death. The field (or *tzykanisterion*) is typically 300 x 200 metres. The game is played by two teams of four players each, all on horseback and armed with long poles with small nets on the end. The aim is to score points by scooping a small leather-covered ball up in the net then hurling down the field towards the opposing team's goal, a pair of posts at each end of the field.

When the game begins, the players line up in the centre of their half of the field. The ball is then placed on a central hill in the playing field by a dignitary and play begins. Opposing team members attempt to hook out the ball when it is being retrieved from the ground, or else check their opponent's horse with their own to either keep him away from the ball or to disrupt his aim. Fouls are incurred by striking another player with the pole (shoving and punching is not against the rules, but is discouraged), or crossing a player (that is, getting in the way of his horse when he has the ball). A fouling player must ride back to his team's goal and touch both posts with his pole before returning to play. Teams change direction of play every time a goal is scored, and the game continues until nine goals in total have been scored.

PANKRATION

Pankration (meaning "all power") is a sporting event popular amongst the lower classes of Constantinople. It is an empty-handed submission sport with scarcely any rules. Pankratiasts use strikes, holds, throws, chokes, and joint locks in order to make their opponent submit. No move is illegal, although gouging at the eyes or genitals and biting are considered dirty fighting. No weapon may be used, although pankratiasts wear gloves or meilichai made of strips of raw hide tied up the arm and under the palm, leaving the fingers bare. These occasionally have small bronze balls sewn into them. Pankration is fought naked or wearing a loincloth – the latter provides purchase for throws and some prefer to forgo it. Pankration makes no distinction for weight classes, but does have separate matches for men (*andres*) and boys (*paides*).

Pankration is fought in a sand-covered ring called a skamma. There is a referee (*alytarch*), whose sole job is to declare a winner. Submission is signalled by raising an index finger, but a victory can also be gained by unconsciousness or death of an opponent (although deaths are rare). Once a winner has been determined, the referee separates the opponents (with a whip if necessary) to prevent further damage to the loser. Matches are elimination bouts; in each round opponents are randomly paired up by drawing lots from a silver urn with matching letters. If there is an odd number of contestants then one lot is blank and its drawer has a bye (*ephedros*). Match winners continue to fight until the final two-man bout, thus the winner is always undefeated. Winning without being an ephedros (*anephedros*) is more honourable than winning with one or more byes.

A match normally has two phases. The Upper Pankration is fought standing and consists mostly of striking and holds. Often a pankratiast has a favoured move such as striking at the legs, a two-footed kick to the opponent's face, or performing acrobatic flips. Once an opponent is thrown or tripped, then the Lower Pankration begins and the opponents wrestle on the ground until a winner emerges.

PANKRATION FIGHTING STYLE

Pankratiasts have a choice what Combat Style Traits they may choose when taking the Pankration Combat Style (see page 61), representing different fighting styles. Those taking Batter Aside or Unarmed Prowess favour strikes; whereas those taking Mancatcher or Immobilise concentrate on grappling, locking manoeuvres, or choke holds. Those with Take Down and Body Slam rely on throws or body checks to initiate the lower game.

THE CALENDAR

The Byzantine week begins with *Kyriake* (the Lord's day, Sunday), and then proceeds through the numbered days of *Deutera, Trite, Tetarte,* and *Pempte*. Friday is called *Paraskeve* ("preparation"), and Saturday *Sabbaton* ("Sabbath"). Both Sabbaton and Kyriake are days of rest, with markets held on the seventh day and worship occurring on the Lord's day. The lower classes work a six-day week, being unable to afford to rest on Sabbaton as well as Kyriake.

Following the Roman pattern, the secular year begins on 1st January. The pattern of months and their lengths are the same as today, both having been established in the Roman period. The sole difference from modern practice is that for leap years, the 24th February is duplicated rather than adding an extra day at the end of the month. Seven seasons are recognised based on the agrarian cycle:

- *Sporetos* ("sowing") begins on 22nd October;
- *Winter* begins on the 21st December, the winter solstice;
- *Phytalia* ("planting") commences on 5th February, the traditional first day of spring;
- *Spring* begins on the vernal equinox, the 22nd March;
- *Summer* starts on the 9th of May when the Pleiades begin their helical rise in the heavens;
- *Opora* ("harvest") commences on the setting of the constellation of Lyra, traditionally on the 11th August;
- *Autumn* begins on the autumnal equinox, 24th September.

The religious year of the Orthodox Church begins on 1st September. Every day of the liturgical year has a saint's feast associated with it. Wednesdays, Fridays, and Sundays are designated fast days; although typically only clergymen observe the Wednesday fast. Religious holidays are days of fasting and worship; Mass is usually attended at dawn, and sometimes extends throughout the day. Processions and holy plays are also popular.

PASCHA

The feast of Pascha (Easter) is the most important event in the liturgical year, commemorating the Passion of Christ on the Cross. All other festivals are secondary to Pascha, necessary but preliminary. Pascha is preceded by a period of fasting called Great Lent, which commences on Ash Wednesday, 40 days (excluding Sundays) before Pascha. The Church might look the other way at those who do not obey other fast days, but ignoring Great Lent is generally not tolerated. Christians fast by abstaining from fat, meat, and eggs.

They involve themselves in charity work within their parish, and are supposed to spend time in prayer. All entertainments are curtailed along with other non-essential worldly pursuits. Holy Friday is the most austere day of all, and most Christians will maintain a paschal vigil throughout the night, ending at midnight. Easter Saturday commences with paschal matins, and then the fast is ended with a celebratory meal. Easter Sunday is marked by reading a portion of the Gospel of Saint John in as many languages as the congregation can manage.

THE 12 GREAT FEASTS

There are 12 Great Feasts (*Dodekaorton*) throughout the religious year of the Orthodox Church, excluding Pascha itself. These feasts celebrate important stages in the life of Christ and the Theotokos (the Virgin Mary). Three of these feasts are moveable, dependent on timing of Pascha. The remaining nine occur on fixed dates:

- *The Nativity of the Theotokos, 8th September*: celebrates the birth of Mary to her previously-barren parents Joachim and Anna;
- *The Elevation of the Holy Cross, 14th September*: commemorates the recovery of the Holy Cross by the Byzantine Empire from the Persians in 629;
- *The Presentation of the Theotokos, 21st November*: Mary was taken to the Jewish Temple and served there until she was married;
- *The Nativity of the Lord, 25th December*: Christmas, the birth of Christ;
- *The Theophany of the Lord, 6th January*: commemorates the baptism of Jesus by Saint John and the beginning of Christ's earthly ministry;
- *The Presentation of the Lord, 2nd February*: recognition of Jesus as the messiah when he was taken as a baby to the Temple in Jerusalem;
- *The Annunciation, 25th March*: The angel Gabriel announces to Mary that she is to become the mother of God's son;
- *Palm Sunday, the Sunday before Pascha*: The entry of Christ into Jerusalem prior to the Crucifixion;
- *Ascension, 40 days after Pascha*: Christ ascends into Heaven in the presence of his disciples;
- *Pentecost, 50 days after Pascha*: the Holy Spirit descends on the disciples;
- *The Transfiguration, 6th August*: commemorates the visit of Jesus to Mount Tabor where he speaks with Elijah and Moses and his divinity is confirmed;
- *The Dormition of the Theotokos, 15th August*: The death of Mary and her assumption into Heaven three days later.

In preparation for these Great Feasts, there are three lesser Lenten seasons:

- *The Nativity Fast*: 40 days prior to the Nativity (commences 15th November)
- *The Apostle's Fast*: from the second Monday after Pentecost until the Feasts of Saints Peter and Paul on the 29th June.
- *The Dormition Fast*: from the 1st August to the Feast of the Dormition.

OTHER RELIGIOUS FESTIVALS

There are five important feasts that are celebrated as Great Feasts but not one of the Twelve:

- *The Circumcision of the Lord, 1st January*
- *The Nativity of Saint John the Baptist, 24th June*
- *The Feasts of Saint Peter and Paul, 29th June*
- *The Beheading of Saint John the Baptist, 29th August*
- *The Protecting Veil of the Theotokos, 1st October*

Each parish church celebrates the saint's day of its patron in a manner similar to one of the Great Feasts, and each guild has its own patron's day. For example, on the Feast of the Holy Notaries (25th October), the clerks of the court don costumes and perform comedic plays and pantomimes; Saint Agathe's Day on 12th March is celebrated by women involved in the textile trade, and so on.

NON-RELIGIOUS FEASTS

There are a few holidays and feast days which are secular in origin. The Orthodox Church disapproves of most of these events (except the Anniversary), but is not so unwise as to try to abolish them.

- *Calends, 1st to 4th January*: the beginning of the secular year, marked by the donning of costumes and the exchange of gifts.
- *Week before Palm Sunday*: the emperor awards honorific titles, grants of (mostly hypothetical) land, and silk costumes to members of his court, whose salaries are also paid on this day.
- *Anniversary of The City, 11th May*: celebrating the inauguration of the city by Constantine the Great; the celebration consists of a grand procession through the streets plus a day of worship; the following day is a holiday for the citizens marked by great revelry and dancing, with races taking place from dawn to dusk. Court salaries are paid on this day.
- *Thesmophoria: 22nd October*: a festival of sowing, condemned as pagan by the church. Seeds are blessed for a good harvest, and it is an auspicious day upon which to conceive a child.
- *Brumalia, 24th November to 21st December*: the harvest festival originating in the Feast of Dionysos. The high point is the unsealing of the first vintages (Pithiogia, literally "jar-opening"). The period of Brumalia is noted by impromptu processions, masquerades, displays of exotic animals, sporting events such as racing, and of course, drinking. This is in contravention of the Nativity Fast (see earlier), and its observance is a testament to one's piety. Brumalia is a feast for the court and the city alike.

FAMILY LIFE

Families in Constantinople are large, typically consisting of a married couple, three to four children, and an extended family of unmarried sisters of the couple as well as possibly their parents as well. It is not unusual for close family friends to live under the same roof: as adopted godparents of the householders' children, they take a role in raising the children cooperatively.

LIFE EVENTS

Birth is a process fraught with danger. Amongst the urban poor, neonatal mortality can be as high as 10%, and maternal mortality up to 3%. Within a week of birth, a child is baptised and given a name by the priest. It is common for a child to be named for the saint's day on which they were born, but names might also run in families. Despite the best efforts of amulets to ward off child-snatching demons and spirits of sickness, infant mortality before the age of five can be as high as 50%. Boys and girls are treated equally as children, and given toys such as dolls, pull-toys, hoops, board games, and knucklebones to play with. Team games such as monks-and-demons (like the modern cops-and-robbers) are popular on the streets of residential areas. At the age of seven a child is given more responsibility, and expected to put aside more childish pursuits. At this age they can assist their parents in their trade or chores, as well as run errands and shop for food. Most will have begun a basic education (see later), and be able to read, write, and count.

Marriage is not supposed to take place before the bride is 12 years old and the groom 15. A marriage is usually a union arranged by the couple's families and the celebrants often do not get a say in the matter. The bride's parents provide a dowry (*proika*) which is matched by a gift from the groom's family. These gifts become the property of the wife within the marriage, and depending on social status could be coin, livestock, jewellery, land, or property. The marriage is formalised with a wedding ceremony, usually held in front of the community so that there can be no doubt that both parties are willing. The couple clasp hands and exchange jewellery, which is often – but not always – a ring. The couple are then carried back to their new home by their friends and family, and a feast is provided to celebrate the happy day.

Divorce can only be sought on occasion of leprosy, murderous assault, the husband's impotence, the wife's adultery, or the wife's madness. If a couple separates, then the woman is entitled to keep her dowry and any investment it has produced during the marriage. A widow inherits all her husband's property and wealth, but also any debts. Only if there is no surviving spouse do the children inherit their father's wealth.

A death in the family is an occasion dominated by ritual. The eyes of the deceased are closed and the mouth secured shut to prevent the entrance of an evil spirit. The body is laid out on a litter, dressed in his best clothing and posed as if in sleep. The residence is carefully swept out, and branches of evergreen trees are brought in to symbolise the hope of resurrection. The doors of the residence are left open for visitors to come and pay their respects. The end of this lying-in period is signified by the breaking of plates and pots by the household, driving out any evil spirits. Bodies are interred in the ground, and public displays of grief are expected. Women will often shear their hair at the graveside. The grave is visited again by the family on the 3rd, 9th, and 40th day after death.

RESIDENCES

Space is something that is not at a premium in Constantinople. Only one in five of all available residences are occupied, although for every habitable residence there is another two that are uninhabitable due to neglect. Apart from the royal districts (Blachernai and Palation), there is no zoning of residence type, and richly-appointed houses can be found right next to an over-crowded city block.

Wealthy urban families live in spacious houses with running water and rooms set aside specifically for receiving visitors and dining. Poorer citizens must make do with occupying space in a multi-storied tenement, although they may have as much room as they wish. Some of these tenements have been occupied by the same families for hundreds of years, and young people often settle close to their own parents for the convenience of babysitting services. This leads to crowded parts of the urban setting despite there being streets of unoccupied homes elsewhere in the city.

Craftsmen and merchants usually rent small shops which have a residential apartment upstairs.

WOMENS' ROLES

In past centuries, women were consigned to secondary roles, even to the extent that they were kept segregated from visitors to the house and were forbidden to pursue any career. Although true equity is still far off, Byzantine women have a lot more choices available to them than many women of the age. Part of this is due to the differing attitude of religion: the Orthodox Church, unlike the Catholic Church, does not hold woman any more responsible for Original Sin than man. Since the Great Schism (see page 31) there has been a softening of attitudes towards a woman's traditional role, and she is no longer a mere chattel of the householder. Women can be found in most professions, although they are rare in the civil service and still barred from the military and the priesthood (although a woman can be ordained as a deacon). Many women choose to take the traditional role of mother and wife, but even then they have a great deal of control over their own lives, managing the household purse and often running a cottage industry such as spinning or weaving. However, there are no legal impediments from preventing a woman from owning a business, renting property, or manufacturing goods; and many have found jobs in more traditional female roles as teachers and nurses.

SAME SEX RELATIONSHIPS

Same-sex relations are supposed to remain within the bounds of dispassionate friendship or *philia*. Homosexual relationships were tolerated in classical Greek and Roman society but are condemned by the church as sinful. The Orthodox Church does its best to prevent same-sex relations amongst the men and women of its monasteries (with mixed success), but in fifteenth century Constantinople religious opprobrium of homosexuality is routinely ignored. The ceremony of *adelphopoiesis*, once used to acknowledge a formal or ritual brotherhood, has become a means by which a same-sex couple can share a household without legal censure. Furthermore, this arrangement sets out how assets are split upon mutual dissolution of the partnership. Adelphopoiesis grants a degree of legal protection and amongst upper classes is socially acceptable, but the majority of Constantinople's populace still take the Church's view that homosexuality is an immoral act.

CHARITY

As an act of Christian charity, the state operates several institutions which serve basic public needs. Perhaps the most important of these to most people is the production of state bread, which is supplied free every day in exchange for a wooden token. These tokens are issued by parish churches free of charge, but a person is limited to receiving just 20 in any given month, and they are supposed to be non-transferable. This bread is low quality 'dirty bread', but it is sufficient to keep a person alive. It is an offence for anyone other than the state-governed Baker's Guild to manufacture this bread, and it is illegal to charge money for it.

There are several hospitals around the city, including Samsun's Hospital (see page 24) and the one attached to the Pantokrator monastery (see page 169). These houses of healing offer their skills without requesting payment, but rely on donations from those able to afford it. Allied to the hospitals are the hospitals that provide care for the long-term ill, the disabled, mentally infirm, and aged. Separate hospices cater to the needs of lepers.

In the past there were many *xenodochia*, free hostels set aside for the poor who visited Constantinople but had nowhere to stay. However, the expense of restocking and maintaining these hospices has been saved since there are so many unoccupied houses in the city that their service is no longer needed.

The final state-run charitable organisation is the *orphanotropheion*, or orphanage. This is actually a governmental ministry (see page 103), which was instituted on behalf of those children of the nobles left orphaned by warfare but in the current age accepts any children left without a family to care for them. Orphanage children are given a good education and found work placements by the orphanage staff, and is supported financially by former residents who have gone on to be successful merchants, businessmen, or courtiers.

Greeks are very fond of dogs, and the city has an abundance of stray dogs as well as countless pets. They consider it an act of charity to leave unwanted food out for the street dogs and ensure that there is sufficient drinking water for them. Some even specifically cook meals for the dogs, which they distribute each evening at a certain spot. Although it would be verging on heresy to admit it, many citizens consider the dogs of Constantinople to be some form of collective guardian spirit that watches over them.

EDUCATION

There are three tiers of education in the Byzantine Empire. Primary education, or the "school of letters" is concerned with the elementary skill of literacy. This *hiera grammata* consists of reading, writing, and basic grammar. This level of education is offered to all children in Constantinople, and was formerly available in all towns and larger villages of the Empire. This teaching is provided by the parish school operated by the church, and the costs of education is born partly by the state and partly by the church. In practice the hiera grammata is only taken up by those families able to afford to have their children in a schoolroom rather than at work. A primary teacher is called a grammatistes

The next tier is the *enkyklion*, and it is dependent on private tutors. The secondary or general education (the "school of grammar") has a more diverse curriculum, concentrating both on *paideia* (teachings in accord with Christian doctrine) and *exosophia* ("outside" – i.e. classical – wisdom) and covering subjects such as classical language, eloquence, logic, arithmetical studies (including music and astronomy), and science (mathema). A secondary school teacher goes by the title grammatikos, a term also used as a soubriquet for any learned individual.

Those who have received the enkyklion are eligible for the highest tier of education (the "school of rhetoric") at the Imperial University (see page 103). The Imperial University consists of three schools: the Patriarchal School, the Law School, and the Pandidakterion. Unlike the lower levels of education, these schools are state-organised and administered through the Pandidakterion, which is a governmental ministry (see page 103). This final level of education is paid for by the pupil, but the university is also a governmental ministry and assistance is offered by the state. A university education covers the higher subjects of theology, philosophy, medicine, and law; and prepares a student for life in the civil service, in the church, or as an academic. Further study can also be arranged privately, such as at the katholikon mouseion, a school of medicine attached to the Petra Monastery; although it is prohibited for law to be taught in private.

At the secondary and tertiary levels, education stems from a contract made between teacher and student. This legal document dictates the schedule of the student, including how much time they are expected to spend in private study. It also details the responsibilities of the master, and the fee he is paid. A master may take on as many students as his contracts permit: they stipulate how much one-on-one and group teaching is permitted and the curriculum he will teach.

All levels of education are available equally to both sexes, which sets Constantinople apart from most European nations. Nevertheless, there is still a male bias at all levels of education, which gets more pronounced the further up one goes. This has nothing to do with legal impediments and everything to do with social expectations on women.

Mathematics and its allied disciplines of astronomy, music, arithmetic, geometry, and optics has been greatly assisted by diligent scholars such as Gregory Chiomiades, who travelled to Persia at the end of the 13th century to bring back works in Arabic and incorporate their advances into the general understanding of the subject.

Natural philosophy still holds onto two great truths of hylomorphism and geocentrism. Hylomorphism holds that everything that is exists first as an immaterial form (hyle) which combines with formless matter (made up of corpuscles of earth, fire, air, and water), to create a physical substance. The doctrine of geocentrism describes how these substances are arranged: the universe is conceived with the habited world at the centre of a series of nested spheres made of aither (the fifth element). The planets are imbedded in these invisible spheres, and they spin around the earth causing the planets to revolve in complex cycles around us.

Interest in moral philosophy has undergone an Aristotelian renaissance in the last 50 years or so after the Summa Theologica written by the western scholar Thomas Aquinas was translated into Greek. Platonism – or rather Neoplatonism – has also been revived by the interest of scholars such as George Gemistos (see page 96).

History as a subject of academic study in its own right has been largely ignored in the west, but the in the fourteenth century no less than four major historiographies were penned, founding a whole new field of scholarly pursuit.

ECONOMY

In the century prior to the Sack of Constantinople, the Byzantine Empire was the wealthiest nation in Europe. It projected an image of luxury and excess; travellers to the capital commented on the wealth accumulated there. Every altar was adorned with gold and gemstones, every building faced with marble, every palace with a gilded roof, and every table laden with exotic fare. It was this ostentatious display of its prosperity that caused the envious eyes of Venice to fall upon it. Latin rule was to see the city stripped bare of its finery. Much of the public wealth was stolen and shipped back to the cities of Western Europe, and the gold held in private hands spent on ransoms. By the time of the Restoration, the republics of the Italian peninsula had taken Byzantium's place as the great trading centre of the Mediterranean, and the state has never recovered. The Genoan colony of Pera in Constantinople's suburbs has an annual revenue over seven times greater than that of the Empire, which at the current time is less than 40,000 hyperpyra.

The empire's fortunes were made in grain and silk. Constantinople has to import about half of its wheat, supplementing what can be grown in the few remaining European territories. The city still has a thriving silk trade, one of the few industries that was not taken over by the Venetians during the Frankokratia due to the unwillingness of the secretive foreign silk producers to deal with anyone except their Greek contacts. Passing through Constantinople are all manner of luxury goods from beyond the Black Sea, and the state collects a tax on that which passes through its markets. This includes perfumes, spices, ivory, wax, salt, precious gems, exotic timber, and slaves. Other imports include oil, wine, fish, meat, linen, wool, and ceramics.

Mythic Constantinople is a cash-driven society. Few citizens are involved in direct production such as livestock rearing and growing crops (with the exception of fishermen), so there are few goods with which to barter. Much of the Empire's food provision is imported into the city, which is then bought by Imperial guilds or private wholesalers and then sold onto the consumer. These additional steps in the supply chain add a premium onto all industries. It is for this reason that some guilds are controlled by the Empire and prices fixed centrally and enforced by law.

A much-hated government tax is the *kommerkion*, or customs tax, which is levied at 10% on all imports, exports, and trade in between. This was a major source of income for the empire when people wanted to come to Constantinople to trade, but now that there are alternate markets it is a yoke around free trade. The imperial guilds have a concession over the kommerkion, and it is not charged on goods grown or manufactured within the empire.

Coinage

Gold coins, for which Byzantium was once famous, are no longer in circulation. However, there is a notational gold coin called the *hyperpyron*, used in accounting but does not actually exist as a physical coin.

Since 1367, the basic coin of the Empire has been the stavraton, a heavy silver coin named after the cross (*stavros* in Greek) on its face, which is worth half a hyperpyron. Coins worth a half-stavraton and an eighth-stavraton (called an *aspron*) are also in circulation; and the Venetian ducat is used as a quarter-stavraton. There are two copper coins for smaller denominations, the tournesion (12 of which make an aspron, and 96 make a stavraton) and the follario (36 to the aspron, 288 to the stavraton).

The Empire has used a confusing array of coins in its long history and defunct denominations are still occasionally used as currency or found in old treasure troves. Some were concave in shape to make them stronger and less easily bent. After the Sack of Constantinople in 1204, debased coins called "*trachea*" (singular "trachy", meaning "short"), were minted. Debased gold is called *electrum*, an alloy of 10-30% gold with the rest made up of silver. Debased silver is *billon*, an alloy of 2–6% silver with copper. In the above table, exchange rates relative to the gold standard are given in parentheses, although bear in mind that gold purity changed over time as did the level of deliberate debasement. Concave coins are indicated with an asterisk.

Coinage

Metal	Period I (fifth to mid-eighth century)	Period II (mid-eighth to late eleventh century)	Period III (late eleventh to late thirteenth century)	Period IV (late thirteenth century to 1367)
Gold	Solidus nomisma (1) Semissis (2) Tremissis (3)	Solidus nomisma (1)	Hyperpyron nomisma* (1)	Hyperpyron nomisma* (1)
Electrum			Nomisma trachy* / aspron* (3)	
Silver	Hexagram (12)	Milliaresion (12)		Basilikon (12)
Billon			Aspron trachy* (48)	Tournesion* (96)
Copper	Follis (288) Half-follis (576) Decanummium (1152) Pentanummium (2304) ummius (11520)	Follis (288)	Tetarteron (864) half-tetarteron (1728)	Trachy* (384) Assarion (768)

Prices

Inflation has driven the cost of everything up within Constantinople. Any imported goods should have the price listed in the Mythras rules doubled, and all other goods and services should be 50% greater due to inflation. If your campaign is set mostly in Constantinople you may instead opt to leave the prices of domestic goods and services the same but decrease income by half.

The prices of firearms and artillery can be found in the description of those weapons on page 74.

The Guilds

Twenty one imperial guilds (*syntechia*) govern key trades still under the control of the Byzantine Empire. These guilds specifically exist to manage the Imperial monopolies; although guildsmen are private business-owners, guild membership grants them the right to trade in regulated goods. This guarantees a steady income, but prevents profiteering since all prices are controlled by the Ministries of the General and Special Fisc (see page 107). Each guild has a complete and often complex list of rules and bylaws which govern the quality and production of their trade. These bylaws establish what is expected of each master guildsman, which usually requires some guarantee of quality: to become a master requires the approval of the other masters in the guild. A master is permitted to sell goods under his own name, and to train apprentices. Each master typically has one or more journeymen as well – craftsmen for whom the apprenticeship has ended, but who are not yet ready for master status.

Constantinople Goods Table

Goods	Cheap	Reasonable	Superior
Amulet to ward against the Evil Eye	5 SP (fake)	10 SP (1 use)	25 SP (1d3+1 uses)
Gunpowder, 100 grams	5 SP	7 SP	—
Opium (one dose of 4 grains)	—	3 SP	—
Potion from a witch or alchemist	5 SP (non-magical)	15 SP	30 SP*
Slave	1200 SP	2000 SP	6000 SP

Constantinople Services Table

Service	Cheap	Reasonable	Superior
Curse laid by a witch	—	—	20 SP**
Curse removal by a witch	3 SP (ineffective)	7 SP	—
Prostitute	2 SP	4 SP	12 SP

**Superior potions have an enhancement of some variety, such as being easy to hide in food or have an unusual delivery method.*

***Multiply the cost by the Money Modifier for the social class of the victim (see Mythras page 24). A curse on a dynatos would therefore cost 100 SP, whereas one on a slave would be only 10 SP.*

THE NOTARIES

The Guild of Notaries draw up contracts, wills, and other legal documents. The guild also covers advocates, graduates of the Magnaura School of Law (see page 155) who can represent a person in the law courts. The Notaries have a close relationship with the Chancellery and the Imperial Archives.

GOLD AND SILVER GUILDS

The Guild of Money-Lenders and the Guild of Silversmiths and Goldsmiths are closely associated with one another. The silversmiths and goldsmiths operate on the easternmost section of the Mese Odos, setting up tables in front of their workshops. They deal with all manner of precious metals, but also pearls and precious stones. Members of the guild are the only merchants permitted to manufacture, sell, and import artefacts made of precious metals and gems. The Money-Lenders are very affluent individuals who multiply their vast wealth by lending it and charging interest. The guild also buys foreign currency for local coinage and operates as a bank, but in the latter it is challenged by foreign banking interests who have been permitted to operate within Constantinople.

CLOTH GUILDS

There are six Imperial Guilds involved in the business of clothing, five of which are concerned with the trade of silk. The Raw Silk Merchants' Guild purchases unprocessed silk from foreigners, and most of it comes from Syrian Arabs. They sell the cocoons to the Silk Spinners' Guild, who turn the cocoons into silk thread. The Silk Weavers' Guild are the final producers of silk cloth, including the weaving and dying of the fabric. The Silk Merchants' Guild then forms the silk cloth into garments and sells them in the markets. The last silk guild is the Silk Importers' Guild, which buys silk cloth and garments overseas and sells it in the market. All five silk trades are required to do business in the Forum of Constantine.

The sixth cloth guild is the Linen Importers' Guild, which comes from Macedonia and Bulgaria. Linen garments may be sold directly to the public, but they also sell to the Silk Merchants' Guild who use it to finish off their silk clothes. The shops of the Linen Importers' Guild are also found in the Forum of Constantine, but limited to the western gate with the Mese Odos.

APOTHECARIES

The Guild of Spicers and Perfumers controls the importation, manufacture, and sale of spices, perfumes, ink, and dyes. They also gather and prepare ingredients for medicines, but are forbidden by law from prescribing medication themselves: this requires authorisation from a physician of proven reputation. The Guild must trade spices and perfumes in the Portico of Achilles between the Chalke Gate and the Milion (see page 149), but can sell other pharmaceuticals and herbs (which are not part of their monopoly) anywhere.

TRADERS GUILDS

These four allied guilds include the Wax Merchants, the Soap Merchants, the Saddlers, and the Grocers. The Wax Merchants are responsible for importing wax, flavouring and colouring it as required, and shaping it into candles and tapers. The Wax Merchants also make votive offerings for those wishing to pray at a shrine for a healing miracle; these commonly take the shape of the emblem of the saint or an effigy of the affected body part. Soap Merchants import and manufacture soap and perfumed oils. The Saddlers' Guild manufacture saddles, reins, and other horse-tack; they also make boots and leather armour. The Grocers' Guild places food in the marketplace, selling butter, cheese, oil, vegetables, and salted fish; but is also responsible for the sale of utensils and building materials such as pitch, oil, nails, rope, and plaster. The workshops of the Soap and Wax Merchants are required by law to be unattached to other buildings for safety purposes; apart from this, there are no regulations as to the trading places of these guilds.

FOOD GUILDS

Five guilds control the supply of food. The Butchers' Guild deals with cows, sheep, and lambs, whereas the Pork Merchants' Guild specialises in pigs. Both guilds are responsible for acquiring their appropriate livestock, slaughtering and jointing, and sale of the meat. Sheep may be sold in the Strategion market, whereas lambs and pigs must be sold in the Forum of the Ox. The Fishmongers' Guild brings fresh fish up from the docks and sells it; they are prohibited from selling dried or salted fish, which is the province of the Grocers' Guild. Wholesale fish purchasing is done at the docks, whereas fish for retail is brought to the licensed stalls of the Megistai Kamarai (Great Vaults) at the Neorion Harbour. The Bakers' Guild is one of the largest in the city; they are responsible for supplying the city with the mainstay of its daily meal. Baking is done in the Artopoleia neighbourhood (see page 145), along the Mese Odos. Finally the Innkeepers' Guild is responsible for the sale of wine, and by extension, hostelry. They must close at night and on Sundays and feast days, and are responsible for regulating the size of their drinking vessels according to the price of wine, which is determined centrally. Inns and wineshops are permitted throughout the city.

INSPECTORS' GUILD

The Guild of Assessors and Inspectors is responsible for making sure that all guilds – Imperial or private – are operating within the law. They regulate the marketplaces, check and calibrate the weights used by vendors, and handle disputes between guilds. They have legal jurisdiction over smuggling, falsification, and counterfeiting, and work closely with the customs officials of the General Fisc (see page 106). The Assessors are also responsible for regulating foreign traders, who often try to undercut the Imperial Guilds. The Assessors ply their business all over the city, but their main offices are at the Forum of Amastrianos

Private Guilds

In addition to the 21 Imperial Guilds are many hundreds of private guilds (or *somateia*). A private guild is set up by a single person or family, but can quickly grow to employ hundreds of people. Several private guilds are as large and powerful as some of the Imperial Guilds, and may maintain a similar monopoly over a given trade. Private guilds are wholly voluntary and the State has no say in their business as long as they fall within the general rules of trading and abide by the standards of the Guild of Assessors and Inspectors.

Private guilds are bound by whatever rules they set for themselves but they are also left to police themselves, having no formal recourse for dispute resolution if both parties have remained within the law. The motivation for forming a private guild varies: it could be about setting and maintaining a professional standard for the customer; as a profit-sharing enterprise for several like-minded craftsmen; or a blatant attempt to eliminate competition. Example private guilds exist for: furriers, builders, furniture-makers, lapidaries, doormakers, plasterers, dyers (of non-silk cloth), tanners, shoemakers, copper smiths, blacksmiths, and armourers.

Most private guilds tend to have the same structure of apprentices, journeymen, and masters as the Imperial Guilds; although the rank of Master is not always a guarantee of a particular level of skill, and may just be an empty title. Caveat emptor.

Crime & Illicit Activities

With its economy in the state that it is, it is perhaps no great surprise that so many citizens have turned to crime. Most organised crime revolves around smuggling in order to avoid the swingeing import duties demanded by the state. The sea walls of Constantinople prove to be the biggest impediment to smuggling, as they restrict entrance into the city to a few points, which the customs inspectors can easily control. Bribing state officials can be risky, so smugglers often rely on alternate strategies. For those with the right contacts, goods can be lifted into the city at night using a crane hidden within a warehouse that backs right up to the wall, and there are rumours that at least one smuggling ring uses the tunnels of the Undercity (see page 188), although this may just be a lie to cover up their real method.

Other than smuggling, there are the usual cutpurses, burglars, con artists, fences, forgers, thugs for hire, and even professional killers for those with the right contacts. Some of these run with gangs, others are sole operators. The Zanconi Family are the largest criminal organisation in the city, mostly involved in loan-sharking, extortion, and running illicit businesses. Star and Crescent are the main suppliers of opium in The City, and also run a smuggling operation. Finally, Dražan's Gang is mostly involved in 'acquisitions', the misappropriation of other people's possessions in all its myriad of forms.

Perhaps the biggest business (illicit or otherwise) in Constantinople is prostitution. Some have estimated that 10% of the city's population is involved in prostitution, either as a sex-worker, brothel-owner, or associated trade. Prostitution is not illegal as long as it takes place in a brothel. Many tabernai and phouskaria double as brothels despite only having one or two house girls. Many skirt the law by hiring out rooms to freelance prostitutes in return for a cut of the fee. There are also dedicated brothels throughout the city, catering to a variety of different tastes. Regardless of the social class of the clientele, many of these brothels are owned and operated entirely by women. A relatively recent trend is for the prostitutes within a brothel to form a private guild (see earlier), and govern themselves according to self-determined rules, which normally involve some form of profit-sharing. The street trade is cheaper but risks the attention of the authorities. Many such prostitutes are slaves and conditions are harsh. Women in need of advertising their trade wear shawls of striped fabric, known as "the devil's cloth", which is a signal that her affections are up for negotiation.

A recent import from the east is opium, and it has quickly found itself at the centre of a black market. This resin or sticky liquid is made from the juice of a particular poppy grown in Arab lands. It has genuine medicinal use, being the most effective analgesic available to surgeons when mixed with other soporific ingredients. However, Arab traders introduced the recreational use of opium: the rich have it prepared as a tincture with saffron, cloves, and cinnamon to counteract the bitter taste, which is then added to water to make a black tea; whereas the poor or the addicted chew the resin directly. Opium produces a powerful sensation of euphoria coupled with vivid dreams-like hallucinations, but is devastatingly addictive. Opium is prohibited by law, and yet it still gets imported to the city by those under its sway; and it is sold at exorbitant prices to addicts in places where other illicit behaviour takes place: gambling dens, gutter phouskaria, and disreputable brothels.

Four grains of opium resin, enough for a single recreational dose, can be bought for 3 SP. This dose might come as a solid resin or else as a tincture dissolved in spirits of wine with spices. Black water is made by adding twenty drops of opium tincture (containing 4 grains of opium) to water. A month's supply of two doses per day (not accounting for tolerance) comes to ½ ounce (there are 480 grains to the ounce) or ¼ pint of tincture (1920 drops).

Governance of the Empire

At the head of the Byzantine Empire is the emperor. He has the ultimate authority over his lands, his people, and his city; none can gainsay him and few would try. However, while the regal power lies within the hands of the emperor, much of the executive control of the empire is handled by persons other than the emperor himself.

The three great powers involved in the governance of Constantinople are the Court, the Church, and the Military. The interplay between these three powers plus the internal politics of each of them is the motive force for most political machinations in the Empire.

OPIUM & OPIUM ADDICTION

Opium is a poison (Mythras, page 74). Consuming opium has varying effects, depending upon the amount taken. A dose can be recreational, medicinal, or lethal. One recreational dose consists of four grains of opium. Ten grains of opium constitutes a medicinal dose, and 200 grains a lethal dose. Habitual users build up a tolerance: for every 1d3 doses within the same month, increase the amount needed to get the same recreational or medicinal (but not lethal) effects by one grain and increase the difficulty grade of the Resistance roll by one. These increases in dose size and resistance difficulty are permanent.

Application: Ingested

Potency: 100%

Resistance: Endurance

Onset time: 1d4+4 minutes

Duration: 1d4 hours

Conditions: All doses cause euphoria and numbness even if the Resistance roll is made. All rolls to resist pain after a recreational dose of opium are Very Easy. For those failing the Resistance roll, a recreational dose of opium causes Confusion and Hallucinations. Medicinal doses cause Confusion and Hallucinations instantly, and Unconsciousness once the onset time expires. A lethal dose is the same but causes Asphyxiation rather than Unconsciousness.

Antidote/Cure: none

***Addiction**: Opium is both physiologically and psychologically addictive. Opium addiction is simulated using the Disease rules (Mythras, page 112). This disease may be 'contracted' after a person has consumed a total number of doses of opium equal to (CON/2)+1d6, rounded up. From then on, the character must roll to avoid addiction every time a dose is ingested. A player should not know how many doses it takes to addict his character.*

Application: Ingested

Potency: 95%, but may be lower if there has been a substantial gap between doses

Resistance: lowest of Willpower and Endurance

Onset time: 1d6+6 hours

Duration: permanent

Conditions: Mania. Addiction causes trembling limbs, a lack of focus, and above all an overwhelming craving. The addiction is represented by a Crave Opium Passion of 30+(21–POW)% and increasing by 1d4% for every dose taken. Unless under the effects of opium, all rolls requiring coordination, willpower, or mental focus are opposed by the character's own Passion. If the Passion wins, then the Skill roll is counted as a failure. If the Passion roll is a critical, then the Skill roll automatically fumbles.

Antidote/Cure: Withdrawal. 2d4+8 hours after the last dose of opium, the character suffers Nausea. 2d4+8 hours after that the symptoms increase to Agony, which persists for 2d4+8 hours before fading away over the same amount of time. The Mania condition (and the Crave Opium Passion) is permanent, but after withdrawal the Passion score is reduced by 1d10% and declines at 1d10% per week until it reaches 30%. If the character takes another dose after completing withdrawal, the Passion score is doubled and Addiction grips the character again.

THE IMPERIAL COURT

The Imperial Court is the name given to the small army of ministers and officials who tend to the machinery of governance. Each is the bearer of a court title or dignity (axia), of which there are two types. Awarded dignities (axiai brabeion) are purely honorific, with only ceremonial duties attached to them, whereas proclaimed dignities (axiai logou) are part of the state bureaucracy. In the past there were two series of awarded dignities, one for the *Ektomiai* (eunuchs) and one for the Barbatoi ("Bearded Ones", i.e. non-eunuchs), but the distinction between these has broken down with the decline of eunuchs in imperial service, and the titles have now been combined into a single list. Awarded titles, in decreasing order of precedence, include: president (*proedros*), master (*magistros*), patrician (*patrikios*), first sword-bearer (*protospatharios*), *kaballarios* (knight), consul (*hypatos*), prefect (*stratelates*), *spatharios* (sword-bearer), *kynegos* (huntsman), *hieraetos* (falconer), doorkeeper (*ostiarios*), "silence-keeper" (*silentiarios*), groom (*strator*). Despite their names, none of these honorary positions entail any duties, although they do permit a person to attend court in the appointed costume and provides a way of ranking courtiers.

Receiving a proclaimed title from the emperor's hand makes one a civil servant, a member of one of the 12 governmental ministries. Each ministry has its own series of titles, and the relative rank of each official within and between ministries is carefully regulated. Much of the intrigue for which the Byzantine court is famous revolves around conflicts between ministries and rivalries over rank.

BANNERS & SEALS OF THE EMPIRE

The tetragrammic cross is the primary symbol of the Empire. The red field is quartered by a gold or silver cross, and four letter betas (B) of the same colour are in each quarter. The left-hand betas are sometimes in mirror image to maintain symmetry. The Bs are said to stand for Basileus Basileon Basileion Basileuousin ("King of kings ruling over the kings"). This symbol is also used as the imperial seal.

The double-headed eagle, again gold on a red background, is the insignia of the House of Palaiologos, and thus the personal symbol of the emperor and his family. The eagle has an amulet around its neck bearing the sympilema or imperial cipher, a monogram of the Palaiologos name.

The crescent and star is the symbol of Constantinople itself. This is the oldest of the insignia mentioned here, belonging to the goddess Hekate Lampadephoros ("light-bearer") who protected The City in pagan days. The horns of the crescent moon point upwards and the star balances between the points. The symbol can be found scratched on many buildings in Constantinople, particularly the oldest ones.

The labarion is the military standard of the Empire. A pole surmounted by the chi-rho symbol of Christ stands above a crossbar that holds the imperial flag. The labarion is richly decorated with gold and jewels.

Various other banners are used on ceremonial occasions: the oktapodion with its eight streamers; images of Saints Demetrios, Prokopios, Theodoros the Recruit and Theodoros the General, and George on horseback; the drakoneion carried by the Varangian Guard, and the image of the emperor on horseback.

THE MINISTRIES OF THE IMPERIAL COURT

The *mesazon* or prime minister is the head of the vast bureaucracy that heads the Imperial Court. The title literally translates to "intermediary", as the mesazon stands between the Emperor and his subjects. Before the Fall of Constantinople, mesazon was simply an honorary title, but the Empire of Nicaea used the role as the chief minister, and when the Empire was restored, the role was carried forward into the reconstituted Imperial Court. The mesazon has no official position within the imperial ranking system, as he speaks with the voice of the emperor. The current mesazon is Demetrios Palaiologos Kantakouzenos.

The 12 ministries, in descending order of precedence, are

- The Army Office or *Scholon*, led by the Grand Domestic Andronikos Palaiologos Kantakouzenos
- The Imperial Household or *Vestarion*, led by the Provestarios Georgios Sphrantzes
- The Naval Office or *Ploimon*, led by the Grand Doux Loukas Notaras
- The Chancellery or *Sekreton*, led by the Grand Logothete Loukas Notaras
- The General Fisc or *Genikon*, led by the General Logothete Theologos Notaras Pylles
- The Office of the Drome or *Dromos*, led by the Logothete of the Drome Thomas Strouthion
- The Imperial University or *Pandidakterion*, led by the Hypatos Michael Komnenos
- The Imperial Archives or *Chartothesion*, led by the Protasekritis Alexios Palaiologos Tzamplakon
- The Special Fisc or *Eidikon*, led by the Special Logothete Konstantinos Sigeros Doukas
- The Military Fisc or *Stratiotikon*, led by the Military Logothete Manuel Palaiologos Iagaris
- The Imperial Library or *Bibliotheka*, led by the Librarian Antonios Chrysoloras
- The Imperial Orphanage or *Orphanotropeion*, led by the Orphanotrophos Michael Serron

More information about these ministries can be found in the Communities chapter.

THE IMPERIAL PROXY

An unusual proclaimed dignity is that of the *Topoteretes* (literally "place-holder") or Imperial Proxy. The Proxy is always someone unrelated to the culture of the imperial court and sometimes a complete stranger. For example, the Proxy of Emperor Michael III of the Amorian Dynasty (r. 842–867) was a Macedonian peasant found in the doorway of Saint Diomedes's Monastery.

An Imperial Proxy's function is to receive all spells directed at the emperor. The two are mystically linked so that any spell targeted at the emperor is automatically retargeted to the Proxy, regardless of the distance between them. Strong magic can still sometimes penetrate this protection: the chance of a spell affecting the emperor rather than his Proxy is equal to its (Magnitude -1) x 10%. A Miracle of Magnitude 5 targeted at the emperor therefore has a 40% chance of affecting him rather than the Proxy. All Folk Magic spells, Sorcery spells without Shaping, and the Evil Eye (which are all Magnitude 1) are always deflected onto the Proxy. Spirits directed to affect the emperor are judged as having a Magnitude equal to their Intensity. The Proxy link specifically protects the emperor against any magic purposefully directed at him from a human or supernatural agency. It is not triggered should the emperor activate an enchantment himself or drink a magical potion, for example. Intent is irrelevant; the emperor is protected from beneficial and harmful magic equally. The mystical link between the emperor and his Proxy works in one direction only; spells cast on the Proxy target the Proxy as normal.

A person becomes the Imperial Proxy as part of the coronation ceremony through a rite practised since time immemorial. Should the Proxy die before the emperor, another can be designated by repeating the coronation ceremony, which is usually done in private. In the past, sorcerers have studied the rite in an attempt to reproduce the effect; however, the rite requires one of the participants to be the emperor, making experimentation virtually impossible. The purpose of the Proxy is not widely known; from the outside the position appears as nothing more than an odd quirk of the court; often the Proxy himself is left entirely unaware of his magical role. The more unpopular an emperor, the more supernatural detritus the Imperial Proxy attracts, and for this reason the Proxy is generally treated well by the Imperial Household: the rank of Topoteretes attracts a salary paid out of the imperial treasury, and their only duty is a weekly meeting with the emperor or his mesazon. Some Proxies have become both rich and powerful due to their access to the emperor. For example, the Proxy of Michael III eventually assassinated the emperor and seized the throne as Basil I the Macedonian.

CITY GOVERNANCE

Civil administration of Constantinople is the duty of the praitor ton demon, whose job is an evolution of the previous title of eparch (eparkhos). This powerful civil servant, who is a member of the Chancellery, operates out of the Praitorion (see page 148). He has three main duties: to maintain order, to dispense justice, and to maintain the structure of the city. To help him he has the Praitorion staff, but also the kephalai – the community leaders of each of Constantinople's districts. The role of kephale is an elected position, although elections are rife with corruption and many bad kephales get re-elected year after year.

The role of the sergeant-at-arms and the chief justice are described below. The tribune is responsible for overseeing the public facilities and spaces of the city. The walls and fortifications need constant attention, the streets need cleaning, and the water supply needs to be maintained. Under the authority of the Praitor, the tribune enforces building regulations and supervises construction. His office also manages the distribution of food, and as commander of the phylakes, is responsible for coordinating the fire service.

CRIME PREVENTION, LAW & ORDER

Each kephale is responsible for organising a *phylax*, which is the district watch. All phylakes are technically under the control of the tribune but many kephalai use them as a private army. Members of the phylax are responsible for preventing crime by apprehending criminals caught in the act, and preventing fires by enforcing curfew and keeping a night-time watch. Every district by law must maintain a storehouse stocked with sand, earth, manure, and liquid (urine and vinegar are believed to have superior fire-quenching abilities). They must also have working hand pumps, and most stock cloaks made of rawhide soaked in vinegar and coated with a fireproof mixture of alum, talc, and gypsum. Some districts even have cloaks of 'salamander wool' (asbestos).

The city's police force is the Vardariotai, under the command of the sergeant-at-arms. The Vardariotai are principally responsible for preventing disturbances in public order. It is also the job of the Vardariotai to keep order at court and to ensure that accused parties attend appointments before judges. The Vardariotai have no remit to investigate crimes – that is the job of the phylakes – but the Vardariotes and the phylakes regularly clash over jurisdictional issues. For more information, see page 110.

THE JUDICIAL SYSTEM

The Byzantine legal system has a pedigree that reaches back to Classical Rome. At its core is the *Corpus juris civilis* compiled under the Emperor Justinian in 534, although in the intervening thousand years the law codes have been amended, altered, and in some cases repealed. The current legislature is labyrinthine in complexity, and doctors of law are greatly sought after to navigate its murky depths. The entire legal system falls under the jurisdiction of the Chancellery (see earlier) and the chief legal authority is its minister, the Grand Logothete.

In general, crimes require that the victim reports the injury or insult committed, and seeks redress. There is no state prosecutor that pursues criminal cases; the plaintiff must personally file claim; although in practice he can hire an advocate trained in law to act on his behalf. The defendant is permitted to do the same. Trials take place before a judge (krita), an official of the Chancellery. The defendant may be imprisoned during the course of the trial but unless this is a capital crime, this is done at the expense of the plaintiff, although he can claim back expenses from the defendant if a conviction is made.

The plaintiff has the right to question the authority and competence of the judge before the trial begins. With that formality out of the way, the plaintiff describes the crime committed and the sentence he seeks. Typical sentences for crimes can be found on the nearby tables. The typical punishment is for first time offences or marginal cases; the maximum punishment listed is for repeat or unrepentant defendants. Should the plaintiff lose the case, he is subject to the same penalty he sought against the accused; this system is designed to reduce frivolous lawsuits and discourages plaintiffs from demanding the maximum sentences. Minor cases are best settled privately without involving the courts.

Witnesses are called to give evidence, either under oath or through ordeal. The number of witnesses required depends on the severity of the crime: one is sufficient for petty theft, but five might be required for a crime that could result in maiming or execution. Witnesses may attest to the character of the accused rather than pertain to the circumstances of the crime. Witnesses need not be actual people: a corpse, a written statement, an animal, or a piece of incriminating evidence can act as a witness, although witnesses who cannot swear an oath are considered weaker evidence than actual living people, and may need their own witnesses to attest validity.

The judge makes his decision based on the evidence before him and the arguments to law; there is no jury, and he decides the penalty immediately. Appeals can be lodged with the chief justice and the emperor can grant clemency; a full month is supposed to pass

OFFENCES AGAINST PERSONS

Offences Against Persons	Typical Punishment	Maximum Punishment
Slander	Flogging and Damages	Maiming (Tongue)
Accidental Killing	Damages	–
Physical Assault	Flogging and Damages	Imprisonment
Abduction	Flogging and Damages	Imprisonment
Abortion	Maiming (Nose)	–
Prostitution	Maiming (Nose)	Maiming (Blinding)
Rape	Maiming (Blinding)	Exile
Crimes Committed While Drunk	Add Short Term Exile to Sentence	
Injury During Another Crime (E.g. Robbery)	Death	–
Premediated Assault, Murder, Attempted Murder	Death or Exile	–
Treason	Death	–
Military Desertion	Death or Exile	–

OFFENCES AGAINST PROPERTY

Offences Against Property	Typical Punishment	Maximum Punishment
Cheating, Underselling Goods, False Measurements and Weights	Flogging, Maiming (Cheek)	Exile
Damage Through Accident	Damages	–
Damage Through Negligence	Damages	Short Term Exile
Damage, Deliberate	Flogging and Damages	Maiming (Hand)
Theft From Home (Burglary)	Flogging and Imprisonment	Maiming (Blinding)
Theft From Person or Marketplace	Flogging	Maiming (Hand)
Looting the Dead	Flogging	Maiming (Hand)

OFFENCES AGAINST THE CHURCH

Offences Against The Church	Typical Punishment	Maximum Punishment
Blasphemy	Confession and Penance	–
Adultery	Confession and Penance	Maiming (Blinding)
Sexual Deviation	Confession and Penance	Cnfinement in Monastery
Sacrilege	Confession and Penance	Confinement in Monastery
Simony	Confession and Penance	Confinement in Monastery
Apostasy	Maiming (Tongue or Blinding)	Confinement in Monastery
Schism	Maiming (Tongue or Blinding)	Confinement in Monastery
Heresy	Death	–

between sentencing and execution to allow time for these procedures to take place. Even the emperor's clemency can only commute a death sentence to exile.

Condemned criminals are scourged and their heads shaved. They are paraded to the place of their sentencing, riding backwards on a donkey. Executions, mutilations, and exile are popular events accompanied by jeering crowds. These public spectacles are often half-day holidays, and there are usually entertainers who act out the criminal's offences for the gathered crowds while food and wine vendors hawk their wares. Executions are normally held in the Forum of Theodosios (see page 146).

- Execution methods vary according to the choice of the judge. Beheading by sword or hanging and impalement are used for common criminals, but high profile cases might have more exotic deaths, like being thrown from the top of the Column of Theodosios, or torn apart by horses in the Hippodrome. Unless the crime is treason, aristocrats can avoid execution by accepting exile.
- Exile involves leaving Constantinople and the Empire or else entering a monastery. Exiles must surrender their titles, property, and assets. One third of his net worth goes to his victim's family, one third to his spouse or own heirs, and the final third either to the monastery that will support him or to the state.
- Maiming involves blinding, cutting off a hand or foot, or slitting the tongue, nose, or cheeks (from the corner of the mouth).
- Imprisonment involves interment in one of the state prisons (The Prison of Anemas or the Noumera). Prisoners must pay for their own food and lodging, although they can rely on the state bread (see page 23). If unable to pay the accrued fees, they can agree to debt bondage (see page 16).
- Damages involve financial compensation to the plaintiff: for offences against property these cannot exceed seven times the value of that lost by the plaintiff; and for offences against persons these cannot exceed the net worth of the plaintiff. Criminals unable to pay damages usually have to resort to debt bondage.
- Flogging is usually ordered in allotments of 12 and applied with a long whip, although the criminal can elect to take half the number with the short knout. Each group of 12 (or six) lashes is applied on separate days with recovery time allowed in between; the criminal is imprisoned for the time it takes to apply his punishment.
- Confession and penance requires public admission of the crime and asking forgiveness. Penance requires compensating the victims of the crime, prolonged fasting, and exclusion from communion.

THE CHURCH

According to Orthodox theology, the purpose of a Christian life is for mankind to attain mystical union with God (known as theosis), both on an individual and a collective level. The entire structure of the church is devoted to realising this goal.

HISTORY

When the Christian Church first formed, it did so under the auspices of five patriarchs, located at Rome, Constantinople, Jerusalem, Antioch, and Alexandria. Rome, the centre of the classical Roman Empire, was granted primacy as 'first amongst equals'. Relations between the five patriarchates was not always cordial, but things really started to break down around the tenth century. Three of the patriarchates were hostages in Muslim-controlled territories, and the remaining two were split between the Greek-speaking east and the Latin-speaking west. The Bishop of Rome claimed ecclesiastical supremacy over the rest of the church rather than mere primacy; and demanded the right to appoint the patriarchs of the other four churches. Further, the Western and Eastern churches argued over an important theological distinction regarding the nature of the trinity. These grievances ultimately lead to the Great Schism, which is usually dated to 1054. The Western or Catholic Church of Rome continued under the supreme authority of the pope, and the Eastern or Orthodox Church composed of the other four patriarchs became a separate entity.

RELIGIOUS CONTROVERSY AND HERESY

The Church has had its fair share of controversy. Throughout the early centuries of the Church, there have been countless heresiarchs (leaders of heresy) who had differing opinions on the nature of God, and many of these served to shape the core beliefs of the modern church through a series of seven ecumenical councils held in Nicaea, Constantinople, Ephesus, and Chalcedon. Arianism (which teaches that Jesus is distinct and subordinate to the Father), Monophytism (which teaches that Jesus has a single nature which is either divine or a synthesis of divine and human), and Nestorianism (which teaches that Jesus existed as two separate persons), all conflict with the official position, decided at the Council of Chalcedon (451), that Christ has a dual nature – one divine, one human – perfectly united in a single person. The Monophysite majority of the Patriarchate of Alexandria seceded to form the Coptic Orthodox Church of Alexandria, although there is still a small Patriarchate of Alexandria that is in accordance with the Chalcedonian position.

In the eighth century and again in the ninth a movement called Iconoclasm came to prominence within the Patriarchate of Constantinople. The iconoclasts believed that images of sacred personages such as the Holy Family and saints were equivalent to the graven idols warned against in the Bible. They believed that these ikons encouraged idolatry: that worship due to God was instead being offered to those represented by the portraits. The iconoclasts went on a rampage through Constantinople, tearing down ikons, smashing statues, and levering up mosaics. Both periods of iconoclasm were brought to an end at church councils held under the patronage of an empress (Empress Irene in the First Iconoclasm and Empress Theodora in the second). The first Sunday in Lent is celebrated as the Triumph of Orthodoxy, commemorating the final defeat of the Iconoclasm movement.

The key doctrinal point in the Great Schism of 1054 that split the Catholic Church from the Orthodox Churches was also about the nature of the trinity. The Pope had formulated the Creed – the central statement of Christian Faith – to state that the Holy Spirit proceeds from the unity of the Father and the Son. However, the four eastern churches insisted that the Holy Spirit had a single origin in the Father alone. This '*filioque*' crisis (named after the Latin phrase for "and the Son") was just one of several points of difference that ultimately resulted in the four Orthodox Churches declaring the Church of Rome heretical, and vice versa. The rift between the two halves of the church had further reaching consequences than religious differences: the Great Schism laid the groundwork for the Sack of Constantinople and the Frankokratia that followed (see page 8); after all, from the perspective of Catholics, all Greeks were unrepentant excommunicates.

A much more recent religious controversy erupted in 1337. Barlaam, the *hegumen* (abbot) of Saint Saviour's Monastery in Constantinople visited Mount Athos and encountered Hesychasts (see pages 53 and 84), for the first time. He was scandalised by their behaviour, likening the mystical tradition to polytheism since it posited the existence of the uncreated light as a separate entity to God yet equally eternal. Gregory Palamas took up the fight on behalf of the Hesychasts. The religious dispute took four synods to resolve, presided over by two different emperors. Rather than a solely academic debate, the controversy led to fighting in the streets between rival groups of monks and their supporters. The matter was eventually settled in 1351 conclusively in favour of Hesychasm, and Palamas was later canonised for the part he played. The anti-Palamites were forced out of Constantinople, and most fled west and converted to Catholicism.

THE UNION OF THE CHURCHES

The Council of Florence, under the auspices of Pope Eugene IV, was part of the seventeenth ecumenical council of the Catholic Church; moved from Ferrara in 1439 to avoid plague. It was attended by a 700-strong contingent of Greek prelates, including Patriarch Joseph of Constantinople, and the matters at hand were the resolution of the theological differences between the Catholic and Orthodox faiths: the processions of the Holy Spirit; Purgatory; and papal primacy. An agreement was signed by the patriarch and all the Eastern bishops (with the exception of Mark Eugenikos of Ephesus), formally ending the schism and uniting the two halves of the Church. However, the structure of the Orthodox Church does not allow the Patriarch to speak for the entire body, and upon arriving home the Eastern bishops found the Union of the Churches, widely rejected by the monks, the populace, and much of the nobility. Furthermore, Joseph II died two days after the signing of the union, and Eugene IV was deposed before the year was out, leaving no strong ecclesiastic support for the union on either side. It has only been the approval of Emperor John VIII and his successor Constantine IX that has kept the fiction of the Union alive despite the doctrine never having been accepted by the Eastern Church.

THE ORGANISATION OF THE ORTHODOX CHURCH

The Orthodox Church is a communion of separate hierarchical churches each with its own patriarch at the head. Each church is autocephalous, meaning that it is self-governing with no higher (earthly) authority, so the Patriarch of Constantinople is free to rule its own flock without interference from any of the other patriarchs.

Each patriarch may have one or more autonomous churches subordinate to them. An autonomous church is also self-governing, except when it comes to finding a new archbishop or metropolitan bishop to head the church. The patriarch exerts his authority to choose the new incumbent, but at all other times has no say on the operation of an autonomous church in his patriarchate. A synod of bishops governs each church through the patriarch or archbishop, who is just one voice amongst the synod and is not considered a higher authority merely because of his rank. This decentralised system contrasts strongly with the doctrine of papal supremacy found in the Catholic Church, which places the whole denomination under the leadership of the pope.

All bishops are sacerdotal equals but they do have ranks for secular administrative purposes. The highest ranked bishops are the seven patriarchs. There were five Ancient Patriarchs, but ever since the Patriarch of Rome split from the church to form Roman Catholicism they have numbered only four, with the Patriarch of Constantinople considered to be the first amongst equals. The Ancient Patriarchs (Constantinople, Alexandria, Jerusalem, Antioch) have been joined by the Junior Patriarchs of Georgia, Bulgaria, and Serbia. The Church of Cyprus is also autocephalous, but under an archbishop rather than a patriarch.

Each patriarch is assisted by subordinate Metropolitan bishops, each of whom is in control of their own diocese. Typically, a diocese covers a city or region. There may also be auxiliary bishops who have no diocese of their own but assist patriarchs or archbishops in their duty. Beneath the bishops are the sacerdotal rank of priest, and beneath them are the deacons and deaconesses.

THE SACRED MYSTERIES

A sacred mystery is a means by which God reaches out to mankind, usually through a medium such as oil, water, bread, wine, etc. These are mysteries because the manner in which they work cannot be explained in human terms but they are the prime means by which a person can touch the divine. Included amongst the mysteries are the blessing of holy water, the lighting of a candle, the burning of incense, the giving of alms, the blessing of food before a meal, and the giving of a priest's tonsure. However, there are seven Great Mysteries that mark important life stages. These are:

- ***Baptism*** is the mystery that cleans away the stain of sin and brings a person new into the church through the use of water;
- ***Chrismation*** is the mystery that confirms a person's reception of the Holy Spirit through blessed chrism (a mixture of oil, salt, and incense);
- ***Communion*** is the partaking of the Body and Blood of Jesus, which are the products of transformed bread and wine;
- ***Repentance*** is the renewal of baptism through the confession and remission of sins via penance;
- ***Unction*** is administered to all in need of spiritual or bodily healing through the medium of holy oil, most if not all receive Unction once a year and if possible it is given to the dying before they pass;
- ***Matrimony*** is the union of man and woman symbolised by betrothal rings and wedding crowns;
- ***Ordination*** is the dedication of a person to a pastoral role as deacon, priest, or bishop. Men and women can be deacons, but only men can become priests or bishops.

THE CLERGY

The clergy are those who have received the Mystery of Ordination and dedicated their lives to the church. There are three ranks of clerics: deacon or deaconess (Greek: *diakon* or *diakonitissa*), priest (Greek: *presbyteros*), and bishop (Greek: *episkopos*). Clergymen cannot marry; although a married man can become a deacon or priest, but a deaconess must be celibate. Bishops are chosen from the ranks of monks, and so can never have married.

The role of a priest is a pastoral one, to act as a shepherd, guiding his flock towards union with God. In this priests are assisted by deacons, who fulfil an administrative role within the church and care for its fabric and possessions.

MONASTICISM

Monks are members of the Orthodox Church, but they are not part of the hierarchy of the church. Each monastery answers directly to the bishop who commands the diocese. There are three models for the monastic life. The eremite is a solitary monk. Some eremites are hermits, but others pursue an active rather than contemplative life. The *coenobite* is a monk who lives in a monastery, which is lead in worship by a *hegumen* or abbot. Finally, the *skete* is a small community of just two or three monks lead by an Elder, who pray privately for the most part but come together for communal prayer on Sundays and feast days. It is normal to enter a coenobitic life first, and then before leaving the novitiate choose to stay or to follow one of the other two paths. Eremitic and sketic service is becoming increasingly rare. Monks are often not ordained; those that are both monks and priests are known as hieromonks.

Mount Athos is a monastic republic consisting of 20 monasteries built on the Holy Mountain in Macedonia. It is currently a vassal of the Ottoman Empire, but also nominally owes fealty to the Patriarch of Constantinople.

HOLY FOOLS

The Fools-for-Christ are monks who employ shocking, unconventional behaviours in imitation of the prophets in order to shame others into right action or to demonstrate their piety. There are many examples in the Old Testament: Isaiah walked naked and barefoot for three years; Ezekiel ate bread baked from the excrement of humans and cows; and Hosea married a wanton harlot to symbolise the infidelity of Israel.

The first Fool-for-Christ was Saint Andreas of Constantinople, and his hagiography reads like a slapstick farce, with all the outrageous antics he got up to, suffering public beatings, being run over by an ox cart, and accidentally set on fire. At his monastery (see page 173), holy fools follow the pattern he established: feigning insanity, pretending to be silly, or provoking outrage by deliberate unruliness. They might engage in public urination, hang bells on their genitals, ride a goat backwards or spout gibberish. It is understood that the holy fools are actually sane, moral, and pious, but they take on the guise of insanity to conceal their perfection and avoid the sin of pride.

THE MILITARY

The strength of the Byzantine Empire has always rested largely in its military structure. Benefiting from the resources of the Roman Empire, it was once the envy of the world. In the current era the military is much reduced; the empire no longer has the land needed to support soldiers with a military contract, and instead most are salaried fighters. The size of the army therefore relates directly to what the empire can afford to pay, whereas in the past it was self-sustaining since the soldiers paid themselves from the farming the land that the state had given them. The military is currently divided between two ministries – the Army Office and the Naval Office – and supported by a third, the Military Fisc.

> **COMBAT STYLES**
>
> *Combat Styles for all the units described in this chapter can be found in the Characters chapter, on page 61.*

THE REGULAR ARMY

The Byzantine army has gone through many reforms in the history of the Empire, changing as the needs and the territories of the Empire changed. Up until the mid-fourteenth century the army was divided into *megala allagia* ("great squadrons"). By this time, all Anatolian territories of the Empire had been lost and the army consisted of six megala allagia:

- Thessalonikaion Mega Allagion of Thessaloniki;
- Serriotikon Mega Allagion at Serres;
- Visyeteikon Mega Allagion at Vizye;
- Moraïtikon Mega Allagion of Morea;
- Adrianopolitikon Mega Allagion of Adrianople; and
- Politikon Mega Allagion of The City (i.e. Constantinople)

Each mega allagion was commanded by a regimental leader called a protoallagator, and was divided into 10 allagia of 300 men each. The current army of the Empire consists of just the Politikon Mega Allagion, since all of the provincial themes that raised the other five units have been lost to the Turks. The role of the protoallagator has been dropped, and the leader of each allagion (called allagatores) now report directly to his supervisor, the prefect of the army (domestikos tou stratou).

At the heart of the army are the *stratiotes* ("soldiers", plural stratiotai). In the past many stratiotai possessed a pronoia, the right to collect the revenue and labour services from a plot of land granted them to support them as professional soldiers. As the Empire shrunk in size, its ability to offer rights to land declined and the pronoia system collapsed. At the current time, soldiers work for pay rather than out of feudal obligation to the empire.

There are four key troop types employed in the Byzantine regular army: the cavalry (*hippeis*) are divided into heavy cavalry (*kataphraktoi*) and the light cavalry (*trapezites*); and the infantry (*pezoi*) are similarly divided into heavy infantry (*skoutatoi*), and the light infantry (*toxotes* and *psiloi*, using bows and slings respectively). Of these troop types, the Empire is perhaps best known for the kataphraktoi, although the skoutatoi are more numerous.

Unit: Kataphraktoi
Role: regular cavalry
Armour: Greek heavy armour
Combat Style: Kataphraktos

Unit: Trapezites
Role: regular cavalry
Armour: Greek medium armour
Combat Style: Trapezites

Unit: Skoutatoi
Role: regular infantry
Armour: Greek heavy armour
Combat Style: Skoutatos

Unit: Toxotes and Psiloi
Role: regular infantry
Armour: Greek light armour
Combat Style: Toxotes

MERCENARIES

A substantial portion of the army is composed of non-Greek mercenaries. Some of these are "imperial mercenaries" with a continuing obligation towards the empire. Others have no such arrangement but are paid a retainer during peacetime to keep them at combat readiness. The empire's enthusiasm for mercenaries has waned in the last fifty years following the revolt of Roger de Flor's Catalan Company. The significant foreign mercenary syntrophiai (brotherhoods or companies) still employed consist of the Cretan light infantry, the Condottieri, and the Latinikon.

The Cretans are the remnants of a military colony composed of refugees from the Venetian conquest of Crete. They were established in Nicea, but when the territory was lost to the Ottoman Turks, it was moved to a colony on the northern side of the Golden Horn. The Cretans are famous for their unswerving loyalty to the empire. The Condottieri are an Italian phenomenon, although most are not actually Italian in nationality but instead are drawn from all nations of Europe.

Condottiere bands formed in Italy to provide military support to various city-states. They were formed initially from amongst the many thousand soldiers left unemployed following the end of the Hundred Years War. Most Condottiere companies have a variety of troop types, but heavy cavalry, heavy infantry, archers, and handgonners are mainstays

The Latinikon are not a single unit, rather a catch-all term for any non-Italic Frankish mercenary brotherhoods. Most of them are French, and while some are specialist infantry units such as crossbowmen (Tzangratoroi) and handgonners, most are heavy cavalry.

Ten thousand Albanians were settled in Morea in the late fourteenth century in exchange for military service. Evenly split between cavalry and spearmen, these forces were used to reconquer Morea in the 1430s and 1440s. However, as a whole they are not available to the Empire as a whole. The Cumans once formed a mainstay of the Byzantine light cavalry and horse-archers called hippotoxotes. This Turkic people from the Eastern European steppes are expert horsemen and superb archers. Unfortunately, the bulk of the Cuman skirmisher unit was loaned to the Kingdom of Serbia in the 1320s and never returned.

The Tauroi Chalkeoi, or "Bronze Bulls" were proud to be at the forefront of the Empire's battle lines in land wars. This mercenary unit consists entirely of minotauroi (page 58) clad in heavy bronze armour and wielding fearsome menaulia (glaives). They are famous for opening charges against the enemy, using both their carried weapons and their horns to devastating effect. While instrumental in the Restoration, in recent years the need for this expensive mercenary unit has been questioned and the Tauroi Chalkeoi have all but disbanded.

Unit: Albanian mercenary
Role: mercenary infantry
Armour: Greek light armour
Combat Style: Halberdier

Unit: Cretan Light Infantry
Role: mercenary infantry
Armour: Greek light armour
Combat Style: Toxotes (using slings)

Unit: Condottiere Pikemen
Role: mercenary infantry
Armour: Frankish heavy armour
Combat Style: Halberdier

Unit: Hippotoxotes
Role: mercenary cavalry
Armour: Greek light armour
Combat Style: Trapezites

Unit: Latinikon or Condotierre Knights
Role: mercenary cavalry
Armour: Frankish heavy armour
Combat Style: Cavalier

Unit: Latinikon or Condotierre Handgonners
Role: mercenary infantry
Armour: Frankish medium armour
Combat Style: Arquebusier or Schiopettiere

Unit: Tzangratoroi
Role: mercenary infantry
Armour: Frankish medium armour
Combat Style: Crossbowman

Unit: Tauroi Chalkeoi
Role: mercenary infantry (minotauroi)
Armour: Frankish heavy armour (bronze)
Combat Style: Chalkotauros

IMPERIAL GUARDS

The Imperial Guard regiments or *phroura* are mercenary units in the permanent employ of the emperor. They usually remain close to the person of the emperor as their primary function is as his bodyguards. However, each also has other functions in the emperor's service. There is fierce competition between the guard regiments, and numerous jurisdictional disputes. The Guard regiments are general considered fiercely loyal to the emperor and virtually incorruptible. It is an adage that they cannot be bribed, and only the foolish would try.

There are four Guard regiments in the mid fifteenth century, in order of precedence these are the *Varrangai* (or Varangians), the *Paramonai*, the *Mourtatoi*, and the *Tzakones*. Some count the Vardariotai amongst the guard units, but they do not have a guarding function, being mostly a police force. More information about these units can be found in Chapter 6.

Unit: Varrangai
Role: guard infantry
Armour: Greek heavy armour
Combat Style: Pelekyphoros

Unit: Paramonai
Role: guard infantry and cavalry
Armour: Greek heavy armour
Combat Style: Kataphraktos

Unit: Mourtatoi
Role: guard infantry
Armour: Greek medium armour
Combat Style: Toxotes

Unit: Tzakones
Role: guard infantry
Armour: Greek heavy armour
Combat Style: Apelatikiaros

THE MILITIA AND THE CITY WATCH

The provincial themata once maintained their own armies under a commander called the doux. With the loss of the themata, the provincial army has been reduced to *katepanika* – a small administrative unit centred on a *kastron* or walled town with a central keep. These are found scattered throughout what remains of the territory of the Empire. A katepanikon is under the command of a kephale or governor, who is assisted by a *kastrophylax* (fortress guard) who looks after the defences of the katepanikon, and a tzaousios who commands the garrison. Most of the members of the garrison are civilian watchmen called *phylakes*, who also man the numerous watch towers (*pyrgoi*) along the borders of the empire. The provincial phylakes receive identical training to the city watch of Constantinople who bear the same name. The one place that crossbowmen are regularly encountered in the Greek armed forces is amongst the garrisons of the militia and the watch.

The Vardariotai are the police force of Constantinople. They began as a guard unit in charge of keeping order at court, a role they still fulfil. Over time their command was transferred to the Grand Logothete, who put them at the service of the city as a whole. They are widely disliked by the people.

Unit: Phylakes
Role: civilian watch
Armour: Greek light armour
Combat Style: Phylax or Crossbowman

Unit: Vardariotai
Role: police
Armour: Greek medium armour
Combat Style: Manglabliaros

THE NAVY

The foundation of the current navy lies in the fleet of 80 ships built by Michael VIII Palaiologos. By the fourteenth century most of this fleet had been disbanded to reduce costs and a fleet was hired from Genoa when needed. Today the Byzantine navy consists of just 10 ships, manned by *Prosalentai* and *Gasmoulai* (marines). Some of these ships are the same ones built by Michael VIII two hundred years ago.

The Prosalentai are primarily oarsmen, but who have been given weapon training. Every bank of oars in a Byzantine galley is supposed to have at least one Prosalentai as well as two or three non-fighting oarsmen.

Aboard ship is the only place that the Gasmoulai have been able to secure a position in the standing military. These Greco-Latin half-breeds are not popular amongst the populace, but they are savage fighters with a point to prove.

In the past, naval battles have seen ships manned with men from the Tzakones Guard, who were originally marines before the fleet was disbanded.

Unit: Prosalentai
Role: armed sailors
Armour: none or Greek light armour
Combat Style: Shipboard Combat

Unit: Gasmoulai
Role: marines
Armour: Greek light armour
Combat Style: Apelatikiaros

PRIVATE UNITS

Many of the dynatoi maintain their own private armies to defend their own property and family against those who would try to take it from them, whether it be Turks, fellow noblemen, or the mob. There are some smaller mercenary bands who will fulfil this role, but many rely on their oiketai and oikeioi. Both these groups have personal obligations towards a lord; the oikeioi are his companions and relatives, who are generally of similar social standing as the lord and he acts more or less as a first amongst equals in their company. The oiketai on the other hand are a lord's retainers who have a social obligation towards the lord; they may be the sons of his tenant farmers or family servants, or his wards or foster sons. Between them these two groups form the retinue of a lord at war.

THE MEDITERRANEAN WORLD

Constantinople is arrogant in her wealth, treacherous in her practices, corrupt in her faith; just as she fears everyone on account of her wealth, she is dreaded by everyone because of her treachery and faithlessness.

~Odo of Deuil, 1147

This chapter describes the world outside the walls of The City. In particular, the other powers around the Mediterranean Sea are considered: the Ottoman Empire, the Italian City States, and the Mamluk Sultanate. Briefer treatment is given to more distant lands: the independent nations of the Balkans, the Turkoman states to the east, and the Frankish kingdoms to the west.

While this book concentrates on the city of Constantinople, the Byzantine Empire is larger than the city – but only just. At its height, the empire claimed as its territory all of Greece including the islands, much of the Balkans, and most of Asia Minor. In the middle of the fifteenth century it is reduced to the very corner of Thrace, and Morea on the Peloponnese. The remaining European cities are important to the survival of Constantinople, since between them there is just enough agricultural land to support the mainland cities (including Constantinople) without relying on expensive foreign imports of grain and meat.

THE EMPIRE IN EUROPE

EPIBATOS

A small town on the Marmaran coast, 50 kilometres west of Constantinople. Epibatos is a popular retreat for those wishing to escape the bustle and the smell of the city, and is surrounded by the villas of the dynatoi families who maintain property here. The countryside surrounding the town is used to raise geese and pigs, which are driven to Constantinople to meet the demand for their meat.

SELYMBRIA

An ancient city founded in the days when Constantinople was still Byzantion. It fell to the Ottomans in 1399, but was returned four years later when the Sultan's forces suffered a disastrous defeat at the hands of Timur the Lame, and was forced to relinquish some of its European holdings. Since then it has been attacked several times by the Turk but has never been reconquered.

Selymbria has an enviable position on the main trade routes around the Black Sea coast and a long natural harbour for taking ships. Rich Constantinople families often have a summer home here amongst the vine-covered hills: Selymbria is famous for its grapes and wine production, and also has the climate for domestic silk production.

The most recent ruler of Selymbria was the Despot Theodoros Palaiologos, brother to Emperor Constantine XI Palaiologos. He died in 1448 with no male heirs, and the city has continued under the rule of his former counsellors until the emperor sees fit to appoint a regent.

MESEMBRIA

From the fifth century onwards an important stronghold of the Byzantine Empire, Mesembria (or, to give it its Slavonic name, Nesebar) has exchanged hands between the Greeks and the Bulgarians since the days of Khan Krum. After five centuries in Bulgarian hands it was finally returned to Greek hands when it was conquered in 1366 by Venetian knights lead by the Count of Savoy. The fortress at Mesembria is on a small, manmade island connected to the mainland by an easily-defendable peninsula.

ANCHIALOS

Like Mesembria, Anchialos has been alternatively a Byzantine and Bulgarian possession, and was ceded back to Byzantium after its capture by the Count of Savoy. Anchialos is important for the production of salt, which is essential for the preservation of meat and fish.

MOSYNOPOLIS

Once a stronghold of the Manichean heresy in the twelfth century, this was stamped out in the Norman invasion of 1185 and the town was virtually destroyed in 1208 by Tsar Kaloyan of Bulgaria. It lay vacant for most of the Frankokratia, but the city was reoccupied in the Palaiologan Restoration and is the breadbasket of Constantinople, providing much of the grain that cannot be grown in the immediate vicinity of the city.

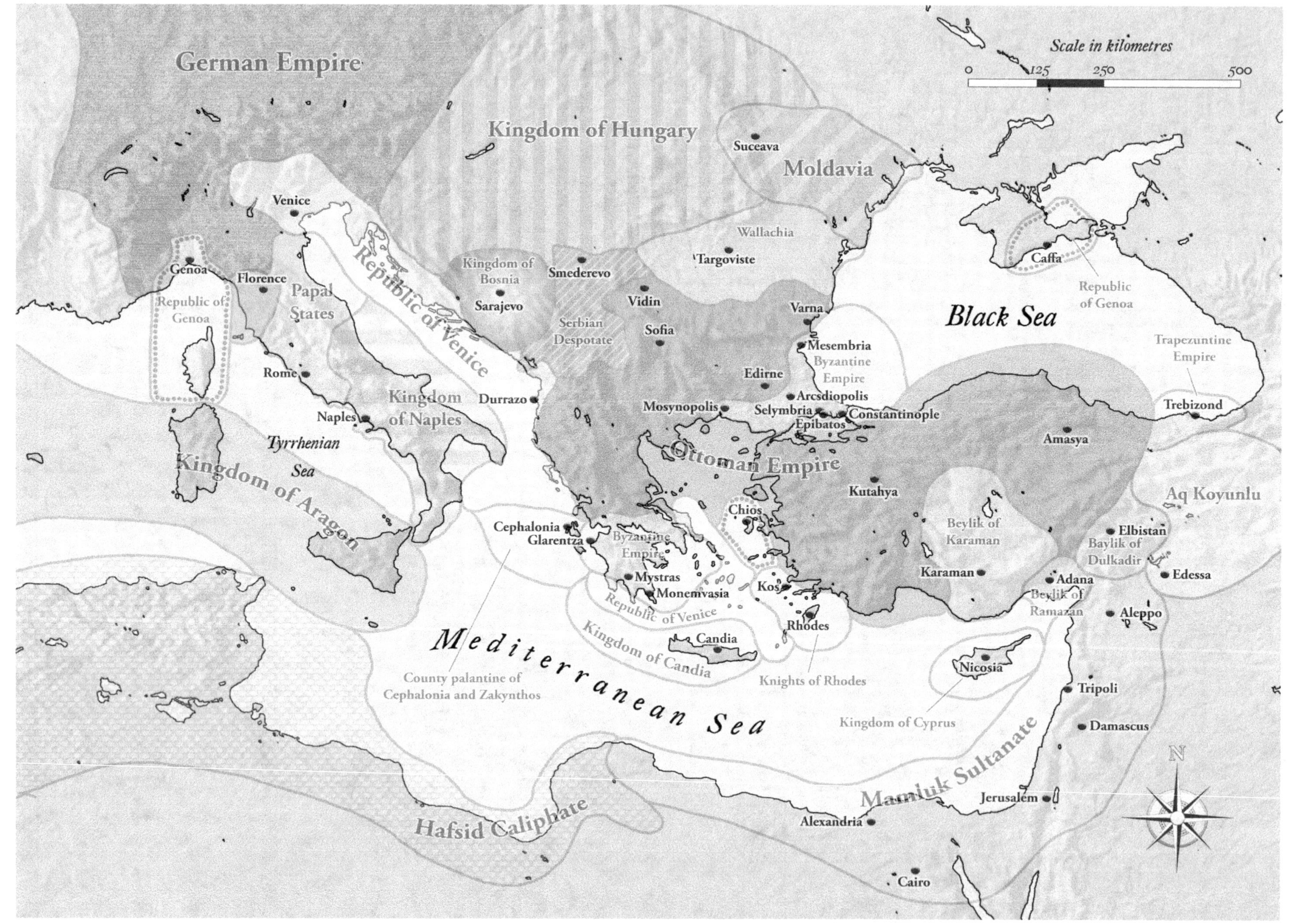
German Empire
Scale in kilometres
0
125
250
500
Kingdom of Hungary
Suceava
Moldavia
Venice
Wallachia
Targoviste
Caffa
Republic of Genoa
Genoa
Florence
Republic of Genoa
Papal States
Republic of Venice
Kingdom of Bosnia
Sarajevo
Smederevo
Serbian Despotate
Vidin
Sofia
Varna
Black Sea
Mesembria
Byzantine Empire
Trapezuntine Empire
Rome
Kingdom of Naples
Naples
Durrazo
Edirne
Arcsdiopolis
Mosynopolis
Selymbria
Epibatos
Constantinople
Trebizond
Amasya
Tyrrhenian Sea
Kingdom of Aragon
Ottoman Empire
Kutahya
Aq Koyunlu
Chios
Cephalonia
Glarentza
Byzantine Empire
Beylik of Karaman
Elbistan
Baylik of Dulkadir
Karaman
Edessa
Mystras
Monemvasia
Kos
Adana
Beylik of Ramazan
Republic of Venice
Rhodes
Aleppo
Candia
Kingdom of Candia
Mediterranean Sea
Nicosia
Knights of Rhodes
County palantine of Cephalonia and Zakynthos
Tripoli
Kingdom of Cyprus
Damascus
Mamluk Sultanate
N
Jerusalem
Alexandria
Hafsid Caliphate
Cairo

ARCADIOPOLIS

Emperor Theodosios I renamed the city of Bergula in honour of his son and heir Arcadios. A battle was fought here in 970 at which the Byzantine army crushed a combined force of Rus, Magyar, and Pecheneg nomads who were hoping to take Constantinople, 160 kilometres to the east.

LEMNOS AND IMBROS

During the Frankokratia the isle of Lemnos was given as a fief to the Venetian Navigajoso family, but under orders from Michael VIII Palaiologos it was won back from the last remaining member of that family in 1282. With the loss of Asia Minor to the Turk, Lemnos has become vital in supplying Constantinople with sufficient grain, and its lordship is generally given to a member of the royal family, although it is currently under the rule of the Grand Domestic, a more distant Palaiologian relative. King Alfonso V of Aragon has demanded Lemnos as part of his price in helping the Byzantines resist the Ottoman Empire, but Emperor Constantine XI Palaiologos is keeping it in reserve for now as a rich prize to offer a more trustworthy ally.

THE DESPOTATES OF MOREA

Michael VIII Palaiologos defeated the Frankish Prince of Achaea, William II Villehardouin at the Battle of Pelagonia in 1259. The Peloponnese thus became the first part of mainland Greece in the Restoration of the Byzantine Empire. The fertile agricultural land and rich fishing waters of Morea have always been a prized possession, but it was John IV Kantakouzenos who, in the mid fourteenth century, reorganised the Peloponnese into a despotate for his son Manuel. A pattern was established that the heir to the Byzantine Empire would be Despot of Morea until his ascension, a wise precaution to split the emperor from his heir as the encroachment of the Ottoman Empire drew ever closer to Constantinople.

In 1427 the despotate was divided into three to accommodate the three sons of Emperor Manuel II Palaiologos. Demetrios received Mistra in the south, Thomas Glarentza in the northwest, and Constantine Kalavryta in the north. Over the next three years the despots defeated and conquered the remaining holdings of the Principality of Achaea. The six-mile long wall (the Hexamilion) that once guarded the Isthmus of Corinth was repaired to ward against the Turk. By the time Constantine became emperor, Morea had acquired Patras, Athens, Thebes, and Boetia with the help of Albanian mercenaries fleeing the Ottomans. In 1446 Sultan Murad II could not allow the conquests of the Morean despots to continue, and destroyed the Hexamilion, opening Morea to invasion. The sultan died before he could exploit this weakness, and his successor Mehmed II has yet to move on the Peloponnese, but it can only be a matter of time.

FORMER BYZANTINE TERRITORIES

Upon the partition of the Byzantine Empire in 1204, various Crusader lords were given control of different parts of the territory. Much of this was reclaimed by the Empire in the Restoration, only to be lost to the Ottomans. Other territories have been swallowed by the Republic of Venice or other states (see later). However, there are still some small independent nations in the region, most notably Cyprus and Rhodes.

KINGDOM OF CYPRUS

Cyprus has been a Frankish Kingdom since the Third Crusade. From the capital at Nicosia the French House of Lusignan has ruled since 1194. The native Cypriot population is ruled over by the *Haute Cour* (high court) of French-descended noblemen. The current king John II, like his forebears, claims the empty title of King of Jerusalem, although it has not been in Christian hands for over a century and a half. The king's life is dominated by two women, Queen Helena Palaiologina (the daughter of the Despot of the Morea Theodoros II Palaiologos) and Marietta de Patras, the king's mistress. The former has given the king a daughter, whereas the latter has produced a much-loved son. Such is the hatred between the two women that, in a public brawl, the queen bit off Marietta's nose.

The population of the towns are mostly of Frankish descent, retaining their French language and Catholic faith. However, the majority of the population is Greek-speaking and Orthodox. The Church of Cyprus is an autocephalous Orthodox community under the authority of an archbishop which achieved independence from the Patriarchate of Antioch in 431. There are currently four Orthodox bishops (including the archbishop), each one under the nominal authority of a Catholic bishop. Despite historical persecutions, the two churches manage to co-exist and even co-operate, partly due to the influence of Queen Helena.

RHODES

The island of Rhodes has been held by the Byzantine Greeks, Umayyad Arabs, Seljuk Turks, and Genoese adventurers, but since 1309 it has been occupied by the Knights Hospitaller. After the fall of the Kingdom of Jerusalem in 1291 to the Mamluks, the Order was forced to move. They initially set up headquarters in Cyprus, but were seeking a more permanent home when they seized control of Rhodes and several nearby islands. The city of Rhodes has been rebuilt and fortified in the manner of a European city, and its legendarily strong walls have withstood a siege by the Mamluks in 1444.

The city of Rhodes is not very large, but has an imposing Palace of the Grand Master, called the *Kastello*, which is partly within and partly outside the city. The harbour is large and well-guarded, with two moles entering the sea. One of the moles is bedecked with windmills. There is a great deal of trade at Rhodes: no ships go to Alexandria, Jerusalem, or Syria without stopping at Rhodes, and the Ottoman Empire is so close it can be seen from the island. The people of the island are Greek and grow much fruit, particularly citrons, lemons, and limes. Most are of the Orthodox faith, and have their own bishop. There are several minotauroi settlements in the territory of the Knights of Rhodes, in particular on the island of Kos.

The Knights of Rhodes are described in Chapter 6. The auberges (headquarters) of the seven subdivisions of the Order are found either in the city or elsewhere on the island.

THE OTTOMAN EMPIRE

Compared with the ancient pedigree of the Byzantine Empire, the Ottoman Empire is an upstart, less than a century old, and yet it occupies a territory that rivals the Byzantine Empire at its zenith. Osman took Bithynia, his first major city, in 1302, and proceeded to conquer the surrounding Byzantine cities over the next twenty years. His descendants continued to expand his emirate from his base in Bursa, crossing the Bosphoros and taking the first European possession at Gallipoli in 1357. Only five years later, the Sultan had taken the great Byzantine city of Adrianople, renamed it Edirne, and made it his capital. Serbia fell to the Ottomans in 1389, Wallachia in 1391, Bulgaria and Albania in 1396. Meanwhile, most of Anatolia has fallen under the Sultan's yoke. Thessaloniki held out until 1430, and Epiros until 1433. Morea is the only holdout on mainland Greece, and, of course, the jewel that is Constantinople.

THE TURKISH PEOPLE

The Ottoman Turks do not have an aristocracy as such. The empire arose from the pre-eminence of a single family – Osman and his descendants – who began as tribal chiefs, just one amongst many. Apart from the sultan and his immediate family, Ottoman society is split into three: the professional class, the common people, and the slaves.

SOCIAL STATUS

Ottoman social structure is a blending of traditional Muslim classes with Turkic elements. There are two basic ways in which people can be divided in Ottoman society: the first divides Muslims from non-Muslims (zimmi), and the second distinguishes those who work for the state from those who do not. By definition, the Muslim is considered superior to the non-Muslim, but in practice people of different creeds are often treated as equals according to their usefulness. Advancement in society is based mostly on merit, but also in part by Turkish blood.

The professional class – who work directly for the Ottoman state – is equivalent to the aristocracy of Greek and Frankish culture but membership is defined by the will of the sultan, not a right of birth. This professional class divides into four major groups: the *mülkiye*, the *kalemiye*, the *seyfiye*, and the *ilmiye*. The first of these groups, the mülkiye, consists of all individuals involved in activities that take place in the imperial palace. This includes a great variety of craftsmen, services, schools for government offices and for the Yeniçeri, the servants of the court, the members of the Divan, the provincial and district governors, and so forth. The kalemiye is the caste of scribes, and is responsible for the financial administration of the empire. The treasurers of the Divan and the tax collectors are members of this group. The seyfiye are the military, strictly speaking the feudal warriors (*timarli*) and the sultan's slave army (the *maasli*); the irregular units are not considered to be amongst the professional class. The structure of the army will be described in more detail in a later section. The final group of professionals was the ilmiye, the religious caste. They are all members of the ulema, the college of Islamic scholars who determine the law for all Muslim members of the empire.

Ranks in the Ottoman Empire are dispensed by the sultan on merit only; they are not inherited and can be withdrawn as easily as bestowed. The basic rank of *bey* ("lord") is used for governors, military commanders, and bureaucrats, although its near-equivalent *ağa* is a military honorific. Above the bey is the *paşa*, which has three grades signified by one, two, or three horsetails decorating their ceremonial standard or *tugh* (the sultan himself has four). The general title for a lord is *çelebi* (or *hanim* for his wife). The only royal titles are those of the sultan himself and his sons who bear the title *şehzade*, or for those who have married an Ottoman princess, *damat* ("bridegroom").

Nine out of every ten subjects of the Ottoman Empire are members of the *reaya* (literally "the flock") who do not work for the state. These are the equivalent of the "free men" of other societies, mostly determined by the requirement for them to pay a land-use tax to the state. This tax must be paid regardless of religion, but each religious group pays different taxes to different officials. The reaya are therefore grouped into millets, social units of organisation based on religion. The majority of the subjects of the Ottoman Empire in the fifteenth century are non-Muslim, and the largest of the millets is the Orthodox millet. This millet contains all members of the Patriarchates of Bulgaria and Serbia, plus those members of the Patriarchate of Constantinople who live in lands conquered by the Ottomans. There are also millets for the Muslims, Armenian Christians, Syrian Christians, and Jews. Each has an appointed ruler called a millet-başi, who reports directly to the Sultan.

SLAVERY

Slavery is even more common in the Ottoman Empire than it is in western lands. A slave (*kul*) is the property of his owner, with no more rights than livestock. It is forbidden under law to enslave a Muslim, although post-slavery conversions are treated with a great deal of suspicion, and the penalty for religious apostasy is death by impalement. The main source of slaves is captives of war and organised slaving expeditions around the Black Sea and, more recently, into Africa to obtain valuable Zanj slaves with black skin. Many European slaves are bought from the Crimean Tatars, Slavic peasants raided from Poland, Lithuania, and the Rus' states. Slaves are traded in dedicated marketplaces called yesir, and the recapture of runaway slaves is performed by the dedicated profession of *yavaci*.

A *cariye* is a concubine, a woman sold into sexual slavery and used as a casual sexual partner by the harem's owner. Slaves enter the harem as an *odalik* (literally "chambermaid") in a virginal state, and many remain virgins, to be given as gifts to those one wishes to honour. Odaliks and cariyes learn to dance, to play musical instruments, and to recite poetry for the entertainment of the harem owner. Only once an odalik is presented to her master for sex does she become a concubine, and from this point she can reclaim some of her former status by becoming a *gözde* or "favourite". She will never hope to become a wife – slave concubines are used for gratification because they have no lineage and any children who result share their mother's status. Circassians, Syrians, and Nubians are considered the most beautiful, and command the highest prices.

Sexual slavery is not limited to girls. Christian boys taken in the *devşirme* may become *köçeks* (cross-dressing dancers), *tellaks* (masseurs), or *saqis* (wine-pourers), mostly in bathhouses (*hammam*). Only those who are young and beardless are exploited in this way; and some are made eunuchs to preserve their youthful appearance.

ASTOMATOI

This race of non-humans can be found throughout the Ottoman territories. They are tall, mouthless humanoids with greenish-tinged skins and immense ears that surround them like a cloak. They do not gather with members of their own race, at least not in Ottoman-controlled lands, but instead form some sort of relationship with the Ottoman ruling class – *sanjak-beys, beys, paşas*, and one is even a vizier on the Divan (see below). There may only be a handful of them in any given city, and they are rarely seen together. The astomatoi are highly secretive and seem to simply stand and observe the human they accompany. The edict from the sultan is that the astomatoi are not to be impeded and that their advice, on the rare occasions it is offered, should be followed – within reason.

Most Ottomans find the astomatoi disconcerting, with their judging stares and their creepy silence. Beys who have questioned the need for them to be around tend to be replaced by the administration. The role that the astomatoi play is as yet unknown; the paranoid say that they are the secretly manipulating – perhaps even controlling – the Ottoman elite to their own ends. Others believe that they are spies for the Divan. Few believe that their motives are anything other than sinister. More about the astomatoi can be found on page 57.

GOVERNANCE

The sultan or *padişah* (lord of kings) is the supreme leader of the Ottoman State. The caliphate (highest Islamic authority) has been claimed by the sultans of the Ottoman Empire since Murad I. The sultan has been a member of the House of Osman since the very beginning of the empire. His personal standard is red with the fabled twin-bladed *zulfikar* sword and four horsetails. The standard of the House of Osman bears a stylised bird with its wings uplifted. The Ottoman Empire's flag is green with three white crescents

The *Divan-i Hümayun* is the ministerial council advising the sultan, headed by the *Sadrazam* (grand vizier or prime minister). It consists of three viziers (ministers), two *kadi'askers* (military judges), the *defterdar* (treasurer), the *nişanci* (chancellor), the *beylerbey* ("bey of beys") of Rumelia, the *Derya Bey* ("bey of the sea", commander-in-chief of the navy), and the *Ağa* of the Yeniceris. The Divan has two subordinate groups. Firstly, it is in charge of the provincial governors and military elite, who in turn control the local administrators who themselves are in charge of the landowners and tax collectors. Secondly, the Divan also oversees the heads of the millets, and thereby exercises executive power over the people of the empire.

The Imperial Harem (*Harem-i Hümayun*) is an important yet subtle force of governance in the Ottoman Empire. It is ruled by the mother of the sultan, the Valide Sultan, and populated by his wives, servants, female relatives and concubines, as well as those of his chief advisors. The Valide Sultan influences the political life of the empire through regulating the relations between the sultan and his wives and children, and by arranging dynastic marriages between foreign hostages and Turkish statesmen. The Valide Sultan also has the best network of spies and agents of the royal court, administered through the army of eunuchs that serve her. Second in rank to the Valide Sultan is the Haseki Sultan, the mother of the sultan's first-born son. There are up to four *kadins* (wives) who rank next, then the eight ikbals (the fortunates). The rest of the harem is made up of the princesses and ladies taken as foreign hostages, and the slave concubines (see earlier). Harem members of kadin rank or higher may use the honorific "*hatun*", meaning "lady".

TERRITORIES

The three provinces (*beylerbeyliks*) of the Ottoman Empire are Rumelia, Andolu, and Rüm. They were created in that order and have that precedence, although the beylerbey of Anatolia is also viceroy of the empire. Each beyerbeylik is composed of sanjaks (districts), each under the command of a sanjak-bey. Most sanjaks are comprised from former territories conquered by the empire. The sanjak-beys are usually non-hereditary appointments who have no family attachments to the area. Each sanjak is further divided into *kazas* (subdistrict). Each kaza typically represents a city, and has a bey (lord) from the military class representing the sultan's executive authority and a *kadi* (judge) representing his legal authority.

Provincial civil and judicial administration is carried out by the bey and the kadi. These two officials keep a check on one another: the executive authority of the bey cannot be exercised without sentence provided by the kadi. Although technically under the authority of the bey and kadi, towns and villages conquered by the empire are self-governing according to the laws of their millet. Each millet is guaranteed to maintain its own laws, traditions, language and practice of religion without forced conversion to Islam.

RUMELIA

The first territory in Europe taken by the Ottoman Empire was Gallipoli in Thrace. In just four decades, the Turkish war machine has inexorably crept across the southern Balkans, and now stretches from the Adriatic to the Black Sea, and from the Carpathian Mountains to the shores of the Aegean Sea. The Beylerbeylik of Rumelia is the administrative division of the empire that encompasses all European holdings of the Ottoman Empire. It is ruled from Edirne, which also serves as the home of the Sultan and thus the capitol of the whole empire.

Despite the change in rulership, life has not changed a great deal for the inhabitants of Rumelia. The millet system is designed to allow conquered people to be self-governing and to avoid disruption of pre-existing power structures. The greatest hardship suffered under Ottoman rule is the *devirşme* (see later). Rumelia consists mostly of people of Bulgarian, Albanian, and Greek origins who now live under the Ottoman Empire. They are culturally Ottoman, although maintain their own Slavic or Greek customs and appearance.

Another consequence of Ottoman rule is the settlement of Turkish people amongst the native population. Many of these are ex-soldiers and their families, but there is also net immigration to Rumelia from Anatolia actively encouraged by the beylerbey. The beylerbey is in charge of the most important military force in the empire outside the sultan's own forces, in the form of the *timariot sipahi* heavy cavalry (see later), and since his capitol coincides with the sultan's, he is included as a member of the divan (ruling council) of the empire.

ANDOLU

The Beylerbeylik of Andolu was the first Ottoman province to be established. It came about in 1393, when Sultan Bayezid I needed to appoint a viceroy to look after his Anatolian provinces while he campaigned in Europe. The beylerbeylik covers most of Ottoman-controlled Asia Minor, save those sanjaks that make up the Beylerbeylik of Rüm. Andolu is ruled from Kütahya. The majority of the people are ethnically Turkish, although some Greeks still occupy the coastal provinces.

RÜM

The third and smallest Beylerbeylik, Rüm was formed from Bayezid I's conquests in northeastern Anatolia. Rüm was the name originally given to the whole of Asia Minor, deriving its name from the Eastern Roman Empire. Rüm was part of the Ilkhanate of Rüm, a successor state of the great Mongol Empire of Genghis Khan. It was entrusted to a governor in 1335 who claimed independence from the Ilkhanate, and the emerging Emirate of Eretna (named after its founder) lasted some sixty years, until it was added to the Ottoman Empire as a new beylerbeylik. It was in Rüm that the Turks first came across the astomatoi, who have since entered into some kind of compact with the Ottoman ruling class.

The Beylerbeylik of Rüm is ruled from Amasya.

VASSAL STATES

To the Ottomans, the world is divided into broad regions or 'houses': the House of Peace (*Dar as-Salam*) consists of countries under Muslim rule where other faiths are left unmolested; and the House of War (*Dar al-Kharb*), where heathens (i.e. Christians) rule and other faiths are persecuted. The House of Truce (Dar al-'Ahd) are vassal states of Muslim nations, lands of non-believers with a treaty of non-aggression in return for a tribute paid to the Sultan.

Much of Rumelia began as tribute states, and this process is ongoing with Serbia and Wallachia forming a buffer region between the Ottoman Empire and the Dar al-Kharb of Hungary and beyond.

THE PRINCIPALITY OF WALLACHIA

Nominally a vassal state of the Ottoman Empire, the principality is riven by civil war between two royal families, the Danesti and the Draculesti.

Vlad II Dracul ascended the throne in 1436, but his son Mircea II took over in 1442 while his father was at the Ottoman court negotiating assistance against the ambition of John Hunyadi in Hungary. Mircea was ousted in 1443 and the Hungarians put Basarab II of the Danesti on the throne, but lost this to Vlad II Dracul a year later with the help of the Ottomans. Dracul paid them a tribute and the sultan held his sons Vlad III and Radu hostage. Mircea II did not support his father's alliance with the Ottomans and led Wallachian forces against the empire. At the Battle of Varna Hunyadi demanded that Vlad II fulfil his oath as a member of the Order of the Dragon and a vassal of Hungary but he refused to join the battle, although Mircea II did. In 1447 the *boyars* (noblemen) in league with Hunyadi rebelled against the Draculesti. Lead by Vladislav II of the House of Danesti, the rebels blinded Mircea with a hot poker and buried him alive, and his father Vlad II was beheaded. Hunyadi placed Vladislav II on the throne of Wallachia. His rule lasted just one year: Vlad III Dracul was released from Ottoman captivity in 1448 and he deposed Vladislav with the help of his former captives. His brother Radu was also released, but he had become a great friend of the sultan's son Murad, and converted to Islam and entered Ottoman service. Vladislav regained control of Wallachia later that year and Vlad III escaped to Moldavia where he stayed with his uncle Prince Bogdan.

The flag of Wallachia consists of a raven holding a red double cross and a red star in its beak, perched on a green juniper.

THE SERBIAN DESPOTATE

The Principality of Serbia became a subject state of the Ottoman Empire in 1389 following the Battle of Kosovo. However, the new prince Stefan Lazarevic was an unwilling ally. In the early years of his reign, Stefan fought on behalf of the sultan, but clearly as an unwilling ally. He styled himself despot after being awarded the title by Emperor Manuel II Palaiologos in Constantinople in 1402, and this spurred him to turn on his conquerors during the Ottoman Interregnum and accept the suzerainty of the King of Hungary, for which he received land including his new capital Belgrade. Shifting alliances forced Stefan to side alternately with Hungary and the Ottomans. He used the rift between the sons of Bayezid I to acquire more territory, assisting one brother (Mehmed) against the other (Musa) when the latter sought to expand his holdings in Rumelia. With Musa dead and Serbia in alliance with Mehmed, the despotate entered a golden age. Its silver mines gave it financial security, and there was a boom in art, sculpture, and poetry.

When Stefan died in 1427, his nephew Durad Brankovic became despot. Serbia has suffered a period of Ottoman occupation between 1439 and 1444, when they were expelled by a coalition of Serbians, Hungarians, and Wallachians. Between 1446 and 1448, Serbia was at war with Bosnia over territory taken from them under Stefan's rule, but with help from his Byzantine allies Durad has forced the Bosnians to retreat. Brankovic's wife is Despoena Irene Kantakouzene, known locally as *Prokleta Jerina* ("Irene the Damned"). She is the sister of George Palaiologos Kantakouzenos and cousin to the Byzantine emperor. Hated and feared because of her many evil acts, including throwing children off her high tower at Smederevo into a river in order to dedicate it to Hell.

The Serbian flag is yellow, with a double-headed eagle in red.

MOUNT ATHOS

The Holy Mountain (Greek: *Agion Oros*) is located on the easternmost leg of the Chalkidiki peninsula in Macedonia which protrudes 50 kilometres into the sea, at no more than 12 kilometres wide. The first monastery was founded here in 958 by Athanasios the Athonite, who built the Protaton (first church) and the Great Lavra Monastery. Nineteen more monasteries followed under the patronage of the Byzantine emperors and its wealth grew considerably. The Fourth Crusade brought Frankish overlords, who were forced to return pillaged goods by the pope. The mountain was returned to the Byzantine Empire upon the reconquest of Macedonia, but when Murad II conquered Thessaloniki in 1430, the monks pledged allegiance to him, and thus gained his protection as an independent state.

The Holy Mountain is run as an autonomous monastic republic under the authority of the Patriarch of Constantinople. It is governed by the Holy Community consisting of a representative from each of the 20 monasteries, and headed by an elected *Protos* ("First"). As well as the 20 monasteries there are numerous dependencies or *sketes* (see page 33). Women are forbidden from setting foot on Mount Athos to make celibacy easier for the monks. When the Serbian Emperor brought his wife here to protect her from the Black Death, she did not touch the ground for her entire stay but remained in a hand carriage at all times.

THE BYZANTINE EMPIRE

Since 1424 the Byzantine emperors have paid a yearly tribute to the Sultan in return for peace, placing the remains of the once-great nation within the Dar al-'Ahd.

OTTOMAN DAILY LIFE

The Ottoman way is to not interfere with the social structure of conquered people apart from where necessary, and the empire has more Rumeli (i.e. ethnically Greek) subjects than it does Turkic ones. However, migration of Turks into the European possessions of the sultan has been actively encouraged and Turks are now a familiar sight in the cities of Rumelia, although they may be entirely absent from the provinces. The people subjected to Ottoman rule inevitably pick up customs from their overlords as a matter of expedience and habit, although some tenaciously cling to their culture.

The currency of the Ottoman Empire is the silver *akçe*, a coin approximately equivalent to the Byzantine aspron, although slightly lighter and worth a little less: 20 akçes weigh the same as 16 Byzantine aspra (i.e. a hyperpyon). The *manghir* (8 to the akçe) is a smaller denomination coin in copper. Three akçe make a *para*, which is the largest denomination currently produced in the Empire.

APPEARANCE AND CLOTHING

The Anatolian Turks are naturally darker-skinned than European Greeks, and have distinctive features of their Seljuk ancestors. However, many generations of interbreeding with non-Turkic subjects of the Ottoman Empire have blurred this distinction, in Rumelia at least.

The basic items of male clothing are a short robe or tunic (*gömlek*) with trousers (*şalvar*), or for manual workers, short trousers (*potur*). All these garments are typically made of linen or cotton. A poor man or slave might own nothing more than this other than a waistcoat (*cepken*). The middle classes augment this basic garb with a sash (*kuşak*); a short fitted inner jacket (*hirka*) or a mid-length long-sleeved inner robe (*entari*); and maybe a short outer jacket (*yelek*) which may be short-sleeved or sleeveless. On the head is a felt or fur high-crowned cap (kalpak) or a turban (*sarik*). A wealthy or important man wears a short-sleeved outer robe (*kaftan*) beneath his yelek, this might be fur-lined and heavily embroidered; furthermore his tunic and trousers are more likely made of silk.

Women's clothing is similar to that of men, although garments tend to be longer than their male equivalents; in particular the gömlek is of mid-calf or ankle length. Even lower class women usually wear a hirka. If worn, the entari tends to be of a single colour, whereas the kaftan is covered in embroidery and made of rich patterned fabric. Both are buttoned only as far as the waist so that the contrasting lining of the kaftan can be seen. Women (with the exception of slaves) cover their hair in public with a veil (*yaşmak*) held in place by a headband (*çeki*), but rarely keep their faces covered.

Either sexes may wear a drab-coloured shapeless overcoat (feraçe) to protect their clothes when moving around town. This has slits in the front through which the hands can be thrust, and may have a hood and (for woman) a face veil.

Turkish people prefer to bathe daily, often in public baths or hammam. They are shocked at the uncleanliness of the comparatively clean Greeks, and appalled by the Franks. Many Ottoman men shave their beards but not their moustaches, although the more devout wear beards, considering shaving to be irreligious (since it alters the appearance that God has determined). Earrings are common in both sexes, as is other jewellery, although wearing gold is religiously prohibited to Muslim men.

FOOD AND DRINK

Bread and rice form the stable of the Turkish diet. Bread may be *has* bread of high quality flour or *harci* bread of poorer quality. The bread is often flavoured with sesame, cumin, or fennel seeds. The Turkish people use clarified butter in preference to oil, and make heavy use of yogurt and fruit even in savoury dishes. All but the poorest tables use honey or cane sugar to sweeten and spices to flavour, although the latter is used in moderation where cost is a consideration.

Mutton is the principal meat; as Muslims they eschew pork, and beef is only used in cured meats. Offal is very popular, particularly in Anatolian households, and sheep heads, feet, liver, intestine, and stomach are all used. Chicken is the province of the upper classes, and consumption of goose, duck, and pigeon is forbidden to all except the elite classes. The poor rely upon beans, lentils, peas, pumpkins, and radishes as well as various cereal crops, eating meat only rarely.

Sweet dishes are far more prevalent than in other Mediterranean cuisines. Sugar is a luxury but not exorbitantly expensive; and honey, fruit juice, and almonds are also used as sweeteners. Halva – made with sesame, almonds, or chestnuts – is popular with all strata of society, and most meals end with *zerde*, a flavoured pudding made of rice, sugar, and milk. Fruit jams and syrups are also common accompaniments, made with apple, pear, quince, cherry, rose, bitter orange, medlar, melon, and citron.

As Muslims, the consumption of alcohol is punishable by law. Other than water, Turkish people drink *hoşaf*, *şerbet*, and *boza*. Hoşaf is a fruit compote, mostly made of figs, grapes, apricots, or pears. Şerbet is a sweet syrup made from flower petals or leaves (rose, water lily, narcissus, violet, mint) and usually drunk diluted. Boza is made from fermented wheat, barley, or rice and is the principal drink in towns and cities. It is very mildly alcoholic but not sufficiently intoxicating to contravene religious law. However, so-called Tatar boza is laced with opium, and illegal. *Kahve* (coffee) is a recent import to Anatolian cities, brought by Yemeni Sufis who used it to remain awake and suppress their appetites during their religious devotions; although it has begun to be drunk recreationally.

PASTIMES

Ottoman pastimes feature the performing arts, including shadow-puppetry (*karagöz*), storytelling, dance, and music. The meddah (storyteller) is a popular figure in market places, employing a wide range of performance tricks such as sudden changes in volume, dramatic gestures, ventriloquism, and pyrotechnics to entertain. Shadow theatre uses the stock characters of Karagöz (from whence its name) and the learned Hacivat, along with a huge cast of regular characters, to tell humorous and bawdy tales often loaded with satire. Both storytelling and shadow-puppetry are employed to publically criticise the government and clerics, and they are not always seen as harmless entertainment by the establishment.

Sports include oil wrestling (*yağli güreş*), competitive archery, and *cirit*. Oil wrestlers wear leather breeches and douse themselves in olive oil; a win is achieved by getting an unbreakable hold on your opponent's breeches. Cirit is an equestrian sport where the objective is to score points by throwing a blunt wooden javelins at opposing players. Teams are made of up to 12 players, starting with the youngest player each rides forth and calls the name of an opponent, throwing his javelin. He then flees while the challenged player gives chase, trying to score with his own cirit.

Opium (see page 27) is forbidden by the religious elite and yet still widely enjoyed. Other intoxicants include tatula and deli bal. The large yellow tatula seeds are imported from Tunisia. When chewed they cause intense and bizarre hallucinations quite unlike anything produced by opium, often leading to violent behaviour. The effective dose can vary widely between plants, and it is easy to poison oneself. Symptoms of tatula poisoning include overheating of the body and severe sensitivity to light. *Deli bal* or 'mad honey' is collected from wild-living bees on the Black Sea coast in Rüm. They make the honey from the toxic blossoms of rhododendron bushes, and consuming the honey causes a feeling of euphoria. The strength of mad honey can vary from year to year, and strong batches or overconsumption can lead to nausea, seizures, and death. Neither tatula nor deli bal are physiologically addictive in the same manner that opium is.

EDUCATION

Muslim children, both boys and girls, may be enrolled in the *sibyan* school system as early as three years old if they have elder siblings attending, although six years old is more normal. This is a state-run system of primary education, teaching children to read the Arabic language and script of the Qu'ran and instilled with the basics of Islam including ethics and the forms of worship. They are also taught simple arithmetic and Turkish grammar. The sibyan school is usually held in a large room attached to the local mosque, and can provide all the teaching necessary to prepare a boy for the *Medrese*, although few go that far.

There are two principal so-called palace schools, founded by a wealthy patron. The Medrese is for members of the Muslim faith only. Here, students are educated in traditional Islamic subjects of theology and law, in preparation for a religious life or else serving at court. The Medrese is expensive to attend, although grants are offered for promising students. The exterior or hariç school is preparatory for the interior or dahil school, where advanced religious topics are studied.

The *Enderun* is a palace school for Christian boys recruited through the devşirme. This is a free boarding school, with salaries for the teachers coming from the palace purse. The children are trained primarily as warriors; a punishing regime of physical effort and swordplay. They are also schooled in Turkish and Arabic, and given a basic education in Islamic theology, grammar, science, and courtly manners. Those who successfully graduate from the school convert to Islam and join the Yeniçeri. Those who fail, or who refuse to convert, become household slaves.

Education for a woman beyond the sibyan system was only provided if she lived in the palace or was raised in an ulema family. In these cases, women learned to read and write Turkish and studied the fundamentals of Islamic law as well as 'womanly' arts of needlework, singing, and playing musical instruments. Ladies of the harem studied Arabic and Persian literature as well as the Qu'ran

RELIGION

The Ottomans are Sunni Muslims, who accept the Prophet's father-in-law Abu Bakr as the first caliph; as opposed to the Prophet's son-in-law and cousin Ali, held to be the first caliph by Shi'a Islam. All Sunni Muslims are united by a common creed that includes a belief in: the Reality of God, the existence of angels, the authority of the books of God, following the prophets, preparation for the Day of Judgement, and the Supremacy of God's will.

The five pillars of faith are mandatory for Muslims: the proclamation of faith (*shahada*), the five daily prayers (*salat*), paying religious tax (*zakat*), fasting during Ramadan (*sawm*), and a pilgrimage to Mecca at least once in one's life (*hajj*). The salat takes place at a mosque (Turkish *mescidi*) under the leadership of an imam. All worshippers must abide by the rules of cleanliness, performing a ritual ablution before worship and abstaining from strong-smelling food until after prayer. Women are expected to cover their heads during prayer. Muslims follow dietary regulations including abstention from intoxicating drinks and from pork. Other actions which are *haram* (forbidden) include adultery, sex between unmarried individuals, usury and interest charges, making an image of a human being, depriving a child of his inheritance, altering one's physical appearance (including tattoos, dying the hair or beard, and wearing wigs), and (if a woman) wearing clothing that fails to cover the body properly, or (if a man) wearing gold and silk. The extent to which these prohibitions are followed varies considerably.

The Qu'ran holds that women are spiritually equal to men, but that women should exemplify femininity and men masculinity. This has led to a separation of the sexes in Islam; with women in charge of the world inside the home and men in charge outside it. Women live segregated lives, at least in larger households – living, eating, and praying in different social spaces to menfolk.

The *şeyhülislam* is the supreme religious authority in the empire, second only to the caliph (a role claimed by the sultan). The şeyhülislam advises the sultan on the teachings of the Qu'ran, but is also the only cleric entitled to issue *fatwas* – written interpretations of the Qu'ran that have authority over the entire millet of Islam. The şeyhülislam is head of the ulema, the college of Islamic scholars and the guardians of the legal and religious tradition of the empire. Each member of the ulema is a graduate of the Medrese, and may have studied in Persia or Egypt as well as (or instead of) within the empire. While some ulema concentrate on accounts of the prophet's life or explanations of religious texts, most are either a *müftü* or a *kadi*. The müftü (or "*mufti*" in Arabic) are scholars of the religious law or *fikh*, whereas the kadis are the judges involved in the practical application of fikh. A müftü is the equivalent of a professor – he is qualified to interpret and expound upon religious law, and provides legal instruction for lords in the same way that the şeyhülislam advises the emperor. A kadi ranks lower than a müftü; not only is the kadi a judge of the Şeriat court but he also presides over secular law and local customs as well. A kadi rules each sub-province hand-in-hand with a bey, adjudicating on criminal and civil matters as well as governing religious properties and acting as the legal guardian for orphans.

Religious law has two expressions: the *Şeriat* and the *fikh*. Şeriat (Arabic Sharia) is the body of law that governs every aspect of a

Muslim's life. It covers crime, trade, politics, economics, morality, dietary matters, sexual relationships, and all daily customs. The Şeriat is considered of divine provenance since it stems directly from the Qu'ran and the sayings of The Prophet. The fikh is the human understanding of Şeriat, the interpretation of the law into a legislative body. There are several schools of fikh (four in Sunni Islam and either two or three in Shi'a, depending upon sect), although in the Ottoman empire, the ulema is governed principally by the Hanafi school.

Islam lacks a religious hierarchy in the manner of Christian faiths. While the ulema fulfils this role to some extent, it is more of a legislative body than say, a synod of bishops, because in Islam there is no separation between religion and law. The müftüs and kadis do not interfere with the day-to-day worship of God, having no authority over the imams who administer each mosque. An imam is similar to a Christian priest in that he leads his congregation in prayer and provides spiritual advice when asked. He has no power to enforce moral behaviour, but can report religious impropriety to the kadi.

ALEVISM

Alevism is a mystical branch of Islam closest to Shi'a Islam but differing from them on several key points. It arose in the 11th century during the Turkish expansion into Anatolia, influenced by pre-Islamic belief of the Turkomans and wandering Sufis of the Bektashiyyah sect. They hold that the last four holy books (the Qu'ran, the Gospel, the Torah, and Psalms) have the same degree of importance in guiding people to the Divine Truth. Alevis do not observe the fast during Ramadan, nor do they count hajj as an article of faith. Alevis are not proselytisers, and membership is mostly inherited through the paternal line. Religious crimes lead to *düşkün*, or shunning, including murder, adultery, divorce, theft, and gossip. Alevis are strictly monogamous and do not practice gender segregation; but are still subject to cultural male-centred attitudes.

The central Alevi communal worship service is called a *cem*. It uses the Prophet's nocturnal ascent to heaven as a prototype, and consists of the singing of spiritual songs, the sharing of wine, ritual dances, and a religious discussion.

Alevism is still strongly influenced by the Bektaşiyyah Sufis (see page 95), in particular the concept of four life-stages or doors: the first is religious law, which is elementary to all, the second is spiritual brotherhood, the third and fourth (which are mostly theoretical), are mystical truth and mystical knowledge.

Alevism is prominent in the Beylerbeylik of Rüm, and is also the dominant faith amongst the Black Sheep Turkomans and the White Sheep Turkomans. Alevism is not recognised by the religious elite, and Alevis have no official representation, but are judged under the millet of Islam. There is a degree of persecution against them as they do not accord with Sunni law, and some consider them to be heathen.

THE MILITARY

In common with most armies of the day, the Ottoman army comes in two main varieties: the infantry (*piyadesi*) and cavalry (*süvarisi*). Those who receive a salary for their military service – in effect, the professional soldiers – are called *kapikulu* (literally "gate slaves"). As well as the kapikulu, the army consists of *timariots*, who hold a fief in return for an oath of military service, and the *azaps* who are conscripts. There are also the irregular units who are neither conscripted nor paid, but who subsist entirely on plunder.

YENIÇERIS

The *devşirme* ("contribution") was introduced by Mehmet I in 1380. Christian lands under Ottoman rule are subject to this tax, which consists of relinquishing young boys aged 7 to 14 for training as soldiers. Each year, about a thousand boys from Christian families are sent from the provinces to the capitol at Edirne. Here they are subjected to intense education and military training. The best are chosen for training as pages of the palace (*iç oğlani*), and the rest are sent to provincial farms where they learn Turkish, convert to Islam, and become Yeniçeris (or *Janissaries*, literally "new troops"), also called the *Kapikulu piyadesi* (professional infantry). Training of the Yeniçeris takes place under the watchful gaze of dervishes of the Bektaşi sect (see page 88).

The Yeniçeris are an elite infantry regiment, divided into *ortas* of 100 men ruled by a *çorbaşi* (literally "chief soup maker"). There are 101 orta in the army, although not all are at full strength; the Ottoman army can field about 6000 Yeniçeris. Each orta has its own insignia, which is placed on flags and tents, as well as tattooed onto the men. They are paid a monthly salary, and live in large communal barracks. Promotion is based on seniority, and retired or injured men are provided with a pension. The Bektaşi dervishes instil a sense of brotherhood and camaraderie similar to a cult: they eat, sleep, fight, and die together, and the importance of the regimental symbol of a cooking pot cannot be overstated. Off-duty Yeniçeri wear a distinctive hat which has a holding place for a spoon; and an orta is called 'a brotherhood of the spoon', symbolising this closeness. When the Yeniçeris disagree with the orders they have been given they will overturn their cooking pots as a sign of rebellion.

Their distinctive uniform includes a white felt cap with a flap that falls over the back of their necks. They are best known for their *yatağan* swords (which they are only issued immediately before battle), but also receive training in either standard missile weapons or in firearms. When employed as palace guards, the Yeniçeris are armed with glaives.

Unit: Yeniçeri
Role: regular infantry
Armour: Turkish heavy armour
Combat Style: Yeniçeri or Topçu

KAPIKULU SIPAHI

Also called the *Kapikulu Süvarisi* (i.e. professional cavalry), to distinguish them from the Yeniçeri (who are also Kapikulu), and the Timarli (who are also Sipahis, or "knights"). There are six units of professional cavalry making up the Kapikulu Sipahi, each lead by a commander or agha. There are about 2000 Kapikulu Sipahi in active service.

The Left and Right *Ulufeciler* ("salaried men") units are formed mostly from the iç oğlani who were specifically chosen at a young age from the devşirme recruits because they showed intelligence and prowess. After seven years of education, concentrating on leadership, military tactics, weapon skills, sciences, and religion, they are subjected to three gruelling examinations. The results determine whether they become Kapikulu Siphai, Kapikulu officers (with the Sipahi or the Yeniçeri), or take up posts as senior military leaders.

The Left and Right *Garipler* ("poor foreigners") originate amongst the ghazi tribesmen of Anatolia. They are more lightly armoured than the other Kapikulu Sipahis, and fight in the same skirmishing style.

The *Sipahi oğlan* ("knight's children") are made up of the male relatives of the Ottoman elite – viziers, pashas, and beys – wanting to distinguish themselves in battle but unable to fight amongst the Timarli Sipahis.

Finally, the *Silahadar* ("weaponbearers") are responsible for guarding the person of the sultan. This last unit is different to the others; any Ottoman soldier could be promoted to this division for a significant deed of prowess or courage, although the entry requirements are more stringent for an infantryman, who has to enlist as a *serdengecti* ("giver of his head"), and survive suicide missions before he is accepted – and even then he will be despised by both his former and his new unit. The Silahadar Agha, who leads this elite unit, handles all the communications to and from the Sultan, and carries his personal sword.

Unit: Ulufeciler
Role: regular cavalry
Armour: Turkish heavy armour
Combat Style: Sipahi

Unit: Garipler
Role: regular cavalry
Armour: Turkish medium armour
Combat Style: Ghazi Tribesman

Unit: Sipahi oğlan
Role: regular cavalry
Armour: Turkish medium armour
Combat Style: Sipahi

Unit: Silahadar
Role: regular cavalry
Armour: Turkish heavy armour
Combat Style: Sipahi

TIMARLI SIPAHI

A *timar* is a fief granted by the sultan in return for an oath of military service. The yearly revenue is not more than 20,000 akçe per year, but larger fiefs such as the ziamet (up to 100,000 akçes) and has (more than 100,000 akçes) exist for officers of the Timarli units. The timariot (i.e. holder of a timar) is expected to be a trained cavalryman, and bring to war with him a number of mounted retainers or cebelu based on the size of the fief. A standard timariot is expected to muster five armed cebelus wearing scale cuirasses. A ziamet-holder is obligated to provide 20 cebelus, and a has-holder the same plus an additional retainer per for every 3000 akçes income. Income also determines the armour that is expected for the Sipahi's horse, and what equipment he must bring on campaign. The cebelus are usually sons, brothers, or nephews of the timariot.

Timarli from Rumelia are expected to be heavy cavalry, equipped with plated chainmail armour and barded horses. They carry lances, swords, and shields. The Andolou Timarli on the other hand are medium to light cavalry, with leather and felt armour, bows, and sabres.

When mobilised, one in ten Timarli Sipahis remain at home to maintain order. The remainder are arranged into local regiments called alays, commanded by an alay-bey. Alays are combined into sanjak regiments commanded by the sanjak-bey. If fighting in Rumelia then the Rumelian Timarli take the honourable right flank and the Andolou Timarli take the left flank; in an Anatolian battle the positions are reversed. The Yeniçeris occupy the middle position between the two flanks. The Timarli Sipahi make up the bulk of the Ottoman army, with approximately 20,000 sipahi and the same number of cebelu.

Unit: Timarli Rumeli
Role: regular cavalry
Armour: Turkish heavy armour
Combat Style: Sipahi

Unit: Cebelu
Role: regular cavalry
Armour: Turkish medium armour
Combat Style: Cebelu

Unit: Timarli Andolou
Role: regular cavalry
Armour: Turkish medium armour
Combat Style: Ghazi Tribesman

YAYA

The *Yaya* are infantry units made up of conscripts, mostly native Turks from Anatolia. Under the azap conscription scheme, every town and village in Anatolia is expected to provide a fully-equipped infantryman in lieu of certain taxes. During military campaigns they are paid a salary, and have the freedom to leave the army whenever they wish. Their military skills are often limited, and they are useful as infantry archers and in support roles, but rarely fielded as the principal troops. Each unit is led by a *yayabaşi*. There are about 15,000 Yaya in the Ottoman army.

Unit: Yaya
Role: regular infantry
Armour: Turkish light armour
Combat Style: Azap Conscript

AKINCI

The *akinci*, meaning "raiders", are employed by the Ottoman army as advance troops, used in guerrilla tactics, or given scout duties. They originate in Anatolian tribal society, and are divided into clans of Turkomen who descend from the warrior ghazis of the first Ottoman ruler Osman I. Prominent families include the Malkoçoğlu, Turhani, Ömerli, Evrenosoğlu, and Mihalli. When they take part in military actions, the Akinci are unpaid, subsisting entirely on plunder. Akincis wear colourful and interesting clothes to confuse and frighten their opponents. They attach eagle wings to their backs and bull horns to their helmets. They might wear coats of leopard skin, and fight with bizarre hooked swords and barbed spears. They have a reputation for recklessness and near-suicidal bravery, outcompeting each other with who can perform the most courageous feat in combat. The Ottoman army can call upon 10,000 akinci.

Unit: Akinci
Role: irregular cavalry
Armour: Turkish light armour
Combat Style: Ghazi Tribesman

BASI-BAZOUKS

The *başi-bazouks* (literally "damaged head"), are notorious for their lack of discipline and their predilection for preying on civilians. They are little more than bandits and adventurers who are armed and maintained by the government but neither salaried nor conscripted. The başi-bazouks do not wear any uniforms or fight under any unified banner. Their motives for partaking in combat is the expectation of plunder. Like the akinci, the başi-bazouks are rarely used for concerted military actions, but instead used for reconnaissance and guard duty. There are about 8,000 başi-bazouks available to the army at any time.

Unit: Başi-Bazouks
Role: irregular infantry
Armour: Turkish light armour
Combat Style: Ghazi Tribesman

NAVY

The main purpose of the Ottoman navy is to transport and support land troops with coastal bombardment from cannons. The empire has a vast coastline, and the Ottoman fleet patrols the Aegean and Ionian Seas, rooting out Christian pirates and blockading enemy ports. The fleet consists of some 90 galleys and some 400 smaller boats, mostly manned by azap conscripts. The Anatolian shipyards of Izmit are responsible for most of the outfitting. The sailors or levents are mostly recruited from Greek, Albanian, and Dalmatian vassals. The kürekçiler (oarsmen) are mostly slaves, criminals, and prisoners-of-war. The Ottomans have a navy of about 5,000 fighting men.

Unit: Turkish navy
Role: armed sailors
Armour: none
Combat Style: Azap Conscript

EASTERN EUROPE

There are still parts of the Balkans that have so far resisted the advance of the Ottoman Empire.

THE KINGDOM OF HUNGARY

The Kingdom of Hungary is the dominant nation in the Balkans, a position due in part to its previous king, Sigismund who reigned between 1387 and 1437. Sigismund was also the Holy Roman Emperor, a prince of the Luxembourg line who married Mary of Hungary, daughter of Louis the Great. His successor Albert II of Germany ruled just two years before his death. Wladyslaw III of Poland was offered the crown by the lords and prelates in fear of an Ottoman invasion, but Elisabeth of Luxembourg, widow of Albert II and daughter of Sigismund, wanted to keep the throne for her unborn child Ladislaus V. She had him crowned but this was declared invalid, and civil war broke out. Wladyslaw died at the battle of Varna in 1444, and the parliament offered to recognise Ladislaus as the next king. John Hunyadi, called "Christ's Champion" by the pope, is a minor Transylvanian nobleman and mercenary leader, with responsibility for the defences of the frontiers of Hungary. His outstanding success against the Ottoman Empire saw him elected regent of Ladislaus and governor of the kingdom by the parliament in 1446.

THE KINGDOM OF BOSNIA

The Kingdom of Bosnia was originally a *banate* (subject nation) of the Kingdom of Hungary, but enjoyed virtual independence since 1290 and crowned its first king Stjepan Tvrtko in 1377. During his reign, Bosnia underwent a period of expansion, annexing Dalmatian territory from the disintegrating Serbian Empire. His successor Stjepan Tomas rules the kingdom, but has a mere fraction of the influence wielded by Bosnia's first king. A recent attempt to reclaim Srebrenica from Serbia ended in defeat.

Most of the population of Bosnia are members of the Church of Bosnia. This is a heretical faith that combines aspects of Bogomolism with Catholicism, holding Michael and Satan as the sons of God. Satan made the world, and Michael was reborn as Christ to redeem the souls trapped within. The ruling house of Kotromanic has always been Catholic, and the Pope is threatening to withhold his support for Bosnia unless forced conversions of the noble and servile classes take place.

THE PRINCIPALITY OF MOLDAVIA

Moldavia is named after the beloved hunting dog Molda of the first *voivode*, Dragos Voda who chased an aurochs across the Carpathian mountains. He reigned in mid-fourteenth century, driving the Tatars out of the land. His grandson Balc was deposed by Bogdan of Cuhea, who was in rebellion against the Hungarian king.

Moldavia has had an extended conflict with the Orthodox patriarchate of Constantinople over control of appointments of its bishop. The patriarch established a metropolitan see for Moldavia in 1394, which was refused by Stephen I. This was resolved by a second appointment of the princely family as bishop. There is a sizable Catholic community (ethnic Germans and Magyars), as well as non-Chalcedonic Armenians. Moldavia is politically close towards Poland, although nominally the vassal of Hungary. The current prince is Bogdan II, uncle of Vlad III of Wallachia.

The flag of Moldavia commemorates its founding by bearing a golden bull's head on a red field. Either side of the head is a rosette and a crescent, and between its horns is a star.

THE ITALIAN CITY STATES

Italy during the fifteenth century consists of the Papal State, the Kingdoms of Sicily and Naples, and a collection of independent city states including Venice, Genoa, Florence, Siena, and Noli.

THE SERENE REPUBLIC OF VENICE

The Most Serene Republic of Venice was established at the end of the seventh century in northeastern Italy as a Byzantine colony. It claimed de facto independence sometime in the early 800s, but really only gained total autonomy in 1084 when the city gained exemption from all taxes owed to the Byzantine Empire in return for intervening in the war between the Norman Duchy of Apulia and Alexios I Komnenos. This exemption contributed greatly to the burgeoning wealth of Venice, who acted as middlemen in the silk and spice trade that passed through its holdings via the Levant and Egypt.

Venice is a representational democracy, where the Major Council engage in legislature on behalf of the people. Membership of the Major Council is automatic for anyone in The Golden Book, a list of all Venetian aristocrats in 1315 (when the book was compiled), and all their direct descendants aged 25 or over; currently consisting of over 1000 noblemen. From the Major Council are elected, each year, the *Quarantia* (a forty-man strong supreme court), and the Council of Ten. Executive control is held by the *Signoria*, a body of government consisting of the *Doge*, the Minor Council (one councillor elected from each district of Venice), and the three leaders of the Quarantia. The Doge is the head of state. His title deriving from Greek doux or 'duke', and he is elected for life by the Major Council. His palace is the Rialto, the commercial heart of Venice located on the Realtine Islands amidst the canals of the city. The secretive Council of Ten have almost unlimited authority over all governmental affairs. They are led by three *Capi*, elected for one-month terms, and who confined to the Doge's Palace during that time to limit political corruption, at least in theory.

The symbol of Venice is the winged Lion of Saint Mark holding a sword, gold on a red background. It can be seen flying throughout the region, proclaiming Venice's dominance over the sea.

STATO DA MAR

The "State of the Sea" is the name Venice uses for its overseas possessions, one of the threefold subdivisions which also includes the Dogado (i.e. Venice proper) and the Domini di Terraferma in northern Italy.

In addition to those mentioned below, included in the Stato da Mar are several colonies on the Adriatic Sea (Istria, Dalmatia, Durazzo, and Albania), and colonies on the Peloponnese (including Modon, Coron, Argos, Lepanto, and Navarino)

Kingdom of Candia: An overseas colony on the island of Crete. Since its conquest in 1204 there have been 14 uprisings of the native Greeks against the ruling Venetian settlers, many of these instigated by the Empire of Nicaea. Since the last major uprising in the 1360s, the kingdom has been mostly at peace and has prospered; and the capital of Chandax has become a haven for artists and musicians. The kingdom is divided into four prefectures arranged east to west.

Kingdom of Negroponte: Originally a Lombard-controlled triarchy centred on the three cities of Oreos, Karystos, and Chalkis, Negroponte became a Venetian colony in 1390 and the three cities given to the de Noë, Zorzi, and Sommaripa families respectively.

Duchy of the Archipelago: A state arising from the partition of the Byzantine Empire, comprising all of the Cyclades Islands. The capital is at Naxos, and has been under the control of the Crispo family ever since they took the duchy by force from the Sanudos in 1383. The current and fourteenth duke Gian Ciacomo is an infant, and his grand uncle William is the regent. The duchy is strategically important to the Republic because of its position, controlling trade routes to Anatolia and the Eastern Mediterranean. Furthermore, Naxite marble is highly prized and exported to Venice.

Ixole Jonie: The seven principal Ionian islands have come under various rule since the partition of the Byzantine Empire after the Fourth Crusade. Corfu passed into the hands of the Despotate of Epiros, and then to the Kingdom of Naples, but since 1386 has been Venetian. The County palatine of Cephalonia and Zante (Zakynthos) encompasses the remaining Ionian islands, and is currently in the hands of the Lombard Tocco family, owing fealty to the Kingdom of Naples.

THE REPUBLIC OF GENOA

Genoa began to gain autonomy from the Holy Roman Empire around the time of the First Crusade. It began in the Compagna Communis, a meeting of all the city's trade guilds and nobles. Genoa's fortunes have particularly flourished since the Fourth Crusade, expanding to take over the exotic trade through the Black Sea and controlling ports on Crimea. They have fought extensively with Venice on both the political battlefield and the field of war.

Genoa is headed by a Doge, elected for life by the Gran Consigilo or ruling council. However, the Doge of Genoa has little executive power, kept tightly under control by the Gran Consiglio, and few rule for more than five years before they are forced to resign or flee for their lives. The council is composed of 28 *alberghi* (singular *albergo*), communes of allied families that provide common economic, political, and military support for one another. Each is centred around one of Genoa's parish churches, and specialises in different trades. Chief amongst the alberghi are the Cybo, Giustiniani, Imperiale, Grimaldi, Fieschi, Doria, Pallavicini, and Spinola families. The dogate has been monopolised by two families, the Adorno and the Campofregoso for several centuries.

The Bank of Saint George (Ufficio di San Giorgio) was founded in 1407, the first of its kind. The governance of the Bank is provided by four consuls from the Houses of Grimaldi and Serra, with the assistance of Jewish agents from the Ghisolfi clan. The Republic is heavily in debt to the Bank.

Genoa's patron saint is Saint George, who lends his insignia of a red cross on a white field to the Republic; although Genoa adds the word *iustiçia* ("justice" in Ligurian) to the top.

As well as its holdings in northwest Italy, Genoa has four colonies on the Black Sea (Caffa, Soldaia, Cherco, and Cembalo), the Greek islands of Chios (see below) and Samos (controlled by the Giustiniani family), the islands of Lesbos, Samothrace, and Thasos and the mainland city of Ainos (all controlled by the Gattilusio family), and Corsica (currently contested by the King of Aragon who also rules Sardinia). Chief amongst its overseas settlements is the suburb of Pera in Constantinople which arose from it being granted a quarter of the city during the Frankokratia. The Republic still controls a fourth part of the city of Trebizond, which it gained in the same period.

CHIOS

Chios was ceded to the Republic of Genoa by Michael VIII Palaiologos in recognition for its help in the Restoration of the Byzantine Empire. The Lordship of Chios was short-lived, lasting just three generations before being ousted by the local population.

In 1346 a chartered company, the Maona di Chio e di Focea, was established to exploit the wealth of Chios and the town of Phocaea in Asia Minor. The controlling interest in the maona was owned by the Giustiniani albergo, who also controlled Samos. Rather than attempting to conquer the island, the maona worked with the local population, and the Genoese now control the trade-posts and warehouses but run the production and manufacture jointly with the Greeks. The chief exports of the island are mastic, alum, salt, and pitch. Mastic in particular is vital to the success of the Genoese colony; this resin can be sourced from nowhere else in Europe and is used as a potent medicine. When chewed it also freshens the breath and prevents tooth decay. Alum is vital for fixing dye and keeping colours bright, and Genoa tightly controls this monopoly as well.

The Kingdom of Naples

The Kingdom of Naples is the remainder of the Kingdom of Sicily after the Byzantine-sponsored revolt of the island of Sicily in 1282. The king Charles of Anjou was forced to leave the island and take up residence on the mainland while Peter III of Aragon took possession of Sicily. Queen Joan I formally renounced claim over Sicily in 1373 at the Treaty of Villeneuve. The kingdom ruled by Charles' successors is still officially called the Kingdom of Sicily despite not actually holding Sicily any more, but most call it after the city of Naples, where the king has held court since the thirteenth century.

Naples has been riven by a dynastic succession crisis. Queen Joan I had no children, and her choice of heir – Louis, Duke of Anjou – lead to a competing claim from her cousin the prince of Durazzo, prompting him to murder her and seize the throne. His own daughter Joan II was in the same childless position as her namesake, and her indecision over a choice of heir prompted Alphonso V of Aragon to conquer Naples in 1442, uniting the kingdom once again as a dependency of Aragon.

The standard of Sicily and Naples is that of the House of Anjou, a blue field scattered with golden fleur-de-lys, with a red label to difference it from the senior line of the Duchy of Anjou. This has since been combined with the arms of the House of Trastàmara to which Alphonso V belongs.

The Republic of Florence

The Republic of Florence originates from a rebellion against the Margrave of Tuscany in 1115, which left the city occupied by a commune. Florence is dominated by the seven Greater Guilds (*Arti Maggiori*) and 14 Lesser Guilds (*Arti Minori*), the first five of which are termed the Middle Guilds (*Arti Mediane*). The Greater guilds are: judges and lawyers, dyers, wool merchants, bankers and moneychangers, silk weavers, physicians and pharmacists, and furriers. The Florentine Arti protect their members from competition, guarantee quality of work, stipulate working hours, run markets, fund holidays, and control many other aspects of daily life.

There are three arms of Florentine government. The Signoria has nine members, six from the major guilds and two from the middle and minor guilds. The ninth member is the *Gonfaloniere*, the titular ruler of the city. Every two months the Signoria is selected by raffle from the ranks of all guild members over 30 years of age. The role of the Signora is to introduce new laws and governance for debate by the other two governmental arms. The *Dodici Buonomini* (the 'twelve good men') and the *Sedici Gonfaloniere* ("standard bearers of the Gonfaloniere") debate and ratify legislation produced by the Signoria but cannot introduce it. Membership of these two councils is limited to those families who had previously held office, making this a hereditary position. The leading family in Florence is the Medici who own the Medici Bank. Their chief rivals are the Houses of Albizzi and Alberti.

The Florentine standard consists of a white flag with a red fleur de lys.

The Papal State

In the eighth century, King Pepin the Younger seized territory from the Byzantine Empire in central and northern Italy. The former Duchy of Rome was given to the Pope as a temporal rather than spiritual domain, granting the papacy financial independence from the surrounding nations. Since that time, more territory has been ceded to the pope, and the Papal State now included not just Rome but also Ravenna, Bologna, Perugia, and the Pentapolis (five Adriatic cities of Ancona, Fano, Pesaro, Rimini, and Sinigaglia). The Papal State also consists of exclaves not continuous with the Italic holdings, most notably the city of Avignon.

The flag of the Papal State (as opposed to the pope's personal flag) is red with four white keys, one in each corner. The flag itself has a swallow tail shape with rounded points.

The Mamluk Sultanate of Egypt

The mamluks were the household guard of the Ayyubid Dynasty that ruled Egypt. Most were Kipchak Turks who were bought as slaves, trained in martial pursuits, courtly ways, and given an education, then converted to Sunni Islam and freed. They were the mainstay of Ayyubid power but staged a coup in 1250, assassinating the last of the Ayyubid sultans. After initial power struggles, Baybars of the Bahri faction rose to prominence, rebuilding the army and expanding into Syria. His successors ended all Christian presence in the Holy Land. The sultanate is currently under the rule of the Burji faction. Its flag is a gold standard with two rounded swallowtails, bearing a crescent moon in white.

The Mamluks broadly have the same administrative, legal, and economic system inherited from the Ayyubids. The sultan wields ultimate authority, delegating power to provincial governors (*nuwwab*, singular *na'ib*), who, in order of precedence, rule Egypt, Damascus, Aleppo, al-Karak, Safad, Tripoli, Homs, and Hama. A council of emirs forms a loose electoral college. The sultan rules through the will of the emirs: if he fails to please them they foment insurrection, delay in their financial or military obligations, or even conduct coups.

The upper class of emirs still speak Turkic, and many of them come from ancient Turkic bloodlines. However, the populace is overwhelmingly Arab and thus Arabic-speaking. The state still imports mamluks from their ancestral lands north of the Black Sea, mostly from Genoese slavers, training and then freeing them, giving them careers in the military. There are three regiments, the Royal Mamluk regiment or *khassakiyah*, the soldiers of the emirs, and the *halqa* (non-mamluk soldiers). The emirs are ranked as tens, forties, and hundreds, with the number indicating how many troops they command on the battlefield. Each emir is awarded an iqta, the right to collect revenue from a fixed territory that provides him with an income and money with which to finance his men. The size of the iqta is directly proportional to his number rank.

Trade is of vital importance to the Mamluk Sultanate. They are one of the great mercantile nations in the region, and maintain an administrative body to oversee the marketplace called the hisbah. Four inspector-generals (*muhtasib*) oversee the *hisbah*, stationed at Cairo, Alexandria, al-Fustat, and Lower Egypt. The primary source of revenue for the sultanate is agriculture; although sugar (from sugar cane) and cotton are also major exports. Goods originating in Persia and further east reach the Mediterranean primarily through Mamluk ports in Egypt and Syria: silk, pepper, cloves, cinnamon, indigo, and opium. These are mostly controlled through a state monopoly which grants the sultan a percentage of all profits.

The Mamluks present themselves as the defenders of Islam. They re-established and protect the Abbasid Caliphate to gain legitimacy to this claim, but the caliph has no real power over the sultan. They are mostly Sunni Muslims, but show no particular propensity towards any one of four schools of jurisprudence (or *madhab*) that form internal divisions within that sect; indeed, the sultan promotes a chief judge from each of the four. The Mamluks embrace and actively promote Sufism, with three orders – the Shadhiliyyah, Rifa'iyyah, and Badawiyyah – enjoying particular prominence. Christians and Jews are protected under the Pact of Umar, which grants them *dhimmi* (protected) status. Egypt is home to two varieties of the Orthodox Church (divided from one another on the issue of monophysitism; that Christ, as the incarnation of the eternal Son or Word of God, had only a single nature which was *either* divine or a *synthesis* of divine and human.)

WESTERN EUROPE

There is no room here to do justice to the other nations of Western Europe that may have influence over the political situation in the eastern Mediterranean Sea. Fortunately, it is relatively easy to get information about these nations from other sources. Here are some brief overviews of the most important nations:

- ***The Kingdom of England*** is currently ruled by Henry VI, who has inherited a war with France that has been going since 1337. Hostilities have just resumed after four years of peace, meanwhile the king faces a popular revolt at home.
- ***In the Kingdom of France***, the king, Charles VII was disinherited (in favour of the English monarch), by his own father, and since gaining the throne has been struggling to maintain control of his feuding vassals. However, there has been an upswelling of French nationalism following the death of Jean d'Arc, and a French victory against the English seems to be inevitable.
- ***The Holy Roman Empire*** currently lacks a ruler; the King of the Germans, Frederick IV of the House of Habsburg has yet to convince all the prince-electors of his legitimate candidacy. The core of the empire has dissolved into a patchwork of petty feuding states.
- ***The Crown of Aragon*** is a composite monarchy ruling Aragon, Valencia, Barcelona, Navarre, and Castile on the Iberian Peninsula, as well as Sicily, Sardinia, Corsica, and Naples.
- ***The Grand Duchy of Lithuania and the Kingdom of Poland*** are united under the rule of Casimir IV Jagiellon. He has made the rights of the Lithuanian nobility equal to those of Poland, and made strong ties with the sovereign of Hungary-Bohemia.
- ***The Grand Duchy of Moscow*** is the dominant principality of the Rus', ruled by Vasily II, who was blinded by his cousin during a coup. The Grand Duke is profiting from the collapse of the Golden Horde by strengthening his hold over subject states.

OTHER NATIONS

There are a few other nations in Anatolia and on the borders of the Ottoman Empire that are worth mentioning.

INDEPENDENT ANATOLIAN STATES

The Ottoman Empire dominates Anatolia, but there are some states who have managed to resist their expansion.

THE BEYLIK OF KARAMAN

Arising from a tribe of Oghuz Turks, the Karamanids migrated from the shores of the Caspian Sea to southern Anatolia following the Mongol invasion of 1230. They established themselves as one of many Turkish beyliks (states ruled by a bey or prince) in Asia Minor, and are one of the few that has stayed independent of the Ottoman Empire thus far. The Empire coverts their territory, but they have allied with the Mamluk Sultanate and have managed to remain independent. In 1444, while the Ottoman Empire was celebrating its victories in Rumelia, Ibrahim Bey, the current prince marched into central Anatolia and destroyed several cities including Ankara and Kütahya. The Empire has yet to respond to this challenge.

THE BEYLIK OF RAMAZAN

A beylik with its capital at Adana. It was formed from the defeat of the Armenian Kingdom of Cicilia. It is allied with the neighbouring Belylik of Karaman, and has resisted attempts at conquest by the Mamluks.

THE BEYLIK OF DULKADIR

A frontier province established by the Oghuz Turkomans and still independent from the Ottoman Empire. Their capital is at Elbistan, famed for its apples. Dulkadir is a buffer between the Ottomans and the Mamluks of Egypt, and have given many brides to the former including the mother of the current Sultan, Murad II and the wife of his son Mehmet II.

THE EMPIRE OF TREBIZOND

Emerging from the breakup of the Byzantine Empire after the Fourth Crusade, the city of Trebizond was seized by the grandsons of the last Komnenian Byzantine Emperor. Alexios and David were given military support from their aunt, the Queen of Georgia. Alexios Komnenos was crowned the first emperor. From its inception, Trebizond was in conflict with the Sultanate of Rüm, and relied heavily on trade from its Venetian and Genoese partners. The empire allied itself with Timur Khan and survived the rampant conquests of Sultan Bayezid. Emperor John IV Komnenos's three sisters are wives of the khans of Trebizond's Turkoman neighbours, the Aq Koyunlu and the Kara Koyunlu; and the current (third) wife of the Byzantine emperor John VIII Palaiologos. The current emperor spent 10 years in exile in Georgia after killing his mother following her adultery. When he returned in 1429, his father Alexios IV was murdered by John IV's over-eager allies, and John IV took the throne. He has so far resisted an attempted invasion by Murad II. The empire has one overseas colony, the Principality of Theodoro on Crimea.

KARA KOYUNLU

The Black Sheep Turkomans are a federation of Oghuz Turkic tribes occupying a vast triangle of land joining the Arabian Gulf in the south with the Caspian Sea and Black Sea in the north. They were once vassals of the Sultanate of Baghdad, but rebelled against the ruling dynasty and conquered their territory, only to be defeated themselves by Timur Khan in 1400. Their ruler Qara Yusuf fled to Egypt, and returned a decade later at the head of an army that captured Baghdad and Tabriz. The first years of their rule of Armenia were peaceful, but in recent years the native people have been ravaged by swingeing taxes and slaving raids.

The rulers of the Black Sheep Turkomans are Shi'a Muslims, and they rule over a mixture of co-religionists, Armenian Orthodox Christians, and Alevis.

AQ KOYUNLU

The White Sheep Turkomans or Aq Koyunlu are a tribal federation that rule lands to the east of the Ottoman Empire. They first acquired land under Timur in 1402, when they were granted the lands of Diyarbakr in eastern Anatolia. They are pressed in by the Black Sheep Turkomans to their east and the Ottomans to their west. The Aq Koyunlu are Alevis, and are ruled by khans taken from the Begundur clan, descendants of Oghuz Khan himself, originator of all Oghuz Turks. They are known as a nation of merchants, but like all Turkic people are trained as warriors from an early age.

CHARACTERS

Of the other Greeks – the high, the lowly, the poor, the rich; of the greatness of the city, of the palaces, and of the other wonders which are therein – will we forbear to tell you further; for no earthly man, though he abode never so long in that city, could number or relate all this to you. And if he were to describe to you the hundredth part of the riches and the beauty and the magnificence which were to be found in the abbeys and in the minsters and in the palaces and in the city itself, it would seem that he was a liar, nor would ye believe him at all

~ Robert de Clari, 1204

Characters in Mythic Constantinople follow a very similar creation process to standard Mythras characters. When creating characters you will need to follow most of the chapters 1 through 3 of the Mythras rules, but note the differences introduced in this chapter. A Mythic Constantinople character sheet can be downloaded from the Design Mechanism website.

CHARACTERISTICS & ATTRIBUTES

These follow the same steps described in Chapter 1: Basic Character Creation of the Mythras rules.

CULTURE & COMMUNITY

Certain decisions need to be set by the Games Master or agreed on with the players:

CHARACTER CULTURE

The Games Master should decide whether he or she would prefer a group of foreigners visiting Constantinople for the first time, a group of residents (Greek or otherwise) who know the city well, or a mixture of both. Many cultures are available to play. The four most common cultures are described in detail in this chapter, although guidance for playing other characters is also provided. Not everyone who comes to Mythic Constantinople is human: if you are interested in playing a non-human then you should discuss this with the Games Master.

RELIGION

The conflict between Christianity and Islam, and the conflicts between Western Catholicism and Eastern Orthodoxy, are very strong themes in Mythic Constantinople. Regardless of religion or sect, most (if not all) people in the Mythic Constantinople setting have a belief in an all-powerful God who created heaven and earth. In the fifteenth century there were members in all three faiths who sought nothing less than the extermination of all who did not believe the same as themselves; but just as common are those for whom religious observation is a social nicety rather than a moral obligation – even although most characters accept the existence of God, there is no requirement for them to be pious. There is little room for atheists or agnostics in a world of magic and miracles, although there are indeed those who worship pagan gods or espouse a Neoplatonist belief in an uncreated universe.

It is entirely possible for you all to have different religious backgrounds, although this would be unusual for the time, and is sure to be a matter for comment. All characters take a Cultural Passion reflecting their religious beliefs, and it is worth ensuring that these do not make it impossible for the characters to interact with one another.

BACKGROUND EVENTS

Mythic Constantinople has its own Background Events table, found on page 66. Every character gains one roll on the table. As an option, you could roll twice and pick the event which appeals to you most.

In addition to the background events, you should consider these things:

- *How long have you been in Constantinople? Are you fresh off the boat, or has your family lived here since at least the Restoration?*
- *Why are you in Constantinople? If you are new here, something must have brought you here. Are you looking for something, or running away from something? If you have been here a while, then why are you still here? The city is in its worst economic slump for centuries, and while there is peace at the moment, the threat of Ottoman invasion is ever present. What is keeping you here?*

A character who has lived in Constantinople for a long time is likely to have more local contacts but less money – inflation has risen steadily for the last few generations. Conversely, a character who is fresh off the boat could know no-one in the city but have a purse full of foreign silver. As an optional rule, a player can decide to exchange starting money for Affiliations (or vice versa) to represent these extremes. Affiliations are explained on page 85. Every character begins with 4d6 SP multiplied by some modifier (Mythras page 21). A player can decide to reduce this wealth by 1d6 in exchange for an additional Affiliation, or else increase it by 1d6 for the loss of an Affiliation. She can do this up to three times. For example, the player of a true-born dyed-in-the-wool citizen decides to roll only 1d6x75 for her starting money, but gains 3 extra Affiliations. Conversely, a Kievan barbarian visiting the city for the first time might instead decide to roll 6d6x50 silver pieces in place of his Contact and career-related Affiliations.

SOCIAL CLASS

Social class can be chosen or randomly determined; which method to use is best decided in conjunction with the Games Master. If characters are of vastly different social rank then some explanation is needed as to why they associate with one another. See the Social Class table on page 59.

PASSIONS

Every character has three cultural Passions with starting values as described in the sections below. Players should also pick one or two other Passions that drive their characters.

Passions can be used to represent the virtues and vices of religious belief. According to Christian doctrine, all human souls are prone to sin due to the existence of Free Will. It is appropriate for a Christian character to pick a Passion that represents a key vice, through which they are tempted to sin. Examples include: Aggrandise Self, Avoid Work, Covet (Person), Deceive Women, Desire Fornication, Gorge on Food, Lust after Wealth, and Resent Insolence.

Similarly, Passions can be used to represent the cardinal virtues, ideals to which Christians should strive. Examples include: Desire Truth, Eschew Luxury, Foreswear Impatience, Observe the Law, Promote Mercy, Espouse Charity, and Uphold Chastity.

Other faiths have concepts similar to the cardinal vices and virtues, although the emphasis might be different. For example, prime Muslim faults revolve around how you treat others rather than how you treat yourself, so cheating, lying, and theft have more prominence than envy, gluttony, and sloth.

CAREERS

The Careers open to characters are culture and class dependent. These are explained on page 60.

GREEK CULTURE

Three defining features make up the subjects of the Byzantine Empire: Greek language and culture, Roman law and tradition,

EXAMPLE GREEK CHARACTER CONCEPTS

- *Agent of the Drome*: A spy employed by the Public Post to maintain the security of the Empire
- *Cemetery Priest*: takes care of a family mausoleum, only parishioners are the dead
- *Consobrin*: a low-level boss in the Zanconi crime family
- *Courtesan*: escort for hire, knows many people. Perhaps now retired (maybe even a nun)
- *Courtier*: a cog in the machine of the Imperial Bureaucracy with access to all kinds of information
- *Exorcist*: member of the Order of Kappa-Pi-Alpha and dedicated to driving out evil spirits
- *Grammatikos*: a scholar or teacher at the Pandidakterion
- *Hesychast*: monk gaining mystical talents as a side effect of beholding the Uncreated Light
- *Holy Fool*: the Fools-for-Christ are anarchist monks who upend social norms to challenge concepts of faith
- *Kataphraktos*: heavily-armed cavalry for which the Byzantine army is famous
- *Pankratiast*: A sportsman who engages in pankration (no-rules unarmed combat), probably for money
- *Pharmakopeia*: a witch, either a herbalist or a worshipper of Hekate
- *Skoutatos*: heavily-armed infantry carrying massive glaives, forefront in all land battles
- *Smuggler*: the city's crippling commercial tax makes this a lucrative business
- *Tekton*: an artisan member of an imperial or private trade guild
- *Tzykanion Player*: a form of polo much loved amongst the upper classes of Constantinople society
- *Vardariotes*: a policeman, generally considered to be corrupt by most people

EXAMPLE NON-GREEK CHARACTER CONCEPTS

- *Barbary Pirate*: a raider from the Arab coast of North Africa, although not necessarily a Muslim
- *Dervish*: a Turkish mystic and spy for the military
- *Divan Spy*: a eunuch devoted to the Sultan's mother, who runs the Ottoman spy ring
- *Dragonist*: member of the Order of the Dragon, a knight and perhaps also a sorcerer
- *Gunsmith*: Serbian manufacturer of handguns or artillery weapons
- *Knight of Malta*: heavily armoured warrior-monk devoted to defending Christendom from Saracens
- *Merchant Venturer*: speculative seller or industrial spy looking for trading futures
- *Spice Merchant*: Genoese trader from the isle of Chios trading in perfumes and medicine
- *Tatar slave*: a barbarian from the Black Sea coast
- *Varangian Guardsman*: an elite bodyguard of Englishmen protecting the emperor

OPTIONAL RULES

STREETWISE VS. LOCALE

City folk are not going to know much about local geography, fauna, and flora, but everyone will know where they can buy the best vegetables or find an apothecary. For characters that grew up in Constantinople (or another city), you may wish to consider making Streetwise a Standard Skill, swapping it for Locale, which now becomes a Professional Skill. References in Culture and Careers to either Skill can be swapped for the other if it makes more sense.

CUSTOMS (BYZANTINE) VS. LORE (BYZANTINE)

It is easy to confuse these two Skills. You should roll on Customs to find out basic information about your culture, but Customs will also contain smatterings of history (particularly events that lead to public holidays or traditions) and politics. The Lore Skill covers historical details and political analysis, as well as the ability to recognise famous and/or important living persons.

and Christian faith. It has been remarked that Greeks are resistant to change, preferring tradition to innovation and forever striving to maintain the status quo rather than moving with the times. Outsiders might describe the Greek culture instead as stagnant and decadent.

This culture is also appropriate for most of the other nations in the Balkans, including Serbians, Albanians, and Bulgarians. They would not self-identify as Greek but there are enough similarities between the cultures to substitute Customs, Lore, and Language Skills for those more appropriate and keeping the rest the same.

The skills for Greek characters are listed below. Distribute 100 Skill Points.

CUSTOMS, LORE, AND LANGUAGE

- Customs (Byzantine) +40% (does not count towards the 100 Skill Points available)
- Lore (Byzantine) +40% (does not count towards the 100 Skill Points available)
- Greek +40% (does not count towards the 100 Skill Points available)

STANDARD SKILLS

Boating, Conceal, Deceit, Influence, Insight, Locale, Willpower

PROFESSIONAL SKILLS (CHOOSE 3)

Art (any), Commerce, Craft (any), Courtesy, Language (any), Lore (any), Musicianship, Streetwise

Distinctive Byzantine choices are:

- Art: Iconography, Sculpture, Enamelling, Ivory Carving
- Craft: Silk Weaving, Gold and Silver Plate, Jewellery, Glassware, Books
- Lore: History, Politics, Architecture, Philosophy, Christian Theology
- Musicianship: Keyboards (pneumatic organ/hydraules), Wind (pipes/syrinx, flute/aulos, horn/salpinx), Percussion (bells/semantra, cymbals/kymbala, rattles/seistra), Strummed Strings (lute/pandoura), Plucked Strings (lyre/kithara)

COMBAT STYLES (CHOOSE 1)

For more details see page 61

- Huntsman
- Pankration, a mixed form of boxing and wrestling with few rules, played for sport.
- Self Defence, for city folk and rural commoners
- Brawling

PASSIONS

- A Passion reflecting religious inclination, such as Respect Church or (rarely) Love God; at 30% + INT + POW
- A Passion explaining why you are still in Constantinople, such as Loyal to City, Loyal to (specific dynatos family), Love Family, or Uphold Tradition; at 30% + INT + POW
- A Passion covering cultural flaws such as Covet Wealth, Covet Luxury, Covet Happiness, or Obey Authority; at 30% + INT + POW

TURKIC CULTURE

The Turkic culture shares many characteristics with the civilised Greek culture, and yet it should not be forgotten that just a couple of generations earlier the Ottomans were ghazi nomads on the plains of Anatolia. The various beyliks that make up the Ottoman Empire were formed from tribal holdings united by the House of Osman, and many of them still hold deep-running enmity for their neighbours born from many generations of raids and warfare. The stereotype of savagery and recklessness is not entirely unfounded.

The skills for Turks are listed below. Distribute 100 Skill Points.

CUSTOMS, LORE, AND LANGUAGE

- Customs (Ottoman) +40% (does not count towards the 100 Skill Points available)
- Lore (Ottoman) +40% (does not count towards the 100 Skill Points available)
- Turkish +40% (does not count towards the 100 Skill Points available)

STANDARD SKILLS

Athletics, Deceit, Endurance, Influence, Locale, Ride, Stealth

PROFESSIONAL SKILLS (CHOOSE 3)

Art (any), Courtesy, Craft (any), Culture (any), Language (any), Lore (any), Survival, Track

Distinctive Turkish choices are:

- Art: Storytelling, Shadow Puppetry, Calligraphy, Poetry, Miniature Painting
- Craft: Tailoring, Carpet Weaving, Sweetmeats, Paper Making, Woodcarving
- Lore: Strategy & Tactics, Science, Islamic Theology

COMBAT STYLES (CHOOSE 1)

For more details see page 61

- ɸ Ghazi Tribesman, for Anatolian nomads
- ɸ Azap Conscript, for town-dwellers in Asia Minor and Europe
- ɸ Brawling
- ɸ Turkish Wrestling, a sport played with both opponents covered in olive oil. The aim is to achieve a grapple from which the opponent cannot escape.

PASSIONS

- ɸ A Passion reflecting religious inclination, such as Obey Qu'ran or (rarely) Love God; at 30% + INT + POW
- ɸ A Passion relating to your family or clan, such as Loyal to Chief; at 30% + POW + chief's CHA, or Loyal to Family at 30% + INT + POW
- ɸ A Passion covering cultural flaws such as Hate Neighbouring Tribe, Espouse Revenge, Act Impulsively; at 30% + INT + POW

FRANKISH CULTURE

To the Greeks, *all* westerners are Franks, regardless of their country of origin. The common thread uniting them is a feudal frame of mind and a reverence for the Catholic Church. Some nations – notably the Italian city-states – have notionally given up feudalism, but they have simply replaced their hereditary nobility with oligarchs drawn from the wealthy middle classes. In contrast to the Greeks, Franks are more accepting of new ideas and more prone to taking risks that could pay off. A Greek is afraid to fail, whereas a Frank is afraid not to try.

Most Franks encountered in Mythic Constantinople will be mercenaries or merchants. The mutual dislike between Greeks and Franks is centuries old, based on both religious schism and the Fourth Crusade, and when Franks come to Constantinople they should prepare for trouble. Each of the nations carries its own stereotype: the English are arrogant, Germans are thugs, Italians are robbers, French are perverted, and so forth.

The skills for Franks are as follows. Distribute 100 Skill Points.

CUSTOMS, LORE, AND LANGUAGE

- ɸ Customs (country of origin) +40% (does not count towards the 100 Skill Points available)
- ɸ Lore (country of origin) +40% (does not count towards the 100 Skill Points available)
- ɸ Native Language* +40% (does not count towards the 100 Skill Points available)

**Typically English, High German, French, Italian, Veneto, Calabrian*

STANDARD SKILLS

Conceal, Deceit, Influence, Insight, Locale, Willpower, and either Drive or Ride

PROFESSIONAL SKILLS (CHOOSE 3)

Art (any), Commerce, Courtesy, Craft (any), Culture (any), Language (any), Lore (any), Musicianship, Streetwise

Distinctive Frankish choices are:

- ɸ Art: Frescos, Sculpture, Illumination
- ɸ Craft: Blacksmithing, Gunsmithing, Linen Cloth, Wool
- ɸ Lore: Agriculture, Christian Theology, Strategy & Tactics, Politics, Animal Husbandry

COMBAT STYLES (CHOOSE 1)

For more details see page 61

- ɸ Code Duello, for the noble born
- ɸ Peasant Levy, for commoners of any feudal nation
- ɸ Huntsman
- ɸ Self Defence
- ɸ Brawling

PASSIONS

- ɸ A Passion reflecting religious inclination, such as Obey Church or (rarely) Love God; at 30% + INT + POW
- ɸ A Passion reflecting your social contract, such as Loyal to Liege; at 30% + POW + liege's CHA
- ɸ A Passion covering cultural flaws such as Hate Islam, or a cultural stereotype such as Despise Disrespect (English), Lust for Women (French), Seek Conflict (German), Covet Wealth (Italian); at 30% + INT + POW

ARAB CULTURE

The Arab culture is dominant in the Holy Land, the Arabian Peninsula, Egypt and North Africa. Arabs are not an uncommon sight in Constantinople, where they come to trade. In general they are neither enemies nor allies of the Ottoman Turks despite sharing a faith. In the past the various Arab states have clashed with the Byzantine and the Ottoman Empires, but currently there is no active warfare between the cultures.

Traditionally the Arabs have been divided into two groups. The *badawi* (Bedouin) originate in Northern Arabia, and are nomads to whom honour, hospitality, courage, and magnanimity are paramount. They revere the camel over all animals, relying on its strength and inexhaustibility to roam the desert. Sharing the Arab culture with the badawi are the *madani*, the settled townsfolk who cultivate crops, usually in close proximity to oases and permanent rivers. Virtually all Arabs are Muslims, although there are several denominations of Islam to which they can belong. The Mamluk Sultanate of Egypt, which covers all of the Holy Land as well as Egypt, is officially a Sunni Islam state, much like the Ottoman Empire.

The skills for Arabs are listed below. Distribute 100 Skill Points.

CUSTOMS, LORE, AND LANGUAGE

- Customs (Arab) +40% (does not count towards the 100 Skill Points available)
- Lore (Arab) +40% (does not count towards the 100 Skill Points available)
- Arabic +40% (does not count towards the 100 Skill Points available)

STANDARD SKILLS

Athletics, Endurance, First Aid, Locale, Perception, Ride, Stealth

PROFESSIONAL SKILLS (CHOOSE 3)

Craft (any), Commerce, Language (any), Lore (any), Musicianship, Navigate, Survival, Track

Distinctive Arab choices are:

- Craft: Swords and Blades, Ceramics, Enamelled Glass, Silk Weaving
- Lore: Science, Islamic Theology, Alchemy, Agriculture
- Musicianship: Plucked Strings (zither/qanun, lute/oud), Wind (shawm/mizmar, double-pipe/arghul)

COMBAT STYLES (CHOOSE 1)

For more details see page 61

- Bedouin Warrior, for badawi nomads
- Huntsman
- Self Defence, for most madani

PASSIONS

- A Passion reflecting religious inclination, such as Obey Qu'ran or (rarely) Love God; at 30% + INT + POW
- A Passion relating to your family or clan, such as Loyal to Chief at 30% + POW + chief's CHA, or Loyal to Family at 30% + INT + POW
- A Passion covering cultural flaws such as Seek Converts, Hate Christians, or Covet Wealth; at 30% + INT + POW

OTHER CULTURES

BARBARIAN

There are few barbarians left in Europe, but the Barbarian Culture (Mythras page 14) is appropriate for the hill tribes of the Balkans, in particular the Vlachs who still pursue a pastoral existence. This culture is also well-suited to the Berbers, the aboriginal people of North Africa who have been mostly conquered by the Arab caliphates.

CIVILISED

The Civilised Culture (Mythras page 14) can be used for most Slavic people, including the Polish and the Russians. The Magyars of Hungary are also members of the Civilised culture, as are the Scandinavians of the Union of Kalmar.

JEWISH CHARACTERS

For characters of the Jewish faith, culture and religion are intricately intertwined. The Jewish diaspora from the Holy Land has resulted in a wide distribution and diverse backgrounds. Each of the Jewish communities has its own religious customs and language, which are reviewed on page 16-17. Regardless of their origin, Jewish characters should use the Civilised Culture (Mythras page 14). Each community has its own language, typically a dialect of their adopted country's language. Most Jews also speak Hebrew (add this to Cultural Skills). Educated Jews may also speak Aramaic (add as an option to Professional Skills).

NOMADIC

The Nomadic Culture (Mythras page 15) can be used for Mongols, Cumans, Pechenegs, Alans, and other nomadic tribes of the Asian steppes. Many of these cultures still follow their ancestral beliefs, although some have adopted Islam or Christianity (often Nestorian Christianity, see page 31).

NON-HUMAN CHARACTERS

In distant lands there are many strange peoples and races. Mythic Constantinople stands at the crossroads of Europe and Asia and it is here that many of these peoples meet up.

ARIMAPSOI

The Arimapsoi come from the Scythian Plains to the east of the Carpathian Mountains. They first came to Constantinople with the Cuman warriors who in the past have served in the Byzantine army. The Arimapsoi have wavy blond hair and stand a little taller than the average human. Their most notable feature is a single protruding eye, larger than a human's and placed centrally on the forehead. Combined with their sloping brows, this gives them excellent all-round vision, and it is exceptionally difficult to catch an Arimapsos by surprise. In their homeland, the Arimapsoi are plagued by griffins that live in the mountains and raid their livestock for food. The griffins gather gold to adorn their nests, and the Arimapsoi occasionally raid these nests to have precious metals with which to trade.

Arimapsoi are not kind or helpful people, even to each other. They avoid social and societal obligations: everyone is expected to do the job assigned them when they reached puberty suited to their skills and aptitudes, and failure or laziness is unacceptable. They do not offer praise or criticism to others – a task is completed satisfactorily or not at all. Likewise, they do not offer assistance and will not accept it, to do so would be to admit weakness or uselessness. They will work cooperatively but only out of necessity, never through altruism.

An Arimapsos character should be created as a human, with the following changes:

- SIZ 2d8+6
- Barbarian culture
- Arimapsoi lack depth perception and rarely use missile weapons; when they do they suffer an additional distance modifier on attack rolls.
- An Arimapsos has almost a 180° field of view, and can also see above his head. Reduce the difficulty of a Situational Modifier by one grade on all Perception rolls, and all Stealth rolls made against them are one difficulty grade harder.
- Cultural Combat Style is Griffin Hunter, which uses longspear, mace, and net and confers the Mancatcher Combat Style Trait
- Cultural Passions are Hate Griffins, Despise Idleness, Hide Weakness

ASTOMATOI

The Astomatoi (as-STOW-mat-ee) are tall, thin, with sunken eyes and hairless skin that resembles green-mottled parchment. They have no mouths, just smooth skin where one might expect one. Their ears are exceptionally long and broad, to the extent that they can wrap them around their bodies like a cloak. It is not well known that Astomatoi can use these ears to fly, albeit clumsily. They do not like to be seen flying, preferring to do so at night.

Their fluting voices – rarely heard – seems to radiate from their heads. Astomatoi do not eat, but subsist on the smell of food. After the odour has been inhaled by an Astomatos, food is bland and lacks nutrition, as if the vitality had been sucked from it. Some allege that they can inhale vitality from living prey as well, although this appears to be slanderous gossip.

Astomatoi originate from somewhere in northwest Anatolia or perhaps the Caucasus Mountains, brought west by the Ottoman Turks. Since the incorporation of the Beylerbeylik of Rüm into the Empire some 50 years ago, Astomatoi have been seen with increasing frequency in the company of Turkish pashas and beys, and there are several lodged in the Sultan's court, including one in the Divan. They apparently serve as advisors, although many have wondered what influence these non-humans have over the Ottoman Empire.

Astomatoi have the statistics of humans, with the following changes:

- CON 2d6+3, SIZ 2d6+9
- Civilised culture
- Astomatoi have the Flying Ability (Mythras page 216). They can fly at 12 metres per round, but flight for them is a Strenuous activity (Mythras page 79); although they can glide (losing 1 m of altitude for every 15 m horizontal movement), which is only Light activity.
- All Astomatoi have a keen sense of smell in general, but each one is attuned to a particular substance. Treat this as a version of the Find Folk Magic spell, which they can cast without needing to make a roll – although it still costs a Magic Point.
- Astomatoi are particularly sensitive to smells, and make Endurance rolls against noxious odours and airborne poisons at a Formidable penalty. They can be left incapacitated with Nausea (Mythras page 75) by strong smells.
- Cultural Combat Style is Concealable Weapons
- Cultural Passions are Protect Secrecy, Desire Political Influence, Fear Strong Smells

BLEMMYAI

The Blemmyai (or Acephali), are a curious race of humanoids found in parts of Africa and India. They have no heads, instead their faces are to be found on their chests. They are driven by the desire to explore the world and to trade with other races. These primitive tribesmen live in lands so rich in gold and gems that they can simply be gathered as simply as picking fruit. However, they have learned of man's greed for such things, and are careful to not reveal where their communities may be found for fear of wide scale raiding. What they actually want is to trade their gold for technology and tools that are not available in their lands or for which they lack the skill to manufacture themselves.

Statistics for the Blemmyai (under the name Acephali) can be found in Mythras (page 225), with the following changes:

- Primitive culture, although they can take Miner as a possible career.
- Cultural Combat Style is Acephaloi Hunter, which uses sling, bolas, bow and grants the Ranged Marksman Combat Style Trait
- Cultural Passions are Loyal to Chief and Love Exploration.
- They have 4d6 x 50 SP starting money, and this is probably raw gold or small gems

KYNOKEPHALOI

The Kynokephaloi, or dog-headed men, can be found in small communities throughout North Africa; and about a thousand live in the Lykos Valley at the heart of Constantinople. They stand taller than a human (about 2 metres on average) although are usually more slightly built. Their heads are those of jackal-like dogs with erect rounded ears. Their fur is black with white and tan patches, and they have a scimitar-shaped tail. They are known as fierce warriors, and some have travelled the Mediterranean Sea in search of work as mercenaries. The Kynokephaloi are famous in Constantinople because one of the popular saints of the Orthodox Church,

Saint Christopher, was a member of the race. His fur turned white on the day he was baptised.

A kynokephalos character should be created as a human, with the following changes:

- CON 2d6+6, SIZ 3d6+6, CHA 2d6.
- Barbarian culture.
- Cultural Combat Style is Barking Raider, which uses longswords, javelins, and bows, and offers the Batter Aside Combat Style Trait.
- Cultural Passions are Loyal to Chief and Enjoy Battle.

MINOTAUROI

The race of minotauroi (pronounced "mee-no-TAFF-ree"), may be descended from the Minotaur of Knossos, but share nothing of its savage nature. They are a coastal race who live in small villages on the Lydian coast and offshore islands around Smyrna, all the way down to Rhodes. Many are accomplished sailors and fishermen. Minotauroi are not a devout race, although they nominally hold a pagan belief in the six children of Rhea: Hestia, Demeter, Hera, Hades, Poseidon, and Zeus. Those raised traditionally take one of the names of these gods as an additional name. Famously, the Tauroi Chalkeoi are a minotaur regiment in the Byzantine army, and is the reason why there are many members of this race in Constantinople.

Statistics for minotauroi and guidance for using them as a player character race can be found in Mythras (page 259). The Tauroi Chalkeoi use the Chalkotauros Combat Style, other minotauroi may learn Brawling or Self Defence (page 61) but may add their gore attack to these styles.

SKIAPODES

Skiapodes originate in Ethiopia. They have come to Mythic Constantinople following a diaspora caused by the Arab invasions of their homelands. Skiapodes have just one leg, which terminates in a single huge foot, easily a metre in length. They otherwise appear similar to Europeans save for a rich brown tan and curly dark hair. Skiapodes are remarkably agile jumpers, and can achieve speeds comparable to a two-legged human, covering ground with mighty bounds. Their name (which means 'shadow foot') comes from their propensity to lie on their backs and use their huge foot as a shade against the sun and a shield against attacks.

Skiapodes are utterly devoted to their spouses and children; infidelity is virtually unknown in Skiapod society. They believe in a strict hierarchy of life, with things with many legs at the bottom along with the no-legs, up to quadrupeds, then humanoids and birds, and with the Skiapodes at the very pinnacle. They treat birds and other two legged creatures as equal to humans, and find eating them as unconscionable as eating human flesh.

Skiapodes have the statistics of humans, with the following changes:

- Civilised culture
- Their huge foot makes rolls to resist exposure from heat one skill grade easier if they can use it to provide shade. When jumping, Athletics rolls are one skill grade easier. Use this modifier to Athletics when determining how far a Skiapod can jump. The leathery skin on the sole of the foot provides cover like a heater shield, but only when the Skiapod is lying on his back.
- Cultural Combat Style is Huntsman (page 61)
- Cultural Passions are Love Family and Disdain for Humans

TRIPITHAMOI

Tripithamoi come from deepest Ethiopia, beyond the burning sands of the Sahara Desert. Arabs and Berbers have traded with the African Empires for years, and occasionally bring back wonders, such as Tripithamoi, who are also known as *Pygmaeoi.* They stand about 1.5 metres high, have black skins, and long, usually braided hair. They are possessed of an inner fire that rages inside them. Their eyes shine red in the dark, and light shines from their open mouths. Their breath is hot enough to boil water. When they are wounded their blood spits and sparks like molten metal; although it is hotter than human blood, it is not hot enough to cause damage. The inner fire waxes and wanes with their emotions; an angry Tripithamos can literally have smoke coming from his ears. Tripithamoi live in villages woven from grass and use weapons made from brass that cannot be damaged by exposure to their inner fire. They war with a race of intelligent cranes and hate all manner of birdlife.

Statistics for Tripithamoi should use those for halflings (Mythras page 259), except as follows:

- Primitive culture.
- Tripithamoi have the Darksight and Immunity (Fire) abilities (Mythras pages 215, 216).
- All Tripithamoi know Folk Magic (add it as a Cultural Skill), and start with a number of spells equal to their INT/3 chosen from Extinguish, Firearrow, Heat, Ignite, Light, and Warmth spells, which are all expressions of their inner fire. Their version of the Firearrow spell is applied to darts that they spit from their mouths rather than throw; treat this as a dart in all respects despite its unusual deployment.
- All Tripithamoi should know the Extinguish spell; their version is restricted to touch range, and the quenched flames are absorbed into the Tripithamos's inner fire, restoring Magic Points equal to the damage the fire would normally inflict. They do not regenerate Magic Points any other way, and if they spend all their Magic Points their inner fire is quenched. Reigniting it is possible, but requires a short quest to find a fire hot enough.
- Cultural Combat Style is Flaming Raider, which uses darts, shortswords, and buckler shields and the Skirmishing Combat Style Trait.
- Cultural Passions are Hate Birds and Love Fire.

BACKGROUND EVENTS

The following background events (see pages 66 to 69) are specific to Mythic Constantinople and should be used in place of those found in Mythras.

SOCIAL CLASS

Social class is a significant determinant of career in Mythic Constantinople. Social class should be determined in conjunction with the Games Master; you could either decide on the career of your character and then choose from an appropriate social class, or else determine social class first (perhaps randomly), and then pick a career from the available options. Certain careers are unusual or impossible for certain social classes: for example, no slave can become a priest, and it would be extraordinary for a member of the aristocracy to practice a manual trade. If your chosen combination of career and class is not present in the table below, discuss it with Games Master: it might still be possible given an unusual background story.

GREEK & FRANKISH SOCIAL CLASSES

Once social class has been decided, use the Civilised Social Class Table (Mythras page 24) to determine money modifiers and background resources. Treat a wealthy freeman as equivalent to Gentry for these purposes.

GREEK & FRANKISH CLASSES

1d100	Class	Common Careers
01–15	Outcast	Agent, Beast-Handler, Entertainer, Fisher, Hunter, Miracle Worker, Mystic, Scout, Sorcerer, Thief
16–17	Slave	Beast-Handler, Courtesan, Crafter, Farmer, Fisher, Herder, Hunter, Labourer, Miner, Miracle Worker, Sailor, Sorcerer
18–70	Poor freeman	Beast-Handler, Courtesan, Crafter, Entertainer, Farmer, Fisher, Herder, Hunter, Labourer, Merchant, Miner, Miracle Worker, Mystic, Sailor, Scout, Sorcerer, Sportsman, Thief, Warrior
71¬–95	Wealthy freeman	Alchemist, Courtier, Crafter, Merchant, Miracle Worker, Mystic, Official, Physician, Priest, Scholar, Sorcerer, Sportsman, Warrior
96–99	Aristocracy	Courtier, Merchant, Miracle Worker, Mystic, Official, Priest, Scholar, Sorcerer, Sportsman, Warrior
100	Royal	Courtier, Official, Priest, Scholar, Sorcerer, Warrior

TURKIC & ARAB SOCIAL CLASSES

Once social class has been decided, use the Nomadic Social Class Table (Mythras page 24) to determine money modifiers and background resources

TURKIC & ARAB CLASSES

1d100	Class	Common Careers
01–05	Outcast	Agent, Beast-Handler, Entertainer, Fisher, Hunter, Miracle Worker, Mystic, Scout, Sorcerer, Thief
6–20	Slave	Beast-Handler, Courtesan, Crafter, Farmer, Fisher, Herder, Hunter, Labourer, Miracle Worker, Sailor, Sorcerer, Warrior*
21–90	Freeman	Beast-Handler, Crafter, Entertainer, Farmer, Fisher, Herder, Hunter, Merchant, Miracle Worker, Mystic, Official, Physician, Sailor, Scholar, Scout, Sorcerer, Thief, Warrior
91–100	Professional/ Ruling	Courtier, Merchant, Mystic, Official, Scholar, Sorcerer, Warrior
96–99	Aristocracy	Courtier, Merchant, Miracle Worker, Mystic, Official, Priest, Scholar, Sorcerer, Sportsman, Warrior
100	Royal	Courtier, Official, Priest, Scholar, Sorcerer, Warrior

**Turkic Culture only, Arabs do not use slave warriors*

NEW CAREERS

CHRISTIAN PRIEST

Bishop, deacon, monk, nun, priest...

Christian priests differ somewhat from the Priest Career offered in the Mythras rules. An Orthodox priest can be a secular clergyman in charge of a congregation of the faithful, or a regular clergyman serving in a monastic community. Playing a priest (in the strict sense) can be challenging to the player and to the Games Master because the duties of a priest in charge of a parish will interfere with the usual life of an adventurer. Playing a monk, nun, or deacon bypasses some of these problems.

The Exhort Magical Skill is not part of the standard training of a Christian Priest. Its possession is a charism – a gift from God – and it cannot be taught to those who have not received this gift. Whether a player character has this gift is a choice that should be made in conjunction with the Games Master. Characters who have this gift and take the Christian Priest Career can develop Exhort under the teaching of other theists within the church. In the Mythic Constantinople setting, the Devotion Skill is not required, but all theists need the Love God Passion; see page 79 for more details.

Note that there is no equivalent priesthood career for Jewish or Muslim characters. Since the fall of the Second Temple, the Jewish faith has not had a professional sacerdotal caste. Instead, religious leaders are rabbis who study the Talmud and the law, and are trained in the interpretation of the Bible. These are best described by the Scholar career. Similarly, the closest thing that Islam has to priests are the imam, who are professors of the faith and judges of holy law and are represented by either the Official or Scholar careers.

STANDARD SKILLS

Customs, Deceit, Influence, Insight, Locale, Sing, Willpower

PROFESSIONAL SKILLS

Bureaucracy, Exhort*, Language (Latin), Literacy, Lore (theology), Meditation**, Oratory, Teach

** See text above*

*** Part of the training for monks, but its magical aspects are only available to Hesychasts*

LABOURER

Carter, Galley Slave, Gleaner, Gravedigger, Janitor, Longshoreman, Mudlark, Nightsoilman, Porter, Stevedore, Striker, Teamster...

Labourers are those who toil in a non-skilled profession. They are generally drawn from the lower classes and complete the jobs that others will not. Some are forced into becoming labourers by personal or economic reasons; many slaves are labourers, performing jobs such as manning the oars aboard a ship or breaking rocks; whereas others take up the job of a nightsoilman (collecting the contents of chamber pots), or become a gleaner (searching refuse piles for anything which can be repurposed, repaired, or sold), because they cannot get any other sort of work. However, labouring can also be honest work in which people take pride, such as gravediggers, stevedores, and teamsters. A labourer may work alongside a craftsman even if they are not involved directly in production; for example, strikers wield sledgehammers for smiths but do not craft the metal themselves.

STANDARD SKILLS

Animal Handling, Athletics, Brawn, Drive, Endurance, Locale, Sing

PROFESSIONAL SKILLS

Commerce, Craft (any), Engineering, Gambling, Lore (any appropriate), Streetwise, Survival

MIRACLE WORKER

Exorcist, Pagan Priest, Oracle, Seer, Street Witch...

Every neighbourhood of Constantinople has their own wonder-worker, whether it be a wise woman who can set bones and ease injuries, a witch who prays to the pagan gods for fertility, or an oracle who has knowledge of future events. They are treated with an equal measure of fear and respect. The hypocrisy is not lost on the Miracle Workers themselves – they make brisk trade amongst the populace seeking their services and yet they are the first to be blamed should misfortune strike.

Each Miracle Worker has one Gift related to the tradition in which they trained; and, if they learn Folk Magic, a selection of spells from which they may learn 1 per 10% (or fraction) of the Folk Magic Skill. More information can be found on page 80.

STANDARD SKILLS

Customs, Dance, Deceit, Influence, Insight, Locale, Willpower

PROFESSIONAL SKILLS
Acting, Folk Magic, Healing, Lore (any), Oratory, Sleight, Streetwise

SPORTSMAN
Athlete, boxer, contender, gymnast, player, racer, wrestler...

In the somewhat effete world of Mythic Constantinople, it is possible for a character to make a living as a professional sportsman. This trend began in the days of the Roman Empire, when chariot-racing was all the rage and it was possible for a skilled charioteer to become exceptionally wealthy. In Byzantium, the sport of choice for the last five hundred years has been tzykanion, a form of polo. This sport is exceptionally popular with the upper classes, although most of the team is made up of professional players. Part of the role of the professionals is to ensure that the guest teammates from a noble family are not harmed or killed during the game; something that is all-to-common with tzykanion.

As tzykanion is to the upper classes, so pankration is to the lower classes. This is a mixed martial art combining boxing, kickboxing, and wrestling. It is popular as a spectator sport, and there is an annual, state-sponsored competition with a cash prize.

As well as tzykanion and pankration, citizens of Constantinople enjoy watching horse-racing, foot races, and weight-throwing. Since they compete for the enjoyment of paying spectators, sportsmen would do well to cultivate a modicum of the entertainers' arts: showmanship is more than just athletic prowess.

STANDARD SKILLS
Athletics, Brawn, Customs, Endurance, Evade, Unarmed, and either Drive, Ride, or Swim

PROFESSIONAL SKILLS
Acrobatics, Acting, Gambling, Lore (Strategy and Tactics), Oratory, Streetwise, Teach

MODIFIED CAREER: WARRIOR
Add the Lore (Firearms and Artillery) Skill to the choices of Professional Skills of this Career for all Greek, Frankish, and Turkish characters. This Skill covers the loading of firearms and cannons, how to set fuses, how to fix jams and misfires, and how to care for their weapons and the powder. Actually aiming and firing a firearm is part of an appropriate Combat Style.

COMBAT STYLES
Members of the Warrior Career specialise in one or more professional Combat Styles determined by their training. The Culture associated with warriors of each type is indicated but it is possible in most cases to have a different origin to the norm for that unit type. For example, most members of the Varangian Guard are culturally Greek, even though they descend from English and Norse ancestors. However, an Englishman (culturally Frankish) who pledges allegiance to the Empire will probably be placed in this unit and can learn the Pelekyphoros Combat Style.

Combat Style Traits marked with an asterisk (*) are described below.

UNIVERSAL COMBAT STYLES
These Combat Styles are available to all characters, regardless of culture.

CULTURAL COMBAT STYLES

BRAWLING
Aggressive back-alley fighting.
Weapons: club, knife, hatchet, unarmed.
Trait: Choose one from Daredevil or Knockout Blow.

HUNTSMAN
For anyone who has pursued game.
Weapons: short bow, hatchet, knife.
Trait: Ranged Marksman.

SELF DEFENCE
Learned by peasants and city dwellers alike.
Weapons: quarterstaff, club, knife, sling.
Trait: Cautious Fighter.

PROFESSIONAL COMBAT STYLES

CONCEALABLE WEAPONS
The staple of thieves and spies.
Weapons: knife, dagger (thrown and melee), garrotte.
Trait: choose one from Assassination, Daredevil, or Hidden Weapons.

SHIPBOARD COMBAT
Used by sailors, marines, and pirates.
Weapons: sabre, buckler shield.
Trait: Excellent Footwork.

BYZANTINE COMBAT STYLES
The average fifteenth-century Greek is not a warrior, leaving the defence of the community to either professional soldiers, mercenaries, or a specialised militia. Cultural Combat Styles are therefore restricted to those available to all characters, plus the sport of Pankration.

CULTURAL COMBAT STYLES

PANKRATION
Greek martial arts.
Weapons: Unarmed.
Trait: choose one from: Batter Aside, Body Slam, Immobilise, Mancatcher, Take Down, Unarmed Prowess.

PROFESSIONAL COMBAT STYLES

APELATIKIAROS
Tzakones Guard, heavy infantry.
Weapons: flanged mace, kite shield.
Trait: Siege Warfare.

CHALKOTAUROS
Minotaur heavy infantry.
Weapons: battleaxe, glaive, hoplite shield, gore.
Trait: Do or Die (using gore).

KATAPHRAKTOS
Heavy cavalry and the Paramonai Guard.
Weapons: longspear, longsword, battleaxe, dagger, buckler shield.
Trait: Mounted Combat.

MANGLABLIAROS
Vardariotoi police units.
Weapons: manglabia, club, unarmed.
Trait: Do or Die.

PELEKYPHOROS
Varangian Guard, heavy infantry.
Weapons: great axe, longsword, dagger, kite shield.
Trait: Shield Splitter or Defensive Minded.

PHYLAX
Provincial militia and town guard.
Weapons: short spear, kite shield.
Trait: Cautious Fighter.

SKOUTATOS
Heavy infantry
Weapons: longspear, glaive, longsword, sabre, kite shield
Trait: Formation Fighting.

TOXOTES
Light infantry archers and the Mourtatoi Guard. Psiloi units exchange infantry bow with sling.
Weapons: infantry bow, longsword, hatchet, solenarion, buckler shield.
Trait: Volley Fire.*

TRAPEZITES
Light cavalry.
Weapons: cavalry bow, javelin, sabre, hoplite shield.
Trait: Skirmishing.

TURKISH COMBAT STYLES

Most Turkish men receive basic training in weapons, allowing them to join the retinue of a timariot as a mounted cebelu or else fulfil the azap conscription obligation of their village. The ghazi are tribal warriors recruited from the Anatolian homelands, who learn to ride and fire a bow from horseback alongside learning to walk and talk.

See page 45 for more details on Ottoman military and conscription.

CULTURAL COMBAT STYLES

GHAZI TRIBESMAN
Irregular cavalry.
Weapons: recurve bow, short bow, sabre or battleaxe, javelin, hoplite shield.
Trait: Skirmisher.

AZAP CONSCRIPT
Conscripted infantry.
Weapons: sabre or mace, light recurve bow, glaive, hoplite shield.
Trait: Defensive Minded.

TURKISH WRESTLING
A popular sport.
Weapons: Unarmed.
Trait: Mancatcher.

PROFESSIONAL COMBAT STYLES

CEBELU
Retainers of Sipahi.
Weapons: hatchet, pike, shortsword, shortspear, hoplite shield.
Trait: Formation Fighting.

SIPAHI
Heavy cavalry.
Weapons: sabre, lance, javelin, mace or battleaxe, hoplite shield.
Trait: Mounted Combat.

TOPÇU
Specialist artillery units.
Weapons: crossbow or handgonne or hook gun, grenado.
Trait: Siege Warfare.

YENIÇERI
Elite infantry of Greek or Frankish origin.
Weapons: yatağan sabre, glaive, javelin, club, dagger, hoplite shield.
Trait: Formation Fighting or Trained Beast (for Segmen).

FRANKISH COMBAT STYLES

The *Code Duello* is a generic term for the fighting style taught to the children of Frankish Lords. It is therefore only available to characters from an upper class background. All Englishmen are required by law to be proficient with a longbow, although in practice actual level of competence varies.

CULTURAL COMBAT STYLES

CODE DUELLO
Reserved for the upper classes only.
Weapons: main gauche, rapier or longsword, buckler, dagger.
Trait: choose one from Do or Die, Excellent Footwork, Swashbuckling, Defensive Minded (This choice represents the wide range of schools of combat in which the Frankish upper classes may train).

PEASANT LEVY
Irregular infantry. All Englishmen, at least in theory, train in the use of a longbow.
Weapons: falchion, pike, shortspear, hatchet, longbow (English only).
Trait: Defensive Minded or Volley Fire (English only – see opposite).

PROFESSIONAL COMBAT STYLES

ARQUEBUSIER
Trained for using firearms in formation.

Weapons: hook gun, shortsword, grenado, buckler shield.
Trait: Daredevil.

CROSSBOWMAN

Often a member of a Crossbow Guild, particularly the Genoese.
Weapons: heavy crossbow, shortsword, tower shield (as a pavise).
Trait: Ranged Marksman.

CAVALIER

Heavy cavalry.
Weapons: Lance, longsword, heater shield, one of: mace, ball-and-chain, military pick.
Trait: Beast-back Lancer.

FOOTMAN

Light infantry constituting the peasant levy or conscripted soldiers.
Weapons: mace, military pick, falchion.
Trait: Formation Fighting.

HALBERDIER/PIKEMAN

Heavy infantry. Includes the Albanian mercenary, German Landsknecht, Swiss Pikemen, Italian Condottiere, and the Spanish Tercio.
Weapons: great sword, halberd or pike or zagaie, shortsword or dagger.
Trait: Formation Fighting.

SCHIOPETTIERE

Italian handgunner.
Weapons: handgonne, rapier or sabre, buckler shield.
Trait: Daredevil.

ARAB COMBAT STYLES

CULTURAL COMBAT STYLES

BEDOUIN WARRIOR

Irregular cavalry mounted on horses or war camels.
Weapons: scimitar or longsword, longspear, dagger.
Trait: Mounted Combat.

PROFESSIONAL COMBAT STYLES

The halqa or 'free army' consisted of Turks and Mongols (using the Ghazi Tribesman Combat Style) and badawi (using the Bedouin Warrior Combat Style).

'ASKARI

The Combat Style of the mamluks, heavy cavalry and infantry.
Weapons: longspear, sabre, battleaxe, dagger, (round) hoplite shield.
Trait: Formation Fighting.

NEW COMBAT STYLE TRAITS

BODY SLAM

After taking a turn of movement, you can engage an opponent with a crashing blow with your arm or shoulder. Make an opposed Athletics roll versus the defender's Brawn or Evade. If you win, then the defender is automatically knocked down with you astride them. He suffers his own Damage Modifier (if any) in damage to a random location from the fall. If your Athletics fails, the defender has weathered or sidestepped the impact. If you win one or more levels of success you may select suitable Special Effects as per normal combat (Bash and Flurry are both popular).

IMMOBILISE

When you have someone grappled or entangled, in lieu of damage you may use your action to try to immobilise the hit location you are grappling. Roll your Combat Style opposed by your target's Endurance; if successful, adjudicate like the Stun Location Special Effect (Mythras page 99), but this does not need a level of success to employ and only lasts for as long as you maintain the grapple.

TAKE DOWN

Using leg sweeps or throws that use the opponent's weight against him, rolls to resist your Trip Special Effect are made at one difficulty grade harder.

VOLLEY FIRE

Requires three or more combatants with the same Combat Style Trait to all be attacking with missile weapons at the same target or targets. As long as at least one of the combatants succeeds in an attack roll, the enemy is affected by the Pin Down Special Effect in addition to any other Special Effects earned from levels of success. This tactic can be used against a group of enemy soldiers of equal or lesser frontage than the archers.

NAMES

Different cultures have different practices when assigning names.

GREEK NAMES

Greek names depend on social status. A slave typically has just a given name. A freeman has a baptismal name plus some other form of identification such as an occupational byname, a locative byname (derived from his place of origin), a nickname, or a patronym (derived from his father's name). Locative names imply that the person originates from outside the local area and go against the general trend that the second names of freemen are not inherited: For example, Mavros's great grandfather may have come from Corinth when it was still part of the Empire, but Mavros is still known today as Mavros Korinthou.

Nicknames or *paratsoukli* are a Greek tradition. They may be purely descriptive (and sometimes cruelly so) or they may instead be humorous reminders of particular incidents in the past. If the paratsoukli is a mock title rather than an adjective, then the definite article "*ho*" is used. Thus Mavros might be known as Mavros Kontos (Short Mavros) if he is particularly short (or, ironically, if he is very tall) or Mavros ho Lagos (Mavros the Rabbit) if he is of a cowardly mien or particularly fond of lettuce or was once bitten by a fox.

Patronyms are uncommon. They occur where two people share a baptismal name and cannot be distinguished by other second names. A patronym is formed by adding "*-idis*" or "*-iadis*" to the father's baptismal name; the suffix "*-opoulos*" is also used, particularly for inhabitants of the Peloponnese. So Mavros might be known as Mavros Iaonnidis (Mavros son of Iaonnes).

The names of women are formed in a similar way to men. A freeborn woman might gain a second name in her own right, but might also take the occupational, locative, or patronym of her husband, or a patronym formed from her father's name if she is unmarried. In either case the name is given a feminine ending (see later). For example, before she is married, Anna might be known as Anna Michaelidou, after her father Michael. After her marriage to Mavros Iaonnidis, she becomes known as Anna Iaonnidou. If Mavros is instead known as Mavros Korinthou, then she may also be known as Anna Korinthou even though her family did not originate in Corinth.

Members of the aristocracy have a different pattern to name-giving. Here, inherited family names are used to indicate one's lineage. An aristocratic name consists of a given name followed by one or more family names belonging to his parents, grandparents, or great grandparents. It is considered crass to use a name from more than three generations ago. These family names have no particular order except that the father's family name is always given last. If the person also has a paratsoukli, this is given before the father's family name or sometimes in place of it. Take the aristocratic name Michael Tarchaneiotes Kamytzes. Michael's father was a member of the Kamytzes family and either his mother, one of his grandparents, or one of his great grandparents was a Tarchaneiotes. If he commits a deed of heroic bravery he might become known as Michael ho Leontidis Kamytzes, or maybe simply Michael Leontidis (the lion's son) if he is very famous.

The names of aristocratic women are constructed in the same way. A woman takes her father's last name as her own and also inherits family names from her descent as middle names. All these family names would be feminised, as per the following table. When a woman marries, she takes her husband's last name (in feminine form), usually appending it to her own. Thus Eirene Karantene Laskarina might become Eirene Laskarina Kamytzina when she marries Michael, and she might also have Karantene (from her own family) and/or Tarchaneiotina (from her husband's) as additional middle names in any order.

Greek Male Baptismal Names

Names given in bold are particularly common.

Alexandros, Alexios, Andreas, Andronikos, Anthes, Asemopoulos, Athanasios, Balsamon, Bardas, Bartolomaios, ***Basileios****, Christophoros,* ***Demetrios****, Dionysios, Ermanes, Foteinos, Gabriel, Georgios, Gerasimos, Gregoras,* ***Ioannes****, Ionnikios,* ***Konstantinos****, Kyriakos, Leo, Leon, Loumbertos, Makarios, Manuel, Mavros, Meletios,* ***Michael****, Modestos, Myristikos, Nikephoros, Niketas, Nikodemos,* ***Nikolaos****, Nikophoros, Niphon, Pantoleon, Paulos, Pelekanos, Petros, Philippos, Prousenos, Romanos, Sabas,* ***Stamates****, Stefanos,* ***Theodoros****, Theodoulos, Theophylaktos, Theotokios, Thomas, Triakontaphyllos, Trifyllios, Xenos*

Greek Female Baptismal Names

Names given in bold are particularly common.

Anna*,* ***Arete****,* ***Argyre****, Cheilou, Christina,* ***Eirene****, Elaiodora,* ***Elene****,* ***Eudokia****, Eugenia, Euphrosyne, Foteine,* ***Georgia****, Ioanna, Ioannousa,* ***Kale****, Kyriakia, Leonto, Margarito,* ***Maria****, Marina, Semne, Siligno, Sofia, Stammatike, Stania,* ***Theodora****, Theodosia, Theofano, Thomais, Triakontaphyllia, Vasilike, Velkonia,* ***Xene****,* ***Zoe****, Zoranna*

Additional female names can be generated by giving a man's name a feminine ending according to the following table:

Convert These Endings	To This
-ios	*-ia*
-os	*-ou or -e or -a*
-as	*-a*
-es	*-e*
-is	*-i or -ou*

Greek Occupational Bynames

A byname for a woman is formed by giving it a feminine ending, as described under the female baptismal names.

Alieos (fisherman), Amaxas (wagonmaker), Chalkeos (copper smith), Chenapios (goose keeper), Diakonos (deacon), Flevotomos (vein-opener, i.e. doctor), Gounaras (furrier), Iereios (priest), Kalaphates (ship's caulker), Kalligas (shoemaker), Kerouras (gardener), Krasopolia (wine seller), Ktistes (mason), Mageiros or Makellares (butcher), Metaxas (silk weaver or dyer), Mylonas (miller), Neropoles (waterseller), Pelekanos (carpenter), Phylax (watchman), Psychoprates (soul-seller, i.e. slaver), Raptes (tailor), Sapouna (soapmaker), Siderourgos (ironsmith), Skiadas (tent or hatmaker), Tzangarios (shoemaker), Tzepeas (hoemaker), Tzykalas (potter), Vagenas (barrelmaker), Xylurgos (carpenter), Yfantes (weaver)

Greek Locative Bynames

Bear in mind that with the current state of the world, many of the places listed here are no longer part of the Byzantine Empire. The original name of the city is given in parentheses.

Avidou (Abudos), Adrianoupoleos (Adrianoupolis), Aleksandroupoleos (Aleksandroupolis), Ankyras (Ankyra), Argous (Argos), Artas (Arta), Athinon (Athina), Constantinoupoleos (Constantinoupolis), Ephesou (Ephesos), Evias (Euboia), Herakleiou (Herakleion), Dramas (Drama), Ikoniou (Ikonion), Kallipoleos (Kallipolis), Kephallenias (Kephallenia), Khalkeos (Khalkis), Khersonesou (Khersonesos), Khiou (Khios), Korinthou (Korinthos), Laodikeias (Laodikeia), Larissis (Larissa), Lesvou (Lesvos), Militou (Miletos), Moreos (Morea), Mytilinis (Mutilene), Nicaeas (Nicaea), Nicomedeias (Nicomedeia), Patron (Patrai), Pigis (Pegai), Philadelphias (Philadelpheia), Philippoupoleos (Philippopolis), Samou (Samos), Serron (Serrhai), Sinopis (Sinope), Thivon (Thevai), Thessalonikis (Thessaloniki), Trapezous (Trapezon)

Locative bynames can also derive from neighbourhoods within Constantinople. Appropriate names by district include:

- Akropolis: Eugeniou, Kynegiou, Manganas
- Kainopolis: Amantiou, Kanikleiou, Chalkoprateias, Argyroprateias, Keropoleias, Sphorakiou, Artopoleias
- Palation: Hormisidou
- Petrion: Dexiokratou, Kyriou, Phanariou
- Platea: Zeugmas, Stauriou, Leomakellou, Heptaskalou*
- Stoudion: Exokioniou, Psamathias, Dalmatou
- Venetian Quarter: none
- Vlanga: 'Elenianou, Eleutheriou, Heptaskalou*, Amastrianas, Olybriou, Kaisariou
- Xerolophos: Lyke, Paradeisou, Olympiou, Elebichou, Tritou

**there are two neighbourhoods with this name in different districts.*

GREEK NICKNAMES (PARATSOUKLI)

A byname for a woman is formed by giving it a feminine ending, as described under the female baptismal names.

Agrios (wild), Akakios (innocent), Alkaios (strong), Aoinos (drinking no wine), Argyros (silver, rich, or mercenary), Arkopudophagos (bear eater), Atychos (unlucky), Choirosphaktes (slaughterer of pigs), Chrysostom (golden-mouthed), Digenis (of two races), Eukratas (abstemious), Eugenikos (courteous), Euthymos (good spirited), Galanis (blue-eyed), Gerontias (old), Geros (elder), Grammatikos (learned), Kalos (good, beautiful), Kaloutzikos (pleasant), Karvounis (coal-like), Katsaros (curly), Katsoufis (never cheerful), Klostogenes (curly beard), Kokkinis (red), Kontos (short), Koutsos (lame), Lachanodrakon (cabbage-dragon), Lagos (rabbit), Leontidis (lion's son), Leventis (brave, honourable), Makris (big), Mavros (black), Mavrovasilas (dark hair), Melachrenos (dark skin), Methysos (drunkard), Monophthalmus (one-eyed), Moros (foolish), Moundis (sulky), Murtzouphlos (scowling eyebrows), Neos (younger), Niketes (winner), Onassis (useful), Pachys (fat), Pantechnes (many skills), Pogonatos (bearded), Prosaites (beggar), Ptochos (poor), Pyrsokomos (fire hair, redheaded), Sfaxangoures (cucumber slayer), Sophos (wise), Spanos (beardless), Strabo (squinter), Tranospetes (big house), Traulos (stuttering), Tychos (lucky), Voulgaroltonos (Bulgar-slayer), Voutselos (barrel), Xanthos or Xanthakos (blond)

GREEK ARISTOCRATIC FAMILY NAMES

Anemas, Apokavkos, Axuchos, Chryselios, Dalassenos, Dasiotes, Dokeianos, Euphorbenos, Gabras, Iasites, Kalamanos, Kamateros, Kamytzes, Karantenos, Kastamonites, Keroularios, Kontostefanos, Makrembolites, Mavrozomes, Metochites, Mousele, Mouzalon, Pegonites, Petraloifas, Philanthropenos, Photios, Rallis [Raoul], Rogerios, Strategopoulos, Synadenos, Syrgiannes, Tarchaneiotes, Taronites, Tornikes

To generate a family name for a woman, convert the name given below to the feminine form according to the following table.

Convert These Endings	To This
-es, -is, -on, and -os	*-ina*
-nos	*-ne*
-tes	*-tissa*
-as	*drop s and add -ina*
-is	*-i or -ou*

GREEK ROYAL FAMILY NAMES

These family names were once like other aristocratic families, but have become associated with the imperial throne either by ascending to the throne or by marriage to an emperor or other royal.

Angelos, Argyros, Asanes, Botaneiates, Doukas, Dragases, Kantakouzenos, Komnenos, Laskaris, Palaiologos, Vatatzes

TURKISH NAMES

Turkish people usually have two names: a byname (traditionally given first) and a personal name. Turkish men sometimes use a patronymic as a byname; this is formed from the father's name with the suffix -oğlu (pronounced oh-luh, and meaning "son of"). Those who descend from a ruling house use the suffix -zade ("of the lineage of"). Otherwise the byname can be occupational or descriptive, both of which tend to be inherited. Turkish women following this pattern do not often have a byname; if they do, it is usually the name of a flower or a bird. Honorifics such as Sultan, paşa, or bey are given after the personal name.

Some Turks have taken to use a naming pattern derived from the Arabs, of a first name and a patronymic, separated with *bin* ("son of") for a man and *bint* ("daughter of") for a woman. Any titles are placed after the first name.

Slaves have no personal names. They are given a new byname when they are enslaved. Harem slaves take on flower or bird bynames, other slaves are named after objects, animals, or professions. Freed slaves and converts to Islam take bin Abdullah ("son of a servant of Allah") instead of a patronymic.

TURKISH MALE NAMES

Abbas, Abdullah, Ahmed, Ali, Aslaan, Aslihan, Avranos, Bekir, Butrus, Dana Halil, Davud, Dilman, Dimitri, Doğan, Dolabci Musa, Erdoğan, Evhad, Halil, Hamid, Hamza, Hasan, Heyreddin, Hizir, Hoşkadem, Husein, Husnü, Ibrahim, Ilyas, Isa, Iskender, Ismail, Istani, Kadri, Karaca, Kasim, Kemal, Kepçi, Kilavuz, Kökcü, Kutbeddin, Mehmed, Mercan, Muharrem, Murad, Musa, Mursel, Mürsel, Nasuh, Nebi, Paşayiğid, Ramazan, Salih, Sinan, Şirmerd, Suleiman, Sunduk, Sun'üllah, Timurhan, Yağci Amca, Yahşi, Yazid, Yunus, Yusuf.

TURKISH FEMALE NAMES

Asul, Ayşe, Behiye, Benefşe, Canhabibe, Dervişe, Devlet, Dilber, Dur-cihan, Emine, Fatima, Gümüş, Hadice, Hafza, Huban, Husni, Inanpaşa, Ine, Islah, Kadem, Kapabaşa, Mansure, Melike, Nar, Nasira, Nefise, Nergis, Neslihan, Paşabeği, Rabiye, Safiye, Şah-huban, Sara, Saruca, Selçuk, Selime, Şerife-bol, Şeruda, Sitti, Surur, Tohin, Zühal.

TURKISH MALE BYNAMES

Aksoy ("white lineage", i.e. famous), Attar (perfumer, herbalist), Avci (hunter), Badem (almond), Balik (fisherman), Bardakçi (glassmaker), Barzanci (shopkeeper), Binici (horseman), Burakgazi (warrior of the faith), Değirmenci (miller), Demir (iron), Demirci (blacksmith), Ekmerkçi (baker), Etci (butcher), Gazzaz (silk-maker), Helvaci (sweetmaker), Kara (black, gloomy, unlucky), Karga (crow), Kartal (eagle), Katirci (mule), Koç (ram), Küçük (small), Marangoz (carpenter), Peynirci (cheesemaker), Reis (captain), Sadik (loyal), Solak (left handed), Teke (goat), Terzi (tailor), Tilki (fox), Tiryaki (addict, stubborn), Tüccar (merchant), Uzun (long or tall), Yilmaz (dauntless)

TURKISH FEMALE BYNAMES

Burçak (vetch), Bülbül (nightingale), Bürke (gull), Çiçek (flower), Çiğdem (crocus), Defne (laurel), Gülbahar (rose-blossom), Gülfem (rose cheeked), Gülşah (rose monarch), Hüma (bird of paradise), Kiraz (cherry tree), Kumru (dove), Lale (tulip), Menekşe (violet), Müge (lily of the valley), Nergis (narcissus), Nesrin (wild rose), Nilüfer (lotus), Papatya (daisy), Sarmaşik (ivy), Turgay (skylark), Turna (crane), Yasemin (jasmin), Yonca (clover)

OTHER NAMES

Naming guides have not been given for Franks or Arabs. Franks can have such a wide range of origins that it would take pages to list names from all possible nations. There are several good websites for which authentic names for fifteenth century Europeans may be obtained. Arab names are complex, having up to five types of elements, some of which can be repeated: the *ism* (birth name), *nasab* (patronymic), *kunya* (son's name), *laqab* (honorific), and *nisba* (byname). An Arab character would typically be known by just two of these, the ism and the nasab, separated by *bin* ("son of") or *bint* ("daughter of"). Again, it is suggested that online sources are consulted for appropriate names.

AFFILIATION

Every character in Mythic Constantinople begins with one or more Affiliations. These are described in more detail starting on page 85.

BACKGROUND EVENTS

BACKGROUND EVENTS

1d100	Event
01	You grew up believing that you have royal blood. No one outright claimed it, but there were enough hints and slips of the tongue. You are determined to find out the truth.
02	A member of your family to whom you are very close is wanted by the authorities. He might be a Bogomil heretic or a common criminal. This association has caused you difficulties in the past, and may do so again.
03	An angel has taken an interest in you. Throughout your life you have been visited, sometimes in your dreams and sometimes when you are awake. It doesn't ever say anything, but you get the feeling that it is trying you guide your life's path – but to what end? Is it even an angel?
04	As a child, your father used to disappear for several months at a time. You were never allowed to ask where he was, although you could tell your mother didn't like it. One day he never returned from one of these trips, and you have always wanted to know what happened to him.
05	You grew up in one of the cities that has been recently conquered by the Ottomans, such as Adrianopolis or Thessaloniki. Your life was spared by one of the enemy soldiers, and you have secretly remained in touch.
06	You have always had a remarkable facility with horses. They trust you implicitly, and if you can make eye contact you can communicate your intent to them. You encountered one magnificent stallion years ago, and know that you are destined to meet that beast again.
07	You were praised excessively as an infant and this attracted the evil eye. You are excessively unlucky and always seem to be narrowly avoiding peril. Could it be that the curse is actually protecting you – there might be a reason why misfortune tends to be deflected on those close to you.
08	Once, when you went to the market with your mother, an old man approached you and gave you a gold coin. Your mother seemed to recognise him although they exchanged no words. The coin has writing in a script you have never been able to identify. You are strangely reluctant to let anyone touch it.
09	You have had the same dream every night for as long as you can remember. You are fighting a group of soldiers with a band of comrades. There is something unidentifiably wrong about your opponents, and you always wake filled with a sense of dread and foreboding.
10	You barely remember your mother and never met any of her family. Your father refused to ever discuss her and you were raised by a gaggle of aunts. All you were ever able to glean is that there was something shameful about her or her background.
11	You have always been remarkably lucky. You have one extra Luck Point, but to regain it you have to perform some ritual obeisance to Tyche (or another deity of luck), which costs you one Experience Roll.
12	You were born with a caul and you still wear it in a pouch around your neck. You can get free passage on any sea-going vessel, for common belief is that people like you will never be shipwrecked.
13	You were very close to a sibling growing up and you used to play together all the time, having many adventures. However, you recently found out that you were actually an only child, and that none of your family and neighbours have any memory of your sibling.
14	You have a curious birthmark, which an old woman once told you marks you for one of the Olympian gods. You have noticed that this god does seem to have relevance in your life without you making any conscious effort. Your career is likely to match a profession favoured by the god whose mark you bear
15	Your father (or another relative) is a revolutionary who seeks to overturn the social order and replace it with something better. You are worried that one day he will get into serious trouble and expect you to bail him out.
16	A relative loaned a substantial sum of money to a neighbour, who promptly disappeared. It turned out that the neighbour had borrowed money from other people as well. Your family was driven into poverty due to this, and you have always vowed to track them down and get what is due.
17	Your grandfather was an alchemist and some say he discovered the trick of turning base metal into gold. As proof of this, you have a half-tetarteron, an old coin struck in either lead or copper, except yours is gold. You also have your grandfather's notes, but it is in a code that has defied all translation.
18	You have always suspected that the people who raised you are not your parents. You bear no physical resemblance to them or to any siblings you might have. This did not affect how they treated you, but you have always wondered what your origins really are.
19	Your first true love was a nymph or godling. It was only after you declared your undying love that you discovered the true nature of your paramour, and flew in fear. To this day, you have not dared to return to the site where you met them in case they hold a grudge for the decades-old abandonment.
20	When you were younger several children in your neighbourhood went missing. No culprit was ever found, although a relative of yours was blamed, and disappeared ahead of the lynch mob. The abductions stopped on that day. Was your relative really to blame, or is there a less obvious explanation?

1d100	Event
21	You are prone to periods of memory loss. These come roughly once a year and last up to a week. During these periods your personality changes and you demonstrate the use of a specific charism (choose one from page 77), something you are usually incapable. Your grandmother used to say that it was a saint working through you.
22	An accident with alchemy as a child granted you great strength (you have the Gift of Perfection: +1d6 STR) but you may never benefit from any other magic that increases your Characteristics or Attributes
23	Your parents are from a higher social class than you are. Perhaps they were wealthy merchants who didn't want another child, so sold you to a poorhouse instead. Alternatively, you could have been sold into slavery as a child to alleviate your parent's debt.
24	You had a mentor as an adolescent who was an important influence on your career. One day you visited him and another man, who you'd seen regularly before, was just leaving. It seemed like they had had an argument. Your mentor then broke off your relationship and suggested you shouldn't see each other again. What could cause him to abandon you like this?
25	Every year your family performed a ritual where you cursed Adam for his covenant with the owner of the earth. Every time at church that the priest said "Jesus", your father would mouth the name "Michael". You thought this was normal behaviour, but you realise now that your family were heretics.
26	Your sister was really sick as a child, and you prayed over her constantly. At one point you offered to give up your life if it would save hers, and you felt within you that the deal had been accepted. She got better. For a few months, you were frightened that you would die in her place but nothing happened. Now, years later, you wonder if you still owe a debt to whoever – or whatever – cured your sister.
27	You have always loved easily. Your first love died in a storm, the second was married against his or her will, the third disappeared under mysterious circumstances, and so on. These setbacks may have disheartened you, or perhaps you are ever hopeful that the right person will come along – and stay.
28	You mastered a skill at an early age, and were somewhat of a prodigy. People would come from miles to witness your talent or buy your products. Now you are an adult, your skills are unremarkable, and you miss the fame that you once had. Perhaps it had something to do with the man who visited your mother before you were born – if you could find him again maybe you would be famous again.
29	During the recent conflicts, your family's patriarch was murdered. Everyone thinks he was killed in enemy action, but you know the truth because you witnessed it: he was killed by a family friend, someone you knew and trusted. Now you want to know why, and to bring his killer to justice.
30	There is someone in the local area who looks a lot like you – sufficiently so that you often get mistaken for him or her. What is worse is that your lookalike is a scoundrel and you often are blamed for things he/she has done. One day you are going to track him/her down and sort it out.
31	You inherited a journal that describes the exploration of ancient ruins located beneath the city streets. There are hints of untold riches and forgotten lore. However, you lack the first page, so you have no idea where the entrance is – or even which city you need to be in.
32	When you were younger you started a fire with a group of other children. It got out of control and burned down several houses before it could be extinguished by the watch. An old woman died and you have always felt guilty.
33	Your family has travelled extensively, which has given you an aptitude for foreign ways. Any improvements in Culture or Language (other than your native tongue) are doubled.
34	You were raised by non-humans. You may have grown up in Africa amongst the Kynokephaloi, amongst the Arimapsoi of the Golden Horn, or even amongst the dogs of Constantinople.
35	One of your parents is (or was) an opium addict. If he or she is still alive this may place an obligation on you to feed the habit, or perhaps you have severed all ties. If he or she has died, you may be in debt to an opium dealer. Whatever your relationship, this has probably affected your attitude towards the drug.
36	When you were a child in Constantinople you explored a cistern under repair and discovered a series of tunnels under the city. You were unable to find your way out and became terrified, but a woman's voice calmed you and guided you to the exit. You will never forget her sibilant tones and exotic accent.
37	You ran away from home as a youngster. While away from your parents you fell in with a group from an entirely different social strata. You lived with them for several months until your father found you, and could still be in touch with some of them today.
38	You have been befriended by a dog from the streets of Constantinople. The creature seems uncommonly intelligent, appearing to listen carefully to everything you say. You have taken to confiding in the dog, treating him or her like a beloved friend.
39	You have an injury that resembles a mutilation imposed as a punishment – a slit cheek, a missing nose, or a half-hand. This leads to many people believing you to be a criminal
40	Your parents left you for dead as an infant in a desolate place. You were found and taken in by an old peasant couple, but they never hid the circumstances of your birth from you. You have several romantic notions based on mythological precedents as to your true origin.
41	A gang of older boys used to bully and beat you; their leader is now an important man in the city.
42	You and your twin were raised separately by family friends and relatives, in order to keep you away from your father, who was corrupted by an evil power.
43	Someone in your family was a terrible judge of character; at least one Contact, Ally, and/or Enemy is really something else entirely (the GM knows which).
44	Your grandfather gave you a lucky charm that allows you to choose the result of any dice throw, coin toss, or similar lot-casting. He warned you that one day it will fail catastrophically and never work for you again (Note that this charm affects the character's dice throws, not the player's!)
45	A merchant sold you three knives, part of an ancient set. When the other four are found, the seven immortals at last may die. Or so the merchant said.
46	You have a non-fatal skin condition, however you conceal it as you are scared people may mistake it for leprosy
47	You were captured by slavers or Barbary pirates, but you were freed after an unknown benefactor paid your ransom.

1d100	Event
48	You are constantly mistaken for and compared with your more successful brother/sister. You have spent your whole life living in his/her shadow
49	Over the last few years you have been aware that people with whom you have contact have died. You have come to believe that you might be the carrier of a curse or a disease, to which you are somehow immune.
50	A traveller from afar stayed with your family and entrusted you with a secret word; he said someday you would need its power.
51	When you were a child you went missing for a week. When you were found, you had no memory of what had a happened but you gained a strange tattoo.
52	You are a half-caste: one of your parents was a foreigner. If you are Greek then you are probably a Gasmouli (one parent was a Frank). You may keep this a secret to avoid prejudice.
53	You've tried to leave the city three times by ship, but each time you were thwarted: the ship was holed in the harbour; the captain was arrested; the boat was commandeered by the navy. Perhaps you're cursed to stay on land?
54	Your parents are from a lower social class than you are. Perhaps they are slaves, and their master freed you on your seventh birthday, although his motives for this are not clear. Or maybe you were fostered in a gentile household and treated as one of their own, although you never lost track of your poor parents.
55	A family curse has left you incapable with a specific activity: choose one Standard Skill; it can never be improved beyond its base score, and any rolls will fumble on any double.
56	When exploring the countryside as a child you found a rock with a curious carving on it. You brought it back to show your family, who reacted in horror. It took a whole week of exorcisms and prayers for the priest to decide that you were free from contamination. They never explained what it was all about. You never admitted to anyone that you can still see the symbol sometimes when you close your eyes.
57	There is someone in the city who looks just like you. You have seen them many times, often copying what you are doing, but always disappears into the crowd before you can confront them. You suspect this doppelgänger is trying to replace you.
58	You are not who you pretend to be. For some reason you have assumed another's life, and fear that one day their past (or your own) will catch up with you.
59	Your grandmother used to talk about her "locked heart", which you took to be an excuse for her cold and sometimes cruel behaviour. When she died, you found a curious bone key in her hand and you now wonder if she was speaking more literally than you thought.
60	Ever since you were a child you have heard the voice of a saint or angel in your head, but the advice she offered was always nonsensical. Why would a heavenly being take the time to give you meaningless advice?
61	You have a relative in a high social position, but you know that he gained that position on the strength of a crime in which you were complicit. You prefer to avoid one another – you could blackmail him, but he has the power to bring you down with him.
62	You have managed to offend a group of people (Jews, Bulgars, Tripithamoi, etc.), but you can't find out what you did or how to set things right. In the meantime, they shun you.
63	Your brother was killed when you were younger, and you have been hunting his murderer since you reached adulthood. You don't know what he looks like, only that he has mismatched eyes and smells of cloves.
64	You have a distinctive appearance: you are an albino, have extra fingers, a tail, or something similar. Do you try to keep this a secret? If not, it is probably the source of a colourful byname.
65	You secretly suffer from an inconvenient but harmless affliction (such as venereal disease, haemorrhoids, or the like). You have tried many cures, but nothing has worked so far.
66	When you concentrate you can occasionally see dead people crowded around you (you gain the effects of the Trance Skill but at a score equal to a Herculean Perception check). They gesture at you, trying to communicate something important.
67	While travelling, a peddler in your company died, and his belongings were divided up between those with him. You received a book, but between its pages were the plans to some gunpowder-fuelled weapon. You haven't yet found a person with sufficient skill to build it, since it appears to be more advanced than anything available today.
68	You somehow acquired a piece of leather with a page's worth of text tattooed upon it. You've managed to determine it is the words of a spell but are unable to decipher it.
69	Ever since a terrifying childhood incident, you have a debilitating fear of burning to death. You are not frightened of fire per se, but are cautious around flames larger than a cooking fire. You should take Fear Immolation as a Passion.
70	A witch stole your heart – literally. She touched your nipple with her wand and your chest opened up, letting her remove it. Its lack doesn't seem to have affected you, but you worry what she intends to do with it, and you want it back where it belongs.
71	Your family dog went missing and as you searched for it you came across a pack of other dogs, along with yours, sitting on a piece of barren ground. They were discussing the emperor. You were never comfortable around your family pet ever since.
72	An old lady once sent you on seven errands, one to each of the seven hills, but she was gone when you returned. She may have been a witch.
73	An annoying kid used to hang around you when you were younger. Your sister ended up marrying him, and he is still hanging around you. What keeps him coming around? Is it hero worship, or does he crave influence or intimacy of another kind?
74	One or more family members were tragically killed in a fire when you were young. You later found out that the Prasinoi were implicated, and you have vowed revenge. You should take Hate Prasinoi as a Passion.

1d100	Event
75	Over supper one night writing suddenly appeared on the dining table. Your uncle, who had been mute for two decades, suddenly spoke forth a cryptic utterance (your Games Master will tell you what was said). He then lapsed back into silence and never spoke again.
76	You inherited a religious ikon from an aunt. It is very old and depicts the Passion, and you have found it brings you good fortune. Just recently a stranger pointed out that while true depictions of the Crucifixion show both feet transfixed with a single nail, your ikon has a blasphemous "fourth nail";. You are concerned that your ikon's luck might be sent from a source other than Heaven.
77	You are strangely linked to the number seven. It crops up everywhere in your life, and you have become slightly obsessed with the number. You look for significance whenever it appears.
78	Your younger brother was snatched from his cradle by a wolf, which stole into your shared room. You watched the whole thing, and have since been deathly afraid of wolves. You should take the Passion of Fear Wolves
79	You would have drowned were it not for the kiss of a nymph. Since then, you have found that you have been able to breathe underwater, although you prefer to avoid the sea since you worry that the nymph will return to claim your life.
80	When you were young you were dedicated to the river Lykos (if male) or one of his daughters (if female). As long as you honour their rites (such as remaining unmarried, if a woman) then you may ask your patron god or goddess for a boon. Your Games Master can find out more information about Lykos on page 185.
81	You have spent some time in prison. Where you a political prisoner jailed with your parents? A juvenile delinquent? Or a victim of mistaken identity?
82	You have an urge to atone for previous wrongdoings. You should decide who you offended (a religious group, a culture, a non-human race, etc.), and how (destruction of a significant site, insulting of an elder, etc.), but your redemption will require reparation, not just forgiveness.
83	An elderly relative of yours whom you respect achieved prestige, for example, as a Paranomos, churchman, or courtier. Your parents' generation was a disappointment, and you feel that it falls on you to uphold the family's honour.
84	You had difficulty making friends as a child. If you find someone whom you feel you can trust, cling onto them and never let them go.
85	According to your cousin's wife's best friend, you will be granted a wish if you walk seven times widdershins around a specific statue of Herakles. But she never told you which statue.
86	You have been trying for years to finish an epic poem. The beginning is the most powerful thing you have ever read, but the inspiration to finish it has fled from you.
87	You have begun to suspect that apparent coincidences that affect your life are not coincidences after all. All the significant people in your life seem to be connected to one another, and you think that some conspiracy is driving you towards some unknown purpose.
88	Like other members of your family, you have a remarkable facility with one Professional Skill. Whenever you spend an Experience Roll on this Skill, you always increase it by 1d4+1%; there is no need to roll over the Skill.
89	Your family are fervent pro-Unionists. They blame the Orthodox Church's intransigence over this issue for all that is wrong with the city. Whether or not you agree with their views, you have a strong opinion on the issue of the Union of Churches.
90	Your family are militant anti-Unionists. They believe the emperor and the patriarch to be heretical, and that God has turned his face from the city because of their blasphemy. Whether or not you agree with their views, you have a strong opinion on the issue of the Union of Churches.
91	Your father or an older brother was/is a Vardariotes. This had a profound influence on the way that you treat law and order (for good or for ill), and you cannot shake the reputation of being associated with the guard unit.
92	You have recently discovered you have a relative you didn't know about. Why did your family keep them hidden? Perhaps your uncle is a Holy Fool, or your elder sister an anchorite, or a cousin a Gasmouli?
93	You have had to make a choice between your own life and that of a loved one. Against all odds, the person you sacrificed survived, and your betrayal has brought them crushing sorrow or burning vengeance.
94	You have always been more comfortable at night when the light doesn't dazzle your sensitive eyes and the sun does not blister your skin. Treat complete darkness as partial darkness, and full daylight as twilight for Visibility (see Mythras page 84).
95	Your mother left you overnight in the arms of a statue of Hermes the god of thieves. You've always felt comfortable around criminals, and improve the chance of success for Influence and Deceit rolls by one difficulty grade, although not above the Standard grade.
96	There is a statue in a forgotten niche. When you place a coin in the pool by its feet, it will speak and offer you advice and counsel. You sometimes wonder if it is your only real friend.
97	You are secretly caring for a trapped or injured monster, such as a chimera, griffin, or giant mantis. You've been bringing it food and you think it has come to trust you. Maybe someday it will become your trusted ally.
98	You found a trove of bronze coins, each one bearing an ox's head on one side. You buried them again, but carry one on you for luck. Sometimes you can hear it whispering to you late at night, telling you the secrets of those who claim to be your friends.
99	As a baby you swallowed an amulet against the evil eye and it lodged itself inside you. You may always cast the Avert Folk Magic spell as a Reaction using Willpower instead of Folk Magic. You may not use this spell as a Proactive Action unless you have the Folk Magic Skill.
00	For some time now you've suspected that a powerful being has been watching out for you, and have come to believe it is one of the Ateleutoi (Immortals) of popular legend. You cannot say why they might be interested in your fate, but you've had several strokes of remarkable fortune that cannot be attributed to luck alone.

MONEY & EQUIPMENT

As discussed earlier (page 25), the coins minted by the Empire include the (hypothetical) gold hyperpyron; the silver stavraton, half-stavraton, and aspron (or eighth-stavraton); and the copper tournesion and follario. Venetian silver ducats are used as quarter-stavrata.

One tournesion is equivalent to 1 CP. For simplicity's sake, the approximate values in the Exchange Rate Table can be used if preferred. Converting to Byzantine coinage isn't necessary; just continue to use GP, SP, and CP on the character sheet.

EXCHANGE RATES

Coin	Approximate value	Exact value
1 follario	1/3 CP	1/3 CP
1 tournesion	1 CP	1 CP
1 aspron	1 SP	12 tournesia = 1.2 SP
1 stavraton	10 SP	96 tournesia = 8 aspra = 9.6 SP
1 hyperpyron	20 SP	192 tournesia = 2 stavrata = 19.2 SP
1 copper piece	1 tournesion	3 follarii = 1 tournesion
1 silver piece	1 aspron	10 CP = 0.8 aspra
1 gold piece	10 stavrata or 5 hyperpyra	100 SP = 10.4 stavrata = 5.2 hyperpyra

ARMOUR & ARMS

NEW WEAPON TRAITS

Flanged – the weapon has blunt metal blades or crowns of blunt spikes that are designed to concentrate the impact against armoured opponents. Ignores a specific number of armour points equal to half the maximum damage capability of the weapon, but only for determining the effects of the Stun Location or Sunder Special Effects. So a flanged mace (1d8 damage) against an opponent with 4 AP can still cause a Stun Location effect even if it 4 or fewer Hit Points damage were rolled.

Puncturing – the weapon has a significant metal spike, usually slightly curved and designed to penetrate stiff armour. Can also apply to ammunition. Ignores a specific number of armour points equal to half the maximum damage capability of the weapon but only against rigid armour. So a puncturing dagger (1d4+1 damage) ignores 3 points of rigid armour.

NEW WEAPONS

MANGLABIA

A whip made of flexible bullhide, 1½ m long. Use the statistics for a chain but add the entrapping weapon trait.

MEILICHAI

Leather fingerless gloves worn by pankratiasts (see page 21). If sewn with bronze beads, increases the damage of unarmed attacks to 1d4.

SOLENARION

A hollow tube held in the place of an arrow on a bow, through which an archer can launch small darts or mues ("mice"). The advantage is that these darts may be used in very close quarters at a rapid rate of fire. Treat as a dart but inflicting 1d6 damage. The solenarion can also fire several darts at a time, acquiring the Scatter Weapon trait (see page 74).

ZAGAIE

A 3–3.7m spear with a blade fitted on both ends. Use the statistics for a longspear with the double-ended weapon trait. Characteristic of Albanian mercenaries

ARMOUR

The Greek heavy armour worn by kataphractoi and skoutatoi consists of a padded gambeson (*kavadion*), over which is a coat of double-layered chain or scale mail (*lorikion*). This usually extends to the lower legs, and may be long or short sleeved. Over the coat of mail is a lamellar cuirass (*klivanion*), with the lathes made of metal or hardened leather. Greaves and gauntlets are common, and a heavy cloth skirt (*kremesmata*) is worn on top. On the head is a tall *casque* helmet, either conical or onion-shaped with a tuft of horsehair in the unit's colours. The helm has either a flat wide brim or a narrow, downward-sloping brim, and no nose guard. Occasionally a coif is worn with the helmet, but more usually a neck guard of mail, plate, or hardened leather is used. Trapezites and Tzangratoros wear Greek medium armour consisting of the casque helmet, kavadion and lorikon, but without the klivanion on top. Light infantry and cavalry troops such as Toxotai, Hippotoxotes and Psiloi wear Greek light armour: just a metal casque helmet and kavadion.

The Franks are famous for their plate armour – the Greeks call them the *siderophoroi* or "iron clads". Frankish heavy armour consists of a padded arming doublet is worn on the torso and abdomen with a mail skirt and a long-sleeved mail shirt. A breastplate is worn on top along with massive pauldrons protecting the shoulders, upper arms, neck, and upper back. The elbows, lower arms, and hands have jointed plate mail. Over the mail skirt is more plate armour. The leg armour is attached to the bottom of the arming doublet: plate coverings protect the thighs, knees, and lower legs, with chain mail fringes to grant protection to the joints. The greaves end in mail socks over which sandals are worn; else plate sabatons are

GREEK WEAPONS

Greek name	Equivalent to...	Notes
Tzikourion	Battleaxe	a single-bladed weapon, usually with a straight rather than curved edge.
Hippotoxon	Bow, recurve	cavalry bow, 1.2 m high, less tightly strung than infantry bows for greater accuracy. Reduce the range to 15/75/150.
Toxon	Bow, recurve	infantry bow, a composite, reflex bow with unbendable horn grip and reinforced wooden bowstave.
Menaulion	Glaive	a heavy spear 2.7 to 3.6 m long used by heavy infantry against heavy cavalry. Tipped with a 50 cm blade.
Pelekys	Great axe	the two-bladed axe characteristic of the Varangian Guard.
Tzangra	Crossbow, heavy	all crossbows are imported from Venice or Genoa.
Peltas	Javelin	a light throwing spear.
Kontarion	Longspear	a 2–3 m long spear with a metal blade.
Spathion	Longsword	a sword with an 80 cm long blade, double-edged and heavy.
Siderorabdos	Mace	a heavy, all iron mace with blunt metal blades. Add the Flanged Weapon Trait.
Paramerion	Sabre	a one-edged sword.
Thyreos	Shield, buckler	A small round shield worn by kataphraktoi attached to the left arm.
Hopliton	Shield, hoplite	often square in form.
Skouton	Shield, kite	A wooden shield the shape of an elongated triangle with a pronounced curve along its width. The sides are straight or slightly convex.
Sphenedone	Sling	

TURKISH WEAPONS

Turkish name	Equivalent to...	Notes
Nacak	Battleaxe	blade shaped like a half-moon, sometimes double-bladed. Typically two metres long.
Menzil	Bow, recurve	a long-range bow, increase the range to 20/150/300 but reduce damage to 1d6+1.
Tirkeş	Bow, recurve	the war-bow, a standard recurve bow.
Puta	Bow, short	a target bow used for hunting, smaller than the tirkeş and less tightly strung.
Çark yayi	Crossbow, light	
Tirpan	Glaive	used by all infantry troops.
Teberzin	Hatchet	the "saddle-axe" is like the battleaxe in form, but smaller, only one metre.
Gönder	Javelin	
Sünü	Lance	
Amud	Mace	a simple iron baton.
Gürz	Mace	like the amud but topped with an iron sphere.
Bozdoğan	Mace	ends in six flanges in the shape of a ball; add the Flanged Weapon Trait.
Külünk	Mace	hammer-shaped.
Harbe	Pike	
Kiliç	Sabre	standard sabre.
Palyos	Sabre	slightly shorter and less curved than the kiliç.
Yatağan	Sabre	reverse-curved blade and no quillons, and is carried exclusively by the Yeniçeri.
Şimşir	Scimitar	
Sipar	Shield, hoplite	a round shield with a distinct convex shape.
Nize	Shortspear	
Hançer	Shortsword	

ARMOUR TABLE

Armour type	Head	Arms	Chest	Abdomen	Legs
Heavy Greek armour	Plated Mail	Mail	Plated Mail	Plated Mail	Mail
Medium Greek armour	Plated Mail	Mail	Mail	Mail	Mail
Light Greek armour	Half Plate	None	Padded	Padded	Padded
Heavy Frankish armour	Art. Plate	Art. Plate	Art. Plate	Art. Plate	Art. Plate
Medium Frankish armour	Plated Mail	Scaled	Art. Plate	Scaled	Art. Plate (left), Padded (right)
Light Frankish armour	Half Plate	Padded	Plated Mail or Scaled	Scaled	Padded
Heavy Turkish armour	Plated Mail	Plated Mail	Art. Plate or Plated Mail	Mail	Plated Mail
Medium Turkish armour	Half Plate	Plated Mail	Scaled	Scaled	Laminated
Light Turkish armour	Padded	Padded	Laminated	Laminated	Padded
Mamluk armour (Arab)	Plate	Mail	Plated Mail	Plated Mail	Plated Mail
Halqa armour (Arab)	Half Plate	Laminated	Scaled	Scaled	Laminated

Note that metal armours are made from steel rather than iron or bronze, so total ENC is multiplied by 0.75 before calculating the Armour Penalty.

worn instead. A visored armet helmet combines head protection with a gorget around the neck. Infantrymen wear Frankish medium armour, a reduced version of this full suit, foregoing the pauldrons and upper arm armour, and wearing leg armour only on the left or leading leg. They also exchange the plate abdominal protection for a padded or plated brigandine over the mail. Frankish light armour consists of a padded or plated brigandine or a two piece Italian style breastplate with attached taces. They usually wear a metal helmet.

Turkish heavy armour is worn by the Yeniçeri and by all Sipahi units except for the Garips. Yeniçeri armour consists of a full-length lamellar cuirass (*prahen ahenin*) over a mail hauberk (*zirh*). Plate vambraces (*kolluk*) and greaves (*kolçak*) are favoured. A mail coif (*zirh külah*) is worn under either a crested helmet (tuğulka) or a turban helmet (*migfer*). The Siphai units wear a plate armour cuirass protecting the chest (*krug*) over the mail hauberk rather than the lamellar cuirass. Turkish medium armour is worn by the Garips and Anatolian timariots. They exchange the cuirass and mail hauberk for a shorter lamellar cuirass (*cevşen*) and leather hauberk (*cebe*). Thick leather cuisses (*budlak*) protect the legs. They wear a metal helmet ending in a point (*işik*). Turkish light armour is worn by all irregular units including the akincilar. It consists of felt armour on all locations, except for the leather cebe. Any other armour they are able to plunder will doubtless be worn.

Mamluk armour consists of a thigh-length shirt of mail (*kazaghand*) with a sleeveless cuirass of velvet lined with scale plates (*qarqal*) worn over the top to protect the torso. Separate plate and mail sections protect the thighs and knees; and heavy cavalry boots protect the lower legs. The helmet is metal with a brim and sliding nasal, with cheek pieces often decorated with symbols of rank. The halqa wear whatever armour is appropriate to their origin; many of the cavalry are ghazi tribesmen and wear the equivalent of Turkish medium armour. The Egyptian footsoldiers typically wear flexible halqa armour: a leather lamellar coat (only occasionally in conjunction with mail), and a metal scale cuirass over the top for superior torso protection. The khud helmet is part solid steel, part leather.

GREEK FIRE

The Byzantine Empire is famous for its use of Greek fire, although the Greeks themselves called it *pyr hygron* ("liquid fire") and the Franks used various translations of "wild fire". The Ottomans used the Arabic term naffata. In the past the recipe was a state secret and unique to the Byzantine Empire; this is no longer true and it is now employed by Arabs and Turks as well, although its use in warfare is limited on both sides.

Greek fire is employed as an incendiary rather than an explosive; that is, it is used to start, spread, and maintain fires. It is manufactured in a number of different consistencies according to its purpose. The most liquid is poured onto the surface of the sea to use against ships (this use is called *pyr thalassion*, or "sea fire"). More viscous versions are poured onto besieging armies through murder holes, used to fill breaches in walls, or thrown in ceramic jars wrapped in cloth which is set alight before throwing, so that the Greek fire ignites when the jar is smashed. The stickiest version is loaded into siphons and squirted onto enemy troops; a burning match at the end of the nozzle turns the siphon into a flamethrower. It may also be deployed unlit and then fired using a flaming arrow. This viscous preparation is the hardest to use; the resins in the Greek fire tend to set solid, and it must be carefully warmed before loading the tanks that supply the siphon.

RULES FOR GREEK FIRE

Greek fire follows the usual rules for fires (Mythras page 79), except as noted here. When lit, Greek fire burns ferociously, hot enough to cause adjacent areas to catch fire. Areas set alight by Greek fire can be doused normally, but the location where the Greek fire is burning cannot be extinguished with water and will continue to burn for its Intensity in rounds even when smothered with heavy cloth or soil. Smothering does prevent the fire from spreading, however.

SPOT RULES

- Most preparations of Greek fire produce an Intensity 3 flame (1d6 damage), affecting the nearest 1d4+1 Hit Locations, and every round (if it has material to burn) spreads to three adjacent locations. Greek fire can ignite cloth and hair with ease and will even ignite skin. Damage is inflicted directly to Hit Points, ignoring Armour Points.
- It takes a crew of four and 10 minutes to load a large siphon, usually used in ship-to-ship combat. These have an inbuilt

burner to warm the Greek fire, and squirt it under pressure in a jet up to 15 metres away. Each siphon holds enough Greek fire for a total of 2d6 rounds, which may be deployed as one or more bouts. A *cheirosiphon* (hand-siphon) is a syringe-like apparatus which can be deployed by one person. It contains enough Greek fire for 1d3 rounds, and has a range of 3 metres. It takes 3 rounds to load a cheirosiphon with warmed Greek fire, and it must be used within 5 rounds or it will solidify inside the apparatus. In both cases the Greek fire is ignited by a nozzle-mounted linen match.

- For the duration of a jet of Greek fire from a siphon, the operator may make an attack each turn. A Lore (Firearms and Artillery) roll is used in place of an Attack roll for siphons and cheirosiphons. The Mechanisms Skill may be used instead at a Hard penalty. Attacks from siphons and cheirosiphons can be opposed by Evade but not parried. Shields can be used to provide cover in the same manner as for missile fire. For crowded battlefields use the rules for firing into a crowd (Mythras rules page 108).
- The preparation thrown in ceramic jars ignites as soon as the jar smashes. A jar can be thrown in the same Action as it is lit. This requires an Athletics roll in place of an Attack and is not opposed. A jar is SIZ 0 for the purpose of range (Mythras page 39). A success means that the jar hits the intended target and smashes, affecting one Hit Location with an Intensity 2 fire (1d4 damage). This fire will spread to two adjacent Hit Locations in the following round if not smothered. A fail causes the jar to miss, but it will probably still ignite. A fumble means that the jar ignites in the thrower's hand.

GUNPOWDER

Gunpowder (or *botane* in Greek) is the explosive power behind personal firearms and artillery weapons. It is a mixture of charcoal, saltpetre, and sulphur in certain proportions. Until relatively recently, gunpowder had to be mixed on the field as it had a tendency to separate out, but a new technique developed around 1420 involves 'corning' the gunpowder by mixing it with vinegar or urine and pressing through a sieve then letting it dry into grains. This not only reduces the risk of the gunpowder separating, it also gives better explosive power. Gunpowder is notoriously tricky stuff: if it is old, too hot, or exposed to moisture, it is likely to spoil; meaning that it has reduced power or fails to work at all. Non-corned gunpowder must be remixed and ground to the correct grain size before use, often on the battlefield.

The Lore (Firearms and Artillery) Skill covers all aspects of gunpowder usage. This Skill permits the character to manufacture his own gunpowder, prepare it on the battlefield if necessary, and store his powder correctly. Gunpowder typically costs 5 SP per 100 grams to buy, 7 SP if corned. This much gunpowder requires 2 SP's worth of sulphur and saltpetre; artillerists usually prefer to make their own charcoal as this greatly affects the performance of the final product.

Fifteenth century gunpowder produces a lot of smoke and artillery units complain about not being able to see their targets after two or three shots. The noise and flash has psychological benefit over inexperienced troops and can terrify horses. Breathing in the smoke causes chronic diarrhoea.

FIREARMS

There are two basic types of firearm employed in the Mythic Constantinople setting. The first is the *handgonne* or hand cannon, which the Italians call a *schiopetto* and the Greeks call a *touphax* (from the Turkish name tufenk). This is simply a metal barrel mounted on a pole, with a touch hole through which the gunpowder is ignited. The handgonne is muzzle-loaded and the projectiles vary from iron or stone balls to arrows, or even (at a pinch) pebbles collected from the ground. Handgonnes must be held in two hands while an assistant applies the source of ignition – a smouldering coal, a slow-burning match, or a red-hot iron. A smaller handgonne can be operated by one person but it is still cumbersome. All handgonnes are inaccurate at range due to their awkwardness in use. Further they are dependent on the quality of the gunpowder used. See later for rules involving firearms.

The second type of firearm is a hook gun or arquebus, called an *archibugio* by the Italians and a *molybdobolon* ("lead thrower") to the Greeks. The hook gun is a development of the handgonne, with a narrower and longer barrel (about 1 metre long) providing better aiming, and a hook or stock which is braced against the shoulder. A hook gun weighs about 5 kilograms. Like a handgonne, the hook gun is muzzle-loaded. Rather than inserting the ignition source directly into the touch hole, the hook gun has a flash pan attached to the side of the barrel which feeds into the touch hole; this has a leather cover to keep the priming powder within it dry until it is ignited with a slow-burning match. An invention coming into usage in the last 10 years or so is a matchlock, where a mechanism (or lock) holds the match away from the flash pan until a lever (or serpentine) is pulled, lowering the match into the flash pan. This lock allows the hook gun to be held in both hands when it is fired, leading to greater accuracy.

RULES FOR FIREARMS

There are additional rules for Firearms for Mythras available from the Design Mechanism website, and Games Masters are encouraged to consult those rules if firearms become a significant part of your Mythic Constantinople campaign. However, fifteenth century firearms are much lower velocity than modern firearms and so combat involving them does not deviate as greatly as it would in a more up-to-date setting and the usual rules for missile weapons are usually sufficient. Some additional rules from Firearms that might be helpful have been summarised below.

SPECIAL EFFECTS FOR FIREARMS

- ***Bleed***: restricted to Critical Success only due to narrow wound paths of bullets
- ***Damage Weapon/Disarm Opponent***: restricted to Critical Success only
- ***Impale***: all ammunition other than grapeshot can impale. However, bullets are too small to impose a difficulty grade penalty, so the main benefit is restricted to the chance of extra damage

ACCURACY OF FIREARMS OVER RANGE

Whilst firearms generally have far greater ranges than missile weapons, they are still subject to the same accuracy issues when shooting at a distance. Due to their short barrel length, less stable firing position, and lack of rifling, handgonnes are typically inaccurate over

Firearms Table

Ranged Weapon	Damage	Range	Firing rate	Ammo	Load	Enc	AP/HP	Cost
Handgonne, small	1d8	10/20/50	1	single	5 rounds	2	4/8	100 SP
Handgonne, large	1d10	10/30/75	1	single	5 rounds	3	4/10	175 SP
Hook gun	2d6	15/50/100	1	single	4 rounds	3	4/8	300 SP

distance. In general, use the following modifiers when using the 'Size and Distance Difficulty Adjustment' table:

- Handgonnes – Increase penalty by 1 step
- Hook guns operated with one hand – Increase penalty by 1 step
- Hook guns with matchlock – no modifier

Remember that as an exception to the normal rule, distance penalties stack on top of other ranged combat situational modifiers.

Reloading Firearms

After spending the time reloading a firearm indicated on the Firearms Table, the player should roll Lore (Firearms and Artillery):

- Critical Success: The weapon may be fired immediately as a Free Action. Alternatively, a fumbled Attack roll can be converted into a fail if a Critical reloading roll was made.
- Success: The weapon can be fired as normal on the character's next Action.
- Failure: The character has not yet completed reloading, reroll Lore (Firearms and Artillery) next Action
- Fumble: roll on the Firearms Mishaps table.

Discharging Firearms

Once the weapon is loaded, the character can make an attack using his Combat Style. This is like any other Attack roll with a missile weapon, except that if a Fumble is rolled, consult the Firearms Mishaps Table, opposite.

A firearm which is continually reloaded and discharged without allowing several minutes for the metal to cool down in between suffers 1d2 damage every time it is fired after the first time. This damage can be repaired by a gunsmith by reannealing the metal in a forge.

If a firearm has zero or fewer Hit Points when it is fired, then the barrel explodes; this also occurs on certain results on the Firearms Mishaps Table. An exploding barrel destroys the weapon. Further, anyone within 1 metre of the firearm takes half of the weapon's damage to each of 1d3 Hit Locations.

Firearms Ammunition

- Gunpowder: usually sold by weight. 100 grams of gunpowder, enough for 10 shots from a firearm, costs 5 SP
- Grapeshot: multiple lead pellets packed with sand. In an emergency, pebbles or nails can be used. Like normal ammunition but with the scatter weapon trait (see below). A bag with sufficient for 10 shots costs 1 SP
- Spear: metal spear with a short wide haft that fits into the barrel of a handgonne. Inflicts normal damage but with the Puncturing weapon trait (see page 70). Each spear costs 5 CP
- Bullet: a sphere of lead or carved stone of the same diameter as the barrel. Each bullet weights about 15 grams. A bag of 10 bullets costs 1 SP

Firearms Mishap Table

1d10	Reloading roll	Attack roll
1–2	Barrel explodes	Barrel explodes
3–4	Premature firing as it is being aimed – targets anyone directly in front of weapon	Misfire – barrel takes 2d6 damage; if this reduces the Hit Points to zero then barrel explodes
5–6	Premature firing as it is being wadded – loader and adjacent units are targets	Misfire – barrel takes 1d6 damage; if this reduces the Hit Points to zero then barrel explodes
7–8	Incorrect loading – must be fully unloaded and reloaded before it will fire again	Weapon damaged – weapon jammed (as below) and requires minor repair before it can be used again
9–10	Incorrect loading – must be fully unloaded and reloaded before it will fire again	Weapon jammed – must be fully unloaded and reloaded before it will fire again

Weapon Traits

Scatter – The weapon or round is made of pellets which spread before they strike, reducing any range penalties by one step and inflicting damage to 1d3 adjacent Hit Locations. This comes at a cost however. Firstly the weapon damage roll for each location is halved; secondly any armour, natural or worn, doubles its Armour Point value against the damage.

Explosives

The art of bombs and explosives is still in its infancy. However, there are numerous technical manuals from the fourteenth and fifteenth centuries that deal with such things. One source suggests filling hollow bones with gunpowder and fitted with fuses, to be strewn behind a retreating force. Primitive grenades (*grenados*, taking their name from their similarity to pomegranates) are employed, typically metal shells filled with gunpowder and nails and fitted with a match fuse. Some inventors have experimented with rockets; using gunpowder to fuel the missile rather than propelling it explosively.

RULES FOR EXPLOSIVES

Most explosive weapons are experimental at best. When dealing with bombs of any variety fumbles occur whenever a double is rolled on the d100 (i.e. 11, 22, 33, etc.), not just on 99 and 00. Bombs can be placed or thrown into melee, but use the same basic rules. Bombs take an action to ready (set the bomb, trim the fuse, etc.) and an action to light the fuse, assuming there is a source of flame available. A bomb has its own initiative and two Action Points. The Strike Rank of a bomb depends on the length of the fuse-match. Use 1d10+10 for a short fuse, or 1d10+5 for a long fuse. On its turn, a bomb has just one Combat Action available, which is to explode. Roll the Lore (Firearms and Artillery) Skill of the person who set the bomb. If it is successful, the bomb explodes. Otherwise, the fuse is still burning, and it has another attempt to explode on its second turn. If it still hasn't exploded, then the bomb is a dud. If either roll is a fumble, the bomb appears to be a dud but is actually still smouldering and could still explode if disturbed. A Fumbled grenado might spew shrapnel in a single direction or even launch themselves from the ground before exploding, allowing the Select Target or Accidental Injury Special Effects. Bombs cannot be parried or evaded when they explode – the trick is to not be near them when they go off.

A bomb that explodes right next to a person inflicts 1d8+1 damage to 1d3 adjacent locations (roll one location and choose the appropriate number of adjacent locations). Any person within 1 metre of the bomb takes 1d6+1 damage to 1d2 adjacent locations.

SPOT RULES

- A *grenado* is a bomb which is thrown into melee. A grenado can be thrown in the same Action as it is lit. This requires an Athletics or Combat Style roll and is not opposed. A grenado is SIZ 0 for the purpose of range (Mythras page 39). Success means that the grenado lands next to the intended target. If the roll fails it is too far away to damage anyone, if it fumbles then the grenado explodes in the thrower's hand. The grenado's initiative is rolled at the beginning of the round following the round in which it is lit. If it has not exploded by the time its target's turn comes round then he may attempt to get away from the bomb with an unopposed Evade roll. Grenados cause Knockback (Mythras page 104): total all the damage rolled and double it before calculating the distance the victim is thrown away from the blast.
- A *petard* is a bomb affixed to a wall or door, and is designed to direct the blast. They normally have a double charge (inflicting 2d8+2 damage) with the Puncturing Weapon Trait (see page 70). If it explodes, the petard gets a free Sunder Special Effect against whatever to which it is fixed.
- Bombs have a psychological effect on men and animals in combat. Use of explosives in melee can warrant Willpower rolls to prevent opponents fleeing the field; for horses the rider must make a Ride Skill check, or the animal automatically fails its Willpower roll. Even with a successful Ride roll, the horse's Willpower still suffers a Formidable penalty.
- A bomb typically uses 50 grams of gunpowder, which costs 2½ SP. Bombs and grenados are not generally available commercially and must be made by the user or commissioned specially.

ARTILLERY WEAPONS

Cannons are muzzle-loaded artillery weapons used principally in sieges to hurl stone or metal balls at the opponent's wall using the explosive power of gunpowder. In Greek they are known as *teleboloi*, or "far-throwers", although the largest are known as *helepoloi*, or "city destroyers", a term also used for the larger non-ballistic siege weapons. Artillery weapons were first used in the region in 1396, when culverins were employed against the Ottomans besieging Constantinople. A culverin weighs about 40kg with a metre-long barrel with a 25-centimetre calibre. When the Turks returned in 1422 they had acquired their own cannons, the larger falconets. A falconet weighs 80 kilograms, has a 1.25 metre long barrel, but the calibre is half that of a culverin and the range is doubled at approximately 1,500 metres. The largest weapons in use are referred to as bombards. The bombard comes in a variety of sizes, with the largest weighing 15 tonnes with a 5 metre barrel and a 50-centimetre calibre barrel. It is rumoured that the Ottoman Empire is interested in acquiring even larger weapons.

One of the few artillery weapons used against field armies is the ribauldi or ribauldequin. This is a volley gun comprised of many small-calibre barrels set up in parallel or in a fan shape on a wooden frame usually attached to a trolley. When the weapon is fired it creates a shower of iron shot. This can be a devastating weapon against soldiers but can usually only be employed once in any given battle due to the short range and high reloading time.

RULES FOR ARTILLERY WEAPONS

Notes about Siege weapons can be found in Mythras page 62. Apart from the ribauldis, artillery weapons cannot be employed in standard melee combat except against colossal creatures. Instead, use the rules for Battles (see page 213). A culverin uses 150 grams of gunpowder per shot; a falconet takes 200 grams; a medium bombard 500 grams, and a large bombard 1 kilograms or more.

An artillery weapon which is reloaded and discharged at its maximum rate, without allowing time for the metal to cool down in between, suffers 1d6 damage every time it is fired after the first time. This damage can be repaired by a gunsmith by reannealing the metal in a forge.

RIBAULDIS

A ribauldi, if fully loaded and range-checked can be a deadly weapon in melee. Versions with nine or 12 barrels are the most common, which defines the frontage (in number of men) who can be affected at the effective range of the weapon. If opponents are closer than the effective range when the weapon fires, then fewer opponents may be targeted. Make Loading and Attack rolls according to the firearms rules given above. A separate attack roll is made for each opponent; these rolls are always at least at the Hard skill grade due to the recoil of the weapon. Note that if there are fewer opponents than barrels, each opponent still only gets one attack against him since the weapon is stationary.

Ribauldis can be loaded with bullets or grapeshot. If loaded with bullets, then bullets that miss their target have the potential for hitting any opponents behind the first line of battle, but at a Formidable skill grade. If loaded with grapeshot use the rules for the Scatter Weapon Trait (see above). There is no significant chance that grapeshot will penetrate more than one rank of an army.

CANNON TABLE

Ranged Weapon	Damage	Range Effective	Firing rate	Ammo	Load	Enc	AP/HP	Cost
Effective	Range	10/30/75	1	single	5 rounds	3	4/10	175 SP
Long	Load	Crew	Size	AP/HP	Cost	3	4/8	300 SP
Culverin	5d6	350 m	750 m	10	2/4	E	8/20	1500 SP
Falconet	7d6	500 m	1500 m	10	2/4	BE	8/25	2500 SP
Medium Bombard	9d6	500 m	1000 m	15	4/8	BE	10/40	5000 SP
Large Bombard	12d6	400 m	800 m	20	6/10	BE	10/60	7500 SP
Ribauldi	3d6	75 m	150 m	20	2/12	E	8/20	3000 SP

MAGIC

The streets of Mythic Constantinople teem with purveyors of miracles, petty charms, and penny wonders. Many of these magicians are charlatans but a few are not, and those in the know are aware who has real power behind their promises and who is a fraud. Those who can actually create magical effects are known collectively as *thaumatourgoi*, literally "wonder workers".

CHARISMATA

A *charism* is a gift from God, and a Charismatic is one who receives one. Charismata are rare, but anyone can receive one; often manifesting before puberty. Most Christian characters will recognise a charism for what it is; they were given to Christ's apostles to help them spread the Word of God, and are mentioned in the Bible (1 Corinthians 12:8-10); but they can manifest in anyone who has a devout belief in God regardless of his or her faith.

Once the gift manifests, a charismatic will usually enter into the care of the Church, typically at a monastery or convent, and be encouraged to use the Gift for good: either to root out evil, spread the Good Word, or administer to the sick. Such characters usually take the Christian Priest or Miracle Worker Career, although it is rare for a charismatic to learn Folk Magic, since there are precious few within the Church who can teach them this Skill.

Using a charism costs the character 1 Magic Point. New Folk Magic spells are indicated in the below table with *, and are described on page 78.

CHARISMATA

Gift	*Effect*
Gift of the Word of Wisdom	When faced with a choice the character can ask God for guidance in making the right decision. The character makes a Love God Passion roll and if it is successful, the Games Master tells the character which option feels right. Note that God's intent for the character does not always match her own desires, but He never recklessly endangers a character or leads them to sin.
Gift of the Word of Knowledge	The character can perceive whether a statement made in her presence is a lie. She cannot sense what the truth is, only that a falsehood has been uttered.
Gift of Discernment	The character can see demons and infernal spirits. He can see through the illusions of a demon without need of a roll and can detect a possessed person with a successful Insight roll. If the possession is covert, then the spirit can oppose this roll with a Stealth roll to remain hidden.
Gift of Polyglossia	The character's speech can be understood by any sentient being; each person hears their native language. The character has no greater understanding of languages spoken in reply, and cannot write in any language foreign to him.
Gift of Panglossia	The character can understand any language spoken to him, although can still only be understood when he speaks in languages he knows. He cannot read an unknown language.
Gift of Speech	When the character speaks, she can compel everyone within earshot to listen. If she pauses for more than a few seconds then her audience is released from the effect. Her voice can be heard over the loudest background noise up to a range of 10x the character's CHA in metres.
Gift of Faith	The character's touch causes agony to a spirit in the material world; including demons, spirits bound in fetishes, and spirits possessing a person. The character should make a Love God Passion roll opposed against the spirit's Willpower: if successful the spirit must flee, which for earth-bound spirits means unbinding them from their fetish or undoes the possession.
Gift of Healing	The character can touch a wounded person and heal him, simultaneously transferring a less serious version of the same wound to themselves. The character immediately suffers half the Hit Point damage of the healed wound to the same location. This Gift does not work once a recipient has died from his wounds and cannot restore missing limbs or maimed hit locations.
Gift of Wonders	The character can reproduce the effects of one Folk Magic spell. The spell is automatically successful. The spell must be chosen from the following list when the Gift is acquired, and once made cannot be changed: Cleanse, Extinguish, Light, Perfume, Phantasm, Repair, Sound*, Tidy, Warmth
Gift of Miracles	The character may learn the Exhort Magical Skill. It does not cost a Magic Point to use this charism.

WHO GETS CHARISMATA?

How a character receives a charism has been left deliberately vague. Possessing such a gift is a defining feature of a character; it should not be taken lightly. A charism is a blessing from God, and comes with responsibilities and duties which; if shirked, may lead to Divine censure or even removal of the gift.

Some Games Masters might demand a price for a charism, to ensure it does not become trivialised. A suitable price is to reduce the character's usual allotment of Experience Points by one.

ALCHEMISTS

Alchemists pursue the "Great Work", their name for the perfection of the union between the physical and spiritual worlds. It is a goal which is believed to lead to immortality through the transfiguration of the soul, and more prosaically to the dissolution of impurities from matter. Alchemists learn many secrets about the nature of the world and the working of magic on this quest for purification. There are two paths to the Great Work. The physical alchemist is seeking mastery over the physical world, one part of which is the transmutation of base metals into gold. Such alchemists might find themselves gravitating towards Sorcery as a means to achieve this goal. The other sort of alchemist is the spiritual alchemist, who instead seeks an inner transformation and a perfection of the soul. These may encounter the Unconcealed Word (see page 84) while on their quest and embark on the mystical path of self-improvement and meditation.

At the option of the Games Master, a character taking the Alchemist Career may learn Folk Magic as a Professional skill; otherwise it must be acquired as a hobby Skill. An alchemist can learn the following spells: *Amalgamate*, Avert, Balm*, Chill, Extinguish, Glue, Grease*, Heal, Heat, Ignite, Light, Perfume, Potion*, Preserve, Rot*, Separate*, Tire, Vigour.*

EXORCISTS

Exorcists specialise in combatting malicious spirits. All are trained by the Order of Kappa-Pi-Alpha (see page 108). The charismata of Discernment and Faith are very useful.

SEERS

A seer is born with the Gift of Oracle. Seers are often rejected at a young age for their uncanny knowledge and the lucky ones end up in monasteries or convents where they can use their Gift to further God's plan. Others become hermits, sick of accidentally seeing someone's tragic fate. A few end up as fortune-tellers, selling secrets to those who would dare know what fate has in store for them.

A seer who learns the Folk Magic Skill (either from the Miracle Worker Career or as a hobby skill) can learn the following spells: *Avert, Calm, Find, Mindspeech, Omen*, Translate, Ventriloquism, Voice, Witchsight.*

PHARMAKOPEIAI

Followers of pagan deities like Hecate or Artemis, *pharmakopeiai* often learn their craft at their mother's knee, continuing an ancient tradition that leads back to ancient times, when pharmakopeiai would conduct mighty rituals to draw down the moon and bewitch the minds of men. Upon initiation into the cult, pharmakopeiai receive the Animal Familiar Gift.

As their name suggests, much of a pharmakopeia's work revolves around the creation of magical drugs and potions (which is achieved through the Potion spell). They are often skilled healers, apothecaries, and/or poisoners through their non-magical skills.

A pharmakopeia who learns the Folk Magic Skill (either from the Miracle Worker Career or as a hobby skill) can learn the following spells: *Avert, Beastcall, Curse, Demoralise, Dishevel, Fanaticism, Glamour, Potion*, Repugnance, Rot*, Spiritshield, Witchsight.*

NEW FOLK MAGIC SPELLS

AMALGAMATE

Touch

Amalgamate causes two different substances to meld together. Their combined weight can be no more than SIZ 1 (less than 10 kilograms, or 3 ENC). The resulting mixture has properties of both the original substances. If both substances are solid then the mixture takes a shape that is intermediate between the two. If both are liquid then the result is a liquid. If one is liquid and the other solid, then the spell creates an amorphous sludge whose consistency is proportional to the relative amounts of the two original substances. The two substances separate at the end of the spell if they cannot naturally exist as a solution or mixture. Therefore, oil and water will separate again when the duration expires, but gold and silver will remain in alloy.

BALM

Touch

Balm provides relief from pain. If a character has failed an Endurance roll to ignore the detrimental effects of pain, this spell allows the character to make another attempt. Used in this manner the spell can restore functionality to a hit location left incapacitated by a Serious or Major Wound, although it does not restore any hit points or stabilise a dying character.

GREASE

Instant, Ranged, Resist (Evade)

Grease coats an object or a surface with a slippery oil or grease. The area covered is quite small (the caster's POW in square metres), enough to lubricate a stuck wagon axle or a millstone's gears. It can also target an object held by another character or else any smooth surface being stood upon or climbed, in which case the character gets a Resistance roll. Walking on a level surface affected by this spell requires an Easy Athletics roll to remain standing, inclined or smooth surfaces make this task at least one difficulty grade harder. Holding a greased object requires a (DEX×5)% roll to avoid dropping. Rolls requiring physical coordination suffer from a Hard difficulty grade due to the grease, such as avoiding the Trip (if spread on the ground) or Disarm (if on a weapon haft) special effects. The grease can be stepped away from or wiped off an object in one Combat Action.

OMEN

Instant, Touch

Omen provides the caster with an inkling of the future. As the spell is cast, the caster must touch the target of the omen and specify a future event about which the target wants knowledge. The event must be specific enough that it includes at least two of the following elements:

- an event (fight, debate, audience);
- a character (Turks, king, judge);
- an item (a knife, an apple, a magical amulet);
- a place (a forest, on a ship, a town);
- an aspect or quality (small, drunk, red);
- a universal (love, death, triumph).

Examples: a merchant on the road, a soldier with a sword, a fight against Turks, if the judge is clearly biased.

The spell reveals a glimpse of the future, which probably means nothing to the target right now, but when the conditions of the event are met they are sufficient to grant the target one Luck Point to be used in the resolution of the event. This event cannot occur sooner than one day after the Omen has been cast, and must occur within POW days of casting else the Luck Point is lost. It is also lost if the event does occur and the Luck Point is not spent. The caster cannot regain the Magic Point spent casting this spell until the Luck Point is spent or lost. An Omen cannot be recast for the same target until POW days have passed since the last casting.

POTION

Special Duration

Potion must be cast in conjunction with a second spell. It delays the casting of the spell, instead imbuing its effects into a solid or liquid form. The effect is triggered by eating, drinking, or applying the potion (as decided when casting Potion). If the imbued spell has the Ranged Trait, then it is treated as Touch instead, affecting the user. The Magic Point used to cast Potion does not return to the caster until the imbued spell is used or until the Potion expires, which occurs after 1 day per 10% (rounded up) of the caster's Folk Magic Skill. Potion is commonly combined with spells such as Balm, Heal, or Vigour to create medicinal potions, with Fanaticism to create love potions, or with Glue, Grease, or Perfume to create alchemical reagents.

ROT

Instant, Touch

Rot causes a perishable object to immediately spoil: milk goes sour, fruit and vegetables become mouldy, and meat generates maggots. Rot cannot affect more durable materials such as wood or cloth. This spell can kill persistent weeds or hasten compost. The caster can affect an amount of organic matter with SIZ equal to his POW divided by 3. The spell cannot be used on living creatures, but against plants it inflicts 2D3 damage to a random location or overall Hit Points. Rot can cancel the Preserve spell, but if used in this way has no further effects.

SEPARATE

Touch

Separate splits a mixture into its component parts and keeps them from mixing until the spell's duration expires, at which point they recombine if still in contact. The targeted substance can be SIZ 1 or smaller (less than 10 kilograms or 3 ENC). This spell can be used to make seawater safe to drink by removing the salt, or to separate an alloy into its component metals. The spell is ineffective if the targeted substance is not a mixture: for example, it cannot divide a brick into mud and ash since the firing process has made these ingredients into a new substance.

SOUND

Instant, Ranged

Sound allows the caster to manifest a single brief noise, as quiet as a whisper or as loud as a shout, originating from anywhere in range. The noise cannot consist of intelligible words, but otherwise appears realistic. Typical sounds created with this affect include a rumble of thunder, a dog's bark, a knock at the door, the snapping of a twig, or a barely audible moan. The sound can last a few seconds at most.

CHRISTIAN MAGIC

Theism stems solely from God. It can only be employed by those with a deep and abiding connection to God, represented in game terms by the Love God Passion. This Passion represents a personal devotion to the Divine which is separate from service due to a sense of duty. It is an unfortunate indictment on the state of the Church to say that few churchmen in Mythic Constantinople have the love for God that is necessary to create miracles.

Not everyone with the Love God Passion is a theist. The vast majority of those with the Love God Passion never develop the Exhort Skill and so remain incapable of producing miracles – even those who enter the priesthood. The Church would love to be able to train cadres of miracle-granting priests, but the ability to develop the Exhort Skill is a charism granted by God and it is impossible to predict who will possess the capacity. Those who demonstrate the skill at an early age are often encouraged to take Holy Orders by their parish priest, and thereby put into touch with another theist who provides the necessary training. The Exhort Skill is therefore part of the Christian Priest Career, even though it cannot be learned by most priests. There are some who possess the natural aptitude for theism who do not take Holy Orders for a variety of reasons that are doubtless part of God's plan. These characters must develop the Exhort Skill as a hobby skill.

DEVOTION

For where two or three are gathered together in my name, there am I in the midst of them. Matt.18:20

It is not enough to possess the Exhort Skill to create miracles. Devotion is also needed, but in Mythic Constantinople this is not a Skill possessed by the theist. Every theist is a member of a congregation of fellow worshippers and it is through the community of devout believers that miracles are worked. If the theist is a monk then the other monks of his foundation provide the devotional backing for his miracles. If he is a secular priest then the congregation who attend his parish church provide the necessary Devotion. A theist who is neither a monk or a priest, or else is a priest subordinate to the celebrant, can draw Devotion merely by being a member of a community worshipping God.

To be a member of a congregation a theist must be a member of the appropriate religious sect (see page 87) in good standing, and must participate in an act of communal worship with that congregation at least once a week. Alternatively, the theist must be specifically mentioned in the intercession prayers of the faithful. These actions provide a Devotion Score of 25%. This score is increased by two factors. Firstly, the more devout congregation is, the more powerful its miracles are. The majority of parishioners will not have the Love God Passion, but in most communities, there will be some truly devout members. The Passion is more likely to be present in monastic communities, which are comprised of people who have heard the call to devote their lives to the service of God; however, monastic congregations are seldom large enough for the base Devotion score to be higher than 25%.

Secondly, if the theist leads the congregation in the worship of God then he gets a bonus according to the size of the congregation. To lead a congregation, the theist must perform the sacrament of the Eucharist on its behalf (which requires the theist to be an ordained priest) or lead them in prayer on a daily basis.

However large and/or devout the congregation is, the Devotion score used by a theist can never exceed the character's Love God Passion.

DEVOTION TABLE

Factor	Devotion
Base Score	25%
Piety: Average Love God Passion of congregation	+1% per 1% of the Passion
Congregation Size (if a priest)	+1% per 50 members, rounded up

Example one: Father Paulos leads a congregation of 115 worshippers (Devotion 25% + 3% for congregation size). Most do not have the Love God Passion, but 10 possess the Passion with an average score of 50% between them. The average Passion score of the congregation is therefore 5%, so Father Paulos can rely on a Devotion of 33%. His own Love God Passion is 58%, so he can use all of the Devotion he is offered.

Example two: Sister Stammata is a member of a small monastic order of 25 nuns (Devotion 25%). All but 5 of the nuns have a Love God Passion with an average score of 60%. The average Love God Passion is therefore 48% for a total Devotion of 73%, but this is capped by her own Love God of 70%.

The Devotion supplied by a congregation does not reflect the standing of the theist or his sacerdotal rank. This is instead determined by his progression in his religious sect (see page 87).

MIRACLES

Devotion also governs the rank of miracles that a theist can derive from the supporting congregation. The miracles which the Christian Faith can offer are as follows:

INITIATE MIRACLES

Aegis, Cure Malady, Dismiss Magic, Fortify, Heal Wound, Lay to Rest, Perseverance, Sacred Band, Shield, Spirit Block, Steadfast

ACOLYTE MIRACLES

Bless Crops, Consecrate, Cure Sense, Exorcism, Fecundity, Heal Body, Heal Mind, Pacify

PRIEST MIRACLES

Excommunicate, Extension, Rejuvenate

MIRACLES TABLE

Devotion	Initiate Miracles	Acolyte Miracles	Priest Miracles
0–24%	No	No	No
25–69%	Yes	No	No
70–109%	Yes	Yes	No
110%+	Yes	Yes	Yes

DEVOTIONAL POOLS

A theist's Devotional Pool has a maximum size equal to one's POW. However, the theist is restricted as to the practical size of the Devotional Pool based on the church where worship takes place (see below).

SACROSANCT LOCATIONS

Shrines, churches, and cathedrals are naturally the sacrosanct locations for Christian theists to recover their Magic Points and refresh their Devotional Pool. Only theists can recover Magic Points on consecrated ground. Any place where Christians gather is suitable for worship, but it must have a consecrated altar to also count as a sacrosanct location. Consecrating an altar requires a ceremony during the foundation of the church, and a relic of the saint who will become its patron. The size of the church determines the Magical Strength it offers.

To recover Magic Points, a theist must worship God at the church for at least an hour. This requires partaking in a service with other worshippers or else (if alone) adopting a prostrate posture on the chancery steps, arms outstretched, for the duration. The magical strength available after an hour of worship is 25%, and this increases by 25% for every additional hour up to the maximum available at that location. Thus after three hours of worship at the Hagia Sophia, a character's Magic Points are raised to 75% of his POW and he can pray for another hour to get the remainder from

SACROSANCT LOCATIONS

Magical Strength	Size of Devotional Pool	Example
25%	¼ of the theist's POW	A small neighbourhood chapel or shrine
50%	½ of the theist's POW	A parish church lead by a priest
75%	¾ of the theist's POW	A monastic church lead by a hieromonk, or district church lead by an archpriest
100%	all of the theist's POW	A metropolitan or patriarchal church lead by a bishop

this 100% source. A character can only recharge his Magic Points in this manner once a day, regardless of how many churches he visits.

Taking communion at a sacrosanct location allows a theist to devote Magic Points to his Devotional Pool. This can take place before or after recovering Magic Points via prayer. For the laity communion is taken once per week on Sunday. Monks and ordained priests receive communion every day. A character may move as many Magic Points as he wishes from his personal store to his Devotional Pool, up to the limit detailed in the Sacrosanct Locations table. Donated points replace the current Devotional Pool rather than add to them.

A lay member of a congregation is expected to attend his own church for communion, and a priest certainly cannot choose to lead communion at a church other than his own. Theists are therefore normally restricted in the practical size of their Devotional Pool by the size of their own parishes. As a special favour, a higher-ranked clergyman might offer the opportunity to attend or lead worship at his own church. Otherwise, a character wanting access to a larger congregation must increase his rank in the Christian Faith and be granted a larger benefice.

Note that the Orthodox Church is not currently in communion with the Catholic Church. This means that an Orthodox character cannot refresh their Devotional Pool at a Catholic church and vice versa because they are forbidden from receiving the Eucharist. If the celebrant at the church is a Pro-Unionist, he will accept Catholic as well as Orthodox Christians, and both denominations may refresh their Devotional Pool. Regardless of doctrine, any Christian may still regenerate Magic Points at an accelerated rate at any church.

NON-CHRISTIAN THEISTS

Theism is exclusively the province of God but not specific to his Christian worshippers. Holy men of Islam and Judaism are also capable of becoming theists, although they are rarer amongst these religions than they are amongst Christians. The main reason for this is the structure of both of those faiths: neither have a formal priesthood that facilitates identification and training of emerging theists. The few Muslim and Jewish theists that exist are mostly self-taught and few are leaders of their religious communities, restricting the Devotion available to them. Another reason for the scarcity of theism in these religions is the prevalence of other magical traditions within both faiths (see later), which tend to attract those with an interest and aptitude in sacred magic. For those non-Christian theists who do exist, use the same rules as for Christian theists.

SORCERY

Sorcery in the Mythic Constantinople setting is a magical tradition driven by dark passions and evil thoughts. Some consider this evidence that sorcery comes from the Devil, although there is nothing to corroborate this hypothesis. Certainly, sorcery predates the Bible, with the earliest records of its practice being found in Egyptian tombs and in Sumerian legends. Some have theorised that this leads to a much older source of sorcery than the Abrahamic concept of mankind's adversary. Perhaps the demons of an older mythology, such as the Children of Tiamat – seven of whom survived the war with the Babylonian gods – might be to blame. The roots of Renaissance demonology can be found in these ancient myths, so why not the practice of sorcery?

Whatever the origins of sorcery, its nature is corruptive. By the time sorcerers master their craft they have embraced their personal demons and are usually willing to serve external ones in exchange for more power. There are no organised colleges of sorcery; these occasionally spring up spontaneously but rarely persist very long – most sorcerers have vile temperaments so sorcerous cults usually implode (and more rarely explode) through bitter rivalries, intense jealousy, and compulsive secrecy.

Sorcery is instead mostly transmitted through spell codices: books encoding a handful of minor spells. The lucky few receive formal training from a master sorcerer and a grimoire of powerful spells to learn. Some may even be taught by summoned entities, although what manner of creature they are – demon, spirit, or something else – is not always clear.

SORCEROUS CORRUPTION

To acquire the Sorcery Skill, a character must have a dark place in their soul. They are consumed by unnatural lusts, strong hatreds, or perverse obsessions. This is not to say that all sorcerers are evil, since they are not compelled to act upon these dark emotions. However, sorcery itself is corruptive and its users are tempted towards a foul disposition. A sorcerer is required to have at least one negative Passion such as Hate, Despise, Destroy, or Torment to represent this dark taint. Furthermore, as sorcery is studied it eats away at the soul: sorcerers either become dispassionate and emotionless or else submit to the dark thoughts that assail their minds. Every time an experience roll is applied to Sorcery Skill, increase a negative Passion or decrease a positive Passion by the same number of percentage points as the Sorcery Skill gains. When a new Sorcery spell is learned, choose an appropriate Passion and adjust it by 1d10%. This applies during character creation as well, so if a character takes +25% to his Sorcery Skill and learns 3 spells, then he must adjust his Passions by a total of 3d10+25%. It is recommended that these adjustments during Character Creation are made to no more than three Passions. The Games Master is final arbiter of what is a negative and what is a positive Passion.

SPELL CODICES

The aspiring sorcerer can find repositories of magic lore relatively easily in Constantinople. Tomes of magical remedies and amulets to manipulate spirits can be found on the shelves of booksellers alongside other volumes of esoteric and obscure lore. Peddlers offer spell codices for sale, guaranteed to attract one's lady love or grant luck in gambling. Mysterious strangers on street corner booths promise to sell the secrets of the universe. Many of these sources are fraudulent or at best teach Folk Magic, but some are genuine sources of Sorcery, called spell codices. Most sorcerers begin their career in a somewhat haphazard manner, picking up a spell codex and learning a handful of spells. Not everyone can learn Sorcery; in addition to the requisite dark passion it requires a great deal of will, effort, and time. First the sorcerer must learn the Invocation Skill unique to the spell codex (which takes 3 Experience Rolls), and then learn at least one spell (another 5 Experience Rolls) before any benefit of all that effort is realised. Those that start on this path often become

RANDOM SPELL CODEX TABLE

1d100	Spell
01–02	Animate Cloth
03–04	Animate Metal
05–06	Animate Wood
07–08	Attract Missiles
09–10	Banish
11–12	Bedevil Humility
13–14	Bedevil Infatuation
15–16	Break Ceramics
17–18	Break Poison
19–20	Castback
21–22	Diminish DEX
23–24	Diminish CHA
25–26	Dominate Horse
27–28	Draw Birds
29–30	Draw Sheep
31–33	Enchant Amulet
34–35	Enhance INT
36–37	Enhance CHA
38–39	Enhance STR
40–42	Enlarge
43–45	Haste
46–47	Hinder
48–50	Holdfast
51–52	Intuition

RANDOM SPELL CODEX TABLE

1d100	Spell
53–54	Mark
55–57	Mystic Hearing
58–59	Palsy
60–62	Perceive Nightsight
62–63	Perceive Earthsense
64–65	Phantom Taste
66–67	Phantom Smell
68–69	Protective Ward
70–72	Project Sight
73–74	Project Hearing
75–76	Repulse Vermin
77	Repulse Dogs
78–79	Sculpt Wood
80–81	Sense Contamination
82–83	Sense Life
84–86	Sense Poison
87–89	Shrink
90–91	Smother
92–93	Spirit Resistance
94–96	Store Manna
97	Summon
98–99	Telepathy
100	Transfer Wound

disillusioned: the easily available sources of magical knowledge hint at great power but offer a random selection of occult knowledge.

Spell codices are relatively common throughout Europe and the Middle East in the fifteenth century. Some are written in foreign languages such as Arabic, Parsi, or Hebrew, but there are many in Greek and Latin. Many of these books claim to contain the knowledge of King Solomon or claim other famous authors such as Nectanabus or even Merlin, although their contents generally have little to do with their title or their authors. A common theme is for the author to claim that this book is distilled from a greater source, and might name-drop one of the Grand Seals (see below).

Each of these spell codices requires the sorcerer to develop a unique Invocation Skill to use the spells within. A month with the book and the requisite Experience Rolls grants the Skill at the base level. The codex may also be used to train the Invocation Skill (Mythras rulebook page 111), with an equivalent Skill level of 50+3d10%. The character may learn also Sorcery spells from the book. Each spell codex contains 1d3+1 spells; these may be determined randomly or chosen from the Random Spell Codex Table. A kind Games Master would allow a sorcerer character, for his first codex, to choose one or more spells from the table and then randomly determine the rest.

Some spell codices contain other lore than just sorcery. Most commonly they contain medicinal information which can be used for training Healing or Lore (Plants). Others are astrological tomes (offering Lore (Astrology) or Navigation) or else alchemical texts (offering Lore (Alchemy)). A rare few also contain Folk Magic.

GRIMOIRES

Grimoires are like spell codices in that they are books of sorcerous knowledge. Each grimoire requires its own Invocation Skill and may be used to Train that Skill (usually with a Skill level of 60+3d10%). The difference is that a grimoire is written with a specific purpose: there are no fake spells or spurious knowledge, and the spells are often designed along a common theme. A grimoire might also contain other knowledge, allowing the sorcerer to Train other Skills (often Lores) or learn Folk Magic spells.

THE KYRANIDES

Textbook of magical medicine. Damage Resistance, Enhance CON, Hide Life, Regenerate, Spirit Resistance plus a tract on the Healing Skill and the Folk Magic spells of *Balm, Cleanse, Find Sickness, and Heal.*

HYGROMANTEIA

A book on water magic. *Abjure Asphyxiation, Animate Water, Evoke Undine, Perceive Echolocation, Sculpt Water, Smother, Transmogrify to Water.*

HAPOTELESMATIKE PRAGMATEIA

A book of practical magic and wonders, allegedly penned by Solomon. *Break Wood, Enslave Horses, Enlarge, Fly, Holdfast, Phantom Sight, Shapechange to Lion, Shrink, Telepathy.*

FOUL BOOKS OF PHOUDOULIS

Evil curses abound in this unpleasant tome. *Abjure Appetite, Attract Magic, Attract Missiles, Bedevil Gluttony, Bedevil Timidity, Draw Vermin, Palsy, Wrack (Pain).*

JOURNALS OF SYROPOULOS & GABRIELOPOULOS

These twin sorcerers were obsessed with instant transportation and transference. Along with records of their travels (which can Train several Culture and Lore (foreign land) Skills), the book contains the spells *Mark, Portal, Project Sight, Project Hearing, Summon, Switch Body, Teleport, Transfer Wound.*

BIBLION SALOMONTEION

A book on summoning the Intelligences, otherworldly creatures that may be demonic. They have names such as Agares, Dantalion, Orobas, and Vapula, and can each Train various Skills or perform certain tasks for the sorcerer. Spells include Dominate Summoned Creature, several copies of Evoke for each specific Intelligence, Imprison, Protective Ward. At least half of the copies of this book have faulty versions of *Dominate Summoned Creature* and/or *Imprison* that are ineffective.

NEW SORCERY SPELLS

The following spells may be learned by any sorcerer with an appropriate source.

BEDEVIL (EMOTION)

Resist (Willpower)

Bedevil inflicts the target with an all-consuming emotion. Should they fail to resist, the emotion overwhelms all their thoughts and they will do their utmost to fulfil its impulses. Rather than directly controlling a target, this spell causes a form of monomaniacal madness that expresses itself slightly differently in each person it infects. Although driven to reckless acts by the spell, the target will do nothing life-threatening, and if in the throes of the spell he has the potential to harm an object of a Passion, he gets another attempt to resist the spell with a Willpower roll augmented by the Passion. Each version of this spell affects a different emotion, and when the spell is cast the sorcerer can qualify the emotion caused. Thus when casting Bedevil (Lust), the sorcerer can specify that the lust is for Eirene Laskaris, for example; or when casting Bedevil (Wrath) she can direct the anger specifically at holy ikons. If a subject of this qualification is not within sight at the time of casting, then the Willpower rolls to resist the spell are made at one difficulty grade easier.

BREAK (SUBSTANCE)

Concentration, Resist (Endurance)

Break causes a non-living substance to crumble, crack, rot, rust, or otherwise fall apart. Each variant of the spell affects a specific type of substance, which can be fairly inclusive, for instance stone, metal, wood, and so on. The affected object is destroyed by the spell, making it useless. The sorcerer can affect a single object with a total number of Hit Points equal to three times the Intensity of the spell. If the object is made up of many parts (such as a wall or suit of armour), only one part is destroyed (e.g. one brick or one piece of armour). For every Turn of Concentration, the target takes damage as indicated by the Wrack Damage Table (Mythras page 177), ignoring any Armour Points. If the targeted object is carried or worn by a living creature, then they may resist the spell with Endurance.

OTHER MAGIC

Animism and Mysticism are rarely found amongst the principal cultures of Mythic Constantinople. However, these magical systems are available to player characters who are from a specific cultural or religious background.

ANIMISM

The Mongols and the Anatolian Turks who have not yet adopted Islam believe in a world thronging with spirits that can influence every aspect of their lives. They interact daily with their ancestor spirits, who are included in all important decisions affecting the family. As the family travels they must be careful not to anger the nature spirits through whose territory they pass, and when they get sick, it is because a spirit has taken against them and possessed the unfortunate victim. Shamans called *böge* intercess between the Upper and Lower Worlds of spirits and the Middle World of mankind. The böge divide spirits into four types: white spirits are peaceful, red spirits are healing spirits, blue spirits are battle spirits, and black spirits are malicious; but generally employ all kinds in their work rather than specialise. All animist practices are used by the böge: fetishes to house beneficial spirits and to imprison evil ones, spirit combat to battle sickness spirits and defeat curse spirits, and summoning to speak with the great spirits of the steppe.

The Arabs of Arabia and Africa also have a native animist tradition. These *sahirs* follow a pre-Islamic tradition of summoning and controlling nature spirits they call jinn. Usual practice is to rely on negotiation to achieve a 'court' of powerful spirits rather than creating fetishes with more minor ones. Occasionally, a jinni is bound into a fetish such as a ring or a lamp and will perform tasks for the possessor in return for the promise of freedom. The user of such a fetish must have the Binding skill to free the jinni temporarily, although anyone can release it permanently by breaking the fetish. The treatment that a jinni receives at the hands of its fetish-owner greatly reflects its demeanour once it gets free.

Jewish mystics who follow the occult tradition of the Kabbalah are often animists. Kabbalah is the study of the sephirot, emanations of the Divine that are the secret structure of the universe. One particular branch of this esoteric field of study is Merkavah Kabbalah, or "Chariot" Kabbalah, the intent of which is to achieve communion with angels. The Chariot Mysteries work in reverse to normal animism; rather than summoning an angel to earth, the Kabbalist enters the Spirit World and is conveyed to the edge of Heaven in order to commune with the divine spirits. Most of the time, this form of animism is used to gain advice or acquire snippets of knowledge about the structure of the universe, but occasionally angels can be persuaded to intercede on behalf of the Kabbalist, such as going into battle against demonic spirits or providing a miracle to the benefit of the Jewish community. Kabbalists never bind angelic spirits into fetishes.

As mentioned earlier (page 78), the Church has an order of Exorcist monks who practice animism. Not all of these holy animists still work within the rules of the church.

MYSTICISM

The Unconcealed Word is a secret cult of philosophers whose expressed Talents are related to their unconventional understanding of the nature of the cosmos. The cult is described on page 95.

Hesychasm is a mystical tradition of the Orthodox Church. Hesychasts retreat inwardly when they pray, shutting off the distractions of the senses in order to experience God. More details can be found on page 89.

Sufis and dervişes are Islamic mystical orders. Sufism is primarily an Arab phenomenon, the tradition beginning in the far south of the Arabian Peninsula. The Derviş orders are principally Turkic, heavily influenced by Persian mysticism. More information can be on page 88.

RELICS

A relic is typically some physical object associated with Christ, Mohammed, or an Old Testament prophet, or else a saint or holy figure. In the Orthodox Church, ikons – painted representations of Christ, the Holy Family, or popular saints – are also considered relics. All relics hold great symbolic importance to the faithful, but some are more than that. Stories abound regarding miracles enacted by relics, and a few rare relics are conduits to a divine spirit who are the source of these powers. The spirit is typically the saint to whom the bodily remains belong, or else an angel set to guard over it. Anyone holding the relic can commune with the divine spirit through its Conjugate Spirit Ability, which allows two-way mental communication. Once this link has been initiated it can be maintained over the spirit's POW in metres, and the spirit is free to use its Spirit Abilities through the character. If these Abilities have a Magic Point cost then this comes out of the owner's Magic Points, not the spirit's, but the character can always refuse to pay the cost (which prevents the Ability from working).

It is not clear whether the divine spirit is trapped within the relic or remains there of its own accord; what is certain is that this is nothing like an Animist Binding. Owning a relic does not grant control over the spirit or its powers. The character must negotiate with the spirit, explaining the purpose of the help requested and how it furthers God's plans. These negotiations take place at the speed of thought and sometimes require a Skill roll (typically Influence, but a Passion or Lore (Theology) might be appropriate). The human might promise to perform some act of charity or good deeds in return for the spirit's aid. An owner that annoys the divine spirit – by acting in a sinful manner, reneging on a promise, asking for help too frequently, or preventing the spirit from using the character as a conduit of its will – finds that these negotiations are made at a difficulty grade penalty of at least one.

The most common Spirit Ability for relic-tending spirits is Spellcasting (Theism), and they can possess any miracle in the Mythras rules, even ones usually denied to human theists.

CHRISTIAN RELICS

The most common Christian relics are body parts of saints. Orthodox belief holds that the righteous soul that inhabited the body of a saint prior to death imprints the power of the Holy Spirit upon it that remains even after the soul has departed. Ikonic representations of the saints are also important relics. The most significant relics are those associated with the life of Christ or the Passion, such as the Crown of Thorns or the True Cross that are impregnated with His blood, sweat, and tears. Even objects He touched during his life have the capacity to become relics. Of course, there are no bodily remnants of Christ Himself, since he ascended into Heaven after death. The Monastery of Saint John at Petra (PT- 7) is the greatest repository of relics in Constantinople, although some of these are claimed to reside in various Frankish cathedrals, stolen during the Sack of Constantinople. The Church of the Virgin of the Pharos (PA- 6) once held the Holy Lance and a part of the True Cross which Saint Helena (Constantine the Great's mother) found in Jerusalem. It was also home to the Holy Mandylion, the Sandals of Christ, the Holy Tile, the Letter of Christ to King Abgar of Edessa, the Crown of Thorns, the Holy Nail, Christ's Clothes, Christ's Purple Mantle, Christ's Reed Cane, and a piece from Christ's Tombstone. These have all gone now, as have the relics held at the Nea Ekklesia (PA-13), which used to house the sheepskin Cloak of Elijah, the Table of Abraham which hosted three angels, the Horn of Samuel which was used to anoint David, the Rod of Moses, and various relics of Saint Constantine the Great.

Much has been made of the multiplicity of relics: at least three heads of Saint John the Baptist are claimed by different cathedrals, and there are enough fragments of the True Cross to make up a whole forest. This does not invalidate the Christian concept of relics, or even create a culture of true versus fake relics: apart from deliberate frauds, all relics are true relics, because they are a focus for human belief. Christian doctrine holds that the physical relic is merely a symbol for the eternal concepts, and their purpose is to inspire and promote faith. Each saint can only be present as a spirit in one of its relics, but angels can attend multiple relics and enable them to produce miracles.

A peculiar Christian tradition is the practice of threatening a saint's relics in order to force him to produce a miracle. This usually involves the whole parish, and the relics are taken from their reliquary and paraded around. They might be publicly shamed, or threatened with injury or destruction. This can be effective if the relic is home to a divine spirit, since breaking the relic will sunder the binding, leaving the spirit unable to fulfil the mission given it by God.

MUSLIM RELICS

In contrast to Christian relics, Muslim relics are never human body parts or depictions of humans, which are haram (forbidden) under Islamic law. Relics instead take the form of things left behind by the Prophet or particularly holy men that followed him, and are attended by angels. Islamic characters can also use Old Testament relics, as long as this does not contravene Sharia law regarding human cadavers.

JEWISH RELICS

Like Christians and Muslims, Jewish characters can contact the divine spirits resident in any Old Testament relics. Relics unique to Judaism are even more unusual than Muslim relics. Some Jewish holy men are able to craft phylacteries that have attendant angels; these spirits can be contacted for advice during meditative prayer.

COMMUNITIES

O how great is that noble and beautiful city! How many monasteries, how many palaces there are, fashioned in a wonderful way! How many wonders there are to be seen in the squares and in the different parts of the city! I cannot bring myself to tell in detail what great masses there are of every commodity: of gold, for example, of silver . . . and relics of saints.

~ Fulcher of Chartres (c. 1100)

This chapter details the social connections between player and non-player characters. Here you will find a new mechanic for explicitly charting the web of social interaction and information through Affiliations, as well as the details of some organisations and societies to which characters may belong. Finally, some important personages are described in the Personalities of Constantinople (page 113).

Not all the information in this chapter is known to all characters, and there are a few secrets in the following sections. If you intend on playing in a game set in Mythic Constantinople, you may want to only read the sections directed by your Games Master.

AFFILIATIONS

In Mythic Constantinople, power is related as much to what you know and who you know as it is to who you are. There are factions and cabals everywhere you look, and everyone is part of a brotherhood, church, guild, or regiment. Characters can use these associations as sources of information and assistance, but Affiliations are a great story resource for the Games Master. Not only can they provide overt story hooks to the player characters – ones which can't really be refused if the character wants to retain the Affiliation – they can also feed rumours and red herrings back to the characters along with the information they wanted.

An Affiliation represents a connection to a specific facet of life in the city. For example, a character whose uncle is a senior official in the Office of the Special Fisc has an Affiliation with this office which he can call upon for help and/or information. Likewise, a character who served in the Byzantine army might have an Affiliation with his former unit.

There are 14 categories of Affiliation, broad descriptors of society that indicate where the character has general knowledge and connections. The Affiliation itself describes the specific link to the

AFFILIATIONS TABLE

Affiliation Category	Definition	Example Affiliations
Academic	Any aspect of teaching or study	philosophy, primary education, Law School
Criminal	Any illicit activity	specific criminal gang, opium trade
Cultural	Any non-Greek culture	Albanian, Bulgarian, Turkic, Vlach
Deviant	Any community outside societal norms	witch-cults, opium users
Family	One's own family or one with which you associate	specific family
Military	Any regiment	infantry, cavalry, guard unit, irregulars
Political	Any politically-motivated unit	Prasinoi, Army Office, Chancellery
Professional	Any guild or trade	silk guilds, craft guilds, inspectors
Religious/Christian	Any aspect of Christianity	Orthodox, Catholic, Monastic
Religious/Muslim	Any aspect of Islam	Sunni, Shi'a, Ismaeli, Sufi
Religious/Jewish	Any aspect of Judaism	Romaniote, Italkim
Rural	Pertains to beyond Constantinople's walls	fishermen, miners, share-croppers
Societal	Any aspect of the Greek people	demoi, mesoi, dynatoi, orphans
Urban	Any aspect of city life	specific district, kephale, Vardariotai

character, which may be further refined to a specific person or area of expertise. The two examples given earlier would therefore be represented as Political (Special Fisc) and Military (7th Allagion) respectively.

AFFILIATIONS BY CAREER TABLE

Career	Affiliation Categories
Agent	Criminal, Deviant, Societal, Urban
Alchemist	Deviant, Professional
Beast Handler	Professional, Rural
Courtesan	Criminal, Deviant, Military, Political, Societal, Urban
Courtier	Political, Societal
Crafter	Professional, Religious/Jewish, Urban
Christian Priest	Academic, Political, Religious/Christian, Urban
Entertainer	Deviant, Professional, Societal, Urban
Farmer	Rural, Societal
Fisher	Cultural, Rural
Herder	Rural, Societal
Hunter	Cultural, Rural
Labourer	Professional, Rural, Urban
Merchant	Professional, Religious/Jewish, Urban
Miner	Professional, Rural
Miracle Worker	Deviant, Rural, Urban
Mystic	Deviant, Religious/Christian, Religious/Muslim, Religious/Jewish
Official	Professional, Political, Religious/Christian, Religious/Muslim, Urban
Physician	Academic, Military, Religious/Jewish
Sailor	Professional, Military
Scholar	Academic, Political, Religious/Christian, Religious/Muslim, Religious/Jewish
Scout	Military, Urban
Shaman	Deviant, Religious/Christian, Religious/Jewish
Sorcerer	Academic, Deviant, Societal
Sportsman	Professional, Societal
Thief	Criminal, Urban
Warrior	Criminal, Military, Societal

STARTING AFFILIATIONS

Every character starts the game with one or more Affiliations:

- A character's Career provides one Affiliation, of a category chosen from the Affiliations by Career Table.
- If the character's Background included any Contacts or Allies, they automatically become Affiliations. These Affiliations can be of any category, but consider choosing them based on culture, family, and/or background events.
- Players may sacrifice starting money for more Affiliations, as detailed opposite.

Players should decide the category of all their Affiliations immediately and probably have a reasonable idea as to the specifics for at least some of them immediately, but with the consent of the Games Master, the details can be filled in once play has started as familiarity with the setting grows.

All Affiliations start with the base score of 40%. An Affiliation can be raised with Experience Rolls and Training in the usual fashion; this represents the character spending time, money, and/or effort to improve their connection to their community. For the purposes of Training, assume a mentor with a Skill of 100%, and the training costs of 20 SP should be multiplied by the character's Money Modifier for her social class (Mythras page 24).

USING AFFILIATIONS

Social rolls made with members of the same Affiliation as a character are usually at least one difficulty grade easier as long as the character has the opportunity to reveal his association. This advantage disappears if the character's actions are aggressive or harmful to the Affiliation.

Whenever a character makes a knowledge-based roll, this is one difficulty grade easier if the subject falls into one of their Affiliation categories. Typical rolls affected by Affiliations are Lore (Byzantine), Customs, and Streetwise. Note that the subject only has to match the Affiliation category rather than the specific Affiliation, since there is an overlap of knowledge within any category. For example: someone with a Criminal Affiliation with the Zanconi Family is also likely to know something about their rival gangs; and an Orthodox priest (Religious/Christian), is likely to know something about Catholic matters as well as those of his own sect.

If a character fails his own knowledge roll, or wants obscure or hidden information from his Affiliation, or to get help or advice from specific members, then he can spend some time talking to his contacts, hunting for rumours, or consulting appropriate repositories of knowledge. This typically takes 1d3 hours and is resolved as an Affiliation Skill roll. This roll can serve many purposes: it might be the probability that Uncle Eugenios is at his office; or the chance that a fence will take the stolen object off their hands. If the character asks someone within the Affiliation to perform a task for her – such as steal a document or craft an exact duplicate of a piece of jewellery – then the Affiliation Skill represents the chance of success. This might be less than the Skill of the person performing the task, but the contact will not always put all his effort into helping out a character, particularly one with weak ties (i.e. a low Affiliation Skill) to his community. The Games Master determines the outcome of the Affiliation's actions; usually a simple roll on the Affiliation Skill but occasionally a task roll (Mythras page 65 or 287). If the contact within the Affiliation is being asked to do something that violates his moral or social code then the Skill roll might be opposed by the contact's Passion. The player may not be aware of whether the action was successful until later in the adventure.

Affiliation Skill rolls are affected by:

- the time given to the contact to hunt down the information required, contact the most skilled individuals in town, or try several times to catch up with a specific person until he succeeds;

- the specificity of the information;
- the willingness of the contact to help the character, based on reciprocation. Characters who abuse their contacts find that they are less likely to expend effort and resources to help them.

These factors are summarised on the Affiliation Skill Table.

Affiliations Skill Table

Situation	Affiliation Skill grade
allow 1d3 hours	Standard
allow 1d3 days	one difficulty grade easier
allow 1d3+6 days	two difficulty grade easier
request falls within Affiliation category but outside specific group	one difficulty grade harder
character hasn't reciprocated since last used	one difficulty grade harder
character hasn't reciprocated several times	two difficulty grades harder

Hitting up an Affiliation is not always free; money might be needed to pay fees or bribes, but the coinage of an Affiliation often is not a physical one. The character have to promise someone an equivalent favour, and this favour might be traded to other members. A character can expect his contacts in the Affiliation to call upon him for help or information on occasion, and there is a social obligation to accept, particularly if the character has used the Affiliation themselves. Typically the Affiliation asks for no more than a character might ask from it. All Affiliations can be refreshed (i.e. reciprocated) with the expenditure of one Experience Roll and a week of downtime, representing the efforts of the character to pay back all of his contacts. Alternatively, each Affiliation can be paid off independently without the need of Experience, but this typically takes more time and/or money.

Faiths, Cults & Brotherhoods

A central feature of the Mythic Constantinople setting is the profusion of cults, brotherhoods, and cabals. It is expected that most player characters will join an organisation for the benefits they offer, and some might join more than one. Even if they do not get personally involved in an organisation, they will encounter many such groups while exploring Mythic Constantinople, and may attract enemies and allies from amongst them. In this section are some faiths, cults, and brotherhoods common in Mythic Constantinople; some are given in some detail and many more are listed in brief form.

ORG-1 Allagion

A typical regiment, the allagion is the basic unit of the Byzantine Imperial army. Each allagion consists of a single troop type. There are four regular troop types, two hippeis (heavy and light cavalry) and two pezoi (heavy and light infantry). There are also some irregular units like the hippotoxotes (horse-archers) or tzangratoroi (crossbowmen). The generic word for "soldier" which covers all these troop types is stratiotes (plural stratiotai).

300 soldiers make up each allagion, and each is subdivided into smaller units: each allagion has three taxeis of 100 men lead by a taxiarchos; each taxa has two phalankes (phalanxes) of 50 men lead by pentekonarchoi; and each phalanx is divided into five syntrophia (companies) of 10 men each lead by a dekarchos. Each allagion has its own colours and standard; they have a tuft of horsehair atop their helmets in the allagion's colours, which are also born on the inside of the shield, along with symbols indicating membership of subunits.

12 allagia make up the Imperial army in the mid-fifteenth century, and none of them are at full strength. At the current time there are two allagia of heavy cavalry, and the bulk of the rest is made up of pezoi.

> **Religious Sects**
>
> *A religious sect is a non-magical version of a theist cult; the organisation exists to regulate its members and bring religion to the masses. A person is usually a member of only one sect. Here, denominations of a religion are considered to be sects, so Catholicism and Orthodoxy are separate sects of the greater Christian Faith.*

Organisation

The commander of an allagion is called an allagator and he reports to the domestikos tou stratou, the prefect of the army within the imperial court (ORG-13). An allagator is equivalent to an Overseer rank; the leaders of the taxeis and phalankes are of Proven rank, the soldiers (and the dekarchoi) are of Dedicated rank, and the trainees and camp followers are Common members of the regiment. There is no equivalent for the rank of Leader in the current army.

Membership

Standard. Recruitment to an allagion typically happens at the age of 16 and a character is trained in the Warrior Career. Only men are officially admitted into the Imperial Army, although it is possible for a woman to join if she keeps her sex hidden or has the collusion of the rest of the regiment. Anyone can join as a lay member if they have a Combat Style which has the same Trait as that taught by the regiment as a whole.

Restrictions

- A stratiotes must eat and sleep at his unit's barracks.
- A stratiotes must maintain his own arms and armour; replacing or repairing at his own expense.
- A stratiotes cannot marry without permission from his unit commander.
- A hippia who loses his horse can no longer be a member of a cavalry allagion. If he cannot replace the beast he must join an infantry allagion instead, if any will have him.

SKILLS

Athletics, Brawn, Endurance, One Combat Style (see below), Lore (Strategy and Tactics); plus a speciality Skill, such as Stealth (for scouts), Lore (Firearms and Artillery), Ride (cavalry units), or a second Combat Style

COMBAT STYLE

- Heavy cavalry: Kataphraktos
- Light cavalry: Trapezites
- Heavy infantry: Skoutatos
- Light infantry: Toxotes
- Irregular units: see page 63

PRIVILEGES, MAGIC, & GIFTS

Joining the army is no light decision in these turbulent times, as the chances of being involved in a battle are high. The chief attraction is a regular salary, a place to live, and a pension. Members are supplied with all the equipment they need, with the exception of providing horses for cavalry units. Much of this equipment is second-hand, but it is more than serviceable. Members receive free training in the regimental skills, and as they rise through the ranks are expected to take part in providing this training. Regimental membership gives a strong sense of camaraderie and brotherhood, and a member can expect help from the members of his syntrophia when they are not on duty.

Despite having to maintain one's own weapons and armour, a stratiotes can purchase replacements from any supplier to the Military Fisc at three-quarters of the listed price. Note that all armour is made from steel, and therefore benefits from a lower encumbrance (Mythras rules page 87).

Allagia do not teach their members any form of magic or provide any Gifts.

ALLIES & ENEMIES

There is a great deal of rivalry between the different types of allagia. The Kataphraktoi were traditionally the elite forces but their numbers have declined sharply as the empire has shrunk, and they can no longer afford their former arrogance. The Hippotoxotes, comprised of Cumans bound in long-term military service, pour a lot of scorn on the regular light cavalry, and in return are disliked because they are foreigners.

LINKS

- The Army Office (ORG-13)
- Psamathia (ST-7)

ORG-2 DERVISH ORDER

A mystical order, Dervishes are a Turkish variety of Sufi (see page 84), most famously members of the Mevlevi and the Bektaşi orders.

NATURE

Instead of the contemplative life of the sufi, a Dervish is employed in practical spirituality, inspiring others to seek God through their example. They live exemplary lives in accordance with Islam, and are involved in conversion and teaching.

The Mevlevi are known as the "Whirling Dervishes" due to their practice of sema, a form of meditation where they spin on their axes whilst executing a circular dance. Their spiritual home is at Konya in Anatolia. They have a blood-relationship with the Ottoman sultans and are favoured at court, producing famed poets, artisans and theologians as well as holy warriors.

The Bektaşi order is also rooted in Anatolia, but has spread throughout the Balkans with the conquest of Rumelia. The Bektaşi maintain close ties with the rural populations and the Yeniçeri corps, and are at the forefront of the conversion of Christians to Islam. The Bektaşi are the spiritual counsellors and teachers of the Yeniçeris, and they inspire them to great acts of courage and devotion in the name of their religion.

ORGANISATION

Aspirants are admitted to either Dervish order at the rank of *aşik*. Following initiation they are known as *muhip*, and having spent time at this rank they may take further vows and become a *derviş*. Above this rank is the *baba*, who is the head of each Dervish *tekke* (lodge). Above the baba are the twelve *dedes*, the most senior of which is called the *dedebaba* and who is the highest ranking authority in the order. The Mevlevi believe that anyone can become a dede, but the Bektaşi hold that only those descended from the Prophet Mohammed are eligible.

MEMBERSHIP

There are no known female-led lodges and therefore all Dervishes are male – in common with Muslim law, women may only be taught by other women. There are rumours of a Dervish lodge within the Imperial Harem that trains women as agents of the Valide Sultan to be spies for the Divan. Such Dervishes would be experts at disguise and subterfuge.

RESTRICTIONS

Dervishes are bound by the outer law of Islam, but have dispensation to make themselves haram (unclean) if it serves a greater purpose, such as perpetuating a ruse or promoting faith.

SKILLS

Combat Style (Dervish), Dance (Mevlevi only), Endurance, Influence (Bektaşi only); Meditation, Mysticism (Dervish)

The Dervish Combat Style employs the scimitar, hoplite shield, and shortsword, and grants the Daredevil Trait.

PRIVILEGES, MAGIC, & GIFTS

As a Dervish advances through the ranks of his lodge, he learns Mystical Talents starting at the rank of Muhip.

TALENTS

- Aşik (Common): none
- Muhip (Dedicated): Augment Dance, Invoke Awareness of Threat, Enhance Fatigue
- Derviş (Proven): Augment Athletics, Invoke Pain Control, Enhance Action Points
- Baba (Overseer): Augment Evade, Invoke Featherlight, Enhance Hit Points
- Dede / Dedebaba (Leader): Augment Combat Style, Invoke Aura of Mastery, Enhance Healing Rate

Dervishes are not taught Folk Magic as part of their spiritual practice, but are under no religious prohibition from learning it from an outside source.

ALLIES & ENEMIES

Dervishes are opposed by all enemies of Islam. Bektaşi dervishes can always find allies within Yeniçeri regiments, who are conditioned to obey the teacher-mystics. The Order of the Dragon has identified dervishes (of either type) as responsible for the spread of Islam, and will stop them wherever it can.

LINKS

- None

ORG-3 HESYCHASM

Hesychasm (from the Greek for "stillness" or "silence") is a mystical tradition of the Orthodox Church. Each monk who embarks on a path towards union with God does so under the guidance of another traveller on that path, although once the first steps are taken, then the character is left to find their own way. There is no taught doctrine of Hesychasm, just a meditative method that leads to a personal experience of the Divine.

NATURE

Hesychasts retreat inwardly when they pray, shutting off the distractions of the senses in order to experience God. They stem from the desert anchorite tradition that gave birth to the monastic movements of both the Orthodox and the Catholic Churches. Most Hesychasts live at monasteries and take part in the sacramental life of a monk, although some live as hermits and seal themselves off from the world. In the past, hermit Hesychasts would climb to the top of tall columns and remain there for years, relying on their brothers to send food up in a basket. Their meditative technique is to shut out the senses one by one, rejecting the tempting thoughts that distract them from their contemplation of the Jesus prayer, which they repeat unceasingly: "Lord Jesus Christ; son of God; have mercy on me, the sinner." Accomplished Hesychasts can maintain this prayer 24 hours a day, seven days a week, having watchful attention of the inner world whilst being separate from the outer world until he spies the Uncreated Light, which is a manifestation of the Holy Spirit.

ORGANISATION

Hesychasts have no ranks or formal cult. They are all members of a monastery and live under its rule, and can achieve rank via this organisation, which does not affect Hesychasm in any way.

MEMBERSHIP

Standard.

RESTRICTIONS

All Hesychasts must hold a rank of at least *Rasophoros* (Dedicated rank) in a monastery, even if it is a *skete* with just a master and perhaps one other monk. They have all the restrictions associated with being a monk plus an additional restriction: they must not commit acts of violence and must seek to prevent harm from coming to others. Failure can result in a temporary difficulty in achieving the Uncreated Light, manifesting as a difficulty grade penalty to the Mysticism Skill. Completing penance is necessary to remove this impediment.

SKILLS

Endurance, Insight, Sing, Willpower; Lore (Theology), Meditation, Mysticism (Hesychasm)

PRIVILEGES, MAGIC, & GIFTS

Hesychasts can develop any of the following Talents in the process of communing with the Uncreated Light: Augment Endurance, Augment Lore (theology), Augment Love God, Augment Willpower; Invoke Aura of Light (works like the Folk Magic spell Light), Invoke Aura of Serenity, Invoke Awareness of Evil, Invoke Denial of Dehydration, Invoke Denial of Starvation, Invoke Indomitable, Invoke Life Sense; Enhance Fatigue, Enhance Healing Rate.

Unusually, Hesychasts can Augment a Passion, specifically the Love God Passion. They can use this enhanced Passion to augment a Skill roll, if the use of that Skill is in direct service to God.

ALLIES & ENEMIES

Hesychasts are allied with the Orthodox Church, in particular the Patriarchate of Constantinople, which has accepted the Palamite position that Hesychasm is a legitimate form of worship and devotion. However, there are still followers of Barlaam's anti-Palamite stance within the church, who are automatically enemies of the Hesychasts. Furthermore, Catholics – who may be tolerant of Orthodoxy since the Council of Florence – are suspicious of Hesychasm.

LINKS

- Monastery (ORG-7)
- Patriarchate of Constantinople (ORG-8)

ORG-4 THE HOSPITALLERS

The Order of Knights of the Hospital of Saint John of Jerusalem – the Knights Hospitaller – a military order of the Catholic Church with a duty to defend Christians, but it is also a hospital order with a duty of care towards the sick and the dying.

NATURE

This order of Church knights was founded in Jerusalem in 1023 in order to provide care and protection for pilgrims coming to the Holy Land. The order received a papal charter in 1099, forming it into a religious and military order where the knights live under a monastic rule. They have held the island of Rhodes as a sovereign domain since 1294.

Like other military orders of the Catholic Church, the Knights of Rhodes take monastic vows and live an austere life in service to God. Their symbol, the eight-pointed cross pattée, represents the eight virtues they hold sacred: loyalty, piety, generosity, bravery, glory and honour, contempt of death, helpfulness towards the poor and sick, and respect for the church. They have a reputation for absolute integrity and even-handedness, and have the respect of all Christendom, despite being an instrument specifically of the Catholic Church.

ORGANISATION

The Order has a host of lay members: farmers who till the land, squires who attend the knights, nuns who nurse the sick, and servants who manage their holdings. Above these members are the postulants (Dedicated rank) who are applying to be full members of the Order. Most postulants spend only a few years at this rank before being raised to the rank of Brother (Proven rank). There are three callings within the Order: the Brother Knights, the Brother Chaplains, and the Brother Sergeants, all of whom must fulfil the requirements of Proven rank.

The Brother Knights are noblemen, knighted by a secular authority who have subsequently devoted themselves to the service of the order. They are the heavy cavalry of the Order, trained to fight from horseback in full plate and chain armour. Those knights who cannot or will not dedicate themselves to the full vows of the Order can remain as postulants indefinitely, regardless of their level of skill. Brother Knights wear a black mantle with a white cross pattée over the heart, or, when on the battlefield, a red surcoat with a white cross.

The Brother Sergeants are the infantry division of the Order, populated by common-born men and required only to swear the vow of obedience. In contrast to other military orders of the church, the Knights Hospitaller make no distinction in their uniforms between the noble Brother Knights and the common Brother Sergeants.

The Brother Chaplains are ordained priests who attend to the spiritual needs of the Order, and who man the hospitals. Most Brother Chaplains do not serve as postulants before swearing vows to the Hospitallers. The Brother Chaplains wear a white habit with a black cross pattée.

Since 1319 the Knights Hospitaller have been divided into seven Langues ("Tongues"), administrative divisions lead by a pilier or baili (Overseer rank). The Langues are based around the ethnic divisions of the knights: Auvergne, France, Provence, Aragon, Italy, Germany, and England. Scandinavian, Hungarian, and Polish knights belong to the German Langue. Each Langue is divided into grand priories who are scattered through their territory; some grand priories have subordinate priories or commanderies. There is a headquarter (or auberge) of each Langue on Rhodes, as well as the Kastello which is the headquarters of the Grand Master of the Hospitallers (Leader rank).

The Grand Council of the Order is made up of the seven piliers, each of whom is also an official of the Order. The pilier of Provence is the Grand Commander; the pilier of Auvergne is the Grand Marshal (in charge of infantry); the pilier of France is the Grand Hospitaller (in charge of charity); the pilier of Italy is Admiral; the pilier of Aragon is the Standard-Bearer; the pilier of Germany is the Grand Chancellor; and finally the pilier of England is the Turcoplier (in charge of cavalry). These seven officers, plus the Grand Master of the Order and the Conventual Prior (the most senior priest), make up the ruling council of the Order of Saint John.

MEMBERSHIP

Standard. Each postulant to the Order must be a member of the Catholic Church and renounce all former allegiances or oaths. Only noblemen may become Brother Knights, commoners become Brother Sergeants instead. Most Brother Chaplains are already priests when they come to the Order; although the Grand Master has an ecclesiastic rank equivalent to a bishop, he cannot ordain the clergy.

RESTRICTIONS

Postulants, Brother Chaplains, and Brother Sergeants are required to take a vow of obedience to the Order. Brother Knights follow a more restrictive monastic rule, taking the triple vow of poverty, chastity, and obedience. Brother Knights are not supposed to attend to fashion or vanity, and are prohibited from wearing fine clothes or cutting their hair or shaving, although practicality permits them to trim their beards. Brothers of the Order are not required to remain within a Hospitaller commissary, but generally need to seek permission of their immediate superior for extended stays away from their home. They are also expected to register with the local commander.

SKILLS

Athletics, Combat Style (Cavalier or Footman), First Aid, Ride, Willpower; Healing, Lore (Strategy and Tactics), Lore (Theology).

PRIVILEGES, MAGIC, & GIFTS

The Order of Saint John caters for all the needs of its members, providing food and shelter, arms and armour, horses, and where needed, medical aid and geriatric care. Free training in all the Order's Skills can be obtained at any Hospitaller commissary.

The Order has no tradition of magic; indeed, the Catholic Church often uses them to back up inquisitors. Occasional members (of any of the three callings) might be Theists, who can call upon the devotion of their brothers. More commonly, Brother Knights may carry relics. The Order owns a small number of true relics and occasionally loans them for high status missions.

ALLIES & ENEMIES

The Mamluk Sultanate is the greatest enemy of the Hospitallers, since they are dedicated to the reconquest of the Holy Land for all Christians. Conflicts with the Ottoman Empire have been infrequent up to now, but are inevitable given the desire of the Sultan to rule the whole of the Middle Sea. The Grand Master of the Order of Saint John does not always see eye-to-eye with the Pope, but can generally rely on assistance from the Catholic Church. There are also good relationships with the Patriarchate of Constantinople and the Byzantine Empire.

LINKS

- Catholic Church (ORG-15)
- Commissary of Saint John (VQ-3)

ORG-5 IMPERIAL GUILD

Typical of Byzantine guilds, the Imperial Guilds are organisations that regulate certain trades. They were instituted to control trade in which the Byzantine Empire has a special interest.

NATURE

There are 21 guilds (or *syntechnia*), that bear the imperial designation. These guilds are the mainstay of the cash flow of the Empire; the Imperial cut of the profits from these key trades fund the military and the court. Guild members are permitted only to sell the prescribed goods of their guild, and they can only sell them in designated market places. In return their trade is protected by Imperial law.

The Imperial guilds are: *Notaries, Money-Lenders, Silversmiths and Goldsmiths, Raw Silk Merchants, Silk Spinners, Silk Weavers, Silk Merchants, Silk Importers, Linen Importers, Spicers and Perfumers, Wax Merchants, Soap Merchants, Grocers, Saddlers, Butchers, Pork Merchants, Fishmongers, Bakers, Innkeepers, Assessors* and *Inspectors*.

ORGANISATION

A master craftsman (Proven member) of a guild is either a sole proprietor of a shop or else a member of a partnership that co-owns the business. Each guildsman has a number of journeymen (Dedicated members) and apprentices (Common members) working on his premises. A Guild Dean is of Overseer rank, and the Guildmaster (exarchos) is the Leader. Deans are responsible for regulating different aspects of their trade, so the Grocers' Guild might have a dean in charge of dairy produce, a dean for utensils, and so forth.

MEMBERSHIP

Standard. A journeyman aspiring to become a master must make a masterpiece, an example of their craft with at least one Enhancement (Mythras page 101). For non-craft guilds, the masterpiece is typically an exclusive trade deal. Deans and Guildmasters tend to be political appointments rather than indicate a particular level of skill, and these characters need only one of the Guild's Skills to equal or exceed 90% or 110% respectively, typically Bureaucracy.

RESTRICTIONS

- A guildsman can only operate from a registered place of work. They are not permitted to work on Sundays or feast days.
- A guildsman's prices are fixed by law. These prices may fluctuate due to availability, but the vendor himself cannot set prices, and bargaining is not possible. The price that may be charged is dependent on guild rank: items made by an Apprentice must use the Cheap column from the Mythras rules (usually ½ to 2/3 of the standard price), Journeymen the Reasonable column (standard price), and Masters the Superior column (usually 2x to 4x more expensive), regardless of actual quality.

SKILLS

Bureaucracy, Commerce, Craft (appropriate to the guild), Customs, Insight, Locale, Streetwise

PRIVILEGES, MAGIC, & GIFTS

The main benefit of Guild membership is a job for life. The Guilds own a great deal of real estate and can loan or lease a workshop and living quarters to its members and their families. Most Imperial Guilds operate as friendly societies, providing injury benefits for those temporarily unable to work, pensions for old age and widows, and pay death duties for their members.

Magic is not routinely applied or taught by the Imperial Guilds except for the Guild of Assessors and Inspectors. About a hundred years ago this guild was headed by a practitioner of Folk Magic who taught many of his secrets to his staff. While learning Folk Magic is by no means mandatory for market inspectors, those that do find great use for the spells they teach, which include: Appraise, Calculate, Find Flaws, Find Underweight Goods, Incognito (for undercover work), Magnify, and Voice.

ALLIES & ENEMIES

Many of the Imperial Guilds are inter-dependent on one another, although they occasionally clash regarding jurisdictional issues. The Guild of Assessors and Inspectors is universally reviled by all the other guilds, despite the work that this guild puts in to protecting the others from the predation of the imperial court. Individual guilds may be allied to particular government ministries: for example, the best customer of the Saddlers' Guild is the Ministry of the Military Fisc, and the various silk trades are kept in business by the Imperial Court's need for ceremonial vestments. All the imperial guilds are administered by officials from the Office of the Special Fisc.

The biggest threat to the hegemony of the Imperial Guilds is the influx of foreign trade. Since the Frankokratia, Venetian influence over trade has been on the rise, and the Genoan presence in the marketplace is almost as big.

LINKS

- Office of the Special Fisc (ORG-28)

ORG-6 IMPERIAL COURT

An example of a college, the imperial court is a sprawling bureaucracy populated by functionaries and eunuchs. While it seems like a well-oiled machine, in truth it is comprised of many petty fiefdoms who all work against each other in order to aggrandise their own importance. Ritual and ceremony attend every court function, and there is a precise order of precedence consisting of more than a hundred ranks of civil servant, each characterised by a specific court uniform. At the heart of the ceremonial dress of the Empire is the *kabbadion*, a brocaded robe that reaches the ankles, with fitted sleeves, buttons down the front, and is secured with a belt. Its colour and decoration is prescribed by the department and rank of the wearer. Headgear is also tightly regulated and comes in a number of forms, from the brimmed skiadion to the domed skaranikon and the inverted cone-shaped *kapasion*.

NATURE

Members of this college are those who bear proclaimed titles rather than honorific awarded titles (see page 28). The holders of proclaimed titles are members of one of the 12 government departments: the Army Office, the Naval Office, the Chancellery, the

Imperial Archives, the Imperial Household, the General Treasury, the Special Treasury, the Public Post, the Military Fisc, the Imperial Library, the Imperial University, and the Imperial Orphanage. More information about these ministries can be found later.

ORGANISATION

At the head of the Imperial Court is the mesazon, who is the chief minister of the emperor. He attends the emperor day and night, and all the other court officials must go through him to reach the emperor, in theory at least. The mesazon must coordinate the other ministers, and he has an office of staff assigned just to assist him in this task. The role of mesazon has been combined with a formerly separate official called the *parakoimomenos* ("one who sleeps nearby"), the high chamberlain who slept in the emperor's bedchamber.

The mesazon holds the rank of Leader in the Imperial Court. The heads of the 12 departments are equivalent to Overseer rank. Each departmental head has his chief deputies and subordinates who hold Proven rank. The bottom layer of petty functionaries constitute the Dedicated rank; there are no Common members of the Imperial Court unless you count servants and apprentices. In each departmental description below the titles of each rank are given, each one a proclaimed dignity. This should not be considered a definitive list; in particular, the court is fond of creating new junior or senior ranks by the addition of prefixes. These might indicate grades of dignitary within the same rank, or promote the individual into the next rank. Thus a *kankellarios* (clerk) and his assistant, a *hypokankellarios* (under-clerk) might both be Dedicated Rank, but the *megas kankellarios* (grand clerk) that oversees them both might be a Proven member.

JUNIOR & SENIOR DIGNITARY TABLE

Junior Prefixes, in ascending order	Senior Prefixes, in descending order
Mikros (lesser)	Basilikos (imperial)
Hypo- (under)	Megas (great)
Deutero- (second)	Sebasto- (honoured)
	Panhyper- (above all)
	Proto- (first)
	Hyper - (above)
	Dis- (twice)

MEMBERSHIP

Joining the Imperial court as a functionary requires being able to read and speak Latin, which is the language of bureaucracy in the Empire. It also requires a sponsor from within the department. Acquiring a proclaimed title is more challenging: it is unusual for someone to be promoted to a titled position from within the civil service since these positions are often given as rewards or bribes.

RESTRICTIONS

- A member of the court has taken an oath of loyalty to the emperor, and held accountable for his actions.
- A member of the court is not permitted to marry without permission from his departmental head.
- An official must obey orders from someone with a superior Rank from the same department, unless they are currently under orders from an equal or superior Ranked individual.

SKILLS

Bureaucracy, Courtesy, Customs, Literacy, and one of Commerce, Insight, Locale, Lore (Byzantine), or Teach

PRIVILEGES, MAGIC, & GIFTS

A member of the court can call upon the resources of his department. Every ministry has a vast amount of paperwork within its vaults, which contains a remarkable amount of information. Searching the stacks allows the character to make an appropriate Skill check at one grade easier in order to find a particular piece of information. All social Skill rolls made with those of a lesser rank, including Affiliation rolls, are also one grade easier.

Training is always available – even encouraged – in the department's Skills. Trainers with at least an 80% Skill are available in all departments, and many of these also have the Teach Skill.

There is no magic or Gifts provided by the organisation; however, certain individuals may well be practitioners of magic (Folk Magic or Sorcery being most common), and contacts made through the ministry.

ALLIES & ENEMIES

The Imperial ministries are rife with cronyism. Any social rolls involving members of the same department is made at one skill grade easier. However, all other departments are hostile to a member of a different ministry, and social rolls involving members of different departments are one skill grade more difficult.

LINKS

- Army Office (ORG-13)
- Chancellery (ORG-16)
- Imperial Archives (ORG-18)
- Imperial Household (ORG-19)
- Imperial Library (ORG-20)
- Imperial Orphanage (ORG-21)
- Imperial University (ORG-22)
- Naval Office (ORG-24)
- Office of the Drome (ORG-25)
- Office of the General Fisc (ORG-26)
- Office of the Military Fisc (ORG-27)
- Office of the Special Fisc (ORG-28)
- Constantine XI Dragases Palaiologos (NPC-6)
- Demetrios Palaiologos Kantakouzenos (NPC-8)
- Great Palace (PA-8)

ORG-7 MONASTERY, TYPICAL

Monasteries of the Orthodox denomination are quite different to the more familiar Western system. Monks and nuns do not live under a formal monastic rule, so there are no orders such as the Western Benedictines, Cistercians, and so forth. Furthermore, there is no division between mendicant monks (friars), cathedral staff (canons), and contemplative monks. Instead, Orthodox monks obey a charter or *typikon* which is an agreement drawn up by the community who founded their monastery; each typikon is a unique document that can be amended through a vote of the current members. Finally, monks can be male or female, although all monasteries are single sex institutions. Monks are most commonly lay members of the Christian faith, although those who are ordained are known as hieromonks.

NATURE

The Orthodox Church measures its health by the quality and quantity of its monks and nuns. Unlike Western monastic practices, the principal purpose of most Orthodox monks is to attain theosis – union with God. However, distribution of alms and care for the needy and the sick is typically an obligation of a monk in order to best emulate the virtues of mercy and compassion, and so Eastern monks do not lock themselves away behind monastery walls as they do in the west. Orthodox monasteries are often found inside cities, and Constantinople is no exception, having three hundred separate institutions.

A monk's life is split into communal worship, hard labour, and private spiritual study and prayer. There is no difference between the expectations on male and female monks, both follow identical paths.

ORGANISATION

A *dokimos* or novice (Common rank) has just recently pledged to the monastery. Depending on the typikon, novices may wear the black inner cassock and soft monastic hat worn by the other monks under their robes, or they may be clad in some other colour or even in normal clothes. The novitiate typically lasts a year or more, until the novice becomes a *rasophoros* ("robe bearer", Dedicated rank), whereupon he receives the tonsure and the outer cassock and cylindrical brimless hat. A rasophoros does not make any formal vows but is obligated to remain within the monastery for the rest of his life. Once the rasophoros has demonstrated an appropriate level of discipline and humility, he may be raised to the rank of *stavrophoros* ("cross bearer", Proven rank). This is symbolised by a wooden cross worn over the heart attached to a square of embroidered cloth worn on the back. The *megaloschemos* ("great schema", Overseer rank) is awarded to those stavrophoroi who show particular devotion and spiritual accomplishment. His rank is symbolised by the analabos, a richly embroidered garment that drapes over the shoulders and hangs down front and back. Each monastery is headed by a *hegumenos* or abbot (Leader rank), who is installed by a bishop. Some hegumenoi are leaders of more than one monastery, in which case they have the title of archimandrites and supervise several hegumenoi.

MEMBERSHIP

Standard. The ranks within a monastery are designed to mirror the spiritual development of the individual; some monks never rise above novice rank whereas others make the Great Schema in under a decade. All monks and nuns must hold at least lay membership in the Patriarchate of Constantinople (or another Orthodox sect).

RESTRICTIONS

- Monks and nuns must be celibate;
- Monks and nuns have no personal possessions: they must relinquish all worldly goods to the monastery;
- Monks and nuns must be moderate in all things. They observe the rules of fasting at all times, avoiding animal meat and fat and breaking fast only after sunset;
- Monks and nuns must observe a strict moral code, leading a sinless life. They must confess and do penance even for thinking about sinful things;
- Monks and nuns must observe the typikon.

SKILLS

Customs, Endurance, Insight, Sing; Literacy, Lore (Theology), Meditation

PRIVILEGES, MAGIC, & GIFTS

Like priests, monks can claim canonical privilege and cannot be prosecuted in a secular court. Their monastery provides them with food, shelter, and training in the college's Skills, but expects a life of selfless devotion and poverty in return.

Monks are not habitually trained in magical arts. However, many discover the Mysticism path of Hesychasm (ORG-3) all by themselves. Furthermore, there is one monastery in Constantinople (The Martyrion of Saints Karpos and Papylos, ORG-30), that trains its members in a form of Animism for the purposes of exorcism.

ALLIES & ENEMIES

Monasteries have no real enemies, unless they have antagonised local landowners with their typikon. Monasteries are hotbeds of anti-Unionist sentiment, so can claim Unionists as rivals.

LINKS

- ɸ Hesychasm (ORG-3)
- ɸ Patriarchate of Constantinople (ORG-8)

ORG-8 THE PATRIARCHATE OF CONSTANTINOPLE

Each autocephalous church of the Orthodox faith constitutes its own sect, although all are practically identical in form (see page 31 onwards for more on Orthodox Christianity). This contrasts strongly with Catholicism, which all falls under the same sect with the Pope as its supreme leader.

NATURE

The purpose of the Orthodox Church is to praise God and to guide people to Christ, thus saving their souls from Hell. In Constantinople, the community of the Orthodox Church falls under the purview of the Patriarchate of Constantinople. This is just one of several patriarchates that together form the Orthodox Church, but since they are autocephalous (independent from one another), they are each treated as a separate sect. For more information on the structure of the Orthodox Church, see page 31.

ORGANISATION

The Patriarch of Constantinople is the head of his church. The greater community of the Orthodox church has other patriarchs, the patriarchate is an autocephalous church with no higher earthly authority. The patriarch is assisted in his role as leader of the church by his fellow bishops. There is no sacerdotal difference between the patriarch and the other bishops, but there is a clear hierarchy for administrative purposes.

The patriarch himself occupies the Leader rank, and his parish is Hagia Sophia. The remaining orders of bishops (*episkopoi*) constitute the Overseer rank of the Orthodox Church. Metropolitan bishops are leaders of the church within their city and district, and they govern autonomously, without the interference of their patriarch. Metropolitans may appoint auxiliary bishops, who have no authority of their own but act as directed by their metropolitan. Most of the metropolitan sees currently lay within Turkish hands, but are still permitted to lead Christians in their worship of God.

Protopresbyteroi (archpriests, Proven rank), and *presbyteroi* (priests, Dedicated rank), fill out the lower orders. Also within the Dedicated rank are those individuals who have taken minor holy orders, such as deacons and exorcists. Finally, the vast lay congregation make up the ranks of Common members.

MEMBERSHIP

To be a Common member of the Orthodox Church one must have been baptised as a child in the Eastern Rite, and then confirmed in the faith as an adolescent.

To rise above the Common rank, a character must be ordained. Ordination is a sacrament of the church that forever marks a person as a vicar of Christ. The sacrament can never be undone: once a priest, always a priest. Further ordinations and investments are required for the rank of bishop. Bishops are required to be monks as well as priests.

RESTRICTIONS

- ɸ Members of the church are expected to abide by the morals outlined in the Bible, including the Ten Commandments. Notorious sinners will be shunned by the community and should expect to do penance before being accepted once more.
- ɸ Individuals are expected to tithe one tenth of all profits to the church. One quarter of the tithe goes to the bishop, one quarter to the poor, one quarter to the priest, and one quarter to the upkeep of the church and its properties.
- ɸ Fasting is required on Fridays, Sundays, and holy days. No practical work or commerce may take place on a Sunday.
- ɸ Only men are permitted to seek ordination as a priest and acquire rank in the sect above Dedicated member. Women can be ordained as a deaconess, but there is no possibility for advancement beyond this.
- ɸ Those of Dedicated rank and higher who are unmarried when they attain this rank must be celibate and can never marry. Married men can be ordained as presbyteroi as long as this is the first marriage for both the priest and his wife. Presbyteroi are expected to fulfil the ministry of their parish, serving God as a teacher, counsellor, healer, and shepherd.

SKILLS

Bureaucracy, Customs, Insight, Literacy, Locale, Lore (Theology)

PRIVILEGES, MAGIC, & GIFTS

There are few prosaic privileges to being a common member of the Orthodox Church; one's reward is salvation from the flames of damnation after death, and the promise of bodily resurrection during the End of Days. It is those who are not members of the church that are treated with suspicion and outright hostility.

Priests have more resources made available to them. Not only can they obtain training in the sect's Skills, they can also consult the libraries of the churches and monasteries around their city. A priest can also use his Status to lever favours out of the faithful; although if he tries this on someone who is not of his own congregation, he can expect to have to justify his actions to the person's priest or their bishop.

Priests can claim canonical privilege and cannot be prosecuted in a secular court. Instead, the Patriarchal court judges members of the clergy who have committed secular crimes, as well as crimes of morality and orthodoxy committed by anyone. The Patriarchal court has different definitions of evidence than the secular courts, and conviction requires that the defendant is notorious – that is, he was caught in the act of the crime and has an eyewitness to speak against him.

Magic is not taught routinely to members of the Church. However, training in Theism can be provided for those with the correct charism and the Love God Passion; see page 79 for more details. Further, the Order of Kappa-Pi-Alpha (ORG-30) provides training in Folk Magic and animism specifically turned towards combatting malign spirits.

ALLIES & ENEMIES

As a vast, multi-continental organisation, the Orthodox Church has its enemies, most of them powerful. The Catholic Church has been in schism with the Orthodox Church since 1054, and can be said to be rivals at best, enemies at worst. Since the Council of Florence in 1437, the two churches are in theory united, but in practice nothing has changed. As a rival faith, Islam is opposed to all forms of Christianity but does not deny its efficacy as a means of achieving heaven, a courtesy which is not offered by Christians to Muslims.

LINKS

- Monastery (ORG-7)
- Order of Kappa-Pi-Alpha (ORG-30)
- Patriarch Gregory III of Constantinople (NPC-14)
- Hagia Sophia (PA-8)

ORG-9 SUFI TURUQ

Sufism or *tasawwuf* is a tradition of Islamic mysticism.

NATURE

Sufis believe that it is possible to draw close to the divine presence in this life, rather than waiting until after death and the Last Judgement. Central to Sufism is the concept of fitra, the primordial state in which everything is done with a burning love for God. Sufis make a distinction between outer Islam (rules pertaining to worship, marriage, judicial rulings, and so forth), and inner Islam (repentance from sin, purging of evil traits, expression of virtues), and focus solely on the latter. Sufis organise into *turuq* (orders), each centred on the teaching of a single *mawla* or grand master. The devotional practices of each order are different, but usually consist of the continual repetition (*dhikr*) of a short prayer, and of meditative contemplation (*muraqaba*) of the soul.

Sufis practice meditation under unusual circumstances. They might balance on one foot for hours, or spend a day walking on their hands.

ORGANISATION

All orders demand that *fitra* can only be sought under the guidance of a master, and students of different skill study together as well as meditate alone. After becoming an aspirant in the chosen order and learning the basic teachings, a Sufi next seeks the rank of *ilhaam* ("unveiling", Dedicated rank), where the sufi's perceptions of things are sharper. The next stage up is called *shahood* ("evidence", Proven rank), where the sufi can achieve knowledge of the universe that others cannot know. Finally, the rank of *fatah* ("victory") frees the sufi from some of the constraints of space and time. Those of fatah rank can teach others within their order. Above the fatah rank is a final secret rank called *qutb*, where the sufi has become a perfect channel of God's grace and has attained a state of sanctity. The qutb is equivalent to the Leader rank, and while they gain no extra talents, they become able to glimpse God. Each qutb is the progenitor of their own turuq, passing on the numinous knowledge they have gained from union with God.

MEMBERSHIP

Standard

RESTRICTIONS

All Sufis must live an exemplary Muslim life, else their master will dismiss them as a student. Women are not considered suitable for inner Islam, and the law prohibits a woman from teaching a man or vice versa. There is no explicit rule against an all-female turuq except for the requirement of a female qutb to found it.

SKILLS

Customs, Insight, Perception; Acrobatics, Lore (Islamic Theology), Meditation, Mysticism (Sufi)

PRIVILEGES, MAGIC, & GIFTS

TALENTS:

- Aspirant (Common): none
- Ilhaam (Dedicated): Augment Perception, Invoke Awareness of Threat, Enhance Fatigue
- Shahood (Proven): Augment Locale, Augment Customs, Invoke Magic Sense, Enhance Strike Rank
- Fatah (Overseer): Augment Acrobatics, Invoke Awareness of Truth, Enhance Action Points
- Qutb (Leader): none

Upon attaining Shahood rank, a Sufi gains the Oracle Gift. Upon coming a Fatah, a Sufi gains both the Swiftness and Youth Gifts as they become freed from time's restraint. Finally, a Qutb gains the Gifts of Cult Evolution, Eternal Life, and Summon Divine Spirit.

ALLIES & ENEMIES

Sufi orders are withdrawn from the world as a whole, and tend to have no enemies or allies.

LINKS

- None

ORG-10 THE UNCONCEALED WORD

NATURE

A mystical order, the followers of the Unconcealed Word, often called Unconcealed Ones (*Aletheioi*), are Platonic philosophers in the mould of Plotinus, Porphyry, Iamblichus, Plutarch, and Proclus. These "neoplatonists" are usually misconstrued as pagans, although this is not entirely correct: they consider gods to be metaphysical constructs of the philosophical concepts in which they believe, and what is interpreted as worship is merely a form of practical philosophy. They use the names of classical gods as a shorthand for complex beliefs.

Neoplatonist philosophy has three key concepts: The One, the Intellect, and the Soul. The One (*Henos*), which they also call Zeus, is the principle of being, the eternal uncreated summation of existence, which contains within itself all being in an undivided state. The Intellect (*Nous*) is the principle of intelligibility, the means by which the One is the cause of everything. Poseidon, symbol of Nous,

NEW TALENTS

APPORTATION

The mystic is able to transport himself instantly to any location within sight. The apportation occurs as soon as the mystic implements this Talent, and has no continuing duration once the change in location has occurred. A mystic who has implemented the Astral Projection Talent can apport to a location within sight of his projection.

MESMERISM

The mystic can catch someone's attention and hold it. The mystic must make eye contact with the target, requiring that she is within two metres of her target. Make an opposed Willpower roll. If the mystic wins then the target can do nothing but stand and gaze into the mystic's eyes. If the target wins the opposed Willpower roll then he has broken eye contact and is now warned of the danger of the mystic's gaze. A mesmerised character remains that way while the mystic maintains eye contact, which makes most physical actions impossible. A mesmerised target is highly suggestible, and the mystic can implant a single compulsion if he can win a social task (Mythras rulebook page 287), with a victim of his gaze involving the mystic's Influence versus the victim's Willpower. The difficulty of the victim's rolls depend on the nature of the compulsion: suggestions that are entirely passive ("forget I was here") have a Hard penalty; whereas those that are dangerous or complex are Easy. Passions augment these rolls as normal. If the mystic achieves greater than 100% in the Task resolution, then he gains one enhancement per 25%. An enhancement allows a permanent alteration of a person's behaviour by adding or removing a Passion or his choice.

is thus perceived as the eldest child of Zeus and is the creator of the heavens and the earth. The Soul (*Psyche*) is the principle of desire, through which things interact with one another. It is symbolised by Hera, first of the Olympian 'gods' who rule immortal life in the heavens. Kronos (time), the third child of Zeus, is first of the Tartarean 'gods' who rule mortal life on earth. Beneath the Olympian and Tartarean gods are further emanations of the One under the agency of Hera, these are the celestial 'gods' who are the source of all mortal life on earth. Their leader is Helios, the sun. The celestial gods are solely good, and their role is to guide all life towards divine order. At the bottom of the divine hierarchy is mankind, but through Neoplatonist philosophy they believe they can climb the ladder and achieve a form of godhood.

Most Aletheioi join the cult later in life, drawn from the ranks of scholars, intellectuals, and seekers of the truth. They learn Mysticism as a means of understanding The One. As they become more skilled, they comprehend that time and space are illusory, everything is The One.

ORGANISATION

The Unconcealed Ones have no leader. There are some who, in the current era, have done much to increase the understanding of The One and whose teachings are greatly honoured; but these cannot be said to be leaders of The Unconcealed Word. One such luminary is George Gemistos Plethon (see page 118), whose membership of the cult is an open secret. As a group of philosophers and scholars, the Aletheioi have no real cult structure, although since comprehension of The One is quantised, the membership naturally devolves into three grades of understanding called hypostases.

Aspirants to the cult (Common Rank) are new to Neoplatonism and have yet to achieve any of the hypostases. They study with a member at a higher grade and develop the cult Skills, particularly Lore (philosophy).

The Hypostasis of Psyche is the first to be comprehended: Students of this rank learn that all life involves desire, but this desire cannot be satisfied except by going outside one's self. Students learn to manipulate the desires of others while becoming impervious to such manipulation themselves.

Disciples of the Hypostasis of Nous understand that the desire of Intellect for union with reality can be eternally satisfied and that other desires are mere distractions. Union with the Intellect allows the character to view heaven and earth as the gods do; potentially nothing is hidden from them.

The Hypostasis of Henos is the highest level of understanding, the closest an incarnate soul can come to union with The One. Masters of this grade understand that everything is The One: time, space, matter, energy, and thought are merely constructs of the Intellect. While their ability to manipulate these things may be limited, they are nevertheless capable of remarkable feats. A Master may demonstrate their understanding of the illusory nature of matter and space by making themselves immune to various types of matter, overcome the force of gravity, and even transporting themselves instantly without passing through the intervening space.

MEMBERSHIP

Standard.

RESTRICTIONS

Unconcealed Ones cannot have a Love God Passion – a deep-seated belief in God is incompatible with the teachings of Neoplatonism.

SKILLS

Customs, Willpower; Lore (Philosophy), Meditation, Mysticism (Unconcealed Word), Teach

PRIVILEGES, MAGIC, & GIFTS

The Unconcealed Ones are mystics. They use their understanding of the world to achieve remarkable feats, and the closer they come to henosis (union with the One), the more Talents they can express. When a character reaches the second and third hypostases, they receive a Gift (see Mythras page 292), either the Gift of Perfection or the Gift of Sagacity in a non-magical cult Skill. They may choose the same Gift twice, but it applies to a different Characteristic or Skill (respectively) each time it is taken.

An Aletheios who knows Folk Magic can be taught spells at each rank, although Folk Magic is not the primary aim of The Unconcealed Word.

STUDENT (HYPOSTASIS OF PSYCHE)

- Talents: Augment Influence, Augment Seduction, Invoke Indomitable, Invoke Mesmerism.
- Spells: Befuddle, Calm, Demoralise, Fanaticism, Voice

DISCIPLE (HYPOSTASIS OF NOUS)

- Talents: Augment Perception, Augment Insight, Invoke Aura of Dispassion, Invoke Astral Projection
- Spells: Calculate, Find Object, Magnify, Translate, Witchsight

MASTER (HYPOSTASIS OF HENOS)

- Talents: Invoke Adhering, Invoke Apportation, Invoke Featherlight, Invoke Immunity (any, can be taken more than once)
- Spells: Extinguish, Ironhand, Mindspeech, Mobility, Protection

ALLIES & ENEMIES

The Orthodox Church is an enemy of The Unconcealed Word, seeing it as rank idolatry at best and devil-worship at worst. In contrast, Sufism (see pages 50 and 84) owes a lot to the early Platonists, as their teachings percolated into Arab lands to influence Islamic mysticism after the sack of the Library of Alexandria.

LINKS

- Georgios Plethon Gemistos (NPC-12)

ORG-11 THE VARANGIAN GUARD

The Varangian Guard (Greek: *Varrangai* or *Englinovarrangoi*) originate from a troop of Scandinavian and Rus' mercenaries who reached Constantinople in the ninth century. By the eleventh century they were firmly established as a distinct unit within the army, and their role gradually altered to that of palace guard. It was supplemented by English members until by the mid-thirteenth century it was staffed almost solely by Englishmen, a tradition that has continued today.

NATURE

Many Varangians are first-generation Englishmen, but some are descended from several generations of resident foreigners. These Greek-born Englishmen (or *Varangopouloi*) are important for they are raised speaking both English and Greek and act as translators for the regiment.

The Varangians still practice certain customs instituted by their Scandinavian forebears. They often tattoo both arms from knuckles to shoulder to indicate a lifelong dedication to the regiment, at a time when tattoos are considered barbaric and only worn by criminals. They carry the pagan symbol of Odin's raven on their shields, and they hold Saint Olaf Haraldsson as their patron. However, the most distinctive 'primitive' feature of the regiment is their characteristic two-handed axe, which is like no other weapon used in the Empire. They carry it on their right shoulder when on duty. The Varangians wear the armour of the Skoutaroi; their ceremonial armour has alternating scales enamelled with blue and yellow on the skirt and shoulders. The *kremesmata* (cloth skirt) and *khlamys* (cloak) are red or purple (the latter for the personal guards of the emperor) and embroidered with gold.

The Varangians are tasked with standing guard outside the imperial bedchamber and in the reception hall. They also hold the keys to the city – in the past, whatever city the emperor happened to be in – and also guard the imperial treasury and the prisons where important guests are held. It is tradition that upon the death of an emperor, each Varangian in active service receives his helmet full of gold in recognition for his service.

ORGANISATION

Common members of the Varangian Guard are the candidates for joining the guard proper. They are admitted to the unit at the age of 12, where they act as squires to the full members for at least four years before they can attempt the tests to enter the guard. If they have not passed the requirements by their twentieth summer they are dismissed. Upon passing the entrance requirements the warrior becomes a guardsman (Dedicated member), and is assigned to a unit to commence training. Once he is considered good enough he is assigned a duty, rising to Proven rank. Those of Overseer rank are called the primmikerioi, and they are the leaders of a unit of guardsmen, usually in multiples of 12. There are currently three units of guardsmen in Constantinople. The *megas akolouthos* is the leader of the whole Varangian Guard, and he has a high rank within the imperial court, above the leaders of the other guard units and only twentieth from the emperor himself.

MEMBERSHIP

To join the Varangian Guard, a number of criteria must be met:

- The candidate must be male and English in the male line for at least four generations, although exceptions have been made for foreigners who meet the other criteria
- They must stand at least 1.8 metres tall (SIZ 15) and be strong enough to hew an upended log with a single blow of the pelekys (Damage Bonus of +1d2 or more)
- They must also pass a test of Endurance, standing in full armour without moving for six days without passing out or falling asleep (make a roll to resist gaining a level of Fatigue every 12 hours, if he gains more than six Fatigue levels he will collapse)

RESTRICTIONS

- The Varangian Guard is expected to live up to a restrictive code of honour, including an oath of obedience to the emperor. They are supposed to be incorruptible.
- A Varangian is not permitted to marry freely. The Megas Akolouthos arranges marriages for his men in order to preserve bloodlines and maintain the strength of his men.
- A Varangian is on duty for at least eight hours of each day, and expected to be off duty but available for another eight.

SKILLS

Brawn, Combat Style (Pelykophoros), Endurance, Insight, Lore (Strategy and Tactics), Perception

PRIVILEGES, MAGIC, & GIFTS

Members of the Varangian Guard receive a handsome salary. Those that marry are given a grant of land in Paradeison (page 187) to support their family. Training to become a Varangian Guard places a lot of emphasis on the importance of relying upon your comrades, and a Varangian unit is usually a close-knit group of friends who act as Contacts and often Allies.

Since the Varangian Guard control access to the emperor, they are seen as wielding substantial power within the palace. They are not permitted to take bribes (although that is not to say this never happens), but they can accrue the favours of members of the Imperial court.

There is no magical skills taught to the members of Varangian Guard, but that is not the same as saying that they have no access to magic. The regiment has a thaumatourgos called Tosti within its ranks who knows some simple Folk Magic appropriate to the battlefield. This magician claims to be a member of a tradition that harks back to the foundation of the regiment, and he casts his magic by drawing angular runes on the targets of his spells. Tosti knows the following spells: Bladesharp, Fanaticism, Heal, Protection, Vigour.

ALLIES & ENEMIES

The Imperial Court prefers to keep the Varangian Guard on their side, as they control who gets to see the emperor and when. The Varangians are resented by the other guard units for their primacy amongst the imperial household (and they are not even Greeks!), which can lead to serious rivalries and occasionally scuffles. The most rancour is dished out by the Vardariotai, who have long-thought that they should be in charge of the emperor's safety rather than a bunch of foreigners.

LINKS

- Army Office (ORG-13)
- Andrew of Killingworth (NPC-2)
- The Brachionion (BL-4)
- Paradeison (XR-9)

OTHER FACTIONS

The following section covers some more factions in Byzantine politics. Some of these might also be brotherhoods of one form or another, but many are just collections of like-minded individuals.

ORG-12 ANTI-UNIONISTS

TYPE

Religious Movement

NATURE

The Anti-Unionists oppose the resolution of the Council of Florence to unite the Catholic and Orthodox Churches. All Orthodox bishops who were present at the council's conclusion signed the Decree of Union, but several have since repudiated that document.

LEADER

The unofficial leader of the Anti-Unionists is the monk Gennadios, religious advisor to the previous emperor, who has gone into seclusion at the Pantokrator Monastery in protest over the Patriarchate's official pro-Union stance. Bishop Akkakios of Derkos has taken possession of Hagia Sophia, and holds anti-Unionist masses there while excluding the Unionists. Amongst their number the anti-Unionists can claim Ioannes Eugenikos (former nomophylax of the Law School), Loukas Notaras, and Demetrios Palaiologos.

WHAT THEY SAY THEY WANT

Keep Catholicism and Orthodoxy separate

WHAT THEY REALLY WANT

Have Catholicism declared heretical

ALLIES & ENEMIES

Naturally, the Catholic Faith is a political foe of the Anti-Unionists, as is the Patriarch of Constantinople. However, there are many priests and bishops within the Patriarchate with sympathy or outright support for the Anti-Unionists. The Notaras family, which controls the Chancellery, is the most prominent supporter, whereas the Kantakouzenos (including the mesazon and the Grand Domestic) are opponents, as too is the emperor himself.

LINKS

- Patriarchate of Constantinople (ORG-8)
- Georgios Gennadios (NPC-11)

ORG-13 ARMY OFFICE

TYPE

Political Guild

NATURE

The Army Office or *Scholon* is the ministry responsible for the army. The Grand Domestic (*megas domestikos*) is the commander-in-chief of the Byzantine army and head of the Scholon. He is the highest ranking of all ministers, coming fifth in the chain of command after the kaisar. His second-in-command is the protostrator. Within the ministry there are a number of other officers, such as the domestikos tou stratou who commands the regular army, and the prefects of the militia, mercenaries, watch, the four household guards, and the Domestic of the Walls. No serving soldiers are members of the upper ranks of the Army Office, which concerns itself with the strategies of war, the campaign against the enemy, and the defence of the city and Empire. Consequentially, the Army Office is stuffed with bureaucrats and military scholars, but precious few that have actual experience in warfare. The Grand Domestic is considering that he will have turn to foreign commanders for the next siege of the city – which intelligence suggests is coming soon.

The Army Office is located within the Konisterion in the Great Palace, although in practice it has relocated to the neighbourhood of 'Exakionion in Stoudion District. The regulation colours of the Army Office are red and yellow.

DIGNITARIES BY RANK

- Leader: Megas Domestikos (Grand Domestic)
- Overseer: *Protostrator*, *domestikos tou stratou*, *megas stratopedarches* (prefect of the militia), *megas hetaireiarches* (prefect of mercenaries), *megas droungarios* (prefect of the watch), prefects of the household guards (*megas akolouthos* of the Varangians,

protoallagator of the Paramonai, *stratopedarches* of the Mourtatoi, and *stratopedarches* of the Tzakones), *domestikos ton teicheon* (domestic of the walls).

- Proven: *taxiarchos* (taxa leader), *pentekonarchos* (phalanx leader)
- Dedicated: *dekarchos* (company leader), *stratiotes* (soldier)

LEADER

The Grand Domestic is Andronikos Palaiologos Kantakouzenos (see Gallery of Rogues, later)

WHAT THEY SAY THEY WANT

Provide the Empire with an army

WHAT THEY REALLY WANT

Reconquer the world for the Empire

ALLIES & ENEMIES

In theory they are allied to the Office of the Military Fisc, but in practice relations are strained as the Fisc can rarely fulfil their requests. Rivalry with the Naval Office – driven mostly by the feud between the Notaras and Kantakouzenos families – exists, but the Navy is very much the junior partner here.

LINKS

- Allagion (ORG-1)
- Imperial Court (ORG-6)
- Andronikos Kantakouzenos (NPC-3)
- Great Palace / Konsisterion (PA-7)
- Exakionion (ST-2)

ORG-14 ATELEUTOI

TYPE

Secret Cabal

NATURE

The Ateleutoi, or "Endless Ones", are a group of immortals who some claim are the true rulers of Constantinople. Their existence is speculated on by various conspiracy theorists, but no one has any proof of their existence and their purported deeds are a running joke amongst the people of the City. Rumoured candidates for membership include: the goddess Hekate; one or more saints (favourites are Constantine the Great, his mother Helena, and Saint Theodosia); the king of the ghouls; the centaur Kheiron; a sorcerer or alchemist who has discovered the secret of eternal life; the ghost of a murdered nun; and/or Theodoros Palaiologos, the brother of the current Emperor.

LEADER

None.

WHAT THEY SAY THEY WANT

The continuation of the City

WHAT THEY REALLY WANT

Varies, each member is presumed to have their own agenda

ALLIES & ENEMIES

Unknown. Even if they exist, the fact that few believe that they do makes it difficult for them to forge alliances or enmities as a group.

LINKS

- None

ORG-15 THE CATHOLIC CHURCH

TYPE RELIGIOUS SECT

NATURE

The dominant faith in Europe. The Catholic Church has the Pope, as Patriarch of Rome, at its head, and a College of Cardinals guides the Pope in political and religious matters. Beneath the cardinals are the archbishops and bishops, who typically rule over regions and cities respectively.

LEADER

Bishop Isidoros of Kiev is the leader of the Catholic Church in Constantinople.

WHAT THEY SAY THEY WANT

Salvation for all humankind

WHAT THEY REALLY WANT

Salvation for Catholics

ALLIES & ENEMIES

Since the Union of the Churches, the Catholic and Orthodox Churches are united in a common cause. As well as the Orthodox Anti-Unionists, there are detractors in Catholic lands as well. The Catholic Church has other opponents too, in the shape of Jan Hus. On the political front, the Catholic Church cannot always rely on the support of Catholic monarchs, and often has to negotiate assistance. The Knights Hospitallers are the Catholic Church's remaining military order of any note.

LINKS

- The Hospitallers (ORG-4)
- Isidoros of Kiev (NPC-17)

ORG-16 THE CHANCELLERY

TYPE

Political Guild

NATURE

The *Sekreton*, or Chancellery, is central to the vast bureaucracy of the Byzantine court. It fulfils three vital functions: the Office of the Treasury, the Office of the Praitor, and the Judiciary. Overseeing all three is the Grand Logothete (*megas logothetes*), who holds a role equivalent to the Chancellor in western nations and ranked ninth in the imperial hierarchy.

The Grand Logothete's chief subordinate is the praitor ton demon, the civil administrator of the city of Constantinople and himself holding the 23rd rank of the court. To assist him, the praitor has the chief judicial officer (*koiaistor*) who commands the judges, drafts legislation, maintains the court of appeals, and is the public trustee for wills. The praitor is also served by the sergeant-at-arms who commands the Vardariotai (see page 110), and the tribounos who is responsible for maintaining the roads, monuments, and buildings of Constantinople. Under the tribunos is a subordinate tribune for each of the city's districts.

Another subordinate of the Grand Logothete is the grand treasurer, who is technically the supervisor of the other logothetes. In practice, each logothete refuses to be managed by the Grand Logothete's office and operates independently. This department is also responsible for minting new coinage (under the authority of the master of the mint), maintaining the imperial estates and religious foundations, and financing the repair of the empire's infrastructure. The port authority is in charge of the seashore and the city's ports, particularly the collection of tolls.

The office of the Grand Logothete is found in the Daphne within the Great Palace, although the Praitor has his own headquarters at the Forum of Constantine. The regulation colours are blue with a white trim.

DIGNITARIES BY RANK

- Leader: Megas Logothetes (Grand Logothete)
- Overseer: Praitor ton demon
- Overseer: *koiaistor* (quaestor)
  - Proven: *krita* (judge)
  - Dedicated: *nomikos* (jurist)
- Overseer: *megas tzaousios* (sergeant-at-arms)
  - Proven: *nykteparchos* (prefect of the night watch)
  - Dedicated: Vardiariotai (ORG-35)
- Overseer: *tribunos* (tribune)
  - Proven: *geitoniarchos* (district tribune)
  - Dedicated: *kankellarios* (clerk), notarios (scribe),
- Overseer: *megas sakellarios* (grand treasurer), *chrysoepsetes* (master of the mint)
  - Proven: *sakellarios* (treasurer), *logariastes* (accountant), *chartoularios* (chartulary), *parathalassites* (port authority)
  - Dedicated: *kankellarios* (clerk), *notarios* (scribe),

LEADER

The Grand Logothete of the Sekreton is Loukas Notaras (see Gallery of Rogues, later). The Praitor is Demetrios Metochites, the sergeant-at-arms Nikephoros Notaras (see Vardariotai, later), the tribunos Leo Barzanes, and the koiastor Petriotes Spyridon.

WHAT THEY SAY THEY WANT

To serve the empire

WHAT THEY REALLY WANT

To rule the empire

ALLIES & ENEMIES

The Chancellery is by definition the enemy of all who would disrupt the law and order of the City and empire. In addition to the various criminal gangs, the biggest enemy of this department is the Prasinoi. The works of the Chancellery are often resisted by those politically opposed to the Grand Logothetes himself (see later). As one of the major political offices in the city, officials of the Chancellery should find allies amongst all hard-working people: in practice many find that the law works for the dynatoi and few others besides.

LINKS

- Imperial Court (ORG-6)
- Demetrios Metochites (NPC-9)
- Loukas Notaras (NPC-20)
- Praitorion (KN-13)
- Great Palace / Daphne (PA-7)

ORG-17 DRAZAN'S GANG

TYPE

Criminal Gang

NATURE

The second largest criminal organisation in Constantinople has no real name other than "Dražan's Gang": the Bulgarian crime boss built his organisation over the last 30 years by taking over the disparate gangs of Vlanga (see page 178). His influence over criminal activities in Vlanga is near total: only a fool would go against a man whose by-name means "the Greek-killer". As well as controlling the gambling, prostitution, and extortion in Vlanga, his two big money-earners are money-lending and theft. Dražan runs an illegal moneylending enterprise, ignoring the Imperial monopoly controlled by the Guild of Moneylenders and Bankers. His interest rates are punishing, and he probably profits more from debt-slavery than he does from the interest. His army of enforcers are also thugs-for-hire for anyone with enough money, and it is widely rumoured that Dražan arranges for people to turn up dead at the behest of rich clients.

Dražan also controls gangs of thieves throughout the City. He takes a cut of much of the city-wide larceny, whether it is house-breaking, mugging, or pick-pocketing. If a freelance thief is spotted and reported by one of Dražan's thieves, he can expect a visit from one of the bosses' lieutenants, a meeting which can only go two ways. Either they become the newest employee of Dražan, paying half of their income to him, or else they lose a limb of their choice. The snitch gets a reward for his efforts.

LEADER

Dražan Romanoktonos maintains an iron grip over his gang. It is small enough for him to oversee most operations directly or with the help of a handful of lieutenants.

WHAT THEY SAY THEY WANT

Maintain current territories and income

WHAT THEY REALLY WANT

Expand current territories and income

ALLIES & ENEMIES

The Vardariotai are Dražan's biggest foe. They are determined to bring him down, but must do this publically and with incontrovertible evidence, else he will wriggle free from their hook like he has so many times already. Dražan has an arrangement with both the Zanconi Family and Star and Crescent, but they are no means allies. His treaty with the Zanconi revolves around the demarcation of territorial boundaries (Dražan gets Vlanga, the Zanconi get everywhere else), and the protection of Zanconi operations from thieves. The Star and Crescent pay a yearly fee to Dražan in return for the right to sell opium in his territory. Neither rival gang have any illusions regarding Dražan's ambition.

LINKS

- Dražan Romanoktonos (NPC-10)

ORG-18 IMPERIAL ARCHIVES

TYPE

Political Guild

NATURE

The Imperial Archives, or *Chartothesion*, is run by the First Secretary (protasekritis), ranked 29th in the imperial hierarchy. He assists the mesazon and is responsible for all the official documentation of the Empire. His chief subordinates are the *mystikos* (literally "secret-keeper") who is the emperor's personal secretary, the dekanos who is in charge of the imperial papers, the keeper of the Imperial Inkstand (which contains the special crimson ink used in all official documents), and the *dikaiodotes* who affixes the imperial seal and issues all imperial commands.

These officers are assisted by an army of senior notaries (*asekritai*), record keepers (*chartoularioi*), and copyists. Most of the neighbourhood of Kanikleion in Kainopolis is given over to the Imperial Archives, providing homes and offices for the cogs in the machinery of the court. The regulation colours are green and red.

DIGNITARIES BY RANK

LEADER

Protasekritis (First Secretary): Alexios Palaiologos Tzamplakon

- Overseer: mystikos (private secretary), *dekanos* (in charge of imperial papers), *kanikleios* (keeper of the inkstand), dikaiodotes (dispenser of laws)
- Proven: *asekritis* (secretary), chartoularios (chartulary), *antigrapheos* (copyist)
- Dedicated: *kankellarios* (clerk), *notarios* (scribe)

WHAT THEY SAY THEY WANT

To administer to the empire's paperwork

WHAT THEY REALLY WANT

To conceal the fact that the Archives cannot keep up with the demands made of it.

ALLIES & ENEMIES

Most other governmental departments have a neutral attitude towards the Imperial Archives – paperwork is a necessary evil of a well-run bureaucracy. Most needs of the department are grudgingly served by the rest of the court.

LINKS

- Imperial Court (ORG-6)
- Alexios Tzamplakon (NPC-1)
- Kanikleion (KN-9)

ORG-19 IMPERIAL HOUSEHOLD

TYPE

Political Guild

NATURE

The Imperial Household (Vestarion) is the ministry that takes cares of the personal wardrobe of the emperor, organise the palace servants and attend to his personal finances. The Vestarion also includes officials who perform the same service for the empress (when there is one). The Imperial Household is responsible for arranging parades, receptions, appointments, feast days, and controlling the imperial calendar. Naturally, this department is located at the Blachernai Palace. Its regulation colours are green and gold.

The Protovestiarios who heads the Vestarion, ranks sixth in the order of precedence. There is a concierge assigned to each of the imperial palaces, responsible for the security, cleaning, and maintenance of the building. Every hall has its own chamberlain, who commands subordinates that attend to heating, lighting, and other amenities. These subordinates are not servants, but dignitary-holders who command the domestic staff. The concierges all report to the grand concierge who attends the emperor at the Blachernai Palace. Amongst the emperor's retinue are other courtiers such as the cupbearer and the domestic in charge of the imperial table.

DIGNITARIES BY RANK

- Leader: *Protovestiarios*
- Overseer: *megas papias* (grand concierge), *papias* (concierge), *minsourator* (in charge of imperial tent on campaign)
- Proven: *pinkernes* (cupbearer), *domestikos tes trapezes* (domestic of the table), *diaitarios* (chamberlain of a hall)
- Dedicated: *loustes* (responsible for baths), *kandelaptes* (in charge of lighting), *kamenades* (in charge of heating), *horologos* (in charge of clocks)

LEADER

The Protovestarios is Georgios Sphrantzes, the emperor's close friend, breaking with tradition that grants this role to a minor relative of the emperor.

WHAT THEY SAY THEY WANT
To serve the emperor

WHAT THEY REALLY WANT
To keep the empire looking strong to outsiders.

ALLIES & ENEMIES
Cash-strapped departments – particularly those lower in the court hierarchy – look enviously at the budget of the Protovestiarios, but do little to curtail it, understanding that the pomp and circumstance that surrounds the emperor is important in maintaining the façade of a thriving and powerful nation.

LINKS

- Imperial Court (ORG-6)
- Georgios Sphrantzes (NPC-13)
- Blachernai Palace (BL-3)

ORG-20 IMPERIAL LIBRARY

TYPE
Political Guild

NATURE
The Imperial Library or Bibliotheka was instituted by Constantius II in the fourth century with a special interest in Holy Scripture. This first imperial library was believed to consist of 120,000 volumes of ancient texts transferred from papyrus to parchment by the army of scribes. However, the library was burnt in 473 and most of the volumes were lost. Over the next 800 years the library was rebuilt, only to be destroyed again in the Sack of Constantinople in 1204 when it was burnt by Venetians and its staff executed. However, learning from last time, the library was not all maintained in one building, and many of the volumes were preserved and smuggled out of Constantinople. When the empire was restored in 1261, the library returned to the city and was rehoused in The Stoudion (ST-9). The head of the department, the Grand Librarian or megas anagnostes, occupies the 51st rank in the court and is ably assisted by readers and scribes, who work diligently to restore the older texts and transcribe knowledge at risk of being lost forever. The preservation of texts is the prime work of the Imperial Library. Not only do they labour to make copies of the vital texts, the readers and scribes reconstruct ancient texts from scattered fragments, and provide grammars, commentaries, and paraphrases of the great works.

Another overlooked function of the Imperial Library is acquisitions, and its agents can be found all over the known world, scouring libraries for texts that the Imperial Library does not have, and acquiring them by whatever means necessary. A staggering proportion of the books in the Bibliotheka have been stolen from the repositories of the Franks, Persia, and even further afield. Life as a librarian is not always dull!

Books are only lent under the most extreme of circumstances; normal procedure is for a book to be consulted, under the supervision of one of the library staff, at an approved location. No naked flames are allowed near the books, and they must be read on a cedar wood bookstand and stored in cedar chests to ward off any pests that might destroy the parchment. The use of cursors (ivory wands used to read lines and turn the pages) are obligatory. This may seem over-cautious but some of these books have been pieced together from fragments over several lifetimes, and library staff make frequent research trips to distant lands in search of unblemished copies of partial texts owned by the Library. Every one is treated like a sacred object.

A trusted reader may make a copy of a book or pay for one to be made. There are stipulations: every copy must be made as a pair, and the library keeps the spare. Further, any copies made from the purchased manuscript belong to the Library, not to the reader or the copyist; and so on for any descendants. These second-generation copies are usually exchanged for books possessed by the copyists that are not already in the Imperial Library. Any duplicate texts are sold to other libraries or exchanged for other texts, and these sales are what allow the Imperial Library to continue its mammoth task of recording all human knowledge.

The regulation colours of the Imperial Library are white with a blue trim.

DIGNITARIES BY RANK

- Leader: *Megas Anagnostes* (Grand Librarian)
- Overseer: *chartophylax* (chief librarian, document-guardian)
- Proven: *logios* (scholar), *antigrapheos* (copyist), *bibliothekes* (librarian)
- Dedicated: notarios (scribe)

LEADER
The Megas Anagnostes is Antonios Chrysoloras

WHAT THEY SAY THEY WANT
To preserve the knowledge of the past and present for the future

WHAT THEY REALLY WANT
To conceal how much knowledge has been lost

ALLIES & ENEMIES
For generations the Imperial Library has considered the other departments of the court to be rivals. Successive Anagnostes have encouraged an atmosphere of paranoia amongst their staff: conservation and restoration being the main orders of business, and scholars wishing to actually study from the books are thieves and despoilers who cannot be trusted to treat a text with appropriate care. By imperial edict, members of the Imperial University are permitted access but this edict is carried out with varying degrees of success and attempts to see it repealed are regularly brought to meetings of the court.

LINKS

- Imperial Court (ORG-6)
- The Stoudion (ST-9)

ORG-21 IMPERIAL ORPHANAGE

TYPE

Political Guild

NATURE

The Imperial Orphanage or *Orphanotropheion* is one of the ancient institutions of the city. The post of Orphanotrophos is 55th in court rank and is typically held by a clergyman, and it carries a high degree of prestige for a charitable position. The city has two main orphanages under the control of this office, one in the acropolis and one near the Gate of Eugenios. The Imperial Orphanage is responsible for any orphaned child up to the age of 20. The Orphanotrophos is their legal guardian and steward of any wealth they may have inherited until that age, unless they marry before that at which point their wealth is released to them. He has several subordinates who administer the secondary houses, care for the finances and for the gathering of alms, as well as teachers who provide tuition for the orphans. As well as orphanages, this office administers all charitable donations of the emperor, including the veterans' hospital and several ptochotrophia or poor-houses. Considering the size and narrow scope of this department, the Orphanotrophos has a remarkable influence over court politics, even despite being the lowest ranking of the twelve ministries. The Office is left to govern itself without governmental interference; managing its own budget and appointing its own staff – even to the extent of choosing its own replacement for the Orphanotrophos on the passing of the previous incumbent. The Orphanotrophos is chosen by the uncontested nomination of the master of the Orphanage of Saint Paul.

The Imperial Orphanage has no office to speak of, but the Orphanotropheion itself in Akropolis is seen as its headquarters. The regulation colours are white with a black trim.

DIGNITARIES BY RANK

- ϕ Leader: *Orphanotrophos*
- ϕ Overseer: *chartoularios tou oikou* (house master), *chartoularios tou hosiou* (secretary of the saint)
- ϕ Proven: *kourator* (curator), *arkarios* (investor), *logariastes* (accountant)
- ϕ Dedicated: *baioulos* (tutor)

LEADER

The Orphanotrophos is currently Michael Serron (NPC-21).

WHAT THEY SAY THEY WANT

To serve the people of the empire

WHAT THEY REALLY WANT

To serve the people of the empire

ALLIES & ENEMIES

The Imperial Orphanage attracts a lot of jealousy from other government departments, particularly for its large budget; which it mostly gives away rather than spend on more 'worthy' causes. One tenth of the emperor's personal income is also donated to the Orphanage, along with uncounted capitals and lump sums offered by former emperors, former residents, and the God-fearing wealthy.

LINKS

- ϕ Imperial Court (ORG-6)
- ϕ Michael Serron (NPC-21)
- ϕ Orphanage of Saint Paul (AK-11)

ORG-22 IMPERIAL UNIVERSITY

TYPE

Political Guild

NATURE

The Imperial University or *Pandidakterion* is a combination of the Roman university founded by Theodosius II in 425 with the School of Magnaura in the ninth century and the Capitol School in the eleventh century. This ministry is responsible for administering three schools, the Pandidakterion proper, the Law School, and the Patriarchal School. The Pandidakterion is by far the largest of the three schools, and the minister in charge of the University is also president of the Pandidakterion.

The main purpose of the university has always been to train bureaucrats for the Imperial court and clerics for the church. The Pandidakterion is headed by the president of the University, the hypatos ton philosophon (ranks 28th in the imperial hierarchy). His principal subordinates are the *nomophylax* (literally the "guardian of the law") who is the president of the Law School, and the maistor rhetoron, who is one of the five teachers at the Patriarchal School (see page 156), although the only one who is appointed by the emperor rather than the patriarch.

The primary curriculum consists of a grounding in the trivium of logic, grammar, and rhetoric, and the advanced quadrivium of arithmetic, geometry, astronomy, and music. Students are expected to learn in both Latin and Greek, and passing the examinations results in a basic or bachelor degree. Advanced degrees – doctorates – may be sought in the faculties of rhetoric, philosophy, medicine,

STUDYING FROM TEXTS

Members of the Pandidakterion are guaranteed borrowing rights from the Imperial Library by imperial edict, although the speed with which a book is retrieved depends very much on its rarity, the status of the borrower, and the personality of the librarian through whom the request is made.

Books can be used as temporary Affiliations: a book serves as a source of information on its subject (usually a Lore), although the Skill level is limited the Literacy and Language Skills of the reader.

Books can also be used to Train a Skill (Mythras rulebook page 73). Each book should be assigned a Skill level, with 50% being a basic introduction, 75% being an intermediate work, and 90%+ being an advanced or comprehensive text. As above, the Skill is limited by the Literacy and Language Skills of the reader. Before studying, the student should make a roll on his current Skill; and the result is interpreted as if the character had made a Teaching Skill roll (Mythras page 73).

and (at Magnaura) law. The students have an individual contracts with each of their assigned teachers detailing the expectations on their time on both sides.

The teachers in charge of the day-to-day education are the *didaskaloi*, who operate under instruction from the kathegetes or professors. The didaskaloi may only hold a basic degree, but all kathegetes hold an advanced degree. There are places for 31 professors but the school has not operated with a full academic board since the restitution of the Empire. The masters are teachers first and scholars second.

Unusually amongst the universities of Europe, the Pandidakterion has equality in education for men and women; Imperial policy is that education is available to all, and Frankish visitors to Constantinople find it scandalous that it has nearly as many female students as it does male ones. Another feature which sets it apart from its Frankish counterparts is the teaching at the Pandidakterion proper is entirely secular and the Church has no say in the curriculum. Consequently, it maintains an active tradition of Platonic and Aristotelian philosophy.

The Kapetolion building at the Philadelphion in Vlanga is the headquarters of the Imperial University as well as the Pandidakterion. The regulation colours are blue and orange-yellow.

DIGNITARIES BY RANK

- Leader: *Hypatos ton Philosophon*
- Overseer: *Nomophylax* (president of the Law School), *Maistor Rhetoron* (secular governor of the Patriarchal School)
- Proven: *kathegetes* (professor)
- Dedicated: *disaskalos* (teacher)

LEADER

The Hypatos is Michael Komnenos, who serves as both the governmental minister in charge of education as well as being the president of the Pandidakterion.

WHAT THEY SAY THEY WANT

To provide an education for the city's elite

WHAT THEY REALLY WANT

To train the next generation of bureaucrats

ALLIES & ENEMIES

The Imperial University is technically at odds with all 11 government ministries, because they are all competing for the same limited resources. There is a theoretical synergies with the Imperial Library and the Imperial Archives, but personal jealousies and grudges tend to prevent these departments from working smoothly with one another. Virtually all the bureaucrats of the state received their education in one of the University's three schools, and their experiences there colour their attitudes today.

LINKS

- Imperial Court (ORG-6)
- Magnaura Palace (PA-12)
- Patriarchal School (PA-15)
- Philadelphion / Pandidakterion (VL-11)

ORG-23 MOURTATOI

TYPE

Irregular Regiment

NATURE

The *Mourtatoi* are a unit of infantry archers and crossbowmen of mixed Greco-Turkish parentage, mostly deriving from an alliance with the Emirate of Aydin in southwest Anatolia in the mid fourteenth century. They have a reputation for savagery, although nominally Christian their behaviour does not suggest this; they have been likened to caged beasts that the Emperor lets loose when there is a bigger threat that needs defeating. They are trained in the use of a bow, and like the Anatolian Turks employ a variety of bows including a long range bow, war bow, and target bow. They also train on horseback, but do not go mounted into battle.

LEADER

The leader of the regiment is the *stratopedarches* of the Mourtatoi, who ranks between the Protallagator of the Paramonai and the stratopedarches of the Tzakones

WHAT THEY SAY THEY WANT

Serve the Empire

WHAT THEY REALLY WANT

Serve the Empire

ALLIES & ENEMIES

The Mourtatoi have a generations-old feud with the Ottoman Turks, who long coveted their ancestral lands and made numerous raids against Aydin. Most members of the Mourtatoi have had a family tragedy at the hands of the Ottomans, and show them no mercy.

LINKS

- Army Office (ORG-14)

ORG-24 NAVAL OFFICE

TYPE

Political Guild

NATURE

The Naval Office or *Ploimon* is in charge of the empire's military fleet. The Grand Doux of the Fleet is the head of the navy and seventh rank in the overall hierarchy of the court. He is assisted by the megas droungarios of the fleet who is in command of the naval officers. An admiral answers directly to the megas doux and is responsible for any foreign ships in the fleet. The captains of each ship occupy the next level of the hierarchy; formerly there was a droungarokomes between the nauarchos and the megas droungarios who commanded a squadron of ships, but with the parlous state of the Byzantine navy, this rank is not currently in use except as the head of the neighbourhood of Dalmaton. The Naval Office headquarters are in the Augustaios of the Great Palace, although most of the officers are stationed in Dalmaton. The regulation colours are blue and gold.

Given that the Byzantine navy consists of just 12 ships, the Ploimon is probably the most over-staffed of the 12 ministries, employing four times as many captains as there are ships.

DIGNITARIES BY RANK

- Leader: *Megas Doux tou stolou*
- Overseer: *megas droungarios, admyriales* (admiral)
- Proven: *nauarchos* (captain)
- Dedicated: *Prosalentes* (sailor)

LEADER

The Megas Doux is Loukas Notaras (see Gallery of Rogues, later), whose double duty as Grand Logothete takes up all his time, and the day-to-day business of the Naval Office (not that there is much) is handled by the Megas Droungarios.

WHAT THEY SAY THEY WANT

Provide the Empire with a Navy

WHAT THEY REALLY WANT

Rebuild the Empire's Navy

ALLIES & ENEMIES

A principal task allotted the Navy is the patrol of the Sea of Marmara, and to protect Byzantine ships from pirates. This has earned them some enemies, not least amongst the corsairs employed by the Republic of Venice.

LINKS

- Imperial Court (ORG-6)
- Loukas Notaras (NPC-20)
- Great Palace / Augustaios (PA-7)
- Dalmaton (ST-1)

ORG-25 OFFICE OF THE DROME

TYPE

Political Guild

NATURE

The public face of the Drome is the public post and ambassadorial wing of the government. Its other role – espionage and state security – is an open secret. It began as the imperial message service, organising the messengers and postal stations across the empire. In the tenth century the Drome assumed control of domestic security and the Empire's foreign affairs, handling intelligence, diplomacy, the reception of ambassadors, and the negotiation of treaties. The Logothete of the Drome is the chief officer of this department, and ranks 27th in the hierarchy of the court. His staff includes the chief of the embassy, ambassadors to foreign lands, translators, messengers, and of course, spies (*praktores*, "agents"). Most of the staff of the ministry are really messengers, translators, and ambassadorial staff: foreign governments would be surprised just how few spies the Logothete of the Drome has at his disposal and how thinly stretched they are.

All Drome agents have an official position in the public side of the ministry, giving them a legitimate reason to visit foreign courts and travel through hostile territory. They are a direct descendent of the *agentes in rebus* (Latin: "those active in matters"), who were the intelligence officers of the Roman Empire. Like their predecessors, praktores of the Drome serve as carriers of military dispatches and letters or supervisors of roads and inns of the Drome, as well as verifying warrants, supervising the arrest of senior officials, escorting exiles out of Byzantine lands, and delivering imperial commands. While conducting these duties they have an imperial mandate to ensure the security of the Empire, and are afforded a degree of latitude in interpreting this mandate. They still go by the name of the *magistrianoi* ("magistrate's men") following the old title of magister for the Logothete of the Drome.

The offices of the Drome are located within the Great palace, in the Triklinos of the Candidatii. Its regulation colours are blue and red.

DIGNITARIES BY RANK

- Leader: *Logothetes tou dromou* (Logothete of the Drome)
- Overseer: *protonotarios tou dromou* (senior deputy of logothete), *kourator tou apokrisiareiou* (chief of the embassy), *presbeutis* (ambassador)
- Proven: *hermeneutes* (translator), kourator (curator), *sakellarios* (treasurer), logariastes (accountant), chartoularios (chartulary)
- Dedicated: diatrechon (courier), mandator (messenger)

LEADER

The Logothete of the Drome is Thomas Strouthion.

WHAT THEY SAY THEY WANT

The security of the empire

WHAT THEY REALLY WANT

The security of the empire

ALLIES & ENEMIES

The main enemy of the Office of the Drome is the spy network run by the Valide Sultan, the mother of the Ottoman ruler. The Paramonai regiment are the 'special forces' of the Drome, a unit of highly trained and swift-moving soldiers whose missions mostly revolve around extracting agents, apprehending political fugitives, and the occasional state-sanctioned assassination.

LINKS

- Imperial Court (ORG-6)
- Thomas Strouthion (NPC-25)
- Apokrisiarion (BL-1)
- Great Palace/Triklinos of the Candidati (PA-7)

ORG-26 THE GENERAL FISC

TYPE

Political Guild

NATURE

The General Fisc or *Genikon* is responsible for general taxation and revenue. It is one of the two treasury departments, the other being the Special Fisc. The General Fisc also tries legal cases of financial improbity. The General Logothete heads the department, he is ranked 18th in the hierarchy. As well as the usual fiscal officers of treasurers, accountants and chartularies, an army of curators of imperial estates, tax collectors, and customs officials serves him. The Counts of the Waters have the important task of maintaining the aqueduct and cisterns of the city. The Counts of the Mines oversee the mines and the bullion. The Genikon is located in the Great Palace, within the Triklinos of Lausiakos. Its regulation colours are green and white.

DIGNITARIES BY RANK

- Leader: *Logothetes tou genikou* (General Logothete)
- Overseer: *komes hydaton* (count of the waters), *komes lamias* (count of the mines), *exochartoularios* (chartulary of a province), *chartoularios tou oikistikou* (chartulary of exemptions), *domestikos tes kouratorias* (domestic of imperial domains)
- Proven: kourator (curator), *dioiketes* (tax collector), *kommerkiarios* (customs officer), sakellarios (treasurer), logariastes (accountant), chartoularios (chartulary)
- Dedicated: kankellarios (clerk), notarios (scribe)

LEADER

The General Logothete is Theologos Notaras Pylles.

WHAT THEY SAY THEY WANT

Administer the finances of the empire

WHAT THEY REALLY WANT

Reverse the crippling state of the empire's finances

ALLIES & ENEMIES

The General Logothete is a puppet (and second cousin) of Chancellor Loukas Notaras.

LINKS

- Imperial Court (ORG-6)
- Great Palace / Triklinos of Lausiakos (PA-7)

ORG-27 THE MILITARY FISC

TYPE

Political Guild

NATURE

The Military Fisc or *Stratiotikon* is the ministry responsible for all financial matters relating to the army and navy, keeping them in a state of perpetual readiness for war. This includes the possibility of living under siege. It is responsible for supplying the army with food, equipment, and horses and for organising the pay and the pensions of the soldiers – although the salaries themselves come from the budget of the Army and Naval Offices. The department is run by the Military Logothete, who ranks 46th in the imperial hierarchy. His two chief officers are the paymaster-in-chief who is in charge of the salaries of the army and navy, and the quartermaster-general who is the chief procurer of military materiel. The Military Fisc is quartered in the Strategion in Akropolis. Its regulation colours are red and white.

DIGNITARIES BY RANK

- Leader: *Logothetes tou stratiotikou* (Military Logothete)
- Overseer: *chartoularios ton thematon* (financial officer of the provinces, mostly defunct), *megas aktouarios* (paymaster-in-chief), *stratopedarches* (quartermaster-general)
- Proven: *aktouarios* (paymaster), *prokourator* (procurer), legatarios (legate), sakellarios (treasurer), logariastes (accountant), chartoularios (chartulary)
- Dedicated: *mandator* (messenger), kankellarios (clerk), notarios (scribe)

LEADER

The Military Logothete is Manuel Palaiologos Iagaris (See page 204), an ambitious man for whom the pressure of meeting the demands of the Byzantine Army and Navy is almost too much.

WHAT THEY SAY THEY WANT

Keep the army battle-ready

WHAT THEY REALLY WANT

Improve political rank

ALLIES & ENEMIES

The Military Logothete sees the Army Office in general and the Grand Domestic in particular as an antagonist, despite the supposed partnership between the two ministries. In his opinion, the Grand Domestic has no idea about the cost of maintaining an army, and is always putting in requests for finances, often for expenditures already made.

LINKS

- Imperial Court (ORG-6)
- Strategion (AK-12)

ORG-28 THE SPECIAL FISC

TYPE

Political Guild

NATURE

The Special Fisc, or *Eidikon*, is one of two treasury departments, responsible for supervising the imperial treasury, consisting of precious materials belonging to the state such as gold, silk, and spices. The Special Logothete ranks 38th in the imperial hierarchy. His officers include the imperial clerk, the guild overseer, and the masters of each imperial factory. The imperial clerk administers the salaries of all state officials and organises all imperial tours and travel. The guild overseer is the supervisor of all masters of imperial guilds, and his army of inspectors administer the imperial guilds and issue licences to private guilds. The imperial factories (ergodosia) are responsible for producing raw materials under imperial control, whether it is ore-processing, livestock rearing, or wine-growing.

The Eidikon is located in the Great Palace, within the Triklinos of Justinianos. Its regulation colours are yellow and white.

DIGNITARIES BY RANK

- Leader: *Logothetes tou eidikou* (Special Logothete)
- Overseer: *basilikos notarios* (Imperial clerk), *archon ton ergodosion* (master of a factory), symponos (guild overseer)
- Proven: kourator (curator), *meiziteros ton ergodosion* (foreman of the factory), *episkeptetes* (inspector), sakellarios (treasurer), logariastes (accountant), chartoularios (chartulary)
- Dedicated: kankellarios (clerk), notarios (scribe)

LEADER

The Special Logothete is Konstantinos Sigeros Doukas

WHAT THEY SAY THEY WANT

Collect monies owed to the state

WHAT THEY REALLY WANT

Take as much money out of private hands and into the state coffers as possible

ALLIES & ENEMIES

The Special Fisc contends with the General Fisc for jurisdiction over some sources of income, which amounts to a turf war at times. As an office they are no more corrupt than any other governmental department, but as they have a great deal of contact with business owners, officers have a reputation for rapaciousness and avarice.

LINKS

- Imperial Court (ORG-6)
- Great Palace / Triklinos of Justianios (PA-7)

ORG-29 ORDER OF THE DRAGON

TYPE

Aristocratic Regiment

NATURE

The Order of the Dragon (Latin: *Societas Draconistarum*, "society of dragonists") is one of the best-known secular military orders. It was founded in 1408 by Sigismund, Holy Roman Emperor and King of Hungary after the Battle of Dobor, which was fought against the Bogomil heresy and the Church of Bosnia. It is a Catholic organisation with many members of German, Italian, Serbian, Hungarian, Polish, and Wallachian descent. The membership includes notables such as King Alphonse V of Aragon, King Ferdinand of Naples, Despot Stjepan Lazarevic of Serbia, Vlad II Dracul of Wallachia, as well as several significant Florentine and English noblemen.

All members of the Order must be knights, and they are divided into an inferior order who have sworn an oath to uphold the aims of the order, and a superior order that have actually fought in battle against "the followers of the ancient Dragon" – Ottomans and other enemies of the Catholic faith. The Order of the Dragon has its headquarters in Nuremberg, from here it plans campaigns against the Turk, both military exercises and political intrigues to motivate Western Europe against the threat they pose. There are rumours that some Dragonists have turned to Sorcery in search of weapons to use against their hated enemy.

The Order uses two symbols: an equal-armed red cross with golden flames issuing from all four ends; and a dragon curved into a circle, its tail winding around its own neck. Both are used by the Superior rank, whereas the Inferior ranks use just the dragon symbol.

LEADER

The Grand Master of the Order was Sigismund and his wife Beatrice. He has yet to be replaced, so the Order is run by the council of 21 masters, the original members or their nominated successors.

WHAT THEY SAY THEY WANT

The stated goal of the Order of the Dragon is, to quote from the oath sworn by all members, *"to crush the pernicious deeds of the same perfidious Enemy, and of the followers of the ancient Dragon, and ... of the pagan knights, schismatics, and other nations of fallen faith, and those envious of the Cross of Christ, and of our kingdoms, and of his holy and saving religion of faith, under the banner of the triumphant Cross of Christ..."*. The "perfidious Enemy" referred to is the Ottoman Empire.

WHAT THEY REALLY WANT

While the order as a whole certainly desires to see the Dragon crushed, individual members are often second, third, or more junior sons who join to get the political influence and military fame not normally meted out to noblemen low down the birth order of their family. As Dragonists, they get to rub shoulders with kings and heroes.

ALLIES & ENEMIES

The Order is the declared enemy of Ottomans in particular and Muslims in general, but also "schismatics" – Orthodox Christians, Nestorians, and the like – as well as pagans. The Order of the

Dragon is on good terms with most European nations, especially Hungary and the Holy Roman Empire who they assist in various crusades against Turkish incursions.

LINKS

- Catholic Church (ORG-15)

ORG-30 ORDER OF KAPPA-PI-ALPHA

TYPE
Animist cult

NATURE
A small monastery in Stoudion dedicated to the saints Karpos, Papylos, and Agathonike (see page 173) is the centre of this cult dedicated to the extirpation of all evil spirits. The Order uses a monogram of the initial letters of its three patron saints, from whence it gains its common name. The order provides its services free of charge. Its members are driven by their own personal crusade against the foot soldiers of the Devil.

The Order accepts anyone who is willing to take on the battle against evil. Many of its lay members are those who it has helped in the past, and it calls upon them for vigilance against malicious spirits and occasionally for support. For those who learn the trade of an animist, the order can offer a small stipend supplied by the Orthodox Church, although it is not enough to live on. The Order teaches Trance for the detection and identification of spirits, Binding for the purposes of spirit combat, and Folk Magic. The cult teaches the spells of Avert, Spiritshield, Witchsight, Vigour, and Voice.

Those ordained as an *exorkistes* (exorcist) gain a minor ecclesiastical rank junior to deacon. An exorkistes can augment his Binding Skill with his Lore (Theology) when fighting in Spirit Combat, and is also able to dissipate spirits that he defeats. Animists trained by the cult but who have not been ordained can still exorcise a possessing spirit or bind it into a fetish, but not dissipate it. Not all members of the Order become exorkistes, mostly for personal reasons such as a dislike for the Church. Characters with the Charisms of Discernment or Faith (see page 77) are particularly sought out by the Order, although it has no means by which these Gifts can be given to its members. The monks at the Martyrion curate the knowledge gathered by the order over the centuries, and train members in relevant skills.

At its core, the Order has four experienced demon-hunters, six monks, a handful of trainees, and perhaps a hundred people across the city who have personal experience of the Order's activities and who count as lay members of the cult.

LEADER
The cult has no official leader. The hegemon (abbot) of the Martyrion of Saints Karpos and Papylos has a dispensation from the patriarch to ordain exorkistes; but it is the experienced demon-hunters who have a say in directing the goals of the Order.

WHAT THEY SAY THEY WANT
Eradication of all evil spirits

WHAT THEY REALLY WANT
Eradication of all evil spirits

ALLIES & ENEMIES
The Order is allied to the Orthodox Church through the Martyrion. However, the church tries to keep the activities of the Order a secret, which causes tension with some of its members. Every infernal spirit is an enemy of the Order, fortunately for its members most spirits are entirely ignorant of its existence.

LINKS

- Patriarchate of Constantinople (ORG-8)
- Martyrion of Saints Karpos and Papylos (ST-4)

ORG-31 PARAMONAI

TYPE
Special Forces Company

NATURE
The *Paramonai* are the least well known of the four Guard regiments, being the smallest and also the most secretive. They are trained as both horsemen and foot soldiers and are best known for their longswords. The emperor uses the Paramonai for sudden, decisive action; they are swift, well trained, and deadly. They are used to apprehend or assassinate fugitives and recover sensitive information from hostile territories. The Paramonai are on permanent secondment to the Office of the Drome, and their chief officer is a member of the Empire's security council. They are housed in the Triklinos of the Excubitores, in the Great Palace.

LEADER
The leader of the Paramonai is called the protallagator, and he ranks just below the megas akolouthos who leads the Varangian Guard

WHAT THEY SAY THEY WANT
Maintain the security of the Empire

WHAT THEY REALLY WANT
Serve the emperor and his instrument the Logothete of the Drome

ALLIES & ENEMIES
The Paramonai are allied to the Office of the Drome. Other than that, they are careful to remain neutral in the politics of the court.

LINKS

- Army Office (ORG-13)
- Office of the Drome (ORG-25)
- Great Palace (PA-7)

ORG-32 PRASINOI

TYPE
Rebellious Gang

NATURE
The *Prasinoi* is a covert political brotherhood intending to topple the government and restore the emperor as the true head of state. Members believe that the emperor has become little more than a puppet ruler on behalf of the noble families who run the Imperial Court. The movement has been simmering away for the last 70 years or so, but it was only after John VIII Palaiologos was forced to become a subject of the Ottoman sultan that the Prasinoi was formally instituted to oppose those who, or so it is believed, manipulated this treaty for their own ends.

Despite having a manifesto drawn up by an anonymous revolutionary, the Prasinoi have never coalesced into a formal organisation. The brotherhood consists of a number of independent gangs who take action on their own initiative to disrupt governmental operations. Those who support the inherent corruption are particular targets: merchants and the officials they bribe, magistrates who punish those who steal to feed their families, slave-owning dynatoi, and the Vardariotai – the very symbols of aristocratic oppression. The Prasinoi particularly like taking action that sets right a social inequality or injustice, or which ridicule the self-important. This can be as petty as slinging mud during public processions right the way up to civil disobedience and criminal activity. They usually stop short of murder, but assault, arson, pillage, inciting riots, and robbery are their stock and trade.

They are self-funding, often conducting thefts in order to gain the materials they need for their activities. Each Prasinoi knows the members of their own gang, and might also know members in other gangs, but they tend to keep away from one another for fear of infiltration by the Praitor's men, and when they do meet tend to wear disguises. There are less than a hundred active members, but thousands of supporters who 'wear the green' – an armband, hat, or scarf of green cloth – as a sign of support.

LEADER
No-one knows anything about the leadership or central organisation of the Prasinoi.

WHAT THEY SAY THEY WANT
To overthrow the government and restore the emperor's direct rule

WHAT THEY REALLY WANT
Create chaos and instability

ALLIES & ENEMIES
The Prasinoi by definition opposes all the government departments, but is most strongly opposed to the instruments of financial and military oppression: The Office of the General Fisc and the Chancellery, particularly the Praitorion. The sergeant-at-arms has long sought for the leader of the Prasinoi without any success. Some have accused the army of colluding with the Prasinoi, although there is no evidence of this. The Prasinoi have a lot of notional support amongst the lower classes, but are despised by the middle and upper classes who are often the targets of their disruption.

LINKS

- ɸ None

ORG-33 STAR AND CRESCENT

TYPE
Criminal Guild

NATURE
The Star and Crescent is a criminal gang, one of the more recent to appear on the scene of Constantinople's underworld. The two founders – Balsamon Astraeios (code-named "Star") and Zayd ibn Tamim ("Crescent") – were originally part of the Zanconi Family. Balsamon used to be a board member of the Zanconi, running the Ufizhio Zhelèste under Clario Zanconi, and in charge of all smuggling operations for The Family. Zayd was his subordinate and in charge of opium supply and distribution. When Clario died, Balsamon refused to work for his daughter Cleope, and mounted his own leadership challenge against her. There was a brief internecine war but the partners were unable to wrest control from Cleope Zanconi, equally she was unable to eliminate her rivals. Star and Crescent split, taking about a quarter of the organisation with them, and set up in business for themselves. Active hostilities between the two gangs have ceased, but they remain fierce rivals.

Star and Crescent operates from the neighbourhood of Zeugma (PL-16), which they virtually own in its entirety. They own and operate a number of private guilds related to the timber industry, including construction, roofing, import of exotic woods, and carpentry. These businesses are kept clean of any criminal activity, providing a legitimate front for the fraternity's other activities; although many of the labourers at the timber mill moonlight as muscle for criminal jobs. Star and Crescent have a stranglehold on all smuggling and illegal import to Constantinople, which is connected to their other main business – the opium trade. They are the main importers and distributors of opium in the city, and own all of the phouskaria and brothels that sell it to addicts. This monopoly is easy to maintain since they control the supply, but they aggressively defend this monopoly against interlopers. The other big money-spinner for Star and Crescent is the adulteration and falsifying of precious metals, including silver coinage. All money that flows into their hands flows out again with a small fraction of its value removed, usually replaced with lead or tin.

LEADER
Balsamon Astraeios and Zayd ibn Tamim.

WHAT THEY SAY THEY WANT
To be the sole distributer of opium in Constantinople.

WHAT THEY REALLY WANT
To eliminate or take over the Zanconi

ALLIES & ENEMIES

The Zanconi Family is both a personal enemy of Balsamon and Zayd as well as a rival organisation, although there is little crossover between the two criminal gangs.

LINKS

- Balsamon Astracios (NPC-4)
- Zayd ibn Tamin (NPC-26)

ORG-34 TZAKONES

TYPE

Imperial Regiment

NATURE

Deriving originally from the fighting men accompanying the Byzantine Navy, with the decline of the fleet during the Palaiologian rule, the Tzakones have been repurposed into guards of the Sea Walls and Land Walls. Their armour is adorned with white lions, these, and their flanged maces, are the identifying features of the Tzakones. They rank lowest of the four Imperial Guard units in the hierarchy of the Byzantine military, and this has fostered a competitive spirit amongst the Tzakones that some have likened to recklessness. There is great social pressure amongst the unit to be unwaveringly brave and support the honour of the unit no matter the cost. They have their barracks at the Tower of Eugenios.

LEADER

The stratopedarches of the Tzakones is a member of the Army Office who is subordinate to the Domestic of the Walls.

WHAT THEY SAY THEY WANT

To defend Constantinople against invaders.

WHAT THEY REALLY WANT

To be heroes

ALLIES & ENEMIES

The Tzakones have an unfriendly rivalry with the Mourtatoi, who are ranked above the unit despite being half-cast Greeks.

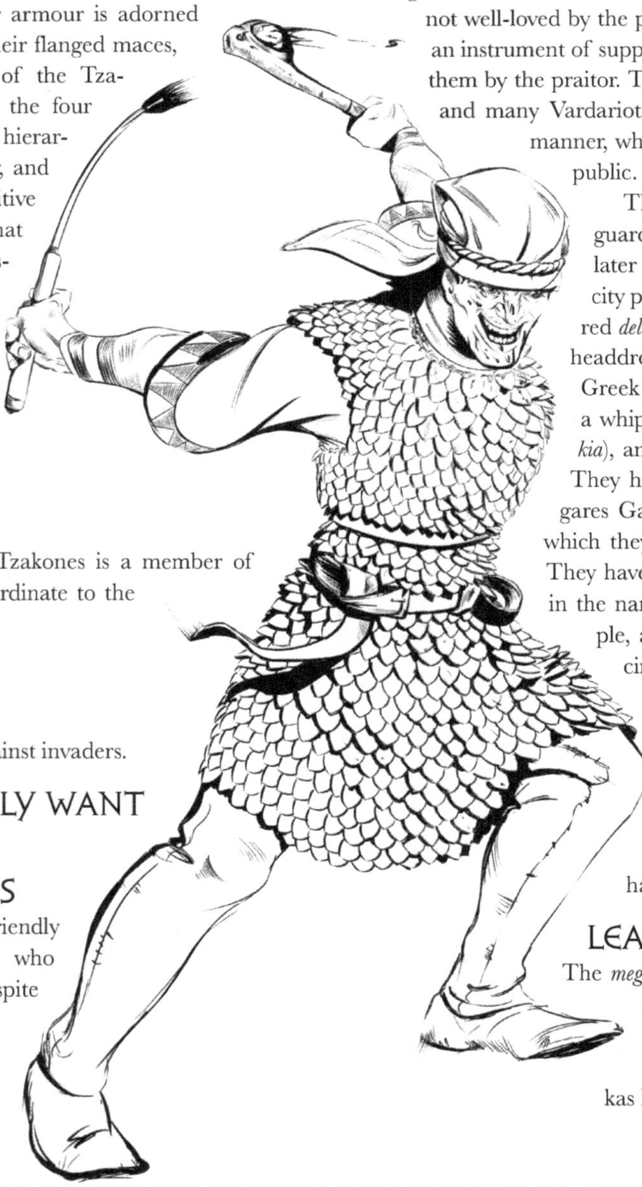

LINKS

- Army Office (ORG-13)
- Tower of Eugenios (AK-13)

ORG-35 VARDARIOTAI

TYPE

Political Regiment

NATURE

The *Vardariotai* (Anglicised to Vardariots) are Constantinople's police force. Their remit is to preserve social order and prevent disturbances in public order. Part of this remit is to prevent crime by bringing perpetrators to justice, although they do not actually investigate crimes, since the onus in Byzantine law is on the plaintiff to provide evidence of wrongdoing. They enact the summons of the courts to defendants, and are supposed to be involved in the greater issue of dismantling organised crime. The Vardariotai are not well-loved by the people of Constantinople, who see them as an instrument of suppression who are abusive of the power given them by the praitor. They are generally considered to be corrupt and many Vardariots supplement their meagre wage in some manner, whether it is accepting bribes or extorting the public.

The Vardariotai were originally one of the guard units of the Imperial Court, but were later merged with the Droungares who were the city police. The Vardariotai uniform consists of a red *delmatikon* and vrakha and a distinctive yellow headdress called an *aggouroton*. They typically wear Greek medium armour. Each Vardariotes carries a whip (*manglabia*) and a red-painted club (*dikanikia*), and usually wear some sort of light armour. They have three fortresses or vigla at the Droungares Gate, in Platea, and at the Praitorion, from which they patrol the streets in a show of strength. They have the power to question and detain anyone in the name of securing the safety of Constantinople, a blanket order that can be twisted to any circumstance. The Vardariotai will certainly stop anyone openly carrying weapons or wearing armour in the streets; claiming that people acting in this manner are generally a threat to public order, and in this they are mostly correct. Some are not above using their general orders to harass strangers or intimidate locals.

LEADER

The *megas tzaousios* or sergeant-at-arms is Nikephoros Notaras. His superior is the praitor Demetrios Metochites, but everyone knows he answers mostly to his uncle Loukas Notaras, who is the praitor's boss.

THE NINE FAMILIES OF THE DYNATOI

There are nine key dynatos families, along with a host of others tied to one or more of these through a complicated web of marriage and descent. Family names can only be claimed for four generations, so the minor families seek to strengthen alliances with repeated marriages. There are two key factions within the nine families: the Kantakouzenos-Komnenos-Doukas alliance which generally supports the emperor; and the Notarades supported by the Laskaris and Iagaris families which seeks power for itself.

Family	Interests and Influences	Allies	Enemies
Doukas	Special Fisc, History, Anti-Unionist Leanings	Kantakouzenos, Komnenos, Palaiologos	Notaras
Kantakouzenos	Army Office, Imperial Court, The Morea	Doukas, Palaiologos	Metochites, Notaras
Komnenos	University, Academia, Anti-Unionist Leanings	Doukas, Palaiologos	Iagaris, Tzamplakon
Iagaris	Military Fisc, Trade With Genoa, Weakly Pro-Unionist	Laskaris	Komnenos, Tzamplakon
Laskaris	Nicaea, Fiercely Anti-Ottoman, Alliance With Western Nations, Anti-Unionist Leanings	Iagaris, Notaras, Palaiologos	
Metochites	Praitoron, Byzantine Hinterlands And Islands, Pro-Unionism	Palaiologos	Kantakouzenos
Notaras	Naval Office, Chancellery, General Fisc, Vardariots, Anti-Unionism	Laskaris	Doukas, Kantakouzenos, Palaiologos, Sphrantzes*
Palaiologos	Imperial Family, The Empire, The Morea, Pro-Unionism, Alliance With Serbia	Doukas, Kantakouzenos, Komnenos, Laskaris, Metochites, Sphrantzes*, Tzamplakon	Notaras
Tzamplakon	Archives, The Church	Palaiologos, Sphrantzes*	Iagaris, Komnenos

**Sphrantzes is an influential name at court, but not one of the Nine Families. They arose from the mesoi in the last century.*

WHAT THEY SAY THEY WANT

Maintain order in the City

WHAT THEY REALLY WANT

Control the City

ALLIES & ENEMIES

Both Dražan Romanoktonos and Star and Crescent are targets of the Vardariotai; although the Zanconi have them in their pocket due to regular 'donations' to the sergeant-at-arms. The Vardariotai get a lot of flak from the other guard units; they are technically part of the military but viewed as the Praitor's bully-boys, and not "real" soldiers. Worse, they are not a guard unit, but a police unit, something to which most of the other phrourata would not stoop.

LINKS

- Chancellery (ORG-16)
- Praitorion (KN-13)
- Vigla (PL-15)

ORG-36 WITCH CULTS

TYPE

Pagan Gang

NATURE

There was a time that every house in Byzantion had a *hekataion* – an altar to Hekate – just inside the entrance, and prayers said to the goddess as the tutelary deity of the city. Those days are long gone and yet worship of Hekate continues to this day in secret amongst the witch cults of Constantinople. Most of these cults claim an unbroken tradition leading back to priestesses of Hekate in pre-Christian days, but in most cases the leaders are mistaken or lying. A new witch cult generally forms through the secession by a charismatic individual from a cult with a domineering leader, and then recruits new members who are told some tale about their ancient lineages. Membership requirements depend on the leader: in ancient times both men and women worshipped Hekate although it was predominantly the latter, but in the surviving cults the membership is almost exclusively female.

Nearly all of the dozen or so witch cults in the city have one or more magician amongst their number, unusually a pharmacopeia who inducts others into Folk Magic. Some cults have formed around sorcerers instead; such cults tend to drift away from the worship of Hekate and focus on darker entities, or else give up all pretence at religious devotion entirely. A typical member is a lower class woman, often one in a menial or undervalued role who has taken up with the cult for a sense of sisterhood and achievement. Some cults are little more than social clubs for women, although there are the occasional true believers who keep the focus on paganism and magic.

At the dark of the moon, members of a witch cult will gather at their sacred place. Temples to the goddess (*hekatesia*) are still dotted around the city, although many were destroyed to make room for other buildings, and still others were converted into churches. Others head into the parks or wild places such as the Lykos Valley or down to at shore. A cult usually meets under the veil of secrecy, wearing masks to conceal their identities, although this is mostly in case outsiders come across them: most members know the identities of some or all of their sister worshippers. In addition to offering worship to the goddess, witches will conduct "sacred business" at the direction of the cult leader; this might include meddling in local politics (often by applying pressure to husbands), vengeance (magical or otherwise) on behalf of wronged women, healing the sick, or acts of sheer malice.

LEADER
Each witch cult has its own leader. More rarely they are triumvirates, with one leader for each aspect of the Triple Goddess.

WHAT THEY SAY THEY WANT
A return to the worship of Hekate and the old gods

WHAT THEY REALLY WANT
To learn magic for weal or woe

ALLIES & ENEMIES
The various witch cult leaders do not cooperate with one another, and often seek to absorb or eliminate rival cults. Naturally, the church is keen to suppress idolatry and pursues the witch cults with zeal. In theory, the cults have the patronage of Hekate, although the goddess's ways are even more mysterious than those of the Christian God.

LINKS

- None

ORG-37 THE ZANCONI FAMILY

TYPE
Criminal Gang

NATURE
The Zanconi (from the Veneto *zanco*, meaning "left handed") or La Famèja ("the Family") is the oldest crime organisation in Constantinople, originating with a Venetian merchant who escaped the Massacre of the Latins by hiding in a barrel. He accompanied the Venetian army on the Fourth Crusade and was one of the men who helped the blind doge of Venice Enrico Dandolo disembark and enter the city. During the Frankokratia Zanconi operated his illegal businesses in the open, such was his political influence; but was forced underground during the Restoration.

The Zanconi have a hand in all manner of illicit activity in Constantinople, from running street prostitutes, to money laundering, gambling and underground fighting pits, and even murder for hire. Their main business is extorting money from businessmen in the form of protection or insurance, or blackmail. They provide thugs to protect income generation, pay bribes to the phylakes, Vardariotes, and petty functionaries, and regulate competing businesses. La Famèja will punish thieves stealing from businesses protected by its sign, a left hand holding a sword. One of the few black markets with which they have no control is the opium trade – a result of the leadership struggle with Balsamon Astraeios (NPC-4) ten years ago.

While the Zanconi style themselves as a family, although most of its members are neither Venetian nor related to the Zanconi by blood. Each enterprise within the organisation – the extortionists, pimps, brothel-keepers, moneylenders and so forth – are called *abiàdegi* ("distant relatives"). Each abiàdego has a contract with a *consobrin* ("cousin") who runs a clearly-defined territory. A census is held each year to determine the fee paid by a consobrin to keep his franchise. La Famèja is administered by the *zhigli* ("uncles", singular *zhio*), a council of five elders who are partners and share-holders in the organisation. At the head of it all is the *capòcia* ("head of family"), who has absolute authority and is always a member of the Zanconi family itself. Members of the Zanconi use Veneto terms for one another: a *fradèl* ("brother") is someone of equal status; the *parón* ("boss") is a term of respect for those of higher rank; and the capòcia is addressed as *paronsón* ("big boss").

LEADER
Cleope Zanconi (NPC-5) has been capòcia of La Famèja since the death of her father Clario.

WHAT THEY SAY THEY WANT
To give the people what they want.

WHAT THEY REALLY WANT
To get rich and to not get caught.

ALLIES & ENEMIES
Star and Crescent arose from a succession crisis and failed coup, and there has been nothing but acrimony between Cleope Zanconi and Balsamon the Star ever since. Relations between Cleope and Dražan are neutral, based on mutual respect for geographical boundaries and as long as Dražan's thieves stay out of Zanconi businesses. However, Dražan's ambitions may bring him into conflict in the future.

The *Çonéto di Palàso* (the guard of the Venetian Quarter) is so corrupt that it can be considered an ally of the Zanconi. The quarter's bailo has publically pledged to crack down on crime, but did not name the Zanconi specifically, and it is inconceivable that he is not taking the family's bribes.

LINKS

- Cleope Zanconi (NPC-5)

PERSONALITIES OF CONSTANTINOPLE

In this section, some of the notable inhabitants of Constantinople are described. While these characters may have significant impacts on the lives of player characters, it is unlikely that any of them will be faced in direct physical conflict. However, as sources of information, influence, opposition and/or manipulation, it may be necessary to know what Skills they have at their disposal. Therefore, rather than giving complete statistics for each of the following non-player characters, each NPC is described as having percentage score in one or more Careers. The character is assumed to have any Skill that falls into one or more of these Careers at the highest applicable base percentage, and 30% in all other Standard Skills. The actual score of each Skill is the base percentage +1d20%. Thus, Andrew of Killingworth can be expected to have an appropriate Combat Style ranging between 91 and 110%

NPC-1

ALEXIOS HO PTOCHON PALAIOLOGOS TZAMPLAKON

ROLE

Protasekritis

Alexios ho Ptochon is the minister of the Imperial Archives, ranked 8th of the 12 departments of the Imperial Court. As First Secretary (protasekritis) he has direct access to the emperor, and divides his time between Blachernai, the Great Palace, and the Archives in Kanikleion (KN-9). His nickname *ho Ptochon* means "the poor man", a soubriquet he earned through constant referrals to the poverty of his department whereas in fact it has one of the largest per capita budgets because of its sheer size. The Archives has one of the largest staffs amongst the ministries of the court, since it employs all the scribes, copyists, notaries, and record keepers that keep the other departments running.

He is the patriarch of the large Tzamplakon family. His maternal grandmother was a minor member of the royal Palaiologos family, and he proudly bears the name as one of his own. His daughter Helena is the wife of the Mesazon Georgios Sphrantzes.

APPEARANCE

Alexios is in his fifty-third year. He is tall but has a perpetual stoop from decades spent hunched over a writing desk. His court costume consists of a green epilorikon over a red overtunic, with a skiadon covered with a silk brocade of white and purple. The hat has a wide band of gold embroidery, and this and the brim is decorated with pearls.

SKILLS

Official 90%, Courtier 70%, Scholar 50%

ALLEGIANCES

He is allied to the Sphrantzes family through his daughter, and while he tries to stay out of court politics, he tends to side with the Mesazon over the Grand Logothete.

OPPONENTS

He is unaware that he has attracted the envy of the Military Logothete and is a target for his scheming. See page 204 for more information.

LINKS

- Imperial Archives (ORG-18)
- Kanikleion / Palace of the Kanikleios (KN-9)

NPC-2

ANDREW OF KILLINGWORTH

ROLE

Megas akolouthos of the Varangian Guard

The head of the Varangian Guard is a position of great trust, being amongst the handful of people allowed within an arm's length of the person of the emperor. Like most of the Guard, Andrew is an Englishman. He came to Constantinople in pursuit of the murderer of his brother, who was also a Guardsman. Upon dispatching the killer and his employer, Andrew accepted his brother's commission in the Guard. That was nearly 30 years ago, and Andrew now runs the regiment. He has a reputation for incorruptibility, although that does not stop people trying to offer him bribes, which he always accepts, notarises, issues a receipt, and announces the gift at court.

APPEARANCE

Andrew only just made the height requirement for the Guard, but still cuts an imposing figure even in his fifties, with a waistline only a little larger than when he joined the Varangians. He has long dark-brown hair that falls beyond his shoulders, and a goatee beard worn with long moustaches. He wears the full ceremonial armour of the Guard, with a white khlamys bearing a purple border, indicating his high rank (which is twentieth from the emperor).

SKILLS
Warrior 90%, Courtier 50%

ALLEGIANCES
Thomas Strouthion (see page 124) has a cautious respect for Andrew, although the two have differing ideas on what is best for the emperor. He and Andronikos Kantakouzenos, his nominal superior, have a working relationship largely based around the Grand Domestic not giving any orders to the Varangian commander.

OPPONENTS
The man that Andrew killed to get vengeance for his slain brother was a member of the Notaras family. Although the man's guilt was not in question, Loukas Notaras has never forgiven Andrew for his 'barbarian justice'. Had the murderer gone to trial he would have been offered exile and his family therefore taken care of out of his estate. As an executed criminal (albeit after the fact), the whole estate went to the crown and the Notaras family became notably poorer (although still fabulously wealthy by anyone else's standards).

LINKS

- Varangian Guard (ORG-11)
- Palace of the Porphyrogennetos (BL-6)

NPC-3

ANDRONIKOS PALAIOLOGOS KANTAKOUZENOS

ROLE
Grand Domestic

Andronikos Kantakouzenos is commander of all of the Empire's soldiers, including the imperial guards, the wall guards, the mercenary units, and the standing army. The army relies upon volunteers rather than conscription, and recent battles combined with poor morale has led to the current parlous state of the army, with a few more than five thousand men. In the past, a career in the army was made attractive by the promise of land, but as the empire shrunk so did that award, and all the Army Office can offer now is three square meals a day and a meagre pay. Still, the cost of maintaining this army is a stretch on the budget his department is paid, and detractors are quick to mock the Grand Domestic for his constant concerns over the numbers of men he can field. He is stereotyped as a warmonger, who wants more men so he can sally forth and kill the Turk, but nothing could be further from the truth. Andronikos knows the number of men that can be fielded by the Sultan and while the rest of the court pretends that a diplomatic solution is possible, he knows there is no other way that the long-term survival of Constantinople is possible, because the army is not up to the task of the city's defence.

APPEARANCE
Andronikos is a tall man well-suited to be the head of the empire's armed forces. He is in his early forties with a barrel-like chest and a voice to match. His hair and beard are black, but with carmine highlights he adds as an affectation. The court regalia of the Grand Domestic is a kabbadion of red and yellow silk with a pearled border. His skaranikon is of the same colours, and bears a portrait of the emperor front and back. His baton is gilded and has a silver chain wrapped around it.

SKILLS
Courtier 70%, Warrior 70%

ALLEGIANCES
Andronikos's father is the current mesazon, Demetrios Kantakouzenos

OPPONENTS
The Kantakouzenoi have a long-standing feud with the Metochites family.

LINKS

- Army Office (ORG-13)

NPC-4

BALSAMON ASTRAEIOS

ROLE
Smuggler and Drug Dealer

Ten years ago, Balsamon was a high-ranking member of the Zanconi crime family. He was in charge of the Ufizhio Zhelèste, which was responsible for all smuggling operations in Constantinople – big business because of the kommerkion. He was a close friend of Clario Zanconi, the *capòcia* (head of the family) and doted on his daughter Cleope. When Clario died, he assumed that he would take over as capòcia, but Cleope saw things differently. The two went to war but ultimately the Family supported Cleope, and Balsamon fled the organisation, taking with him several key associates who remained loyal to him. The Zanconi were never able to recover a viable smuggling operation, and Balsamon's new gang – named Star and Crescent – have cornered the market there.

APPEARANCE
He is a tall, broad-shouldered man with the stance of a pit fighter. His long, thick beard is combed into two forks. He wears a quilted blue kabbadion brocaded with many eight-pointed stars, a pattern his tailor guarantees is unique to him. He also wears an indigo fez wrapped in a white turban. On his left hand he has a tattoo of seven stars. His nickname is "Star"; his name, Astraeios, means "starry".

SKILLS
Agent 90%, Thief 50%, Warrior 50%

ALLEGIANCES
Balsamon's closest ally is Zayd al-Ghassani, with whom he runs Star and Crescent. He has a business arrangement with Dražan Romanoktonos, but they could not be considered allies.

OPPONENTS

Balsamon's perceived betrayal by Cleope Zanconi has turned their former affection into mutual hatred. In Balsamon's case this has become a form of madness. Simply hearing her name will drive him into a frothing rage, and he plots cruel and elaborate ways to despatch her should she ever fall into his clutches.

LINKS

- Star and Crescent (ORG-33)

NPC-5

CLEOPE ZANCONI

ROLE

Crime Boss

Cleope is a Gasmouli, the daughter of a Venetian father and a Greek mother. She is equally despised by both cultures, but she cares little for this, for she is one of the most powerful crime-bosses in Constantinople. She inherited the rulership of the Zanconi Family (ORG-37) from her father Clario; having no surviving brothers left her to inherit her father's fortune and enterprise when he died. One of her father's lieutenants Balsamon (NPC-4) was like an uncle to her, so his betrayal cut deep when he tried to seize control of The Family from her. She had less to do with Zayd (NPC-26), the other conspirator, but his departure was a major blow with a high cost, both financial and otherwise. She would dearly love to make Zayd and Balsamon pay for tearing the Zanconi in twain. She has proven to her detractors that she is more than capable of filling her father's shoes, but she will always be in his shadow. To make matters worse, Cleope has never married. She has five children, all daughters. Their fathers are a matter of conjecture, but all are dead so it is of little consequence. The eldest is Colleta, who is already running her own enterprise in Platea at the age of 16.

APPEARANCE

Cleope is average in nearly all respects. She has dark blonde hair, but often uses dye or wigs; and she is adept at disguise and can pass for plain or pretty with just a few strokes of make-up. She enjoys using disguises to keep her underlings on their toes or her enemies off guard.

SKILLS

Official 70%, Agent 90%

ALLEGIANCES

Cleope does not make friends, partly due to her inability to trust anyone. She has an agreement with Dražan regarding territory, but assumes (rightly) that he either intends to break it or has already.

OPPONENTS

Cleope's hatred of Balsamon Astraios has cooled to a seething need to see him suffer. She is aware that he is obsessed with seeing her dead, and is planning to exploit his madness.

LINKS

- Zanconi Family (ORG-37)

NPC-6

CONSTANTINE XI DRAGASES PALAIOLOGOS

ROLE

Emperor of the Romans

Constantine was born in 1405 to Emperor Manuel II and Helena Dragaš, third son of the six that survived to adulthood. Of all his brothers he was closest to the eldest John; together they shared the despotate of Morea and wrested it from the control of the Latin princes who ruled the Peloponnese. Before assuming the throne, he was regent for John before once again becoming despot in the Morea. During his second stint on Morea he conquered the Duchy of Athens, eliciting a response from Sultan Murad II to whom the duke had paid tribute. With his brother Thomas, Constantine held Morea against the sultan until 1446 when they were eventually beaten and forced to pay tribute.

When John died without an heir Constantine and his brother Demetrios disputed the throne. Demetrios was supported by the anti-Unionist nobility, but it was the support of his mother Helena that secured him the throne when she interceded with Sultan Murad II, technically the suzerain of the Byzantine empire. He was crowned emperor on 6th January 1449.

Constantine has been married twice; both his wives died following complications giving birth and neither produced him an heir. After a brief engagement to Mara Brankovic (daughter of Durad Brankovic of Serbia and widow of Murad II) to which some of his counsellors (and Mara herself) objected, the emperor is currently seeking betrothal from either a princess of the Emperor of Trebizond or the King of Georgia.

APPEARANCE

The emperor is 45 in 1450, and in fine health. He has a prominent nose and dark hair and beard, both neatly coiffured and oiled. In full court regalia, the emperor has several garments unique to his rank. He wears a long tunic (or *rhoukon*) of red or purple with a pearl-decorative hem and fitted sleeve, and over this a second, looser tunic with wide sleeves called a *sakkos* in black. He wears a cloth-of-gold loros, and a red khlamys (occasionally white bordered with purple). The crown or stemma has the form of an inverted cone of gold decorated with gems and pearls, surmounted with triangular tines. Only the emperor wears black or purple.

SKILLS
Courtier 70%, Warrior 50%

ALLEGIANCES
At court the emperor's most trusted friend is Georgios Sphrantzes and also relies heavily on Thomas Strouthion. Of his two surviving brothers, Constantine has always had a friendly relationship with the youngest Thomas.

OPPONENTS
In theory he can rely upon the support of all 12 of his chief ministers, but everyone is aware of the growing rift between the emperor and Loukas Notaras, an outspoken opponent of the Union of the Churches. Constantine's brother Demetrios is perhaps his strongest opponent, although he is far away in the Morea.

LINKS

- ϕ Imperial Court (ORG-6)
- ϕ Demetrios Kantakouzenos (NPC-8)
- ϕ Palace of the Porphyrogennetos (BL-6)

NPC-7

DEMETRIOS ASANES PALAIOLOGOS

ROLE
Despot in the Morea

The younger brother of the current emperor, Demetrios Palaiologos is perhaps the most troublesome of the six sons of Emperor Manuel II Palaiologos who survived to adulthood. He has always been the most ambitious of his brothers; something that has brought him into direct conflict with his family. He was given lordship of Lemnos in 1422 but refused to live there, and fled instead to the court of Sigismund of Hungary. He reconciled with his brothers by 1427, and accompanied John VIII to the Council of Florence. Unlike his brother he was a fierce anti-Unionist, and left without his brother's consent, for which he was forced to surrender Lemnos, and compensated with Mesembria instead. Demetrios retaliated by allying with the Ottomans in a failed attack against Constantinople in 1442. When John VIII died in 1448, Demetrios attempted a coup, which failed partly due to the intervention of his mother, who favoured Constantine. In 1449 he was given co-rulership of Morea with his brother Thomas to remove him from the vicinity of Constantinople. His current wife is Theodora Asanina, and they have a daughter Helena. His byname of Asanes honours his wife's family and one of his paternal great-grandmothers.

APPEARANCE
Demetrios has a strong family resemblance to the emperor, but has a flushed face and red nose which might hint at a problem with drink. Demetrios has not been seen at court since his appointment to the Morea, but is entitled to the same regalia as worn by his brother Thomas.

SKILLS
Warrior 70%, Official 50%

ALLEGIANCES
He counts the Ottoman Sultan amongst his allies, although it is certain that Murad II merely finds him a useful tool rather than a true ally. He supports the anti-Unionists, but this may be because they oppose the emperor rather than through any religious conviction.

OPPONENTS
Constantine and Thomas – his surviving brothers – are perhaps his greatest rivals, and he would not hesitate to have either killed if it was expedient.

LINKS

- ϕ Anti-Unionists (ORG-12)

NPC-8

DEMETRIOS PALAIOLOGOS KANTAKOUZENOS

ROLE
Mesazon (prime minister)

Mesazon (and cousin) of Emperor Constantine XI, and probably the second most important person in the Byzantine Empire. He was imprisoned by Sultan Murad I for three years when he carried envoy from the court of John VIII Palaiologos to the sultan, since the emperor had supported Murad's uncle Mustafa during the Ottoman Interregnum. His daughter Eirene is married to Durad Brankovic (see page 42), and his son Andronikos serves as the Grand Domestic.

APPEARANCE
Demetrios has an uncanny resemblance to his son Andronikos, and could pass, if not for his twin then certainly his brother. Behind his back, his enemies whisper at some sort of sorcery employed to keep himself young. As mesazon, his court regalia consists of a floor-length tunic of red cloth, and a red khlamys bordered with gold. His skiadon is also red brocaded with gold. He wears hose and boots of sky blue.

SKILLS
Official 90%

ALLEGIANCES
Demetrios's son Andronikos is the Grand Domestic of the empire. The Doukai and Kantakouzenoi have always been closely allied families.

OPPONENTS

The Kantakouzenos and Notaras families have long feuded with one another; and the Metochites are also long-standing enemies of the Kantakouzenoi.

LINKS

- Constantine XI Palaiologos (NPC-6)
- Imperial Court (ORG-6)
- Palace of the Porphyrogennetos (BL-6)

NPC-9

DEMETRIOS PALAIOLOGOS METOCHITES

ROLE

Praitor ton Demon

The Praitor ton Demon of Constantinople is the civil administrator of the city. Metochites was formerly governor of Lemnos in the absence of its despot Demetrios Asanes Palaiologos, which he successfully defended against Turkish attack. He was promoted to praitor in 1449. Demetrios has a terrible secret: his mother is a living vampire (or broukolak); he has her imprisoned in a disused tower and fed on a diet of pig's blood. Although he has shown no signs of the affliction himself, he is convinced he will one day inherit his mother's affliction.

APPEARANCE

Demetrios Metochites is a small man who does not like to be towered over, and will often stand on steps to equal out any differences in height. He shaves his moustache in the manner of the island Greeks, but wears a full beard. His court dress is a kabbadion of the regulation silk with a skiadon of white and yellow. He carries a baton of polished wood.

SKILLS

Official 70%, Sailor 50%

ALLEGIANCES

Metochites's direct superior is Loukas Notaras, although he cannot be truly considered an ally.

OPPONENTS

As the figurehead of the city administration, Metochites attracts a great deal of misplaced opprobrium. The demoi hate him because of poverty and crime; and the dynatoi hate him because they have to witness the poverty and crime. The mesoi hate him because of the kommerkion and the state monopolies (neither of which are in his control). When he tries to impose order through the Vardariotai he is hated even more. There is a pharmakopeia on staff at the Praitorion whose main job is to avert the Evil Eye from the person of the Praitor; barely a day goes passed when he is not cursed.

LINKS

- Chancellery (ORG-16)
- Loukas Notaras (NPC-20)
- Praitorion (KN-13)

NPC-10

DRAZAN ROMANOKTONOS

ROLE

Crime Boss and Master of Thieves

Dražan (first syllable rhymes with "barge"), surnamed "The killer of Greeks", is a local criminal. He is a second-generation Bulgarian immigrant, fluent enough in Greek although he still affects a thick Slavic accent that encourages people to underestimate him. He has methodically absorbed or eliminated his competition, leaving him the most powerful crime-boss in Vlanga, ruling through several trusted lieutenants, mostly misfits and foreigners such as himself. He demands a cut of all illicit income that goes on in Vlanga, and most fall in line with those demands – he didn't get his nickname for nothing. Most of his income comes from thievery. He also owns numerous brothels and gambling houses in Vlanga, and charges rent on a substantial number of the tenements despite not actually owning them. He runs an illegal money-lending operation, and is not above the protection racket. For the moment Dražan keeps his business activities confined to Vlanga although his thieves operate city-wide.

APPEARANCE

Dražan is in his sixties, and still cuts an impressive figure. He is tall and built like a bull, with a huge dense beard which is now dyed black out of vanity.

SKILLS

Warrior 70%, Thief 50%

ALLEGIANCES

Dražan has made arrangements with both Star and Crescent (ORG-33) and the Zanconi family (ORG-12), with which they are content for now. Star and Crescent are permitted to sell opium in Vlanga under licence from Dražan, who charges them a single yearly fee rather than a percentage of profits.

OPPONENTS

Like all criminals, Dražan has both the phylakes and the Vardariotes as enemies.

LINKS

- Dražan's Gang (ORG-17)

NPC-11

GEORGIOS GENNADIOS KOURTESIOS SCHOLARIOS

ROLE

Religious gadfly

Georgios Kourtesios Scholarios, often known simply by his religious name of Gennadios, is a pupil of the famous teacher Mark of Ephesus as well as Plethon, Georgios Scholarios became the theological advisor to John VIII Palaiologos and accompanied him to the Council of Florence in 1437. He initially supported the Union, but was opposed to the Latin approach to the Trinity, which was primarily Aristotelian. This brought him into conflict with his former teacher Plethon, who is a fervent proponent of Aristotle's philosophy. Since both philosophers were laymen, neither could directly take part in the discussions of the council. Scholarios abandoned the council early and never signed the decree of Union. He returned to Constantinople and resumed his theological studies, maintaining an irreconcilable attitude against Union. Upon the death of John VIII in 1448 he entered the Pantokrator Monastery, taking "Gennadios" as his religious name. A note pinned to the door of his monk's cell reads: "O unhappy Romans, why have you forsaken the truth. Why do you not trust in God, instead of in the Italians? In losing your faith you will lose your city."

APPEARANCE

Gennadios is in his late forties and hale – although his new asceticism is taking its toll. He wears the garb of a stavrophoros, or full monk. He has not been seen since his seclusion.

SKILLS

Christian Priest 70%, Scholar 90%

ALLEGIANCES

Demetrios Palaiologos uses the anti-Unionist stance to further his campaign against his brother the emperor; Gennadios realises that Demetrios is using the cause for political rather than religious reasons, yet still counts him as an ally. Loukas Notaras is a more useful contact; not only does he hold high court rank, he is also fervent in his opposition to Catholicism.

OPPONENTS

his former teacher Georgios Gemistos is an intellectual foe, being both a supporter of the Union and having pagan leanings. Gennadios has become obsessed with his former master, to the point of madness.

LINKS

- Anti-Unionists (ORG-12)
- Monastery of Christ Pantokrator (PL-10)

NPC-12

GEORGIOS PLETHON GEMISTOS

ROLE

Secretly-pagan philosopher

Born in 1375, Plethon (as he is commonly known) is a prominent scholar, responsible for the reintroduction of Platonic philosophy into both the Greek and Frankish intellectual worlds. Plethon has studied in Edirne in the Ottoman Empire, as well as Cyprus and Palestine, and now lives in Mistras in Morea while making regular trips to Constantinople. He has authored books on philosophy, astronomy, history and geography, as well as translating the works of classical philosophers. He is a proponent of establishing a Platonic republic with political, legal, and economic reforms. He attended the Council of Florence, where his friendship with Cosimo de' Medici lead to the establishment of a Platonic Academy in Florence. Plethon has attracted accusations of heresy – not least from his former pupil Georgios Scholarios – due to the presence of pagan idols at his school in Mistras, and rumours regarding his resurrection of the mysteries. The truth is that Plethon is a leading figure in a Neoplatonic cult called the Unconcealed Word (see page 95), having achieved the rank of Master.

Plethon is a ruthless manipulator and master of intrigue. He can persuade people to reveal their secrets then make them forget they ever talked to him. He can witness private conservations unobserved, and change people's minds and allegiances. He can be a formidable enemy or a useful ally, but either way he is a dangerous man. His biggest failing is perhaps his arrogance.

APPEARANCE

In his mid-seventies, Plethon cuts an impressive figure, with long white hair and snowy beard. His clothing harks back to an earlier era, preferring flowing robes. When he speaks, it is difficult to turn away, and he has a compelling demeanour.

SKILLS

Scholar 90%, Mystic (Unconcealed Word) 90%

ALLEGIANCES

Plethon is loyal to the empire. He cares little who is on the throne (although has a personal dislike for Demetrios Palaiologos), as long as they are Greek: having spied extensively on the sultan, he is sure that his dream of a Platonic republic would be impossible under Ottoman rule.

OPPONENTS

Plethon's biggest opponent is Gennadios, who has grown convinced that his former teacher has been possessed by devils. His insanity has been subtly encouraged by Plethon's mystical Talents, to make him appear a fool, giving his words less weight.

LINKS

- The Unconcealed Word (ORG-10)

NPC-13

GEORGIOS SPHRANTZES

ROLE

Protovestarios

Georgios Sphrantzes has served as protovestiarios to both John VIII and Constantine XI Palaiologos. He grew up with the current emperor and is a close personal friend and advisor. Georgios accompanied Constantine to the Morea when he became despot, and was made governor of Glarentza and later Mistras.

Georgios Sphrantzes is not currently in Constantinople. He has been placed in charge of finding a new wife for the emperor, and is visiting the Kingdom of Georgia and the Empire of Trebizond to interview prospective candidates. He returns in 1451 upon hearing of the death of Sultan Murad II, which leaves behind his widow Mara Brankovic, a very suitable candidate for empress. She is the daughter of the Serbian despot Durad Brankovic and his wife Irene Kantakouzene, who is herself the daughter of Demetrios Kantakouzenos the mesazon. Unfortunately, the lady has vowed not to marry again.

APPEARANCE

Georgios Sphrantzes is in his early forties and is as fit as a soldier despite never having served. His skin has a healthy tan – unfashionable at court – and his brown hair and beard are somewhat bleached by the sun. As a high-ranking member of the court, Sphrantzes's formal wear consists of a kabbadion made of green and gold silk covered with a green khlamys, green boots and headgear (either the tall skaranikion or the brimmed skiadon). He carries a baton of gold decorated with green enamel.

SKILLS

Merchant 90%, Courtier 50%

ALLEGIANCES

Georgios Sphrantzes has the ear of the emperor himself, which puts him in a much envied position. His wife Helena is the daughter of Alexios Tzamplakon, which allies him with the protasekritis.

OPPONENTS

Sphrantzes and Loukas Notaras loathe one another. Sphrantzes considers Notaras to be a self-serving and vain man. Jealousy over Sphrantzes's friendship with the emperor has cost him other potential alliances.

LINKS

- Imperial Household (ORG-19)
- Blachernai Palace (BL-3)

NPC-14

GREGORY III MAMMAS MELISSENOS

ROLE

Patriarch of Constantinople

Tonsured in 1420 and made patriarch of the Orthodox church in 1442, Gregory III is the senior clergyman of the Orthodox Church. He is a native of Crete; his nickname 'Mammas' ("grandmother") is a mocking reference to his concerned, sometimes patronising tone and fussy manners. He is a supporter of the Union of Churches, having participated in the Council of Florence, but is struggling to reconcile the regular and secular clergy with the agreement of that synod, and tension is rising for him to resign (he does so in 1451, going into exile in Rome). He has never been comfortable in his role as patriarch, preferring the life of a theologian and monk to the political whirl of court, a game for which he has little talent.

APPEARANCE

The Patriarch is unmistakable in his finery; when on occasion he dons a monk's robe and walks the streets he goes entirely unnoticed. Gregory III is gaunt, with sparse hair and sunken eyes. Those who see past his vestments might consider him to be sick with consumption, although he has no such disease.

SKILLS

Christian Priest 90%, Scholar 70%

ALLEGIANCES

The patriarch has the support of the emperor, but few others will ally with him, even other pro-Unionists. Gregory III is viewed as a toxic ally whose days are numbered. He often seeks out the company of Isidoros of Kiev, and enjoys debating theology with him.

OPPONENTS

As a Unionist, the patriarch is opposed by all the prominent anti-Unionists such as Gennadios, Demetrios Palaiologos, and Loukas Notaras. His subordinate Akkakios, Bishop of Derkos, has possession of Hagia Sophia and barred entrance to the Patriarch and other known Unionists.

LINKS

- Patriarchate of Constantinople (ORG-8)
- Hagia Sophia (PA-8)

NPC-15

HELENA DRAGAŠ

ROLE

Empress Dowager

More correctly Sister Hypomone ("Patience") since entering the Monastery of Kyra Martha in Elebichon, Helena was the daughter of a Serbian lord, the wife of Emperor Manuel II Palaiologos, and the mother of two further emperors. She took the veil 25 years ago upon the death of her husband, but has not retired from public life. She has sponsored many charitable works, most notably a home for the elderly called "the Hope of the Despaired" at the Monastery of Saint John at Petrion. She still counsels her son, and is widely honoured for her piety and wisdom. Her biggest regret is having favourites amongst her sons, and her rift with Demetrios is probably unsalvageable.

APPEARANCE

Helena was well-known for her beauty, and at the age of 78 she has aged gracefully, with a shadow of that former beauty still with her. She wears the Great Schema that marks her amongst the most spiritually-enlightened of monks.

SKILLS

Courtier 90%, Christian Priest 70%, Mystic (Hesychasm) 70%

ALLEGIANCES

Helena is devoted to her son Constantine. Her blessing is sought by ministers and magnates, who know that her approval can make or break a venture.

OPPONENTS

Helena is universally loved, only her son Demetrios can only really be considered an opponent, and even he is not truly an enemy.

LINKS

- Constantine XI Palaiologos (NPC-6)
- Demetrios Palaiologos (NPC-7)
- Thomas Palaiologos (NPC-24)
- Elebichon / Kyra Martha (XR-3)

NPC-16

ILLARIO DORIA

ROLE

Podestà of Pera

The Lord Ambassador of the Republic of Genoa to the Imperial Court, and also the Podestà (ruler) of the colony of Pera, Doria is an influential man in the region. The empire has had an inconstant relationship with Genoa, sometimes allies, sometimes enemies, but Doria believes that an alliance between the two cities is the only way to fight the Ottoman threat. His masters in Genoa don't see it the same way; a truce has been negotiated with Mehmet II, whose intentions towards Constantinople when he becomes sultan are widely known. Doria has orders to remain neutral when Mehmet comes for the City in order to preserve Pera; and has yet to decide where his loyalties lie.

He suspects that one of his council is a spy from Genoa, sent to ensure that he obeys their instructions, but has yet to discover who it is. Doria is remarkably intelligent, although he is careful not to let it show. He doesn't care much for politics, but his family chose him for this role and he is loyal to a fault.

Doria is married to Isabella Palaiologina, illegitimate sister of Emperor Constantine IX, whom he loves very much.

APPEARANCE

In contrast to many Genoese, Doria affects a Greek mode of dress, often wearing a turban and epilorikon. He is slightly portly in stature, with auburn hair worn in a queue and a clean-shaven face.

SKILLS

Merchant 90%, Courtier 70%

ALLEGIANCES

Although his city disapproves, Doria is a personal friend of Constantine and Georgios Sphrantzes, and occasionally dines with one or both of them. They rarely talk politics at these get-togethers.

OPPONENTS

Doria is disliked by Loukas Notaras, who assumes that his friendship with the emperor is an attempt to manipulate him. Although he is yet to realise it, Valeri Giustiniani (PR-6) is the spy for Genoa and a potential enemy should Doria show any signs of betraying the Republic.

LINKS

- Palazzo del Commune (PR-7)

NPC-17

ISIDOROS OF KIEV

ROLE

Orthodox Bishop of Kiev and Catholic Cardinal

Born in Monemvasia and educated in Constantinople, he became abbot of the Monastery of Saint Demetrios and earned fame as a theologian, which lead to his inclusion in the Council of Florence as a fierce pro-Unionist. In 1437 he was appointed Metropolitan of Kiev and all of Rus', and his role was to bring the Russian Orthodox Church into the Union. Furthermore, the Pope appointed him cardinal and legate for Ruthenia, an ecclesiastic province including Lithuania, Livonia, Rus', and Poland. He returned to his see at Moscow in 1441 only to be imprisoned by Grand Prince Vasily II of Moscow who opposed the Union. He escaped prison two years later and fled to Rome, where he was sent to Constantinople as the representative of the Latin Church.

Isidoros is secretly addicted to opium. He first took the drug to ease the pain of the long-term damage inflicted during his confinement, but now finds he cannot do without it. A loyal servant procures what he needs.

APPEARANCE

Formerly a portly man, but his years in a Muscovy prison rid him of all his body fat. His saggy skin belies his former shape, and he is wrinkled beyond his six decades. His hair is greying from black, and he wears his beard short in the Roman style. He tends to wear the scarlet robes of a Catholic cardinal despite also being an Orthodox bishop.

SKILLS
Christian Priest 90%, Official 50%, Miracle-Worker 30%

ALLEGIANCES
Isidoros has a working relationship with Patriarch Gregory III, although they still clash over points of doctrine.

OPPONENTS
As leader of the Unionists, Isidoros has an enemy in Loukas Notaras.

LINKS

- Catholic Church (ORG-15)

NPC-18
KAMOS KAKOTYCHOS

ROLE
Imperial Proxy

Kamos is a commoner from the Morea. When Constantine was hurriedly crowned emperor two years ago in Mistras, Kamos was called in to be one of the witnesses to the ceremony. When the new emperor left for Constantinople, Kamos couldn't believe his luck when he was included amongst the Imperial entourage and expected at any time to be discovered as an imposter and sent back to the provinces. Instead, he was given an imperial title and a salary, in exchange for which all he is required to attend a weekly meeting at Blachernai Palace with the emperor to give the view of the common man. The imperial salary means that he does not have to work, and he has a modest house in Phanarion. Amongst his many friends and neighbours he is known for his legendary bad luck. Accidents and illness often befall him, even dogs dislike him, and although he loves gaming he is sure to lose any game he plays – his nickname literally means "shitty luck". Nevertheless, Kamos is cheerful and believes himself blessed.

Kamos is blissfully unaware of the true nature of his job as the Imperial Proxy (see page 29). His terrible luck is not his own, it is born from all the ill wishes directed towards Emperor Constantine XI. The accidents and illnesses result from curses that the emperor's enemies have paid to have laid on him.

APPEARANCE
Kamos is of average height, with long dark hair and a beard. He has a perpetual wheezing cough that renders him unfit. It is not unusual to come across him with a broken ankle, eye affliction, or upset stomach. Kamos dresses according to his purse, but his fine clothes always seem to get ripped or stained within a few days.

SKILLS
Labourer 50%, Merchant 50%

ALLEGIANCES
Kamos is kind and generous has a wide circle of friends. Some have tried to befriend him purely to get access to the emperor, but he has become good at spotting such false friends. His most unusual ally is the emperor and by extension, the Imperial Household. Although they are not friends, Constantine shows a great interest in his life and has always sent him help: the best physicians money can buy when he fell ill, soldiers to fix up his house when the upper storey collapsed, and so forth.

OPPONENTS
Kamos has no enemies; he always pays his debts and is generous to those who suffer misfortune around him.

LINKS

- Constantine XI Palaiologos (NPC-6)

NPC-19
LEONTES DIKTUOPLOKOS

ROLE
Prisoner and fixer

Leontes is a fixer, a go-between for the various shady and downright criminal inhabitants of Constantinople. He has an office in the Noumera (PA-14), where he meets with clients and makes deals. What few realise, at least the first time they meet him, is that Leontes is an inmate of the Noumera. It is not clear what his crime was, but it has kept him incarcerated for at least the last 10 years, although this might be by design. Thanks to a generous 'rent' he pays directly to the prison's governor, he has a great deal of freedom for a prisoner. The guards show clients to and from his office and provide a complementary bodyguarding service. He has a servant who sees to his needs and acts as personal secretary. At the governor's insistence, Leontes is escorted back to his (somewhat luxurious) cell every night and locked up, for appearance's sake.

Leontes has a reputation for knowing everyone in the city, and is the person to go to for those looking for goods and services that cannot be obtained through legitimate channels. He specialises in matching freelance criminals of all varieties with potential clients, which is from where he got his epithet, meaning "netmaker". He extracts a fee from both parties for making the introduction. He likewise puts thieves in touch with fences who can hawk their stolen goods, connects clients with particular sexual tastes with underground brothels, and finds mercenaries for more violent or dangerous enterprises. He has sufficient incriminatory material on members of the dynatoi and the Imperial Court that he is virtually untouchable; although he is careful to not involve himself in the negotiations between clients and hires so he cannot be considered an accessory to any crimes committed by either party.

APPEARANCE
An enormously fat man, dressed in clothes typical of a middle-class man of wealth and taste. His hair and beard are kept immaculate and on trend by weekly visits from a barber. He favours a turban dyed a pale rose in colour, and those who work for him identify themselves with a matching garment.

SKILLS
Merchant 90%, Entertainer 50%

ALLEGIANCES

No one has fully divined the extent of Leontes' network of contacts. He never commits anything to writing, relying instead on his prodigious memory. Few as yet have managed to make a request of him that he cannot fulfil, although it might take time and a lot of money.

OPPONENTS

Leontes has no real opponents; his influence is sufficient that people stay on his good side. That said, he doesn't really have contact with people except in a positive manner, so he has few opportunities to make enemies.

LINKS

- ɸ Noumera (PA-14)

NPC-20

LOUKAS LASKARIS NOTARAS

ROLE

Megas Doux and Grand Logothete

Born in 1402 to the powerful Notaras family, Loukas has served the last two emperors as interpreter and emissary, negotiating treaties with Sultan Murad II and working hard to secure Catholic aid for the failing empire. He is heavily opposed to the Union of the Churches, famous for saying, after the Council of Florence, that "I would rather see a Turkish turban in the midst of The City than a Latin mitre". He is the rival and personal enemy of Georgios Sphrantzes. It is rumoured that the Notaras family are fabulously wealthy, sufficiently so that they could bail out the empire were they so minded.

APPEARANCE

Loukas Notaras is tall with an imposing beard that reaches mid-chest level, streaked with grey. His eyes are large and protruding, and behind his back he is known as *ho Batrachos* ("the frog"). His court regalia consists of a blue kabbadion with a white trim and a red skiadon or skaranikon with gold stripes. His khlamys is a matching colour to his headgear. Notaras chooses to carry the baton of the Megas Doux rather than go emptyhanded as is traditional for the logothetes; the baton has engraved gold bosses and has a silver chain wrapped around it.

SKILLS

Official 90%, Scholar 50%

ALLEGIANCES

Notaras controls the Chancellery and the Navy Office, and as one of the most powerful of the emperor's ministers has no end of sycophants and hangers-on. The only true alliances he has are with the Laskaris family, to whom he is related through both of his parents.

OPPONENTS

Notaras despises Georgios Sphrantzes. He resents Sphrantzes' high position despite his (relatively) low birth, and considers him an upstart and social climber. He publically opposes the emperor on several issues, and clashes between Constantine IX and his chief minister are the topic of market gossip.

LINKS

- ɸ Anti-Unionists (ORG-12)
- ɸ Chancellery (ORG-16)
- ɸ Naval Office (ORG-24)
- ɸ Great Palace/Daphne (PA-7)

NPC-21

MICHAEL SERRON

ROLE

Orphanotrophos

Michael Serron is the head of the smallest of the 12 departments in the Imperial Court, the Office of the Orphanotropheion which cares for the City's orphans and administers other charitable activities of the crown.

Michael Serron is perhaps one of the most well-informed people in Constantinople, with the possible exception of his rival the Logothete of the Dromos, Thomas Strouthion. Whereas the latter is seen as a shadowy figure who lurks behind a web of intrigue, the Orphanotrophos is known and loved in the city for his diligence and hard work. His network of informants is drawn from the ranks of the many children who have passed under his care in the long years of his career, and who have found themselves in a position to provide their former caretaker with information. There is camaraderie in being an orphan and despite their very different fates, all those who have sat at his table feel nothing but affection towards their brothers and sisters.

APPEARANCE

Michael Serron is in his eighth decade, but is remarkably spry for his age. He is a little shorter than average, and is stick-thin. His hair and beard are both snow-white. His court garb consists of a kabbadion or epilorikon of regulation white silk with a black trim. His truncated cone-shaped skaranikon is covered in red silk and has a small red tassel. He rarely wears his kabbadion outside of court (which he rarely attends in any case), but is fond of his skaranikon and wears it constantly.

SKILLS

Scholar 90%, Official 90%

ALLEGIANCES

Serron has countless connections forged from amongst the orphans formerly under his care. He is likely to have an informant in every government department, all imperial guilds and many private guilds as well. He does not have any criminal contacts, since he tries to find honest jobs for his charges.

OPPONENTS

Michael Serron has a professional rivalry with Thomas Strouthion, although it is about point-scoring rather than having any true heat, and they share information (eventually) that is in the empire's interest.

LINKS

- Imperial Orphanage (ORG-21)
- Zotikos (IMM-3)

NPC-22

ORBAN OF BRASSÓ

ROLE

Gunsmith and artillerist

A Hungarian iron-founder and master craftsman. Orban has a business in Kainopolis making the finest firearms in the city, although his real love is for making bombards. Orban has made some of the largest bombards known, and has plans to make even bigger ones. He employs a pair of brothers from Dubrovnik who craft most of the handgonnes and arquebuses, and a team of forge men, powder-grinders, and the like.

APPEARANCE

A short Hungarian man with short hair, patchy beard, and fire-reddened face. He has lost the last two fingers from his right hand, a testament to his dangerous profession.

SKILLS

Crafter 90%, Merchant 70%

ALLEGIANCES

Orban can rely on support from Andronikos Kantakouzenos, with whom he is negotiating for supplying new artillery towards Constantinople's defence. The bombards are expensive, but Orban is known for the quality of his work. The Grand Domestic has promised that the money will be forthcoming, and the moulds for a gun called "Basilike" have already been made. He promises that this bombard will be the largest that the world has ever seen

OPPONENTS

Orban has no rivals in gun manufacture in Constantinople.

LINKS

- Andronikos Kantakouzenos (NPC-3)
- Chalkoprateia (KN-5)

NPC-23

ORHAN ÇELEBI

ROLE

Şehzade (Prince) of the Ottoman Empire, Byzantine hostage

Şehzade Orhan Çelebi is an Ottoman dignitary and political hostage. He is the grandson of Süleyman Çelebi who was brother to Mehmet I; and other than Sultan Murad II and his son Mehmet II (with whom he shares a great grandfather), he is the only surviving member of the House of Osman. Orhan's father was kept in Constantinople as surety for the agreement between Emperor Manuel II Palaiologos and Mehmet I, when the Byzantines assisted Mehmet in taking the Ottoman throne from his brother Musa. After Mehmet I gained the throne he agreed to pay the Byzantine Empire to keep Orhan's father imprisoned, preventing him from mounting a challenge to the Ottoman throne. This sum, 3000 aspra per year, became the upkeep of Orhan and his sister Fatma upon the death of their father. However, since Mehmet II's ascension the upkeep has not been paid, and Constantine XI has threatened to release Prince Orhan unless the payments resume.

Orhan has a legitimate claim to the Ottoman throne. Although primogeniture is not a rule in Ottoman inheritance, birth order does add weight to any dispute, and Orhan is descended from the first son of Bayezid I rather than his youngest son, from whom Murad II and Mehmet II descend. The prince was born in Constantinople and considers it his home. He is not actively seeking to rule the Ottoman Empire, although the Turks who live permanently in the city are fiercely loyal to the prince and would support him if he did. This loyalty is a matter of no small concern to the Imperial Court, as Orhan poses a potential risk to the city's security. For now he seems content to live amongst his own people and act as liaison and advocate for the rights of Turkish citizens.

Orhan is hospitable and generous: despite the lack of support from his empire, he has personal wealth from which to draw. Those who deal with him find him personable and scrupulously honest, and his good looks are a favourite with Byzantine ladies. He is a keen tzykanion player, and a favourite amongst the fans.

APPEARANCE

Orhan is dashingly handsome. He is prideful of his hair: long, silky, black, and anointed with perfumed oils. He goes clean-shaven. He often combines Greek and Turkish clothing, but it is always impeccably tailored.

SKILLS
Sportsman 70%, Warrior 70%, Courtier 50%, Entertainer 50%

ALLEGIANCES
Orhan has a loyal following amongst the Turks who reside in Constantinople. There are five hundred soldiers who have sworn to protect the prince no matter who the enemy, Turk or Greek,

OPPONENTS
the Ottoman prince is aware that he is being watched by the spies of the Valide Sultan, and does his best to be aware of whoever is the current spy of the Office of the Drome. He is more concerned over the Turkish spies than the Greeks – as soon as he becomes a political nuisance he has no illusions that his cousin on the Ottoman throne will order his death, and he cannot be sure that his Byzantine handlers will risk their lives to save his. Orhan's sister Fatma has become addicted to opium, and the prince's investigations has revealed that Zayd al-Ghassani deliberately targeted her to obtain leverage over the Turks. He has vowed to gut the Syrian drug-dealer, but not until his sister can be cured.

LINKS
- Mitaton (PL-9)

NPC-24
THOMAS PALAIOLOGOS

ROLE
Despot in the Morea

The youngest surviving son of Emperor Manuel II Palaiologos and brother to the current Emperor Constantine XI. He became despot of Morea in 1428 with his brothers Theodoros and Constantine. When Constantine became emperor Thomas shared the lordship of Morea with his elder brother Demetrios, with Thomas ruling the northern half of the peninsula from Glarentza. Thomas has a fiercely anti-Ottoman position, despite having to concede Turkish dominance of the province. He is married to Catherine Zaccaria, daughter of the last Latin Prince of Achaea; and they have four children: Helena (married to Despot Lazar II of Serbia), Andreas, Manuel, and Zoe (who is betrothed to Grand Prince Ivan III of Russia). The two boys are the only male issue amongst the grandchildren of Manuel II.

APPEARANCE
Thomas is in his thirties but appears younger, untouched by the worries of statehood. His hair and beard are brown, unlike his darker brothers. His court dress is a red rhoukon like that of the emperor, with a kabbadion of purple and red and a red khlamys. His skiadon is covered in pearls, and he wears red hose, and purple and white boots with pearled eagles.

SKILLS
Courtier 70%, Warrior 50%

ALLEGIANCES
Thomas always had a good relationship with his brothers John and Constantine, which put him immediately in conflict with his other brother Demetrios. Thomas was schooled by Plethon, and maintains a good friendship with the aged philosopher.

OPPONENTS
Apart from his brother Demetrios, Thomas has no real opponents; he spends precious little time at court to attract any rivals.

LINKS
- Constantine XI Palaiologos (NPC-6)

NPC-25
THOMAS STROUTHION

ROLE
Logothete of the Drome

Thomas is widely believed to be an imperial bastard although rumours vary as to whether he is John's or Constantine's son. Either way he has been shown favour by the current emperor, but has earned his trust through hard work. His nickname means "little sparrow", a term also used for agents of the Drome, because they can be anywhere and are always watching what is going on. His personal sigil is a sparrow in the same posture as the Palaiologian eagle. Thomas is young for such an important position (being in his thirties), but has proven himself to be both capable and loyal.

APPEARANCE
Medium height with a short beard and black hair. His hair is longer than is fashionable, partly to conceal the port-wine birthmark on his forehead. He dresses according to his status but without being ostentatious. He only occasionally attends court; when he does his regalia consists of a blue

and red epilorikon rather than a kabbadion, with a skiadon made of white silk and decorated with pearls. Like the other logothetes he does not carry a baton.

SKILLS
Agent 90%, Official 50%, Courtier 50%

ALLEGIANCES
Thomas Strouthion takes his role very seriously. He has become an ally of Georgios Sphrantzes

OPPONENTS
The Little Sparrow is disliked by most of the ministers of the court, in particular Loukas Notaras. As a rumoured bastard (albeit an unacknowledged one), he has an enemy in Demetrios Palaiologos, who is the next in line while Constantine has no appointed heirs.

LINKS

- ɸ Office of the Drome (ORG-25)
- ɸ Paramonai (ORG-31)
- ɸ Great Palace/Triklinos of the Candidati (PA-7)

NPC-26

ZAYD IBN TAMIM AL-GHASSANI

ROLE
Alchemist and Falsifier

A Syrian Arab by birth, although Zayd has not been in his homeland for many decades. Once the employee of Balsamon Astraeios, Zayd is now his partner, and between them, they run the Star and Crescent, one of the larger criminal organisations in Constantinople.

Zayd is an alchemist by trade, and has invented several new preparations of opium and other recreational drugs, changing the potency, the addictive properties, and the effects on the user. He is an accomplished magician, and is favourite means of smuggling is to use the Amalgamate spell to hide the smuggled matter (such as pure opium resin) inside another innocuous substance and bring it through customs, paying duty for what it appears to be. Most of his contraband originates in Asia, and might come aboard a ship on the Black Sea or else smuggled across the Bosphoros at the dead of night.

APPEARANCE
Zayd is in his late sixties, although his alchemical preparations have kept him hale. He dresses in a striped burnoose, a green turban and a headscarf. The colour of his turban indicates to other Arabs he is a descendent of the Prophet.

SKILLS
Alchemist 90%, Miracle-Worker 70%

ALLEGIANCES
Balsamon Astraeios is Zayd's business partner; while Balsamon considers them bosom friends, Zayd considers Balsamon to be no more than a useful ally. He would not hesitate to betray his partner if the circumstances warranted it.

OPPONENTS
Zayd has nothing but distaste for all farangi (westerners, including Greeks), but does his best to hide his opinions of their decadence. He has made an enemy of Orhan Çelebi by addicting his sister to one of his alchemical drugs, although he is the only one who knows the formula to make her specific preparation, thus safeguarding himself from the prince's vengeance.

LINKS

- ɸ Star and Crescent (ORG-33)

CONSTANTINOPLE IN DETAIL

Constantinople is squalid and fetid and in many places harmed by permanent darkness, for the wealthy overshadow the streets with buildings and leave these dirty, dark places to the poor and to travellers; there murders and robberies and other crimes which love darkness are committed.

~ *Odo of Deuil, 1147*

From this chapter onwards only the Games Master should proceed. If you are going to be the player in a Mythic Constantinople game, please stop reading now.

This chapter describes in detail the Great City of Constantine. Each of its nine districts and two suburbs will be taken in turn, giving an overview of the people who live there, the characters with whom to interact, and the key locations to be found. Unlike a standard fantasy city description, of which there are several fine examples, a different approach is given here.

CITY NODES

There is no detailed street-level map with the locations and characters indicated thereon. Rather, Mythic Constantinople is described as a network of interlinked elements. Each place or person of interest is a node on this network, and has links to further nodes. Some of these nodes are geographically connected, so a character conducting a chase through the city will travel between successive nodes; but some of the nodes are social connections, requiring the characters to interact with people to pass from one node to another. The geographical nodes are organised in a hierarchal fashion: several nodes make up a neighbourhood, which themselves make up a district.

NODE NOMENCLATURE

Each node has a designation for quick reference.

- Nodes that have two letters and a number (for example, VL-4) are found in this chapter, since they link to a specific location or person within the city.
- Nodes with a three letter designation (for example, NPC-22) are found in the previous chapter (for people and organisations) or next chapter (for events in a greater plot).

Following the node's name, the description of each node begins with a list of Affiliation categories; a character might come to this node thanks to the information supplied by one of his Affiliations of this type, or else a character can use an appropriate Affiliation to find out more information about the node. The description of each node ends with a list of Links. Interacting with this node can reveal none or more of these leads (depending on character actions), and each lead contains a cross-reference to the section to which it points.

The nodes are arranged into sections for each of the districts and suburbs of Constantinople. As well as the node descriptions, each section also has local knowledge and Local Rumours relevant to that district. Local knowledge requires a Skill roll to determine what the characters know about the area. Rumours are just that; they can be picked up from any person with whom the characters have a significant interaction, or they can be obtained from a Streetwise roll while visiting the public areas of the district. Also in each district or suburb section is a list of Descriptive Elements, which can be used when characterising the district to the players. These might be features or landmarks found in the district, types of people that populate the streets, or adjectives that give the general demeanour and appearance of the district.

DESCRIBING THE CITY

Constantinople is too large to provide a comprehensive map of its streets. A million people lived here at its height, and although only a portion of that population lives here today the City is vast enough to make detailed maps excessive. Characters often simply pass through neighbourhoods to get between locations in which they are interested, without worrying about which route they take or what they see on the way. Sometimes however it is necessary to know exactly what is in the local area.

This section offers a means by which the Games Master can generate a node in less than five minutes. This node should be treated just like the nodes described in this chapter, and it is worth keeping notes on the nodes you develop yourself, since once they are created they should be the same if the characters decide to go back there. The method below can also be used to add context to one of the locations described in this chapter, which typically include just one building in their description.

PLACES OF WORSHIP

Constantinople has a lot of churches and monasteries, some of which are described below. At the head of each description are three statistics that are of interest to theists:

- *Congregation Size: the average number of parishioners. This can swell to two or three times as many on religious festivals or saints' days;*
- *Piety: the average Love God of the congregation;*
- *Magical Strength: the percentage of a theist's MP that can be recovered here and the size of a theist's Devotional Pool as a percentage of his POW.*

RANDOMLY GENERATING A CITY NODE

To create a node, you will first need to know what district and neighbourhood it is in. Find the neighbourhood in the appropriate section below; the connections assigned to it will let you know:

- Typical societal level (dynatos, mesos, demos)
- Characteristic professions practised here
- Cultural mix, if not Greek

The description will also tell you if it is a crowded neighbourhood or more sparsely populated than average.

Next, roll 1d6, 1d8, 1d10, and 1d12 on a piece of paper, and consult the ***Random Buildings Table*** to determine what type of buildings are present at the node. The actual locations of the dice on the page represent the relative placements of these buildings. You can use more or fewer dice if you wish, but these four are a good starting place. If you are creating your location around a known place (such as the taberna that the player characters are currently inside, or one of the nodes described later on in this chapter), then include 1d4 in with the dice when you throw them to find out where it is in relation to the other buildings.

Draw lines between some or all of the dice to determine where the streets and alleyways go, fashioning T-junctions, dog-legs, central courtyards, and the like as the fancy takes you. The streets do not necessarily have to cross at right angles. Next, draw boxes (not necessary four-sided ones) around the dice to determine the relative positions of the buildings around the streets. The proximity of the dice on the page determines how close the buildings are: if the dice are (virtually) touching, then so are the buildings; if they are far apart then a park or a forum might separate them.

Pay attention to these combinations of numbers:

- If ***two*** dice roll the same number, then there is a *feature* here. Choose or roll on the ***Random Feature Table***, and pay attention to the descriptive elements of the district when fleshing it out. The feature is situated somewhere between the two buildings partaking in the double.
- If ***three*** dice roll the same number, then there is an *event* going on at this intersection right now. The die not included in the triple indicates the building in or near which the event is happening. Choose or roll on the ***Random Events Table***. You may also add a feature if you wish.
- If all ***four*** dice roll the same number, then something *disastrous* is happening right now, or has occurred in the recent past and its after effects are still obvious. Choose or roll on the ***Random Disasters Table***. You may also add a feature if you wish.

RESIDENCES

The typical residence of a low class neighbourhood is the tenement. These have 2d3 storeys around a square courtyard with one exit to an alleyway. Each storey consists of up to four apartments, each big enough for a married couple and children, although this is crowded. Many families occupy multiple apartments. Depending on the neighbourhood and district, tenements might be overcrowded or mostly vacant, and they might be well looked-after or on the verge of collapse. It is quite common for the ground floor apartments to be places of business, and many neighbourhood tabernai are located in these locations.

The typical residence for a middle class neighbourhood is a house, often with a workplace or shop on the ground floor and a residential apartment on the first floor. These houses are often terraced in blocks, and usually face onto a street. They often have upper storeys which hang over the streets, flouting city ordinances about the width of streets.

The typical residence for an upper class neighbourhood is a villa. These occupy an entire block, and are usually surrounded by a wall enclosing a small garden. The entrance leads into an enclosed courtyard which stands in front of the main house.

If the size of any family matters then you can use the Family Tables (Mythras rulebook page 25) to generate random families. During the day the men of the household are likely to be at work.

See page 132-133 for samples of typical dwellings.

BUSINESSES

A business may be a simple, family-run enterprise or it may be a place of work for several unrelated workers. There are many possible trades in the city, some more common than others. Many neighbourhoods have workers of similar trades gathered together (as indicated by the Professional Connection listed under the neighbourhood description), and most businesses will belong to that or a related trade. However, there are always other trades mixed in with the more characteristic ones, so a Business Table is provided on page 131 for you to choose or determine randomly the trade of any business at a node. This is not meant to be representative of the frequency of any trade in the city, merely a source of inspiration. You may wish to first determine what type of business (common or specialist) based on the neighbourhood social class: a lower class neighbourhood has a 5 in 6 chance of a specialist business; a middle class neighbourhood a 4 in 6 chance; and an upper class neighbourhood a 3 in 6 chance.

A business typically has a proprietor and 1d3−1 assistants. These may be family members or hirelings.

CHURCHES & MONASTERIES

Constantinople is crowded with churches and monasteries. Most churches will be simple cross-in-square design with a priest in charge and 3d20+10 parishioners. If there are more than 50 parishioners the priest probably has a deacon to assist him. During mass, most of these parishioners will be present, but at other times only 3d6–6 (minimum 0) parishioners will be present. The Magical Strength is 25% and the Piety is 1d6%.

Small neighbourhood monasteries have 2d6 monks (equal probability of them being all male or all female). The Magical Strength is 50%, and the Piety is 3d20+10%.

Choose or roll a dedication for the church or monastery from the ***Random Saints Table***. About half the churches and monasteries in Constantinople are dedicated to the Virgin Mary, not for nothing is the city nicknamed "Theotokopolis".

See page 132 for samples of a typical church.

OCCUPANTS & BYSTANDERS

As well as the characters, there will be other people present at the node. Assume that all buildings have a normal number of occupants, as detailed above. Outside there are two types of people: street occupants who tend to remain present in the streets for some time; and passers-by who will be here fleetingly.

Use the ***Random Street Occupants Table*** to generate the first type, rolling d100 and consult the appropriate column. If this is a highly populated area, make multiple rolls on this table. If it is night time, then subtract 30 (to a minimum of 01) from the value rolled before looking up on the table.

Passers-by are on their way elsewhere, or else they are customers of the businesses, visitors of the residents, or worshippers at the church. Either way, they are disinterested in the characters and will hurry away if approached. If you need to know how many passers-by are present, use the following method for each hour. For every residence at the node, roll 1d6. For every business, roll 1d10. For every church roll 1d4. Monasteries do not attract any additional people. There is one passer-by for each point of the total of these dice. Apply the largest of the following modifiers that applies (minimum of zero passers-by):

- Crowded neighbourhood: no adjustment
- Average neighbourhood: subtract 10
- Sparse neighbourhood: subtract 20
- Any neighbourhood at night: subtract 30

If the player characters remain at a node for any length of time and the occupants of the street matter to them, then the Street Occupants hang around for 1d6 hours. There will be a different number of passers-by every time the characters emerge from a building, or every half-hour.

CONNECTING THE NODE

As an option you may wish to add Affiliations to the node. If it is a one-off location which probably won't feature again in your campaign then this is not necessary, but otherwise choose or randomly determine 1d3 Affiliations as well as the Societal Affiliation that matches the node's neighbourhood. If you wish, determine the specific Affiliation within each category; this will allow you to characterise the node better and get an idea regarding its inhabitants.

The last stage in generating a node is to link it to other nodes. You already know in which neighbourhood it located, so you can add that link immediately. Next, have a look at the neighbourhood map, and decide whether the node is connected to other neighbourhoods in the same district or adjacent ones. Make at least one link to a node that already exists, either one detailed in this book or one that you have created yourself. You can make as many other links as you see fit.

Give your new node a name, and if you want, a designation based in its home district. You are done!

All the tables used for generating nodes can be found on pages 130 to 131.

EXAMPLE OF GENERATING A NODE

The player characters failed to apprehend their target during the recent fight, but they did manage to break his rapier. Realising that there are aren't many craftsmen capable of making such a fine weapon, they use their connections to track one down and stake it out. The Games Master approves of this clever plan and decides it will give them another chance to catch the mysterious Venetian they are chasing, but since they are setting up an ambush at a hitherto undescribed location, he needs to generate a node.

The node is located in the Venetian Quarter, a middle-class neighbourhood associated with fancy wares. The Games Master gathers up the four dice, adds a d4 to represent the location of the weaponsmith, and rolls them. He draws on a street and a narrow alleyway between buildings. Because two dice show a number 2 he rolls for a feature, and places a fountain in some parkland between the two residences. Next he draws around the dice to get the shape of the buildings, and starts to add details.

- *The residences take the typical Venetian design, overcrowding the street below. Each is occupied by a single family.*
- *The other business is a cordwainer*
- *The church is dedicated to a Catholic saint rather than an Orthodox one. Rather than rolling, the Games Master decides that it is the Church of Saint Luke the Evangelist.*
- *The fountain is surrounded by a small formal garden.*

To populate the node, the Games Master rolls twice on the Random Street Occupants, using the middle class column. This produces one street entertainer (a juggler) and 3 locals gossiping on a street corner. There are two businesses, two residences and a church at the node, and therefore (2d10 + 2d6 + 1d4 – 10) passers-by, resulting in 9 potential witnesses for anything the characters wish to do.

The node has just one Affiliation other than Societal (mesoi), and it is a Criminal one. The Games Master decides that the Zanconi have a hold over the priest of Saint Luke's.

RANDOM BUILDINGS TABLE

1d12	Building
1–3	Residence appropriate to the neighbourhood's societal level
4	Residence other than the neighbourhood's societal level
5–6	Business appropriate to neighbourhood
7–8	Business other than that appropriate to the neighbourhood
9–10	Church
11–12	Monastery

RANDOM FEATURE TABLE

1d20	Feature
1	Statue of an animal (horse, lion, dolphin, elephant, eagle, goose, fly, rat, snake)
2	Statue of historical figure (emperor, patriarch, patrician)
3	Statue of mythological figure
4	Statue inhabited by a spirit (see page 219)
5	Fountain (reroll for Platea)
6	Arch
7	Shrine
8	Column
9	Portico
10	Fire tower
11	Marketplace
12	Remains of a palace
13	Derelict house or shop
14	Animal pen
15	Garden
16	Stone cross commemorating a saint
17	Burned-out or ruined church
18	Sewer opening (reroll for Xerolophos)
19	Above-ground cistern
20	Abandoned monastery

RANDOM EVENTS TABLE

1d20	Feature
1	A robbery in progress
2	A wedding procession
3	Mourners attending a funeral or memorial
4	Discovery of a body
5	A foreigner in distress
6	Mistreatment from the phylakes or Vardariotai
7	A street preacher or holy fool harangues passers-by
8	A horde of rats throng over an object
9	An argument between two individuals or groups
10	Someone is about to vandalise another's property, or has already done so
11	The religious procession of an ikon held aloft followed by a crowd of the faithful
12	Herd of sheep or pigs loose in the streets

RANDOM EVENTS TABLE (CONTINUED)

1d20	Feature
13	Backed-up sewer overflowing into streets
14	Someone is about to disturb a huge swarm of bees
15	Locals are in the middle of felling a tree causing a nuisance
16	Characters become potential targets for pickpockets
17	Characters are accused of or framed for a crime that has just occurred
18	A political rally consisting of a small mob lead by a demagogue
19	An upset cart blocks the street, its contents scattered everywhere
20	A Very Important Person (minor royal, patriarch, minister) passes through with entourage

RANDOM DISASTERS TABLE

1d20	Event
1	Fire affecting one or more adjacent buildings
2	Riot sparked by taxes, religion, politics, etc. Vardariotai might already be on scene
3	Lynching of a perceived criminal or foreigner
4	Words are mysteriously appearing on a wall, and they speak of doom and dark times
5	Minor earthquake affecting whole neighbourhood
6	An act of terrorism perpetrated by Prasinoi (see page 109) intended to disrupt and frighten
7	One of the buildings or features suffers catastrophic collapse
8	Most of the locals are currently suffering from a mysterious illness
9	A bizarre localised thunderstorm striking buildings and people with lightning
10	The seasons turned around: snow in summer, baking heat in winter
11	Night becomes day and day becomes night
12	A malevolent spirit lurks nearby, preparing to have its evil way
13	A terrible beast runs rampant, attacking indiscriminately
14	The restless dead (ghouls) roam the streets, hungering for flesh
15	A source of water (fountain, overflowing sewer, tap) has turned to blood
16	A pillar of blazing white fire blocks the street
17	Noxious gases have emerged from a building or the sewers; people have begun to succumb
18	Shadows reach out and grab at people's clothing and limbs
19	All base metal tarnishes and rusts in an instant; a wall supported by scaffolding is in peril
20	A demon (see page 220) is about to manifest from an innocuous mundane animal

RANDOM BUSINESS TABLE

1d100	Common Business	Specialist Business
01–04	Apothecary or herbalist	Architect and Mason
05–08	Baker	Armourer and/or crossbow maker
09–12	Barber	Book and parchment maker
13–16	Basket weaver and/or broom-maker	Book and/or map seller
17–20	Brothel	Brickmaker and/or tile maker
21–24	Butcher (lamb and beef)	Button-maker and/or thread-maker
25–28	Butcher (pork)	Clockmaker
29–32	Candlemaker and oil distiller	Confectioner
33–36	Carpenter	Cutler (blade maker)
37–40	Clothier	Glassmaker and/or glassblower
41–44	Cobbler (shoe repairs)	Goldsmith*
45–48	Cordwainer (shoe maker)	Gunsmith
49–52	Fishmonger*	Hostel
53–56	Grocer (dried food)	Linen merchant*
57–60	Grocer (fresh food)	Milliner (hat maker)
61–64	Grocer (small goods)	Moneylender*
65–68	Leatherworker	Notary and/or advocate
69–72	Pankration ring and training field	Perfumier*
73–76	Potter	Physician
77–80	Phouskarion	Rug-maker
81–84	Ropemaker and/or Netweaver	Silk merchant*
85–88	Sailmaker	Silversmith
89–92	Smith (iron, copper, or brass)	Wheelwright
93–96	Taberna	Wiredrawer and needlemaker
97–00	Warehouse	Witch, prognosticator, seer

**Required by law to trade in a specific marketplace (see page 11), so possibly operating illegally.*

RANDOM SAINTS TABLE

1d100	Dedicated to...
01–03	Theotokos Kecharitomene ("Full of Grace")
04–06	Theotokos Glykophilousa ("of the Sweet Kiss")
07–09	Theotokos Eleousa ("The Merciful")
10–12	Theotokos Panagiotissa ("All Holy")
13–15	Theotokos Paregoretria ("Giver of Solace")
16–18	Theotokos Platytera ton Ouranon ("Wider than the Heavens")
19–21	Theotokos Hagiaskepe ("The Sacred Protection")
22–24	Theotokos Ponolytria ("The Deliverer from Pain")
25–27	Theotokos Aeiparthenos ("Ever Virgin")
28–30	Theotokos Pantanassa ("Queen of All")
31–32	Theotokos Pammakaristos ("All Blessed")
33–34	Theotokos Eleutherotria ("The Liberator")
35–36	Theotokos Giatrissa ("The Healer")
37–38	Theotokos Gorgoepekoös ("The Quick-to-Listen")
39–40	Theotokos Chrysopege ("The Fountain of Gold")

RANDOM SAINTS TABLE (CONTINUED)

1d100	Dedicated to...
41–42	Theotokos Kataphyge ("The Safe Haven")
43–44	Theotokos Angeloktiste ("Built by Angels")
45–46	Theotokos Nerantziotissa ("of the Bitter Oranges")
47–48	Theotokos Kyriotissa ("Enthroned")
49–50	Theotokos Panachrantes ("Immaculate")
51–52	Saint Barbara: patron of military engineers, artillerymen, and gunpowder
53–54	Saint Michael: first of the seven archangels and patron of the fight against evil, carries a spear with a white banner and a green palm branch
55–56	Saint Georgios: patron of cavalry, farmers, shepherds, and against skin diseases
57–58	Saint Theodoros Strateletes: "the General", patron of soldiers, specifically the commanders
59–60	Saint Demetrios of Thessaloniki: patron of soldiers (see page 179)
61–62	Saint Theodosia of Constantinople: most beloved native saint, patron of the infirm, lame, deaf, and mute (see page 163)
63–64	Saint John the Forerunner: has more churches dedicated to him in Constantinople than any saint other than Mary.
65–66	Saint Euphemia: her relics repudiated Monophysitism at the Council of Chalcedon
67–68	Saint Constantine Isapostolos: "Equal-of-the-Apostles" due to role in spreading Christianity
69	Saint Helena: mother of Saint Constantine, discoverer of relics, including the True Cross, the Nails of Crucifixion, the Holy Tunic, and the Burning Bush
70	Saint Polyeuktos: patron of vows and treaties
71	Saint Theodoros Tyron: "the Recruit", patron of infantry and the recovery of lost articles
72	Saint Stephen the Protomartyr: patron of masons and headaches
73	The Holy Unmercenaries: The Anargyroi are those saints who refused renumeration for their charitable acts. Patrons of the poor and the desperate
74	Saints Kosmas and Damianos: twin brothers and patrons of surgeons, barbers, orphanages, and confectioners
75	Saint Gabriel: second of the seven archangels and the instrument of divine revelation, carries a lamp (revelation) and a mirror of green jasper (mystery)
76	Saint Nicholas: patron of thieves, pharmacists, and sailors
77	Saint Panteleimon: patron of physicians, lotteries, loneliness, and against witchcraft
78	Saint Menas: patron of peddlers and the falsely accused
79	Saint Raphael: third of the seven archangels and fount of healing, carries an alabaster jar full of the healing waters of Paradise
80	Saint Lavrentios: patron of chefs, miners, tanners, librarians, and comedians
81	Saint Moses the Black: larger-than-life patron of non-violence
82	Saint Abo of Tiflis: patron of perfumers and converts from Islam
83	Saint Uriel: fourth of the seven archangels and embodiment of God's understanding and guidance, scientists and seekers of truth. Carries a sword in his right hand and fire in the left
84	Saint Thaïs the Harlot: patron of prostitutes
85	Saint Tryphon: patron of geese, gardeners, and vine growers
86	Saint Elizabeth the Dragon-slayer: patron of menstruating women

RANDOM SAINTS TABLE (CONTINUED)

1d100	Dedicated to...
87	Saint Khristophoros the Dog-Headed: patron of travellers and bachelors
88	Saint Anastasia the Pharmakolytria: "Deliverer from Poison", patron of weavers and the poisoned
89	Saint Apollonia: patron of dentistry and toothache
90	Saint Basil the Ouranophantor: patron of courtiers, administrators, and exorcists, "revealer of heavenly mysteries"
91	Saint Selatiel: fifth of the seven archangels and angel of worship, overcomer of obstacles. Depicted with arms folded and eyes downcast in prayer.
92	Saint Theophilos the Penitent: made a deal with the devil for his bishopric, saved by the Theotokos
93	Saint Monica of Hippo: patron of difficult marriages and abuse of alcohol
94	Saint John the Compassionate: patron of the poor and of religious tolerance
95	Saints Agape, Chionia, and Eirene: three sisters from Thessalonkiki whose names mean "Love", "Purity", and "Peace".
96	Saint Jegudiel: sixth of the seven archangels, angel of leadership and patron of hard work. Carries a wreath (reward) and a three-tailed whip (punishment)
97	Saint Polykarpos of Smyrna: patron against dysentery and earache
98	Saint Barachiel: seventh of the seven archangels, angel of the family, guardian of worldly success. Carries a white rose, or a staff and breadbasket
99	Saint Vitus: patron of dogs and comedians
100	Saint Gregory the Wonderworker: patron against thieves and of desperate causes

RANDOM STREETS OCCUPANTS TABLE

	Lower Class	Middle Class	Upper Class
No-one	01–10	01–20	01–30
Prostitute	11–20	21–27	31–33
1d2 drunkards	21–25	28–30	—
1d4 ne'er-do-wells	26–30	31–32	34
1d4+1 urchins	31–38	33–36	—
Pack of 2d6 dogs	39–48	37–46	35–44
1d4+1 phylakes	49–53	47–49	—
1d6 locals	54–67	50–59	45–49
1d4 locals plus 1d6 servants	68	60–63	50–59
1d4+1 Vardariots	—	64–65	60–66
Beggar	69–76	67–68	—
Messenger or courier	77–80	69–75	67–80
Street performer	81–85	76–80	81–82
Delivery, with handcart or wagon	86–89	81–88	83–88
Tinker or peddler	90–93	89–93	89–92
Food vendor	94–97	94–97	93–95
Wine or water seller	98–00	98–00	96–00

RANDOM AFFILIATION TABLE

1d20	Affiliation category
1–2	Criminal
3–4	Cultural
5–7	Professional
8–9	Family
10–11	Military
12–13	Religious/Christian
14	Educational
15	Political
16	Urban
17	Deviant
18	Religious/Muslim
19	Religious/Jewish
20	Rural

TYPICAL CHURCH

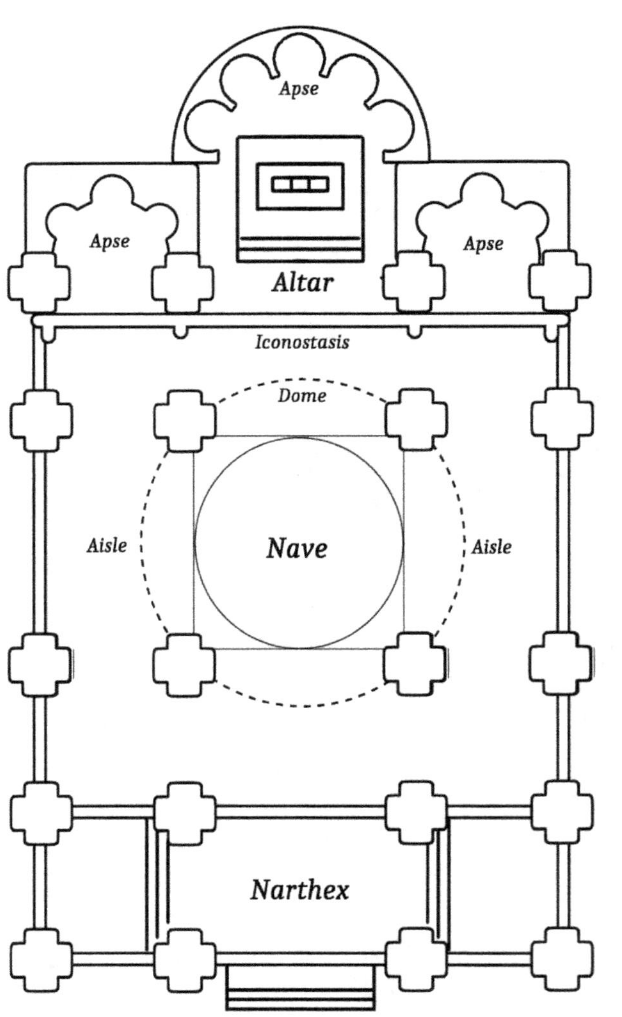

TYPICAL TENEMENT

1st Floor

Yard

2nd Floor

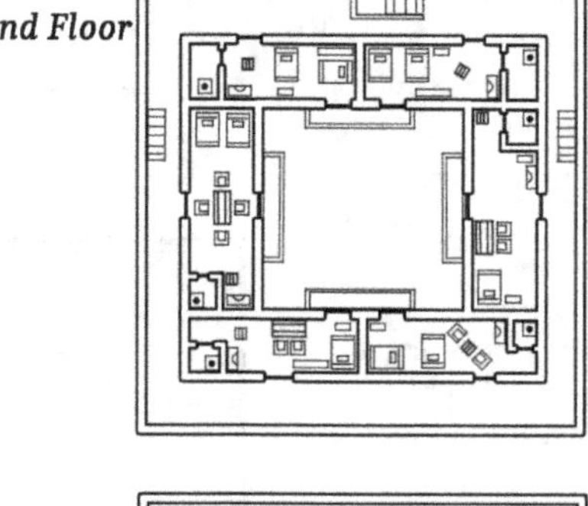

3rd Floor

Roof

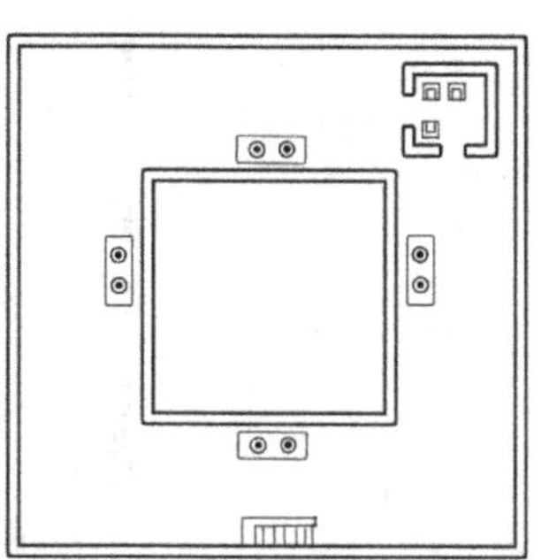

TYPICAL HOUSE

2nd Floor

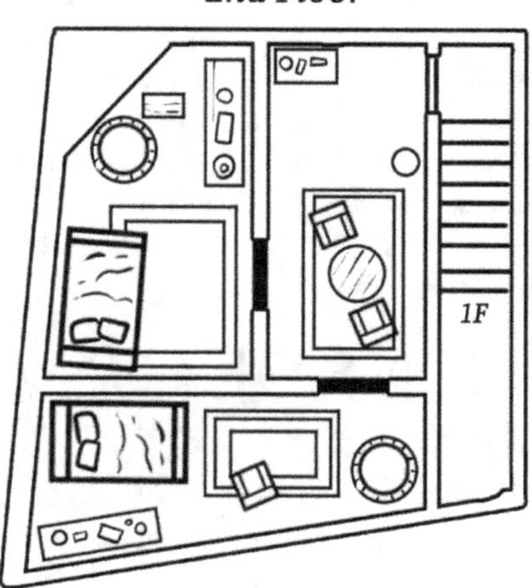

First Floor

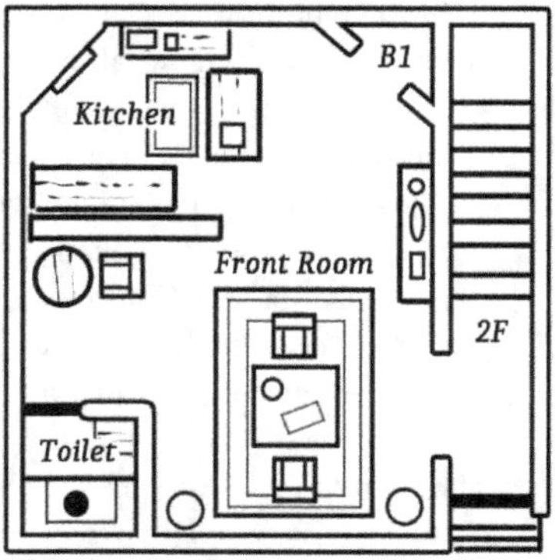

Basement

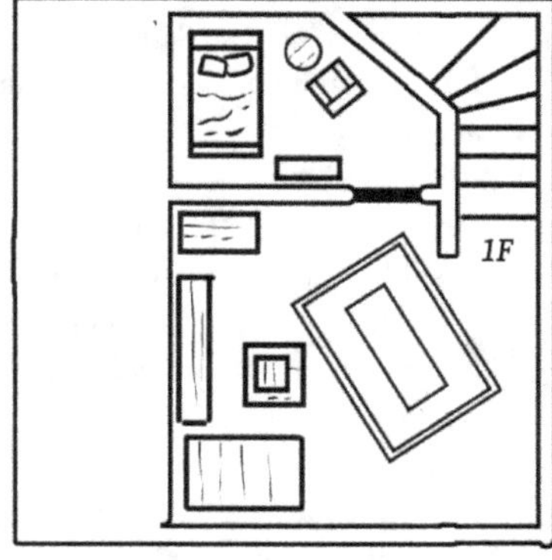

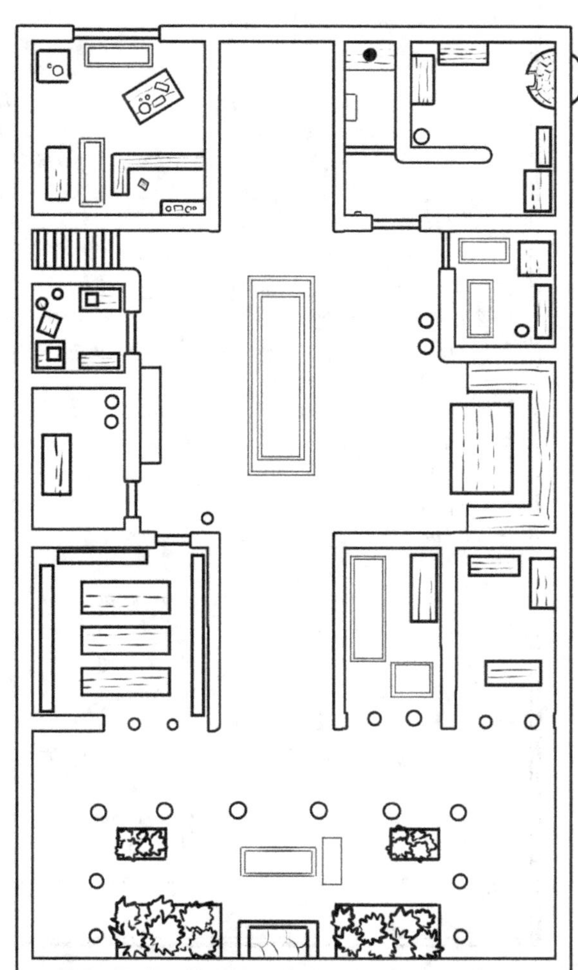

TYPICAL VILLA

NAVIGATING CONSTANTINOPLE

The Streetwise Skill governs a character's knowledge of Constantinople. With each of the following districts and suburbs described below there is a local knowledge section revealed on a successful roll of that Skill, and other Skills where relevant. This section deals with questions asked of The City as a whole. See the Common Questions and Answers Table on page 135 for some typically posed questions about the city.

TOPICS OF CONVERSATION

The following things are discussed by inhabitants of Constantinople:

- The kommerkion, or customs tax, levied at 10% on all goods coming in or going out of Constantinople and on all transactions with imported goods in between. This swingeing tax is a major source of wealth for the government, and in the days that the empire was at the centre of the world, it was highly lucrative, encouraging affluent merchants to come here to trade. Now it is a yoke on an already cash-poor society, especially since foreign merchants have been offered concessions and exemptions. The kommerkion is only 4% in the Embolo, and it is not charged at all in Pera.
- The health of the Empress Helena Dragaš is a matter of great concern to the populace. The empress dowager is greatly loved, but rumours abound that she had a bout of sickness during the winter.
- The Union of the Churches was enacted 13 years ago, but is still a matter of great contention in Constantinople. The emperor and patriarch are pro-Union, but many of the emperor's ministers, including the Grand Logothete, are fervent anti-Unionist. It is a great scandal (to both sides) that the Patriarch has been denied access to Hagia Sophia by the anti-Unionists.
- Rumours have been circulating that Theodoros Palaiologos, older brother of the emperor, is still alive. Theodoros was a possible heir to the throne, and the rumour is that rather than dying of plague two years ago as widely reported, he faked his own death in the wake of an assassination attempt from one of his brothers.
- The city dreads the day that Mehmed II becomes sultan. Murad II has been a benign suzerain, but his son showed his true colours in the two short years of his first reign (1444–1446), and there is no doubt he desires the conquest of Constantinople.
- Several murders have occurred where the victim's hands and feet have been removed. Reports on the number of victims vary, but it is currently less than 10. Most of the victims were found in Vlanga.
- The Vardariotai are becoming more partisan. They are rarely seen at all in some areas of the city, and rebellion is brewing there. It seems like the only place you see them these days is near the businesses of the mesoi who pay the largest bribes.
- The Prasinoi (or Greens) are denounced as anarchists by their detractors and royalists by their supporters. They seek to bring down the imperial bureaucracy and restore direct rule to the emperor.
- The streets of The City are not safe. Cutthroats and robbers abound, as do much more sinister creatures. There are persistent rumours of *broukolakes*, horrific creatures that prey on the blood of their victims; quite apart from the flesh-eating *strigoi* (ghouls) who used to haunt parts of Platea.

INHABITATED STATUES

Constantinople is filled with statues, and some of them have a life of their own. People say that they are inhabited by demons that cause them to speak, move, seduce women, and injure people. All classes of society approach statues to reveal faithless spouses, restore sexual potency, foretell future events, or heal a particular complaint.

These inhabited statues each contain a spirit rather than a demon. They were created by the Ktistes (IMM-8), an ancient guild of statue carvers. Each statue is the focus of a Location Binding (Mythras page 135). The bound spirit usually inhabits the statue, and since it has the same appearance as the statue itself the spirit remains undetected for the most part. Occasionally, those addressing the statue will see its eyes move or its expression change, but what they are actually seeing is the spirit. The spirits have a range of different Abilities, which determines what it can do. Half of all inhabited statues have an Intensity of 1, the remaining half have an Intensity of 1d2+1. They have one Spirit Ability per point of Intensity from the following list:

- *Animate Stone or Bronze: spirits with this Ability can animate their own statue. They can move their limbs, gesture, form the shape of words with their mouths, and even walk – although they cannot go more than their POW in metres from their plinth. An Inhabited Statue has the statistics of an earth elemental with a volume equal to twice its Intensity, in cubic metres. The statue is not necessarily that volume, but is made of dense stone or bronze, which is as resilient and damaging as a much larger volume of earth.*
- *Glamour: spirits with this Ability can speak by forming phantom words, either aloud or in someone's mind. Talking statues may pretend to know the future.*
- *Healing: spirits with this Ability normally have the power to cure a specific illness. Since spirits cannot regain Magic Points while bound, healing statues normally require a sacrifice (see Mythras page 117 for typical MP value of animal sacrifices)*
- *Passion (Truthfulness): spirits with this Ability can force a person to tell the truth. If the spirit wins an opposed Willpower contest, then the victim is forced to answer questions put to him or her truthfully. A given spirit might only force truth over certain questions such as marital fidelity or else it might permit all manner of questioning, depending on its personality.*
- *Domination (single pest species): spirits with this Ability take the form of the species they can affect, typically a rat, fly, beetle, scorpion, or snake. They were designed to keep the city free from such pests. Any pest of the appropriate kind coming within POW metres of the statue is ordered to flee, and those with INS rather than INT continue to flee even after leaving the spirit's range of effect.*

COMMON QUESTIONS AND ANSWERS TABLE

Where can I find ...?	Answer
a place to stay	Most districts have a *xenodocheion* (hostel) where the room is free but you pay for food and service. There is a famous one in Petrion.
a place to eat and/or drink	The tabernai of Sporakion are the highest quality, followed by those on the Mese Odos. Back-alley tabernai are more for the budget-minded.
a place to get drunk	Potent *phouska* can be bought in most districts, but Vlanga has the cheapest
gambling	Most tabernai in Eleutherion for games of chance
spectator sports	The Skamma of Eumachos for pankration
The Tzykanisterion for tzykanion	Religious/Christian
The Hippodrome for foot and horse racing	Educational
a library	The Stoudion Monastery
a scholar	The Pandidakterion
a lawyer	The Law School of Magnaura
official records	Kanikleion
opium	Any of the brothels owned by Star and Crescent
hired companionship	Prostitution is rife; Platea has numerous brothels, Vlanga has Thaïs Alley and plentiful street trade
mercenaries	Psamathia currently houses the empire's soldiers
a thief for hire	Amastrianon
a moneylender	Guild moneylenders trade on the Mese Odos. If you have poor credit history then there are reportedly Venetians who will make secured loans

AKROPOLIS (DISTRICT)

The District of the Akropolis is the oldest in the city. There are buildings here whose foundations date back two thousand years, when Byzantion was just a colony of Megara. The ruins of the old wall which went around the base of the First Hill can still be seen in places, particularly where they mark the district's southern border. The Harbour Road divides Akropolis from Kainopolis. The central road running from the Eastern Gate to the Milion, and then later extended between the Great Palace and the Hippodrome into Hormisidon is called the Pelargoi ("the storks") due to the birds that roost along its length. Many of the churches in Akropolis used to be temples to the pagan gods, or else built over them. Artemis, Aphrodite, Apollon, Hekate, Demeter, Poseidon, and Zeus all had prominent altars in Kynegion and Mangana; the most famous example being the Church of Saint Menas, which used to be a temple to Poseidon. A few minotauroi in Constantinople still come to the former shrines of Demeter, Poseidon, and Zeus to worship their gods.

Akropolis is famous for its *ptochotropheia*, or alms' houses. These institutions, supported by state and private charity, provide clean clothes, a dry bed, a square meal, and basic medical services to anyone in need, with no questions asked. Monks run many of these institutions, but often have women volunteers from dynatos or rich mesos families.

Everyone knows that the Orphanotrophos Michael Serron (see page 122) really runs Akropolis, regardless of who is elected kephale.

LOCAL KNOWLEDGE

STREETWISE

- Akropolis is famous for the parks of Kynegion on top of the First Hill, its gunpowder factories in Mangana, and its alms' houses.
- The Imperial Orphanage is located in Akropolis; responsible for all state-sanctioned charity
- The Office of the Military Fisc is to be found on the Strategion

LORE (BYZANTINE)

- Many of the buildings here are built on top of pagan temples from the days of Byzantion

LOCAL RUMOURS

- "Don't fall asleep in the streets! A cousin of my brother's friend got too drunk to go home and he woke up to find himself in a basement with a robed and masked physician standing over him with a scalpel. There were jars of organs all around and some of them were still moving! He escaped but that doctor is still out there."
- "My cousin's wife saw a group of witches at the Prosphorion Harbour at night. You wouldn't get me going anywhere near there at night!" (actually only true on nights of the full moon)
- "I heard that there are monsters living under the First Hill! They come out at night and search Kynegion for people to eat."
- "Don't ignore the signal horns of Mangana! When they blare out, look to the skies and find shelter. My friend's uncle's brother-in-law was killed by a misfired rock from one of those war machines."

DESCRIPTIVE ELEMENTS

Ancient moss-covered architecture, beggars and cripples attended by scrawny dogs, weed-choked streets, vine-clad buildings, smell of gunpowder (in the east of the district), trees growing through flagstones.

AK-1 CHURCH OF SAINT CYPRIAN

Congregation Size: 100; Piety: 8%; Magical Strength: 25%

AFFILIATIONS

Deviant (magicians), Political (Imperial Library), Religious/Christian

Cyprian was a fourth century sorcerer who employed his magic against Saint Justina, a holy virgin. Three times he was foiled by the saint's piety until he saw the error of his ways and converted to Christianity, eschewing his sorcery forever. Cyprian eventually became Bishop of Antioch, with Justina at his side as abbess. Both were seized on the orders of Diocletian, tortured in Damascus and executed by beheading at Nicomedia. They were later proclaimed martyrs of the faith and were favourites of Constantine the Great, who had the relics of Saint Cyprian brought here.

The priest in charge is always uncommonly versed in magic, although the incumbent is not himself a practitioner. The church is the repository for books on magic owned by the Imperial Library. Most are treatises on the theory and taxonomy of magic, and have no practical magical learning (instead offering Lore (magic)), but amongst these there are a few books on Folk Magic and several spell codices (see page 81).

The relic of Saint Cyprian is his mummified body, kept in a silver-decorated casket. Since he was martyred through decapitation, it might strike some as unusual that the relic still has the head attached.

LINKS

- ɸ Mangana (AK-8)
- ɸ Imperial Library (ORG-20)

AK-2 COLUMN OF THE GOTHS

AFFILIATIONS

None

Located in the same park land as the Orphanage of Saint Paul, the Column is the oldest monument in the whole of Constantinople. The Column of the Goths is an 18.5 metre pillar of marble with a Corinthian capital. It commemorates the victories of Claudius II Gothicus from the time when the City was just an outpost of the Roman Empire. It stands on the site of an even older monument, the Tyche (statue of the goddess of luck) erected by Byzas the Megaran when he founded the original city of Byzantion.

The Column of the Goths is the best place to contact spirits in Constantinople. All Binding and Trance rolls are made at one difficulty grade easier while standing near the column's base.

LINKS

- ɸ Kynegion (AK-7)
- ɸ Orphanage of Saint Paul (AK-11)

AK-3 EUGENION

POPULATION

1400

AFFILIATIONS

Cultural (Pisan, Amalfitan), Political (customs officers), Professional (architects, masons), Societal (demoi)

Originally the Genoese quarter, before they relocated to Pera (see page 157). The Palace of Botaneiates in the southwestern side of the Strategion was the home of the Genoese commander. During the Frankokratia this neighbourhood was added to Perama to make the Venetian Quarter, and the expanded Perama was taken over by the Genoese upon the Restoration of the Empire. However, when the Genoese vacated Perama the city for Pera across the Golden Horn, the empire separated Eugenion from Perama once again. As a consequence of this changing of hands, Eugenion has some of the newer buildings of the Akropolis district, and many of them are constructed in an Italian style. The parish church is dedicated to Saint Demetrios.

The Tower of Eugenios is part of the gate in the sea walls of the same name. It is the southern terminus of the great chain that crosses the mouth of the Golden Horn as a defence against invasion. The tower contains a mechanism for the raising and lowering of the chain and is permanently under guard. During the day there is a customs official stationed here, who admits or denies trading and passenger vessels.

STORY HOOK

The characters stumble into a small courtyard. Before the faceless statue of a goddess, three semi-naked witches circle a brazier burning foul-smelling herbs. They turn to stare at the characters, their expressions unreadable behind their animal masks. Do the witches curse the characters, or offer them a quest?

LINKS

- ɸ Kynegion (AK-7)
- ɸ Strategion (AK-12)
- ɸ Sphorakion (KN-14)
- ɸ Perama (VQ-7)

AK-4 HAGIA EIRENE

Congregation Size: 500; Piety: 5%; Magical Strength: 50%

AFFILIATIONS

Religious/Christian

Upon the inauguration of Constantinople as holy city and centre of the Empire, Constantine the Great founded three churches dedicated to God's virtues: Hagia Eirene ("Holy Peace"), Hagia Sophia ("Holy Wisdom"), and Hagia Dynamis ("Holy Power"). Of these, Hagia Eirene was the first, and was the church of the Patriarchate until Hagia Sophia was completed in 360. The church was restored in 548 after it was destroyed during the Nika Riots (see page 15), and again after an earthquake in the eighth century. The Roman style basilica has a nave and two aisles separated by marble pillars. There is an atrium at the front, and the narthex has a half-dome with twenty windows. The whole interior is richly decorated with mosaics and frescoes.

It is customary for those settling disputes or ending feuds to receive a blessing at this church to symbolise the cessation of hostilities. The Empire solemnifies peace treaties with its political and foreign enemies in the same fashion.

LINKS

- Mangana (AK-8)

AK-5 HODEGON MONASTERY

Congregation Size: 50; Piety: 15%; Magical Strength: 50%

AFFILIATIONS

Religious/Christian (Barlaamite, Patriarch of Antioch)

Formally the Monastery of the Panagia Hodegetria, this monastery was founded by Saint Pulcheria in the fifth century. Unusually, this monastery is part of the estate of the Patriarch of Antioch. It gets its name from the Ikon of the Hodegetria ("She who shows the way"), which was painted by Saint Luke the Apostle. This ikon depicts a full-length image of the Virgin Mary holding the Child Jesus in her left arm while pointing to Him as the source of salvation with her right hand.

Every Tuesday, 20 monks bring out the ikon for the adoration of the gathered crowd, and this is considered one of the most spectacular sites of the city. In turn, each monk, robed in red linen, holds aloft in turn the four-sided pyramidal reliquary in which the ikon resides and walks 50 times around the square, chanting praises to God. It is said that the piety of the monk determines the weight of the relic, and it is certain that some have greater trouble carrying the huge reliquary than others. The Hodegetria is particularly famous for healing blindness and other eye-related illnesses.

Hodegon Monastery has become a centre of anti-Palamism. Those priests who could not accept the Palamite position taken by the Orthodox Church in Constantinople were given a choice: leave the Orthodox church or enter into seclusion in a monastery. For the few that took the latter option, Hodegon monastery became the cloister of choice, since it does not come under the authority of the Patriarchate of Constantinople. Although they are meant to be in seclusion, the Barlaamite monks have congress with the rebellious anti-Palamite congregation in Elebichon.

LINKS

- Mangana (AK-8)
- Elebichon (XR-3)

AK-6 THE KERATEMBOLON

AFFILIATIONS

Cultural (Minotauroi)

A statue called the *Keratos* stands on a bronze vault looks out to sea, it depicts a man with four horns on his head. The portico in which this stands is called the *Keratembolon* ("marketplace of the horns") after this statue. Its provenance has been forgotten, and several attempts have been made to remove the statue because of its presumed pagan depiction. Each time it has strode back to its plinth and once more gazed out to sea. The Keratos is an inhabited statue (see page 134).

The Keratembolon is a significant location to minotauroi, and a small community has established itself here. They are led by Spiros, a priest of the Six Kronides (the gods worshipped by the minotauroi, see page 58) who holds services at the Keratembolon. Many of the minotauroi are employed as porters, stevedores, and shipwrights serving the nearby Neorion Harbour. Here too is the headquarters of the Tauroi Chalkeoi, the disbanded mercenary regiment (see page

34). Former members still meet here socially, and there is a training ground where minotauros warriors are still trained to fight in their archaic bronze armour. The pankration skamma, used exclusively by minotaur pankratiasts, draws big crowds on match nights.

LINKS

- Eugenion (AK-3)
- Neorion Harbour (AK-9)

AK-7 KYNEGION

POPULATION

150 (sparse)

AFFILIATIONS

Professional (coopers, box-makers), Societal (demoi), Urban (actors)

Kynegion ("menagerie") was originally a private park filled with exotic animals. Some were displayed as wonders to be gazed upon and admired. Various emperors kept camelopards, unicorns, ostriches, and elephants. Other creatures were kept in cages for beast contests or executions in the Hippodrome. Such animals included lions, leopards, bears, crocodiles, and even griffins (with their wings clipped). There are even rumours that more horrifying creatures were once imprisoned here during the seventh century, such as manticores, basilisks, and gorgons.

Kynegion today is mostly parkland build on the steep slopes of the First Hill. There is an amphitheatre built into the hillside that still hosts plays, mostly tragedies, put on by a local troupe. There are clusters of houses close to the Propontis Walls and along the Kynegion Street (which starts at the Kynegion Gate and runs into Palation), but the eastern slopes of the First Hill are heavily forested. The parish church is the Church of Saint Menas.

When the shows at the Hippodrome stopped many of the ferocious beasts kept at Kynegion were killed, but others were simply let free. Most perished, but there are deep tunnels and caves beneath the First Hill, and who knows what lurks there still? (see the Undercity, page 188)

LINKS

- Eugenion (AK-3)
- Mangana (AK-8)
- Tower of Eugenios (AK-13)

AK-8 MANGANA

POPULATION

1250

AFFILIATIONS

Military, Professional (gunsmiths, armourers), Political (Military Fisc), Societal (mesoi)

The neighbourhood of *Mangana* ("arsenal") is on the eastern side of the First Hill. Most of the neighbourhood is given over to the production of the materiel of war, including siege engines, weapons, armour, Greek fire, and in particular, gunpowder. The neighbourhood has workshops and warehouses that make and store equipment to supply the army, although these days it is mainly made for trade since the empire is impoverished. The smoke from charcoal burners and armourers' forges hangs heavy over the district, blended with the hellish stench of sulphur. Partway up the east flank of the First Hill is a staging post for testing new war machines; when the horns of Mangana sound, everyone should be aware that there is the potential for misfires, explosions, or poorly-guided missiles, and the residents usually duck for shelter.

The neighbourhood has a famous monastery dedicated to Saint George, one of the three principal warrior saints and the patron of artillerists amongst other warlike professions. It sits within a great court filled with orchards, terraced gardens, and houses, where the monastery's old-age home and hostel for army veterans is situated. The monastery receives an annual visit from the Emperor on Saint George's feast day (23rd April).

Mangana is under the control of the kourator ton Manganon, who is an officer of the Military Fisc (see page 106). He resides in a five-storey mansion built by the ninth century emperor Michael I Rhangabe and still owned by the throne.

LINKS

- Church of Saint Cyprian (AK-1)
- Kynegion (AK-7)
- Chalkoprateia (KN-5)
- Great Palace (PA-7)

AK-9 NEORION HARBOUR

AFFILIATIONS

Urban, Professional (fishmongers), Cultural (Italian city-states)

The Neorion was the first harbour built after Constantinople was founded, but it was preceded by Byzantion's Prosphorion Harbour. The Neorion is overlooked by the First Hill, which protects it from the heavy storms of the Marmara Sea.

The area around the harbour is surrounded by many storehouses, although many of them lay empty since the migration of the Genoese to Pera. However, being next to the Venetian Quarter has helped its fortunes, and the Neorion is an important shipyard and commercial port. It services the smaller trade ships carrying expensive commodities such as silk and spices. The vaults at the west side of docks by the Gate of the Neorion – called the Megistai Kamarai – are the only place where it is permitted to sell fish wholesale to mongers rather than private customers.

The Neorion used to have the statue of a bull that, once a year, used to bellow loudly. It caused such a fright to the wife of the Emperor Maurice (reigned 582–602) that he had it thrown into the sea. For the last nine centuries, it has been heard lowing on days of the full moon in the astrological month of Taurus.

STORY HOOK

A ship is eagerly awaited at the docks. It left Egypt several months ago, bringing cheap grain, slaves, spices, and gold. The customs agents of the General Fisc (see page 106) and the merchants working for the Special Fisc are expecting a much-needed boost to their coffers. When it fails to arrive, the characters are hired to find out what happened to it. Who diverted it, and to where? When they catch up with it floating adrift in the sea, the more pertinent question is what happened to the crew?

LINKS

- Eugenion (AK-3)
- Prosphorion Harbour (AK-10)

AK-10 PROSPHORION HARBOUR

AFFILIATIONS

Criminal, Deviant (witches)

The original harbour of Byzantion, this harbour now lies deserted. In the past it was the landing place for all ships originating in the Black Sea, and the warehouses were stocked with exotic goods. Since the stranglehold of the Ottoman Empire has put an end to most of such trade, the Prosphorion has been closed. Its sole remaining use is a landing place for the Emperor's own ship when he sails from Blachernai to visit Hagia Sophia.

The harbour gets its name from a cult name of the goddess Hekate, who was witnessed helping the defenders of Byzantion when the harbour was besieged by Philip of Macedon. The goddess of witchcraft still has a presence here; on nights of the full moon witches come here to perform their rites of purification and adoration of the Bitch-Queen.

STORY HOOK

A player character awakes to find a witch standing over his bed. She touches his left nipple with her wand, and while he lies paralysed his chest opens like a flower and she removes his heart. While there is no sign that the witch was ever there, the character has no heartbeat and is slowly starving to death. Another witch can tell him that he must retrieve his heart and eat it, else when he dies of starvation he'll rise from the dead as a horrible revenant under the witch's control.

LINKS

- Eugenion (AK-3)
- Neorion Harbour (AK-9)
- Strategion (AK-12)
- Witch Cults (ORG-36)

AK-11 ORPHANAGE OF SAINT PAUL

AFFILIATIONS

Societal (demoi, dynatoi), Religious/Christian, Urban

The orphanage is situated at the very top of the First Hill, overlooking the confluence of the Golden Horn and the Bosphoros. It is one of the oldest foundations still standing in the city, having been first founded by Zotikos, a minister of Emperor Justin II in the late sixth century. Around the central three storey square building, amidst a cultured woodland, is a township of makeshift accommodation for the blind, crippled, diseased, lamed, war veterans, and elderly incapable of caring for themselves. The orphanage is a state-sponsored charitable organisation as well as a governmental ministry. Its business has long been considered by the court as a home and school for the care of orphaned nobility, however its chief minister the Orphanotrophos has always suborned this expectation by caring for every child brought to its gates, whether they come with an inheritance or not.

Although the Orphanotrophos is the actual head of the orphanage, its day-to-day running is overseen by the master of the house (chartoularios tou oikou). A treasurer looks after the charitable donations to the house as well as the endowments of the orphans themselves, and an army of curators look after the orphans themselves: feeding and bathing the youngest; providing tuition in academic subjects, manners, and religion; and finding work placements for those who are not due to inherit money. The master of the orphanage also has the older children care for the sick and elderly outside the orphanage at least once per day, tending to their wounds and serving them food.

STORY HOOK

Heno is a guest of the orphanage although he is approaching his majority (16). The characters might meet him in the course of his work placement. He claims to be the heir to lands on Lemnos: his father was dispossessed and executed by the Emperor's estranged brother Demetrios Palaiologos; Heno came here as an infant with his sister and older brother. He wants to know the truth about his brother's sudden death, and help in reclaiming his family estates. He has a substantial amount of money in trust, although the master of the house will be cautious about handing this over to a group of mercenaries.

LINKS

- Kynegion (AK-7)
- Office of the Imperial Orphanage (ORG-21)
- Michael Serron, the Orphanotrophos (NPC-21)

AK-12 STRATEGION

AFFILIATIONS

Political (Military Fisc), Professional (sheep merchants), Societal (Demos), Rural (sheep farmers), Urban (market)

A public square that is home to a daily market. There is an arcaded portico which runs around the square and there are upper storey windows which look over it. The Strategion is packed on all days except Sundays and feast days; with traders operating out of the booths in the portico, and iterant grocers selling vegetables, fruit, caviar, and drinks in small disposable pots. The city's only sheep market is held in the Strategion every market day. Many of the permanent traders here are Venetian or Pisan, as the Strategion marks the eastern extent of the foreign neighbourhood around the Neorion Harbour.

One side of the Strategion sits on the Maurianos Embolos, a porticoed street that runs from the Gate of Eugenios to the Forum of Constantine. On the northeastern end is the headquarters of the Ministry of the Military Fisc, which gives its name to the whole square. Opposite the headquarters used to sit the Palace of Botaneiates, the home of the ruler of the Genoese Quarter in the twelfth century. After the Restoration the palace was dismantled brick by brick and shipped back to Genoa where it was reconstructed to form the Banco de San Giorgio, Genoa's principal financial institution.

STORY HOOK

The Office of the Military Fisc would pay handsomely for enough brass to make a huge bombard similar to the ones that the Sultan is reported to be building. All of its supplies however have been adulterated, and cannot be cast without cracking. A fortune in brass is rumoured to lie within the Leaden Vault in Pera (PR-5), although the city is unlikely to simply give the brass to Constantinople.

LINKS

- Eugenion (AK-3)
- Neorion Harbour (AK-9)
- Office of the Military Fisc (ORG-27)

AK-13 TOWER OF EUGENIOS

AFFILIATIONS

Military (Tzakones), Political (General Fisc), Urban (customs inspectors)

Attached to the Gate of the same name, the Tower of Eugenios is the southern end of the great chain or boom that can be raised to prevent egress to the Golden Horn. The northern end is controlled in the Great Tower in Pera. The Tzakones use the tower as their barracks, charged as they are with the defence of the sea walls.

Just outside the Gate of Eugenios is the main customs post of the imperial tax office of the General Fisc. Perpetually staffed by kommerkiaroi – customs inspectors – all ships intended to dock at or depart from a Constantinople harbour are expected to report here and pay the dues owed: the much-hated kommerkion.

STORY HOOK

One enterprising member of the Tzakones has made a small fortune collecting a bribe to distract the kommerkiaros on duty in order to smuggle goods – and occasionally whole cargoes – past the customs post. The player characters are hired to investigate a past incident or to negotiate a fee (depending upon their proclivities) just as one of the guard's rivals in the Mourtatoi decides to expose his scam. The player characters risk getting caught up in the fallout.

LINKS

- Kynegion (AK-7)
- The Great Tower (PR-4)
- Tzakones (ORG-34)

BLACHERNAI (SUBURB)

A suburb in the very northwest of the city on the northern flanks of the Sixth Hill. After the Restoration of the Empire, the Palaiologian emperor had no desire to return to the Great Palace (PA-7) of his forebears, or occupy the Boukoleon Palace (PA-2) used by the Latin emperors, so he made Blachernai Palace his home. The suburb has long been the province of the very rich and moving the focus of the royal court here has done nothing to dispel this. Blachernai is dominated by the imperial palace and residence, but also bears the mansions of those select families in favour with the emperor. These are usually his oikeoi or those of previous emperors. There is temporary accommodation for visiting ministers and officials, but the majority of the machinery of government still resides at the Great Palace.

The Walls of Blachernai connect with the northern terminus of the Theodosian Walls at the Palace of the Porphyrogennetos and surround the whole suburb. The walls are 12 to 15 metres high for most of their length and have closely spaced towers. There are several sections of wall built at different times; and four key gates: the Kaligaria Gate, the Gyrolimne Gate, the Blachernai Gate, and the Xyloporta.

As a suburb of Constantinople rather than a district, Blachernai does not have a kephale. Instead, the commander of the Varangian Guard, Andrew of Killingworth (NPC-2), is responsible for keeping law and order in Blachernai.

LOCAL KNOWLEDGE

STREETWISE

- (Success): Blachernai is the royal district; here one can find the emperor's personal residence and the principal palace from which he rules. The Imperial Household and the Regiment of the Varangian Guard are also located here.
- (Success): the most important locations are the Palace of the Porphyrogennetos, where the emperor lives, and the Blachernai Palace, from where he rules.

LORE (BYZANTINE)

- (Success): the name of the district derives from a small Vlach settlement here in the fifth century.
- (Success): The Church of Saint Mary of Blachernai is the site of one of the city's few springs, supplying fresh water to the city

LOCAL RUMOURS

- "There's a prisoner in the Tower of Anemas for the first time in over two hundred years. There's no record of him, but he's been heard screaming at night."
- "The screams at night aren't coming from Anemas. They are from the Apokrisiareion. There's a new guest – some Wallachian princeling called Vlad Draculesti. He wants support

to reclaim his homeland from the usurper that murdered his family. The night-time screaming started when he arrived."

- "Someone has been robbing the villas in Blachernai. No-one knows how they get in and out, but they leave wet footprints on the floors."

DESCRIPTIVE ELEMENTS

Steep terraced hillside, kept neat and tidy by an army of servants, marble steps and numerous statues, tamed vegetation cultured into formal gardens, fountains. Pampered and well-fed dogs being walked by servants.

BL-1 APOKRISIAREION

AFFILIATIONS

Cultural, Political (the Drome)

A grand palace which houses foreign envoys. Foreign relations are vitally important to the Empire at the current time, and the quarters in which ambassadors are lodged are sumptuous in order to make them feel welcome.

The Apokrisiareion is under the command of the kourator tou apokrisiareiou, a high-ranking official in the Office of the Drome (see page 105). He has a staff servants to cater to the whims of his guests, as well as a cadre of translators capable of speaking many different languages. It may be presumed that at least some of these staff are spies reporting directly to the Drome.

LINKS

- The Office of the Drome (ORG-25)

BL-2 BLACHERNAI

POPULATION

350 (sparse)

AFFILIATIONS

Professional (shoemaking), Societal (mesoi)

The suburb of Blachernai is about the size of a city neighbourhood and has fewer than 400 residents, most of whom are civil servants of one department or another. The Imperial Household is the biggest individual employer. There are no tenements in Blachernai and remarkably few villas; instead, groups of houses are located in clusters around the many parks and formal gardens of the suburb.

The parish church is that of Saint Thekla at Blachernai, next to the Anastasia Gate. Prior to this becoming the royal district, Blachernai was famed for its cordwainers and cobblers, and it is still home to long-lived shoemaking businesses, as well as allied trades, such as lace-makers and those which make small leather goods out of the offcuts. Blachernai boots are considered the finest on sale in the city.

LINKS

- Kyrion (PT-5)
- Phanarion (PT-9)

BL-3 BLACHERNAI PALACE

AFFILIATIONS

Military (Varangians), Political (Imperial Household), Societal (dynatoi)

Built at the end of the fifth century, the palace was the favoured residence of the Komnemian emperors but fell into disuse after the Fourth Crusade when the Latin Emperors installed themselves in the Boukeleon Palace. It has been returned to use since the Restoration, not as a royal residence but as an instrument of the state. The emperor holds his privy councils here, comprising of himself, the mesazon, and the twelve departmental heads and their chief aides. For all but the highest of state occasions, the business of ruling is conducted from the Blachernai Palace and the great bureaucracy that puts the emperor's orders into practice is run from the Great Palace.

The Blachernai Palace is the domain of the protovestiarios Georgios Sphrantzes, who is in charge of the imperial household. Nothing occurs here of which he is unaware due to his highly efficient system of pages who wait in pairs in all rooms. Should something occur that Sphrantzes should know, one page is sent to inform him, and messages from the pages always take precedence over all other business except the emperor's.

The vast palace complex has undergone extensive remodelling in its thousand years. It has been built on a number of terraces on the flank of the Sixth Hill. The palace consists of a series of triklinoi or halls, each named after the emperor who built it or after the distinctive features of its decoration.

- The Triklinos Anastasiakos (Hall of Anastasios)
- The Triklinos Okeanos (Hall of the Ocean)
- The Portikas Iosephiakos (Portico of Joseph)
- The Triklinos Danoubios (Hall of the Danube). A series of staircases lead downhill to the Church of Saint Mary
- The Triklinos Eireniakos (Hall of Eirene)
- The Polytimos Oikos (House of Valuables)

LINKS

- Georgios Sphrantzes (NPC-13)
- The Imperial Household (ORG-19)
- Church of Saint Mary of Blachernai (BL-5)

BL-4 THE BRACHIONION

AFFILIATIONS

Military (Varangian)

A section of the Walls of Blachernai that consists of a pair of walls some 25 metres apart forming a fortified enclosure known as the Brachionion ton Blachernon or "bracelet of Blachernai" in which the Gate of Blachernai is set.

The Brachionion contains the principal barracks of the Varangian Guard, who are tasked with the defence of the emperor. The Brachionion is built like a fortress, with reinforced walls and its own well. If the emperor is under threat, he is brought here to wait out the danger. The keys to the Brachionion are a metre long with an intricate ward; the sergeant-at-arms owns one and the commander of the Varangians owns the other.

LINKS

- Paradeision (XR-9)
- The Varangian Guard (ORG-11)

BL-5 CHURCH OF SAINT MARY OF BLACHERNAI

Congregation Size: 50; Piety: 12%; Magical Strength: 75%

AFFILIATIONS

Religious/Christian

Saint Mary's of Blachernai is the church that serves the royal court. The church complex consists of three principal sites: the Church of Saint Mary proper, the Chapel of the Reliquary (Hagia Soros) and the Sacred Bath (Hagion Lousma).

The Church of Saint Mary is a large basilica with the form of a cross, decorated with columns of green jasper and white marble. The ceiling is decorated in multi-coloured enamel and gilt. The walls are covered with colourful marble panels joined by a silvery mortar. Above eye level are mosaics representing the life of Christ. A famous ikon of the Virgin, the Blachernitissa, resides here; it is credited with protecting the city from attack. It has been paraded along the ramparts of the Theodosian Wall or plunged into the sea in order to invoke this protection. During the Iconoclastic period the Blachernitissa was hidden under a layer of silver mortar, but it was uncovered again in the eleventh century and resumed its protection of the shrine and the city. The ikon is normally kept covered by a veil, but at sunset on every Friday the veil moves up on its own accord to reveal the face of the Virgin, and descends again at sunset a day later. This habitual miracle ceased during the Latin occupation.

The Chapel of the Reliquary sits to the right of the church. This round chapel was built to house the dress and the robe of the Virgin as well as her veil and a part of her girdle. The relics are kept within a gold and silver casket. The dress and robe were actually both destroyed during a fire of 1434; this has been kept secret from the people of the city to prevent them losing faith in the power of the Blachernitissa.

The Sacred Bath lies to the right of the chapel. It consists of a robing room, the pool itself, and the hall of Saint Photinos. The pool is surrounded by ikons, and the water is poured into the bath through the hands of a statue of the Virgin. Once a year on the 15th August (The feast of Dormition) the emperor comes to the Sacred Bath and immerses himself three times.

There is also a fountain of holy water or hagiasma contained within a small shrine. The shrine has the words "*nipson anomemata me monan opsin*", a palindrome in Greek which means "wash the sin not only the eye"; reflecting the practice of bathing the eyes in the hope of miraculous cures. The water of the hagiasma falls into an underground gallery, which by tradition connects to the Church of Saint Mary of the Spring.

LINKS

- Blachernai Palace (BL-3)
- Zoödochos Pege (XR-11)

BL-6 PALACE OF THE PORPHYROGENNETOS

AFFILIATIONS

Family (Palaiologoi, Kantakouzenoi), Societal (dynatoi)

A recent annex to the Blachernai Palace, built about a hundred years ago when the walls of Blachernai were built to join up with the Theodosian Walls. Its name means literally "born to the purple", and refers to children born to a reigning emperor. The palace is the residence of the Emperor and his family; whereas the Blachernai Palace is the place from which the emperor rules, the Palace of the Porphyrogennetos is where he lives. The mesazon and his family are also housed in the Palace of the Porphrogennetos.

The Palace is a three-storey building located between the inner and outer fortifications of the Theodosian Walls. The exterior walls are decorated in an elaborate geometric design picked out in white marble and red brick. The ground floor is an arcade with four arches that opens into a courtyard. This courtyard has a central fountain and a formal garden with fruit trees and delicate flowers. Songbirds throng in the foliage, filling the air with their sweet music. The first floor has five large windows that look onto this courtyard. The top floor projects over the level of the Theodosian Walls and has windows on all four sides. A balcony faces east to catch the morning sun, and affords a view over the Golden Horn.

LINKS

- Blachernai Palace (BL-3)
- Andrew of Killingworth (NPC-2)
- Emperor Constantine XI (NPC-6)
- Demetrios Palaiologos Kantakouzenos (NPC-8)
- The Imperial Household (ORG-19)

BL-7 PRISON OF ANEMAS

AFFILIATIONS

Cultural, Military (Varangian), Urban (prison)

This large structure forms part of the Walls of Blachernai. It is named after the first prisoner interred here, Michael Anemas; since then it has been the cell of four emperors, as well as various ministers, generals, and clerics who have displeased the emperor. The prison is not used for common criminals (for whom justice is all-to-often summary) but rather for noble (or royal) locals and foreign hostages.

The prison's outer wall is 23 metres high and up to 20 metres thick. The interior space is divided into 12 chambers by buttresses; each one is three storeys high and connected with spiral staircases. On the upper two storeys there is a corridor which runs down the middle of the compartments, separating each into two and providing access to each chamber. The ground floor compartments have no natural light, but the upper storeys are lit with small openings in the western wall. As a whole, the prison should be considered to be two rows of 12 three-storey towers joined together with an outside wall. On the ground floor, the internal "towers" are connected in pairs. Depending on the social standing of a prisoner and the current capacity of the prison, an inmate might have one room, one tower, or one double-tower to themselves and possibly their family.

At the front of the building on its right are two larger towers, added to the prison after its construction and at different times. One is the Tower of Isaac Angelos, an emperor who built it as a residence and a fort, which is now used by the prison staff. The other is the Tower of Anemas, now reserved for high-status "guests".

The Prison is under the auspices of the Varangian Guard, who have a permanent presence here as well as commanding the prison staff. In general, prisoners are well cared for and gently treated, tending to be victims of political circumstances rather than actual criminals. This is not always the case: the father of the current emperor was imprisoned here as a child with his brother and father during the reign of the usurper Andronikos IV.

LINKS

- Varangian Guard (ORG-11)

KAINOPOLIS (DISTRICT)

The "new town" (as opposed to the Akropolis, or "old town") is only new in comparison to the age of the city. It was the first district to be established outside the Severan Wall, and comprises the chief mercantile region of the city. Kainopolis is centred around the Mese Odos, the middle street which runs from the Milion (PA-1) through Kainopolis, Vlanga, and Stoudion until it connects to the Via Egnata at the Golden Gate. Most of the district is located to the north of the Mese Odos, with Vlanga occupying the southern side except in the very east. Kainopolis is the domain of the middle class: here are found most of the businesses, public companies and Imperial Guild workshops. The neighbourhoods are mostly named after their dominant trade although these are less clear-cut than they were in previous centuries.

Here more than anywhere else are the city ordinances obeyed; regarding road widths, keeping sewer entrances clear, and permitting access to public fountains. Much of Constantinople's private wealth is bound up in the streets of Kainopolis, and the accusation is that the Praitor spends the bulk of his budget here to the neglect of more densely populated but poorer districts such as Vlanga and Platea.

LOCAL KNOWLEDGE

STREETWISE

- (Success): Kainopolis is the main mercantile district of the city.
- (Success): The neighbourhood of Kanikleion is wholly given over to the Imperial Archives.
- (Success): If you get lost, look up. The watchtower above Artopoleia is distinctive, as is the Column of Constantine

LOCAL RUMOURS

- "Don't get your bread from Krages! My uncle's cousin's wife got sick from eating his state bread, and I hear that others have too."
- "There's a con game being run in Kainopolis. People buy an expensive item from a boutique, but later get a visit from the Vardariotes who tells them that the item is counterfeit. They take it away, leaving a receipt, but both the receipt and the Vardariotes are bogus, and working with the boutique."
- "There's going to be an execution tomorrow! Someone said it was a minotauros – should be a good spectacle. Claims it is innocent too – that it had nothing to do with that robbery where the householder was killed. Magistrate Kamyztes issued the sentence, and he's usually pretty inventive with his execution methods. Make sure you turn up early at the Forum of Theodosios, there is sure to be a crowd!"
- "I saw a rat the other day that was the size of a small dog, I kid you not! It squeezed itself out of a storm drain then sauntered down the street, cool as you like. Last I saw of it was near the door to Stauros's taberna.

DESCRIPTIVE ELEMENTS

Crowded streets; noisy both day and night; alleyways filled with waste from markets; disposable crockery from the wine-vendors discarded in the streets; women carrying small dogs; raucous gulls stealing from stalls, with urchins shooting at them with slings; pitted and damaged architectural features

KN-1 AMANTION

POPULATION

1850 (crowded)

AFFILIATIONS

Deviant (Prasinoi), Professional (fishermen, netweavers, ropemakers), Societal (demoi)

Probably the most highly populated of Kainopolis's neighbourhoods and without doubt the poorest. The parish church is dedicated to Saint Andrew the Fisherman, and Amantion is home to many who draw their income from the Sea of Marmara: fisherman, ferrymen, shipwrights, but also oystermen, mussel-gleaners, and crab-mongers. These professions were always traditionally associated with the Venetoi circus faction ("The Blues"), although there is currently an upswelling of Green sentiments in Amantion it tends not to be among the traditional Blue trades.

The last manufacturer of imperial purple dye (porphyra) lives in Amantion. He collects the murex shells from a secret location, and the process by which he extracts the vibrant purple colour is unknown but almost certainly involves an alchemical process. The Imperial Purpler has a standing order for a wide range of reagents, although he only uses a selection of those he buys – the rest are to throw people off the scent if they try to recreate his process. Since there is a limited market for purple dye, he also makes other rare pigments such as carmine, crimson, and scarlet (from kermes grain) and *indikon* (indigo).

LINKS

- ϕ Argyroprateia (KN-3)
- ϕ Artopoleia (KN-4)
- ϕ Kanikleion (KN-9)
- ϕ Hormisidon (PA-10)

KN-2 ANEMODOULION

AFFILIATIONS

None

This structure, whose name means "the servant of the winds" stands on the meeting place between the Mese Odos and the Makros Emblos, the two busiest streets of Constantinople, occupying the north east corner of the junction. The Anemodoulion is a four-sided arch (from which it gets its other name of "Tetrapylon") with a steep pyramidal roof. It is decorated with bronze reliefs depicting the eight winds. The roof bears a weather vane in the shape of Nike, the winged goddess of victory. The Anemodoulion was erected in the reign of Theodosius I in the late 300s and while it suffered terrible damage during the Sack of Constantinople, it has since been repaired.

The eight wind-gods depicted on the Anemodoulion have the torsos of men but the tails of snakes instead of legs:

- ϕ Boreas the North Wind with shaggy hair and beard, wearing a billowing cloak and carrying a conch shell
- ϕ Kaikas the North East Wind, a bearded man with a blindfold carrying a shield filled with hailstones
- ϕ Apeliotes the East Wind, a clean-shaven man with a cloak filled with fruit and grain
- ϕ Euros the South East Wind, a bearded man with a heavy cloak
- ϕ Notos the South Wind who pours water from a jar
- ϕ Lips the South West Wind who holds onto the stern of a ship
- ϕ Zephyros the West Wind depicted as a beardless youth scattering flowers
- ϕ Skiron the North West Wind, a bearded man tilting a cauldron

The Anemodoulion has a place of great affection in the hearts of the Byzantine people. Folk will brush their hands against one of the bronze panels as they pass, as a charm against ill luck. This ritual causes the loss of 1 Magic Point, but protects the person for the day as if they had an Avert spell with the Trigger trait.

The sorcerer Kyprianos is fascinated by the Anemodoulion. He is convinced that there is something hidden beneath the monument, but has not been able to find a tunnel in the Undercity that goes anywhere near the location – it is almost as if this is deliberate. He has yet to make any connection with the sixth oracle of the Prophecy of Leo the Wise (see page 208), which refers to the monster that slew the south-west wind. There may not even be a connection since the prophecy is riddled with allegory, but it is a curious puzzle nonetheless.

LINKS

- ϕ Artopoleia (KN-4)
- ϕ Kyprianos (IMM-9)

KN-3 ARGYROPRATEIA

POPULATION

500

AFFILIATIONS

Professional (goldsmiths, silversmiths, moneylenders), Societal (mesoi)

The neighbourhood of the money-makers is one of the richest in the entire city. It is the first neighbourhood on the Mese Odos, traditionally occupying the stretch between the Augustaion and the Forum of Constantine. The parish church of the neighbourhood is that of Saint Euphemia at the Hippodrome, although many of the wealthier merchants will attend the Hagia Sophia instead.

Argyroprateia is the only neighbourhood where the Guild of Silversmiths and Goldsmiths may operate. Their goods are laid out for all to see under the shade of the porticoes of the Mese Odos, which are kept in good repair due to contributions made by the guild. The Vardariotai are more numerous along this stretch of the Mese Odos than in other parts of the city (in part due to bribes paid by the guild), nevertheless many shops employ their own guards to watch over their wares. Once the working day is done and the shops pack up, an army of gleaners come creeping from the surrounding neighbourhoods. They sort through the spoil of the day, searching for any scraps of precious metal they can find. They will even scrape out the drains and the sewage gutters and pan it for gold dust. These fragments of metal are sold back to the guild.

STORY HOOK

The characters witness a mugging and the victim implores them for help. Once rescued he claims to be the heir of a vast fortune, but has been cheated out of it by his sister's husband. However, when the characters see their new friend talking to one of the muggers that they saved him from, they might question what his game really is.

LINKS

- ϕ Amantion (KN-1)
- ϕ Chalkoprateia (KN-5)
- ϕ Church of Saint Euphemia (KN-6)
- ϕ Keropoleia (KN-10)
- ϕ Great Palace (PA-7)
- ϕ Hormisidon (PA-10)

KN-4 ARTOPOLEIA

POPULATION

1750 (crowded)

AFFILIATIONS

Professional (bakers, cookhouses, brewers), Societal (demoi)

The neighbourhood of the bakers lies to the north of the central portion of the Mese Odos, just behind the shops and businesses that make up the portico. The buildings here are made of brick with tiled roofs, and do not connect to any other buildings. A fire watch station sponsored by the Imperial Guild of Bakers stands high over the neighbourhood, a tower that forms a landmark by which to navigate the city. The parish church of Artopoleia is the Church of Mary Diakonissa.

The ovens operate day and night, collectively producing over fifty thousand loaves of bread every day. They are all owned by the Bakers' Guild and operated directly or under contract to private companies. The ovens require a phenomenal amount of fuel every day, mostly charcoal but also wood harvested outside the city walls. Bakers displaying a sign with the imperial seal (a cross with four Bs) are purveyors of the state bread which is a right given to all citizens (see page 23), although those who can afford not to rely on it do not.

LINKS

- Amantion (KN-1)
- Kanikleion (KN-9)
- Keropoleia (KN-10)
- Konstanton (PL-7)
- Kaisarion (VL-8)
- Olybrion (VL-10)
- Perama (VQ-7)

KN-5 CHALKOPRATEIA

POPULATION

650

AFFILIATIONS

Professional (blacksmiths, coppersmiths), Societal (mesoi)

The neighbourhood of the bronzesmiths now houses other varieties of smiths, including those who work in iron (blacksmiths), tin and lead (greysmiths), and copper and brass (redsmiths). The whitesmiths, who deal with gold and silver, have a neighbourhood of their own. The parish church is that of Saint Mary of Chalkoprateia.

Chalkoprateia is a solid, middle-class neighbourhood, heavily occupied but not crowded. The Maurianos Embolos, which runs between the Forum of Constantine and the Eugenios Gate and bisects the neighbourhood, is well-maintained but uncobbled, making access easy for the horses that visit the makers of horseshoes.

STORY HOOK

A lamia stalks the alleyways of Chalkoprateia at night. It has the torso of a beautiful woman and the body of a snake in place of legs. Use the Statistics of an Ophidian (Mythras page 254), with the Ability to entrance a victim which works like the Domination power of a vampire (Mythras 271). The lamia is a servant of the Divan (the Ottoman high council, see page 41), and they are seeking to acquire a spy who cannot be corrupted.

LINKS

- Argyroprateia (KN-3)
- Keropoleia (KN-10)
- Sphorakion (KN-14)
- Mangana (AK-8)
- Great Palace (PA-7)
- Orban of Brassó (NPC-22)

KN-6 CHURCH OF SAINT EUPHEMIA IN THE HIPPODROME

Congregation Size: 100; Piety: 12%; Magical Strength: 50%

AFFILIATIONS

Political, Societal (dynatoi), Religious/Christian

A hexagonal church built in the northernmost corner of the hippodrome. It was built from the remains of a fifth century palace belonging to Antiochos, a Persian eunuch who rose to great power due to his influence over the under-aged Emperor Theodosios II. The church was built during the seventh century and dedicated to the martyred virgin. During the Iconoclasm (see page 31) the building was converted into a manure store; the emperor ordered that the relics of Euphemia be cast into the sea. Two monks rescued them and smuggled them to Lemnos, from whence they were returned in the ninth century upon the restoration of the church.

LINKS

- Argyroprateia (KN-3)

KN-7 FORUM OF CONSTANTINE

AFFILIATIONS

Professional (silk trades, linen merchants), Societal (mesoi), Urban (market)

Built at the foundation of the city, this forum is the central point of Constantinople. The forum is circular, with a monumental gate to the east and the west which exit onto the Mese Odos. The Makros Embolos and the Maurianos Embolos also pass through the forum. A portico surrounds the forum, and there is a market here on all days except Sunday.

The Column of Constantine marks the centre of the forum, although the statue of the emperor has been replaced by a cross after the statue was blown down in a gale in 1150. The Sack of Constantinople (see page 8) did more damage: a fire started by the invading Franks damaged many of the surrounding buildings, and the statues decorating the forum were melted down. More statues have been removed in recent years; as a valuable source of bronze for the crafting of bombards in Mangana.

All the silk merchants of Constantinople are required by law to operate from the Forum of Constantine. Many of the shops beneath the portico are involved in the spinning, weaving, and dyeing of silk thread, the tailoring of silk cloth, or the sale of silk garments. Those who work here can often be distinguished by their permanently dyed hands and forearms. The importers of Syrian linen also trade from shops around the western gate of the forum.

Sights at the Forum might include:

- A trio of prostitutes proposition the characters from their street corner. One is a Blemmye. Their muscle lurks in a nearby doorway, a hulking yet hornless female minotauros.
- A young boy pipes music for a cobra, which sways in time to his tapping foot. The snake rises higher and higher until it is balancing on the very tip of its tail.
- A man leads a remarkable bird on a leash. It is taller than a man, with long legs, a long neck and small head. He swears it is a roc chick, and that its parents were big enough to carry off elephants.
- A Syrian silk merchant struggles under his massive burden of cloth; city ordinance prohibits him from setting down his load in a public place. His cloth is excellent – finer than from the native guilds – but pricey.

LINKS

- Amantion (KN-1)
- Keropoleia (KN-10)
- Mese Odos (KN-12)
- Praitorion (KN-13)

KN-8 FORUM OF THEODOSIOS

AFFILIATIONS

Urban (market)

Originally called the Forum of the Bull because of a statue that resided here, which was later moved to Neorion Harbour (AK-9) when the forum was rededicated to the Emperor Theodosios I. No sign remains of the triumphal arch that lead from the Mese Odos into the forum from the west, although the centre of the forum is still home to the column (but not the statue) commemorating its namesake. The column has a spiral staircase within it and the column has been used for public executions, hurling the condemned man from its summit. Most notable of those executed in this way was Emperor Alexios V in 1204. Execution through other means usually takes place in this forum, and execution day is always a spectacle.

The staircase inside the column also leads underground, but the way is blocked with a locked gate and the Praitor has the only key. This leads directly into Nekropoleia in the Undercity.

LINKS

- Artopoleia (KN-4)
- Nekropoleia (UC-8)

KN-9 KANIKLEION

POPULATION

900

AFFILIATIONS

Political (Imperial Archives), Professional (scribes, archivists), Societal (mesoi)

This neighbourhood gains its name from the Palace of the Kanikleios built in the ninth century. The kanikleios is a high-ranking imperial dignitary, the keeper of the imperial inkstand (the kanikleion, which takes the shape of a small dog, or canicula in Latin). The ink in this inkstand is scarlet in colour, and is used exclusively to sign state documents. Since the Restoration of the Empire, the role of kanikleios has gone hand in hand with the office of the First Secretary, and the Palace of the Kanikleios – indeed, most of the neighbourhood – is occupied by the Imperial Archive.

The parish church of Kanikleion is the Church of Saint John of Patmos, who is the patron of authors and scribes. The Palace of the Kanikleios is the central storage house for the Imperial Archive, as well as being the home and offices of the First Secretary Alexios Tzamplakon. Most of the other residences belong to the Sekreton and are loaned out to its members, with the senior secretaries getting well-appointed houses, right down to junior scribes who share tenement buildings. Various supporting trades have grown up around the demands of the Archives, and there are ink makers, ink grinders, paper makers and bookbinders. Most of the parchment is brought in from Hormisidon (PA-10). Paper is an interesting innovation: the availability of cheap linen and cotton garments – particularly undergarments – has led to a proliferation of waste cloth, making the manufacture of paper from shredded rags economically viable.

STORY HOOK

The characters are asked to help by a local family. They have been given notice of eviction by the Praitor's office on the basis of deeds that show the family neither own or pay rent for their home and it is needed for another purpose. The document has the correct seal and signature, but as the characters examine it, the words animate as the ink flows back to their original form before manipulated with sorcery – a completely unrelated document. The ink-wizard who performed this magic (using Animate Ink; he also knows Animate Parchment and Break Parchment), is selling his skills to the highest bidder, and he could destroy the integrity of the Imperial Archives single-handedly.

LINKS

- Amantion (KN-1)
- Artopoleia (KN-4)
- Kaisarion (VL-8)
- Alexios Palaiologos Tzamplakon (NPC-1)
- Imperial Archives (ORG-18)

KN-10 KEROPOLEIA

POPULATION

600

AFFILIATIONS

Professional (soapmakers, candlemakers), Societal (mesoi)

Two allied Imperial Guilds dominate this neighbourhood: the Wax Merchants (after whom the district is named) and the Soap Merchants. City ordinance stipulates that both industries must take place in buildings unconnected to others, in order to minimise the danger of fires. The pallor of boiling animal fat hangs heavy in the air, and anyone spending time here gets covered with a thin layer of grease. As well as handling, dyeing, and shaping imported beeswax, the Wax Merchants make inferior grade tallow candles from rendered fat, and also have a contract from the Ministry of the Military Fisc to produce match cord for its firearms and artillery.

The manufacture of soap at an industrial scale is a dangerous business, involving the use of noxious lye and producing acrid – and occasionally flammable – vapours. The waste is thrown into the back alleys to evaporate in the sun, resulting in an impossibly slippery surface. Characters would be advised against conducting a chase through Keropoleia.

The parish church of Keropoleia is the Church of the Theotokos Pammakaristos.

LINKS

- Argyroprateia (KN-3)
- Artopoleia (KN-4)
- Chalkoprateia (KN-5)
- Sphorakion (KN-14)
- Perama (VQ-7)

KN-11 KONTOSKALION

AFFILIATIONS

Professional, Cultural, Criminal (smugglers)

As one of the oldest and most active harbours of Constantinople, the Kontoskalion has borne many names: The Harbour of Julian, the Portus Novus ("New Port"), and the Harbour of Sophia. It lies on the Marmaran Coast, at the southern end of the valley of the Hippodrome. Facing the tempestuous Sea of Marmara causes problems: not only is the harbour undefended from the storms of the southwest wind, it is also prone to being clogged up with sand brought in by these storms and therefore needs dredging on a regular basis. This has been partly alleviated by the wall built across the harbour mouth by Emperor Michael VIII Palaiologos, and his successor Andronikos II added an iron gate and deepened the basin.

The Kontoskalion today is a busy port, bringing in goods originating from all over the Mediterranean Sea. It holds the meagre fleet of Constantinople (see page 36), although there is room for over three hundred galleys. The sea walls of the harbour are lined with artillery weapons, both ballistae and cannon.

LINKS

- ф Amantion (KN-1)
- ф Kanikleion (KN-9)

KN-12 MESE ODOS

AFFILIATIONS

Urban (market)

The "Middle Street" runs from the Milion westwards to the Philadelphion, where it splits and heads towards two of the city gates: the Gate of Charisios in the northwest and the Golden Gate in the southwest. The first section, as far as the Forum of Constantinople is called The Regia and is the imperial processional way to the Hagia Sophia and the Great Palace. This is the province of the Imperial Guild of Silversmiths and Goldsmiths. Between the Fora of Constantine and Theodosios is the neighbourhood of Artopoleia, named after the bakeries of the Imperial Guild.

The Mese Odos is 25 metres wide and for much of its length is lined with colonnaded porticoes that hold shops and booths. Large flagstones form the road's bed; the original marble flags still exist in places but they have tended to have been replaced with cheaper stone. The sidewalks beneath the porticoes bear intricate mosaics; these have to be maintained by the proprietor of the shop that they sit outside, but since they act as signposts, most do not mind this added expense. Over the centuries, some of mosaics have been altered, and now tell comic stories, local history, or blatantly advertise a merchant's wares.

LINKS

- ф Augustaion (PA-1)
- ф Forum of Constantine (KN-7)
- ф Forum of Theodosios (KN-8)
- ф Philadelphion (VL-11)
- ф Forum of the Ox (VL-6)
- ф Forum of Arkadios (VL-5)
- ф Sigma (ST-8)

KN-13 PRAITORION

AFFILIATIONS

Military (Vardariotai), Political (Law), Political (Praitor), Urban (civil administration, prison)

The Praitorion is a three storey building occupying the southwest quadrant of the Forum of Constantine. It has a flight of marble steps leading up to the entrance, flanked with columns of porphyry. During the Frankokratia the building was used as a palace for the Catholic bishop of Constantinople, but after the Restoration it was returned to its original function as the administrative hub of The City itself (as opposed to the Empire, which is run from the Great Palace).

The Praitor ton demon is a high-ranking member of the Chancellery, and is the civil administrator of Constantinople. His office maintains law and order, maintains the water supply and sewage systems, repairs the roads and public buildings, and is responsible for city planning. He and his three subordinates – the koiaistor, the megas tzaousios, and the tribunos – have departments here in the Praitorion.

The main headquarters of the Vardariotai is located at the Praitorion under the command of the megas tzaousios, or sergeant-at-arms Nikephoros Notaras. Behind the Praitorion building itself are their barracks, as well as one of the city's prisons. The cells here are used mainly for criminals being brought to trial, or those arrested for public order offences; not for long-term incarceration.

LINKS

- ф Demetrios Metochites, the Praitor (NPC-9)
- ф Vardariotai (ORG-35)
- ф Amantion (KN-1)
- ф Chancellery (ORG-16)

KN-14 SPHORAKION

POPULATION

100 (sparse)

AFFILIATIONS

Professional (luxury goods), Societal (dynatoi)

Sphorakion is one of the richest neighbourhoods in Constantinople. Amongst its parks one can find the villas of some of the wealthiest dynatos families, including the Komnenos, Bryennios, Botaneiates, Doukas, Kamateros, Kantakouzenos, and Angelos. Each villa is surrounded by a high wall, and most have a household guard (*oiketai*) even if there is no one at home. The local phylakes are comprised from members of the oiketai, so tend to be professional warriors, unlike typical members of the watch. The parish church of Sphorakion is the Church of Urbicus.

The businesses of Sphorakion are boutiques of the highest calibre, selling luxury goods to the wealthy and privileged. Many of these goods are imported, and bear a hefty premium as well as the import tax.

LINKS

- ф Chalkoprateia (KN-5)
- ф Keropoleia (KN-10)
- ф Eugenion (AK-3)

PALATION (DISTRICT)

Palation District is the south-easternmost region of the city. It is dominated by the Great Palace (mega palation), a structure of nearly twenty thousand square metres contained behind a single wall. However, the district is more than just the Great Palace, it also contains the Hippodrome, Law School, Hagia Sophia, and several other palaces and public areas. Palation has some of the most impressive architecture in Mythic Constantinople despite its general poor state of repair.

The Great Palace is the seat of government for Constantinople, and was once the place of governance for the whole Empire. It consists of numerous separate structures and pavilions joined by covered walkways and stairs and surrounded by a great wall. The Great Palace is built on the southeast-facing slope of the Second Hill. It is built on a series of six terraces that bring the palace from its heights at the Chalke and Hippodrome down 33 metres to sea level at the Boukoleon Palace. The main entrance to the Great Palace is via the Chalke at the Augustaion. This opens first into the barracks of the palace guards, and from there into various reception halls and palaces.

LOCAL KNOWLEDGE

STREETWISE

- (Success): Palation is the home of government. The Offices of the Chancellery, General Fisc, Special Fisc, the Drome, the Army, and the Navy are all located here

LORE (BYZANTINE)

- (Success): the Boukoleon Palace was home to the emperor up until the Frankokratia, but it was considered 'defiled' by the Latin Emperors.

LOCAL RUMOURS

- "The Daphne Palace is haunted by a nymph who inhabits the statue of Daphne they brought from Rome. She's been trapped in stone for centuries, and has gone mad."
- "The Army Office is looking to hire anyone who can bring them useful intelligence on Boğazkesen ("The Throat Cutter") – a fortress that the sultan is building about 10 kilometres north of Pera."
- "The Special Logothete always needs people to guard the income being brought into the City from the Imperial estates. Not all of the raiders who attack the wagons are human, or so they say."
- "Nothing can be said within the Great Palace without the Logothete of the Drome hearing it."
- "My cousin Vini and his best friend are scallop divers. The friend says that their boss saw a huge pile of gold on the sea floor. Reckon it must be the gold thrown into the sea in place of Saint Euphemia's relics. Never did manage to find that gold again."

DESCRIPTIVE ELEMENTS

Cool and shaded; fountains in hidden courtyards; colonnades beside meticulously-tended gardens; marble streets and staircases; dogs lying in the shade on cool marble; petty bureaucrats in formal costume hurrying between departments; ministers in richly-embroidered robes and assortment of headgear; hushed voices; echoing footsteps; suspicious looks and whispered conversations as the characters pass by; cracked marble walls; incomplete mosaics; fire-damaged frescoes.

PA-1 AUGUSTAION

AFFILIATIONS

Profession (apothecaries, perfumers)

Originally a public market, the Augustaion is one of the oldest parts of Constantinople, built when the city was a tribute state of the Roman Empire and called Augusta Antonina. It is a closed courtyard lined with porticoes, entered through the Melete Gate from the west or the Pinsos Gate from the south. The Augustaion is the property of Hagia Sophia, although it has not been repaired since the earthquake of 1344 and is mostly in ruins.

The Melete Gate connects the Augustaion to the Mese Odos. To the north is the Hagia Sophia, and to the east is the Magnaura next to the Chalke Gate which leads into the Great Palace. The southwest side is occupied by the Baths of Zeuxippes. At the western end of the square is the Column of Justinian, a 30-metre tall column of marble standing on steps topped with a bronze statue of the Emperor Justinian astride a horse holding aloft a golden orb, with a group of three barbarian kings kneeling before him in tribute. Remarkably, the statue still stands despite the sorry state of the rest of the Augustaion, although the statue is attached to the column by four iron chains.

Directly outside the Melete Gate is the Milion. This monument is the starting place for all distances measured from Constantinople. It is a domed building resting on four large arches, decorated with statues of past emperors and paintings of scenes from the Hippodrome. It is crowned with a statue of Constantine and his mother Helena looking towards the east; a statue of the Tyche (Fortune) of the City stands behind them. On its base is inscribed the distances of all the main cities formerly part of the Empire from Constantinople.

The Portico of Achilles is the name given to the Augustaion's southernmost colonnade. Here are the workshops and stalls of the Guild of Spicers and Perfumers, and the air is filled with the heady scents of pepper, cinnamon, aloe, ambergris, sandalwood, and other exotic substances.

LINKS

- Chalke Gate (PA-3)
- Hagia Sophia (PA-8)
- Magnaura (PA-12)
- Noumera (PA-14)
- Mese Odos (KN-12)

PA-2 Boukoleon Palace

Affiliations

Political (Imperial Household)

The lowest part of the Great Palace, this grand residence sits right next to the sea walls. The palace has its own harbour reached through the Gate of the Lions which leads directly into the palace; so named for the two stone lions that flank the gate. The palace has a balcony looking out to sea above the seaward walls. Before the Fourth Crusade the palace was a favoured imperial residence, and was the principal home of the Latin Emperor during the Frankokratia (see page 8). Upon the empire's restoration, the Palaiologian dynasty was loathe to use the residence so associated with the usurpers, and the imperial residence was moved to Blachernai. No-one lives here now except for caretakers; it is occasionally used to house important foreign visitors, such as the Ottoman Sultan.

The Boukoleon is home to the Porphyra (see page 15); only a prince born here can call himself *Porphyrogennetos* and lay an undisputable claim to the throne. An empress usually spends the last month of her pregnancy living at the Boukoleon, other than that it is mostly empty.

Links

- Hormisidon (PA-10)

PA-3 Chalke Gate

Affiliations

Military (palace guards)

The Bronze Gate is the principal ceremonial entrance to the Great Palace complex. It stands at the eastern end of the Augustaion. It is a rectangular building with four piers supporting a central dome, which themselves rest on four barrel arches. There are two chambers on the north and south sides, each featuring a vaulted dome. The gate gets its name from the gilded bronze tiles used on its roof and the massive bronze doors that separate the palace from the rest of the city. There is a small chapel to Christ Chalkites built atop the gatehouse which used to bear the Ikon of Christ Chalkites, one of the city's major religious symbols before the Iconclastic Crisis (see page 31). A mosaic ikon now graces the wall of the chapel since the Ikon was destroyed.

Links

- Augustaion (PA-1)

PA-4 Chrysotriklinos

Affiliations

Political (Imperial Household)

The "Golden Hall" is the main ceremonial hall of the Great Palace. Important visitors are still received here, imperial dignities are conferred here, and religious festivals and banquets are held here. The Chrysotriklinos is octagonal in form, consisting of a dome supported by eight arches each with two windows. The dome is decorated with sumptuous mosaics of Christ, the Virgin Mary, various Emperors and Patriarchs, and the Heavenly Court with angels and martyrs. The arches create eight apses leading from the central chamber. The imperial throne occupies the eastern apse. The north-eastern apse holds the imperial crown and relics when the court is present, including the Rod of Moses. The northern apse has a silver door, and leads to the (former) imperial bedroom in the Daphne Palace. The north-western apse is the steward's room, where his keys are kept. The western apse leads to the hall of the Lausiakos, and beyond that the Justinianos. The south-western apse opens to a courtyard called the Horologion due to the sundial within it; this is used for the emperor to speak in private with his guests. The southern apse is a waiting room for officials. The south-eastern apse opens onto a portico that leads to the Church of the Virgin of the Pharos.

Light is provided by the windows and great chandeliers, the imperial regalia and relics displayed under their own lights to set them off in all their glory. During banquets, two silver and two gold organs are placed in the porch, and the choir of the Hagia Sophia is brought in to regale the guests with heavenly music.

Links

- Church of the Virgin of the Pharos (PA-6)
- The Great Palace (PA-7)

PA-5 Church of Saints Sergios and Bakchos

Congregation Size: 600; Piety: 3%; Magical Strength: 75%

Affiliations

Religious/Christian

One of the most important churches in the early centuries of the Byzantine Empire, ranking behind Hagia Sophia and the Holy Apostles. It sits south of the Hippodrome in the Hormisidon neighbourhood next to the Iron Gate. Sergios and Bakchos were fourth century Roman soldiers, model soldiers, inseparable friends (or *erastai*, "lovers'). They were held in high favour until their secret Christianity was revealed. They were publically humiliated by being dressed in women's clothing and paraded around town. Bakchos was beaten to death and Sergios was beheaded. They are always venerated as a couple, and their friendship is evoked in the *adelphopoiesis* (brother-making) rite (see page 23).

When Justin I was emperor, his nephew Justinian was due to be executed for plotting to usurp his uncle. The two saints Sergios and Bakchos appeared before the emperor and vouched for his innocence; in gratitude Justinian built this church to their honour. It is a classic Byzantine style cross-in-square design, the first of its kind and the pattern of many future Byzantine churches, including the Hagia Sophia restored by Justinian. It has a dome in 16 compartments with alternating flat and concave sections supported by eight pillars. There is a two-storey colonnade running around three sides of the building, bearing a poetic inscription to Justinian, his wife Theodora, and Saint Sergios (but curiously no mention of Saint Bakchos). The columns alternate red and green.

LINKS

- ɸ Hippodrome (PA-9)
- ɸ Hormisidon (PA-10)

PA-6 CHURCH OF THE VIRGIN OF THE PHAROS

Congregation Size: 50; Piety: 5%; Magical Strength: 25%

AFFILIATIONS

Religious/Christian

Named for the Tower of the Lighthouse (Greek: *pharos*) next to the church, this church was the chief palatine chapel of the Byzantine Emperors before the Fourth Crusade. It is a small church with a ribbed dome, three apses, a narthex and an atrium. The interior was decorated in red porphyry. As the palatine chapel the church held the important relics of the empire, including important artefacts relating to the Passion (see page 84). The priest in charge held the imperial title of *skeuophylax*, "keeper of objects". Unfortunately, all of these valuable relics were taken during the Sack of Constantinople. Many of them were eventually acquired by King Louis IX of France (r. 1226–1270), who built his own version of the Church of the Virgin of the Pharos.

The church and the lighthouse were both heavily damaged during the Sack of Constantinople, although have been rebuilt since the Restoration.

LINKS

- ɸ Chrysotriklinos (PA-4)
- ɸ Hormisidon (PA-10)

PA-7 THE GREAT PALACE

POPULATION

400 (sparse)

AFFILIATIONS

Political (Army Office, Naval Office, Drome, Chancellery, General Fisc, Special Fisc), Professional (advocates, notaries, teachers, scribes), Societal (mesoi)

The principal neighbourhood of Palation district is the Great Palace itself. This is a vast complex consisting of separate palaces and halls located around courtyards and connected via covered walkways. Each courtyard has a unique signature feature, which is an aid to navigation for the novice: various statues, fountains, pools of water, rose gardens, apricot orchards, and the like make each distinctive. The Nea Ekklesia is the church of choice attended by most palace residents.

The Great Palace contains many separate halls (triklinoi), each one a virtual palace unto itself. These have been occupied by the various ministries of government, and usually consist of a grand reception hall, several smaller halls, a large office for the departmental minister, and progressively smaller offices for each rung in the ministry hierarchy. Every bureaucrat with an office bears a dignitary, some of which have become preposterously grandiose over the centuries. Several sections of the Grand Palace lay in ruins, with the government lacking the funds or the inclination to restore them.

- ɸ Chalke Gate: see PA-3
- ɸ Triklinos of the Scholai: this hall is home to the palace guards. Day-to-day these are provided by the Army Office, but when the emperor visits this hall is occupied by the Varangian Guard for the duration.
- ɸ Triklinos of the Excubitores: The Paramonai Guard (see page 108) are housed in this hall.
- ɸ Triklinos of the Candidati: Home to the Office of the Drome. Thomas Strouthion (see page 124) maintains an office here.
- ɸ Delphax or Tribunal: a courtyard where imperial dignitaries and demerits are offered. To the southwest a flight of stairs leads up to the Daphne Palace. To the northwest is the Triklinos of Nineteen Couches, to the southeast is the Augustaios.
- ɸ Triklinos of Nineteen Couches: a long dining hall with nineteen apses or niches, each with a semi-circular couch and table
- ɸ Onopodion: A small semi-circular courtyard in front of the Augustaios
- ɸ Augustaios: formerly the throne room and crowning hall, now taken over by the Naval Office. Like the Army Office it is a warehouse of documents but has no high-ranking staff, since most are at the alternate barracks in Vlanga
- ɸ Daphne Palace: Built by Constantine the Great, this was the main residence of the emperor up until the eighth century when it was abandoned in favour of the Boukoleon Palace. It is now occupied by Ministry of the Chancellery. The Grand Logothete occupies the former personal imperial quarters, and uses the coronation hall to meet with his chief subordinates. The Oratory of Saint Stephen, once the private chapel of the emperor, now lies vacant, although the stairway leading to the imperial box in the Hippodrome is still used by the Grand Logothete.
- ɸ Konsisterion: the main audience hall of the early palace, now used by the Army Office. There is only a skeleton staff here since the Grand Domestic spends his time at the Blachernai Palace and his subordinates are with the army in Stoudion (see page 171)
- ɸ Chrysotriklinos: see PA-4
- ɸ Triklinos of Justinianos: The Office of the Special Fisc occupies the hall built by Justinian II.
- ɸ Triklinos of Lausiakos: The Office of the General Fisc is right next to its rivals in the Special Fisc. Very little actual coin or bullion is held here; the money that exists in the ledgers of the department of taxation is actually deposited in a secret vault.

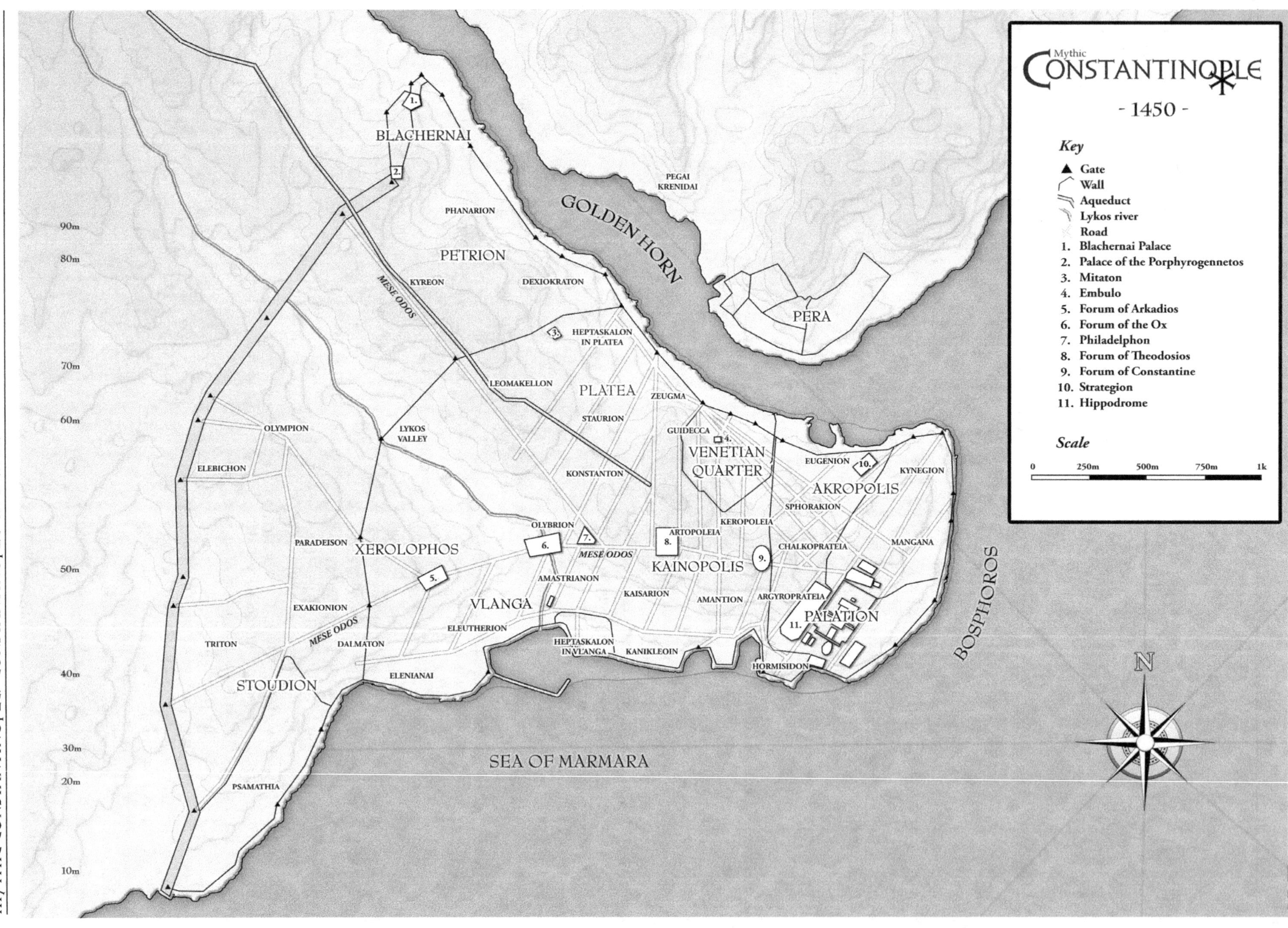

Mythic
CONSTANTINOPLE
- 1450 -
Key
▲ Gate
Wall
Aqueduct
Lykos river
Road
1. Blachernai Palace
2. Palace of the Porphyrogennetos
3. Mitaton
4. Embulo
5. Forum of Arkadios
6. Forum of the Ox
7. Philadelphon
8. Forum of Theodosios
9. Forum of Constantine
10. Strategion
11. Hippodrome
Scale
0
250m
500m
750m
1k
N
90m
80m
70m
60m
50m
40m
30m
20m
10m
BLACHERNAI
PEGAI
KRENIDAI
GOLDEN HORN
PHANARION
PETRION
KYREON
DEXIOKRATON
MESE ODOS
PERA
HEPTASKALON IN PLATEA
LEOMAKELLON
PLATEA
ZEUGMA
STAURION
LYKOS VALLEY
OLYMPION
GUIDECCA
VENETIAN QUARTER
EUGENION
KYNEGION
ELEBICHON
KONSTANTON
AKROPOLIS
SPHORAKION
OLYBRION
KEROPOLEIA
ARTOPOLEIA
PARADEISON
XEROLOPHOS
MESE ODOS
CHALKOPRATEIA
MANGANA
KAINOPOLIS
AMASTRIANON
KAISARION
VLANGA
AMANTION
ARGYROPRATEIA
EXAKIONION
PALATION
ELEUTHERION
TRITON
MESE ODOS
DALMATON
HEPTASKALON IN VLANGA
KANIKLEOIN
BOSPHOROS
HORMISIDON
ELENIANAI
STOUDION
SEA OF MARMARA
PSAMATHIA

THE GREAT PALACE

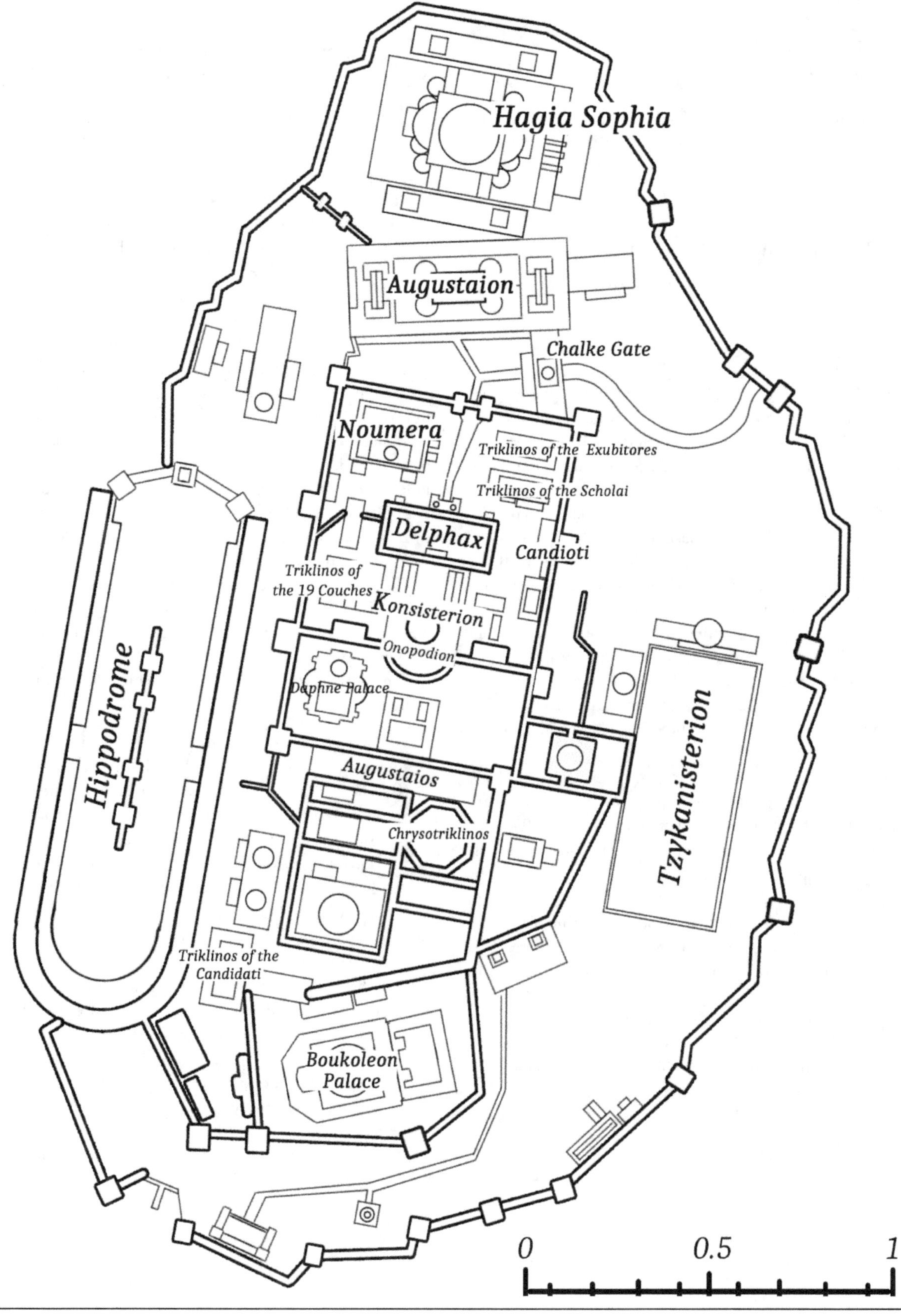

LINKS

- Hormisidon (PA-10)
- Noumera (PA-14)
- Mangana (AK-8)
- Argyroprateia (KN-3)
- Paramonai (ORG-31)
- Office of the Drome (ORG-25)
- Navy Office (ORG-24)
- Army Office (ORG-13)
- Office of the General Fisc (ORG-26)
- Office of the Special Fisc (ORG-28)
- The Chancellery (ORG-16)
- Loukas Laskaris Notaras (NPC-20)

PA-8 HAGIA SOPHIA

Congregation Size: 3,100; Piety: 5%; Magical Strength: 100%

AFFILIATIONS

Deviant (anti-Unionists), Religious/Christian

The current Church of Holy Wisdom is the third building of that name on this site. The first was founded by Constantine the Great upon the dedication of the city but was burnt down in 404 following a riot prompted by the exile of Patriarch John Chrysostom. The church was rebuilt, but perished during the Nika Riots (see page 15) in 532. The current church was inaugurated in 537, and despite numerous earthquakes and fires has lasted for nine hundred years. The church was ransacked and desecrated during the Fourth Crusade, and was rededicated as a Catholic cathedral during the Frankokratia. The tomb of Enrico Dandolo – the Doge of Venice who orchestrated the Sack of Constantinople – lies within the current church, and is still regularly cursed and spat upon by the congregation. Emperor Andronikos II ordered the most recent major restoration of the church in 1317, although the earthquake of 1344 caused damage to the dome, which forced its closure for another 10 years.

Hagia Sophia is a vast church with a complex interior. At the heart of the church is the great dome over the nave, over 55 metres above the nave floor and 30 metres in diameter, resting on 40 arched windows. There a two half domes of the same diameter to the east and west, each with three smaller half-domes, creating an interior 75 metres long. The interior of the nave is sheathed with green and white marble, purple porphyry, and gold mosaics. An upper gallery forms a horseshoe shape around the nave as far as the apse. This gallery is reserved for the use of the empress, and is decorated with many fine mosaics.

The Hagia Sophia is currently occupied by anti-Unionist monks and priests, lead by Bishop Akkakios of Derkos. They deny the access of the Patriarch to hold Mass at his own church. The patriarch is seeking to end this siege peacefully, but is determined to perform the Pascha Mass here and will take whatever means necessary to gain access to his church.

LINKS

- Augustaion (PA-1)
- Patriarch Gregory III Mammas (NPC-14)
- Patriarchate of Constantinople (ORG-8)
- Anti-Unionists (ORG-12)

PA-9 THE HIPPODROME

AFFILIATIONS

None

The Hippodrome lies in a deep valley in the Second Hill. It is a racetrack and circus that was once the social centre of the Roman Empire, hosting sporting events and spectacular displays of athletic superiority. It now lies mostly in ruins, with half the track overgrown and used by enterprising citizens to grow grape vines. The other half of the U-shaped racetrack is still used for horse races and foot races, and occasionally for jousting.

The track is nearly 400 metres long and 130 metres wide. The main entrance is to the north, which is also where the traps for the chariots are found. The two sides of the track are separated by a partition called the spina, which bears several monuments – and used to hold more, before they were taken during the Sack of Constantinople. The stands have over 30 stepped rows of marble seats and could hold up to 100,000 spectators; at the northern end there are a number of boxes owned by aristocratic families, and the emperor had his own private lodge on the eastern side which could be reached from within the Great Palace.

The track was lined with bronze statues of gods, heroes, emperors, and famous charioteers and horses. Some of the Prasinoi are known to meet here amongst the statues to plan their moves against the government.

The monuments of the spina include (from northeast to southwest)

- The Obelisk of Thutmose III: carved from pink granite, it was taken from the Temple of Karnak at Luxor.
- The Tripod of Plataea: a column of three intertwined snakes; their heads raised at the top to support a golden bowl. This tripod was brought from the Oracle of Delphi. The golden bowl went missing during the Sack of Constantinople
- The Obelisk of Constantine VII Porphyrogennetos: stands in the centre; it was originally covered in gilded bronze plaques and topped with a golden ball, but they were looted in the Fourth Crusade.
- The Monuments of Porphyrios: seven monuments erected in honour of a famous charioteer. They are stone blocks carved with his image in relief, along with his patrons Nike (Victory) and Tyche (Luck). The names of his horses are also inscribed. Two of the monuments were raised by the Blues, and the remaining five were raised by the Greens when he switched sides.
- The Statue of Herakles Trihesperos by the famous sculptor Lysippos

LINKS

- The Daphne Palace (PA-7)
- The Prasinoi (ORG-32)

PA-10 HORMISIDON

POPULATION

800

AFFILIATIONS

Professional (bookbinders, pecumenaries), Societal (mesoi)

Emperor Constantine the Great gave sanctuary to Prince Hormizd of Persia who was persecuted by his brother-in-law, King Shapur II. The prince was given a palace overlooking the Sea of Marmara, and the neighbourhood became called Hormisidon after him. The parish church is the Church of Saints Sergios and Bakchos.

Hormisidon is an uncrowded neighbourhood and home to many mid-level bureaucrats who work in Palation but are not of sufficient status to get to live there. It is not well known as a commercial district, although some of the best parchment-makers (*pecumenaries*) and bookbinders can be found here.

LINKS

- Boukoleon Palace (PA-2)
- Church of Saints Sergios and Bakchos (PA-5)
- Church of the Virgin of the Pharos (PA-6)
- Great Palace (PA-7)
- Amantion (KN-1)
- Argyroprateia (KN-3)

PA-11 HOSPITAL OF SAMPSON

AFFILIATIONS

Academic (medical arts), Professional (nurses, surgeons, physicians), Urban (hospital)

Attached to the Hagia Sophia, this hospital was founded by Justinian I and named after the distinguished physician who first ran it. During the Frankokratia, the Catholic monks that ran it organised into the military Brothers of Saint Sampson, who fled to Corinth after the Restoration.

The prime purpose of the hospital is to provide medical care to those without the financial capacity to hire a physician; however, the hospital does not distinguish between social class or wealth, and treats anyone who comes to its doors. Those who are able to pay are asked to make a donation, which is used to support the charitable work of the institution, which otherwise runs on a small budget from the Orphanotrophos.

In addition to treatment of the sick, the hospital also provides accommodation for the destitute and long-term care for those with disfiguring and debilitating conditions.

STORY HOOK

The Brothers of Saint Sampson return in secret, intent on retrieving secrets or treasure they hid in the chapel when they fled. The player characters are at the hospital when these highly trained warriors try to infiltrate it.

LINKS

- Orphanage of Saint Paul (AK-11)

PA-12 MAGNAURA PALACE

AFFILIATIONS

Academic (law), Professional (lawyers, advocates)

Lying to the east of the Augustaion and north of the Great Palace, the Magnaura was formerly the Senate building, but since the ninth century has formed part of the Imperial University. The building is accessed through a marble gate leading into a courtyard. The palace itself consists of a basilica with three naves.

Magnaura houses the law chair of the University. Its principal business is the training of the next generation of courtiers and civil servants. It caters mostly to a male student base, unlike the greater university. The Law School of Magnaura is headed by the nomophylax ("guardian of the law"). This president of the school is tasked with being the final authority on the law of Constantinople, and has usually served as a magistrate. It is also the job of the law school to provide accreditation for lawyers and advocates, and has the power to arrest and imprison those who practice law without such accreditation.

LINKS

- Augustaion (PA-1)
- Philadelphion (VL-11)

PA-13 NEA EKKLESIA

Congregation Size: 300; Piety: 6%; Magical Strength: 50%

AFFILIATIONS

Religious/Christian

The "New Church" was built in the ninth century by Basil I in the south-eastern corner of the Great Palace on the site of the former Tzykanisterion. The church has a large central dome dedicated to Jesus Christ surrounded by four smaller ones dedicated in turn to the archangel Michael, the Prophet Elijah, the Virgin Mary, and Saint Nicholas. These are covered on the outside with brass, and on the inside decorated with stars picked out in gemstones. Inside, the church is faced with multi-coloured marble panels and the pavement is a mosaic depicting the various divine figures to whom the church is dedicated. The riches with which the church was adorned – gold, silver, and pearls – did not survive the Sack of Constantinople, and have not been replaced.

Two porticoes on the north and south of the church head towards the Tzykanisterion; the sacristy lies to the south. To the east there is a garden called the *mesokepion* ("middle garden").

LINKS

- Chrysotriklinos (PA-4)
- Tzykanisterion (PA-16)

PA-14 NOUMERA

AFFILIATIONS

Criminal, Military (Vardariotai), Professional (silk guilds), Urban (prison)

The Noumera is the main prison for civilians in Constantinople. It occupies the northwest corner of the Great Palace, on a site that used to house the famous Baths of Zeuxippos, which was itself formerly a temple to Zeus. The public baths had the typical Roman arrangement of cold, tepid, and hot baths; women bathed in the morning and men in the afternoon. The western end of the former baths is rented by the Imperial Silk Guilds as a workshop and storehouse; the rest is given over to the prison.

The Noumera is under the control of the Vardariotai, unlike the Prison of Anemas that caters to important prisoners and is guarded by the Varangian Guard. Considering the population of the city (even at its currently reduced size), the Noumera is not a large prison, having a capacity of just 250 at its most crowded. Most convicted criminals are not imprisoned; justice tends to punitive, corporal, or capital rather than penitentiary in nature. Those convicted to a spell in prison are usually put here due to owing money to the plaintiff, where the sum involved is not sufficient to evoke debt slavery. Prisoners must pay for the privilege of being imprisoned; they pay rent on their cell and must purchase food from the prison cooks if they do not have family who can bring them meals. A prisoner is permitted to run up a line of credit if they are likely to be able to repay it; but if the debt grows too great then they may be sold into slavery to cover their imprisonment fines. The prison is also used for defendants awaiting trial who cannot be trusted to appear before the judge when called. By the Code of Justinian a person cannot be held on remand for more than 13 months, but few prisoners know this, and some have languished for years in gaol because their case has been lost in the system.

The prison consists of four dozen multi-occupancy cells, designed for four people but often holding three times that while other cells remain empty. If the appropriate bribes are paid to the guards a prisoner can have the run of the interior during the day, but the governor insists that everyone returns to their cells at night. The walls of the Noumera are over four metres thick, and both of the doors into the prison interior have double locked doors with a guarded vestibule between, providing safe zones that prevent the prisoners from rushing the doors. There are also quarters for the Vardariotai who guard the prison, and a plush apartment for the governor. Some chambers still show evidence of the building's former usage, with mosaics on the wall and drains in the floor.

Leontes Diktuoplokos is a famous, if atypical, prisoner.

STORY HOOK

A player character is falsely accused of a crime by an enemy. Due to his adventuring lifestyle, the character is judged a flight risk and remanded in the Noumera. The accuser then pays the Praitorion to lose the paperwork, consigning the character to a life in prison or as a debt slave. The player character must rely on his comrades to resolve the legal tangle, or perhaps he plans an escape.

LINKS

- Leontes Diktuoplokos (NPC-19)
- Vardariotai (ORG-35)

PA-15 PATRIARCHAL SCHOOL

AFFILIATIONS

Academic (sacerdotal), Political (Imperial University), Religious/Christian (Orthodox)

The Patriarchal School was founded by Alexios I in 1107. It is located within the bounds of the Hagia Sophia, and its main purpose is the training of theologians. Most priests begin their education at the Patriarchal School, but the full curriculum is for the professional scholar of church doctrine, not for parish priests. There are five masters of the school: the didaskaloi of Gospel, Apostle, and Psalter, the maistor rhetoron, and the dikaiophylax (who arbitrates over matters of canon law). The maistor rhetoron ("master of rhetoric") is the only one who is an appointee of the government (specifically the Imperial University); the others are chosen by the patriarch and are all deacons.

LINKS

- Augustaion (PA-1)
- Philadelphion (VL-11)

PA-16 TZYKANISTERION

AFFILIATIONS

Professional (horse breeding), Societal (various dynatos and mesos tzykaniasts)

A stadium to the east of Palation for the playing of tzykanion, a form of polo (see page 21). This game has always been popular with the Byzantine nobility and that is as true today as it ever was. The game is dangerous: deaths are not uncommon, and even one emperor has met his end on the Tzykanisterion.

The playing field consists of a large flat field of grass save for a central raised hill where play begins. There is stadium-style seating along the western edge of the field, and the northern end is occupied by extensive stables and a stud farm.

STORY HOOK

The Tzykanisterion is haunted by the ghost of Emperor Alexander, who was killed while playing the sport in 913. He was a lazy, lecherous, and malignant drunk who made sacrifices to pagan altars. Perhaps it is no surprise that his restless spirit came to reside in his tzykanion pole, which now decorates the clubhouse. The wraith acquires a new Spirit Ability with every death it causes, and it can now cause accidents (using Telekinesis), spook horses (using Spellcasting: Demoralise), and cause clumsiness (with Curse: Ride). Characters might encounter the wraith when attending (or participating

in) a Tzykanion match, or else be asked in to investigate when someone is injured or killed.

LINKS

- Great Palace (PA-7)
- Nea Ekklesia (PA-13)

PERA (SUBURB)

Around 1150 the Genoese were first given permission to settle on the north shore of the Golden Horn in the ruins of a Justinian-era settlement. The new town was attacked and nearly destroyed in 1171; the Venetians were blamed and Manuel I Komnenos used the attack as a pretext for what became called the Massacre of the Latins. As a prelude to the Sack of Constantinople all 2,500 Jews living in Pera were put to death by the Latin army; and during the Frankokratia the city became occupied by the Venetians.

The current suburb of Pera was founded after the Restoration of the Empire. Genoese grandees petitioned the Emperor for permission to build a new settlement in order to avoid violent confrontations with Venetian competitors who had become established in the city during the Frankokratia. Michael VIII Palaiologos agreed, perhaps suspecting it would afford him more control over the Genoese. The precise terms of the foundation were stipulated in 1303 and the inhabitants were forbidden from expanding or fortifying the settlement, both of which have been ignored with no reprisals from the Empire, and Pera is now a thriving independent city. The name "Pera" simply means "Across" in Greek, signifying both its proximity to Constantinople and its separation from it by the Golden Horn.

The suburb takes the form of a fortified town or citadel, divided into five wards, each with its own wall. The wards represent the four phases of growth of the settlement: the Magnificata represents the original Genoese settlement in 1303, which was then extended up the hill to form the Tower Ward in 1349. The North Ward was added in 1387, and the West Ward in 1397. Finally, the Ward of Saint Benoit was enclosed on the east side of the city in 1400.

Pera's ruler is called the *podestà*, who is elected by the metropolis for life. The podestà is the permanent Genoese ambassador to the Byzantine court, and governs all the trade affairs of the colony with the assistance of a council of 24 members. The podestà of Pera also wields authority over the consuls of Genoa's colonies in the Black Sea: Varna, Chilia, Lykostomo, Moncastro, Kaffa, and so forth. In 1450, the podestà is Illario Doria (NPC-16); the Doria albergo (Genoese commune) has dominated the position for the last six generations.

The population of Pera – about 5,000 souls – is primarily Genoese, but there are substantial numbers of Amalfitans, Tuscans and Ragusans, as well as a small community of Venetians living amongst their traditional enemy. The principal language spoken here is Italian, although many inhabitants also speak Greek. Most of the inhabitants are employed by Genoese magnates who have settled in Pera and operate banks, trading houses, and notary offices. Most of the inhabitants and all the churches in Pera are Catholic, under the authority of the archbishop of Genoa.

LOCAL KNOWLEDGE

STREETWISE

- (Success): Pera is an independent city from Constantinople, and part of the Republic of Genoa.

LORE (BYZANTINE)

- (Success): Pera was originally called Galata after the Galatai people who settled here before they became the Galatians of central Anatolia. Justinian II resettled it and named it Iustianopolis, and it later became the Jewish quarter. The Genoese first occupied the site around 1150.

LOCAL RUMOURS

- "Have you heard about the ghost at the Great Tower? It wears a long white robe and a turban. Supposedly it points the way to hidden treasure, but can only be seen on nights of the new moon."
- (From a Greek) "The Franks of Pera are planning to betray us to the Ottomans. Their council has met with the Grand Vizier, and a Turkish general has a permanent residence near the palace."
- (From a Genoese) "The Greeks are planning to blockade our harbour. They are jealous of our Republic's success in a few

short years; whereas their centuries of greed have led to nothing but cheated merchants and stagnant markets."

DESCRIPTIVE ELEMENTS

New buildings with the occasional ancient structure wedged between them; Genoese-style architecture; narrow terraced streets with few alleyways; statues from Classical period; western-style cross-shaped churches with bell towers instead of domes

PR-1 CHURCH OF SAN BENOIT

AFFILIATIONS

Religious/Christian (Catholic)

This church is located at the top of a long staircase built into the Galata Hill. It is situated on a terrace surrounded by a garden. The church has a single dome over the central nave, with an interior decorated with mosaics. At odds with Orthodox churches found in Constantinople, the church has a bell tower, which is also used as a watchtower. The grounds include a large Byzantine-era cistern still supplies water to this part of the city

The church was founded by a Benedictine monk from Genoa in 1427, established just inside the new rampart wall built in the most recent expansion of Pera. It is dedicated jointly to Saint Benedict and the Virgin Mary, and is occasionally known as Santa Maria della Cisterna.

LINKS

None.

PR-2 CHURCH OF SAN PAOLO

AFFILIATIONS

Religious/Christian (Catholic)

Built during the Venetian occupation of Pera during the Frankokratia, the Church of Saint Paul became a Dominican possession in 1325 when it was enlarged and renamed the Church of San Domenico, although residents continue to call it San Paolo. The church remains a Dominican foundation, and the black-robed friars can be seen throughout Pera preaching against the heresy of the anti-Unionists.

The church takes a classic Italian form, a ribbed vaulted roof with a bell-tower and a pair of side chapels to form a cross-shape. The chapels contain shrines maintained by Genoese noble families.

STORY HOOK

A Catholic flagellant cult comes to Pera, and takes the ferry to Constantinople every day. These monks have a nihilistic message about the End of Days, and whip themselves with scourges to purge sin. They are initially made the object of ridicule, but their masochistic form of worship appears to be contagious and soon the craze is sweeping the city. The characters get involved when someone they know is swept up in the religious fervour. One of the original monks carries a jar of ointment, which is really a fetish containing several hundred spirits of madness. Whenever he anoints someone he releases the spirit. Is this deliberate, or accidental? If the former, to what purpose?

LINKS

None.

PR-3 GALATAS HARBOUR

AFFILIATIONS

Professional (stevedores, warehouse owners, merchants, shipowners), Urban (market)

This busy harbour has three times more commercial activity than any harbour in Constantinople, estimated at over 200,000 ducats per year. The majority of the business is in receiving trade goods from the Black Sea colonies, the mouth of the Danube, and from Trebizond, and shipping it to Genoa. The goods traded include wheat, tallow, wax, raw and processed silk, fine textiles, alum for dyeing, fur, salt, and of course slaves.

LINKS

- The Slave Market (PR-9)
- Zeugma (PL-16)

PR-4 THE GREAT TOWER

AFFILIATIONS

Military, Political (customs officers)

The Kastellion was an imposing fortress that guarded the northern shore of the Golden Horn. Now, only the Great Tower (Megalos Pyrgos in Greek) remains, an edifice rising over 30 metres from the Galatan shore. It is the northern terminus of the great chain that crosses the Golden Horn, controlling the passage of ships and serving as a customs station. Once the toll has been paid, a section of the chain is lifted via a mechanism housed in the tower to allow passage.

The rest of the Kastellion was besieged during the Fourth Crusade, and eventually taken by Baldwin of Flanders. With the fortress and the tower under Crusader control, their ships could enter the Golden Horn and commence the Sack of the city.

LINKS

- The Leaden Vault (PR-5)

PR-5 THE LEADEN VAULT

AFFILIATIONS

Cultural (Arab), Deviant (ghosts)

Near to the former site of the Kastellion is an underground temple converted into a prison during the days of Emperor Tiberius II. In the first Arab siege of Constantinople, a soldier Sufyan bin Uyeyne was imprisoned here, where he was tortured to death. During the Second Arab siege, when the Umayyad Caliphate made another attempt to take Constantinople, Sulayman ibn Mu'ad commanded the Arab fleet on behalf of the Arab commander Maslama ibn Abd al-Malik. He made landfall at Galata, guided by a Sufi who had been visited in a dream by Sufyan bin Uyeyne. They remained in the area for seven years, but the winter of 718 proved their undoing. There was a great famine brought about by heavy snowfall, and the soldiers first ate their horses and camels before turning to bark and boiled leather. Eventually they resorted to cannibalism. Over three hundred thousand Arab soldiers died during the famine, some of whom were interred in the vault. When they abandoned their campaign and returned to Damascus, they left their valuables in the vault and closed off the entrance with lead.

There is no visible opening to the buried temple, and people have searched for decades to uncover an entrance and enter the vaults, believed to be filled with riches. It is likely that there are a fair few cannibal spirits within the vaults too.

STORY HOOK

The spirit of Sufyan bin Uyeyne is a haunt who infects people with the treasure-hunting obsession through the Passion Spirit Ability. People have found themselves unable to leave the supposed site of the Leaden Vault, frantically searching for its hidden treasure to the neglect of all else. The spirit is actually trying to have its mortal remains (located within the vault) uncovered and buried properly so it can find rest.

LINKS

- The Great Tower (PR-4)

PR-6 MAONA DI CHIO E DI FOCEA

AFFILIATIONS

Professional (merchant)

The maona (chartered company) operates – indeed, rules – the island of Chios, but it has an office here in Pera. There are two principal trade goods, mastic (which is grown on Chios) and alum (which is mined in Focea, a Genoese-controlled town on the Anatolian coast).

The controlling interest in the maona is owned by the Giustiniani family, and Bartolomeo Giustiniani mans the offices here in Pera. Bartolomeo has been tasked by Genoa's Gran Consiglio to watch over the city-state's interests in Pera. There is a general feeling back home that the podestà Illario Doria has "gone native", and is too closely allied with the Palaiologans; and Giustiniani is his nominated successor should this prove to be the case.

In preparation for his takeover of Pera and possibly Constantinople, Giustiniani has covert links with the Prasinoi. More information can be found on page 109.

LINKS

- Prasinoi (ORG-32)

PR-7 PALAZZO DEL COMMUNE

AFFILIATIONS

Cultural (Genoese), Political (podestà)

The palace of the podestà was built in 1316 by Montano de Marinis as an identical copy of the Palazzo San Giorgio in Genoa. It is a grand building that serves as both the residence of the podestà and the centre of Pera's government. The ruling council of 24 worthies meets once a week; each member represents a Genoese commune with an interest in Pera or the Black Sea ports; although some communes have more than one representative, reflecting the magnitude of their interest in the city.

LINKS

- Illario Doria (NPC-16)

PR-8 PEGAI KRENIDAI

AFFILIATIONS

Cultural (Arimapsoi)

About half a kilometre from Pera is a region where several natural springs form a series of pools and cascades. Amongst these lives a small community of Arimapsoi (see page 56). They migrated to Constantinople in the eighth century as mercenaries, and settled here rather than return to the plains of Skythia. Their homes are conical constructions made of a wooden frame covered with reeds, and each family maintains a small herd of semi-wild horses by which they measure their wealth. There are about 500 families of Arimapsoi living at Pegai Krenidai. There are nests of harpies in the hills above the settlement that are a constant threat to the hunter-gatherers.

Their chief wears the skull of a griffin as a headdress, decorated with feathers from the same beast; whom he slew himself to confirm his elevation to head of the tribe.

LINKS

None

PR-9 THE SLAVE MARKET

AFFILIATIONS

Cultural (Tatar, Turcomen, Armenian, Slav), Professional (slave traders), Urban (market)

The slave market next to Galatas Harbour is the largest in the Christian world. It is overseen by the Office of Saint Anthony, a branch of the Genoese government that has an impressive marble-faced building overlooking the market. A tax is levied on every ship carrying slaves, and the Office has jurisdiction over all trade east of Candia (Crete), maintaining a Genoese dominance of the slave trade to the Muslim nations.

The slaves come mostly from the Black Sea, and are principally Tatars, Armenians, and Slavs, although many other races are traded including some non-human ones. There are three principal destinations for slaves brought to Pera. Many will end up being sold in the

Ottoman Empire as servants, labourers, and concubines. The Mamluks want Turcomen for their armies, particularly boys and young men; although they will also buy exotic slaves for resale to more distant nations. The rest are mostly purchased by Venetian merchants who will onsell them in the markets of Europe, principally Prague and Venice itself.

A healthy male slave can sell for 100 hyperpyra. Female slaves rarely earn more than half of that, but those that are exceptionally unusual or beautiful can achieve much higher prices, particularly to Turks. Each slave costs 4½ ducats to convey across the Black Sea and the same again to feed; although slave-traders do not need to pay for those that perish en route.

STORY HOOK

A non-Greek player character hears a girl's voice speaking in his native tongue. She is a prostitute, illegally enslaved but bought legitimately by the brothel or taberna at which she works. When she realises someone can understand her, she pleads for help finding her brother. She was bought at Pera's slave market, and assumes that he was as well. She claims that they are the children of an important nobleman, who can recompense the character. Can the characters find the boy before he is shipped to his destination?

LINKS

- Galatas Harbour (PR-3)

PR-10 THE TOWER OF CHRIST

AFFILIATIONS

Urban (city watch)

The Tower of Christ (*Christea Turris* in Italian) was built in 1348 at the highest point of the citadel, in defiance to the Byzantine edict against such structures. It is nearly 70 metres tall, and is located on a hillside 35 metres above sea level, making it taller than any of Constantinople's buildings. The internal diameter is nine metres, with walls that are nearly four metres thick at the base. The conical roof sits on a rotunda with 12 columns supporting arches, with a walkway on top, used for spotting fires.

LINKS

None.

PETRION (DISTRICT)

Petrion occupies the northern part of the City, between the fifth hill and the Golden Horn. It is named after the Monastery of Saint John at Petra, a prominent monastery high on the hills. The region is exposed to a chill wind from the north, and in the summer denied the cooling breeze from the south. Furthermore, the hills block out the sun from mid-afternoon onwards, bringing early dusk to the main residential area of Petrion. This early darkness is not entirely natural: scholars have calculated that the hills are not high enough for dusk to occur as early as it does. An old legend states that the hills of Petrion are actually a giant, whose head forms the sixth hill and his body is the fifth. When the giants rose up against the old gods, he challenged Helios for control over the sun but lost. He has lain here in darkness ever since. He can only be killed by the club of Herakles wielded by a mortal's hand, but should his body be exposed to the light his strength will be restored.

The district is mostly middle class, bridging the gap between overcrowded Platea to the south and the Imperial suburb of Blachernai to the north. Petrion is dominated by churches and monasteries, many of which are on the northern flanks of the Fifth and Sixth Hill that separate Petrion from other districts.

The neighbourhoods of Petrion are more recent than most of Constantinople and in general are in better repair. There is little Classical architecture and no statues of pagan gods or mythological beings.

LOCAL KNOWLEDGE

STREETWISE

- (Success): Famous for its beacon, Petrion is overlooked by monasteries and churches
- (Success): Phanarion is virtually nocturnal, with many of its people sleeping during the day and going out to work at night.

LOCAL RUMOURS

- "They're an odd lot up in Petrion. Sleep during the day, then come out at night like owls. Their skin is pale like a lizard's belly, rarely touched by the sun."
- "The light of the Phanarion banishes all enchantment. No witch can live in Petrion"
- "During the day, the hills dream of being mountains. That's why Petrion gets dark so early."
- "I heard from my priest's wife that at a funeral recently, the deceased came back from the dead and started attacking the mourners! It seems that the negligent family had failed to hold the funeral soon enough, and an evil spirit had gotten in."

DESCRIPTIVE ELEMENTS

Dark comes early due to shadow from the hills; either bitterly cold in winter or stiflingly hot in summer; dogs huddle in doorways or pant on porches, nearly all of them have upwards-curving tails; buildings mostly in good repair; monks or nuns travelling (in pairs) to places of study or on missions of mercy; (at night) the light of the Phanarion.

PT-1 THE BEACON

AFFILIATIONS

Deviant (spirits), Urban (Tribunos)

The Beacon (Greek: *phanarion*) gives its name to the main residential district of Petrion. The Beacon has a keeper, who is responsible for lighting the beacon at dusk and keeping it burning all night. For this he receives a stipend from the imperial treasury and a budget with which to buy wood. He lives in a house adjacent to the beacon, which is a sturdy tower wider at the bottom than the top, which

is 50 metres above the ground. A bronze-cowled cage at the summit protects the beacon from the weather. Although it might appear that this structure directs the light out to sea, that is not the case at all. The beacon is the focus of a location binding for an aspect of Hekate Phosphoria, the Bringer of Light. This aspect is a separate spirit from the goddess, and manifests as a being of pure light. Phosphoria can manipulate light to produce a narrow beam or a gentle pervasive glow, and even create shadow images by controlling where its light falls and doesn't. In this form, it can reignite the beacon and even take the place of the mundane flame and be seen in even the worst of conditions.

Most residents hold that the light from the beacon is inimical to magic. This is true to some extent: Phosphoria can cast the Avert Folk Magic spell, which will cancel any Folk Magic spell and remove the Evil Eye. It can also use the Neutralise Magic Sorcery spell up to Magnitude 5, at a cost of 3 Magic Points per Magnitude. The duration of the spell is one day per point of the spirit's POW. The spirit is Intensity 5 (INT 15, POW 33, CHA 18), and has the Spirit Abilities of Animate Light, Demesne, Eternal, Manifestation, Persistent, and Spellcasting. Given that these spells are costly for the spirit – who does not naturally recover Magic Points while bound – a person must petition Hekate for her favour. There is a shrine to the triple goddess built into the bottom of the beacon tower, and those offering a dove as a sacrifice may hear the goddess's voice demanding a certain service, after which she will instruct her servant to exercise her power. The tasks set by Hekate are often mysterious and confusing, but ultimately will be revealed to be to the benefit of Constantinople. For example, she might ask that a person move a pile of stones from one part of the city to another; these will be later be fortuitously found by a slinger and used to take down a spy escaping the city with vital documents.

The keeper's family has served the spirit of the beacon for generations. They are cultists of Hekate, and although some of them are witches, none have any power over Phosphoria. Once a year, on the night of the third new moon after the Winter Solstice (a day sacred to Hekate), the keeper conducts a rite to replenish the Magic Points of the spirit of the beacon. In the previous months, he has identified the most despicable and notorious villain he can find. He then brings this individual to the beacon by trickery or by force on the appointed night, and at midnight slits his victim's throat and spills the sacrificial blood into the fire. The spirit gains a number of Magic Points equal to the victim's POW.

STORY HOOK

To an outsider, the activities of a player character might seem more typical of those of a wandering serial killer – their deeds are what becomes public, not their motivations. If the player characters have gathered a reputation for violence in any way, then they may attract the attention of the keeper of the beacon, and find themselves on the wrong side of his knife one winter.

LINKS

- Phanarion (PT-9)

PT-2 CHURCH OF SAINT MARY OF THE MONGOLS

Congregation Size (church): 800; Piety: 8%; Magical Strength: 50%
Congregation Size (monastery): 32; Piety: 51%; Magical Strength: 25%

AFFILIATIONS

Religious/Christian

A small, single-storey church and monastery commissioned by Isaac Doukas, uncle of Michael VIII Palaiologos, it was originally dedicated to the Theotokos Panaghiotissa ("All-Holy"). However, 20 years after its foundation Maria Palaiogina – illegitimate daughter of Michael VIII and widow of Abaqa Khan of the Mongol Ilkhanate – retired here along with a small community of nuns. The monastery thereby acquired its current epithet (Mouchliotissa in Greek). The monastery complex lies behind a high wall next to the church, and consists of a central cylindrical tower surmounted by a central dome. Under the church there is an underground passageway which emerges close to the Hagia Sophia. The church is the parish church of Phanarion, and is tended by the nuns who live next door.

STORY HOOK

Recently, heirs of Maria Palaiogina have discovered an imperial chrysobull (edict) amongst their ancestor's belongings which certifies the purchase of the nunnery by the Palaiogina, and have used it as proof of ownership. Under their governance, the nunnery has been run into ruin. No repairs have been made, and the owners have even raised a mortgage on the property. The nuns are in danger of losing their monastery, but with the heirs owning the chrysobull, neither the Patriarchate nor the Emperor will make a ruling in their favour. The hegumina is certain that it is a fake, but has been unable to verify this. She asks the characters if they will assist her prove that they are being cheated by ruthless charlatans.

LINKS

- Phanarion (PT-9)
- Hagia Sophia (PA-8)

PT-3 CISTERN OF AETIUS

AFFILIATIONS

Urban (Tribunos)

This immense covered tank for water storage was constructed at the same time as the Valens Aqueduct, and it acts as a reservoir for that pipeline should the canal's source become broken or dry up. The cistern lies parallel to the northern branch of the Mese Odos on the Sixth Hill, just inside the Gate of Charisios.

The cistern is 244 metres long by 85 metres wide, and is on average 11 metres deep. Valves and pipework connect it to the moat of the Theodosian Walls, allowing the ditch to be flooded during a siege. Should the cistern be emptied, these pipes are wide enough for a man to walk through, and represent a breach in the security of the walls.

LINKS

- Kyrion (PT-5)

PT-4 DEXIOKRATON

POPULATION

1100

AFFILIATIONS

Professional (tailors, hatmakers), Societal (demoi)

Many of the houses here belong to the Dexiokrates family, thus the name of the neighbourhood. Although a lower class neighbourhood, Dexiokraton is not overcrowded, and most of the homes are well-appointed, with people apparently taking pride in their appearance. However, upkeep of the premises is mandatory in the lease agreement with the Dexiokrates, and they have successfully had fines levied by the courts on householders who fail to maintain standards of external neatness demanded by the exacting family. Despite these rules, Dexiokraton is an aspirational neighbourhood for those currently living in the slums. The parish church of Dexiokraton is attached to the Monastery of Saint Theodosia.

A Skiapod family has developed a reputation amongst the hatmakers of Dexiokraton as producing the highest quality headgear. They are petitioning the Office of the Imperial Household for the right to supply the emperor and his court. Naturally, the current holder of this benefice is not best pleased.

STORY HOOK

A private guild of hatmakers wants to destroy the skiapodes who are competing for their business. They have commissioned the creation of a magical construct from a sorcerer, a golem-like creature made of quicksilver (a substance used extensively by milliners). It has orders to kill anyone with only one foot, but on its first outing it was distracted by an army veteran and now returns to the hostel every night hoping to claim another victim. Its handlers have tried unsuccessfully to herd it into Dexiokraton to fulfil its mission, with mixed success. During the day, the inactivated golem's body is stored in a disused cistern.

LINKS

- Kyrion (PT-5)
- Monastery of Saint Theodosia (PT-8)
- Phanarion (PT-9)
- Leomakellon (PL-8)
- Heptaskalon in Platea (PL-5)
- Lykos Valley (XR-4)

PT-5 KYRION

POPULATION

900 (sparse)

AFFILIATIONS

Academic (primary and secondary education), Professional (nurses, gravediggers, teachers), Societal (mesoi)

Named after the high concentration of churches (kyria) in the neighbourhood, Kyrion is a large, sparsely-populated neighbourhood on Fifth and Sixth Hills. Most of the population lives in one of the many monasteries or the communities that serve them, and are therefore clustered in the north and east of the neighbourhood rather than on the barren flanks overlooking the Lykos Valley in the west. The parish church for the laity is the Church of the Theotokos Kecharitomene ("full of grace"), also known as the Theotokos in the Rock. In its crypt this church has a fresco of the Virgin Mary surrounded by angels; it is said to move on its own accord and even speak to the devout.

The largest concentration of sanctified soil is within the compound that encloses the Monastery of Saint John in the Rock, the Monastery of the Holy Saviour in Chora, the Church of the Theotokos in the Rock, the Monastery of Manuel, and the Church of Saint George. This complex also contains auxiliary chapels, cemeteries, hospitals, and schools, and the whole compound is considered to be a place of particular sanctity.

LINKS

- Monastery of the Holy Saviour in Chora (PT-6)
- Monastery of Saint John at Petra (PT-7)
- Dexiokration (PT-4)
- Phanarion (PT-9)
- Xenodocheion of Maurianos (PT-10)
- Lykos Valley (XR-4)

PT-6 MONASTERY OF THE HOLY SAVIOUR IN CHORA

Congregation Size: 75; Piety: 35%; Magical Strength: 50%

AFFILIATIONS

Religious/Christian

When built, this monastery, one of the oldest in the city, was outside the city walls, so its name *tou Chora* or "in the country" made more sense. Emperor Theodosios incorporated the fabric of the monastery into his great land walls and it became heavily fortified. The central building, Chora Church (as it is often known), consists of three main areas: the body of the church has three domes; the entrance hall has two domes; and the side chapel has one dome. After the Restoration the monastery was endowed with many mosaics, depicting scenes from the Old Testament and the New Testament, as well as the legend of the Theotokos and her family. These are some of the finest mosaics in Constantinople.

LINKS

- Kyrion (PT-5)

PT-7 MONASTERY OF SAINT JOHN AT PETRA

Congregation Size: 210; Piety: 12%; Magical Strength: 75%

AFFILIATIONS

Religious/Christian, Academic (medicine and surgery), Professional (physician)

This is one of the largest monasteries of Constantinople, with room for 300 monks, although it is currently at just over two-thirds capacity. The entrance to the compound is through an elegant cupola rising above four arches, the outside of which is decorated with a superb mosaic of Saint John the Baptist. The inside of the cupola has more intricate designs. Passing through the cupola leads to a large court surrounded by porticoes backed with buildings. The court has many trees, mostly cypresses. Across from the entrance is a white marble fountain covered with a second cupola, this one supported on eight marble columns. The Church of Saint John has a cross-in-square design, with columns of green jasper supporting the domed roof. The nave ceiling bears a mosaic depicting God the Father, and the walls and floor have further mosaics of saints and the Holy Family. The monastery is home to numerous relics, many of them the instruments of the Passion of Christ. These include:

- A sop of bread from the Last Supper, which Judas was unable to swallow.
- The rod with which Christ was struck when He stood before Pilate
- The Holy Vestment, for which the servants of Pilate cast lots
- Hairs from the beard of Christ, plucked out when he was crucified
- The head of the lance of Longinus which pierced Christ's side
- A morsel of the sponge used when the gall and vinegar was given Him on the cross
- Some of the blood of Christ which was shed when wounded by Longinus
- A piece of the stone slab upon which his body was laid

These relics are kept locked in a red-painted chest and sealed with white wax; the emperor has the only key. Another key relic, not kept with those of the Passion but left on display, is the burnt left arm of Saint John the Baptist (its partner is at the Church of Saint Mary Peribleptos, ST-6). It has a gem-encrusted band around the wrist, and is kept in a reliquary made of silver and crystal.

The Petra Monastery (as it is also known) is also home to the Hospice of the Kral and the Katholikon Mousaion, a renown school of the medical and surgical arts. The hospice was founded by Stefan Uros II Milutin, a fourteenth century Kral (king) of Serbia.

STORY HOOK

The monks of Petra would dearly like to unite the two arms of Saint John, and are not above forgery and larceny to get it. Their plan involves obtaining a corpse and burning it, after wrapping the right arm in salamander wool (i.e. asbestos). They then plan to substitute this arm for the real one. The characters might get involved when they rescue the monks from a pack of ghouls attracted by the smell of cooking flesh. Alternatively, if they are of a shady kind, they may be asked to perform the switch.

LINKS

- Kyrion (PT-5)

PT-8 MONASTERY OF SAINT THEODOSIA

Congregation Size (church): 750; Piety: 5%; Magical Strength: 50%
Congregation Size (monastery): 54; Piety: 55%; Magical Strength: 25%

AFFILIATIONS

Religious/Christian

During the Iconoclasm, Leo III the Isaurian ordered the removal of the famous image of Christ over the Chalke (PA- 3). A group of women tried to stop the soldier carrying out this order, and one – a nun called Theodosia – shook the ladder causing him to fall to his death. Theodosia was executed for his murder by having a ram's horn hammered through her neck in the Forum of the Ox. Upon the Triumph of Orthodoxy Theodosia was recognised as a martyr and a saint, and her body was taken to the Church of Saint Euphemia in Dexiokraton and the dedication changed to Saint Theodosia. The monastery came about from a grant by Basil I, whose four daughters became the first nuns.

Saint Theodosia is one of the most venerated saints in Constantinople and has many miracles associated with her name, mostly curing the infirm of their various woes. The monastery is covered with wild-growing roses that blossom in all seasons, which is also accounted to be a miracle.

The central church is a typical cross-in-square Byzantine design, and is the parish church of the Dexiokraton neighbourhood.

STORY HOOK

Ottoman agents have their hands on the ram's horn used to execute Theodosia. It is infested with evil spirits, and they plan to use it to slay the saint – the divine spirit itself – and thus rid the City of one of its supernatural defenders. They are reliant on an outsider to control the spirits of the horn, and he is willing to betray the Ottomans if the Greeks can offer him more money. The characters are asked to negotiate with the turncoat magician on behalf of the church.

LINKS

- Dexiokraton (PT-4)

PT-9 PHANARION

POPULATION

1300

AFFILIATIONS

Professional (fishermen, rat-catchers), Societal (demoi)

This residential neighbourhood at the bottom of the hills is named after the beacon (phanarion in Greek) that stands atop a column overlooking the Golden Horn. The neighbourhood is therefore never really in darkness, since the great beacon acts as an immense streetlight despite its glow being mostly directed towards the water.

The popular belief that residents of Petrion are nocturnal really only applies to Phanarion. Many of Phanarion's residents are fishermen who ply the Golden Horn at night for squid and cuttlefish and are guided home by the Beacon. Other professions that operate at night (such as nightsoilmen and rat-catchers) gravitate towards Phanarion, and the district's businesses are often open throughout the night.

The parish church of Phanarion is the Church of Saint Mary of the Mongols.

LINKS

- The Beacon (PT-1)
- Church of Saint Mary of the Mongols (PT-2)
- Dexiokraton (PT-4)
- Kyrion (PT-5)
- Blachernai (BL-2)

PT-10 XENODOCHEION OF MAURIANOS

AFFILIATIONS

Political (General Fisc), Rural (petitioners)

A xenodocheion is a hotel provided for the use of poor travellers and wayfarers who do not have the means for hiring a room in an inn. They were found throughout the countryside of the Empire, provisioned with dried food and a few other essentials and periodically restocked by the Office of the General Fisc. The Xenodocheion of Maurianos was founded by Emperor Romanos I Lekapenos (r. 920–944) specifically to house those poor who lived in the provinces and who had to visit the capitol for their affairs. It is integrated into the old Prodromos Gate in the Walls of Constantine, and unlike the provincial xenodocheia, this one has a warden who is responsible for attending to the needs of the guests, who are expected to stay no more than three days. A stipend is provided by the state for the purchase of provisions, but the wardenship of the xenodocheion is prone to attracting those who pocket the cash and provide a few scant secondhand crusts of bread.

STORY HOOK

The xenodocheion is taken over by a slaver who abducts his guests and sells them as debt slaves with forged documents produced by a corrupt friend in the judiciary. When a friend or relative of one of the player characters fails to arrive, they may uncover the man's tyranny, but is it already too late for their friend?

LINKS

- Kyrion (PT-5)
- Office of the General Fisc (ORG-26)

PT-11 XEROKEPION

AFFILIATIONS:

The Xerokepion ("dry garden" in Greek) lies on the eastern slope of the Fifth Hill, overlooking the Golden Horn. It was formerly called the Cistern of Aspar, but the north-east wall of the cistern collapsed many years ago. The cistern was square in plan, with walls over 150 metres a side, 10 metres high, and 5 metres thick, and when in use would have held more than twice the capacity of the Basilika Cistern. It is now mostly filled with soil and someone — no-one knows who — has planted it with flowers and vegetables and carefully tends it. A small sign encourages people to help themselves to the food or flowers if they need them.

When in use would have held more than twice the capacity of the Basilika Cistern. It is now mostly filled with soil and someone – no-one knows who – has planted it with flowers and vegetables and carefully tends it. A small sign encourages people to help themselves to the food or flowers if they need them.

STORY HOOK

The hunt for a missing girl turns up a new statue in the Xerokepion that looks remarkably like her. Investigation will reveal the girl was raiding the garden's bounty to sell to feed her opium habit. Unfortunately, she encountered the garden's secret caretaker: Stheino (IMM-2). The gorgon enjoys the relaxation of gardening by moonlight, but was incensed by the girl's plundering of the garden's bounty for profit. If the characters want to confront the killer, they will need to track her down to her lair in the Undercity.

LINKS

- Church of Saint Mary of the Mongols (PT-2)
- Dexiokraton (PT-4)
- Hagia Sophia (PA-8)
- Nekropoleia (UC-8)

PLATEA (DISTRICT)

Platea is found in the region between the third and fourth hills, from the Gate of the Droungaries as far as the course of the Constantinian Wall. Its name ("Flat") is a reference to most of the district being at sea level. Platea is primarily a residential area, and several neighbourhoods are densely populated. The people of Platea are mostly Greek, unlike the more cosmopolitan Vlanga (see page 178) to the south. Visitors to The City might be surprised to see Turks in the streets, but there is a small community of them near the Mitaton and they are the kephale's biggest headache. The Turks are peaceful enough, and their Prince Orhan is a reasonable person. However, there is tension between the Christian Greeks and the Muslim Turks, particularly seeing as Platea has a large proportion of refugees from parts of the Byzantine Empire that are now controlled by the Ottomans. The kephale and Orhan both have to work hard to keep a lid on the natural friction.

Platea has no underground water supply. The Valens Aqueduct runs through the district, but its purpose is to carry water over Platea and to the eastern parts of the city. No springs emerge on this side of the city, and there is no pipework under the streets. Inhabitants must rely instead on rainwater – which is gathered in vats on roofs – or on the numerous water-sellers.

The Droungares Gate is a major hub of the city: seven streets radiate from this point, and the Vardariotai maintain an office within the gate's structure as a back-up to their main headquarters at Vigla.

LOCAL KNOWLEDGE

STREETWISE

- (Success): Over half the populace of Constantinople live in Platea
- (Success): It is the only district that does not have a public water supply
- (Success): Leomakellon is the Turkish Quarter, home to merchants, envoys, mercenaries, and families loyal to a hostage prince. There are undoubtedly spies as well.

LORE (BYZANTINE)

- (Success): The catacombs beneath Platea have been used since the days of New Rome to bury the bodies of those killed in earthquakes, plagues, fires, riots, and the Latin invasion.
- (Success): During the Year of Seven Deaths, a purge was conducted in Platea to rid the tunnels beneath the district of strigoi (ghouls)

LOCAL RUMOURS

- "The judges have finally found someone who'll stand up to Megeiras in court. He's been robbing the people of Konstanton for months and boasting about how he can never be caught. Let's hope the judge sees sense and orders an execution! Assuming the Vardariotai can hold onto him long enough for him to reach trial – they have a habit of letting criminals escape..."
- "Did you hear about those nuns they found dead in a Konstanton gutter? There was no sign of what killed them, but both had scratch marks on their ankles."
- "I hear that there's a hidden crane in Staurion that can lift things clear over the Golden Horn Walls. The smugglers who run it can assemble it in just one hour, and break it down in half that time. They use it to get things in or out of the city that they don't want customs to see."
- "Red Maria was a prostitute who killed her clients and was eventually killed by one of them. She still haunts the streets, looking for victims."

DESCRIPTIVE ELEMENTS

Crowded buildings; wide streets with wagons; the raucous shout of the water-seller, who balances two immense leather sacks of water on a yoke; well-fed dogs resting in groups in the entrances to buildings; fire-scarred monuments and broken statues, mementoes of riots and the Sack of Constantinople; the muezzin calling the Islamic faithful to prayer five times each day.

PL-1 CHURCH OF THE HOLY APOSTLES

Congregation Size: 2000; Piety: 3%; Magical Strength: 75%

AFFILIATIONS

Religious/Christian

The Church of the Holy Apostles stands at the summit of the Fourth Hill. As well as a church, it is the Imperial Polyandreion (cemetery), and is the final resting place of most of the Byzantine Emperors beginning with Constantine I in 337 and ending with Constantine VIII in 1028; lacking space, subsequent emperors were interred at other monasteries and churches across the city.

This is probably the busiest church in Constantinople, situated along the Mese Odos in one of the most heavily populated regions of the city. Second in size only to Hagia Sophia, it was built by Constantine the Great and dedicated to the Twelve Apostles of Jesus. It was the intention to gather relics from all of the Apostles in the church, but only six are represented, plus Saints Luke and

Timothy, several Church Fathers including John Chrysostom, and various other saints. The church's most prized relic is the Column of Flagellation, to which Christ was bound and flogged before the Crucifixion.

The church has been rebuilt and expanded several times in its existence. It began as a rotunda of vast height, overlaid with marble slabs and the domed roof covered with gold inside and brass outside. Four transepts were later added giving the whole church its current cruciform shape, with a dome above each arm of the cross. Like many churches in the City, it was looted and stripped of much of its gold and gems during the Sack of Constantinople. The western arm extends further than the others, forming an atrium at its far end. The sarcophagi of the emperors, made of purple porphyry, adorn the grounds around the church. Other sarcophagi made of white marble denote the resting places of the wives and children of the emperors.

In front of the main door of the church of the Holy Apostles stands a tall column surmounted by a very large bronze statue of the archangel Michael. At the feet of the angel was the kneeling figure of the Emperor Michael VIII Palaiologos holding a model of the city of Constantinople in his hands. This column was commissioned by the emperor it depicts, an offering to his patron and namesake in thanks for the reconquest of the city and for its continued protection.

STORY HOOK

One day the statue of Michael is missing. This is particularly perplexing given the massive size of the statue. Then, reports come in of sightings of the angel flying high above the city, apparently engaging with something too small to see from the ground. Is the angel a creation of the Ktistes (IMM-8)? Is it actually the Archangel himself, or a statue animated with the Awaken miracle? From what is the angel is defending the City?

LINKS

- Leomakellon (PL-8)

PL-2 CHURCH OF SAINT POLYEUKTOS

Congregation Size: 500; Piety: 6%; Magical Strength: 50%

AFFILIATIONS

Religious/Christian

Commissioned in the sixth century by a noblewoman of the Julii family, an ancient lineage of the Western Roman Empire. It was intended as a protest to the ruling dynasty, which was perceived as low born and of common stock. It was perhaps this challenge thrown down by Aemilia Juliana that prompted Justinian I to reconstruct Hagia Sophia as the largest and most expensive church in the city, which hitherto had been this one. The rivalry between Juliana and Justinian was legendary; when he commanded her to contribute a portion of her vast wealth to the state, she had the gold melted down and fashioned into adornments for the interior of the church, thus protecting it from the emperor's greed. This gold has long since been looted, but most of the rest of the church's decoration has been maintained.

The church is laid out according to the plan of the Temple of Solomon as detailed in the Bible. The basilica is square with a central nave and two aisles, with a large atrium and narthex. The interior has two storeys, with colonnades below and galleries above. The walls are covered in white marble panels and the roof is gilded with Juliana's gold. The narthex has a depiction of the baptism of Constantine the Great. The sculptures that adorn the church are inlaid with ivory, amethyst, and coloured glass, and depict in ten relief plaques images of Christ, the Virgin, and the Apostles. Two remarkably large peacocks, painted in blue, green, and gold stand opposite one another in front of the narthex, their tails fanned out.

STORY HOOK

The player characters need to consult some carvings commissioned by Aemilia Juliana around the nave of the church. However, it has been occupied by anti-Unionists who refuse to allow anyone entrance until the Patriarchate abandons the agreements made at the Council of Florence. The occupiers have at least one theist with them, although the congregation he can call upon is small, it is fervent. The populace is denied the spiritual solace of the Church, and infernal spirits are gathering.

LINKS

- Konstanton (PL-7)

PL-3 COLUMN OF MARCIAN

AFFILIATIONS

None

A column carved from red-grey granite and standing on a base of white marble. It was erected in 452 in honour of the Emperor Marcian, and his statue adorns the top of the column, angled so that he faces the Church of the Holy Apostles. On three of the four faces of the base are carved medallions, on the fourth an image of the world as a globe is supported by two winged images of the goddess of victory, Nike.

Marcian hid a great treasure in the plinth of the column. Although the mechanism is now stiff, pushing on the medallions causes them to recess. Each has three depths, and only by pressing them in the right order will they recess all the way, allowing the vault to be opened by twisting the wings of the Nikes. The existence of the treasure has been long-forgotten, and the combination languishes somewhere in the Imperial Library without a clue to what it refers.

LINKS

- Konstanton (PL-7)

PL-4 THE GREAT NYMPHAION

AFFILIATIONS

Deviant (pagan), Political (diplomatic corps of the Drome), Societal (dynatoi), Urban (Tribunos)

A monument dedicated to the nymphs, dating to Classical times. It consists of a rotunda supported on seven arches, one for each of the seven hills. A circular pool in the centre of the rotunda bears an impressive fountain at its centre, from which water cascades from seven carved lion heads. The Nymphaion is at the downhill terminus of the Valens Aqueduct, and from here water is ferried underground into the city's network of pipes and cisterns. Mosaics surround the pool, and it is a popular place for the wealthy to sit and gossip while their children play amongst the statues.

In pagan times the Great Nymphaion was used to celebrate marriages, as well as to provide a sanctuary where violence was forbidden on pain of divine retribution. In the Christian era, the Nymphaion has been a place of diplomacy and reconciliation. Here was the agreement made that ceded Pera to Genoa, and Constantine XI met with his brothers after Demetrios's failed rebellion and negotiated his fate.

STORY HOOK

A diplomatic exchange between the Drome and the Divan ends with three dead and collateral damage to various dynatoi who were visiting the Great Nymphaion. What went wrong? Was it a tragic misunderstanding, vile treachery, or the calculated intervention of a third party who had no interest in a concord between the Byzantines and the Ottomans?

LINKS

- Konstanton (PL-7)
- Valens Aqueduct (PL-14)

PL-5 HEPTASKALON IN PLATEA

POPULATION

1700 (crowded)

AFFILIATIONS

Professional (carpentry, shipbuilding), Societal (demoi)

A crowded neighbourhood overlooking the Golden Horn and the seven wharfs that give it its name, which is not to be confused with the Jewish quarter of the same name in Vlanga. The Walls of Constantine that bounds the neighbourhood to the north are mostly complete, and on the other side of the seawalls, between the Gates of Eis Pegas and Platea, are shipbuilding yards for which this neighbourhood is famous. The parish church is the Church of Saint Lavrentios, who is patron of cooks and comedians.

LINKS

- Leomakellon (PL-8)
- Staurion (PL-13)
- Zeugma (PL-16)
- Dexiokraton (PT-4)

PL-6 THE HOUSE OF APRICOTS

AFFILIATIONS

Criminal (opium dealers), Deviant (opium addicts), Urban (prostitutes)

Signified solely by the pale orange colour of its door, this house in Staurion is one of the busiest brothels in Constantinople. Visitors who make it past the bulky bouncer at the door will be shown to a comfortable sitting room and offered wine and apricots. The madam is Maria (by tradition, this is a pseudonym), who entertains clients, appraises their worth, and hears their preferences before fetching a selection of prostitutes for approval.

The House of Apricots is a legal establishment providing just the standard services, although Maria is not above arranging more exotic entertainment for wealthy clients, but never on premises. Nearly all the sex workers are in the pocket of Star and Crescent, selling opium and other drugs to their clients for a cut of the profits. Maria pretends not to notice, but she knows which girls are on the take, and charges them higher rent. There are 20 rooms on the upper storeys of the house, and a working staff of about 30; mostly women and nearly all slaves. There are no non-human prostitutes at the House of Apricots. Each of the rooms has a false wall concealing a passageway, allowing someone to check in secret on all of the girls through cleverly concealed spy holes. One of the rooms has a Protective Ward holding Neutralise Magic, cast by a sorcerer on retainer, to ensure privacy from scrying spells. This room is occasionally used for clandestine meetings that do not involve sex.

The House is frequented by important clients who want anonymity that they would not get from a more upper-class establishment. Maria wields the power of her client list with subtlety, never overtly blackmailing her patrons but using the information to exert minor influence. The working girls are sometimes less subtle, although those that antagonise clients tend to find their career in the House cut short.

LINKS

- Staurion (PL-13)
- Star and Crescent (ORG-33)

PL-7 KONSTANTON

POPULATION

3250 (crowded)

AFFILIATIONS

Criminal, Deviant (Prasinoi), Professional (labourers, servants), Societal (demoi)

One of the most densely populated neighbourhoods in Constantinople. The region is infamous for its soaring crime, endemic poverty, and for the strength of its phouska (these three things are not necessarily unrelated). Many of the servants who work in richer areas such as Sphorakion or Blachernai live here in Konstanton.

The parish church of Konstanton is the Church of the Theotokos Kyriotissa ("Enthroned"). During the Latin occupation, this church was rededicated to Saint Francis of Assisi, and frescoes depicting the Catholic saint still adorn its walls. The priest is in charge of an impoverished flock, but cannot even get enough state bread – deliveries regularly come up short, and he is faced with making difficult decisions. Meanwhile, three-day old crusts from richer districts are selling for a tournesion apiece.

STORY HOOK

The priest of Konstanton is desperate enough to raid the church coffers to hire mercenaries (i.e. the player characters), to escort the state bread the short distance from Artopoleia to the bakeries in his parish. The first few days go without a hitch, but on the fourth day a heist is attempted, by a bunch of Konstanton residents. What need for the bread do the would-be thieves have that is greater than feeding their own families?

LINKS

- Leomakellon (PL-8)
- Staurion (PL-13)
- Artopoleia (KN-4)
- Olybrion (VL-10)
- Venetian Quarter (VQ-7)
- Lykos Valley (XR-4)

PL-8 LEOMAKELLON

POPULATION

2000

AFFILIATIONS

Cultural (Turkish), Professional (imported goods, mercers and mongers), Societal (demoi), Urban (market)

This neighbourhood is named after its most prominent feature, a covered market or makellon. There used to be the statue of a lion on a rooftop overlooking the market, but this now stands in the centre of the marketplace. Many thin columns supporting barrel vaults hold up the roof of the market, and stalls are set up around each column, allowing customers to pass between. The parish church of Leomakellon is the mighty Church of the Holy Apostles atop the Fifth Hill.

Leomakellon is home to about 500 Turkish households, and a hundred or so more can be found scattered in adjoining neighbourhoods. Each household is led by a warrior pledged in service to Şehzade Orhan Çelebi. Most are clustered around the mitaton, and Leomakellon has a reputation as the city's "Turkish Quarter" despite them making up less than a third of the population in total.

Leomakellon is the home of a Blemmye called Farooj who is the only merchant in Constantinople that has a supply of dragon's blood (vegetable cinnabar) and olibanum (frankincense), two much-desired incenses employed in ritual magic and church services alike. Despite promises of great wealth and threats of terrible violence, he refuses to reveal his sources. He sells his wares through a shop in the Portico of Achilles (PA-1).

STORY HOOK

Farooj's daughter is sick, and he has promised that the person who cures her will gain the secret of his incense business. The characters are hired to fetch the antidote on behalf of their principle, who wishes to remain anonymous. He is one of the merchants who has threatened Farooj in the past, and the characters have to wonder how he just happens to know the correct antidote to the girl's sickness.

LINKS

- Church of the Holy Apostles (PL-1)
- Heptaskalon in Platea (PL-5)
- Konstanton (PL-7)
- Mitaton (PL-9)
- Staurion (PL-13)
- Dexiokraton (PT-4)
- Lykos Valley (XR-4)
- Orhan Çelebi (NPC-23)

PL-9 MITATON

AFFILIATIONS

Cultural (Turkish, Arab), Professional, Religious/Islam, Urban (market)

The Mitaton is the official hostelry for commercial traffic between Constantinople and the Islamic world, established by Isaac II as a gesture towards Saladin at the end of the twelfth century. It began as a simple inn for Arab traders, but over time warehouses to store trade goods were added, along with further residential properties. It has now grown to be a walled complex in the Damascene style consisting of a central covered market surrounded by two storeys of small homes and workshops. Originally, permits to stay and trade in Constantinople were granted for only three months, but this scheme has been abandoned for all except silk merchants (mostly Syrians) at the insistence of the Imperial Guilds.

There was originally a mosque immediately outside the sea walls, but this was burned by Venetians immediately before the Sack of Constantinople. A second mosque – the Dar al-Balat close to the Noumera – was also destroyed during the Latin occupation. Upon the Restoration, Michael VIII Palaiologos almost immediately ordered the building of a new mosque, this time next to the Mitaton. It was outfitted in lush style by Mamluk Sultan Baybars I of Egypt. While the mitaton was originally intended for Arabs, it is now dominated by Turkish traders. Since the days of Bayezid I, the mitaton has had a qadi (judge) who claims authority over its inhabitants, but he is ignored by the kephale of Platea.

STORY HOOK

Demetrios Palaiologos (NPC-7) arrives in the City as an emissary of the Sultan. This provokes widespread anti-Turk feeling; combined with the final defeat of a very popular pankratiast leads to a riot that culminates in a siege of the Mitaton. The player characters are swept up in the affray, and end up trapped inside the Turkish quarter with individuals that in other circumstances they might consider to be their enemies.

LINKS

- Orhan Çelebi (NPC-23)
- Leomakellon (PL-8)

PL-10 Monastery of Christ Pantokrator

Congregation Size: 154; Piety: 43%; Magical Strength: 50%

Affiliations

Religious/Christian

One of the larger monasteries in Constantinople, housing over 150 monks. It was established by Empress Eirene Komnenos around 1120. During the Frankokratia, the monastery was used as the headquarters of the Venetian see in the City.

The church has a central dome, beneath which is a beautiful mosaic floor, with coloured marble tiles worked in a cloisonné technique depicting humans and animals. Unusually for a Byzantine church, the windows are made of coloured glass and depict images of the saints. As well as the central church and accommodation for the monks, the monastery also has a famous hospital and is a significant repository of books for the Imperial Library. A second church dedicated to the Theotokos Eleousa ("The Merciful") is staffed by lay clergy and acts as a parish church. The monastery is the mausoleum for many Komnenoi and Palaiologoi, including the last four emperors (Andronikos IV, John VII, Manuel II, John VIII), and their close kin. One of the more recent sarcophagi is that of Theodoros Palaiologos, elder brother of Emperor Constantine XI, although if the rumours are true, the coffin is empty because Theodoros faked his own death. As it happens, the coffin is empty, but because the body was stolen by an elder ghoul called Dandolo (IMM-5), who has used it to take the shape of Theodoros Palaiologos.

Links

- Pantokrator Hospital (PL-11)
- Basilios Astephanos (UC-2)
- Staurion (PL-13)
- Imperial Library (ORG-20)

PL-11 Pantokrator Hospital

Affiliations

Professional (physicians, surgeons), Religious/Christian (monks), Urban (hospital)

Attached to the Pantokrator Monastery and staffed by its monks, this hospital is the most famous centre for the treatment of disease and injury in Constantinople. The hospital is an imperial foundation by John II Komnenos (r. 1118–1143) and his wife Eirene. The hospital is divided into five departments: general diseases; chirurgy; ophthalmology; gynaecology; and palliative care. Each has several attending physicians (*iatroi*) and a staff of *diakonisses* (deaconesses) trained in the care of patients. Many of the staff received their instruction at the Pandidakterion (VL-11). There is also a space for the burial of patients who pass away without relatives to receive their corpses.

Story Hook

A physician in the ophthalmology department shows remarkable skill in performing cataract operations. All his patients recover their sight, what's more, many of them report feats of sight that they didn't have before, such as seeing long distances clearly, perceiving illness, seeing magic, and the like. The physician is a Disciple of the Unconcealed Word (ORG-10), and has found a means to grant people an unparalleled view of the universe. One woman is driven mad by the presence of the ghosts she can now see, and the player characters are asked to uncover the cause of her visions. How is the physician able to grant these Folk Magic-like abilities?

Links

- Monastery of Christ Pantokrator (PL-10)
- Staurion (PL-13)

PL-12 Ptochotropheion

Affiliations

Political (Orphanotrophos), Religious/Christian, Urban (the destitute)

Literally "a place for the poor", the Ptochotropheion is a charitable institution operated under the Office of the Imperial Orphanage. Byzantine law distinguishes between the passive poor (*ptochoi*) who are unable to find work due to disability and the active poor (penes) who have been made poor by circumstances. The latter are provided for through the provision of state bread (see page 23), and institutions like the Ptochotropheion exist on behalf of the former.

The poor house is built on the outer side of the Golden Horn Walls, not far north from the Droungares Gate, built up against the defensive wall. It has enough room for two dozen beds, although patients are afforded no privacy at full occupancy. There is a separate kitchen and infirmary at one end. The ptochotropheion is staffed by a monk from the Monastery of Saint Stephen in Zeugma, plus one to three volunteers, usually the wives of mesoi displaying Christian charity or doing penance. Once per week, a physician from Pantokrator Hospital pays a visit. The patients are usually those with a terminal illness; many are old, and dementia is not uncommon. There is no attempt to separate those with contagious illness from the others – the germ theory of medicine is about four centuries in the future. Patients are kept clean, warm, and fed; but this is not considered a place one goes to get better. There is no graveyard; the deceased are usually interred in the municipal koimeteron in Nekropoleia (UC-8).

Story Hook

It is not unheard of for the ptochotropheion to suffer from the presence of a haunt, but this current one is most persistent, and the Order of Kappa-Pi-Alpha (ORG-30) needs help. Although none knew it when he was alive, the patient was a patrilinear descendent of Michael VIII Palaiologos, and had an important message for his distant cousin on the throne that he was unable to deliver during his life.

LINKS

- Pantokrator Hospital (PL-11)
- Zeugma (PL-16)
- Imperial Orphanage (ORG-21)

PL-13 STAURION

POPULATION

950

AFFILIATIONS

Criminal (pickpockets), Professional (ironmongers), Societal (demoi), Urban (urchins, beggars)

Staurion ("The Cross") is the neighbourhood into which the body of Saint Stephen was brought after disembarking at Zeugma. His body was brought to Constantinople by Aemilia Juliana, who also commissioned the Church of Saint Polyeuktos. It is marked by a simple stone cross set on a column in an open space near the waterfront. Staurion – and this cross in particular – is a popular meeting place for people rendezvousing in Constantinople, since most passenger boats dock at the Zeugma and this is out of the crush of the dockside itself. When boats dock, Staurion is crowded with street urchins offering their services as guides, porters, or guards; although the visitor should be aware that not all of them can be considered trustworthy.

The parish church of Staurion is the Church of Saint Theodoros the Recruit, one of the military saints, unlike his namesake Saint Theodoros the General he is depicted as an infantry soldier with a clean-shaven face.

STORY HOOK

Floods drive ghouls up to the streets of Platea from Nekropoleia (UC-8). They seem to be on a recruitment drive, more concerned with biting as many victims as possible rather than sating their hunger.

LINKS

- Heptaskalon in Platea (PL-5)
- House of Apricots (PL-6)
- Konstanton (PL-7)
- Leomakellon (PL-8)
- Zeugma (PL-16)

PL-14 VALENS AQUEDUCT

AFFILIATIONS

Urban (Tribunos)

Built in the Classical period, this aqueduct is still responsible for supplying most of the water of the city. It is nearly a thousand metres long, spanning the gap between the Fourth Hill and the Third Hill. Water is brought to the northern terminus by a canal running parallel to the northern branch of the Mese Odos. It is delivered to the basin of the Great Nymphaion, from whence it enters a system of buried pipes, which distribute the water throughout the city. The aqueduct was built from the stones of the city of Chalcedon, whose

walls were pulled down in punishment for their revolt against Byzantine rule. At its highest point, the double-arched bridge section stands 30 metres above Platea's plain. There have been no wide-scale repairs to the aqueduct since the days of Andronikos I Komnenos, but the water still flows.

The komes tou hydaton (the "count of the waters") is a city official working for the Chancellery who is in charge of the City's water supply. Modestos Latax is highly efficient at this job, mostly due to a spell codex teaching the Sorcery spells of Animate Water, Sense Water, and Transmogrify to Water, which has been passed down from komes to komes since time immemorial. These spells can be used to locate water, break through blockages, and even transport one's self through the drainage system.

STORY HOOK

Latax has travelled too far and too deep in his exploration of the water passages, and has been trapped in a Protective Ward by a more powerful sorcerer. His captor wants to know the secrets of the waterways – what better way of gaining access to any house in Constantinople? The player characters get involved when Latax is reported missing and the Praitor hires people to find him.

LINKS

- The Great Nymphaion (PL-4)
- Konstanton (PL-7)
- The Cistern of Aetius (PT-3)

PL-15 VIGLA

AFFILIATIONS

Military (Vardariotai)

A station of the Vardariotai, located on the slopes of the Third Hill. The Vigla is an impressive fortress with four towers, one in each corner. There is usually a guard stationed in each tower on the lookout for fire. It is intended as a rallying point if the city erupts into riot and is kept stocked with food for a week-long siege. The order is that stale food be donated to the poor, but the Vardariots regularly sell it instead.

STORY HOOK

When a riot breaks out, the standing order for the Vardariotai is to assemble at the Vigla to receive instructions. The instigators of the riot know this all too well – the riot is just a means to trap as many Vardariotai inside the fortress as possible, leaving the streets undefended. The player characters might be called upon to break the siege before the guard starves, or else might profit from the situation themselves.

LINKS

- Zeugma (PL-16)
- Vardariotai (ORG-35)

PL-16 ZEUGMA

POPULATION

2000 (crowded)

AFFILIATIONS

Criminal (Star and Crescent), Professional (construction, timber), Societal (demoi)

The neighbourhood known as Zeugma runs outside the Golden Horn Walls down as far as the wharfs of the Venetian Quarter as well as on the inside of the city walls. The parish church is the Church of Saint Akakios. This is the neighbourhood of the timber-merchants, and at the easternmost extent, the fish market of the Neorion. The Street on this side of the wall is called Droungares Street (from the Gate where it starts) and goes as far as the Gate of the Perama, and is lined with two rows of houses, the southern side back directly onto the walls.

The wharf at Zeugma is where most passenger transports dock, and where most people embark for Pera; where the Golden Horn narrows to just 400 metres in width.

Zeugma is almost entirely controlled by the Star and Crescent criminal fraternity. They either own the warehouses outright or the owners pay them protection. The timber industry is a front to give the fraternity an air of respectability. All the houses on Droungares Street are rented from Star and Crescent. Even the customs house is rented to the government through an intermediary, and a fair few of the inspectors are in the employ of the smugglers.

STORY HOOK

The player characters witness a boatload of Turks land in Constantinople – perhaps they are even on the same craft with them. They are keeping their faces covered, and only one speaks Greek. They head straight for the Mitaton, where they get into an argument by Orhan Çelebi. The Turks then disperse into the population. What were they planning, and why did Orhan disagree so vehemently?

LINKS

- Star and Crescent (ORG-33)
- Heptaskalon in Platea (PL-5)
- Konstanton (PL-7)
- Staurion (PL-13)
- Vigla (PL-15)
- Galatas Harbour (PR-3)
- Venetian Quarter (VQ-7)

STOUDION (DISTRICT)

Stoudion lies to the southwest of the main metropolis of Constantinople, but remains connected to it via the Mese Odos. It is best known for The Stoudion, a famous monastery from which the district takes its name, but the district has become a military enclave as most of the army is now resident here. Parts of Stoudion District have become overcrowded with soldiers; the former inhabitants evicted – sometimes forcibly – and have mostly moved to nearby Xerolophos or Vlanga.

The Mese Odos forms the north boundary of Stoudion, and the Sea Walls bound it to the south. At the protests of the monks the whole district has been surrounded by a substantial stockade, and every gate and entrance into the district has armed sentries. Needless to say, neither the Vardariotai nor the city watch patrol Stoudion, but the kephale has a regiment of military police under his command to help keep order.

The kephale of Stoudion is also archon tou allagion, a mid-ranking position in the army and deputy to the prefect of the army (see ORG-13). Unlike other districts, the kephale was appointed by the Grand Domestic rather than elected from amongst the residents.

LOCAL KNOWLEDGE

STREETWISE

- (Success): Stoudion is named after the great monastery of Saint John and famous for its erudition. The Imperial Library is based at the Stoudion.
- (Success): The district is currently used to billet the city's land army.

LOCAL RUMOURS

- "The Emperor is coming to inspect his troops. They say we are finally going to take the war to the Turk!"
- "This is the God-Guarded City. The walls have never failed us – over 20 sieges and not one has succeeded. Constantinople will last forever!"
- "Best to be within the stockade after dark. People have gone missing – swallowed up by the earth or just vanished save for a pair of bloody footprints."

DESCRIPTIVE ELEMENTS

Soldiers conducting drills reciting chants to keep pace; smell of horses from the cavalry quarters; cool sea breeze; the fine white sand which gets into everything; large white dogs peculiar to Stoudion; architectural features infrequent but huge scale — at least half the height again than in other districts.

ST-1 DALMATON

POPULATION

1400

AFFILIATIONS

Military (navy), Professional (tavern-keepers, victuallers), Societal (demoi)

When not at sea, the sailors of the Byzantine navy occupy this coastal village. Dalmaton's population is about two-thirds sailors and marines; the rest run the businesses that the sailors need: tabernai, phouskaria, brothels, flop-houses, and so on. The neighbourhood is ruled by a droungarokomes, an otherwise extinct naval office that ranks higher than a ship's captain but lower than a fleet commander.

Compared to the army in cramped quarters in Stoudion, the sailors have quite luxurious accommodation since there are only ten ships in active service. Only two to three ships are at sail at any time, patrolling the Marmaran coast and the Bosphoros. Half of the sailors as Gasmouli marines, the rest are Greek oarsmen. The navy buys the contracts of debt slaves to fill the ranks of oarsmen. The sailors of any given ship are divided into companies of ten (or fewer) men, each one comprised half each of Gasmouli and Prosalentai. Each company is collectively responsible for responding to any muster: if any man is missing then they share the punishment. This keeps runaway slaves to a minimum.

The parish church is dedicated to the Theotokos Panachrantes.

STORY HOOK

A company is one man down after one of its debt slaves got himself killed in an argument with one of his bench-mates. The order to muster for exercises has been issued for the morning and they need to turn up with a full complement else they will all be punished. How they pressgang a player character (or a beloved NPC) is up to the Games Master: they might abduct someone with stealth, violence, or strong drink; but the first thing he is aware of on the following day is the gentle bobbing of the waves aboard ship. The remaining characters are probably keen to rescue their comrade, but the company that took him has a fearful reputation and are actually heading out on a mission to the Peloponnese.

LINKS:

- 'Exakionion (ST-2)
- Psamathia (ST-7)
- Triton (XR-10)
- Naval Office (ORG-24)

ST-2 'EXAKIONION

POPULATION

100 (sparse)

AFFILIATIONS

Political (Army Office), Professional (vintners), Societal (dynatoi)

Located on the slopes of the Seventh Hill, bounded to the east by the remnants of the Constantinian Wall. This small, scantily-populated neighbourhood is dominated by wild grapevines, which have escaped from monastic gardens and run rampant over the region as far south as the Place of Judgement (see the Monastery of Saint Andrew in Krisei, XR-6). The parish church is dedicated to Saint John the Compassionate.

The name of this region comes from the previous Golden Gate that pierced the Constaninian Walls, which was also known as the 'Exakionion, which means "with six pillars". The gate still stands, unlike most of the walls, and consists of two immense towers flanking the entrance itself, which has two storeys. The walls of the upper storey on both sides are decorated with six columns and niches. The gate is adorned with the bronze statues of four emperors. The building is used as a funeral chapel for the dynatoi, and the interior is decorated with religious frescoes.

This neighbourhood has long been the location of the district's richer residences, benefitting from the milder weather of the Marmaran coast. Since the occupation of Stoudion by Constantinople's army, 'Exakionion has become the home of dignitaries from the Army Office. The Grand Domestic (supreme commander of the army) is resident in Blachernai (BL-2), as befits one of the most important men in the empire, but his general staff reside here under the command of the protostrator, who is the second-in-command and senior general of the army. Also resident here are the other senior officers: the commander of the regular army, the prefects of the militia, the mercenaries, the watch, and the four guard units, and the Domestic of the Walls (responsible for the city's defences).

LINKS

- Paradeison (XR-9)
- Army Office (ORG-13)

ST-3 GASTRIA MONASTERY

Congregation Size: 75; Piety: 56%; Magical Strength: 50%

AFFILIATIONS

Religious/Christian (Orthodox)

The first monastery ever founded in Constantinople. When the Empress Helena, Constantine the Great's mother, returned from Jerusalem with the True Cross, she entered the city though the Gate of Psamathea and left at this site some vases (*gastria* in Greek) containing incense she discovered on Calvary. This became the basis for a small monastery populated by female monks and lead by a *ktetorissa* ("foundress"). As well as the holy vases – containing the oil and incense used to anoint the body of Christ when he was taken down from the Cross – the monastery is also home to relics of Saint Euphemia and Saint Eudokia. The monks have recreated the incense recipe from Helena's vases, and manufacture and sell it.

It has the shape of an irregular octagon with a cross-shaped interior oriented towards the east. The masonry is alternate bands of red brick and white ashlar.

STORY HOOK

A jar of incense prepared at Gastria is accidentally broken, and the smell attracts a small crowd of astomatoi, more than was ever believed to live in Constantinople. The non-humans simply stand downwind of the monastery inhaling the scent, apparently enraptured by the smell. When the smell dies down, most astomatoi depart, but some remain and aggressively demand more. The player characters, perhaps attracted by the spectacle (particularly if they have encountered astomatoi before), may have to intervene to protect the nuns.

LINKS

- Dalmaton (ST-1)

ST-4 MARTYRION OF SAINTS KARPOS AND PAPYLOS

Congregation Size: 6; Piety: 67%; Magical Strength: 25%

AFFILIATIONS

Deviant (exorcists), Religious/Christian (monastic)

Endowed by the Empress Helena, mother of Constantine the Great, this commemoration of the martyrdom of the saints was attended by a small monastery of nuns, who continue to care for the shrine today. The martyrion proper lies under the church. It consists of an underground rotunda, with an inner circle of columns supporting a domed roof. A horseshoe-shaped chamber surrounds the rotunda, and connects its entrance at its east end to the spiral staircase at the west end that leads up to the church.

The dedicants Karpos and Papylos were martyred along with Papylos's sister Agathonike for refusing to eat meat that had been offered to idols, realising that it would open their spirits to possession by pagan spirits. They were hanged over a pit by the neck, and clawed apart alive by beasts. Agathonike committed suicide rather than follow the same fate. The three martyrs (Agathonike, as a suicide, was not canonised) have become patrons of exorcists and those under spiritual possession, and the Orthodox church's cadre of animists specialising in hostile spirits is dedicated to them.

The existence of the martyrion was kept secret during the Frankish invasion, and since the restoration has been largely forgotten about by the Orthodox Church. This suits the purposes of the Order of Kappa-Pi-Alpha who use it as their base of operations. The six monks of that order are the only permanent residents, but the buried rotunda acts as a hospital, hostel, library, and laboratory for its lay members.

LINKS

- Psamathia (ST-7)
- Order of Kappa-Pi-Alpha (ORG-30)

ST-5 MONASTERY OF SAINT ANDREAS HO SALOS

Congregation Size: 42; Piety: 46%; Magical Strength: 50%

AFFILIATIONS

Deviant (the mad), Religious/Christian (monastic), Urban (sanatorium)

Saint Andreas of Constantinople, more commonly called Andreas the Fool (*ho salos*), was the slave of an Imperial bodyguard. He later became the first Fool-for-Christ in Constantinople (see page 33), a devotion still practised at his monastery. During a siege of the city by the Rus' in the tenth century Andreas had a vision of the Theotokos in her church in Blachernai (BL-5), where her protection was cast over the city by angels accompanying the Holy Virgin. After this vision, the city was saved, and this inspired the feast of the Protection of the Theotokos.

Less than a dozen of the monastery's residents are Holy Fools but any monk from whatever monastery who hears this calling may call Saint Andreas home. The monastery is also a sanatorium for the insane, helping those who have had a temporary lapse in their sanity and taking care of the incurably mad. Violent inmates are imprisoned, using restraints if they are liable to harm themselves.

LINKS

- 'Exakionion (ST-2)

ST-6 MONASTERY OF SAINT MARY PERIBLEPTOS

Congregation Size: 310; Piety: 32%; Magical Strength: 50%

AFFILIATIONS

Religious/Christian (Orthodox)

A large monastery sitting on a plateau overlooking the sea, home to some 300 monks. It has its own water source, a rare thing in Constantinople. It is the tradition of the imperial court to come to Peribleptos for the Feast of the Presentation in February, a custom resurrected by the Palaiologians. The church is a typically cross-in-square design with a central hemispherical dome supported by eight multi-coloured columns of jasper. The outer walls are decorated with paintings of the castles and towns that have been endowed to the monastery, although most of these now belong in Ottoman hands. The monastery's refectory has a fresco depicting the Last Supper, and the complex contains gardens and vineyards. The most precious relics of the monastery is the right arm of Saint John the Baptist (unburnt despite his martyrdom by fire, because it was this hand that touched Christ during baptism) and the body of Saint Gregory.

Saint Mary "the Conspicuous" (*Peribleptos*) was founded by Romanos III Argyros in the eleventh century, and he was heavily criticised for the cost. It was converted to a Venetian Benedictine monastery during the Frankokratia, but upon the restoration Michael VIII Palaiologos gifted the monastery with money for an expansion, and the refectory has a mosaic of the emperor and his family. The main church was struck by lightning in 1402, which started a fire that ravaged many of the wooden buildings. During the epidemic and Ottoman siege of 1422, Manuel II Palaiologos took refuge at the monastery.

LINKS

- ɸ Dalmaton (ST-1)

ST-7 PSAMATHIA

POPULATION

5850 (crowded)

AFFILIATIONS

Military (regular infantry), Professional (victualling, weapon-making, armourers), Societal (demoi)

A neighbourhood of Stoudion located near the Marmaran coast and named after the sandy (Greek *psamathion*) nature of the soil. The first monastery of Constantinople, Gastria, was founded here in 383, although at that time it lay outside the walls of the city.

The regular infantry of the Byzantine Army currently occupy Psamathia. While the Psamathia Road is lined with houses, they only extend into a proper neighbourhood on the south side of the road. These houses differ from the more typical inner city tenements in that most are only two storeys high, and some city blocks are occupied by a single grander residence. These latter houses are reserved for the officers of the taxeis and allagia, whereas the rank-and-file men have to share quarters with their company leaders. Each of the four apartments within a tenement building is assigned to a company of 10 men, who have to live in the space normally given to a single family. Buildings tend to be given to four companies of the same phalanx to reduce inter-regiment rivalry, although there are inevitably some mixed billets.

As well as the few hundred tenement buildings occupied by the soldiers, the Army Office has also commandeered warehouses for the storage of food and materiel, and workshops for the repair of equipment. Because of the risk of fire, gunpowder is forbidden within Psamathia: the army's supply is stored in Mangana at the opposite end of the city.

The parish church of Psamathia is the Church of Saint Menas, although many of the soldiers of Psamathia attend other churches, notably Saint Demetrios in Vlanga and Saint Theodoros in Platea.

LINKS

- ɸ Dalmaton (ST-1)
- ɸ Martyrion of Saints Karpos and Papylos (ST-4)
- ɸ The Stoudion (ST-9)
- ɸ The Monastery of Saint Diomedes of Jerusalem (XR-7)
- ɸ Triton (XR-10)
- ɸ The Army Office (ORG-13)

ST-8 THE SIGMA

AFFILIATIONS

None

A semi-circular portico marks a significant crossroads. The Xylokerkos Road (west), Mokios Road (north), and Mese Odos (east and south) all meet at this monument, which gets its name from a passing resemblance to the Greek letter sigma. There is a hekataion (altar to Hekate) here, in her role as the Goddess of the Crossroads, and some travellers still sometimes surreptitiously spill a bit of wine as they pass in libation to the goddess. A common method of cursing a rival is to inscribe an invective on a lead sheet, fold it, hammer nails through it, and bury it at a crossroads. Anyone placing a curse under the hekataion (where there are many thousands of others) can place the Evil Eye (see page 18) on their target deliberately.

No matter what the weather, there is always a dog at the Sigma. It is not always the same animal, but it takes great interest in anyone entering the Sigma from the west or south roads.

LINKS

- ɸ Dalmaton (ST-1)
- ɸ 'Exakionion (ST-2)
- ɸ Psamathia (ST-7)
- ɸ Triton (XR-10)

ST-9 THE STOUDION

Congregation Size: 500; Piety: 35%; Magical Strength: 75%

AFFILIATIONS

Religious/Christian (monastic), Religious/Christian (Orthodox)

More fully the Monastery of Saint John the Forerunner at Stoudion, this is the most important monastery in Constantinople. The Stoudion was founded in 462 by a Roman patrician, Consul Flavius Studius, who had settled in Constantinople. Its monks are commonly surnamed "Stoudites", which is seen as a mark of distinction of both academic rigour and spiritual development. The monastic school is renowned for its calligraphy and for its religious poetry. The monastery currently houses 500 monks, although this is but two-thirds of its full capacity. The Stoudites have always been staunch opponents of Iconoclasm, for which they were temporarily expelled from the city in the middle of the eighth century. Like many parts of the city, the Stoudion was destroyed by Crusaders in 1204 and most of its monks put to death; it was restored in 1290 upon the orders of the emperor.

The Stoudion has been home to the Imperial Library since its restoration under the Palaiologians. Given previous losses of the contents of the library to fire and theft, the Imperial Library is no longer stored in a single location. While the Librarian or Anagnostes (the minister for the Imperial Library) lives as a guest of the monastery and employs the monks here as copyists and illustrators, the texts stored at The Stoudion are not the substance of the library. Instead, they are ledgers which list in detail the contents of any given book of the library, and crucially in which other building it can be found. These ledgers are written in a secret code known only to the Librarian and his most trusted advisors, plus a single member of the Imperial Archives. The actual books – of which there may be nearly 70,000 – are stored in several hundred locations across Constantinople. Most are stored in monasteries, others at churches, private residences, and even in secret vaults.

The most prized possession of the Stoudion is The Suda, an encyclopaedia begun in the eleventh century and added to ever since. The librarians who tend The Suda are the most trusted by the Anagnostes; its purpose is to be the repository of all knowledge known to man and its guardians are masters at cross-referencing and annotation. Its opening sections are a dictionary and grammar of the Greek language, and there are no less than fifteen indices to The Suda covering a variety of themes. The Suda is constantly growing; as new lands are discovered, new knowledge comes to light, and the backlog of its librarians grows ever greater.

STORY HOOK

The characters come into possession of an old text, which, if they have it appraised or take it to a scholar for translation, attracts the attention of the Imperial Library. The book's title is "The Secret Book of John", and it purports to chronicle the secret knowledge of Jesus as reported by John the Apostle. It claims a very different origin story than that in the Bible, where one of God's sons creates the world and rules it as the Devil; and is a central text of the Bogomil heresy. While a scribe tries to persuade them to donate the book, another makes a clumsy attempt to steal it. They work for different factions in the Library, one seeking to preserve all books, and the other wanting to destroy heretical notions.

LINKS

- The Imperial Library (ORG-20)
- Psamathia (ST-7)

VENETIAN QUARTER (DISTRICT)

The Venetian Quarter is officially called *Perama* (meaning "The Crossing"), but no one ever calls it this. The Venetian Quarter was established at the end of the eleventh century under Alexios I Komnenos. During the Frankokratia, Venice was awarded a quarter and half a quarter of The City and The Empire. The Venetian "Quarter" – now expanded into surrounding districts – was ruled by a podestà, who was foreign minister for the whole Latin Empire as well as commander of the merchant and military navy. Upon the Restoration of the Empire, the Venetians who had not already fled were evicted and the area given to the Genoese who had assisted Michael VIII Palaiologos in his conquest of the city. The Genoese occupied the district for just 40 years before migrating across the Golden Horn to found Pera. Venetian merchants slowly returned to Perama, and it became a Venetian Quarter once again; although the merchants do not enjoy all the same privileges that they did in the past. This quarter has the only Catholic churches in the City.

Today, the Venetian Quarter occupies much the same territory as it did under the Komnenoi: the area south of the Droungares Gate, the Gate of the Forerunner, and the Perama Gate. Landward it is defined by the slopes of the Third Hill to the north and west, and the line of the old Severan Walls to the south and east. Unusually, the Venetian Quarter is surrounded by its own wall, which incorporates some elements of the Severan Wall. The Makros Embolos, one of the major commercial streets, arises at the Venetian Embulo before passing south into Artopoleia.

Instead of a kephale, the Venetians elect a bailo, who is governor of the community as well as envoy of Venice to Constantinople. Girolomo Minotto is the current holder of this position. The bailo is assisted by a council (*conségio*) of six advisors, five magistrates, and two treasurers. His court meets publically three times a week at the portico of the Church of Santa Maria de Embulo to settle disputes between merchants. The council meets once per week in the gallery at the palace of the bailo. The bailo must manage the property of deceased Venetians, maintain the revenues of the community, monitor the cargo of the galleys, and implement the directives of the Signoria of Venice. The Venetian Quarter has no phylakes or Vardariotai; instead the Çonéto di Palàso are responsible for the safety of Venetian residents and visitors to Constantinople as well as serving as palace guard and private army of the bailo.

Prominent Venetian families in the Quarter include Falier, Geno, Beccaro, Salmaza, Ziani, and Mastropetro. There are many Gasmouli (offspring of Frank-Greek marriages) in the Venetian Quarter, since they struggle to find acceptance elsewhere.

LOCAL KNOWLEDGE

STREETWISE

- (Success): The only remaining foreign quarter in Constantinople; Venetians are still disliked by the Greek population.
- (Success): The Venetian Quarter is run as an exclave of the Serene Republic and routinely ignores Byzantine law and the Praitor's authority

LORE (BYZANTINE)

- (Success): Since the bailo is the ambassador of Venice to Constantinople, interfering with his rule of the Venetian Quarter could cause a diplomatic incident

LOCAL RUMOURS

- "We Venetians have to pay a fee to trade in Constantinople. The cheek of it! Let the Ottomans come, I say! The sultan will pay us to come back!"
- "Never trust a Greek, even when he comes bearing gifts. That's how the old saying goes, isn't it? And it's not wrong!"
- "You can buy anything in the Embulo – anything! Do you want someone dead? Do you want to be 20 years younger? All you need to know is which door to knock on."

DESCRIPTIVE ELEMENTS

Distinctly different (Venetian) architecture; narrow houses painted gaudy colours; heavily-accented voices speaking Veneto or other Italic dialects; an absence of dogs; no porticoes or arches but plenty of fountains, often moved here from other parts of the city during the Frankokratia; Byzantine churches repurposed as Catholic churches.

VQ-1 CHURCH OF SAINT AKYNDINOS

Congregation Size: 500; Piety: 4%; Magical Strength: 25%

AFFILIATIONS

Professional (bakers, notaries), Religious/Christian (Catholic), Urban (inspectors)

The Church of Saint Akyndinos is the oldest in the quarter, dating back to before this was Venetian territory. A large bakery is attached to the church, which produces a range of different qualities – inhabitants of the Venetian Quarter are not eligible for state bread, so the Church of Saint Akyndinos performs a similar function.

The church holds the official weights and measures used by the Venetian merchants, which are different from the units of measurements used elsewhere in the city. All priests of Saint Akyndinos are also legal notaries, and they can judge on disputes regarding weights and measurements as well as witness legal documents.

LINKS

- Perama (VQ-7)

VQ-2 CHURCH OF SANTA MARIA DE EMBULO

Congregation Size: 750; Piety: 4%; Magical Strength: 50%

AFFILIATIONS

Religious/Christian (Catholic), Urban (court)

The Church of Saint Mary-at-the-Market is a rededicated church of the Theotokos, and is a typical Byzantine cross-in-square design, but with an added bell tower. In front of the church is a portico, continuous with that around the Embulo, which is the site of a public court held three times a week. The bailo sits in judgement, supposedly to mediate in trade disputes, although he also hears criminal cases in defiance of the Praitor's authority. These cases are decided according to Venetian rather than Byzantine laws, although the bailo is careful to pass over cases to the Chancellery where a Greek is the accused.

Venetian sumptuary laws are designed to equalise a community by fining persons who pursue an individual style in terms of hair length, beards, or extravagant clothing. The laws insist that persons must dress according to their status, with prescribed values for clothing for each level of society. It is not unusual for women to wear the maximum permitted for their status, leading to wildly-impractical clothing with yards of silk and tottering platform shoes.

STORY HOOK

An enemy of the characters lures them into the Venetian Quarter, where a corrupt officer of the Çonéto awaits to arrest them based on violation of the sumptuary laws. He is deaf to any pleas that they are not Venetian – the bureaucracy involved in jurisdictional disputes could take months to untangle, during which time the characters could be on a slave ship bound for Venice due to non-payment of fines (since they will not be permitted to leave the Quarter to obtain funds).

LINKS

- Embulo (VQ-4)
- Perama (VQ-7)

VQ-3 COMMISSARY OF SAINT JOHN

AFFILIATIONS

Religious/Christian (Knights Hospitaller)

The Venetian Quarter houses a small religious house dedicated to the Knights of Saint John. The Master of the house – equivalent in rank to an abbot – is also the official ambassador for the Grand Master of Rhodes. There is usually one or two knights in residence, mostly individuals passing through the city. The Master has his own Brother-Chaplain, and three Brother-Sergeants on his staff.

STORY HOOK

One of the Brother-Knights staying at the Commissary is a wanted criminal. The player characters are hired (either by the authorities or the victim) to extract him so he can face justice.

LINKS

- The Hospitallers (ORG-4)

VQ-4 EMBULO

AFFILIATIONS

Criminal (smugglers), Professional (merchants), Urban (market)

The Embulo (or Embolon in Greek) is the heart of the Venetian Quarter. One of the main arterial roads of the City, the Makros Embolos, runs straight through the Embulo on its way from the Gate of the Forerunner. The porticos lining the Makros Embolos divide to run around the perimeter of the Embulo, an open-air marketplace. The church of Santa Maria sits on the western side of the Embulo.

The centre of the square is filled every day except Sunday with stalls selling various imported wares – all trade performed in the Embulo is taxed at only 4% rather than the usual 10% of the kommerkion, and circulation (that is, on-selling of imported goods) is not taxed at all. Many of the houses that line the Embulo are actually narrow passages that lead to larger covered markets behind the building facades, each dedicated to specialist goods: ivory, dried fruit, sugar, gold bullion, gemstones, art works, relics, and so forth. Each of these covered markets has its own door and some are closed to walk-in trade, accessible only by appointment. These covered markets trade under the fiction that they are part of the Embulo, and therefore subject to the same taxation laws.

There are rumours of covered markets that sell even more exotic goods, such as treasure maps, books on magic, caged monsters, memories, and even human souls. You just need to know the right door to open...

LINKS

- Church of Santa Maria de Embulo (VQ-2)
- Perama (VQ-7)

VQ-5 THE GUIDECCA

AFFILIATIONS

Cultural (Italkim), Professional (pawnbrokers, precious metals), Religious/Jewish

The Guidecca is the Venetian Quarter's own Jewish ghetto, comprising about 250 souls located to the west of Droungares Street. All the houses in the Guidecca are owned by the bailo and rented out to the families that live there. By Venetian law, Jews are not permitted to live in Christian neighbourhoods, and are required to wear badges of yellow cloth on all their clothes. The Italkim have always been associated with money; although they are not allowed to run a bank, they can exchange currency, run pawnbrokers' shops, trade in precious metals, and convert gold and silver into pure bullion. For the right cut one could also find someone willing to adulterate pure gold to increase its apparent value.

LINKS

- Perama (VQ-7)

VQ-6 PALÀSO DI BAILO

AFFILIATIONS

Cultural (Venetian), Political (Republic of Venice)

This grand building in the style of a Venetian palace overlooks the Makros Embolos and Embulo from the slopes of the Third Hill. It is surrounded in formal gardens planted with trees and flowers. It serves as the Venetian embassy to Constantinople as well as the personal home of the bailo (who is also the ambassador) and his family. Attached to the palace are the headquarters of the Çonéto di Palàso. A prominent feature of the palàso is a loggia, an open gallery where the bailo meets with his governing council.

The Logothete of the Drome (ORG-25) has the palàso under close surveillance, and always has more than one agent amongst the staff – some of whom are deliberately more obvious than others to allow the bailo's security staff to think they have identified all the spies. The Drome would really like to listen in on the weekly council meetings, but these take place in closed sessions with guards stationed nearby to prevent eavesdroppers.

LINKS

- Embulo (VQ-4)
- Perama (VQ-7)

VQ-7 PERAMA

POPULATION

3050 (crowded)

AFFILIATIONS

Cultural (Venetians, Gasmouli), Professional (trade, tailors), Societal (mesoi)

The only neighbourhood of the Venetian Quarter is Perama, named after the point where the crossing to Pera was made; although the primary crossing point is now further west in Zeugma. This is a crowded quarter, made up of about two thirds Venetians and the remaining third divided equally between the Gasmouli and other Franks, mostly French and Spaniards (the Germanic Franks prefer Pera). A large proportion of the inhabitants make their living in trading, whether they are importing goods, speculating on shipments from far afield, or mediating between the land trade through Anatolia and Syria.

Warehouses are crowded in amongst the cramped accommodations, which are typically houses rather than tenements. The typical Venetian house is long and thin, with a narrow frontage to the street and three or four storeys. Many rent out the ground floor as storage space while living in the higher storeys. The parish church is the Church of San Marco, the favourite Venetian saint. Next to the church is a large spice market, and just outside the Gate of Perama is a fish market that competes with the Megistai Kamarai of Neorion (AK-9).

Perama is policed by the Çonéto di Palàso, who are the bailo's personal guard as well as the quarter's watch and police. They are trained halberdiers and wear Frankish medium armour on guard duty, which is usually stripped down to light armour on patrol. The Çonéto also have a unit of arquebusiers and schiopetterieri.

LINKS

- Eugenion (AK-3)
- Artopoleia (KN-4)
- Keropoleia (KN-10)
- Sporakion (KN-14)
- Konstanton (PL-7)
- Zeugma (PL-16)

VQ-8 SAINT MARK'S WHARF

AFFILIATIONS

Professional (merchants, stevedores)

Saint Mark's Wharf (*Scala Sancta Marci* in Veneto) is the principal wharf and landing stage of the four that serve the Venetian Quarter, located between the Perama Gate and the Gate of the Forerunner. The other three in order east to west are the Wharf of St Marcianus, Droungares Wharf, and the Great Wharf. Ships sailing up the Golden Horn bring goods from Venice's trading partners and vassal states, including silk from the Levant, cotton, precious stones, timber, wheat, and spices in large quantities.

STORY HOOK

As the hold of a merchant ship is opened, a creature leaps forth. It is a manticore, which has been stalking the crew members since the ship left Acre. The monster now rampages through the crowd, heading into the city if it can. Here, it will find an abandoned building and set up a lair.

LINKS

- Perama (VQ-7)

VQ-9 TOWER OF EIRENE

AFFILIATIONS

Military (Çonéto)

The square Tower of Eirene is 25 metres tall and made of alternating bands of red and white bricks. It is surmounted by a copper-plated bronze bell. There are always two members of the Çonéto on guard here at all times, on watch for fires. As a courtesy, if they spot a fire in the rest of the city they send a runner to the Vigla to inform them of this, but only take action against fires within the walls of the Venetian Quarter. A secondary function is to keep watch for riots, armed men, or civil insurrection. The Venetian Quarter has suffered the anger of the Greek people before, and they are ever mindful of the threat. Should the bailo be in danger, an underground tunnel passing through Nekropoleia has been prepared, emerging near the Great Wharf in order to make escape. Prominent Venetian families will also be warned, although they must make their own arrangements for safety and/or escape; many have strongrooms beneath their residents in which they can wait out any city-wide disruption.

LINKS

- Perama (VQ-7)
- Vigla (PL-15)
- Nekropoleia (UC-8)

VLANGA (DISTRICT)

Vlanga is the main industrial district of Constantinople. It sits at the mouth of the Lykos valley and has the highest population density of the whole city and the bulk of these people live south of the Mese Odos. Vlanga houses the largest commercial port (the Eleutherion), used primarily for bulk shipments of livestock and grain rather than passengers or trade goods. Most of the fish landed at Constantinople is brought into Vlanga. Despite being right next to the sea, the high sea walls block the view of it for most of the district.

The thing that strikes people about the district first and foremost is the smell. The "Vlanga Stench" is infamous, a combination of rotting fish, manure, the debouching of the sewer system, and the tannery yards all contribute to a stink that is almost tangible. It lingers in the mouth and nose, and can be smelt on clothes for days afterwards. Those that live here are inured to the smell but it to new visitors it counts as an inhaled poison (Mythras page 74) that causes Nausea with a duration of 1d6 hours. The Potency varies according to the weather: at its worst, on hot still days, it is 80%, and it is mildest in the winter when it drops to 20%. After 2d6 days of living in the stench characters become immune to further exposures where the Potency is less than their Endurance.

Vlanga has the most diverse mix of cultures of any city district. Many provincial Greeks, Albanian Vlachs, and Bulgarians fleeing the Ottoman advance ended up in Vlanga, being unable to find work in other districts. They have been joined by Wallachians, Bosnians, and Serbs fleeing civil war. Vlanga is also home to the largest community of Romaniote Jews. Being one of the poorer districts it is also subject to a great deal of crime, much of it perpetuated by non-Greeks. This has not helped the attitude of the people of Constantinople to immigrants.

Unsurprisingly, Vlanga is rife with supporters of the Prasinoi (ORG-32), and many openly wear a green armband in defiance of the emperor's government. This dismays the kephale, who has ordered the district watch to make a note of all who wear the green. Of course, many watch members have Green sympathies, so this tactic has not worked. The kephale's list is populated with fictional names or the names of businesses who collude with the government to fix prices. Actual membership of the revolutionary-minded Greens is much lower than generally believed; businesses in Vlanga make it a point to ignore (or even show preference for) workers wearing the green, in fear of reprisals.

STORY HOOK

One of the character's neighbours is found suffocated in his sleep. If they investigate his death they discover that he was secretly a sorcerer, and that other sorcerers across the City have died in a similar fashion. On certain days of the year, the Vlanga Stench condenses an air elemental, and a rival sorcerer has learned the Dominate Sylph spell and uses it as a tool to murder his rivals. The sylph's size is one cubic metre per 20% of the Stench's Potency, and it radiates an aura of Nausea (like the parent Stench) with a range equal to the size of the sylph.

LOCAL KNOWLEDGE

STREETWISE

- ɸ (Success): Vlanga is the industrial district of Constantinople. Most goods intended for consumption in the city are landed here, and the district teams with labourers, conveyers, and stevedores.
- ɸ (Success): Avoid Vlanga on hot days. The stench has been known to kill people.
- ɸ (Success): Crime is highest in Vlanga than any other district.
- ɸ (Hard Success): chief amongst Vlanga's criminals is a Bulgarian called Dražan Romanoktonos

LORE (BYZANTINE)

- ɸ (Success) Every riot in Constantinople's history has begun in Vlanga.

LOCAL RUMOURS

- ɸ "If you see someone lying in the gutter it is best to draw your knife before asking if he needs help. My neighbour's cousin didn't, and the man jumped up and stole all his money."
- ɸ "Mengene is sure to win the pankration match tomorrow. I'd put money on him before the bookmakers discover his opponent has a weak knee and shorten the odds."
- ɸ "Help me! My son! My son has been taken! I put him to bed last night, but when we woke he was gone! Please, won't somebody help me?" (see VL-10)
- ɸ "There's a killer on the loose in Vlanga. Three people have been found now with both hands and feet removed."

DESCRIPTIVE ELEMENTS

The Vlanga Stench; raised voices speaking many languages; The Vlanga Stench (it is worth mentioning more than once); dogs chasing rats amongst the refuse; drunken laughter from a phouskarion; the sound of a prostitute singing to attract custom; an opium addict lying insensate in a gutter.

VL-1 AMASTRIANON

POPULATION

2300 (crowded)

AFFILIATIONS

Criminal, Professional (inspectors), Societal (demoi)

A public square and surrounding neighbourhood to the south of the Mese Odos. The forum is rectangular in shape and is delimited by a fence of short marble columns surmounted with crescents. Behind this fence are statues of Zeus, Helios, and a sleeping Heracles, oddly untouched when most pagan statues in the city have been removed. Statues of ducks and tortoises can be found in groups around the square. In the middle of the forum stand two statues of a nameless Paphlagonian and his equally nameless slave, which are perpetually covered in litter and excrement. These strange statues lead most people to avoid the square, believing it to be haunted by devils.

The only building of note on the Amastrianon is called the Modion. Four columns support a pyramidal roof displaying two bronze hands set on spears. This is the headquarters of the Imperial Guild of Assessors and Inspectors, and the bronze hands are a reminder to the mutilation that faces those who cheat customers with false measures. The Modion houses a silver standard for the modios, the basic unit of dry measure.

The sinister reputation of the Amastrianon, coupled with several high-profile deaths occurring here —both executions and murders — has lead to only the bravest souls making their homes in the neighbourhood. It is well-known as a haunt of thieves; those looking to hire a house-breaker or thug make the Amastrianon their first port of call. It is a tradition of the local thieves to smear filth on the Paphlagonian statues for luck in larcenous endeavours, although this is custom is kept a secret within the criminal fraternity.

LINKS

- ɸ The Eleutherion (VL-4)
- ɸ Forum of the Ox (VL-6)
- ɸ Heptaskalon in Vlanga (VL-7)
- ɸ Kaisarion (VL-8)
- ɸ Myrelaion Monastery (VL-9)
- ɸ Olybrion (VL-10)

VL-2 CHURCH OF SAINT DEMETRIOS

Congregation Size: 250; Piety: 8%; Magical Strength: 25%

AFFILIATIONS

Religious/Christian, Military

Demetrios of Thessaloniki is one of the warrior saints of the Orthodox tradition along with Saint George, Saint Theodoros the General and Saint Theodoros the Recruit. He is depicted as a mature, bearded soldier on a red horse, unlike the youthful Saint George on a white horse.

Saint Demetrios's entire body is interred at his church in Vlanga. Its authenticity was under question by the archbishop of Thessaloniki, but the relics were declared genuine after they began to emit a liquid with the strong smell of myrrh, a miracle for which Demetrios is known as Myrobletes, the myrrh-streamer. This church is popular with the army: many of the rank-and-file worship here despite mostly living in Stoudion. The Military Fisc pays a yearly stipend to the priest.

AFFILIATIONS:

- ɸ Kaisarion (VL-8)
- ɸ Office of the Military Fisc (ORG-27)

VL-3 'ELENIANAI

POPULATION
100 (sparse)

AFFILIATIONS
Professional (servants, caretakers, gardeners), Societal (dynatoi)

'Elenianai is the westernmost neighbourhood of Vlanga. Most days in the summer the wind blows from the southwest, keeping the Vlanga Stench away, and one could almost forget that one was just next to the slums of Eleutherion. The neighbourhood consists of houses for the wealthy, arranged in several rows parallel with the sea walls. Some of the houses have been built on artificial terraced slopes. Most houses have an unobstructed view of the sea, and are built with a balcony on the upper floor so that their residents can enjoy the healthy air. Aristocratic families maintain a house here, particularly if they cannot afford a place in the countryside this is a close alternative. Those dynatoi who have fallen on hard times live here all year around. Each house has a generous garden and a permanent staff to care for it and the house, in case the family decide to pay a visit.

'Elenianai has no parish church of its own since it was destroyed in a fire. Most visit the Church of the Theotokos Panachrantes in Dalmaton.

LINKS

- ɸ Eleutherion (VL-4)
- ɸ Forum of Arkadios (VL-5)
- ɸ Dalmaton (ST-1)

VL-4 ELEUTHERION

POPULATION
5400 (crowded)

AFFILIATIONS
Cultural (Slavic, Frankish), Professional (labourers), Societal (demoi)

The Eleutherion is the southern harbour and port of Constantinople, and the neighbourhood immediately adjacent to it. The harbour wall built by Emperor Theodosios continues the line of the sea walls from the Gate of Saint Aemelianos across the whole harbour, leaving only a comparatively narrow entrance next to the Jewish Gate. A smaller wall divides the enclosed harbour into two but does not connect with either the sea walls or the harbour wall. Incoming ships use the western passage closest to the harbour wall whereas outgoing ships use the landward passage to the east. The outer harbour is used as a waiting area for ships without an assigned quay. Agents of the harbourmaster use small skiffs to travel between ships issuing orders. Captains who ignore these orders might find themselves without a berth for their ship.

The surrounding neighbourhood contains the offices of the port authority, quays and cranes for unloading ships' holds, warehouses for storing goods; pens for holding livestock, and, mixed in with all this chaos; residential houses and businesses. The housing in Eleutherion is little better than slums, occupied by foreigners who are not tolerated in other districts as well as the poor who can afford nothing better. These tenements may be four or five storeys high, built adjacent to the city walls and relying upon them for support. The parish church of Eleutherion is Saint Stephanos, patron of masons and labourers.

The water in the Eleutherion is partly responsible for the Vlanga Stench, and it is strongest in this neighbourhood than elsewhere. All unwanted refuse from the docks is dumped in the water and the harbour walls prevent currents from taking it away. Several tons of rotted fish guts blend every day with the contents of the city's sewer system (which also debouches into the harbour) to create a toxic stew with the effluent from the tanning factories of Heptaskalon. Anyone falling into the harbour is advised to keep their mouth shut, and if rescued alive should make a donation to Saint Polykarpos, patron against dysentery and the bloody flux. About 20 years ago a resolution to dredge the harbour was made; when the first load of sludge was brought to the surface it caused a miasma which led to over a thousand deaths. The dredging was quickly abandoned.

STORY HOOK

Posing as a Prasinoi cell, a group of Bektaşi dervishes (ORG-2) have established in the district. They are all fervent Muslims and Greek or Slav converts, trained as Yeniçeris as well as mystics. The player characters stumble across them by accident, and cause them to splinter and scatter. Having nothing to take to the city authorities, the player characters must track down these religious zealots before they get to enact whatever scheme they have planned.

LINKS

- ɸ Amastrianon (VL-1)
- ɸ 'Elenianai (VL-3)
- ɸ Forum of the Ox (VL-6)
- ɸ Heptaskalon in Vlanga (VL-7)
- ɸ Kaisarion (VL-8)
- ɸ Olybrion (VL-10)
- ɸ Skamma of Eumachos (VL-12)
- ɸ Thaïs Alley (VL-13)

VL-5 FORUM OF ARKADIOS

AFFILIATIONS
Professional (slave trade), Criminal (slavers), Urban (market)

The last of the public fora on the Mese Odos, and marking the westernmost limit of Vlanga. It once had a world-wide reputation as a slave market and although slaves are still sold here, most of the trade now takes place in Pera. It still does some specialist business in the trade of female slaves, mostly Circassians and Tatars.

In the centre of the forum is a 50 metre tall column decorated in spiral bands of bas relief sculpture depicting the triumphs of

Emperor Arkadios. The mounted statue of the emperor that once surmounted the tower was dislodged by an earthquake in 704. The immense head of the horse still lies at one end of the square; attempts to move it resulted in several accidents, including one fatal; and it was decided to leave it where it lays.

LINKS

- ɸ Eleutherion (VL-4)
- ɸ Forum of the Ox (VL-6)
- ɸ Dalmaton (ST-1)

VL-6 FORUM OF THE OX

AFFILIATIONS

Political (judiciary), Professional (butchers, pig merchants), Urban (market)

The Forum of the Ox (ho Bous) lies on the Mese Odos in the middle of the Lykos Valley. It is 300 metres long and 250 metres wide and surrounded with porticoes richly carved in bas-relief. Niches hold statues of every emperor who ordered a person executed in this forum, for that has been its main use since before the time of the Tetrachy.

The forum is named after a huge bronze statue of an ox's head that was brought here from the city of Pergamum in Asia Minor. The hollow statue was a furnace used to roast executed criminals alive. Saint Antipas was the first to die in this manner when the statue was still in Pergamum, but it was still used in this fashion after its transportation to Constantinople during the rule of Julian the Apostate (reigned 361–363). It continued to be used to incinerate people until the tenth century, but this was not the only means by which people were executed in the forum. Saint Theodosia (PT-8) was executed here by having a ram's horn hammered through her neck. Others have been trampled by horses, suspended in a sack filled with live cats, thrown from buildings then pelted with rocks, and other cruel and unusual deaths. Patriarchs, usurpers, and saints have all met their fate here.

The bronze ox head no longer exists. It was melted down to mint billon coins to fund various wars of the empire. These coins are occasionally still found in ancient treasure hordes; they are aspra trachea ("short asprons" because they are made of billon rather than pure silver), concave in shape, and marked with the image of a ox's head.

This forum is the only legal market for the sale of lambs by the Butchers' Guild and pigs by the Pork Merchants' Guild. These animals are landed at Eleutherion and driven up Ox Street.

STORY HOOK

A fraction of the Ox Head coins contain the tortured souls of those who were executed in the ox head. When the characters come into possession of such coins, they may be possessed by the haunts. If all characters are possessed, they might be taken back in time to relive the circumstances of the execution through the memories of the haunts, and maybe set right an ages-old injustice.

LINKS

- ɸ Forum of Arkadios (VL-5)
- ɸ Olybrion (VL-10)
- ɸ Forum of Theodosios (KN-8)
- ɸ Lykos Valley (XR-4)

VL-7 HEPTASKALON IN VLANGA

POPULATION

800

AFFILIATIONS

Professional (leather or fur trade), Religious/Jewish (Romaniote), Societal (demoi)

Named after the seven wharfs (skaloi) on the sea wall, this is one of two neighbourhoods in Constantinople called Heptaskalon (the other is in Platea); a source of some confusion to visitors. The Vlanga Heptaskalon is surrounded by its own wall made by barricading the alleyways between tenements. The Eleutherion road marks the north of the neighbourhood; the only entrances to Heptaskalon is via the Amastrianon Road which goes through the neighbourhood to the Jewish Gate in the sea walls.

Heptaskalon in Vlanga is home to a community of about 750 Romaniote Jews. The walls were built in a period where segregation of Jews was mandatory, a position that has since lessened although the Jewish communities are still disadvantaged by the law. Those in this neighbourhood are mostly involved in the tanning, leatherworking, and furriers' trade. The turning of animal skins into leather is a laborious and smelly business. Children are sent into the streets in the morning to gather dog faeces, which are rubbed into the skins before they are soaked in urine gathered from nightsoil along with various noxious chemicals. The fumes from this process are a contributor to the Vlanga Stench, and the waste is emptied straight into the harbour mouth through the Jewish Gate. The products made by the Jews of Heptaskalon are much sought-after for their quality. As well as rawhide and leather supplied to the Saddlers' Guild, workshops in this district supply shoes and garments of leather and fur, including hats and fur linings and trim for garments made elsewhere. They also make satchels, water bottles, book covers, and sundry other leather goods; but are forbidden in making horse tack or leather armour by the imperial monopoly controlled by the Saddlers' Guild.

The unofficial leader of Heptaskalon in Vlanga is Rabbi Daoud ben Daoud, who has the ear of the kephale due to some sound advice in the past.

LINKS

- ɸ Amastrianon (VL-1)
- ɸ Eleutherion (VL-4)
- ɸ Kaisarion (VL-8)

VL-8 KAISARION

POPULATION

1950 (crowded)

AFFILIATIONS

Criminal (fencing stolen goods), Cultural (Bulgarian), Professional (prostitution), Societal (demoi)

The tenements of Kaisarion are not much better than the slums of Eleutherion. Dražan Romanoktonos has claimed ownership of all the buildings here and demands rent from the inhabitants which is little more than protection money. The buildings are in a shoddy state of repair: the city governance has had them due for restoration for many years, but the motion is never tabled – it is not in Dražan's best interests and he pays heavily to keep the item off the agenda. The kephale of Vlanga gets a cut of the rent. Since there are vacant buildings in other parts of Constantinople, residents are really paying for the convenience of a home so close to the two districts with the most employers: Kainopolis and Vlanga. For those who are unable to pay, Dražan is willing to accept rent in other forms of currency than hard coin.

The parish church is Homonia Church, dedicated to Saint Panteleimon, patron of physicians and victims of witchcraft.

STORY HOOK

A man is dragged from a house by two men and taken into an alleyway. A third man waits, ready to break their victim's legs. The assaulters could be the brothers of a girl abused by their victim. Alternatively they could be heavies employed by Dražan Romanoktonos to punish a thief trying to avoid paying him his cut.

LINKS

- ɸ Amastrianon (VL-1)
- ɸ Church of Saint Demetrios (VL-2)
- ɸ Dražan Romanoktonos (NPC-10)
- ɸ Amantion (KN-1)
- ɸ Artopoleia (KN-4)
- ɸ Kanikleion (KN-9)

VL-9 MYRELAION MONASTERY

Congregation Size: 97; Piety: 23%; Magical Strength: 25%

AFFILIATIONS

Religious/Christian

Originally a palace built in the tenth century by Emperor Romanos Lekapenos, intended to be a new centre of government to rival the Great Palace. It was built on top of a giant rotunda some 50 metres in diameter, which Romanos converted into a cistern. This substructure brought the palace that was built atop it to the same level as a new church, which became the shrine of the Lekapenos family. Since the Restoration of the Empire, the Myrelaion (literally the "place of myrrh") has been a monastery populated by nuns.

The church consists of a central nave surmounted by a dome, with four side naves radiating out in a cross shape covered by barrel vaults. The cross is contained within a square outside wall made entirely of bricks, and has a narthex attached to the west and a sanctuary in the east. There are many openings in the walls covered with glass admitting light into the structure.

The myrrh stored at the Myrelaion is centuries old and has lost none of its scent. Anyone smelling the sacred incense finds that their memory is greatly improved, particularly for matters around death and dying. The myrrh is occasionally used in judicial proceedings to assist the power of recall of witnesses.

LINKS

- ɸ Amastrianon (VL-1)
- ɸ Forum of Constantine (KN-7).

VL-10 OLYBRION

POPULATION

1850 (crowded)

AFFILIATIONS

Academic (students), Deviant (alchemists), Professional (brewing, distilling, glassblowing), Societal (demoi)

The commercial hub of the Mese Odos peters out after the Forum of Theodosios, and by the time the street reaches Olybrion it has lost most of its glory. The neighbourhood of Olybrion is on the west-facing slope of the Third Hill, sloping down towards the Forum of the Ox. It is dominated by the Imperial University at the Philadelphion, and many students live in Olybrion. With much of their money going on tuition, the tenements of Olybrion are overpopulated, often accommodating twice their ideal occupancy. Cut-price tabernai provide cheap meals with substandard ingredients; still, many students rely upon the state bread to sustain their bodies while they nourish their minds.

The parish church of Olybrion is the Church of Saint Euphemia.

STORY HOOK

At the edge of Olybrion, as it fades into deserted ruins, is the xenodocheion of Saint Laurentios. It is operated by a pair of living broukolakes (page 217). Their original scheme was to prey upon the visitors to the city who would not be missed. This was a successful if horrifying scheme; however, their bloodthirst is now too strong for the meagre supply of visitors to satisfy it, and they have extended their reach into the districts of Stoudion and Vlanga. Anyone following the pattern of missing persons will be able to narrow down the problem to the neighbourhood of the xenodocheion; alternatively the player characters might follow a fresh trail of blood and footprints. The broukolakes, who pose as brothers, are only just able to pass as human, but will almost certainly lose control in the presence of fresh blood. They will try to lure the player characters alone into dark places where they can transform. The gnawed bones of former victims half-fill the hostel's dry well.

LINKS

- ф Amastrianon (VL-1)
- ф Eleutherion (VL-4)
- ф Philadephion (VL-11)
- ф Artopoleia (KN-4)
- ф Konstanton (PL-7)

VL-11 PHILADELPHION

AFFILIATIONS

Academic (secular subjects), Political (Imperial University), Professional (teachers)

A public square in the western part of Kainopolis, at the point where the Mese Odos splits: the northern branch heading for the Gate of Charisios and the southern branch heading for the Golden Gate. The name of the forum, which means "the place of brotherly love", is derived from a statue that used to stand here depicting Constantine's three sons embracing one another after the emperor's death. This statue, along with several others, is now incorporated into Saint Mark's Basilica in Venice, having been taken there after the Sack of Constantinople.

At one end of the forum sits a grand building called the Kapetolion, which houses the Pandidakterion (the Imperial University). The Kapetolion was originally a pagan shrine, but upon the inauguration of New Rome by Constantine the Great, it (like all pagan temples) was closed down. A monumental cross on an obelisk of porphyry was erected in front of the steps. A colonnade supported by pillars of porphyry flanks the gate. Within is a courtyard containing the restored temple, now serving as a lecture hall. Surrounding the courtyard are two-storey buildings, accommodation for higher students below and masters above. As well as lecture theatres and academic offices, the Kapetolion is the headquarters of the government ministry responsible for overseeing all education in Constantinople.

LINKS

- ф Olybrion (VL-10)
- ф Mese Odos (KN-12)
- ф Imperial University (ORG-22)

VL-12 SKAMMA OF EUMACHOS

AFFILIATIONS

Societal (demoi), Urban (pankration)

This is the most famous of the numerous Pankration rings in Constantinople, and responsible for organising the city-wide tournaments. As well as the ring itself, which has seating for three thousand people around the sand floor, the complex has a training hall or palaistra, where trainers (*gymnastai*) provide specialist training for fighters of different levels of skill and technique. Training falls into three main categories: endurance, speed, and strength. There are punching bags filled with fig seeds, dummies to spar against, and weights to train with. Each paying trainee is provided personalised advice from a qualified physician, who advises on exercise and nutrition according to Galenic philosophy. Attending the palaistra can provide Training (Mythras page 73) in Athletics, Brawn, Pankration, Evade and Acrobatics, and also provide facilities for increasing the Characteristics of STR, DEX, and CON by sacrificing Experience Rolls (Mythras page 72).

There are several types of pankration match:

- ф Training bouts, which are usually public events
- ф Open calls, where anyone can take part. These are usually fought against junior pankratiasts, with the intent to identify some new talent
- ф Rank matches are called by a competitor against a pankratiast with a higher ranking. The winner takes or retains the highest rank. These are highly theatrical bouts, but great crowd pleasers. The top rank cannot be challenged in a rank match
- ф Contests are the big event, usually witnessed by crowds of thousands. They are held on the eve of a Great Feast, and they establish the rankings of all the registered pankratiasts. The four fighters who make it to the semi-finals are the top ranking champions and are treated as equals regardless of the order they were knocked out, although anephedroi (who reached the semi-finals without a bye) rank ahead of the others.

Pankratiasts usually adopt or acquire nicknames based on their signature moves. For example Akrochersites ("Fingertips") breaks the hands of his opponents during Upper Pankration; 'Alteres ("Jumping Weight") throws his enemies backwards while trying to twist their ankles out of their sockets; Leon ("Lion") regularly bites his opponents, and Mengene ("the Clamp") has an unbreakable vice-like grip. One particularly nasty competitor (Kakomachos, or "dirty fighter") urinates on the faces of his grappled opponents in order to force submission.

Polos is a gymnaste and alytarch (referee) who is also a pharmakopeios. He discretely offers pharmaceutical help to fighters; these take the form of Folk Magic spells such as Might, Heal, and Bludgeon prepared as a potion (using the spell of the same name). These come in the form of an oily paste that is smeared on the skin; when the fighter wants to activate its effects he simply licks off the potion. The first of these potions is offered for free, "between friends" but as the competitor becomes dependant on them to win, the price steadily increases.

LEADS

- ф Eleutherion (VL-4)

VL-13 THAÏS ALLEY

AFFILIATIONS

Urban (brothels)

This alley in Eleutherion running between Ox Street and Elenianai Street is crowded with brothels and phouskaria. It has no official name, but is known locally by the name of its small church dedicated to Saint Thaïs the Harlot, patron of prostitutes.

The women (and men) that work Thaïs Alley have incorporated into a private guild for mutual protection and profit. They all receive a fair wage from the guild and are at liberty to refuse clients

or even stop work and receive a pension. The guild is the brainchild of Zsara, an ageing women of half-Greek ancestry who is still possessed of an exotic beauty. She was born a slave and began the guild following the death of her pimp (possibly at her own hands) and subsequent emancipation aided by the political connections she had made through her work. Dražan Romanoktonos (NPC-10) has made several attempts to take control of the women of Thaïs Alley, but they have managed to resist his advances thus far.

LEADS

- Eleutherion (VL-4)

XEROLOPHOS (DISTRICT)

Xerolophos (literally "dry hill") is the most sparsely populated of Constantinople's districts. The district covers the Seventh Hill, taking up about a third of the total area of the city and yet holding less than a twentieth of its population. The people who live here are found mostly in discrete communities – Elebichon, Olympion, Paradeison, Triton – separated by expanses of seared earth and spiny vegetation. The looming presence of the Theodosian Walls dominates much of the landscape of Xerolophos, although much of it shows signs of wear, particularly along the mesoteichion (the "middle wall") around the Pempton Gate.

Instead of a kephale, Xerolophos has a council of five members, one seat for each of the four communities and one for a representative of the praitor. However, the fifth seat has been vacant for over 50 years since the praitor last bothered to appoint someone. A delegate from the Kynokephaloi of the Lykos Valley may attend the meetings but is not given a vote. The council meets irregularly; it is supposed to be every month but it is generally only called when there is a matter that involves two or more of the neighbourhoods. Otherwise, law and order within the neighbourhood is dealt with at a local level. This is in clear contravention of the charter of Xerolophos and the rules of the Praitorion, but few care.

LOCAL KNOWLEDGE

STREETWISE

- (Success): Xerolophos is where the City's home-grown food is produced. There are four hamlets where most of the people can be found, and the rest of the district is fields and orchards.
- (Success): The uncultivated Lykos Valley is home to a tribe of Kynokephaloi. They expect gifts in exchange for safe passage through their territory: meat, salt, and weapons are good choices.

LOCAL RUMOURS

- "I wouldn't go out at night in Xerolophos, even on the roads. There are things that live in the caves of the Seventh Hill, and they come out at night to hunt."
- "If you have to travel through the Lykos Valley, take meat for the dog-headed men. They have a taste for horseflesh, so make sure you have something to ransom the life of each horse with you."

DESCRIPTIVE ELEMENTS

Dry stunted vegetation peaks from between cracked flagstones; soil is blasted and crumbly; packs of rangy dogs watch the characters with suspicion; twisted olive trees.

XR-1 CHURCH OF SAINT MAMAS

Congregation Size: 700; Piety: 5%; Magical Strength: 50%

AFFILIATIONS

Religious/Christian (Orthodox)

This is the parish church of Triton, largest of Xerolophos's neighbourhoods. Saint Mamas was a child-martyr from Caesarea. He became an orphan when his parents were executed for being Christians, but he preached the Word from an early age and was tortured. He escaped with the help of an angel, but was recaptured. He was thrown to the lions but they became docile, and he took to riding on one's back. This did not earn him a reprieve; he was killed with a trident to his belly and was carried to heaven by an angel. The bones of his lion companion are interred here at the church.

STORY HOOK

Some supernatural agency has raised Mamas' lion from death, and it stalks Triton at night as a skeletal lion (see Mythras page 253 for the statistics of a lion, but modify according to the rules for skeletons page 265). Even if slain, the lion reconstitutes itself, borrowing bones from other corpses to replace those it has lost. Is this some divine justice for some secret sin, or is it the action of an evil spirit or sorcerer?

LINKS

- Triton (XR-10)

XR-2 CISTERN OF MOKIOS

AFFILIATIONS:

Saint Mokios shares his holy day with the birthday of the City, May 11, and a small church dedicated to him high on the Seventh Hill gives its name to the nearby cistern, the largest in the city. Mokios, also known as the Holy Hieromartyr, preached against the worship of Dionysius, and for this he was cast into a red-hot oven. He came through unscathed and was instead thrown to wild beasts, who refused to eat him. He was eventually sent here to Byzantion, where he was beheaded.

The cistern named after him is the only one in the western half of the city, and supplies water to the districts of Xerolophos, Stoudion, and Vlanga. It is open to the air and has sides 170 metres by 147 metres, averaging 15 metres deep. It can hold 374 million litres of water.

LINKS

- Paradeison (XR-9)

XR-3 ELEBICHON

POPULATION

300 (sparse)

AFFILIATIONS

Deviant (religious), Professional (goat herding, cheesemaking), Religious/Christian (Barlaamite, anti-Unionist), Societal (mesoi)

A small neighbourhood surrounding the Romanos Gate in the Theodosian Walls. The parish church of Elebichon is dedicated to the Holy Martyrs Menodora, Metrodora, and Nymphodora. A small monastery attached to the church called Kyra Martha is the home of Sister Hypomone, more commonly known as the Dowager Empress Helena.

Two religious groups call Elebichon home, both of them deviants from Orthodoxy. The anti-Palamites are those followers of Barlaam (see page 32) who rejected Hesychasm but who did not want to join with the Catholic church as most did. The Barlaamites at Elebichon maintain that Palamas described a heretical division in the Trinity that was close to polytheism, and the hesychast principle that man can become like God through theosis without comprising God's transcendence is magic, not religion.

The anti-Unionists fiercely reject conciliation with the Catholic Church. Forced out of their parishes and monasteries by the Unionist patriarch, they see a spiritual leader in the curmudgeonly Gennadios (NPC-11).

Neither of these groups have common ground. Many of the anti-Palamites are Unionists and all of the anti-Unionists are Hesychasts. Unable to secure funding for a new church, the two fight over access to the parish church. The goatherds who live here ignore these religious divisions, and will hear mass from whichever group of priests has gained control over the church.

LINKS

- Olympion (XR-8)
- Paradeison (XR-9)
- Triton (XR-10)

XR-4 LYKOS VALLEY

POPULATION

1150 (sparse)

AFFILIATIONS

Cultural (Kynokephaloi)

The Lykos River lends its name to a mostly uninhabited neighbourhood between the Seventh Hill and the Fourth to Sixth Hills. For the most part the Lykos Valley is overgrown with bushes and trees, which thin out on the flanks of the hills. These are hardy, dry-adapted plants such as thyme and rosemary, rich in fragrant oils that give the valley a distinctive scent. The only permanent residents of the Lykos Valley are the monks of the Monastery of Libos and the three Kynokephalos clans; however refugees displaced from other parts of the Empire have created a tent city to the south of the neighbourhood, near where the Lykos dives underground.

The Kynokephaloi have lived in Lykos since the eighth century, but they do not mingle with humans very much, and it is easy for people to forget that they are here. They hunt the wild boar and wild ass that live in the valley, although are careful not to predate the populations too heavily, and may go outside the walls to supplement their diet. However, Kynokephaloi eat every part of their prey except the bones and hair, even chewing the hide, and they can get by with eating only once or twice every week. Kynokephaloi have no concept of fatherhood; to them, the production of whelps by a mature female has nothing to do with sexual intercourse. Whelps are raised communally by the family; there is no sense of ownership by the birth mother. This gives them a great sense of community, but a failure to appreciate ancestry and inheritance. Clan gatherings are noisy affairs, with much excited chatter mixed with yelps and barks. The three clans have clearly defined territories, but are not hostile to one another as long as those boundaries are respected, and for the most part they are.

The dominant clan is the Lykos clan, taking its name from the river, which itself means "wolf" in Greek. The Lykoi number about 450, and live mostly in the central region. The Teichos, or "Wall" clan is the smallest with only 100 members, and lives mostly to the northwest of the valley, near the Theodosian Walls. Finally, the Speleion or "Cave" clan lives in the hills on the northeast bank of the Lykos, where deep gullies form a series of interconnected caves. There are about 200 Speleioi in total. Kynokephaloi religion is animist in nature, there is usually just one shaman in each clan at any time, assisted by one to three apprentices. The Kynokephaloi honour Lykos the River God (UC-7), and have friendly relations with Nature Spirits (Rivers, Caves, Wild Asses, Wolves) and Elemental Spirits (Earth and Water).

LINKS

- ф Monastery of Libos (XR-5)
- ф Olympion (XR-8)
- ф Paradeison (XR-9)
- ф Konstanton (PL-7)
- ф Leomakellon (PL-8)
- ф Kyrion (PT-5)
- ф Eleutherion (VL-4)

XR-5 MONASTERY OF LIBOS

Congregation Size: 170; Piety: 27%; Magical Strength: 50%

AFFILIATIONS

Religious/Christian

The site of a double monastery. Constantine Libos, a Grand Doux of the tenth century first founded a nunnery here dedicated to the Theotokos Panachrantos ("Immaculate"). After the Restoration of the Empire, the widow of Michael VIII Palaiologos established a second monastery dedicated to Saint John the Baptist, to be the burial place of several members of her family. She also restored the nunnery, which had fallen into ruin.

The nunnery is home to 50 nuns, and has a xenon for 15 laywomen. The monastery houses 75 monks and 30 laymen. The North Church, that of the Theotokos, is a cross-in-square style with four columns supporting the central dome. It is home to the relics of Saint Eirene. The South Church, dedicated to Saint John, is a simple square room surmounted by a dome. The brickwork has been laid with great artistry, making patterns of arches, hooks, sun crosses, swastikas, and fans.

LINKS

- ф Lykos Valley (XR-4)

XR-6 MONASTERY OF SAINT ANDREW IN KRISEI

Congregation Size: 163; Piety: 16%; Magical Strength: 50%

AFFILIATIONS

Military (discipline), Religious/Christian

The monastery dedicated to Saint Andrew of Crete is located at Krisei ("Judgement" in Greek), where military tribunals are held. When originally founded by a sister of Emperor Theodosios II, the church was dedicated to Saint Andrew the Apostle, but so popular was the martyr to Icondulism called Andrew of Crete that after the Triumph of Orthodoxy the dedication of the church was changed. The church was refitted from damage inflicted during the Sack of Constantinople by Theodora Raoulina, niece of Michael VIII Palaiologos, and it became an Orthodox monastery once again. She spent the last 15 years of her life in the monastery, and is buried here.

The military tribunal hears cases of desertion and spying, but also deals with matters of internal discipline such as insubordination, unruly behaviour, and assaults against civilians.

There is a cypress tree in the grounds of the monastery with a chain hanging from one of its boughs. If the chain is set swinging by two people who disagree over a matter of fact, the chain will hit the person who is telling the truth.

LINKS

- ф Triton (XR-10)

XR-7 MONASTERY OF SAINT DIOMEDES OF JERUSALEM

Congregation Size: 34; Piety: 44%; Magical Strength: 25%

AFFILIATIONS

Religious/Christian (Orthodox)

Saint Diomedes was a physician from Tarsus who was martyred under Diocletian at Nicaea. The emperor was brought his decapitated head, and all members of the court who were present were struck blind, and this blindness persisted until his head was returned to his body. It is generally believed that this miracle can be repeated with the saint's relics, both of which are possessed by the monastery.

Saint Diomedes is one of the Holy Unmercenaries, and his monks follow his example, caring for the sick free of charge. This monastery is supported by the Office of the Orphanotrophos. In the ninth century the abbot was sent a dream by the saint, and found an impoverished peasant curled up in the doorway of the monastery. He was clothed and fed, and he never forgot the kindness offered by the monastery, even when he became Emperor Basil I.

LINKS

- ф Triton (XR-10)
- ф Imperial Orphanage (ORG-21)

XR-8 OLYMPION

POPULATION

350 (sparse)

AFFILIATIONS

Military (cavalry), Professional (fruit growers, labourers), Societal (demoi)

The slopes of Olympion are covered with orchard trees, growing figs, olives, apples, citrons, quinces, pears, pomegranates, and other fruit. The orchard tenders encourage the wild dogs of the Seventh Hill to live amongst their trees with gifts of meat; in return they keep the deer from destroying the fruit trees and their crops.

The northernmost section of Olympion, near the Romanos Gate, is the headquarters of the City's two allagia of cavalry. The horses are stabled in paddocks and most of the men are billeted in houses abutting the Theodosian Walls. To the disgust of the foot soldiers billeted in Psamathia, each company of 10 men has a house to themselves, whereas the infantry regiments are crowded eight to a room in crumbling tenements. The cavalrymen also have an army of squires to tend to the horses and their tack. Conflicts occasionally occur between the cavalrymen and the Teichos clan of the Kynokephaloi, who have a love for the taste of horseflesh. Raiding into Olympion has been stopped, but should a horse stray into Teichos territory it is unlikely to survive.

The parish church is dedicated to Saint Tryphon and Saint Georgios; dedication to the latter was added when the cavalry units were first billeted here a century ago, but since Georgios is also patron of farmers, there was little argument from the demoi.

LINKS

- ɸ Elebichon (XR-3)
- ɸ Lykos Valley (XR-4)
- ɸ Paradeison (XR-9)

XR-9 PARADEISON

POPULATION

500 (sparse)

AFFILIATIONS

Cultural (English), Professional (weaving), Societal (demoi)

A small neighbourhood centred around its parish church of Saint Mokios and bisected by the Mokios Road. This is a small English enclave with a smattering of other Germanic nations, and belongs to the Varangian Guard. The parents, wives, and children of members of the Guard farm the land here; the boys train in weapon craft, practice their skill with a longbow every Saturday, and dream of being accepted into the famous unit. Were it not for the weather one could almost think one was in England: the houses are built in an English style, and English is spoken here to the exclusion of all other languages – many of the people here have never learned more than a few words of Greek.

While Saint Mokios is the official parish church, the English attend their own Catholic church, called the Panagia Varangiotissa, dedicated to the Virgin Mary and Saint Olaf Haraldson. The sword of the great Scandinavian saint hangs over the altar. The land here is dry but fertile; and with much irrigation from the cistern, the village is able to sustain itself in wheat. All of the land assigned to Paradeison is under the stewardship of the Varangian Guard, and a member who gets married is given a gift of a farm, servants, and land by the megas akolouthos on the understanding that he will raise his sons to try out for the guard. Should he die in service, the land remains with the widow but is not inherited by any children unless they themselves are guardsmen. When a man retires from the Varangian Guard, he keeps his farm until his death, but the widows of retired guardsmen cannot remain on the land and usually retire to the Monastery of Saint Eudokimos, which is supported by the Guard.

LINKS

- ɸ Cistern of Mokios (XR-2)
- ɸ Lykos Valley (XR-4)
- ɸ Triton (XR-10)
- ɸ ‘Exakionion (ST-2)

XR-10 TRITON

POPULATION

850 (sparse)

AFFILIATIONS

Professional (agriculture, horticulture, livestock rearing), Societal (demoi)

The largest of Xerolophos's four villages is Triton, and has half of the population of the whole district. Triton is a farming community that contributes to the feeding of the city. Some of the fields and orchards are inside the Theodosian Walls, but the greatest part of them are outside. The parish church is the Church of Saint Mamas, and the majority of the family residences are clustered around the church in the west of the neighbourhood. Each day, the farmers head out the Gate of the Spring to tend to their crops.

LINKS

- ɸ Elebichon (XR-3)
- ɸ Paradeison (XR-9)
- ɸ ‘Exakionion (ST-2)
- ɸ Psamathia (ST-7)
- ɸ Zoödochos Pege Monastery (XR-11)

XR-11 ZOÖDOCHOS PEGE MONASTERY

Congregation Size: 8; Piety: 43%; Magical Strength: 75%

AFFILIATIONS

Religious/Christian (monastic)

The Monastery of the Mother of God at the Spring, more commonly called Zoödochos Pege or “the Life-Giving Spring” lies about half a kilometre outside of the Theodosian Walls. There has been a Christian shrine here since the fifth or sixth century, although the healing springs at the spot were famous for centuries beforehand. It has suffered damage due to earthquakes and from armies attempting to besiege the city, but as one of Constantinople's most significant holy sites, each time it has been damaged or destroyed it has been restored out of the Imperial purse. The complex of the monastery sits some way back from the church of the Holy Spring. The whole monastery is built on swampy land and is surrounded by lush vegetation and hearty trees.

The church is a rectangular basilica, partially subterranean. The dome of the basilica glitters with pure gold. To reach the source of the spring, one must descend two flights of marble stairs, each of 25 steps, and all the light from outside is concentrated on the spring itself. The water falls from the *hagiasma* (holy fountain) into a marble basin, and channels cut into the floor distribute it to various pools around the inside of the church. These pools have fish living in them

that are spontaneously generated by the life-giving properties of the holy water. The water originates deep beneath the earth, and also supplies the Church of Saint Mary at Blachernai.

The Life-Giving Spring, as an aspect of the Theotokos, has its own feast day, on Bright Friday – the Friday after Pascha. It is the only feast day that may be celebrated in Bright Week. The waters are considered to be a sacred mystery, a means by which mankind can reach God directly; and they have been the cause of many miracles. Using the water from the Zoödochos Pege permits anyone with the Love God Passion to use its score in place of both Exhort and Devotion when requesting a healing miracle. Acolyte miracles impose a Hard penalty to the Passion for the purposes of substituting for both these Skills, and Priest miracles impose a Formidable penalty. The water does not even have to come from the hagiasma, even mud from the nearby swamp carries the healing properties of the shrine. A person can only ever be healed once by the spring, and water taken away from the spring has no healing power.

LINKS

- ɸ Triton (XR-10)
- ɸ Church of Saint Mary of Blachernai (BL-5)
- ɸ Sister Zoë (IMM-6)

THE UNDERCITY

Unknown to most of Constantinople's inhabitants is that there is an extensive underground network of tunnels and chambers. No one really thinks about the sunken cisterns that store water, the sewers built many centuries ago, or the crypts in which the dead are interred. Those in the know call this the Undercity (Hypopolis), and venture here with trepidation. It is divided between several fiefs each controlled by a dangerous individual.

The bulk of the Undercity is found beneath the city's hills and largely absent in the valleys between. There are three chief areas of the Undercity. The densest concentration of the Undercity is the complex beneath the First, Second, and Third Hills, which is called simply "Underground" or Nerterion. Another domain is that beneath the Fourth, Fifth, and Sixth hills, thinly connected to the eastern complex by a few tunnels. This area is called Nekropoleia ("Deadtown"), for it has long been used to store the victims of the various disasters that have struck at Constantinople: plagues, fires, earthquakes, riots, and invasions. The last complex, called Batheia ("The Deeps") is in the southwest of the city beneath the Seventh Hill and is not known to be connected to either of the other two complexes, although there are some deep tunnels that have not been extensively explored.

The bulk of the Undercity is made up of the architecture of water management. When the foundation of Constantinople was made, and each time the city has been expanded, new growth began with the laying of systems to keep the city supplied with fresh water and systems to remove the city's waste. Constantinople has few natural springs, and nearly all the water used by the city is either brought from outside by a series of aqueducts, or else stored rainwater. This is something that few inhabitants of the city think about: water has always been available at public fountains, and the fortunate have it piped under pressure directly into their homes. Many city blocks have a buried cistern that is dipped into as if it were a well, although it is fed not by ground water but by a series of pipes that brings river water from far beyond the city. Indeed, old men will sit with fishing lines and catch their supper, without giving a thought as to how the water – and the fish – gets there. Most of these pipes are of insufficient size to contribute to the Undercity, but the main trunk lines are a metre in diameter allowing egress to the nimble. However, there are hundreds of cisterns and settling tanks in all but the lowest-lying areas of the Venetian Quarter and Platea, and the mostly uninhabited Xerolophos. Many of these have been poorly maintained and are now dry, or hold a fraction of their former capacity. Water pipes get choked with weeds and refuse, or else collapse through improper maintenance, meaning that otherwise intact water chambers have gone dry.

The main conduits of the Undercity are the sewers. All of the major streets of the City have a sewer underlying them that is big enough for two men to stand abreast. These are fed by gutters alongside minor streets and pipes leading from private residences. The gutters and pipes are flushed with rainwater reservoirs and tend to be in working order: the well-known connection between bad smells and rampant disease soon gets the populace complaining to the Praitorion if sewers get blocked. As long as the weather is dry, the sewers are safe to traverse, but they can quickly become raging torrents once rain starts to fall. The sewers disgorge into the sea, usually away from the main harbours, with the notable exception of the Eleutherion (VL- 4). The water supply system was in general installed above the water removal system, so if there is a breach between the two it results in a failure in the supply rather than a contamination of the drinking water with sewage.

RANDOMLY GENERATING AN UNDERCITY NODE

In a similar manner to generating a city node, this section describes a simple method to generate a small part of the Undercity. This method should be repeated to grow a complex, adding each section to the previous one. Characters may be in search of adventure and simply exploring the depths of the city below The City, or they may be searching with a specific goal in mind.

To create a node, you will first need to know what part of the Undercity it is in: Batheia under the Seventh Hill, Nerterion in the east, or Nekropoleia under the north west of the city. Next, roll a d6, d8, d10, and d12 onto a piece of paper. If you are in Nerterion or Nekropoleia, also include one or two d4s.

Consider the d4s (if you rolled them) first. These dice represent sewer lines. Choose a point on the d4 to indicate the path of a sewer line, going in both directions. This should be the line that goes nearest to another die; if you have multiple options, head towards the die showing the lowest number. If you rolled multiple d4s then mark the point where the two sewer lines intersect if it occurs on your map. If any sewer line goes near or through another die, then compare the numbers. If the d4 shows a lower number then the sewer goes underneath that location. If the d4 shows a higher number, then the sewer goes overhead. If the numbers match, then the sewer intersects with the corresponding location. You can now remove the d4s from your page.

Next, compare the values on the remaining dice on the appropriate column of the Subterranean Location Table (see page 190) to determine what type of chambers, voids, or hollows are present at the node. The actual locations of the dice on the page represent the relative placements of these spaces. The numbers showing on the dice also represent the relative depth in the earth of the locations as well as the type: the lower the number, the deeper it is. These numbers are also relative to the sewers (if any). If you are creating your location around a known entry point (such as basement that the characters have entered) then include a d20 in with the dice when you throw them to find out where it is in relation to the other spaces.

Next, join up the locations. If the dice are virtually touching, then the locations themselves are adjacent. Otherwise, draw a connection between any two adjacent dice. This represents a tunnel, water pipe, fissure, or some other means by which characters can traverse from one location to another. Connect the third die to one of the first pair, or instead to the connector between them. Connect the fourth die to any of the three other dice or either of the two connectors. This gives you your basic map of the node. You can draw the shape of the location around each of the dice.

You should decide the nature of the connectors based on the locations at either end. Typical connectors include buried streets, main water pipes, overflow pipes, natural fissures, and gallery crypts from abandoned monasteries. Compare the numbers (i.e. the relative depths) on the dice you have connected. The difference between the numbers determines the steepness and type of connector, which is usually related to one or both of the locations on either end:

Difference between dice	Connector is...
1–4	flat or slightly inclined, like a street, gallery crypt, or water pipe
5–8	up to 30 degrees, like a street, or a set of steps
9–12	45–90 degrees, like a fissure in the rock, a flight of stairs, or a ladder

Before you remove the dice from the page and start filling in some details, make note of these things:

- If two dice roll the same number, then there is a feature here. Choose or roll on the Subterranean Feature Table (see page 190). The feature is situated somewhere between the two locations partaking in the double, or in the connecting feature if there is one.
- If three or four dice roll the same number, then there is an event going on at this intersection right now. Choose or roll on the Subterranean Events Table (see page 190), using a d12 if you rolled a triple or a d20 if you rolled a quadruple. You may also add a feature if you wish.

LOCATIONS

Constantinople is prone to seismic activity, and as a result has many caves. These are not like caves in other parts of the world, carved out by water and featuring stalagmites and stalactites. Instead they are formed by violent earth tremors, and may have uneven floors, jagged rocks, and strewn with rubble. In Batheia one finds artificial caves dug out by the troglodytai (see page 221).

Under the eastern end of the city one finds buried houses underneath the current streets – often still connected with alleyways and streets – where city planners have simply built over the old structures. Some of these buildings are still inhabited. The most common underground structures are connected to water storage and removal. There are hundreds of cisterns buried across the city, rectangular chambers typically 20 metres on one side and 15-18 metres on the other, with the roof supported by four rows of six pillars. The locations of many of these have been forgotten, and they have not been maintained since before the Frankokratia. Only half are still capable of holding water, and fewer still actually have a working feed of water to supply them. Alongside the cisterns are settling tanks, which hold the water to allow particulate matter to settle out, or else are involved in the hydraulics of the pressured water in the city. Other tanks perform a similar settling function for sewer water, but at a lower level.

Crypts and cemeteries often mark where churches used to stand, but after their destruction at the hand of riots, fires, or earthquakes they have not been rebuilt, and the land repurposed. Most of the time the bodies that lay in these crypts have long crumbled to dust. Similarly, houses or businesses may have cellars that they have long forgotten about, or are unaware have connections to the Undercity. Finally, sinkholes are formed from a void forming beneath a structure which then falls into the hollow. They are usually close to the surface, but old sinkholes tend to be built over.

SUBTERRANEAN LOCATION TABLE

Location	Nerterion	Nekropolcia	Batheia
Artificial cave	–	–	1–3
Natural cave	–	1	4–8
Buried house	1–3	2–3	–
Cistern or sewage settling tank	4–7	4–5	9
Crypt, mausoleum, or cemetery	8–9	6–10	10
Cellar	10–11	11	–
Sinkhole	12	12	11–12

SUBTERRANEAN FEATURES TABLE

1d20	Feature
1	Obstacle in connector: rubble, tree roots, chasm in floor
2	Partially-collapsed ceiling, but not so much as to block movement
3	Stream cuts across floor, probably a leak from nearby water pipe or sewer
4	Alcove cut into a wall, perhaps containing a jar or shelf for an ornament
5	Shrine containing an ikon or statue; may be votive offerings
6	A scant blanket and meagre clothes belonging to a down-and-out (not currently present)
7	Partially submerged chamber, 1d6 x 10% full of water
8	Stored goods, either contraband or forgotten
9	A thief's hoard, probably well hidden
10	Thick layer of sludgy sewage over floor
11	One or more corpses, may be discarded or interred in coffins
12	Architectural rubbish thrown down from street level: broken statues, columns, etc.
13	Animal bones with signs of being chewed
14	Passage deliberately blocked with barricade, rock, or crude door
15	Chamber filled with detritus brought here by a flood; could be something valuable hidden in junk
16	A shaft to the surface letting in dim light
17	A trickle of natural gas has ignited to form a single flickering flame
18	A cache of munitions and/or weapons has been left here; explosives may be unsafe
19	The air here is thin or foul, make an Endurance roll every 5 minutes or gain a level of Fatigue
20	This area is crossed by a gantry or bridge

SUBTERRANEAN EVENTS TABLE

1d20	Event
1	A swarm infests the area. Choose from: bat flock*, insect swarm, leech shoal* (sewer only), rat swarm*
2	Storm surge brings torrent of water or sewage through node
3	A person is sheltering here: could be a vagrant, a thief, a man on the run, a holy fool
4	A miasma carrying disease (or Sickness spirits) rises up from the depths
5	The floor of one chamber at the node will collapse once a person is 1d4 metres in
6	A will-o'-the-wisp, which is actually a glamour caused by a haunt or wraith
7	A band of dangerous criminals
8	Strange echoes can be heard from a distant chamber; possibly even audible conversation
9	A blessed font has been abandoned; it may have magical properties
10	A glowing trail is visible on the walls or maybe even floating in the air
11	Someone has laid a trap around a feature (roll on Subterranean Feature Table)
12	Minor earthquake causes loose rubble to fall from ceiling
13	A creature lairs here. Choose from: baboon, bear, giant beetle, carnivorous ape*, giant centipede*, crocodile, lion, giant snake, giant spider
14	An undead horror lurks here. Choose from: broukolak (see page 217), ghoul, mummy (guardian), skeleton, zombie
15	An Elemental spirit (earth or water), either passing through or making its home here
16	A human (or humanoid) denizen of the Undercity, possibly inbred or warped
17	Area flooded with flammable marsh gas; naked flames very dangerous
18	A spy or invader is sneaking into the city
19	A madness spirit roams the area
20	This site is impermeably dark; torches will not illuminate this magically dimmed place

** see Monster Island for the statistics of these creatures, otherwise statistics can be found in Mythras*

OCCUPANTS

As indicated on the Subterranean Events Table, parts of the Undercity are occasionally home to all manner of beasts and other inhabitants. The regions closer to the surface are sometimes frequented by the homeless and the destitute, although most do not stay long, partly due to the other occupants occasionally found here. The Hippodrome used to be the scene of fights against exotic beasts and such creatures were also used to execute criminals. These, and the emperor's menagerie, were let loose during the Sack of Constantinople, and their descendants – particularly creatures like crocodiles and giant snakes – dwell here still. Stories of bears and lions living beneath the city have been around since Classical times; these reportedly come out of the Undercity at night to stalk human prey. Finally, the Undercity is a perfect lair for sorcerers pursuing magics they would rather keep secret from the neighbours, and their experiments can linger long after their death. Due to the influence of strange spells and the lurking presence of primal evil, you may wish to add a Chaos Feature (Mythras rulebook, page 275), to some of the creatures (or people) encountered in the Undercity.

EXTENDING THE NODE

To build a larger subterranean complex, simply add 2d3-2 other exits from each location. Then repeat this process for each exit, throwing a d20 with the other dice to represent the start point each time. Large nodes can quickly become confusing with many interlinked layers, and it is best to represent each one on a separate piece of paper and then decide upon their orientation later.

LOCAL KNOWLEDGE

STREETWISE

- (Hard Success): there are tunnels beneath the streets of the city's heart, these join up to form a maze of chambers and passageways
- (Formidable Success): there are rumours that the Undercity is divided into fiefs, each with a king

LORE (BYZANTINE)

- (Success): When New Rome was built on the ruins of Byzantion, it was literally built on top of the ruins. Many streets and buildings were buried
- (Hard Success): Beneath Platea and the Venetian Quarter are mass graves, and beneath Akropolis are buried pagan temples

LOCAL RUMOURS

- "You don't want to go into the Undercity. Nobody but criminals and the dead use those tunnels."
- "Watch out! My cousin's friend's sister said that there were [pick one: giant albino crocodiles/mole men/golems/vampires] living down there!"
- "The Emperor Without a Crown lives in an underground palace. He was a former ruler who has turned into marble by two angels, so his wisdom would not be lost; and he's now back to seize the throne from the usurper Constantine."
- "On the dark of the moon creatures leave the tunnels under the City in search for blood. You'll know them by the chittering noises they make."

DESCRIPTIVE ELEMENTS

Varying levels of darkness – locations near surface may have some natural light; phosphorescent fungi; dry musty smell (Batheia), damp putrid smell (Nekropoleia), wet fungal smell (Nerterion), cramped narrow passages, low ceilings; distant groaning or rumbling sounds, dripping water, detritus caught in tree roots.

UC-1 BASILIKA CISTERN

AFFILIATIONS

Political (praitor)

The largest of hundreds of cisterns dotted around Constantinople to supply fresh potable water to its citizens. It was originally located beneath the Stoa Basilika, a large public square just inside the wallsof Byzantion. The basilica faced the Hagia Sophia and consisted of gardens and a colonnaded walk, but was destroyed in the Nika Riots of 532 and has since been built over.

The cistern is nearly 140 metres long by 64 metres wide, and can hold 100,000 tons of water. The ceiling is supported by 9-metre tall marble columns arranged in 12 rows of 28 columns spaced five metres apart. One of the columns is inscribed with tears, commemorative of the seven thousand slaves who constructed this immense underground chamber. Two of the columns have capitals in the form of the head of Medousa, although one is upside-down and the other is sideways, and both are at the bottom of the column rather than supported by it. This deliberate misplacement was done to gain the Gorgon's protective power but allay her curse. The water is supplied by the Valens Aqueduct (PL-14) which channels water from outside the city to the Great Nymphaion (PL-4), from where it is carried underground.

LINKS

- Chalkoprateia (KN-5)
- Nerterion (UC-9)
- Stheino (IMM-2)

UC-2 BASILIOS ASTEPHANOS

AFFILIATIONS

Deviant (political imposter)

The "Crownless Emperor" is a moniker that has been given to a revolutionary figure who lurks beneath the streets of Petrion. He has met with representatives of the noble families and carefully selected court officials, and rumours have been permitted to circulate as to who he really is, and what he wants. They say that Theodoros Palaiologos, the emperor's elder brother, did not die of the plague two years ago as was commonly reported. Instead, so the rumours claim, he survived two assassination attempts and decided to go into hiding for his own safety

Theodoros was appointed as despot of Morea at the age of 10, the traditional role of the heir-apparent. However, when his father died, it was John VIII who became emperor, and Theodoros was under no illusion that John would pick his favourite Constantine to be heir. Sure enough, Theodoros suffered the ignominy of having to share Morea with Constantine, and later their youngest brother Thomas. He turned to the Franks for counsel and friendship, marrying the pope's niece and becoming a companion of the Venetian Count of Epiros. For this he was punished by having his beloved Morea stripped from him in return for rulership of the city of Selymbria, where he was forced to then faked his own death when two of his younger brothers – Constantine and Demetrios – each tried to have him killed. Both Palaiologoi wanted to take him out of contention to inherit the throne of the empire, figuring that, as the next eldest of Manuel II's sons, he had a stronger claim than theirs.

Theodoros courts anyone who will help him depose his family. There are many power-hungry nobles and courtiers in Constantinople who stand to gain from being involved in a regime change, and Theodoros will have to make concessions to win their support. He has set up his base of operations in a large underground warehouse in the northern section of Nekropoleia, which has been bedecked in stolen finery. The prospective emperor dresses as if his schemes had already succeeded, and insisted that he is addressed appropriately. He favours the byname Porphyrogennetos to emphasise his royal birth and suitability for the throne

All of this is a lie. Theodoros really did die in 1448, and was interred in the Pantokrator Monastery. The Basilios Astephanos is actually Dandolo, a shapeshifting undead creature called an elder ghoul, who has taken the appearance and memories of the royal prince.

LINKS

- Dandolo (IMM-5)
- Pantokrator Monastery (PL-10)
- Nekropoleia (UC-8)

UC-3 BATHEIA

AFFILIATIONS

Cultural (troglodytai), Deviant (broukolakes)

Batheia ("The Deeps") is the name given to the Undercity beneath the Seventh Hill. The hill is riddled with caves, some exist just on the surface, whereas others lead to deeper fissures and chambers at the heart of the hill. The central, deepest region of Batheia is the home of the Troglodytai, and is called The Hive. The Troglodytai have spent generations widening natural tunnels and carving out new chambers. They bring water up from the depths to nourish huge tubers, some the size of a room, which is one of their principal sources of food. Other chambers are filled with snakes and lizards, which they also eat.

Other parts of Batheia have different inhabitants. On the east-facing flank of the Seventh Hill, overlooking the Forum of Arkadios, is a series of caves. Large slabs of hard rock were once separated by soft sandy rock in a series of layers, but the softer stone has eroded away leaving voids between the larger slabs like a block of flats. These voids extend deep into the earth, and the original Thracian inhabitants of the region used to bury their dead here. They are now home to a nest of broukolakes (vampires).

LINKS

- Cistern of Mokios (XR-2)
- The Hive (UC-6)

UC-4 CISTERN OF PHILOXENOS

AFFILIATIONS

None

The second-largest buried cistern in Constantinople (after the Basilika Cistern UC-1). It can hold less than half the water of its rival at 40,000 tons. Two hundred and twenty four marble columns hold up the roof, supporting arched vaults. It lies beneath Argyroprateia near where the East Sophiae meets the Mese Odos. The Palace of Lausos is connected to the Cistern of Philoxenos by a fissure that opened up during the last earthquake.

LINKS

- Argyroprateia (KN-3)
- Palace of Lausos (UC-10)

UC-5 HAGIA DYNAMIS

Congregation Size: 1; Piety: 0%; Magical Strength: 75%

AFFILIATIONS

None

Constantine the Great founded three churches dedicated to the peace, wisdom, and power of God. The first two are the Hagia Eirene and Hagia Sophia respectively; Hagia Dynamis was built underground but all records of this are lost, and it is commonly believed destroyed in the great earthquake of 869.

Hagia Dynamis is located under the highest point of the First Hill, the position of its altar forming a perfectly straight line with those of Hagia Sophia and Hagia Eirene, but because of the rise of the hill, 30 metres beneath the surface. It can no longer be reached directly from the surface; instead one must negotiate the maze of buried streets, find the temple to Poseidon built in the days of Byzantion, and climb up through the roof to reach the cellar of the church. The church has a single inhabitant, a crazy old man who yells incoherently at anyone who tries to get into the church.

LINKS

- Kynegion (AK-7).

UC-6 THE HIVE

AFFILIATIONS

Cultural (troglodytai)

The Hive is the colloquial name given to the tunnels of the troglodytai (see page 221) in Batheia. No one knows what the troglodytai call it. The Hive consists of a maze of twisty little passages, all alike. There are caverns, most of them laboriously excavated by miner caste troglodytai. There are caves set aside for nurseries; the rearing of snakes and lizards for food; cultivation of house-sized tubers; sleeping (which they do in heaps); and, at the very bottom, a brood chamber where the matriarch lives.

Troglodytai are rarely found alone in these tunnels. Soldier caste patrol in squads, and there are usually 1-3 soldiers guarding each mining gang or group of workers. Old tunnels are marked with scent but trapped to deter invaders; typical traps include deadfalls, collapsing ceilings and pits filled with venomous reptiles. The tunnels near the surface often lead to false passages armed with these traps.

LINKS

- Batheia (UC-3)

UC-7 LYKOS THE RIVER GOD

AFFILIATIONS

Deviant (spirits)

Lykos is a *potamos* or River God who has been largely forgotten by the people of Constantinople. The river is only visible in its upper reaches since the last two kilometres of the river – from the Monastery of Libos onwards – is underground. The process of burying the river began in Constantine the Great's day, undercutting the river so that it ran deeper and then bridging the span to allow the Mese Odos to cross it. As the city expanded, more and more of the river was covered, and now it runs under Vlanga without anyone giving it a second thought. This process also buried the shrine where pagans used to bring their boys in order to seek the protection of the god.

LYKOS, INTENSITY 6 NATURE SPIRIT

Characteristics	Attributes
INT: 14	Action Points: 5
POW: 41	Spirit Damage: 2d6
CHA: 15	Magic Points: 41
	Initiative Bonus: +15

Abilities: Animate Water, Bless Luck Points, Demesne, Endowment (Aquatic), Eternal, Manifestation

Skills: Spectral Combat 106%, Willpower 132%

LYKIDES, INTENSITY 3 NATURE SPIRITS

Characteristics	Attributes
INS: 4	Action Points: 3
POW: 22	Spirit Damage: 1d10
CHA: 18	Magic Points: 22
	Initiative Bonus: +11

Abilities: Animate Water, Glamour, Eternal

Skills: Spectral Combat 90%, Willpower 94%

Today Lykos is only remembered by the Kynokephaloi of the Lykos Valley and a handful of human pagans. To those who can perceive spirits, Lykos appears as a bull-horned man with a long eel-like body instead of legs.

Lykos has three daughters, collectively called the Lykides, nature spirits like him but of lower Intensity. He exerts little control over these spirits, who are favourably inclined towards women but have a hatred for all men. Admete ("unbroken") protects unmarried women from being forced into marriage, Zeuxo ("yoked") guards married women against abusive spouses, and Androperseis ("destroyer of men") targets sexual predators for death by drowning. The Lykides appear as beautiful women carrying bundles of green rushes.

LINKS

- Lykos Valley (XR-4)

UC-8 NEKROPOLEIA

AFFILIATIONS

Professional (gravediggers), Religious/Christian (chancellery priests)

Nekropoleia or "Deadtown" lies beneath the Venetian Quarter and Platea, taking in some of the surrounding areas of Vlanga and Petrion. For centuries the dead have been interred underground here in Nekropoleia in koimeteroi or cemeteries. Each has a small chapel with an extensive crypt beneath. Wealthy dynatoi families have their own koimeteron and have their own chancellery priest to say Mass for the dead and to keep grave robbers away. There are also municipal koimeteroi for those without a family graveyard.

The more sinister parts of Nekropoleia are the mass graves (polyandreioi). Throughout its history, Constantinople has been struck by disasters such as plague, earthquakes, disease, riots, and massacres. These events tend to leave many dead in their wake, and it is not possible to give each one a personal burial. In such cases, a suitable area in Nekropoleia is identified – an unused cistern or settling tank, for example, and the bodies are stacked up and then sealed in.

Ever since the Frankokratia, Nekropoleia has had a persistent problem with ghouls. The problem got so bad that in the fourteenth century a band of brave adventurers conducted a purge of Nekropoleia, although they did not find the elder ghoul.

STORY HOOK

Some cemetery priests have as much trouble keeping the dead in as keeping robbers out. One family has a good chance of contracting the ghoul disease at an early age, and as many as half of all their dead family members become undead. Now that a priest's daughter has married into the family, he is keen to know whether his own grandchildren will become ghouls, and contacts the player characters for help discovering the truth.

STORY HOOK

A family inflicted with the ghoul curse keeps all their undead relatives in an underground cellar. They occasionally kidnap shiftless wanderers in order to keep them fed.

LINKS

- ɸ Basilios Astephanos (UC-2)
- ɸ Cistern of Philoxenos (UC-4)

UC-9 NERTERION

AFFILIATIONS

Urban (vagrants)

Nerterion is the easternmost complex of the Undercity, found under the first three hills. The First Hill in particular has an extensive undercity that derives from the Classical Roman habit of building directly on top of a pre-existing structure. Entire sunken streets and buried houses exist on this hill, extending underneath the Great Palace and as far as Argyroprateia. This underground town peters out further west. Vagrants who brave enough to venture below ground sparsely populate Nerterion. While the streets below ground might offer shelter from the cold and the rain, the entrances are few and far between, and rumours abound regarding what lurks beneath.

LINKS

- ɸ Basilika Cistern (UC-1)
- ɸ Palace of Lausos (UC-10)
- ɸ Stheino (IMM-2)

UC-10 PALACE OF LAUSOS

AFFILIATIONS

Deviant (Ktistes)

No evidence remains above the surface of this palace, which once stood next to the Church of Saint Euphemia (KN- 6). It was built upon the order of Lausos, a eunuch of high regard in the court of Theodosius II. The palace was renowned for the vast collection of mythological statues housed within its walls. He collected these from sacked pagan shrines, though he was purportedly a devout Christian.

Lausos' palace and his public collection were destroyed in the great fire of 475, and a later earthquake swallowed what remained and sealed up all access. The palace can no longer be reached from the surface, but must instead be reached through the crypts adjoining the Cistern of Philoxenos. These crypts are filled with statues in marble and porphyry, including some of Lausos' most famous acquisitions, including the Zeus of Olympia, the Aphrodite of Cnidos, the Hera of Samos, and the Athene of Lindos. Along with these mythological statues are countless others, all remarkably lifelike and wearing clothes from all ages of the city.

The Palace of Lausos is home to the Ktistes, a cult of animists who preserve heroes in marble, and wake them when the City is in need of their particular talents. The Ktistes are a tiny cult of six individuals, plus one who resides in stone form. All are employed in stoneworking trades. The palace is always occupied by one or more members, and they have several Inhabited Statues (see page 134) amongst their works that act to protect the collection.

LINKS:

- ɸ Chalkoprateia (KN-5)
- ɸ Cistern of Philoxenos (UC-4)
- ɸ Nerterion (UC-9)
- ɸ The Ktistes (IMM-8)

MYTHIC CONSTANTINOPLE ADVENTURES

And all these marvels which I have related to you, and still many more which we cannot relate to you, did the Franks find in Constantinople when they had conquered it.

~ Robert de Clari, 1204

This chapter is intended to assist the Games Master to create a campaign set in Mythic Constantinople. Firstly there are some campaign themes, independent from any stories but providing the framing narrative for a campaign in Mythic Constantinople. Secondly there are details on the secret rulers of Constantinople, and some secrets about the ubiquitous dogs of the City. Four extended campaign arcs are presented next, these can form the framework of a game in Mythic Constantinople peppered with other stories. Some rules for conducting military campaigns – specifically those involving the fall of Constantinople – come next. Finally, a short bestiary covers a few creatures specific to the milieu.

CAMPAIGN THEMES

The theme of a campaign in Mythic Constantinople intersects with the reason that characters are in the Queen of Cities in the first place. The Games Master might choose the theme based on her players' choices of characters, or she might guide the players into certain backgrounds based on the theme she has already chosen.

THE CITY OF ADVENTURE & WONDER

This is the default campaign theme for the Mythic Constantinople setting; or, rather, it is the absence of an overt theme. In campaigns of this type, Constantinople exists as a place for the player characters to explore. There are plenty of opportunities for fun, profit, and/or danger within its walls. There are no restrictions on character choices: everyone has their own reason for being in the Golden City, and connections between the characters should be decided either as part of the characters' background or else in the first few sessions of play.

Adventures arise from the characters interacting with the city. Every district has its own secrets, and exploration can lead to uncovering some of the bigger schemes at play in the city. This kind of play is sometimes referred to as a "sandbox" campaign, where the players have the agency to decide what storylines they pursue.

> **A BASE OF OPERATIONS**
>
> *A simple way for player characters to know one another is to have them share the same tenement building. Place a tabernai on the ground floor, to encourage the characters to socialise with other characters (player-driven or otherwise), in the neighbourhood. The players can be left to generate the neighbourhood randomly using the method at the beginning of the Constantinople in Detail chapter.*

SAVIOURS OF THE CITY

Implicit to any campaign set in Mythic Constantinople is a sense of impending doom due to player knowledge that the Byzantine Empire meets its end on 29th May 1453 after a six week siege. Even though the characters do not know the imminence or details of its fall, there is a sense in the city that it is only a matter of time before the Ottoman war machine turns its attentions back to the last corner of Byzantium it has been unable to conquer. Rules later on in this chapter allow the Games Master to plan the events that characters might face in this campaign.

However, there is nothing to say that history in your campaign will follow the course of history in our world. The two principal differences between Mythic Constantinople and historical Constantinople are i) the existence of magic; and ii) the presence of player characters. The assumption is that the reality of magic has so far failed to change the course of history from that which we know from our history books, at least not in a significant manner. A magician must be present at a pivotal time, powerful enough to effect a change, and be sufficiently invested in the matter to bother in the first place. Even a well-placed Folk Magic spell has the capacity to change the world, but the identification of pivotal events is much easier in hindsight, and magicians of any kind are rare. Furthermore, animists are mostly barbarians, mystics are introspective and passive, sorcerers are too obsessive or corrupt to intervene in world affairs, and theism is hindered by the ineffability of God.

What really makes the difference is the inclusion of player characters. In this campaign theme, player characters are endowed with the true quality to alter the course of the world. When they do not intervene then history tends to follow its ordained path, but when player characters get involved then the course of fate is permanently altered. This is especially true with supernatural forces in the mix: persons who wield magic are over-represented in the set of player characters.

This campaign theme is perfect for player characters who would like to save Constantinople. Their intervention might only delay the inevitable for a few months or years, or it might entirely change the course of history. For this campaign theme to work, the player characters have to be in a position to make a real difference. The player characters could be the commanders of a mercenary company that comes to the defence of Constantinople. They might mobilise a Catholic army where other diplomats failed, or bring a contingent of Knights of Rhodes into the city. The Byzantines were outclassed in the field of artillery: unable to afford the massive bombards offered by Orban of Brassó, he sold them to the sultan instead. However, player characters might see it a priority to acquire those guns and use them in defence of the city.

CONSEQUENCES OF SAVING THE WORLD

The impact of a Constantinople that does not suffer a final demise in 1453 is greater than merely saving tens of thousands of Christian lives. The Fall of Constantinople was a major contributory factor to the European Renaissance: Western Europe – the Italian city-states in particular – saw an influx of Greek science, philosophy, art, and culture as people fled the Ottomans. They also brought with them books written in Greek, Arabic, and Persian: translations of Classical texts thought lost. This gave a much-needed intellectual boost that allowed the full flowering of the Renaissance to take place. Had all this intellectual talent remained in Constantinople, then we may never have had da Vinci, Galileo, or Bacon.

With the loss of Constantinople, the last hopes of regaining the Holy Land died. Without it, there was no opportunity for a Crusader army to resupply en route to the eastern Mediterranean. Had Constantinople held out a few more decades then it is possible that Christians once more could reclaim Jerusalem. The fall of Constantinople also indirectly contributed to the rise of Protestantism: Jan Hus and Martin Luther viewed the inability of the Pope to mount a counter attack against the heathen Ottomans a sign that they were God's punishment for the sins of Rome.

ON HIS IMPERIAL MAJESTY'S SECRET SERVICE

For this story arc, the player characters all work for the Office of the Drome (ORG-25) in some capacity. This government ministry is the postal system and diplomatic corps, as far as its public face goes. However, the Office of the Drome is also responsible for the internal security of the Byzantine Empire. It is a combination of the foreign secret service and homeland security, and this campaign theme gives the player characters the opportunity to play a team of spies (or "sparrows"), both at home or in neighbouring countries. One week they might be negotiating the guild politics of the Republic of Venice, and the next searching the streets of Vlanga for terrorists determined to bring down His Majesty's government.

This campaign theme is very much driven by the Games Master, who must provide the player characters with missions given them by their superior. The degree to which they have a license to act autonomously depends on experience and past performance. Naturally, most of the threats to the security of the empire come from the Ottomans, and the Games Master might want to introduce a counter-agency run by the Valide Sultan to provide suitable antagonists.

Characters can be anyone loyal to the Empire. It is more likely that these will be native Greeks, and characters may have semi-permanent cover identities. Varangian Guardsmen or the Paramonai are a natural choice to provide muscle.

OTTOMAN HEROES

The assumption has been so far that the player characters are Greek – or at least, Christian – but this need not be so to adventure in Mythic Constantinople. The Empire is technically a subject state of the sultan, and Turks have freedom of movement through its territory. There is even a Turkish community resident in the city. It is therefore entirely possible to take the alternate view, that the player characters are Ottomans: either Turks or their subjects. Due to the shared religion, Arabs would fit well into such a party as well.

To Turks, the Greeks are gavuriye (infidels) who partake in a godless culture. They over-indulge in alcohol, eat pig-meat, bathe infrequently, and their women concern themselves with the affairs of men. From the Ottoman perspective, the desire to conquer Constantinople is a desire to purge these decadent behaviours and remove a corrupt emperor from the throne. In the Ottoman way the people will be free to continue in their faith after their subjugations; indeed the Orthodox Church will be made the arbiter of the law over the Christians of the empire, forcing them to adhere to the Christian code of morality or else suffer the penalty prescribed by holy law. This belief in a post-conquest utopia is not just indoctrination on the behalf of the Turks: in Rumelia there is plenty of evidence of the benevolence of Ottoman rule.

THE ATHANATOI

As described later in this chapter, there is a cult of animists called the Ktistes who can preserve worthy individuals in marble and awake them centuries later, none the worse for wear. They have done this throughout the existence of Constantinople, in order to safeguard its talent and provide a potent backup of heroes if things look dire. In a campaign of this ilk, the characters can be drawn from any period of history, and were preserved by the Ktistes at the height of their power. They have no memory of the intervening years, so usually require a précis from the cult member who awakens them.

A particularly dramatic way of implementing this campaign theme is to have the characters all wake up in the Palace of Lausos to find themselves under attack. They have no knowledge of who or what is assaulting them. After the battle they discover that they are from different periods of history, and were woken by the Ktistes before their demise as the best hope in combating the evil that has destroyed the cult and now threatens the City. Since the characters have no memories of the intervening time, they may initially struggle to fit in with Constantinople in the current era.

If the player characters are all Athanatoi, then they should be at the peak of their professions and abilities. This might be an opportunity to roll up true heroes. Consider giving each character four (or more) points to spend on the following table.

ATHENOI STARTING BENEFITS

Benefits	Cost
+50 Bonus Skill Points	1 point
+1d6 to one Characteristic, but no higher than the species maximum	2 points
1 Gift (Mythras page 202) or Charism (page 77)	3 points

THE IMMORTALS (IMM)

Constantinople has been called The Immortal City, but it is equally accurate to call it the City of Immortals. There are at least two groups that can rightly claim the title of immortal, although they are not explicitly associated with one another.

IMM-1 TO IMM-7 THE ATELEUTOI

There are no less than seven truly immortal beings that live within its walls, all of whom have a keen desire to see Constantinople thrive. They all achieved immortality through different means, but over the years have gradually become aware of each other's existence. Clashes between them in the past have caused upheavals that have threatened the security of the city, and for the last five hundred years or so, they have all agreed to abide by a loose code that prevents them from interfering with each others' plans where that interference might result in the city's downfall. Together they are the Ateleutoi, or Endless, and some would characterise them as the true rulers of the city.

The nature and character of the Ateleutoi are very different from one another, but they are of one mind concerning the importance of Constantinople. That is not to say that all the Immortals are supporters of the Empire – some would love to topple the Palaiologians or else have no interest in the current rulers at all – but they all agree that the city must persist.

IMM-1 HEKATE

The Goddess Hekate is the eldest of the Ateleutoi, and the architect of the pact that limits them. She has been present in The City from the very beginning: hers was the first temple to be established on the Akropolis, and she has watched over it ever since. Her symbol – the crescent moon and the star – is the oldest symbol for the city itself, and can be found engraved on every building, ancient and modern. She is the goddess of witchcraft and the underworld, daughter of the titans Perses ("Destruction") and Asteria ("Starry One"). Hekate was old when the gods took Olympos, but unlike the other titans she did not war with them, and for this she earned recognition as a goddess. She has a number of cultic epithets, including Phosphoros (light-bearer), Skylakagetis (leader of dogs), Nyktipolos (Night Wandering), Aidonaia (Lady of the Underworld), Enodia (Lady of the Crossroads), and Brimo (the terrible one). She has a triple-aspected form, sometimes depicted as a woman with three faces or in monstrous form with the heads of a dog, lion, and horse. Her familiars are a dog and a polecat.

Most of the old gods have gone, abandoned by their worshippers and unable to reach mortals after the destruction of their temples and statues. Hekate survived through the secret devotion of a cult of witches that continued to offer her worship despite persecution. She spends much of her time with her sentience distributed amongst the city's dogs in a form of passive possession, which gives her remarkable knowledge of the affairs of her beloved City. When she needs to deal more directly with others she overtly possesses the body of a (willing) member of her witch cult. Those taken over by Hekate see it as a great blessing, despite being incapable of remembering anything while being used in this manner. On the rare occasions that she takes spiritual form, she should be considered an Intensity 10 Ancestor spirit.

Hekate's interest in The City is simple: she has been its patron since the founding of Byzantion and wants to see it persist under Greek ownership. She is reluctant to intervene directly, since Zeus had strict rules on divine interference when he was King of the Gods and old habits die hard. However, she is not above subtle manipulation, using dogs or witches as her intermediaries.

HEKATE

Characteristics	Attributes
INT: 24	Action Points: 9
POW: 66	Spirit Damage: 1d8+1d6
CHA: 24	Magic Points: 66
	Initiative Bonus: +24

Spirit Abilities: Bless, Curse, Eternal, Puppeteer, Sagacity (Folk Magic, Invocation, Lore (occult), Shaping), Shapechange, Spellcasting (Folk Magic), Spellcasting (Sorcery), Subjugate, Persistent, Warding, Wither

Skills: Folk Magic 148%, Invocation 148%, Lore (occult) 148%, Shaping 148%, Spectral Combat 140%, Willpower 182%

IMM-2 STHEINO

Stheino is one of the original gorgons, being the eldest sister of Medousa. She migrated here sometime in the Classical age, and is the ruler of Nerterion in the Undercity. She claims to be the daughter of the gods Phorkys and Keto, and sister to Medousa, the original gorgon. The myths say that the three sisters were once exceptionally beautiful but Medousa was violated by Poseidon in Athena's temple, and the outraged goddess turned her and her sisters into hideous monsters of such terrible aspect that they could turn flesh into stone. Medousa was slain by Perseus over three thousand years ago but of the three sisters only Medousa was mortal, so it is possible that Stheino, eldest of the three, is who she claims.

The gorgon's main home is the Basilika Cistern, a palace grand enough for the goddess she claims to be. Although she is monstrous in form she is not a monster in personality, although she is imperious and expects due reverence. She keeps her nature secret using her magic and a hooded cloak, and any who succumb to her Gaze attack are sunk into the dark waters of the cistern. Despite her caution, most denizens of the Undercity know her as a person to be avoided, and, if needs be, obeyed. She has vast knowledge as a consequence of her great age and is aware of many of the plots, motivations, and in some cases secrets of the main players in Constantinople. Stheino

prefers to keep away from all intrigues, and aggressively resists all attempts to involve her in schemes; while she can be induced to give away some of the secrets she knows, she will not do so for free.

If the characters end up fighting Stheino, then they will find her a tough match. She is a gorgon with maximum Characteristics (Mythras rulebook page 247). Unlike lesser gorgons she has a human body (albeit a large one), with a pair of black feathered wings. The snakes that take the place of her hair have red scales and she has flared nostrils and huge boar-like tusks – and yet despite this her voice is pure silk and honey. Her hands are brass, and end in vicious hooked talons. In addition to the other powers of a gorgon, Stheino has command over Folk Magic, and may still be able to access some of her former powers as a priestess of Aphrodite. Given her age and abilities, she may have discovered a way to permanently reverse the effects of her Gaze attack and could withhold this knowledge to gain control over the characters. The poisonous ichor that runs in her veins in place of blood will bring her body back to life 1d6 days after her death, her body healed of all damage done to it.

Stheino wields the Harpe of Kronos, the adamantine sword with a hook-like protrusion that Perseus used to decapitate her sister. This weapon is unbreakable and never dulls; furthermore, it was designed

STHEINO

Characteristics	Attributes
STR: 24	Action Points: 4
CON: 21	Damage Modifier: +1d10
SIZ: 24	Magic Points: 18
DEX: 24	Movement: 6 metres, 18 metres (flying)
INT: 21	Strike Rank Bonus: +23 (–5 for armour) = +18
POW: 21	Armour: Hoplite armour on upper body, scales elsewhere
CHA: 18	Abilities: Flying, Gaze Attack, Immunity (poison, disease, old age), Terrifying, Venomous
	Magic: Folk Magic 120% (any Folk Magic spell)

1d20	*Location*	*AP/HP*
1–3	Right Leg	2/9
4–6	Left Leg	2/9
7–9	Abdomen	2/10
10	Chest	5/11
11–12	Right Wing	2/7
13–14	Left Wing	2/7
15–16	Right Arm	5/8
17–18	Left Arm	5/8
19–20	Head	2/9

Skills
Athletics 78%, Brawn 88%, Deceit 62%, Endurance 82%, Evade 68%, Flying 88%, Insight 72%, Locale (Constantinople) 125%, Lore (city intrigues) 150%, Lore (mythology) 150%, Perception 82%, Seduction 79%, Stealth 62%, Track 72%, Willpower 82%

Passions
Crave Solitude 90%, Uphold Neutrality 80%, Hate Insolence 65%

Combat Style & Weapons
Combat Style: Gorgon Horror (Harpe, Talons, Snake Hair, Gaze, and Bow) 88%

Weapon	Size/Force	Reach	Damage	AP/HP
Harpe	M	M	1d8+1d10	Unbreakable
Talons	L	M	1d6+1d10	As for Arm
Recurve Bow	L	L	1d6+1d10	4/8
Snakes	S	S	Venom	As for Head
Gaze			Special	

by the gods to be able to cut anything, physical or otherwise. Its powers include (but are not necessarily limited to):

- The harpe ignores any natural or worn Armour Points;
- If it causes a wound, inflicts the Bleed Special Effect in addition to any other Special Effects;
- On a critical Attack Roll, the harpe decapitates its target and severs the bond between body and spirit (as per a Sever Spirit Miracle of Intensity 10);

- If a fetish is destroyed by the harpe then the spirit within is dissipated;
- The harpe's touch severs any magical effect or enchantment (as per a Dismiss Magic Miracle of Magnitude 10).

Stheino's overriding goal is to be left alone. She still grieves her sister's death and would love revenge on Perseus, but Zeus put him in the stars and therefore forever beyond her reach. Unable to achieve vengeance, she wants solitude. She doesn't care if people inhabit the city above her, and certainly doesn't care if they are Catholic Franks, Orthodox Greeks, or Muslim Turks. As long as they leave her alone, she'll permit them to dwell there. What she cannot allow is the violation of her subterranean home.

IMM-3 ZOTIKOS

Zotikos has no idea how he became an immortal. Unlike all of the other Ateleutoi, Zotikos' long life appears to be a cosmic accident. He was a minister during the reign of Justin II (r. 565–578). He established the Orphanage of Saint Paul, and the Office of the Orphanotropheion was established to continue his good work. The last thing he expected was to find himself present as a spirit at his own funeral. Experimentation taught him that he can animate dead flesh and possess the living, but his biggest breakthrough was when he observed a death for the first time. As a person's soul leaves its body, Zotikos can slide in and become the new soul within the body as if it was its natural inhabitant. Zotikos can use his Healing Spirit Ability on any body he inhabits, but not those whom he merely possesses. Practically, this means that Zotikos can assume a new body by inhabiting the freshly dead and healing it of its cause of death. If he cannot find a suitable dying person, he can animate a corpse or control a living person until he finds one.

Over the last nine hundred years, Zotikos has lived many people's lives. Some he has had for a long time, others for just a few years. In some of these lifetimes, despondency or anger have ruled and in others he has lived a venial and hedonistic life in the hope that this might bring an end to his endless reincarnation. Over the last century or so he has made peace with himself and with God (who he holds responsible for his condition), and has only taken bodies with the consent of their natural owners: people suffering from fatal wounds, critical diseases, or with incurable pain. Although he gets to live out the rest of their lives, he promises he will do so with respect, and bring honour to their memory.

Since the very beginning of his unnatural lives, Zotikos has served as the Orphanotrophos. When he assumes a new identity, he approaches the Master of the Orphanage of Saint Paul and identifies himself as the new Orphanotrophos using a pass phrase devised by the "last" holder of the post. He is a masterful politician. More than many, he has the capacity for the exercise of patience, sometimes planning his schemes over lifetimes. He builds relationships amongst the city's orphans, using them as sources of information and leverage. He cares deeply for people – not just those of his flock – and while he might use people, he never exploits them. All of his intrigues now are for the betterment of mankind and the preservation of lives, and this occasionally puts him at odds with the other ministers. His investments have made him very rich but the profits all this wealth is poured into the running of his office, maintaining a modest lifestyle for himself.

Zotikos currently inhabits the body of Michael Serron (NPC-21), and has done so for the last 40 years. He is aware that this body is wearing out, and is looking for a suitable replacement.

IMM-4 'ELIOU SKOTIDES

'Eliou is the leader of the vampires (broukolakes, see page 217) of Xerolophos. He was born in the middle of the ninth century, the unwanted son of a prostitute who forced 'Eliou into her trade, selling him from a young age to the perverted appetites of the city's elite. Everything changed for him during the great earthquake of 869. The tremors opened a fissure in the Seventh Hill, and released a long-trapped creature calling itself Akhkhazu the Seizer, an ancient broukolak imprisoned underground before the building of Byzantion. The withered and broken creature offered 'Eliou eternal life and boundless power in return for his soul, and the youth was eager to accept. He took the epithet Skotides, meaning "son of darkness" as a tribute to his patron and to counteract the irony of his birth name (which means "of the sun"). Akhkhazu was an animist dedicated to the worship of the primordial darkness, who he claims had spoken to him during his long years of imprisonment. After teaching 'Eliou his secrets, Akhkhazu disappeared. 'Eliou started to prey on the local populace and spreading fear, targeting particularly children who had a happy home life. He began to gather to himself any living broukolakes he discovered and instilling in them a reverential fear of himself. Those who refuse to worship him are destroyed.

The worship of Erebos the Primordial Darkness is 'Eliou's principal interest. He teaches Folk Magic and rudimentary Animism to some of his broukolak 'children' while they are still alive, choosing only the most pliable of his brood. 'Eliou is paranoid about maintaining his dominance over the cult. He can only directly control his minions through his Domination Gaze Attack, and this requires effort and Magic Point investiture he would rather avoid. He chooses his disciples carefully, selecting those with the least ambition and will (typically those of below-average INT and POW), a policy that results in substandard but easily controlled sorcerers. He limits what his disciples learn and keeps them fighting amongst themselves for his favour, preventing them from uniting to challenge him. Finally, he is not above dispatching any of his disciples who grow too strong. To 'Eliou's frustration, someone is teaching priests how to lay a living broukolak to rest permanently; and he has yet to identify this as the Order of Kappa-Pi-Alpha (ORG-30). Where he can he interferes with this process, possessing individuals who then spread false information about the procedure.

In appearance 'Eliou is a handsome young man of perhaps 19 or 20 years, dressed in the simple garb of a moderately wealthy man. He has short black hair and dark skin; his blue eyes are unusually intense. Unusually for the current age, he is clean-shaven. His age is occasionally betrayed by archaic speech and mannerisms, particularly when being courteous. In his spiritual form he is equivalent to an Intensity 6 spirit.

Ultimately, 'Eliou's goal is to bring eternal night to Constantinople by blocking out the sun with sorcery. He believes that the Prophecy of Leo speaks of this very circumstance. With no light, he can walk the streets with impunity and, more importantly, he can summon forth Erebos the Primordial Dark.

If 'Eliou is expecting trouble, he will bring his Animism to bear. He should be considered a high shaman who can bind up to 17 spirits each with up to POW 42 (Intensity 6). Favourite tricks include

'ELIOU SKOTIDES

Characteristics	Attributes
STR: 24	Action Points: 4
CON: 11	Damage Modifier: +1d6
SIZ: 13	Magic Points: 44
DEX: 30	Movement: 6 metres
INT: 15	Strike Rank Bonus: 23
POW: 44	Armour: none
CHA: 17	Abilities: Allergy (Sunlight), Darksight, Gaze Attack (Domination), Immunity (mundane weapons), Undead, Vampiric, Vulnerable (black hawthorn)
	Folk Magic: Bladesharp, Calm, Darkness, Demoralise, Glamour, Incognito, Tire

1d20	Location	AP/HP
1–3	Right Leg	0/5
4–6	Left Leg	0/5
7–9	Abdomen	0/6
10-12	Chest	0/7
13–15	Right Arm	0/4
16–18	Left Arm	0/4
19–20	Head	0/5
17–18	Left Arm	5/8
19–20	Head	2/9

Skills
Skills: Acting 49%, Athletics 69%, Brawn 67%, Courtesy 57%, Deceit 92%, Endurance 62%, Evade 115%, Insight 59%, Language: Lydian 85%, Language: Latin 75%, Language: Venetian 55%, Literacy 55%, Locale (Constantinople) 115%, Lore (Cryptography) 88%, Perception 79%, Willpower 128%, Stealth 85%, Streetwise 81%, Teach 72%, Track 56%
Spiritual Skills: Spectral Combat 141%
Magical Skills: Folk Magic 101%, Binding 135%, Trance 114%

Passions
Passions: Crave Blood 41%, Fear Usurpers 91%, Hate Life 96%, Reject God 137%, Serve Erebos 141%

Combat Style & Weapons
Psilos (sling, longsword, hatchet, hoplite shield; Skirmisher) 94%, Unarmed 124%

Weapon	Size/Force	Reach	Damage	AP/HP
Bite	M	T	2d6	As for Arm
Talons	M	M	1d4+1d6	As for Arm
Longsword	M	L	1d8+1d6	6/12
Sling	L	-	1d8	1/2

spirits that can Bless him with 2 extra Action Points, 3 extra Luck Points, up to 6 Armour Points, a movement rate of up to 12m, or the Adhering Ability. He also utilises bane and curse spirits as booby traps, placing them in easily-broken fetishes scattered through his lair. If he can choose the location of an encounter, he'll prepare a location binding of a Darkness Elemental, otherwise he might embody the creature.

IMM-5 DANDOLO

Dandolo is an elder ghoul, an intelligent undead creature able to create and control ghouls (see page 218). After the Sack of Constantinople the city's dogs were more than happy to tear apart the bodies of the Franks, but hundreds of thousands of Greeks lay dead in the streets and the dogs would not touch them. The Venetians brought Dandolo here in chains and made a deal with him for his freedom. He was put in a building with a hundred prisoners, and soon had an army of ghouls to consume the bodies of the dead. Then, according to the pact with the Venetians, he and his army disappeared into the Undercity and kept away from its new rulers. No such pact exists with the Palaiologians, and Dandolo has had free reign since the Restoration

When the ghouls of Nekropoleia were discovered, gangs of hunters were sent into the Undercity to eliminate them. Dandolo and a handful of regular ghouls survived this purge, and he has been keen to keep their numbers down to escape notice. The name Dandolo is a curse on the lips of the modern Greek, since Enrico Dandolo was the Doge of Venice who orchestrated the Sack of Constantinople. What relationship Dandolo the ghoul has to the doge is unknown.

For the last two years, Dandolo has been masquerading as the Basilios Astephanos (UC-2), which he has managed to keep secret from the other Ateleutoi. Elder ghouls usually adopt another's persona for a short time in order to trick their foes, and this long-term disguise has started to affect him in unexpected ways; taking on some of the personality of Theodoros Palaiologos. He pursues revenge against the Empress Helena who loved Constantine more than any of her other sons; and also hates Demetrios Palaiologos, who now rules in Morea after a failed coup against Constantine. Dandolo can revert to his native form when he wants, as he has preserved the flesh of Theodoros and only needs a mouthful each time to resume his form. He has avoided taking any other forms while maintaining this disguise, so he doesn't muddle up the memories he obtained from the dead prince.

Dandolo's long-term plan to become emperor will be in ruins if The City is lost to the Ottomans before he bring it to fruition. Were he to sit on the throne he believes that he can hold the city against the Turkish Empire through the simple act of creating thousands of ghouls from the city's inhabitants.

IMM-6 SISTER ZOË

Zoë is the youngest of the Ateleutoi, having attained her immortal status just 150 years ago. She is a nun at Zoödochos Pege Monastery (XR-11) and became a Hesychast early in her novitiate. During one of her meditations she experienced a vision where she was brought into the presence of the Light of Heaven by a golden chariot with fiery wheels. When she awoke from this ecstatic experience, she discovered that her cell had been bricked up: she had been meditating for over 17 years, and her sisters believed her to have died while enraptured. She has not aged a day since she entered that meditative trance and still has the appearance of a young woman in her mid-twenties, despite being over 175 years old. She believes that her exposure to the Light of Creation burned away her mortality, and that she is a sign for the Second Coming, where all Christians will be resurrected in incorruptible bodies such as hers.

Sister Zoë is accompanied at all times by a Divine spirit, whom she addresses as Selatiel, which is the name of the archangel of worship and prayer. Her conversations with this numinous being can be disconcerting to those who can only hear the earthly side of the discussion.

The nun views Constantinople as the bastion of Orthodoxy. She does not believe that the faith will persist if the city falls, and acts to keep it in Christian hands.

IMM-7 KYPRIANOS

The sorcerer who goes by the name Kyprianos was born to the Kantakouzenos family in the Empire of Nicaea, before the Restoration. He changed his name when his family disowned him after discovering his sorcerous studies, but he harbours no specific ill-will towards them. He named himself after Saint Cyprian in the naïve hope that this saint (himself a sorcerer before converting to Christianity) would guard his soul against the dark taint of magic. In his seventy-sixth year he had finally scraped together enough lore to achieve a grand working, and made himself effectively immortal through magic. He no longer ages, and though he still has the appearance of an old man (at least when he doesn't use an illusion), he suffers from none of the debilitating conditions of extreme age.

Kyprianos has amassed a vast library on magic, and has even written a spell codex of his own. His name has influence amongst the magical cognoscenti (although few suspect he is still alive), and there are at least four spell codices attributed to him that he did not write, and are of substandard quality. He destroys copies of these fakes whenever he finds them. The Games Master can assume he has access to all Folk Magic spells: those he does not actually know he can learn in a week from one of his many spellbooks.

Kyprianos's immortality recipe consists of a Combined spell of Abjure Old Age (which keeps him from growing any older), Abjure Senility (which saves him from mental degradation), Abjure Decrepitude (which keeps his body unaffected by the passage of time), and Enchant. The enchantment is protected by as many points of Magnitude that he can afford, in case a rival discovers his secret and tries to unweave his magic. Should the spell fail, then Kyprianos will suddenly gain all the effects of ageing that he has abjured for centuries. His backup plan is to cast Abjure Senility on himself to restore his mental facilities and then escape to a secure location using Teleport (this secret haven has an Enchanted Mark). He is never without a reservoir of Magic Points via Store Manna, and has several other enchantments.

Kyprianos believes that there are secrets hidden beneath the city that will allow him to ascend to godhood. He has determined that the Anemodoulion (KN-2) is the key to his ascension, and is not prepared to let the city fall until he has plundered its secrets.

IMM-8 THE KTISTES BYZANTEION

This is a small and highly secretive animist cult who have existed in The City since it was called Byzantion. Their name literally means "Builders" or "Masons", but it is used metaphorically for those who found cities or build nations. The surviving Ktistes are the remnants of a cult of magical architects and sculptors who were responsible for creating the inhabited statues (see page 134) that are dotted across the city. They rarely create such bindings now, but still practice their non-magical trades of masonry and statuary whilst curating their most important workings, the Athanatoi.

An Athanatos is a person who has been given a form of immortality in return for agreeing to serve the city. The person is turned into a marble statue, which preserves her indefinitely. An Athanatos can be woken up when she is needed and returned to her stone sleep when the need has passed. She is unaware of the passage of time between her waking periods, each of which typically lasts just a few months. An Athanatos's lifespan is no longer than any other human, but her life is not lived continually, but rather split into short chunks of living separated by long stretches of not living.

It is not clear how many enmarbled heroes the cult has at its disposal, but there are some who are many centuries old. Their goal is to preserve the best and the brightest of the city, preserving knowledge and skills in marble. The Ktistes are choosy in picking their targets for their brand of immortality: in the past they chose mighty warriors because the threats to the city were from barbarian raids and pirates but since the Frankokratia they have chosen all manner of worthies, recognising the need for diplomats and politicians, and men and women of faultless morality as well as soldiers. If the city is under threat then the Ktistes awaken members of their collection to aid in its defence. Should the City ever be lost, then the heroes can remain asleep, safe against the day that the City is restored to glory. They only ever immortalise one of their own number at a time, as insurance against their knowledge being lost. The majority of their collection is housed in the sunken Palace of Lausos (UC-10), although caution has led them to make other caches of Athanatoi across the city.

Enmarbling (*marmaromenos*) is achieved through two spirit bindings. The soul of the living person is drawn into the Spirit World by the High Shaman of the cult, and the first binding is to have an earth elemental spirit inhabit the vacated body, converting it into incorruptible marble. Most Athanatoi adopt a supine posture when enmarbled, as if they were a graven image on a sepulchre, but some prefer to become statues and strike a dramatic pose. The second binding unites the disembodied soul with an amnesia spirit, thus keeping it safe from boredom and resulting madness. With the body preserved in marble and the soul preserved in the Spirit World, the person can survive for centuries. Restoration can be performed by even the lowliest adept, releasing the two bindings and restoring the person to flesh by summoning him using his name. For the restored individual, no time will seem to have passed. If the statue is ever destroyed – which is difficult due to the occupying elemental spirit – then the person has no body to which to return and they cannot be restored.

IMMORTAL STORIES

- The player characters are exploring the Undercity and they stray into Stheino's territory. She has no desire to harm them, but employs scare tactics (with the help of her magic) to make it clear they are not welcome.
- The player characters find a ghoul lurking around Kyra Martha in Elebichon (XR-3), acting in a very un-ghoullike manner. It is currently directly controlled by Dandolo. The elder ghoul is suffering from memory leakage from his assumed persona, and has started to wish personal ill on the Dowager

Empress – a sentiment from Theodoros Palaiologos, not his own – and is planning a raid on her monastery.

- Sister Zoë begins a public religious movement seeking to process the most holy ikons of the Theotokos through Constantinople's streets. Her aim is to remind people of their beliefs and to bolster faith, but she attracts the attention of various unsavoury characters who would rather that their people's consciences remained unpricked. The characters might get involved when they uncover a plot to murder the nun, without realising she has no reason to fear assassinations.
- Kyprianos seeks a magical enchantment buried in a deep vault; and he employs the player characters, disguised as a scholar, to retrieve it for him. They must be careful that he doesn't simply dispose of them once they've done what he asks.
- The Ktistes found an enmarbled statue that was not in their ledgers. A junior cult member awoke the man, only to be promptly killed. The man is a blackguard who had conned a previous generation into preserving him to escape justice. This man out of time is now loose in the city, causing trouble for the player characters.

THE REPUBLIC OF DOGS (DOG)

The people of Constantinople are very fond of their dogs. The city has a great number of them; most are feral and spend their days on the streets and in the hills. Others luxuriate at home with doting owners. Many live both lives; staying with humans when it suits them – especially during the winter – and roaming free at other times. Those families that do not have a family pet of their own put out scraps for the numerous feral dogs that roam through all districts.

The affection that the citizens have for dogs is said to go back to the time of Byzantion. The pagan goddess Hekate (IMM-1) was the first patron of the city, and one of her familiar creatures is the dog. It is said that Hekate alerted the militia against a surprise night attack by Philip of Macedon by causing the city's dogs to start barking. This is still an important role that both house dogs and feral dogs perform; once one animal is disturbed at night the others in the neighbourhood will start up such a noise that it will startle housebreakers and villains of all description. The dogs also remove any edible refuse from the streets and control the rat populations. Food is not the only thing that the dogs clear away: after wars or plagues, they have been seen removing human bodies as well. After the Sack of Constantinople, it was noticed that the dogs of the city did not eat the corpses of the slain Greeks, but they attacked the bodies of the fallen Franks with great viciousness, seemingly unsated by the flesh they consumed.

The affection that the citizens have for dogs is said to go back to the time of Byzantion. The pagan goddess Hekate (IMM-1) was the first patron of the city, and one of her familiar creatures is the dog. It is said that Hekate alerted the militia against a surprise night attack by Philip of Macedon by causing the city's dogs to start barking. This is still an important role that both house dogs and feral dogs perform; once one animal is disturbed at night the others in the neighbourhood will start up such a noise that it will startle housebreakers and villains of all description. The dogs also remove any edible refuse from the streets and control the rat populations. Food is not the only thing that the dogs clear away: after wars or plagues they have been seen removing human bodies as well. After the Sack of Constantinople, it was noticed that the dogs of the city did not eat the corpses of the slain Greeks, but they attacked the bodies of the fallen Franks with great viciousness, seemingly unsated by the flesh they consumed.

Unknown to virtually everyone, Hekate still looks after the city through its dogs. Most of the time, the goddess fragments her consciousness amongst all of the city's canine residents, making each one a little smarter. When they congregate together, this consciousness shares information that they all know, and they are more intelligent as a pack than each individual would be alone. By using messengers between packs, Hekate can quickly learn what any of the dogs in the city know, and if she reconstructs her intellect again she can pass this information to mortals.

HOUSE DOGS

Greek families in Constantinople often keep dogs as companions. Dogs frequently accompany their masters on errands, providing company and protection. They are used as alarm dogs and/or guard dogs against housebreakers. Many act as both playmates and protectors for the household's children. Dogs have also been trained as service animals for the blind and assistants to the infirm and crippled. In more rural settings they may be flock guardians or herding dogs, or used for hunting.

These house dogs lodge permanently with a family. They may be descendants from pets kept by the human's own ancestors, or they might one day adopt a family by wandering into a house. There are few Greeks that would turn away such an offer, believing that a house with a dog is particularly blessed. Not everyone has a dog, and not everyone who wants a dog can keep them. The dogs are discerning: some people cannot get a dog to stay with them no matter what they do. The neighbours of such people likely mutter about them when they go by.

Companion dogs exhibit characteristics of specific breeds, such as small white lapdogs, lean rangy hunting hounds, and broad-shouldered dark guard dogs. The most common breeds seen in Constantinople are:

- The *alopekis* is similar to a slightly-built modern corgi, with pricked ears, wedge-shaped head, short legs and a strong body. They typically weigh 4-8 kg (SIZ 1d2) and are usually white or light fawn, occasionally with brown and black patches. The alopekis is used for hunting and as cow-dogs.
- The *kangal* originates in Anatolia. It is a sturdy dog used as a flock guardian, with a solid tan coat of short hair and a black mask. The kangal has a wide head and typically weighs 50–80 kg (SIZ 1d6+9).
- The *kokoni* is a small to medium-sized dog (4-8 kg, SIZ 1d2) with dropped ears, a short muzzle, and curved tail. They have long wavy hair that is usually either black and tan or cream and white. They make great companion animals, being cheerful and affectionate; they also make great alarm dogs because of their deep bark for their size.
- The *kressa kyon* or Cretan Hound is a hunting breed originating on Crete but spread throughout the Aegean. They

are exceptionally swift and excellent for hunting hares and birds. The kressa kyon is slender (15-20 kg, SIZ 1d2+2) with a wedge-shaped head, pricked ears, and a long and upwards-curving tail. They are mostly tan or fawn in colour, sometimes brindled.

- The *molossos* of Epiros is an impressive dog at 70-100 kg (SIZ 2d4+12). It is the ancestor of many European Mastiff breeds, and was bred as a livestock guardian and war dog. They have massive heads, wide and short muzzles, and a heavy dewlap, and are typically white or fawn, sometimes with a black mask.
- The *poimenes* or Greek sheepdog is an all-purpose dog good at herding and protecting sheep from predators. It is similar in body shape and hair length to a modern Newfoundland; but smaller at 30-50 kg (SIZ 1d4+5). Their coats are made from dense fur of black and white patches.

STREET DOGS

The feral dogs of Constantinople take a number of different forms, some clearly deriving from the specific breeds mentioned earlier. However, unrestricted breeding often means that the dogs start to blend features and while all types can be found, there are many who have a common set of characters: small to medium sized animals with either tawny coats and darker muzzles and feet or else white with black and/or liver-coloured patches. They are quite friendly to city residents but wary of strangers.

These dogs organise themselves into packs based on residence in a particular area. They do not discriminate by appearance, and a pack – typically four to 10 animals – may be all shapes and sizes. While the packs have their own territories, there is rarely any aggression between visitor and resident dogs; only if a pack makes a concerted effort to move into another's territory is there any squabbling. Dogs lucky enough to live in a neighbourhood with abundant food will not object to other packs coming onto their territory to eat once the pack has had its fill, but they had better wait their turn if they want to avoid being nipped.

ARCHIKYONA

Amongst the many dogs of Constantinople there are a few that are possessed of a humanlike intelligence. How this comes about is unknown and follows no discernible pattern — intelligent dogs will have pups of normal intelligence and vice versa. There is also no apparent preference for intelligence amongst feral rather than companion animals, although there are proportionally more of the former, and thus more intelligent dogs are street dogs.

Each archikyon is intelligent (roll INT on 3d6 rather than assign an INS score), but cannot speak and does not use tools. They can understand Greek (and possibly other languages as well), but are careful not to make this too obvious. An archikyon can be taught how to use a human invention such as a door handle or a cart, but cannot grasp the concepts behind tools, and must learn its use as a 'trick' much like a normal dog. If faced with an unfamiliar device it cannot divine its purpose. Thus an archikyon can learn to open a specific door using the handle, but cannot apply that learning to an unfamiliar door with a different handle. An archikyon has a lifespan commensurate with a human's.

The archikyona appear to be leaders of dog kind, and some have dubbed this the Republic of Dogs, with the archikyona taking the role of Plato's philosopher-kings. The following archikyona are examples of the 20 or so that live in Constantinople.

- Stitke ("Spot"), a large dog similar to a poimenes but solid white except for a single black spot on his ear. His constituents are the large white dogs particular to Stoudion district.
- Myia ("Fly"), a small fawn and white kokoni who is the companion (and guardian) of a nun. She gets her name from her constant activity.
- Antheos ("Blossom"), an immense molossos who is as gentle as a lamb.
- Krauge ("Yelper") is a scrappy medium-sized mongrel with a short tan coat. One of her ears is pricked, the other dropped. She represents the dogs of the Lykos Valley.
- Iaspis ("Jasper") an all-black mongrel who looks like a large kokoni. He has the powers of a Mystic.

DOG STORIES

- A dog has adopted the player characters and taken to following them around. One day she starts to bark ferociously at someone, either a friend of the characters, or perhaps even one of their number. She won't attack, but whimpers and flinches if her target gets too close. The person in question is an imposter: maybe a mortal sorcerer using illusions or shape-shifting, or else a malicious spirit possesses the person instead. Does the dog spoil the infiltration attempt, or is the imposter able to front it out? What is the motive of the imposter?
- A rat swarm has systematically been killing all the dogs in the neighbourhood. What agency is in control of the swarm, and why has it taken such an exception to the canines?
- A horrific creature has been brought into Constantinople via ship, a hyena. The local dogs are eager to see it gone, and will do their best to herd the player characters toward it, as long as they are armed appropriately to deal with it. Worse still, upon its death the hyena returns as a ghoul. For the statistics for a hyena, use those of a wolf but increase SIZ and STR by 3. If it manages to Grip its prey then on subsequent turns it can spend an Action Point to automatically inflict damage without needing the Attack Action as it tears at its prey.
- A dog trots up to a player character and drops a human hand at his feet. The dog will lead them to the hidden corpse of a man in the brocaded silk of a courtier.
- A dog is digging around a cobblestone. If a player character inspects the stone, she will find a gold coin beneath it. Now it has been uncovered, the dog is content and will saunter off. What is the significance of the ancient coin? Why does everyone the character meets try to possess it?

NAMES FOR DOGS

Asbolos ("soot"), Atkis ("sunbeam"), Bremon ("growler"), Dromas ("runner"), Harpalos ("seizer"), Ichnobates ("trail-follower"), Kanache ("gnasher"), Khara ("joy"), Lachne ("shaggy"), Lakon ("Spartan"), Phonax ("butcher"), Spherkon ("speedy"), Thoös ("swift"), Thymos ("plucky"), Turbas ("topsy-turvy").

THE SILKEN WAR (SLK)

Out of 12 governmental ministries, the Department of the Military Fisc is ranked tenth. This rank is indicative of the budget it receives from the Chancellery, and yet it is expected to outfit the entire army and navy, hire the mercenaries that the Army Office is increasingly relying upon, and maintain the military food stores at a state of readiness. A substantial drain on resources are the bombards and gunpowder demanded by the emperor. Failure to meet the obligations of the office would be a huge disgrace for the Military Logothete, the minister who heads the department.

THE SCHEME

Two years ago, the Serbian Despot Durad Brankovic donated a large amount of money towards the repair of Constantinople's walls despite being a vassal of the Ottoman Empire. The wheels of government run slowly, but the Office of the Military Fisc has been finally authorised to spend this gift on its intended purpose. The emperor has commanded the repair of the Land Walls of Theodosios, in particular the section called the mesoteichion (the "middle walls") that cross the Lykos Valley between the Romanos Gate and the Charisios Gate.

Unfortunately, the Military Logothete Manuel Iagaris no longer has the money. Some of it was used to pay off the huge budget deficit that Iagaris had inherited upon taking the post and the rest was lost on a series of ill-advised investments and failed ventures. Not daring to admit his mistake, he seeks to create a cover-up scandal in a rival department while he finds some way to replace the money. His target is the Imperial Archives; partly because they rank higher (and thus have a larger budget) than his own ministry, and secondly because his family have long feuded with the Tzamplakontes who currently control the Archives. Iagaris has never been able to understand how a department of pen-pushers and ink-monkeys could ever warrant a larger budget than his own.

Fortuitously, an acquaintance of Manuel Iagaris, a monk called Neophytos, has come up with precisely the right scheme, which preys on the social ambition of Constantinople's inhabitants. Every year, at the Anniversary of The City ceremony on the 11th of May, the emperor confers awarded dignities onto selected subjects. These dignities are honorary, but are indicators of status and permit the individual to attend court, where he might make contacts and find opportunities for social climbing. Traditionally, these dignities have been difficult to obtain, but Iagaris and Neophytos have colluded to make them available for sale to all comers. They have been doing this through a dupe in the Imperial Archives, who has access to the scarlet ink and the imperial seal. Better still from Iagaris' viewpoint, the dupe is Nikolaos Tzamplakon, the dim-witted son of the First Secretary.

The scam has a limited life. Once the Anniversary of The City comes around and the fake dignities are not conferred by the emperor, the deceit will become known. However, all evidence will point to Nikolaos Tzamplakon as the author of the scheme. The Imperial Archives will be shamed, and their demotion can only benefit the Office of the Military Fisc – plus the money troubles of Iagaris will be over.

THE CONSPIRATORS

MANUEL PALAIOLOGOS IAGARIS, MILITARY LOGOTHETE

Manuel suffers from having two brothers who are much more accomplished than he is. The eldest Andronikos distinguished himself in the Morea, orchestrating the restoration of the Hexamilion wall at the entrance to the Peloponnese. His second brother Markos is the most famous of the three, he was prefect of the militia and protostrator under Emperor John VIII, and for a short time served as mesazon, making several ambassadorial visits to the Pope and to Venice. Both Andronikos and Markos qualified as oikeioi of the emperor, an honour that Manuel – despite bearing the Palaiologos name – has never been awarded. Although he has risen to be one of the emperor's 12 cabinet members, he could barely be more politically distant from the emperor, ranking 46th in the hierarchy. Needless to say, Iagaris is embittered and disillusioned with his lot in life.

Manuel Iagaris is short and unassuming. Now entering his sixth decade his waistline has expanded somewhat in recent years. A fondness for Turkish sugar has left him with rotten teeth and the siphon disease (diabetes) which sometimes leaves him overcome with profuse sweating and occasional fits of mania. He keeps his greying beard trimmed closer than propriety permits, and has his head shaved daily by his house slave. As a logothete, Manuel wears a red epilorikon and white overtunic rather than a kabbadion, and a turban on his head rather than one of the various court hats. The constant pain from his carious teeth leaves Manuel in a perpetual bad mood, something that is not helped by having three wayward children (their mother died young, it is said, purely to spite Iagaris).

MANUEL IAGARIS BRYENNIOS, DOMESTIC OF THE WALLS

Manuel Bryennios is the son of Manuel Iagaris' sister. His uncle Markos found him a commission in the Army Office, and through his connections he has risen far. As Domestic of the Walls, Bryennios is responsible for the landward defences of The City. Assistance in this task is supposed to be forthcoming from the Stratopedarches of the Tzakones (ORG-34), who technically reports to Bryennios. The young officer, a scion of the Komnenoi, is as unhelpful to his commanding officer as he can be without being insubordinate.

Manuel Bryennios ranks at the 58th place in the empire's hierarchy of proclaimed titles. This puts him a dozen places beneath Manuel Iagaris, and his namesake uncle is keen to use this as well as their familial connection and their difference in age to browbeat his nephew into a subordinate role, despite the fact they are in different government department. Bryennios was brought in to give his uncle plausible deniability; Iagaris will not hesitate to allow his sister's son to shoulder all the blame should the con be uncovered, and has been cautious to ensure that there is no paper trail which leads back to himself. Bryennios is largely ignorant of his uncle's scam; he knows that the old man is up to something, but prefers to stay out of it.

Manuel Bryennios is in the prime of life, and keeps himself in shape with weapons training. He maintains a short soldier's hairstyle and beard, and his day clothes have a military cut; for example he prefers the soldier's short cape (sagion) instead of the more typical khlamys. His kabbadion – when he must wear one – is in the red and yellow of the Army Office, accompanied by a skaranikon with a red tassel. His honorary rank of spatharios is indicated by a white cloak with a purple tablion and a sword with a gilded scabbard.

NEOPHYTOS OF RHODES

A hieromonk of stavrophoros rank who is co-conspirator – indeed, he is the architect of the scheme – of Manuel Iagaris. Neophytos (born under the name Nikodemos) has been an inhabitant of the Monastery of Christ Pantokrator (PL-10) for many years. He is a fervent anti-Unionist and close personal friend of the Notarades and godfather to two of Loukas Notaras' children. However, should anyone bother to check, they will find no record of his birth or monastic training in Rhodes; indeed, the whole persona of Neophytos is a sham. Neophytos is actually an astomatos (see page 57), trained as a sorcerer and master of the Shapechange to Human spell. It has been left to the Games Master to decide how far-reaching its plans go: has this creature always been Neophytos, or has it adopted this disguise after murdering the original? Do its plans stop at getting rich, or is its more nefarious goal to prevent the repair of the mesoteichion – a situation that would greatly benefit Mehmed II when he becomes Sultan and enacts his plan to take Constantinople.

Neophytos' main role in the running of the scheme is to procure clients who wish to buy a dignity. He negotiates the price and then introduces them to Nikolaos Tzamplakon. He then collects the money that he deposits with Manuel Bryennios (who believes it is destined for the repairs).

Neophytos has all the hallmarks of an Orthodox monk: a great black bushy beard, long dark hair, and a heavy black robe with a wooden cross sewn over his heart. He has unusually intense amber-coloured eyes, and is missing the top joint of one of his fingers. He carries a silver nosegay filled with a subtle perfume; nourishment to the mouthless monster that he really is inside.

NIKOLAOS ALEXIADIS TZAMPLAKON, HYPODIKAIOTES

The youngest son of the Protasekritis Alexios Palaiologos Tzamplakon. Nikolaos has never shown any sign of his family's legendary intelligence, and his father despairs that he will ever find him a vocation to which he is suited. In the meantime, he has found him a job in the Imperial Archives as assistant to the dikaiotes, whose job it is to issue all imperial proclamations. It is an important but dull job, and Nikolaos is easily bored. His co-workers in the Archive recognise his inappropriateness for the role, thus his byname "Alexiadis" which acknowledges that he is only here because he is the boss's son.

Nikolaos plays the key part in the scam, although as far as he is concerned the selling of dignities is perfectly legitimate. He knows where the carmine ink used in imperial proclamations is stored, and where the dikaiotes keeps the imperial seal. Persuaded by the silver tongue of Neophytos, he saw nothing wrong with reducing the workload of his superior officer by preparing the award documents himself (did we mention that Nikolaos is a bit stupid?).

STORY PATH

SLK-1: A DIGNIFIED INDIVIDUAL

The player characters discover that dignities are available for sale from the Imperial Archives. This can happen in a number of ways: if they come into money (perhaps as a result of LEO-1, for example) then Neophytos might approach them directly. Alternatively, they might want to or need to improve their social standing – in order to attend the right party, attract the right patron, or gain the attention of an extremely selective courtesan. They might also be investigating for a friend or contact who seeks a dignity for their son.

> **BASED ON REAL EVENTS**
>
> *The chronicler Leonardo di Scio records that a "Manuel Iagari" and "Neophytus of Rhodes" were charged by Constantine XI with overseeing the restoration of the walls of Constantinople. They embezzled approximately 20,000 florins (=aspra) and left a treasure of another 70,000 florins in a clay jar for the Turks to find.*

Either way, they encounter Neophytos, who makes the introduction to Nikolaos Tzamplakon and, if they are purchasing a dignity, takes their money and departs. The hypodikaiotes then fills in all of the paperwork, writes the award, and affixes the seal. It costs 60 hyperpyra (about 1200 SP) to be made a strator (groom), right up to 300 hyperpyra (about 6000 SP) to become a deuteropatrikos (deputy patrician), the highest rank on offer.

Soon after purchase, there will be a test of the authenticity of the dignity. Perhaps they are at that fancy party and they are challenged to a duel of etiquette when it is discovered that the title has already been awarded to another individual. Maybe the courtesan has heard of people purchasing rank in this manner and she is scornful of its mettle. Although the award has yet to be made (the emperor will confirm all dignities on the 11th of May, the Anniversary of The City), it stands up to scrutiny. In confirming the dignity however, the characters approach Neophytos again, and during this process they may overhear a conversation, find some legal document, or financial ledger that suggests that not everything is entirely on the level.

SLK-2: THE GOD-GUARDED CITY

In order to keep up appearances, Manuel Iagaris arranges for the restoration of the Pempton Gate, which sits in the middle of the mesoteichion. Manuel Bryennios is responsible for organising work, and assembles a team of workmen. Through some fortuitous mix-up in the Imperial Archives, the holder of the dignity amongst the player characters is assigned as an imperial overseer of the works. While at the Walls, the characters find that the soldiers that Bryennios assigns them as workmen to be unimpressed by their rank, having heard the rumours around the barracks. Furthermore, a priest arrives to cause trouble: he is a scholar who has studied the legend of the Girdle of the Theotokos (see page 12), and is convinced that the divine protection of the city will cease if the Pempton Tower is pulled down. His interference might seem like an annoyance – certainly Bryennios has no time for fairy tales – but the Tzakones disagree. The doctrine of the Theophylakteopolis ("God-guarded city") is a honoured tradition in their unit, and they take up the cause of the priest.

While the characters try to calm matters down, disaster strikes. The demolition already wrought by the work crews has already damaged the Pempton Tower enough, and it collapses. The Girdle is destroyed, and mere moments later a creature stirs. Imprisoned beneath the mesoteichion was an earth elemental that was causing earthquakes, but the Girdle of the Theotokos rendered it incapable of harming its prison and thus effecting an escape. Now it is free, and it desires vengeance on the humans who trapped it.

SLK-3: THE SCENT OF TROUBLE

In order to thank the player characters for their help at the Pempton Gate, Manuel Bryennios invites them to a party. It will be a good opportunity for them to mingle with the dynatoi, mostly from the Notaras-Laskaris-Iagaris faction amongst the Nine Families. They will see their old friend Neophytos again, but this time he is conspiring with Manuel Iagaris. The last time they saw him he was working for the Imperial Archive, which is opposed to Iagaris' department much as Iagaris himself is at odds with the Archive's chief minister.

If the characters do not already have suspicions about the hieromonk, they should do now. Neophytos has not been particularly conscientious about hiding away incriminating evidence. It should be a simple job for anyone snooping around in his affairs to connect him and Iagaris as the recipients of the money for the dignity-selling enterprise – which is looking more and more like a scam. If the characters trail Neophytos, it is possible that they will witness him transforming back to his natural form and flying away.

What the characters do now is up to them. They could approach the Imperial authorities and report the conspirators. More discretely, they could take the matter to the First Secretary who runs the Imperial Archives. Or, they could attempt to blackmail either (or both of) Neophytos or Manuel Iagaris.

SLK-4: FISC OF FURY

If the player characters have not themselves spoken to the First Secretary of the Imperial Archives, he discovers the scam some other way. He quickly realises that the Military Logothete was trying public shame the Tzamplakon name and the Imperial Archives. Since the Military Fisc won't admit it was defrauding citizens and the Imperial Archive won't own up to the mistakes of a junior member, a covert war between the two ministries begins. The player characters might be affected by these events, or they might just be part of the backdrop of other stories.

- There is an embargo on the ingredients for gunpowder, particularly the difficult-to-procure Hazelwood, used to make charcoal for the highest quality powder. The Military Fisc is no longer able to supply the army what it needs.
- Army engineers "accidentally" demolish an Archive building to make room for a new military storehouse.
- The Imperial Archives "misplace" all the purchase orders issued by the Military Fisc; as a result there is no meat in the soldiers' daily ration. Since pork (and beef twice a week) is guaranteed by the contract they hold with the government, the soldiers go on strike. If this situation persists too long, there may be a riot.

SLK-5: TWO WAY DOUBLE-CROSS

With his fraud in tatters, Manuel Iagaris is left with a dilemma. He now has the funds to repair the mesoteichion, but he also has access to the most money he has ever seen. Over 90,000 aspra were collected, and the temptation is finally too great – Iagaris decides to steal it and abscond to Italy. Unfortunately for him, Neophytos has the exact same idea. This is also the response if the characters try to blackmail either one of them.

There is no way that Manuel Iagaris will risk trying to take all the cash with him. He takes 20,000 aspra and hides the rest in a clay jar in the new foundations of the Pempton Gate, planning to return for it later. He asks his nephew to find him some guards to help him out the city, and it is possible that the clueless Bryennios will ask the player characters to help get his uncle as far as Epibatos, where he intends to take a ship to Milan. If the characters are instead trailing Iagaris, they'll witness him concealing the money at the Pempton gate.

At some point – in the interests of dramatic necessity, when the player characters are present – Neophytos will catch up with his partner, intending to double-cross him just as he is himself being double-crossed. The false monk will have summoned some help, a flock of harpies summoned from outside the city (most likely from Pegai Krenidai, PR-8), with a combined usage of the Draw Harpies and Enslave Harpies spells. A battle royale follows, and to the winner goes the spoils.

Assuming that the player characters prevail, they must decide what to do with the money stolen from so many families. If they report the affair to the emperor, they'll lose the money but might get their dignity legitimised as a reward. Regardless, the mesoteichion is still in disrepair and the Girdle of the Theotokos banished, which was perhaps Neophytos' plan all along.

REBELLION! (REB)

Dissatisfaction with the empire has never been higher amongst the populace of Constantinople. The demoi feel trapped in the city, surrounded by enemies on all sides, and the government is bribing the Ottomans rather than fighting them. Rabble-rousers within the market places and tabernai are spouting invective against the rulers, exhorting the people to rise up as they have done in the past. None of this ire is directed at the person of the emperor, who has been cast as a man manipulated by the false counsellors that populate his court. What is needed, so say the demagogues, is for the bureaucracy of governance to be washed away and for the emperor to be given back control of his empire. This new Constantine should be recast in the role of his illustrious namesake, first of his name, and he should lead the empire to victory. The fomenters of rebellion have taken on the name and symbolism of the Prasinoi or "Greens", the circus faction of several hundred years ago who represented the will of the common people. Allegiance to the Prasinoi is demonstrated by wearing a green band on the arm, a green sash around the waist, or a green hat around which the white turban is wrapped.

THE PRASINOI

Information about the Prasinoi as a faction can be found in Chapter 6 (ORG-32). They are characterised as anarchists by the establishment but their stated aim is strongly monarchical. They want to bring down the government and restore authority to the emperor. Their main targets are the Office of the General Fisc (which is responsible for taxation – see page 106), and the Chancellery (particularly the Praitorion) as the instrument of government most commonly wielded against the common people. The Imperial Archive is another common target: under the (largely accurate) belief that without records, the government cannot function correctly. Due to the military-like precision of some of their actions, an accusation of collusion by the army (if not the Army Office itself) has been levied.

The Greens started their overt terrorist actions during the reign of the previous emperor, but since the ascension of Constantine XI, they have stepped up their attacks on the state machinery. Examples of their activities include:

- ϕ digging up the Mese Odos the night before market day
- ϕ releasing a savage bear in the Forum of Constantine
- ϕ concerted violence against Hungarian merchants after the battle of Varna
- ϕ numerous fires in government warehouses
- ϕ personal attacks against minor bureaucrats
- ϕ attempt to destroy the Praitorion with a huge gunpowder charge (this was discovered by accident and defused before it could do any damage)

THE INSTIGATORS

The disorganised nature of the Prasinoi is at least in part due to multiple forces instigating their actions. Each of these instigators seeks to use the Prasinoi for its own purposes.

THE KANTAKOUZENOI

It seems odd for one of the dynatos families to support a group whose stated aim is to bring down the basis for their own power. However, the Kantakouzenoi – who control the Army Office – have tried legitimate means to shake the hold of the Notaras-Laskaris alliance over the Imperial Court to no avail. The scheming is in the hands of Philippos Kantakouzenos, cousin of the Grand Domestic and an allagator in the Army Office. Andronikos Kantakouzenos has given tacit approval of his kinsman's meddling, although he is maintaining a professional distance.

One of the most successful of Philippos' plans is to get veteran soldiers, particularly those with experience of scouting or munitions, to infiltrate Prasinoi cells and lend their expertise. Most Prasinoi have no training in the skills necessary for a successful terror campaign, and before the Kantakouzenoi got involved, many of the Prasinoi managed to harm themselves or get themselves caught; success rates have greatly improved since. There has always been a degree of sympathy between the army and the common people: in the days of the circus factions, the original Prasinoi were traditionally allied with the Rousioi (the Reds) who represented the interests of the army, and many of these army veterans were chosen for this role because they believe in the goals of the Prasinoi.

The Kantakouzenoi are entirely unaware of the other two influences on the Prasinoi.

BARTOLOMEO GIUSTINIANI

An influential Genoese statesman, Bartolomeo Giustiniani represents his albergo on the inner council that runs Pera. He is also first cousin to the ruler of Samos, and a major shareholder and board member of the consortium which runs Chios and its valuable trade in mastic and alum. His intent is to destabilise Constantinople just when it needs its strength the most, allowing an independent Pera to eclipse the city and take its place as the trading capitol of the world. He is acting on the instructions of the Genoese government, although Ilario Doria (NPC-16), the podestà of Pera, is unaware of this plan, and would be horrified were he to find out

For their truly outrageous schemes the Prasinoi need money, and Giustiniani has been bankrolling them for some time. He knows several groups involved in Prasinoi actions, and an intermediary in a military satchel delivers the money. Occasionally, suggestions as to how they spend the money are offered. Giustiniani has provided no means for the Prasinoi to contact him, and no clue that he is supporting more than one cell. Bartolomeo is aware of the influence of the Kantakouzenoi in the Prasinoi, and has exploited this knowledge well, always careful to leave a trail back to that family rather than himself should anyone uncover his scheming. The intermediary he uses is always Greek, and briefed by a Gasmouli co-conspirator rather than Giustiniani himself, and the intermediary is lead to believe that the instructions are coming from the Kantakouzenoi, the Army Office, or both.

Giustiniani is ignorant of the third player in the game; he has heard the rumour of the survival of Theodoros Palaiologos and his designs against the throne, but does not realise his true nature nor connected Theodoros to the Prasinoi.

THE EMPEROR WITHOUT A CROWN

Some of the Prasinoi are being manipulated by the ghoul Dandolo (IMM-5), masquerading as the emperor's brother Theodoros Palaiologos, otherwise known as the Emperor without a Crown (UC-2). This group, located primarily in Platea, believe the lie that Theodoros faked his own death after two assassination attempts, one from each of his surviving brothers. The aims of these Prasinoi are at odds with the others since they seek to replace Constantine XI with his brother.

Dandolo is aware of the influence of the Army Office over other groups within the Prasinoi, and has also detected Genoese support for the revolutionaries, although he has yet to identify the principal.

THE GOVERNMENT'S RESPONSE

The running conflict between the Vardariotai and the Prasinoi is the hot topic of discussion around the public fountains, and has even been the subject of songs intended to rile the Praitorion by making its employees look like foolish bully-boys. However, it is the job of the Office of the Drome to deal with internal security of the Empire, and after a conspicuous attack by the Prasinoi, the first question asked at court is "where were the agents of the Drome?". The Grand Logothete has accused the Logothete of the Drome for failing in his duty. The Drome refuses to respond to these accusations, ostensibly to preserve the secrecy of ongoing missions of his agents. The implication is that there are spies within the ranks of the Prasinoi, although only Thomas Strouthion knows the extent of the infiltration.

The mesoi are threatened by the rise of the Prasinoi. Of all the groups that will suffer if the populace rise up in rebellion, it will be the businesses of the middle class that will suffer the most. They depend on the current political system and an obedient work force. As a response, there is a movement to oppose the Prasinoi by the resurrection of the Venetoi, or Blues. This circus faction was the traditional rivals of the Greens, and the Venetoi is akin to a neighbourhood watch scheme. Those businesses who have taken the pledge, and who display the blue and white chequerboard flag, have promised to share information and keep a watchful eye on each other's property. Those wearing the Green are not welcome in these establishments. Some feel that the Venetoi are denying themselves business and making themselves targets, so not all shops are signed up to the Blue Pledge.

STORY PATH

This story path may need some adaptation depending upon the attitudes of the player characters. As written, the characters start as innocent bystanders that get involved on behalf of an acquaintance. However, the characters may have a prior connection to the Prasinoi (either sympathetic to their struggle or appalled by their methods), or they may develop these feelings as the story develops. The Games Master should encourage this engagement with the setting.

If the player characters have a vested interest in either the Prasinoi or its opponents, then you might consider running encounters like a military campaign (see later), with the Prasinoi's objective to accumulate so many Minor successes that there is a city-wide rebellion against the Chancellery.

REB-1: ARSON INVESTIGATORS

The player characters are in their favourite taberna one evening when it is set on fire. They may be alerted by the smell or by shouts from outside. The front of the property has been daubed in green paint. The owner – a friend or acquaintance of the player characters – asks them to investigate so he can bring arson charges and perhaps recoup his losses. Clues gathered by the characters implement some discharged soldiers, who are suddenly protected by a wall of bureaucracy. However, the crime was actually instigated by Giustiniani as a hit against Perios, an inspector of the Special Fisc who regularly drank at the taberna (and may have been rescued by the player characters). The agent had been investigating irregularities in the tax payments of a Genoan-owned business.

REB-2: THE BURNING ISSUE

The characters hear about another fire, this time in the neighbourhood of Kanikleion. This would be unremarkable except that it affected a storehouse of the Imperial Archive which just so happened to have the written report of Perios' investigation. If the characters are still looking for the responsible party in the previous fire, they might investigate. This time, one of the men left behind some incriminating evidence, allowing him to be tracked down and captured, although not without a fight. All he can reveal is the fake story he was told, but he does know of another Prasinoi cell that uses a hideout in the Undercity.

REB-3: THE DEATH OF COCK ROBIN

Following the lead given by the captive in the last story, the player characters know where a group of Prasinoi meet. They might seek to join or infiltrate the group, but they will find these are revolutionaries of a whole different variety. They are followers of the Basilios Astephanos, and their activities go beyond terrorism. When the player characters first encounter them, they believe that one of their number is an agent of the Drome and is preparing to execute him. The man is not a "sparrow", this is a setup by Dandolo to test the mettle of those he has working for him. He doesn't want those who would baulk at murder. If the characters are joining (or pretending to join) this group, the dilemma might be left to them: is their cover worth executing someone in cold blood, even if the victim is a terrorist? Of course, there is always the possibility that the potential victim is a sparrow after all...

REB-4: DOUBLE TROUBLE

If the characters are ensconced within Dandolo's cell, then they will be invited to help plan and execute a dramatic attack against the establishment. There is about to be a very important wagon train enter Constantinople: the Count of the Mines is bringing gold bullion that is to form the wages of the court ministers. This unusual collaboration between the General Fisc and the Special Fisc is a perfect opportunity to strike at the government. Unfortunately, another Prasinoi cell has exactly the same thought, and the characters will find themselves opposed by a military-trained unit sponsored by the Kantakouzenoi.

During the activity or its planning, the player characters should also have the opportunity to realise that their boss is Theodoros Palaiologos – or even that he is masquerading as him but actually something altogether more sinister.

REB-5: SMOKE ON THE WATER

The characters learn of a Prasinoi plot to set fire to the Byzantine fleet on Saint Andrew's feast, which coincides with a naval inspection by Emperor Constantine. They may pick this up from an informant, or else be amongst "Theodoros'" agents chosen to do it. The risk posed to the emperor is contrary to Prasinoi aims, so whether the player characters are for or against the Prasinoi, they will want to stop this plot. This is in less than a day's time, and the characters do not have the time to convince the authorities of the plot if they want to save the ships. One ship is loaded with gunpowder, and linked to the others with oil-soaked ropes to spread the flames. Is this a cover for an assassination attempt on the emperor by his "brother" Theodoros? Or is it a Genoan plot to leave Constantinople defenceless by sea?

THE PROPHECY OF LEO THE WISE (LEO)

Leo VI, called "the wise" because of his education, was an emperor of the Macedonian dynasty. He was the youngest son of Basil I, a common-born man who usurped the throne from Michael III. Copies of The Prophecy of Leo the Wise began to circulate only a few years after his death in 912, although it is not clear whether they were actually penned by the emperor himself.

The prophecy attributed to Leo VI consist of 13 to 15 individual oracles, depending on how they are divided up. Each prediction consists of a symbolism-laden illuminated image and accompanying text. Copies of these books are popular throughout Europe although, because The Prophecy of Leo the Wise is quite short, copyists and booksellers have frequently interpolated the text or included text from other prophetic works (such as The Vision of Daniel) or fictionalised histories (most commonly The Tale of the True Emperor), in order to charge a higher price from their customers.

What is not commonly known is that the prophecy itself is sentient. It has an existence separate from the written text, and an awareness of events around it. The best current theory from human scholars is that the prophecy is Metatron, the literal Voice of God – an entity of a different order to angels that came into being when God first spoke the Words of Creation. As a supernal being, concepts like time and space are meaningless, allowing it to both speak prophecy and be present in several locations simultaneously, although it is by no means omniscient. Since it has no material or spiritual manifestation, it cannot be perceived and is immune to all magical and mundane phenomena. The prophecy communicates with chosen individuals, although because of the means of its communication (see below), its intentions in doing so are not clear. Is it trying to alert people of the disasters it has foreseen? Alternatively, is the prophecy trying to bring about the events it describes; that is, fulfil itself? If this is a true prophecy emanating from God (as is commonly believed) then doesn't this contradict the doctrine of Free Will, and suggest a mechanical universe of ordained events?

The prophecy has two powers. It can cause writing (in Greek) to appear on any unpatterned surface: on parchment, tiles, plastered walls, flagstones, wooden boards (as long as the grain pattern is not prominent), even on exposed human skin. The words have a consistent handwriting style and have the appearance of being written with a quill on parchment regardless of the surface they appear on. The words persist as long as desired by the prophecy; some of its words have lasted over a hundred and fifty years.

The prophecy's second power is to cause anyone within sight of its text to begin to recite what is written, even if they cannot normally read or understand Greek (although they must be capable of speech). The reciter can stop at any time – there is no compulsion to read out the words of the prophecy – but if they do so the prophecy can cause another person (if there is one available) to immediately take up the recitation without pause. It takes a trivial amount of concentration to stop the prophecy using one's voice once one is aware of the prophecy's presence, but most people affected by this power for the first time are too startled to stop, and it usually gets a sentence or two before quelled.

When writing and speaking in these manners, the prophecy may only use words that have been used within the corpus of its individual oracles (as found in an unadulterated copy of The Prophecy of Leo the Wise). This gives it a lexicon of about five hundred words, although many of these words are somewhat specialised and archaic. Those communicating with the prophecy can find it frustrating to understand due to this restricted vocabulary. For example, it can use the numbers from one to 12 (with the exception of six), and also 15, 40, and a thousand. All other numbers must be reached through arithmetic using the numbers it can use. It lacks many common adjectives and all proper nouns. Thus merchants are "lucre-seeking men", Turkish soldiers are the "war-men of the sunrise empire", and Franks are "those who follow in the Antichrist's wake". The prophecy can refer to all the letters of the Greek alphabet and might use these to identify individuals or qualify its meaning. So "the lucre-seeking men of the second letter not the third" might mean specifically Venetian merchants, representing them with beta, the second letter of the Greek alphabet (pronounced 'v'), rather than the third letter gamma which would be used to refer to the Genoese. The corpus does not contain the pronouns "I" or "me" and the prophecy rarely refers to itself.

The communications of the prophecy should be seen as utterances rather than conversations. It occasionally engages in dialogue and can understand words that it cannot itself use – and while it communicates in Greek it seems to understand all languages. However, the prophecy does not indulge in idle words and if questioned will more often remain silent than respond.

THE ORACLES

Scholars have argued about The Prophecy of Leo the Wise since the book was first circulated. It is widely believed that each of the individual oracles within the book consists of an illustration and corresponding text; this is certainly true of some of the chapters but

THE ORACLES

Oracle	Illustration	Sample of Text
1	A she-bear with the head of a griffon nursing four dog-like cubs	"You fawn, suckle and rejoice in a miserable way, holding out your hands and curling your toes...how will any word you utter ever benefit The City? What kind of good could you do, you shameless dog, you who are closely attached to a foreign sting."
2	Two crows biting a snake	"you alone are the wretched serpent, the bear-killer. Oh, how you will fall prey to horrible ravens! [...] You, mightiest of the birds, having assumed power from the south, you will end your days on a horse when the morning star is in the centre of heaven's vault."
4	King holding a sickle in one hand and a rose in the other, crowned by an angel. He stands on the severed head of a child	"In wet places you will fail unexpectedly, for in you the beginning and the end is a horn. [...] The cow is the fifth in line and the end of the bear-feeder. Its shape shows its place and its character."
6	Fox with three standards thrust through its body, those of the Empire, the Pope, and Saladin.	"Oh, wretched and woeful city [...] when K will have reigned for a long time: for blood and murder there will be within you. When the eleventh has been shut in, it will not come to an end and the five choicest of the empire will break the monster that killed the south-westerly wind."
8	Throne with a dismembered arm below	"Scythe-bearer, I give you four months then the choicest will all perish by the sword. For a short while you will erect temples for idols. Having lived three times three lifecycles, old man, go to Hades, leaving two in the middle."
9	Diptych of i) Unicorn with a crescent moon on its haunch; ii) Angel bearing the imperial crown	"That first letter will cut off a rose: see, it is the M, that letter, for [...] he will not spare you, you who remain true to imperial power. Look to him, he starts harvesting."
12	The Emperor hand in hand with the Pope	"May you live, you the dead one with the deeply sad face. After bringing all the best together you will scatter the illegal trophy of injustice. But when the biggest star will appear black then go back naked deep into the bowels of the earth."
13	Embalmed emperor with an angel above and two monsters below	"For when a column predestined by fate will be seen in the sky, an invisible messenger will call thrice in a loud voice: hasten to the western part of the City of Seven Hills and there you will find a man. Lead him to the palace, him whose skull is shaped like a half moon [...] and once again, O City of seven hills, you will obtain the power." "When the even number of suns doubles an even number of times, he will return dead into the rock."

then there are some images that seem to have no relevance to the words ascribed to them. It may be that the text and the images have become muddled by copyists, and the situation is further confused by adulteration with text from similar books. Neither the illustrations nor the text are numbered, and some of the images that were diptychs in earlier works have become separate images in later copies. The table on the previous page gives the most likely reconstruction of some of the original oracles; the others are left for the Games Master to invent.

The images in the text are not mere illustrations; they are as much part of the prophecy as the text. They are richly detailed with symbolism, although not all has been retained in cheaper copies. As well as images and text, the oracles also consist of cryptograms, anagrams, and cross-like diagrams bearing letters. The significance of these has not yet been interpreted, but scholars believe that they are key to understanding the text.

The Legend of the Enmarbled Emperor

Several oracles feature the enmarbled emperor (*marmaromenos basilios*). This legend is given within the text of the oracles, but it is the subject of a popular tale widely known in Constantinople. The legend states that there is an emperor who everyone believed was killed in battle, but instead he was taken up by angels and turned into marble. He sleeps in this form in an underground chamber beneath the Old Golden Gate (or perhaps the Sigma). Confusingly, a version of the story says that this has not yet happened but will come to pass.

The legend also holds that in the fortress of the New Golden Gate, beneath the roots of an ancient fig tree sleeps an old man with a long white beard. His name is John, most versions of the legend call him Saint John the Evangelist, but some say he is John V Palaiologos. He holds a book in his hands that contains a list of all the sins of man. He mumbles in his sleep: "the time has not yet come. The hour has not yet arrived. The remission of sins has not come to pass". While he sleeps, the Gate to the city is closed.

On one day some time in the future, when the city is overrun with the enemy, John will awaken and fling open the Golden Gate, and the armies of seven nations will storm the city and slaughter the occupying enemy. The bloodshed will last three days, until John leaves the Gate, bringing calm in his wake. He walks up the triumphal way, and stops at the Old Golden Gate to awaken the sleeping emperor from his stony slumber. People will recognise the true emperor although they will have never seen him before. During his reign the City of Seven Hills (the prophecy's name for Constantinople), will regain its former glory and the whole empire will prosper as it did in days of yore. The emperor will guide his people onto the righteous path, for he is the embodiment of all that is good.

One version of the legend ends with the eternal reign of the true emperor. Another says that a dark star will appear, and the true emperor will become the target of envy. In the last days he will return naked to his rock and be considered to be dead as he was before.

A Conspiracy of Words

There are several individuals in Constantinople with first-hand experience of the Prophecy of Leo the Wise that have gone on to make its study their life's work. They pursue any reported occurrences of the prophecy, document eyewitness accounts, and transcribe any remaining text. They are led by a scholar of the Imperial Library by the name of Moses, who has the demeanour of a modern day conspiracy theorist. He sees hidden connections amongst the web of intrigue across the city, and while many of his guesses stray far from the mark, he and his cohorts has amassed an amazing amount of information about the more bizarre side of the city. Moses originated the theory that the prophecy is Metatron; he believes that it is aware of future events and aware of a crisis on the horizon which it cannot stop, but is taking steps to secure the future of the Empire. He claims to have evidence that this crisis, whatever it will be, is imminent – the prophecy's manifestations have increased steadily over the last few years, convincing people to perform random and seemingly innocuous tasks which are all somehow connected to one another. For example, it convinced someone to put a bucket of sand in a church porch. Four years later, another pronouncement had people at vigil at the church, and they were able to extinguish a fire using the sand that could have burned down an orphanage. One of those orphans was later adopted, again at the insistence of the prophecy.

The characters are likely to encounter Moses once they have had a first-hand experience of the prophecy. They may find their steps dogged by his cronies, or they may encounter him when they seek information about their experiences with it. Moses has only personally heard the prophecy speak once, long after he started to study it, and even then he only witnessed the end of its pronouncement. If the characters have regular communications with it, he'll likely try to stay close to them. The other scholars at Stoudion treat Moses as a figure of fun and the butt of many jokes, and the credibility of those who associate with him is stretched.

The Ktistes (IMM-8) may be the prophecy's willing agents. They have long been guided by its proclamations, having recognised their own activities in the legend of the enmarbled emperor. Their concern is that by their records, they have not yet preserved an emperor, suggesting that this task is still in the future.

Story Path

Stories involving the Prophecy of Leo will usually start with the prophecy making a pronouncement. This could happen at any time: in a crowded bar all the patrons start speaking in unison; in the middle of a fight an opponent spouts the words of the prophecy as the text runs over his skin like a tattoo; in church the priest's sermon is suddenly targeted at the player characters. Given the prophecy's unique mode of speech, the Games Master can prepare the pronouncement ahead of time, making sure it is archaic in tone, convoluted in nature, and never straightforward in meaning.

The characters might resist working for an agent that will neither reveal why it has chosen them, explain its motives, nor speak clearly. Given its powers, the prophecy has the ability to pester the characters like no other, but it is not above offering some incentive. The prophecy has a limited view of the future, so it can arrange coincidental meetings, offer investment advice, or give clues regarding hidden information.

Leo-1: Treasure Hunt

In the characters' first brush with the prophecy, it announces to a crowd that the "wealth sacked from an empire of crows is beneath the beast of four feet in the forum of the emperor". The announcement, heard by many, sets of a fever of treasure hunting: it is 'well known' that there are caches of gold throughout the city. The mob heads for the Forum of Constantine. However, the characters stand right next to the written text, and notice that the version spoken aloud misses the crucial phrase "of the eighth". The eighth letter of the Greek alphabet is theta, and Theodosios is the only emperor with a forum whose name begins "th". While the forum has statues or many four-footed beasts, only one of them has all four feet on the ground; a lion. Further, all the other animals have the same foot – the left foreleg – raised. Naturally, the left foreleg of the lion is a lever that operates a trapdoor leading into the Undercity. The way there has been made perilous with time, but the path leads to a vault containing the Treasure of the Bulgars (the "empire of crows").

LEO-2: THE ADRIATIC EAGLE

The prophecy gives the characters some time with their newfound wealth, but it is not going to let them keep it for long. The prophecy's next pronouncement takes them to a shipyard, where a merchant is touting for investors. He's a Serbian magnate who in desperate to bring refugees from the recent Bosnian and Ottoman conflicts, including his own wife and family. Amongst the refugees is Orban of Brassó (NPC-22), who has been caught up in the fighting on a visit to his home. The Serbian needs money for refurbishment of his ship and to hire a crew. Investors are welcome – nay, encouraged – to accompany him.

The Adriatic Sea is rife with Ottoman warships and Barbary slavers, presenting ample opportunity for action on the high seas. One of these adventures leads to the recovery of a Greek slave Theophilos, who claims to be the nephew of Georgios Sphrantzes (NPC-13). To those with keen eyes, he could easily be the son of Emperor Constantine XI, and his birth certainly matches up with the years that Constantine was despot of the Morea and Sphrantzes and his sister lived in Glarentza. When his mother died he ended up in a Constantinople orphanage, at least until it was destroyed in a fire. Only a well-placed bucket of sand saved his life. He was apprenticed to an architect, but was captured by the Ottomans when scouting the islands of the Sea of Marmara for sources of marble.

LEO-3: KNUCKLING DOWN

Returning to Constantinople with Theophilos, he announces his intent to get close to his uncle, and asks the characters to help him achieve this. The Protovestiarios is stunned at the similarity between Theophilos and his friend the emperor, and the polite fiction is that he is a distant cousin. Theophilos is soon ensconced as an oikeios of Constantine, which permits him to use the name Palaiologos. The player characters now have a friend in a high place indeed.

The prophecy makes another intrusion into the characters' lives. It warns them that "the seed of the twin-headed eagle sleeps in stone through dawn." Theophilos – unknown to the player characters – was more than just an apprentice architect, but was also an apprentice Ktistes (IMM-8). He was on the Marmaran Sea looking for marble spirits, and the one he found has now taken over his body (following a fumbled Trance roll). He is out of Magic Points and cannot retake control of his body. The hapless animist is trapped in his body as the elemental spirit hijacks it for its own purpose. It is homing in on the Anemodoulion (KN-2), a place strongly associated with its opposing element of air, possibly with the intent to destroy it. The embodied spirit can phase through solid stone and hide in plain sight as a statue, albeit one of Theophilos. What ultimately is the spirit's goal? Does it have something to do with the sixth oracle's "slayer of the southwest wind" which is supposed to lie beneath the monument?

LEO-4: ABOUT FACE

Assuming the characters have studied the prophecy by now, they may have connected the legend of the enmarbled emperor with the activities of the Ktistes, to whom they have been introduced by Theophilos. The prophecy has gone a long way to place Theophilos at the side of the emperor, and should Constantine's life ever be in danger, Theophilos has orders from the Ktistes to add their first emperor to the collection under the Palace of Lausos. So why, after all this effort, does the prophecy order Theophilos to travel to Venice – using quite clear and unambiguous terms for a change? Is this really the prophecy, or has another agency found a way to mimic its strategy? If so, what is their ultimate plan? Is this a scheme of the Ottoman Divan to break the power of the Palaiologoi?

THE VAMPIRES OF XEROLOPHOS (VAM)

On the eastern slope of the seventh hill, there are some hidden caves that are home to a nest of broukolakes or vampires. Greek vampires do not transmit the curse of vampirism; instead, they are born as living vampires, a kind of half-vampire that has some powers and a craving for blood. Upon death, a living vampire is reborn as an undead vampire. Statistics for living and undead broukolakes are given in the Bestiary later in this chapter.

There are about a dozen of undead vampires living in Xerolophos, with another 20 scattered throughout the deserted places of Constantinople. There are also untold numbers of living vampires (see below) living undiscovered amongst the people of the city. The broukolakes are ruled by the iron will of an old evil by the name of 'Eliou Skotides.

A WORLD OF DARKNESS

'Eliou's plan is to plunge the city into perpetual darkness. His people would then no longer fear the burning rays of the sun, and would be free to walk the streets with impunity. He envisages the day that he is seated in the Blachernai Palace, ruling over a court of broukolakes. Humans would be farmed for their blood, and he would bring the rulers of nearby nations to him quaking in fear. Soon, the primordial darkness will spread into neighbouring lands, taking Wallachia and Moldova, Anatolia and Trebizond; and he would rule it all, forever.

His plan is to summon Erebos, the primeval darkness that preceded even the gods. This fearsome spirit can only be summoned under a specific set of circumstances, the most important of which is total darkness. The plan is to summon a number of skotoi – spirits of darkness – beneath the earth, and then have them issue out of their underground havens during an eclipse. This should provide the right conditions to bring Erebos from the Tartarean depths in which it dwells, and have it blot out the sun above Constantinople.

EREBOS

One of the creation myths of the Greeks states that Chaos was the first thing that existed, and from Chaos sprung Nyx and Erebos, and from them came Hemera and Aither. Aither was the pure blue air of heaven; Chaos was the churning mass of breathable air that surrounded the earth, and Erebos was the lower air choked with darkness that filled the underworld. Nyx was the night and Hemera was the day. These primordial beings produced everything else: while Aither and Hemera were the progenitors of Mother Earth, Father Ocean, and the Sky; Nyx and Erebos spawned Death, Doom, Old Age, Discord, Misery, and the Fates, along with a host of other abstract beings.

If Erebos were to rule on earth, all of its dark progeny would be released from the hellish prison of the Greek underworld Tartaros. Bane spirits, death spirits, and passion spirits would gain the ability to manifest in the material world, and cause havoc and misery to mankind. Creatures of darkness like the broukolakes would become more common, and chaos would reign.

STORY PATH

As the player characters encounter the broukolakes in these and other stories they will discover their fascination with astronomical information. They steal astrolabes and orreries from houses, collect ephemerides, and even capture astrologers. They are under orders from 'Eliou to discover the date of the next solar eclipse, something that only the best scholar of the heavens can calculate.

VAM-1: FORTY DAYS LATER

There is a terrible natural disaster in a neighbourhood such as a building collapse or a fire. Many people are killed, including people that the player characters know. It is customary to visit the graves of the dead after 40 days have passed, out of respect for the deceased. So many died on the same day that there is a crowd of people at the cemetery when the dead start to crawl out of their graves. A dozen or more of the deceased were living broukolakes, many of them occupying the same slum and mourned by none. Now they are undead broukolakes, and they begin to feast on the mourners. The cemetery priest is well-versed in the lore of the undead, and at his prompting the player characters may be able to corral the creatures, but their efforts will be hampered by an elder broukolak who has come to check on his brood and bring them to his nest in Xerolophos. The player characters should be left wondering why so many of the creatures – usually loners – were in the same place.

VAM-2: BRINGERS OF DARKNESS

A contact of the player characters asks for help. He lives near the Phanarion in Petrion (PT-1), and every night there is a disturbance outside his house. He thinks he is being followed, and finds that things around his house have been moved or disturbed. Unknown to their contact, his son is a living broukolakes. Every night, when vampires travel past his house, they pause and call to the child vampire. The broukolakes are fulfilling a mission for 'Eliou, who has commanded them to extinguish the Beacon – he cannot summon the primeval darkness while it remains. Eager to ensure it cannot be relit, the broukolakes are demolishing the lighthouse one stone at a time.

VAM-3: THE VEIL OF NIGHT

Leads discovered in other vampire-connected adventures bring the player characters to a buried pagan temple near the summit of the Fifth Hill; a nyktesion dedicated to the sister-wife of Erebos, black-cloaked Nyx. The place is crawling with broukolakes, both living and undead. The whole complex can be treated as a classic dungeon-crawl, with passages leading to similar temples under the Fourth and Sixth Hills as well. If the characters delve deep enough they may discover the giant who is supposedly buried under the hill after fighting with the sun god (see page 160). The characters are just in time to prevent (or try to prevent), a ritual lead by an animist-broukolak designed to summon a powerful elemental of darkness and bind it into a shard of obsidian. In two days' time, as the shadow of a solar eclipse sweeps over the city, the vampires will break the fetish and release the skotos. The same ritual is being conducted at six other temples, one on each of the hills of Constantinople. If all seven skotoi are released, the pall of darkness will hang in a continuous sheet over the city: a perfect environment from which to summon Erebos, the Eternal Darkness.

VAM-4: THE COMING OF ETERNAL SHADOW

The solar eclipse comes, but thanks to the player characters, not all of the nyktesia are able to release their elemental of darkness. There are gaps in the cloud of darkness above Constantinople, preventing 'Eliou from immediately summoning Erebos. However, the unnatural darkness grows as the skotoi seem to draw nourishment from the fear and chaos in the City below. The broukolakes boldly walk the streets in the tenebrous districts, doing their best to enhance the terror of the citizens. Some of the weaker spirits of Erebos – passion spirits, but also some bane spirits – have leaked through and are possessing innocents while 'Eliou sits on his throne of skulls in Xerolophos. The player characters must find the master sorcerer and put an end to him before he can complete his hellish plan.

MILITARY CAMPAIGNS

This section presents some simple rules for the planning and adjudication of large-scale military campaigns towards some tactical objective, such as the conquest of a city, capturing a key strategic location, or breaking a fleet. Military campaigns may stand alone, or they might be part of some greater strategic planning in a war.

This system is specifically designed to highlight the actions of player characters in the grander scheme of things, and permit a small band of adventurers to have a real impact on events that can involve thousands of individuals. The first stage of any planning for the Games Master is to decide on the composition and objectives of each military campaign. Typically, a campaign has a single overarching objective, which can be broken down into smaller individual components whose success contributes to the goals of the campaign. Some of these components will be battles, but others will involve espionage, resupply, bombardment of walls, and so on.

The key parts of a military campaign are a series of martial events that lead to clear outcomes. Each campaign has a set of victory conditions that determine success or failure for the belligerents.

The next section shows this system in action, with two campaigns that lead to the historical Fall of Constantinople. The Ottoman assault on Constantinople's formidable defences constitutes one campaign, which is a necessary prelude to the second – the conquest of the city itself.

The guidelines given here focus on grading the impact of martial events on the overall military objectives of a campaign. It does not deal with the resolution of martial events; this is tackled through a number of different mechanics in the Mythras rules:

- Skill rolls (either opposed or simple)
- Task rounds (Mythras page 65)
- Combat
- Battle Actions, using the *Ships and Shield Walls* supplement
- Adventure combining several of these

For military campaigns involving player characters, it is often best to mix and match the different mechanics to resolve different martial events. A duel against an opposing leader might be resolved with combat, but digging mines to bring down a curtain wall might be better as Task Rounds. The same type of event need not be resolved in identical manners either. For example, there will be several skirmishes that prelude the main assault, but the player characters only lead one band of soldiers. For their skirmish, the full Battle rules are employed, but to model the success of the other skirmishes, the Games Master decides on opposed Task rounds on Lore (Military Tactics) for the two commanders.

Belligerents

The belligerents are the opponents involved in military campaigns. Most campaigns have two belligerents – even if one side is made up of a combined force, if their objectives and victory conditions are the same then they count as a single belligerent.

Martial Events and Outcomes

Martial events are at the heart of the resolution of a military campaign. Each event consists of units from one or more of the belligerents involved in the campaign.

The outcomes of martial events are graded on a four-point scale according to the impact they have on the victory conditions: Inconsequential success, Minor success, Major success, and Decisive success. Minor and Major successes are partial victories. Inconsequential successes never contribute towards victory, but might be important propaganda or morale-boosting events. Decisive successes, as the name suggests, decide the outcome of a campaign. Often a Decisive success is only possible if certain other actions have resulted in (usually Major) success.

Sometimes it is necessary for martial events to accrue successes towards a specific objective. For example, during a siege, each section of the walls subjected to bombardment might have its own tally of successes. These successes still count towards the resolution of the military campaign as a whole. The third, sixth, ninth, etc. Minor success gained towards a specific objective is a Major success instead. The opposing belligerent may be able to perform counter-actions to reduce an objective's successes: each Minor success can downgrade a Major success to a Minor or remove a Minor success; and each Major success in a counter-action can remove either all Minor successes or one Major. This system for the accumulation of successes and the reduction due to counter-actions is not suitable for all actions. A Minor success from a battle, for example, cannot be converted into a Major success following the outcome of a different battle. Rather, the accumulation mechanic should be used for actions where success builds on success, such as pushing through a pass choked with enemy soldiers, overcoming a defensive wall, or resupplying a beleaguered force.

The Games Master should provide list of martial events contributing to the military campaign, ensuring that there are sufficient events to meet the Victory Conditions of both sides. When grading the outcome of a martial event, you must take into account the impact of the event on the overall aims of the campaign, not the difficulty of the task. A battle where the defenders are outnumbered 20 to 1 might count as a major victory for the player characters involved, but it might only be an Inconsequential success towards the campaign as a whole. Conversely, casting the Heal Wound miracle might be a simple task for a theist, but it could turn abject defeat into success if the target is the king.

The events provided by the Games Master should not be seen as a proscriptive set: often players will suggest other martial actions during play and group should agree on the outcome level if the event is resolved satisfactorily (and also, if applicable, the outcome for the enemy if it fails). The Games Master is the final arbiter of outcome levels.

Victory Conditions

The victory conditions vary according to the objectives of the campaign. Some campaigns can be won with a single battle that eliminates the leader and/or crushes the opposing army. Other campaigns are wars of attrition, where one force nibbles away at their enemy through guerrilla actions and surgical strikes. Victory conditions will often be different for each belligerent. A martial event that results in a Decisive success is always a victory for the winning side. However, many campaigns can also be won through an accumulation of a certain number of other successes. So, the victory conditions might be "one Decisive success OR three Major successes OR ten successes." When any of these conditions are met, the belligerent has won. Not all victory conditions are in terms of successes. Victory can be won by resisting one's opponent for a certain amount of time (until relief arrives, at which point a different campaign starts), or if individual military actions kill or rout all of an enemy's forces, rendering them incapable of achieving their own victory conditions.

Note that while the victory conditions for each side in a conflict may be similar, the ease at which those conditions can be achieved vary between the belligerents, with things such as troop numbers, training, equipment, terrain, and a whole host of other factors playing a role.

Spot Rules

Sieges

- The attacking belligerent accumulates a Minor success for every week they maintain the siege (or every day if the defenders have no water supply). As these convert to Major successes, the enemy comes closer and closer to starvation.

The fourth accrued Major success counts as a Decisive success: the besieged force have starved or run out of water.

- If the defending belligerent gains successes by receiving supplies or conducting raids then they may count these successes as counter-actions against the siege. Defenders may also gain successes by reducing the number of mouths they have to feed: negotiating the release of civilians, securing their escape, or simply killing them.

BOMBARDMENT AND SAPPING

- The aggressor can gain successes by inflicting damage on the walls. A day's bombardment can be simulated with Task roll (taking 2 hours each) on Lore (Firearms and Artillery). Similarly, three days of sapping is a Task roll on Lore (Sapping). Success in four rounds is a Minor success. Exceeding 100% success is a Major success.
- Check that the siege weapons used can actually damage the walls. The average damage of the weapon should do more damage than the Armour Points of the walls, and if the total difference of all siege engines employed is less than 5% of the total Hit Points of the wall section, then all successes should be downgraded one level.
- The defender can shore up damage if they have sufficient material and are not under bombardment. Each day of repair is a Lore (Architecture) Task roll as a counter-action. Likewise, counter-mines against sapping attempts are a Lore (Sapping) Task roll, as long as the defenders know the location of the attacker's mines.

THE END OF AN EMPIRE (END)

You know well that the hour has come: the enemy of our faith wishes to oppress us even more closely by sea and land with all his engines and skill to attack us with the entire strength of this siege force, as a snake about to spew its venom; he is in a hurry to devour us, like a savage lion. For this reason I am imploring you to fight like men with brave souls, as you have done from the beginning up to this day, against the enemy of our faith.

~ *Constantine XI Palaiologos, before the siege in 1453*

In 1451, Murad II Sultan dies, and his son Mehmet II becomes sultan for the second time. Ibrahim of Karaman takes the opportunity to conquer parts of central Anatolia and instigate revolt against Ottoman rule. However, this is a mere distraction to Mehmed II's true desire: the conquest of Constantinople. He has vowed to add this jewel to the Ottoman diadem and make the rule of his empire absolute.

In late 1452, Mehmet musters his army at his capital of Edirne, and marches down the newly repaired road after the worst of the winter weather, arriving at the City in the middle of March 1453. In all, the Ottoman army consists of approximately 80,000 soldiers, with perhaps 120,000 camp followers and support crews. They face a muster of about 7,000 defending soldiers (of whom 2,000 are foreign mercenaries), although the civilian militia consists of about 33,000 citizens, monks, and merchants armed with makeshift weapons.

Modern military scholars accept that the Fall of Constantinople was not as inevitable as the numbers might seem. The Walls of the city survived two months of near continuous bombardment by the Turkish artillery, and when they did finally breach it was in just one or two places. Waves of attackers at these breach points were fought off time after time and – if contemporary accounts are to be believed – it was the actions of a few individuals that turned the tide in favour of the Ottomans. Maybe if those few individuals had been player characters armed with Luck Points and magic, then the outcome would have been different.

If you intend to run these military campaigns as part of a game set in Mythic Constantinople, then there are plenty of good narratives of the battles available that collate eyewitness evidence in more detail than can be provided here. Particularly recommended are:

- Nicolle, David, *Constantinople 1453: the End of Byzantium.* 2000, Osprey Publishing
- Runciman, Steven, *The Fall of Constantinople 1453, 1965,* Cambridge University Press

The campaign descriptions below concentrate on the historical information, and do not consider successes in martial actions involving the mythical part of Mythic Constantinople. For example, the Tauroi Chalkeoi is a disbanded regiment of minotauroi in heavy armour, but there are still a hundred combat-ready members of this unit still living in the City. If this elite force could be reformed, it might sway the tide of battle. On the Ottoman side, all paşas and beyli have astomatoi advisors put in place by the Divan. These flying inhumans could organise aerial spies to report on troop deployments, which could speed the success of the Ottomans.

CAMPAIGN ONE: SIEGE OF CONSTANTINOPLE

The Ottoman army was in place at the Land Walls of Constantinople, with a fleet in Diplokionion north of Pera, by the last week of March 1453. The Ottoman army relies on slave soldiers who are not needed for agricultural purposes, and the siege could in theory last for years without economic detriment to the Ottoman Empire.

The successes of the Ottoman bombardment of each section of the Land and Sea Walls should be tracked as separate objectives. Historically, the batteries were aimed at the mesoteichion and Blachernai walls. Once the Ottoman fleet attained access to the Golden Horn on 22 April, ship-mounted bombards attacked the Sea Walls, but to little effect. If the great Basilike bombard is being used, then a successful day of bombardment causes a Minor success against an undamaged wall (i.e. one with no successes against it), but a Major success against any wall section that has taken damage. This gun requires a cart drawn by 60 oxen to move it, needs 200 men to manage it, and can only be fired 7 times a day without danger of cracking it.

Note that if the Girdle of the Theotokos (page 12) is active, only the Basilike bombard has any real hope of damaging the walls. Any bombard doing less than 6d6 damage cannot damage the wall at all, and even the Basilike will take an average of over 40 shots to create a breach, and it can only fire once every 2 hours. All Ottoman successes should be downgraded by one magnitude. Even without the Girdle, to breach the Theodosian walls the Ottomans must destroy a section of the outer and the inner walls; although the Byzantines cannot safely repair the outer wall due to the presence of the enemy army.

The prime Byzantine tactic is to wait out the Ottomans. The longer the siege can be maintained, the greater the chance of a diplomatic resolution or the greater the chance that the sultan will be forced to abandon the siege and recommit his forces to a different military campaign: such as a combined force of Catholic monarchs, or a revolt in Anatolia. However, the city has a limited supply of food, and without the capacity to resupply can last a maximum of three months.

Byzantine Forces

Commander	Troops	Position
Constantine XI (Byzantine)	Overall commander	Mesoteichion
Michael Bryennios, Domestic of the Walls (Byzantine)	Civilian force to repair walls	Theodosian walls
Andronikos Komnenos (Byzantine)	250 Tzakones	Golden Horn walls
Maurizio Cateneo (Genoese)	200 Tzangrataroi	Pegai Gate
John Grant (Scottish)	50 Sappers	Romanos Gate
Alviso Diedo (Venetian)	26 ships (10 Byzantine, 5 Genoese, 5 Venetian, 3 Cretan, 3 others)	Golden Horn
Zuan Venier (Cretan Venetian)	3 Cretan galleys	Chain across Golden Horn

Ottoman Forces

Commander	Troops	Position
Mehmet II Sultan	Overall commander	Maltepe Hill, opposite mesoteichion
Zaganos Paşa	Commander of the siege	north of the Golden Horn
Voivode of Jaksa (Serbian)	150 Serbian sappers	
Bey of Artillery	3 batteries of bombards	Blachernai
Bey of Artillery	6 batteries of bombards	mesoteichion
Bey of Artillery	3 batteries of bombards	Pege Gate
Bey of Artillery	2 batteries of bombards	Golden Gate

Ottoman Victory Conditions

- Any Decisive Ottoman success; by surrender, breaches in the wall, or starvation.

Byzantine Victory Conditions

- Deny the Ottomans a Decisive success.

Martial Events in 1453

Date	Event	Outcome	Notes
Winter 1452	Prevent/undo repair of Edirne road	Major Byzantine	Halves accumulation rate of Ottoman siege successes
23 Mar	Bombards face the Land Walls	Minor Ottoman	See Ottoman Forces table for historical deployment
23 Mar	Basilike placed at Blachernai	—	
2 Apr	Chain raised across Golden Horn	Minor Byzantine	Stops Ottoman ships moving troops and guns
6 Apr	Bombardment of walls begins	Minor Ottoman	See bombardment spot rules. Martial action every other day
7 Apr	Shoring up of damage done to walls	Minor Byzantine	See bombardment spot rules. Martial counter-action every other day
9 Apr	Raid against Chain across Golden Horn	Minor Ottoman	Makes ships available for troop and bombard movement; in reality failed
20 Apr	4 ships from Chios break blockade	Major Byzantine	Siege counter-action
22 Apr	Portage of Ottoman ships across land into Golden Horn	Major Ottoman	Makes ships available for troop and bombard movement
28 Apr	Fire ships attack Ottoman fleet in the Golden Horn	Minor/Major Byzantine	Destroys enemy ships, in reality didn't succeed
2 May	Basilike repaired	—	
3 May	Bombard Ottoman ships from Golden Horn wall	Minor Byzantine	Damages enemy ships
6 May	Basilike moved to Romanos Gate on mesoteichion	—	
10 May	Ottoman mines under Blachernai wall	Minor Ottoman	Each attempt takes 3 days
16 May	Byzantine counter-mines	Minor Byzantine	Counter-action against sapping
21 May	Ottoman ambassador offers life of emperor in return for surrender	Decisive Ottoman	In reality, offer was rejected on 24 May
23 May	Capture officers commanding the mining operations, find all locations	Major Byzantine	Removes all minor successes from mining
24 May	Breach in the Blachernai walls	Decisive Ottoman	See bombardment spot rules, in reality failed
26 May	Breach in the mesoteichion	Decisive Ottoman	See bombardment spot rules
27 May	12 Venetian ships arrive in city	Major Byzantine	Siege counter-action
5 Jun	Constantinople starves	Decisive Ottoman	See spot rules for sieges; in reality didn't occur

CAMPAIGN TWO: BATTLE FOR THE CITY

On 21 May, the Ottoman ambassador entered Constantinople under a flag of truce. The Sultan offered to lift the siege if the emperor surrendered the city. The emperor and any other inhabitant would be free to leave with their belongings, but anyone remaining behind would have their safety guaranteed. Finally, Constantine XI would be made governor of the Peloponnese. The emperor gave his answer three days later during a lunar eclipse. He recognised the sultan as the rightful owner of all lands he had seized thus far, but refused to surrender the city. "Giving you the city depends neither on me nor on anyone else among its inhabitants; as we have all decided to die with our own free will and we shall not consider our lives".

The Battle of Constantinople commences when Ottoman forces penetrate the Walls and begin attacking the defending Greek units. Some martial events are possible prior to the breaches in the Walls, but this campaign cannot result in an Ottoman victory until they have first achieved a victory in the siege. Mehmet II planned the assault in three waves, using his başi-bazouks (spurred on by whip-wielding military police) and the Timarli Andalou to exhaust the defenders before sending in his elite Yeniçeri troops at dawn. The defenders are heavily outnumbered, but remember that in the early battles before dawn, the attacking Ottomans could only enter through relatively narrow choke points.

The sea-battle in the Golden Horn and Bosphoros could be run as a separate campaign. The Ottoman fleet consists of 126 ships (6 large galleys, 10 ordinary galleys, 15 small galleys, 75 rowing boats, 20 horse-transporters). Assuming that the martial action of the 22 April succeeded (see Siege of Constantinople, above), 70 of these ships are in the Golden Horn.

OTTOMAN VICTORY CONDITIONS

- ϕ Ottoman victory in siege AND
- ϕ five or more Major Ottoman successes

BYZANTINE VICTORY CONDITIONS

- ϕ Decisive Byzantine success OR
- ϕ Five or more Major Byzantine successes OR
- ϕ defeat of all Ottoman forces inside the city

BYZANTINE FORCES

Commander	Troops	Position
Constantine XI (Byzantine)	1000 Skoutatoi, 300 Kataphractoi, 200 Toxotes, 100 Varrangai, 5000 Civilian militia	mesoteichion
Giovanni Giustiniani Longo (Venetian)	300 Venetian condottieri pikemen, 400 Venetian latikon	Charisian Gate
Bocchiardi Brothers (Genoese)	400 Albanian mercenaries, 3000 Civilian militia	Blachernai, Palace of the Porphyrogennetos
Girolamo Minotto (Venetian)	300 Venetian latikon	Blachernai palace
Theophilos Palaiologos (Byzantine)	50 Sappers	Romanos Gate
Maurizio Cateneo (Genoese)	700 Skoutatoi, 400 Trapezites, 200 Tzangratoroi, 50 Hippotoxotes, 100 Genoese condottiere pikemen, 5000 Civilian militia	Pegai Gate
Filippo Contarini (Venetian)	200 Venetian latikon, 200 Genoan latikon, 5000 Civilian militia	Pegai to Golden Gate
Demetrios Kantakouzenos (Byzantine)	300 Kataphractoi, 500 Skoutatoi, 100 Cretan light infantry, 1000 Civilian militia	Southern part of Land Walls
Jacobo Contarini (Venetian)	100 Venetians, 3000 Civilian militia	Stoudion
Orhan Çelebi (Turkish)	500 Turks	Eleutherion in Vlanga
Pere Julià (Catalan)	200 Catalan condottiere pikemen, 100 Genoese condottiere pikemen	Palation
Isidoros of Kiev (Byzantine)	200 archers	Mangana in Akropolis
Gabriele Trevisano (Venetian)	200 Venetian sailors, 300 Genoese sailors, 250 Tzakones, 1000 Civilian militia	Zeugma and Perama
Loukas Notaras (Byzantine)	250 Mourtatoi, 5000 Civilian militia	Kyrion in Petrion (reserve)
Nikolaos Goudeles (Byzantine)	500 Phylakes, 100 Toxotes, 100 Albanian mercenaries, 5000 Civilian militia	Leomakellon in Platea (reserve)
Alviso Diedo (Venetian)	26 ships (10 Byzantine, 5 Genoese, 5 Venetian, 3 Cretan, 3 others)	Golden Horn

OTTOMAN FORCES

Commander	Troops	Position
Mehmed II Sultan	6,000 Yeniçeri, 2,000 Kapikulu Sipahi	Maltepe Hill, opposite mesoteichion
Karadja Paşa	12,000 Timarli Rumeli, 14,000 Celebu	Blachernai walls
Ishak Paşa	6,000 Timarli Andolu, 6,000 Celebu	Rhesios Gate to Golden Gate
Zaganos Paşa	15,000 Yaya	North of Golden Horn
Hamza Bey	70 ships in Golden Horn, 46 ships in Sea of Marmara, 5,000 Turkish Navy	In Golden Horn and Sea of Marmara
(Many individual leaders)	10,000 Akinci	Behind front lines
(Many individual leaders)	8,000 Başi-bazouk	Behind front lines

MARTIAL EVENTS IN 1453

Date	Event	Outcome	Notes
15 Jan	Giustiniani Longo arrives with 700 condottieri, becomes commander	Minor Byzantine	
10 Apr	3 Genoese ships dispatched by pope arrive	Minor Byzantine	In reality were delayed at Chios by storms
17 Apr	Night raid by Ottomans	Minor success for winner	In reality, Byzantine success
28 Apr	Burn Ottoman ships in Bosphoros harbour	Major Byzantine	In reality failed; would have reduced Hamza Bey's forces
8 May	Night raid by Ottomans through breach in Romanos Gate	Major Ottoman / Minor Byzantine	Requires major success at mesoteichion, in reality, Byzantine success
27 May	12 Venetian ships arrive in city	Minor Byzantine	
29 May			
01:30	Başi-bazouks versus Constantine and Longo at the mesoteichion	Major success for winner	In reality, Byzantine success
01:30	Ishak Paşa versus Filippo Contarini and Demetrios Kantakouzenos at the southern walls	Minor success for winner	In reality, Byzantine success
02:00	Hamza Bey versus Orhan at Eleutherion	Minor success for winner	In reality, Byzantine success
03:00	Karadja Paşa versus Bocchiardi brothers in Blachernai	Minor success for winner	In reality, Byzantine success
03:00	Zaganos Paşa versus Girolamo Minotto in Blachernai	Minor success for winner	In reality, Byzantine success
03:30	Ishak Paşa versus Constantine and Longo at the mesoteichion	Major success for winner	In reality, Byzantine success
05:30	Yeniçeri versus Constantine and Longo at the mesoteichion	Major success for winner	In reality, Ottoman success and entered city; Constantine XI killed
07:30	Karadja Paşa versus Bocchiardi brothers at Blachernai	Major success for winner	In reality, Ottoman success and entered city
08:00	Zaganos Paşa versus Girolamo Minotto at Blachernai	Major success for winner	In reality, Ottoman success and entered city
08:00	Hamza Bey versus Gabriele Trevisano in Platea and Venetian Quarter	Major success for winner	In reality Ottoman success and entered city
10:00	Ishak Paşa (outside walls) and Kapikulu Sipahi (inside walls) versus Filippo Contarini and Demetrios Kantakouzenos at Pegai Gate	Major success for winner	In reality, Ottoman success and entered city

MARTIAL EVENTS IN 1453

Date	Event	Outcome	Notes
10:00	Hamza Bey versus Jacobo Contarini in Stoudion	Minor success for winner	In reality, Byzantines surrendered, Ottomans entered city
11:00	Hamza Bey versus Orhan in Vlanga	Minor success for winner	In reality, Ottoman success and entered city
11:00	Akinci versus Pere Julià in Palation	Minor success for winner	In reality, Ottoman success
11:30	Zaganos versus Loukas Notaras in Petrion	Major success for winner	In reality, Ottoman success
11:30	Timarli Andalou versus Nikolaos Goudeles in Platea and Kainopolis	Major success for winner	In reality, Ottoman success
12:00	Kill Mehmet II Sultan as he enters city	Decisive success for Byzantines	In reality did not happen
13:00	Başi-bazouks versus Isidoros in Akropolis	Minor success for winner	In reality, Ottoman success

BESTIARY

BROUKOLAK

Greek vampires vary from the classical type in a few key ways. Firstly, a broukolak cannot turn a human into a vampire; a broukolak is born, not made. Those destined to become a vampire are born under inauspicious circumstances, such as in a graveyard or at a crossroads on a Saturday. They are usually born with some physical deformation, such as extra fingers, a full pelt of hair, or differently coloured eyes. These children become living broukolakes when they reach puberty, able to transform into a hideous man-wolf hybrid form whenever out of the sun's light. When in this form they gain the following benefits:

- Double both STR and DEX.
- Immune to non-magical attacks except for those inflicted by weapons made from black hawthorn.
- Gain Bite and Claw natural weapons appropriate to SIZ (Mythras page 222).

Living broukolakes also suffer from the following penalties:

- Forced back into human form if more than half their body is exposed to sunlight.
- An aching thirst for blood in either form, represented by the Crave Blood Passion which begins at 30% + POWx2 and increases by 1d10% every time it is slated with a human's life. They take no penalty if unable to drink blood: it is an addiction but not a dependence.

Some living broukolakes naturally develop Folk Magic and are drawn to Animism, typically learning directly from 'Eliou Skotides (IMM-4). Their craving for blood makes it increasingly difficult for a living vampire to keep its nature hidden, and many meet their end at the hands of a lynch mob.

When the living broukolak dies, they rise after 40 days as an undead broukolak (i.e. a vampire). Only precise treatment of the body after death can prevent this; if any one of seven steps is omitted or performed incorrectly, the vampire rises. An undead broukolak has the following benefits of other vampires:

- Gains the Darksight, Undead, and Vampiric creature abilities.
- Double both STR and DEX, not just when in bestial form.
- Increase POW by 1 for every 21 years of existence.
- Gains a Gaze attack allowing it to dominate humans and sapient animals (Mythras page 271).
- Immune to non-magical attacks. Even weapons made from black hawthorn inflict minimum damage
- Shape-Shift into monstrous man-wolf form, gaining Bite and Claws as above.
- Shape-Shift into spirit form – an animate shadow. This form cannot cross areas of bright light, nor enter a light-tight room, but it can slip under doors and jump from shadow to shadow by withdrawing its Manifestation power and travelling as a spirit. Use the Statistics of a wraith (Mythras page 153), but can initiate Spirit Combat on any person wholly in partial or deeper darkness, and on a win will often possess the individual.

They have the following vampiric weaknesses:

- Must consume blood once a week like a regular vampire, and can only recover spent Magic Points if this blood is human. Their Crave Blood Passion no longer increases with each blood meal.
- Susceptibility to sunlight, suffering 1d6 Hit Points damage per round to each location it contacts.
- An undead broukolak only suffers from the catatonic weakness of other vampires from sunset Friday to sunset Saturday, they otherwise have no need for sleep although must still avoid the sun during the day.

Broukolakes typically do not rest in their graves, although they may store the bodies of their most recent victims in them. Many undead vampires work to control and reduce their Crave Blood Passion, freeing them from its savage yoke even though they now rely on blood to survive.

LAYING A BROUKOLAK TO REST

To prevent a living vampire from becoming a broukolak, the following steps must be taken:

- *An iron nail must be driven into every place where the corpse's body laid before burial;*
- *The hands, feet, eyes, and tongue must each be pierced with a black hawthorn thorn;*
- *The hands of the corpse must be bound behind the back;*
- *A red-hot needle must be driven through the corpse's heart;*
- *Salt must be placed in the mouth, ears, and navel;*
- *The coffin must be wrapped with wild roses and buried at a crossroads on a Saturday;*
- *Strands of red thread and millet seed must be scattered over the grave.*

ELDER GHOUL

Elder Ghouls are like standard ghouls (known as strigoi in Greek), but much more terrible because of their intelligence and their command over other ghouls.

Use the statistics of a regular ghoul (Mythras page 244) except for the following:

- Elder ghouls retain their INT, POW, and CHA from life;
- An elder ghoul regenerates at the rate of 1 Hit Point per location per round;
- An elder ghoul can shapeshift into a perfect replica of any person whose flesh they eat. This shape can be maintained indefinitely. They acquire memories as well: all the memories of a fresh corpse (or living person), but memories decay along with the flesh. A year-old corpse has just fragmentary impressions left. Acquired memories gradually fade once the shape is abandoned;
- An elder ghoul can control any normal ghouls it created. They can be taught commands much like training dogs; but for more complex control the elder ghoul must spend a Magic Point to permanently make a ghoul into a thrall. The elder ghoul can choose to see through the eyes of any of its thralls, take control of their actions or voice through a mental link, or give them complex tasks to perform.
- Elder ghouls do not regenerate spent Magic Points naturally; instead they must consume the heart of a magician (of any tradition) to gain whatever Magic Points she had upon death.
- The bite of an elder ghoul infects the victim with the same curse as a regular ghoul. No one knows how elder ghouls come about.

SPIRIT, DIVINE

A divine spirit is a servant of God. The best-known divine spirits are angels, but there are all manner of other kinds of divine spirits. The celestial hierarchy is classically divided into nine orders, which in decreasing closeness to Heaven are: seraphim, cherubim, dominations, thrones, principalities, potentate, virtues, archangels, and angels. There are any number of minor orders to supplement this hierarchy and also three categories that were once human: innocents, martyrs, and confessors. These last three are commonly referred to by the collective name of "saints", whereas the others are "angels".

The main business of divine spirits is to worship God and to oversee Creation. The affairs of mankind are but a small part of this, and most divine spirits have nothing to do with the mortal realm. However, saints, angels (in the strict sense), and archangels are specifically set to watch over humans, and it is these with whom most characters will interact.

Saints are the most likely to offer help to mortals. Innocents are the souls of spiritually pure humans who were taken from the world before their time was due. Most innocents appear as children, and offer succour in the form of Folk Magic (such as Dry, Heal, Vigour, Warm). Martyrs are the souls of humans killed for their faith in God, and then canonised by the procedures of the Church. Martyrs usually create miraculous effects on behalf of those they wish to help. Confessors are doctors of the Church singled out for canonisation by the Church due to their great knowledge and intelligence. Typically, they assist mortals with advice and guidance.

DIVINE SPIRIT

Characteristics
INT: 1d6+18 (22)
POW: As per Intensity
CHA: 1d6+18 (22)
Spirit Abilities: Conjugate plus 1d3 + Intensity choices from: ϕ Sagacity ϕ Spellcasting (Folk Magic) of 1d3 spells ϕ Spellcasting (Theism) of a number of miracles equal to Intensity. Devotion is automatically 25%+(Intensity x10) ϕ Healing ϕ Discorporate at 50% + POW + INT ϕ Manifestation
Skills: Spectral Combat 50% + POW + CHA; Willpower: 50% + (POWx2)

Angels are set over a particular thing in which God has a special interest. This might be a place, a person, or an object. Angels rarely communicate with mortals even if they have been placed to watch over them, instead they act in their defence without warning. Angelic intervention is usually subtle, operating through chains of coincidence aided by their foresight of immediate events.

Archangels are the protectors of entire concepts rather than individual things. There is an archangel of the church, an archangel of Constantinople, an archangel of love, and so on. Most archangels have a high Intensity and command great power; furthermore, each has many angels under its command. When an archangel is moved to intervene then it will do so through employing major supernatural powers, such as the Call Winds, Earthquake, Elemental Summoning, or Sunspear miracles. There is nothing subtle about archangels, and they should be rightly feared.

Only angels and archangels have the Discorporate Skill. Contrary to most other spirits with this power, it is used on allies rather than enemies, loosing their souls from their earthly shackles and enfolding them in their great wings, a balm to all pain, fear, and distress. While being enfolded, a character's body is placed in suspended animation. If wounded it will not get any worse while enfolded, and it is protected as if it had both the Reflection and Shield miracles, each with an Intensity and Magnitude of 10. When the character is returned to her body, the protective miracles cease. If she was formerly suffering the ongoing adverse effects of failed Endurance (such as from a Serious Wound) or Willpower (such as fear) rolls, these are now considered to have passed; although enfolding cannot remove Fatigue levels already gained or cancel spells already in effect.

Angels and archangels can dissipate or sunder a spirit that they defeat in Spirit Combat, although they will never do this to a human soul even if the soul is thoroughly evil.

SPIRIT, INFERNAL

Infernal spirits are a class of malicious entities that seek to do harm to humans. Like other spirits, they are normally undetectable without the use of magic, existing as intangible beings capable of observing the mundane world but being unable to interact with it in this form. In order to meddle in mortal affairs, infernal spirits have two options. They can either possess a human and directly control them, or they can use a demon. Possession is typically used for reconnaissance and infiltration; although has the disadvantage that the spirit does not have access to their host's memories, and so it can be easy for a possession to be uncovered amongst friends and family. Infernal

INFERNAL SPIRIT

Characteristics
INT: 1d6+12 (14)
POW: As per Intensity
CHA: 1d6+6 (10)
Spirit Abilities: Covert, Manifestation, plus 1d3 choices from ϕ Deadly (Sunder) ϕ Discorporate ϕ Miasma ϕ Subjugate ϕ Telekinesis
Skills: Spectral Combat 50% + POW + CHA; Stealth: 50% + INT + CHA; Willpower: 50% + (POWx2)

Intensity	SIZ	Bite: Size / Reach / Dam	Claw: Size / Reach / Dam	Average Spirit Damage
1–2	1d6+6	S / T / 1d4	S / S / 1d3	1d8
3–4	1d6+12	M / T / 1d6	M / M / 1d4	1d10
5–6	1d6+18	L / S / 1d8	L / M / 1d6	1d10
7–8	1d6+24	H / M / 1d10	H / L / 1d8	2d6
9–10	1d6+30	E / M / 1d12	E / L / 1d10	2d6 or 1d8+1d6
11+	1d6+36	C / L / 2d6	C / VL / 1d12	see Mythras p.131

spirits will therefore often take possession of someone with no local connections; favouring strangers and foreigners.

Infernal spirits use demons for direct action against mortals. A demon is formed when an infernal spirit possesses a small animal – with a SIZ no greater than the spirit's Intensity – such as a cat, goat, toad, lizard, or rat (although never a dog) with an insignificant Willpower with which to oppose the possession. The spirit then manifests its demonic form by warping the body of its host, causing it to grow massively in strength and size.

To randomly generate the appearance of a demon, take a d6, d8, d10, and two d12s and roll them all together. Consult the following tables; note that each demon gets two features, one from each d12 result. If the two d12s come up with the same result, then the demon has two of the indicated feature, an enhanced version of the feature, or (if a weapon) one which has a Size, Reach, or Damage one step larger than indicated.

To determine a demon's physical attributes:

- Use the Action Points and Initiative Bonus of the Infernal Spirit;
- Manifested spirits use their MP instead of HP, and have no hit locations (like an elemental);
- Use their Spectral Combat Skill for their Combat Style and for any other physical actions;
- Use the Demon Statistics Table to get the equivalent SIZ, and natural weapon statistics;
- Instead of a Damage Bonus, demons inflict spiritual damage at the same time as inflicting physical damage. Each blow that inflicts physical damage also inflicts the demon's Spirit Damage on the same location, but this spiritual damage ignores worn armour;
- All demons have the Terrifying Ability.

When all Magic Points are exhausted, the demon's body loses integrity and dissolves, leaving behind just the mangled body of the possessed creature. Killing a demon harms but does not destroy the infernal spirit that generated it. It is incapable of producing another demon for a number of months equal to its Intensity while it recovers.

DEMON SCORPION VENOM

- *Potency: 20%+demon's POW x 2*
- *Resistance: Endurance*
- *Onset Time: 1d3 rounds*
- *Duration: 1d3 +6 days*

Conditions: *Agony is instant in the affected limb, lasting the entire duration. After a day, the unrelenting pain leads to Mania, causing the victim to lash out wildly at anyone in sight. At the end of the Duration if the victim remains untreated he becomes a mindless ravening beast, killing and eating anything he can find.*

Antidote/Cure: *The pain cannot be ameliorated through mundane means except by amputating the affected location. Exorcists know a healing prayer, every day match the exorcist's Willpower against the venom's Potency. After four successes the symptoms cease. This prayer is ineffective once the victim has become a ravening beast. Once that has happened, a Heal Mind miracle is needed with a Magnitude greater than the spirit's Intensity.*

DEMON COMPOSITION

1d6	Head of a …
1	human
2	eagle
3	lion
4	reptile
5	bull
6	No head; bite attack located elsewhere

1d8	Forelegs of a …
1	matching body
2–3	eagle
4–5	lion
6–7	human
8	No forelegs

1d10	Body and hind legs of a …
1	scorpion
2	dragon
3	snake
4	bull
5	bull-centaur
6	fish
7–8	lion
9–10	human

1d12	Additional features	Benefit
1	scorpion's sting	Stinger attack; treat as Bite attack but at +3 Range categories plus Venomous Ability.
2	feathered wings	Flying and Diving Strike Abilities
3	extra pair of arms	Multi-Limbed Ability
4	protruding tusks or fangs	Bite attack is one step larger than indicated and can Impale
5	horns	Horn attack appropriate to SIZ
6	snake's head for a tail	Grappler Ability
7	extra head	Multi-Headed Ability
8	oversized hind legs	Leaper Ability
9	reversed ankles and wrists	Adhering Ability, but can move at full speed
10	scales	Armour Points equal to Intensity
11	scintillating colours	Fascination* instead of Terrifying
12	varies	Chaos Feature

* *Fascination: costs the demon an Action point. Make opposed Willpower rolls, if the demon wins then the victim cannot take her eyes off the demon. If the demon does anything on its Action other than concentrate on the victim then the victim gets another chance to break the effect. If the demon attacks the victim then it gets Surprise but the effect is automatically broken*

SPIRIT, SKOTOS

A *skotos* is akin to elemental spirits, except that they are incarnations of darkness rather than one of the classic elements. Like other elemental spirits (Mythras page 148), skotoi can animate a suitable volume of darkness or else manifest within a person; however, only undead animists (such as broukolakes) can survive embodying a skotos: when the darkness spirit is done with a human she is left a withered husk, drained of all vitality. When animated or embodying a person, the spirit has the statistics of an elemental of 2 cubic metres per point of Intensity. The damage inflicted by a skotos is a withering and drying of flesh that leaves deep tissue scars.

Skotoi take damage from light. Assign an Intensity to the light source: a standard lantern (or the Light Folk Magic spell) is Intensity 2, whereas direct sunlight is Intensity 5. Use the light's Intensity as if it were fire (Mythras page 79) on a manifested skotos, although these elementals do not take damage from light Intensities that are less than its own Intensity. The Darkness Folk Magic spell restores 1d6 Hit Points to a skotos. The natural enemy of a skotos is a spirit of light (or photos), these are rare but a skotos will immediately initiate Spirit Combat against such a spirit, and can feed on any Magic Points it acquires from its opponent.

SKOTOS - DARKNESS SPIRIT

Characteristics
INS: 2d6+Intensity
POW: As per Intensity
CHA: 1d6
Spirit Abilities: Animate Darkness, Cannibalistic (spirits of light only), Covert, Demesne
Skills: Spectral Combat 50% + POW + CHA; Stealth: 50% + INS + CHA; Willpower: 50% + (POWx2)

TROGLODYTES

A troglodytes (pronounced "trog-LOW-thy-tace", and meaning "cave-dweller"), is a humanoid creature standing slightly shorter than a man, but is possessed of a wiry strength that far exceeds them. Their arms are long, reaching to their knees, and their hands huge and spade-like. They have little in the way of necks and are completely hairless, covered in pale pink wrinkled skin. All troglodytai are functionally blind: they have eyes but they are entirely concealed by folds of skin. Troglodytai have pronounced incisors in both upper and lower jaws, which meet outside their lips. All troglodytai are mentally connected with one another; each individual can project its thoughts a number of metres equal to their POW x POW. A troglodytes rarely allows itself to get more than 120 metres away from its fellows.

Troglodytai work as a pack. They prefer to surround their opponents and attack from all directions, relying on their superior communication and Earth Sense to gain an advantage in their home tunnels. They have the capacity to tell light from dark; and while they don't fear the light, they understand the tactical advantage that darkness affords them, so against interlopers from the surface they eliminate sources of light first. They dislike being on the surface because their senses don't work at a distance and they are prone to sunburn. Troglodytai are immune to pain: they always pass their Endurance rolls after taking a Serious Wound and do not lose attack actions because of them. Major Wounds affect them normally.

Each troglodytes has a caste based on age and size. Small and young individuals are worker caste, gathering food for the whole tribe, disposing of refuse; and catching and raising snakes and other reptiles, which are eaten raw since they have no use for fire. They also grow huge starchy tubers that can be the size of a house; and the worker troglodytai chew this into a pulpy paste for the others to eat. Larger troglodytai are members of one of three mature castes: the soldier caste involved in defence of the colony; the miner caste who dig the galleries that grant access to the tubers and excavating new home caves with their spade-like hands and chisel-like teeth; and the reserve caste who spend most of their time lazing in the nest caves

TROGLODYTES

Characteristics	Attributes
STR: 2d6+12 (19)	Action Points: 2
CON: 3d6 (11)	Damage Modifier: +1d2
SIZ: 2d6+4 (11)	Magic Points: 11
DEX: 3d6 (11)	Movement: 6 metres
INT: 1d6+6 (10)	Strike Rank Bonus: 11
POW: 3d6 (11)	Armour: none
CHA: 1d6 (4)	Abilities: Burrower, Communal Mind, Earth Sense, Formidable Natural Weapons, Immunity (pain)
	Magic: None

1d20	Location	AP/HP
1–3	Right Leg	0/5
4–6	Left Leg	0/5
7–9	Abdomen	0/6
10-12	Chest	0/7
13–15	Right Arm	0/4
16–18	Left Arm	0/4
19–20	Head	0/5
17–18	Left Arm	5/8
19–20	Head	2/9

Skills
Athletics 50%, Brawn 70%, Endurance 62%, Engineering 40%, Evade 52%, Navigation (underground) 41%, Perception 51%, Stealth 56%, Survival 42%, Track 54%, Willpower 47%

Passions
Protect and Obey Queen 120%

Combat Style & Weapons
Tunnel Rat (Claws and Teeth; Formation Fighting) 65%

Weapon	Size/Force	Reach	Damage	AP/HP
Spade Claws	M	L	1d6+1d2	As for Arm
Chisel Teeth	S	T	1d8+1d2	As for Head

but who can take on any role as needed. The troglodytai are ruled by a queen, who lurks at the deepest part of their hive, surrounded by her fanatically loyal subjects. Amongst the sexless race, she is the only one who breeds, and is the mother of all current tribesmen. The queen is a huge (SIZ 40), bloated individual barely capable of movement. She rules her people with an iron fist, and they would gladly die for her.

GENERIC NPCS

The skill templates provided below assume average Characteristics (13 for INT and SIZ, 11 otherwise) and include only 100 Bonus Skill Points. Feel free to add 2d10% (or more for older or more experienced NPCs) to any Skill.

GREEK CRAFTSMAN, MERCHANT, SCHOLAR, PRIEST, THIEF

Attributes

Action Points: 2

Damage Modifier: None

Magic Points: 11

Movement: 6 metres

Strike Rank Bonus: +12 (–4 for armour) = +8

Armour: Medium Greek Armour (ENC 27/2)

Abilities: None

Magic: None

1d20	Location	AP/HP
1–3	Right Leg	0/5
4–6	Left Leg	0/5
7–9	Abdomen	0/6
10–12	Chest	0/7
13–15	Right Arm	0/4
16–18	Left Arm	0/4
19–20	Head	0/5

Skills (No Career)

Athletics 32%, Brawn 34%, Commerce 54%, Conceal 32%, Craft 42%, Deceit 44%, Endurance 27%, Evade 37%, Customs 66%, Greek 62%, Influence 37%, Insight 34%, Locale 41%, Lore (Byzantine) 66%, Streetwise 37%, Willpower 47%

Skills & Passions (Artisan)

Athletics 32%, Brawn 39%, Commerce 64%, Conceal 37%, Craft (primary) 67%, Craft (secondary) 37%, Deceit 64%, Drive 27%, Endurance 37%, Evade 37%, Customs 66%, Greek 62%, Influence 52%, Insight 54%, Locale 46%, Lore (Byzantine) 71%, Streetwise 62%, Perception 44%, Willpower 62%

Respect Church 54%, Loyal to Guild 54%, Aspire to Perfection 54%

Skills & Passions (Official, Merchant)

Athletics 32%, Brawn 34%, Bureaucracy 49%, Commerce 74%, Conceal 32%, Courtesy 39%, Customs 76%, Craft 42%, Deceit 59%, Endurance 27%, Evade 42%, Customs 66%, Greek 62%, Influence 57%, Insight 49%, Literacy 41%, Locale 41%, Lore (Byzantine) 66%, Perception 46%, Streetwise 57%, Willpower 57%

Respect Church 54%, Loyal to Family 54%, Covet Luxury 54%

Skills & Passions (Scholar)

Athletics 32%, Brawn 34%, Commerce 54%, Conceal 32%, Craft 42%, Customs 76%, Deceit 44%, Endurance 27%, Evade 37%, Customs 66%, Greek 72%, Influence 42%, Insight 39%, Latin 44%, Literacy 41%, Locale 51%, Lore (Byzantine) 66%, Lore (primary) 56%, Lore (secondary) 41%, Oratory 39%, Perception 39%, Streetwise 37%, Teach 39%, Willpower 57%

Respect Church 54%, Loyal to Family 54%, Crave Respect of Peers 54%

Skills & Passions (Priest)

Athletics 32%, Brawn 34%, Bureaucracy 44%, Commerce 54%, Conceal 32%, Craft 42%, Customs 76%, Deceit 49%, Endurance 27%, Evade 37%, Customs 66%, Greek 62%, Influence 62%, Insight 54%, Literacy 49%, Locale 46%, Lore (Byzantine) 71%, Lore (theology) 51%, Oratory 39%, Sing 39%, Streetwise 47%, Willpower 67%

Respect Church 64%, Loyal to Parishioners 54%, Conceal Shame 54%

Skills & Passions (Thief)

Acting 37%, Athletics 52%, Brawn 39%, Commerce 54%, Conceal 32%, Craft 42%, Deceit 69%, Disguise 37%, Endurance 27%, Evade 47%, Customs 66%, Greek 62%, Influence 47%, Insight 49%, Locale 41%, Lockpicking 32%, Lore (Byzantine) 66%, Perception 34%, Sleight 44%, Stealth 42%, Streetwise 57%, Willpower /47%

Fear Hell 54%, Obey Gangleader 54%, Envy the Wealthy 54%

Combat Style & Weapons

Self Defence (quarterstaff, club, knife, sling; Cautious Fighter) 50%
(thief only) Concealable Weapons (knife, dagger, garrotte; Daredevil) 42%

Weapon	Size/Force	Reach	Damage	AP/HP
Club	M	S	1d6	4/4
Knife	S	S	1d3	5/4
Dagger	S	S	1d4+1	6/8

VARDARIOTES, CITY WATCH, STREET THUG

In a fight a Vardariotes attacks with his club and parries or wards with the manglabia (which has the Defensive trait), If he gets a Special Effect while attacking he uses Flurry (from the Do or Die Combat Style Trait) to follow up with the manglabia, hoping for an Entangle. Special Effects gained from parrying are used to Pin Weapon.

Attributes
Action Points: 2
Damage Modifier: None
Magic Points: 11
Movement: 6 metres
Strike Rank Bonus: +12 (–4 for armour) = +8
Armour: Medium Greek Armour (ENC 27/2)
Abilities: None
Magic: None

1d20	*Location*	*AP/HP*
1–3	Right Leg	6/5
4–6	Left Leg	6/5
7–9	Abdomen	6/6
10-12	Chest	6/7
13–15	Right Arm	6/4
16–18	Left Arm	6/4
19–20	Head	7/5

Skills & Passions

Athletics 47% , Brawn 44%, Commerce 54%, Conceal 32%, Craft 47%, Deceit 49%, Endurance 43%, Evade 62%, Customs 66%, Gambling 36%, Greek 62%, Influence 47%, Insight 49%, Locale 37%, Lore (Byzantine) 66%, Lore (Strategy and Tactics) 31%, Oratory 31%, Perception 37%, Streetwise 56%, Unarmed 31%, Willpower 52%

Vardariot: Respect Church 54%, Loyal to Praitor 54%, Covert Respect 54%

City Watch: Respect Church 54%, Loyal to Commander 54%, Loyal to City 68%

Street Thug: Fear Hell 54%, Envy the Wealthy 68%, Enjoy Violence 60%

Combat Style & Weapons

Self Defence (quarterstaff, club, knife, sling; Cautious Fighter) 60%.

Vardariotes: Manglabliaros (manglabia, club, unarmed; Do or Die) 52% OR

City Watch: Phylax (short spear, kite shield; Cautious Fighter) 52% OR

Street Thug: Brawling (club, knife, hatchet, unarmed; Knockout Blow) 52%

Weapon	Size/Force	Reach	Damage	AP/HP
Mangalabia	M	M	1d4	8/6
Club	M	S	1d6	4/4
Knife	S	S	1d3	5/4
Hatchet	S	S	1d6	4/6
Shortspear	M	L	1d8+1	4/5

This Template can also be used for the city watch by reducing the armour to Light Greek Armour and exchanging the Manglabiarios Combat Style for Phylax. It can also be used for a Street Thug by removing all the armour and giving the Brawling Combat Style instead of Manglabiaros.

INDEX

A

B

C

D

F

K

L

M

Q

R

S

www.ingramcontent.com/pod-product-compliance
Lightning Source LLC
Chambersburg PA
CBHW081141300726
48982CB00006B/1032
9781989028162